SAMRAJ

"You do not know my name," the voice whispered. "You don't know your brother's either. Do you know your own?"

Because of the familiar voice, for a moment she thought he was teasing her. Then she felt the black space in her mind for the first time. Her heart began to pound.

"But you do know you have a brother. A twin brother."

She nodded, tears in her eyes. She turned her head to look again at this twin brother.

"You don't recall his name?"

She nodded again. Her brother groaned and rolled on his side. The light fell on his face. His dark, handsome features were framed by waves of shining black hair—all exactly like herself, she knew. "What have you done to us?" she whispered.

"Your name is Draupadi now."

"No—"

"You are fifteen years old. You are King Drupada's new daughter."

"Where have I come from?"

"In a moment you will come from your new father's sacrificial fire."

"No! Before!"

"'Before' you have been made to forget." The shrouded head bowed. "I am sorry."

About the Author

Elaine Aron and her husband Arthur, who live in Santa Cruz, California, were enchanted by *The Mahabharata* when they first read it ten years ago. Five years later, Elaine Aron began researching and writing *Samraj*. She is now working on the two further novels which will complete the epic of Yudishtira and Draupadi.

SAMRAJ

ELAINE ARON

NEW ENGLISH LIBRARY
Hodder and Stoughton

Printed and bound in Great Britain
for Hodder and Stoughton
Paperbacks, a division of Hodder
and Stoughton Limited, Mill Road,
Dunton Green, Sevenoaks, Kent
TN13 2YA. (Editorial Office:
47 Bedford Square, London
WC1B 3DP) by Cox and Wyman
Limited, Reading, Berks. Photoset
by Rowland Phototypesetting
Limited, Bury St Edmunds, Suffolk.

British Library C.I.P.

Aron, Elaine N.
  Samraj.
  I. Title
813'.54[F]

ISBN 0-450-50950-8

To Veda Vyasa
who first wrote this story
and who always seemed so near.

And to Art
To retell the epic was his idea.

The interpretation was ours.

And I wrote it down.

But above all, what follows is
the result of his unfailing support.

It is the fruit of our love.

ACKNOWLEDGMENTS

For their comments and encouragement I wish to thank Elizabeth Gilmore, Christine De Vault, Bob Tager and John Leavit. For his sure-footed guidance along Himalaya paths, Satish Khanduri of Garhwal Mandal Vikas Nigam's Mountaineering and Trekking Division.

For their knowledge of ancient India, I am grateful to Dr K. P. Nautiyal of Garhwal University and Dr Arundhoti Banerji of the Archeological Survey of India. For their scholarly research, the authors of several hundred volumes, a selection of which are listed at the end of this book. For permission to quote J. A. B. van Buitenen's beautiful translations, the University of Chicago Press.

For his honest feedback and countless creative additions, I offer my loving gratitude to my son, Elijah Aron. And for their professional skills and personal support, three of publishing's most brilliant women: Lynn Franklin, my agent; Carolyn Caughey, my editor; and Clare Bristow, my publisher.

CONTENTS

THE KURU FAMILY

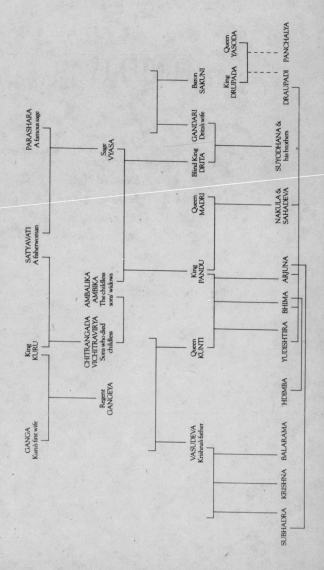

The *Mahabharata* has been retold in many forms, from dramas to comic books. Nevertheless, I hope those who have cherished India's great epic since childhood will be patient with this reshaping of the traditional story into a modern historical novel. What follows (including the perspective taken in the Historical Note) is a modest attempt, by someone far from India, to make some of the essence of the epic more accessible to those in my own culture. And for them, "a new river is best explored in a familiar boat."

HISTORICAL NOTE

Four thousand years before the Christian era, Europe, the Middle East and the Indian subcontinent were inhabited largely by settled communities of farmers who had little need for weapons and worshipped a pantheon of goddesses. Then a vast change began. A people now called the Indo-Europeans started to migrate outward from the steppes between Europe and Asia. These wanderers measured their wealth in cattle and their worth in the conquests they made from their chariots. They were patriarchal, and they worshipped male sky-dwelling gods: the Thunderbolt Wielder, the Sun in His chariot, the Lord of Wind, the Messenger dwelling in fire.

The Indo-Europeans came in a number of waves over the next two thousand years, and it is not clear whether they always conquered, or were sometimes assimilated by the peoples they disrupted. But however it happened, the same Indo-European language, religion, and values are found at the roots of numerous dynamic and assertive cultures: the Greeks, Romans, and iron-discovering Hittites; the Vikings, Celts, Angles, Saxons, and all the Germanic tribes; the Slavs, Russians, Armenians, Albanians, and Lithuanians, two Chinese subcultures; and, in Iran, a branch which produced both the Persian civilisation and a people who called themselves the Arya, "the noble ones".

Around 1500 BC these Arya moved southeast into the subcontinent, first settling the open plains of the Indus Valley and then crossing the Yamuna to the lands drained by the Ganges river system, the heart of today's India. Here these lovers of empty sky and grassy steppes found a world they could only have known from their nightmares—a land of extreme heat and rainfall, dense forests, and strange tropical animals.

But the earth was exceptionally fertile, so the Arya stubbornly burned the forests, built their forts, and brought in their cattle herds.

There was another obstacle, however—those the Arya called the Dasyu, the dark-skinned "demons". Some of these may have been remnants of the ancient Indus Valley civilisation, whose cities had endured unchanged for a thousand years. Others of these Dasyu were people inseparable from their dark woodlands, people who left no stone monuments to explain themselves. Nor did they seem to have the Arya inclination to lay claim to owning the things of Earth. These contrasts between Arya and Dasyu produced an enmity, and an attraction, that were mutual and intense. It also produced a great culture.

By 900 BC (one possible date for this story, based on historical records which appear to describe certain of its events and characters) Egypt was beginning its decline and Homer was composing his poems about the exploits of the first Indo-Europeans in Greece. In northern India the Arya had created a network of kingdoms—islands of cleared land in a sea of shadows. Eventually they called their nation Bharata, a name for India still used. But this Bharata seems to have been as unlike the later India of caste, karma and reincarnation as King Arthur's Britain was unlike today's England. Neither Bharata's men nor its women were ready to accept their fates passively. For example, far from acquiescing to an arranged marriage, an Arya princess could select her husband from a parade of warriors at a "bride's choice", a right guaranteed her by law—unless she eloped or was carried off under a prince's arm.

But law usually prevailed, for the Arya knew it was all that could bind such strong-willed people. They obeyed no mere human law, however, but *dharma*—eternal law. It was tradition, duty, the laws of nature and of human nature, and the particular work one was born to do. But for those who understood it, it was even more. Ultimately dharma could only be known from Veda, Pure Knowledge—the fluctuations within Unbounded Awareness cognised by the Vedic seers.

It was this Unbounded Awareness which was the essence of

the Arya. Most Indo-European deities possessed the attributes of strength, beauty, generosity, wisdom, blazing light, and omnipotent creativity. But in Bharata these bright qualities were merged and transcended—to become the Unbounded Oneness of Brahman, which the Arya maintained the human mind was uniquely designed to experience.

To perfect that experience and gain knowledge and power from it, certain Vedic seers had chosen to dwell in the silence of the very forests their fellow Arya had sought to clear. Some even say it was from this encounter with the Dasyu "darkness" that the one-sided Indo-European worship of light and power was transformed into an integrated understanding of human consciousness and cosmic creation—an all-inclusive cognition which would profoundly affect the world.

Yet even as Bharata flourished, it is said that it, and the entire world, were poised on the brink of a long-prophesied and inevitable decline. Seers had had visions. They had seen creation passing through a cycle of four long ages, from birth to dissolution. The last of these was imminent, and would last thousands of years. Dharma would be scorned, devastating wars fought, the land overcrowded and poisoned, and the Vedic knowledge garbled by ignorance. But later Arya sages also gave comfort: In the same way that fresh seeds fall to earth even as the main plant dies, at the hour before the dawn of this evil age, at the time of a cataclysmic battle, a faint but sustaining light had been lit by a king and queen. He was the son of Lord Dharma himself, the god of righteousness. She was born out of a sacrificial fire. And their lives were remembered in the *Mahabharata*, "Great Bharata"—an epic which has been retold in many versions over these thousands of years, and in one more here.

SAMRAJ

A samraj is an illusion created when one of us reflects too well the light in the eyes of the rest.

PART I
A KNOTTED NET

1

The great fire at the beginning of the dawn has sprung
aloft . . .

Rig Veda

Some say I wrote the *Mahabharata*. Except, of course, there
is the problem that the first version was written centuries
after the events, and I lived through them.

Vyasa *

Ushas, Dawn, opened her doors, and petals of pink lotus-light
flared up from the horizon. The mist over the Ganges glowed
as if on fire. The braided waters beneath changed from silver
to gold.

Behind Kampilya's log palisades the trellis-laced city warmed
under the sun, and vapours rose off her shingle roofs and
fancy-carved balconies. The city was empty—the people lined
the river road, waiting for a response from the gods to events
one league south. There Ushas was blessing a clearing in the
forest with her first light, signalling the start of the largest
sacrifice Kampilya had ever dared.

The suppliant was the king himself and the preparations had
taken months. The wood once growing in that auspicious place
was now carved, kiln dried and geometrically stacked on the
hearths to the height of a horse, with the excess under thatched
roofs supported by decorated columns. Behind the hearths a
tent had been erected in the night. In front of them, on a
carpet of sacred grasses laid down stalk by stalk, were gold

---

* Except when the source is italicised, these quotations are fictional.

9

dishes containing the finest offerings of grains, cakes, curds and clarified butter. Now the king, queen and a hundred privileged others from the priest and warrior classes were gathered in expectant silence.

With this first caress of the dawn, Kampilya's finest singer of the sacred hymns of *Veda*, Eternal Knowledge, took a torch from among the coals brought from the city's perpetual altar fire and implored Agni, the Young and Hungry, the Messenger of the Gods, to come among them. The torch dipped into the wood.

For a moment there was only smoke. Then Agni's yellow flame licked at the tinder and found it acceptable. The dry wood exploded into a tower of fire. King, queen, priests and warriors all drew back from the heat. And so the gods forbore to listen again to our needs, and it began.

She glided to him from somewhere beautiful. The features of the place were crowded out by the sensations of waking, so that now all she remembered was the light. The beauty was only an abstraction; the harmony a mere sense that what happened there was always just. But she knew that world to be in some way more substantial than this one to which she woke.

She opened her eyes and said, "I must tell my brother."

The head above her was not his, however. Through a white shroud she thought she saw the features of an old man. "Do you recognise me?" he asked.

The voice was almost familiar. But she shook her head. "Where is my brother?"

The shrouded head nodded to her left. Through netting she saw her brother, also stirring. An oil lamp made his long body glow like dark gold. She wanted to call to him, but some strange uncertainty made her hesitate. She looked around her instead.

They were in a tent of hides that admitted light only around the floor and entrance flap. This light seemed cold blue, like early morning, but the air was almost hot. In the shadowed corners people worked at tasks she could not grasp. When two stopped to stare at her, a third urged the pair back to work. She could hear they worked with water, pouring it on to something that muffled its fall. Over this sound she heard chanting, confused by the snapping noise of fresh, hungry flames.

"You do understand my words though," the shrouded man persisted.

The voice was gentle, but made no sense. She nodded.

"You do not know my name," the voice whispered. "You don't know your brother's either. Do you know your own?"

Because of the familiar voice, for a moment she thought he was teasing her. Then she felt the black space in her mind for the first time. Her heart began to pound.

"But you do know you have a brother. A twin brother."

She nodded, tears in her eyes. She turned her head to look again at this twin brother.

"You don't recall his name?"

She nodded again. Her brother groaned and rolled on his side. The light fell on his face. His dark, handsome features were framed by waves of shining black hair—all exactly like herself, she knew. "What have you done to us?" she whispered.

"Your name is Draupadi now."

"No—"

"You are fifteen years old. You are King Drupada's new daughter."

"Where have I come from?"

"In a moment you will come from your new father's sacrificial fire."

"No! Before!"

"'Before' you have been made to forget." The shrouded head bowed. "I am sorry."

She closed her eyes and lay still, willing herself to use her intellect. Who was he? The shroud meant he did not want her to know. "Made to forget"? How? *Why*?

The voice interrupted. "You wished to tell your brother something."

The memory had been like smoke anyway; now it seemed ruined by her frantic beating against these new walls in her mind. "I was coming from some place else when I woke," she said flatly, not opening her eyes.

"What was this place, Draupadi?"

11

"Don't call me that!"

"What was it?"

"I don't know. You gave me some herb, didn't you?"

"Many take herbs, but they seldom go where I think you have gone."

She turned away from him. "It was real," she said. "Not a dream. Not just your herb's doing."

"Then tell your brother, Draupadi." The shrouded man took her hands and pulled her upright, turning her to face her twin. Her feet were on cool earth, a reassurance.

"Address your brother as Panchalya—'belonging to this kingdom of Panchala'. Now tell him, Draupadi."

She heard that the man said these lies of names with difficulty. She shook her head. She would not.

"If you wish I will not listen. But today a word of it would mean very much to me also."

She shrugged, trying to hide her emotion. Oddly, his plea had moved her, even though her brother's eyes were filling with a confusion and pain worse than that from any wound. So he also felt the injury in his mind, and searched for her name in the gaping hole of his memory.

"Brother?" She would not torture him with this 'Panchalya'. "I think somehow they have taken our memories."

He did not seem to hear her. She rushed on regardless. "I have been somewhere while my body slept. I can't recall it now. It was so different from anything else—I—I had to tell—" Tears choked off the words.

Strong arms encircled her. She cried into the shroud. "Please forgive us," the voice whispered in her ear. "But be grateful too. Where you went in your awareness is real. Never forget your shred of it. It is a great gift, provided to help you now." Then the voice and the arms drew away. "Now stand, Princess."

The voice left her no choice. She stood. Her brother was also being helped to his feet. Sheepskins were slung up to his broad shoulders and she heard the splatter of water. In a moment the weight of wet skins staggered her also, covering her white cotton shift. More water was poured over his head, then cold wetness ran down her own head and face, soaking into her hair where it was caught under the high cowl of damp wool. Boots of wet sheepskins were pulled on to him, and on to her.

"Now listen carefully, Draupadi. Your life begins on the other side of those two fires out there. For your safety, never speak of this tent or of me. See that your brother does not either. You are royalty now, and much, much more. You will have to learn, or relearn, many things. But for all your ignorance, by seeing their world freshly you, Princess Draupadi, will become their teacher. Do not let their stupidity make you arrogant. Control your temper. But whatever else you hear, believe this: You are one of two born to staunch Bharata's bleeding. You and another who will come for you."

The tent flap was drawn back, revealing a blinding triangle of blazing sun and two blazing fires.

"Walk between the hearths," the voice said from behind. His hands gently pushed her; her brother lurched forward too. "Fear nothing. Go with Brahma."

She stepped towards the space between the flames, leading her brother, as she sensed she often had Before. The heat singed her lashes and burned her lungs. But she obeyed the voice—she felt no fear.

"A daughter!" someone shouted.

"So be it."

"Such dark skin."

"But such beauty. Agni be praised."

Her brother stumbled against her from behind. "A son also!"

"Twins! A grown warrior of a son. Praise Indra, may this one be the death of my enemy. May Guru Vaja feel his wrath. May the gods protect us—*it has happened.*"

The shouts merged into a hymn of praise: "'Agni, bless these progeny, bless the institutor of this rite, may he live a hundred autumns, may all of us behold the sun a hundred autumns'— a warrior prince at last!"

Behind the fires the shrouded figure turned his back on his odd midwifery and went back into the tent. His name was Veda Vyasa, Collector of Veda.

In the tent's gloom Sage Vyasa faced west, away from what he had done, and waited for something more. It came, a new shout above the delirious praising. It was King Drupada's personal priest, and Vyasa knew by the inflections that the words were being wrenched from the priest by the gods: "She shall in time accomplish the purpose of the gods. This woman will lead the warriors of her generation to their doom."

The shrouded man stood rigid in the dark tent. But as he both expected and feared, the shouts of joy drowned out the prophecy. The hymns of praise welled up again.

He shook his head. "Mindless as frogs after a storm. Brahma spare them unnecessary pain."

He removed the shroud, loosened a tent flap, stepped out through the rear of the tent and lost himself in the surrounding forest.

There was a net across Bharata. The knots were one hundred small kingdoms, each allied or opposed to the others, and the ropes were men and women, containing threads of both good and evil, serenity and obsession. One of these kingdoms was Panchala, which was ruled by King Drupada and had its capital at Kampilya. Another was its neighbour to the north, a kingdom belonging to the Kurus and having its capital at Hastinapura. King Drupada had recently lost the northern half of Panchala to Guru Vaja, the weapons-master to the Kuru princes at Hastinapura.

Guru Vaja was a man who frightened children, and some grown men as well. Although born into the priestly class, he had dared to take up the arts rightfully belonging only to the warriors—those who defended and ruled Bharata. This transgression meant that he brought to battle the awesome single-mindedness of those born to weave spells and converse with the gods. The great Vaja, however, had studied weaponry for only one purpose: to defeat King Drupada.

As boyhood playmates Vaja and Drupada, the son of a priest and the son of a king, had vowed to share everything, all their lives. The years passed, and Vaja inherited the poverty endemic to priests who choose to pursue knowledge rather than perform tedious rituals for the rich, while Drupada inherited his father's kingdom. Thus when Vaja was struck by a dire need he lacked the wealth to meet, he went to his childhood friend for help.

But Drupada scorned him, telling him "like should associate with like" and "the poor should not seek out the rich".

At that moment, although Vaja knew nothing of fighting or weapons, he inwardly vowed revenge. For it is said that a warrior is quick to anger but as quick to forgive, but an angered priest is angry for ever. So Vaja began his years of patient study and practice of warfare. When he knew his skill exceeded that of any warrior in Bharata he presented himself at Hastinapura. In spite of his poverty and priestly ancestors he was immediately made weapons-master to the Kurus' princes.

Vaja asked only one fee for his teaching: When his pupils had become the best in the land, as he would see they were, they would fight King Drupada of Panchala and take half of his kingdom. Only half. Drupada would yet learn to share.

When the princes were grown the deed was easily done, for at Hastinapura the sons of not one but two great kings were growing up. Under Guru Vaja's leadership, in one glorious day they proved that the Kuru kingdom was the most powerful in Bharata. And Panchala—suddenly merely Southern Panchala—was proven the most vulnerable.

Thus it was that King Drupada had nowhere to turn but to the gods. He needed warrior sons to fight for him and, even more important, womanly daughters who could make good marriages of alliance. For if he could only unite his family with one of Hastinapura's princes, the Kurus would have to defend South Panchala rather than swallow it or let it be swallowed. Unfortunately, so far, his sons had seemed like daughters and his daughters like sons.

Although in some respects King Drupada was a shallow and pompous man, he was also pious and full of faith in Indra, Agni, Brahma and all the Heavenly Company of Thirty-Three. And so, in hope of receiving more useful offspring, King Drupada had performed suitable austerities, paid his priests, and performed the morning's sacrifice with pitiful eagerness. Still, even he did not expect the gods to provide him with such an immediate and mature response.

It was not the staring eyes or cacophony of amazed voices that Draupadi noticed first, but the peculiar sky. It pressed down in a pale arch rising from a round horizon which, although fringed with trees, seemed to be almost at her feet.

Next she noticed it was strangely, unbearably hot. And the chariot horses, she thought. They are so large and smooth-coated. The grass. Brown, yet it is too warm for frost last night. *Where am I?*

Hints. Concentrate. Before the tent I knew my brother and the man who woke us. The sky was bluer, the air cooler, the horses smaller—

I must do something. Run. Demand an explanation. *Who am I?*

Instinctively she turned towards her brother, "Panchalya". Gifts were being piled at his feet. Weapons. Bows, quivers and arrows—she recognised the types of these. But the other weapons—what were they?

We don't know. Yet my brother is being called a "warrior prince".

That is what they want to make him. Why do I doubt he is equal to it?

The fear rose again. "Draupadi"? Who is that?

My name, he said.

I must escape.

No, attend to everything. You can't escape—you don't even know where you are.

I don't know who I am.

Attend.

She began to categorise by dress and bearing the persons pushing in around her. The ones called "King" and "Queen". Finely dressed but too fat. The weapon-givers, in ornamented leather clothing. Obviously to protect them in battle. The men singing. They sing those hymns too loudly.

Then I have heard such singing Before. Watch the singers.

Some wear rich weavings and gold ornaments. But what of these barefoot men in bark-cloth? They chant with grace and confidence.

They are familiar.

The singing stopped. The finely dressed, loud hymn-singers threw handfuls of grain and ladles of fat into the fires, which flared up as they cried, "Swaha!" The king and queen approached her and her brother.

"Bow before your parents, Princess Draupadi," one of the loudest hymn-singers ordered from her left. He wore gold coins down to his navel and smelled like rotting sandalwood leaves.

"A gift from the gods does not bow to any king or queen of this world," instructed a soft-spoken hymn-singer on her right. He was one of those in bark-cloth. Horse dung clung to his bare feet.

"Bow!" was the command from her left.

The one they wished her to submit to had been addressed as King Drupada. The fat king. Drupada. And my name is Draupadi, she thought—I am truly supposed to be this man's daughter.

The king was smiling inanely at her and spreading his arms, obviously waiting for her to rush to him. She glanced at the man on her right and allowed her eyes to plead. He would not meet her gaze. She vowed not to look for help again.

King Drupada stepped closer. He smelled of dead flowers. A little pouch of flesh jiggled between each armpit and elbow as he waited for her to rush to his breast. But she could not bear to touch him.

"I greet you, King Drupada." She quickly bowed her head, pressing her palms together in front of her face in an awkward imitation of something in her mind from Before. The priest on her left had stiffened with anger. On her right, the other had sighed.

The queen pushed in front of her husband, clearly trying to cover up the awkward moment. "Ah, my beautiful daughter. At last. Please call me Mother."

Draupadi choked back a cry. Her trembling hands were still in front of her face. From their shelter she whispered, "I greet you, Queen."

The queen turned angrily towards the richly dressed man on Draupadi's left. "You said I'd be her mother. You said everyone would call me her mother."

"Everyone but her," were the words from Draupadi's right. "Your Draupadi is the daughter of burning truth."

The queen looked the girl over doubtfully. Then her attention moved on to what obviously mattered to her. "Panchalya, 'Our Panchala's'. So tall and fearless."

17

"He'll be invincible when he is properly trained," the king said, standing back. Draupadi thought she had seen such a calculating look Before—but only given to horses. Her brother, however, was doing his best to take a posture suited to their words. She hoped some of his manly frown was at the weakness of these people who claimed him.

The king reached tentatively for her brother's hand. "Come, ride in my chariot, Panchalya?" Her brother glanced at her but allowed himself to be led away.

The sudden separation, and his allowing it, so stunned Draupadi that she hardly noticed the queen's hand on her own arm.

The sage Vyasa travelled by elephant as far as the Gates of the Ganges, then borrowed a horse to pass through the foothills. At the first wash-out of the trail along the gorge he turned the beast loose and sent it home, making the last three days of the climb on foot with only his contentious inner voices for company.

He had become what he most detested—a meddler. And for what? To steal the memories of Bharata's most precious child in order to create "Draupadi". In order to create the difficult problem of her brother, "Panchalya".

True, it had seemed to be the only answer. But the scheme was a gamble and he did not care for that, even if he also knew this was the timid judgment of what he called his small-self— the self that saw only the narrow view, the problems, and the dangers to his mortal body and personal interests.

When would this small-self give up its last, feeble hold on him? He still thanked all the gods that his teacher had tempted, tricked and cajoled him through those long years of withdrawal from the senses—years of living among boulders, caves and clouds, eating bland food or none at all, and meditating every day for more hours than he had spent with his eyes open. But the long rest in the embrace of the Unbounded had finally reassured his small-self, and allowed it to mostly surrender to what he had come to call his large-self. This Self, guided by the gods and the needs of the times, "the Self moving within Itself", had calmly done its work down there behind him at

Kampilya. Others spun mysteries about such a Self and such guidance, but he knew it as ordinary fact.

Still, as he climbed he could not stop his recurring thought that this time the gods' gamble was dangerous. At these moments he would glance west. It was always from the west that he felt this uneasiness emanating. Every year, more traders coming from the west, going to the west. Arabians, Hebrews, Egyptians, Phoenicians. Were the forces of the Destruction bringing in reinforcements?

No, reinforcements could be everywhere, he would remind himself. As for the west, we came from there ourselves—a handful of daring Arya pushing southeast from the Seven Rivers of Indus, choosing territories, sons choosing new territories, until a hundred kingdoms flourish now, and new sons look for someone or something much greater to conquer. There is the face of the trouble. To look only west for it guarantees an attack from behind. Or from inside.

Finally he would set his mind firmly back on the trail, telling himself that all this searching for causes was only due to his rapid ascent, which could make anyone's mind chase foolish thoughts. Better to observe butterflies. Count monkeys and eagles.

On the final afternoon he climbed up out of the last stand of stunted fir trees and traversed the rock slide, where the path was glistening boulders beside the cataract. And, finally, the blessed silence came down to still his thinking. The blessed silence of the hermitage at Badari.

As the sun set behind rock and cloud on his left and lit the other wall of rock and clouds on his right, Vyasa knelt there where the ground levelled out into the broad Badari valley and thanked Brahma for this place. Peaks continued up all around him, as high again as he had climbed all these days, and at the end of the valley he could have followed the river far deeper into Himalaya, Winter's Place. But this was the windswept plain chosen by the first of their seers. This was the only place on earth where the small-self surrendered to large-self merely by closing or by opening the eyes, either one. This was his heart's home.

There on his knees he noticed that the night's silence was

deeper and purer than he had ever felt. Such pure calm could only mean a gathering. The hermits from the caves on the ridges were making one of their rare visits, or students from the valleys had been called to return.

He hurried on up through the boulders and berry bushes, eager again. Suddenly he saw them—at least a hundred people, and not hidden in the huts and caves scattered near the slope above the common hall of the hermitage, but gathered around her hut.

His surprise was nothing compared to the annoying, deep disappointment that assailed him, even after all these years. How much he had wanted and needed to speak to Aditi alone.

He braced himself. This was a good reminder: she was no longer his student. Rather, if the flow of Knowledge were unrestricted by empty courtesies, it would now flow from her to him.

Vyasa joined the group of supplicants who sat or stood on either side of the path from the one-room stone house. Looking down, Vyasa saw that the path to Aditi's door was strewn with flowers.

Beside him someone said, "Five years ago today, Aditi healed my sister."

Another said, "I was here the day she revealed herself. She wasn't named after the goddess then, but was just 'the dark girl'. I'd come here to see the envoy from Chine. No one could speak with him. But she came forward and in half a day— really, no more—she could understand him. It was the same the next day with the Bactrian."

"And her so dark too, just like an ignorant Dasyu." When the speaker noticed Vyasa's own dark skin, the poor man averted his eyes in embarrassment.

"She came from the gods," another corrected. "How else could she have known so much Veda?"

"Vyasa taught her," yet another said, not recognising the newcomer.

In his mind Vyasa saw a clearing and heard Aditi chanting *Rig Veda* as no one else before.

A woman near the door began weeping. Vyasa had already

sensed the sorrow here. Now he was afraid his dulled mind had missed the cause.

"She lives," someone said, as if he had voiced his fear. "But she is dead to us. Last night at this hour she took the vows of silence and went to hide herself on the mountain. She would not say if she would ever return."

His heart hurting as if under a heavy stone, Vyasa looked up the steep slopes into the clouds. Yes, he thought, she is up there.

My small-self is consuming me. I perceived that she wasn't in the hut, yet couldn't bear the awareness of it.

So we all gather here at her door, helpless from missing her.

He wanted to cry out: Aditi, why couldn't you wait until we had spoken? Just once more?

But he knew the answer. Try as she had, she had not been able to resist punishing him for taking her children.

Vyasa turned around, feeling weary in every quarter of his body. He sat down beside the north wall of the hut, facing her mountain, and closed his eyes to sink into the silence the others had created. He himself had none.

But, in time, he found he could go further again, into the awareness he had been deepening and expanding since boyhood. There, her voice suddenly came to him:

I am grateful you chose to return, Beloved Teacher. You will need our strength.

Forgive me, Aditi.

Forgive yourself, as I must forgive myself.

Aditi, it was my decision in the end.

No, Vyasa. Teacher, you can not save me, or I you. There is only one source of love and strength without limits.

Her words stopped, but they had released a fountain of energy in his body. It rushed up through him. His small-self was gone, spread to the four corners, and only pure being remained.

He opened his eyes. All those who had been standing or sitting by the path were now seated facing him in the chill half-darkness.

"Beloved Vyasa," one said, "we did not recognise you. Thank Brahma for the serenity of your presence tonight of all

21

nights. Please tell us—if we are worthy of the comfort—why have they taken Aditi's beautiful twins?"

"I myself sang songs with them on this very spot a month ago," another said.

"And who, revered sage, is the one Aditi praised last night through her tears? Who is this Yudishtira?"

2

May Brihaspati defend us from a malignant foe coming from behind or from above or from below; may Indra defend us from foes in front and in the middle.

Rig Veda

Black rain clouds walled off the north and east. From the earth to the top of the sky, storm clouds bulged in angry billows frozen by distance. Prostrate beneath them was the forested plain, its rivers snaking languidly southeast. In all directions to the horizon tangles of sala, acacia and rose-apple trees, almost leafless from drought, whipped in the chaotic winds that would bring the storm season, that would bring the healing rain.

Along the gravelled bank of an ancient abandoned river bed three horsemen galloped. Their mounts moved unevenly, tense in the gusting winds. But the young riders pushed them on, striking foaming flanks with bare palms. The country was unfamiliar to them and its forests hid a tiger known to prefer human prey. Therefore, as they had been taught, they were countering fear with boldness.

The rider in the lead reined his mount, giving all his attention to a shallow cave under the left bank of the low ridge on which the three were cantering. Although the lair was mostly hidden by bamboo, sala trees and creepers, he knew this was the place they sought.

"Yudishtira, be careful!" the second rider shouted ahead.

The admonition was unnecessary. This one called Yudishtira, "Steadfast in Battle", was studying the undergrowth intensely. Indeed, intensity was an expression already fixed on his eighteen-year-old face by his deeply set eyes under straight brows, his forehead creased so early with two faint horizontal lines and his lips so obviously accustomed to a tight line of forced silence.

Otherwise his face was the classic Arya's—long, oval and pale, with a firm jaw and thin nose. His dark red-brown hair was tied back and coiled in a knot on his neck. He wore loose muslin leggings and nothing above the waist except a strand of gold coins at his neck and a fine red cotton mantle that he now tossed impatiently back over his shoulders. His body had the perfection of a young warrior's, but with the subtler lines of one who had prepared his muscles for conflicts but preferred to resolve them with words.

The second rider, Yudishtira's brother Bhima, finally brought his horse alongside. Bhima, "The Terrible", was only seventeen—a year younger, but already the biggest man in Arya memories. This "terror", however, had wrinkles from laughter around his blue eyes and enthusiastic red hair that sprang out about his ears no matter how tightly he tied it back. He too was half naked in the summer heat, his skin scarlet from the sun and from his thin pelt of red hair. Now his face was also flushed, from his struggle to stay mounted on a long-legged, iron-grey stallion with ears habitually laid back in anger.

"I think this demon," Bhima panted, "wants to carry me back to Hell with him."

When Yudishtira did not appear to hear, Bhima shrugged and turned to watch their younger brother join them. This was Arjuna, "The Silver One". He was sixteen, with pale blond hair that moved soft as river foam to the rhythm of the nervous, prancing colt between his thighs. A graceful warrior, Arjuna wore his bow and quiver like wings.

"Sorry you had to wait," Arjuna said. "I didn't want to wind him."

Yudishtira only nodded. Arjuna's colt was, in fact, too young for such a long ride. But he was Arjuna's favourite, the prettiest foal of the herd when it was born two years ago.

"As always, you have led us straight to the goal, Yudishtira," Arjuna said.

Yudishtira nodded again, wanting silence in these circumstances but choosing not to ask for it. The wind blowing from behind them paused. Yudishtira felt his filly tense under him, her ears pointed towards the cave under the left slope. He strained to see his prey among the swaying trees. A phrase ran through his mind, one they said about the coming decline of the world, the Age of Kali, of Strife: "The wise will be called fools and the hunters become the hunted."

The young mare's nostrils quivered, trying to be certain of some faint scent.

Suddenly Bhima's stallion reared. It twisted away from the direction of the lair, oblivious to the crumbling of the right edge of the ridge. For a moment Yudishtira saw his brother hanging in the sky above bouncing rocks and striking hooves.

Then it was over. Horse and rider were upright on sound legs, halfway down the slope.

Yudishtira turned away to let Bhima recover in dignity. How casually Yama the Fetcher has toyed with one of us, he thought. The god is travelling with us, then.

Yama escorted to Hell's penance, then on to Heaven's City of the Ancestors. Yet Yama was also the most potent preserver of life. Yudishtira fingered the gold at his neck, another guard against an early end. Not that he hadn't seen youths die with their parents' gold covering them from head to foot.

"I tell you," Bhima called as he climbed the slope and remounted, "horses should only pull chariots. Whoever heard of stalking a tiger without elephants or bush beaters?"

Yudishtira felt them both waiting for his answer, but he had nothing to say. It could not be denied—their uncle, King Drita, had taken an extraordinary risk with their lives merely to impress a Dasyu headman. Nor was it the first time their uncle had put them in danger. As usual, on the surface King Drita had had good cause. The black-skinned leader of the Nishada—the Dasyu people most prevalent in Drita's conquered lands—had arrived at the palace in Hastinapura the morning before, begging his Arya masters to rescue his village from a tiger. Which could only have meant that the villagers were desperate. Until now the Nishada had stubbornly ignored the advantages Arya rule could offer. They only complained endlessly about being moved about a little in their infinite forests. So it was at least true that the hunt was a fitting opportunity to make the local Dasyu properly grateful.

But why hadn't his uncle proposed a full hunt? Instead, after the Dasyu headman had pleaded before the assembly, the blind King Drita had turned to his nephew Yudishtira and said, "Why, it is the perfect task for you, our next king. Of course leave the young twins here—Sahadeva and Nakula should be with your mother. But take your brothers Bhima and Arjuna. The three of you will become great Nishada heroes."

The joke about "great Nishada heroes" had earned King Drita a long, loud laugh from his eldest son, Prince Suyodhana. Then the others present had joined in. The assembly's opinion of the safety of three youths hunting this tiger alone on horseback had not been solicited. Nor was it easily offered in the face of the blind King Drita's enthusiasm for the project.

As he recalled the moment, Yudishtira's fists clenched knuckle-white over his mount's mane. Dharma, duty, demanded obedience to one's elder, one's kin, and one's king— Drita was all three to Yudishtira.

But dharma, the eldest swore to himself, does not demand I put my brothers in the path of this absurd danger.

Arjuna snapped his reins at the rump of Bhima's stallion, giving his brother another kick to ride out. "We'll surprise this tiger. Show him *men's* faces, after all those Nishada women they've sacrificed to it."

Arjuna is trying to make jokes, Yudishtira thought. But his voice is too tense. And he is the most experienced hunter of the three of us.

"Couldn't they give it deer instead?" Bhima muttered. "A stupid idea anyway—trying to satisfy a meat-eater with your own people. Why do they make gods out of them? Snakes, tigers—gods should be protectors, not enemies."

Yudishtira dismounted and tied his mare facing into the wind. The other two imitated him. "Arjuna, I will approach the lair and you—"

Arjuna whirled. "You mean 'we'—we will approach it together."

"I mean," Yudishtira said quietly, "that in case our prey slips by me, Bhima will wait down in the clearing where it will have

26

to pass, and you, Arjuna, will stay up here where you can make the best shot if you must help us."

"An excellent plan of course, eldest brother, but—"

"Smell the rain on the wind?"

Arjuna hung his head. The tiger waited on his own ground —Arjuna would not cause delays until his brother had the disadvantage of rain too, when vision and hearing would be impaired. Yudishtira pulled on his wrist guards.

"Wait." Bhima's voice was almost panicked. "Send me instead."

"A future king who lets his younger brother kill his tigers for him—is that what you want them to say?"

The oblique reminder of their situation at the palace in Hastinapura silenced the two younger brothers. Arjuna took his stance on a jutting rock; Bhima followed Yudishtira down the slope. At the bottom Bhima made one more silent, pleading gesture, but Yudishtira walked away as if he had not seen it.

At the edge of the undergrowth that hid the lair Yudishtira strung his bow and selected two arrows—one he nocked, ready to shoot; the other rested between his fingers, ready to follow the first "like an ardent lover". A quiverful more were on his back, within a reach that had been honed until it was a reflex.

He took a step towards the thickets, then stopped. His trembling shamed him. It did not console him that he was only eighteen and in grave danger. Not going into those trees before him also did not enter his mind. His refusal to allow his uncle and cousins to call him a coward was his least reason. He would go because this hunt was his elder's wish for him. It was dharma.

His father's face was before him. He heard the vow again: "For you, Father, I now make dharma my friend, my shield, my only recourse. My obedience to dharma will be without flaw."

His brothers had not been asked to vow. They could err. It was enough that they saw dharma as tradition, law, the order of nature, one's personal vocation. Only Yudishtira was reared to see dharma as Master.

"Honesty is dharma's essence." Yudishtira could hear his teachers speaking. "And there is no dharma at all without self-honesty."

I am afraid of the animal in there.

And *I will kill it!* My uncle will *not* have his way.

Control. I have been prepared for today.

He aimed his mind: "Be still, be in harmony with the prey." Then he followed a rivulet into the trees.

The smell of tiger stung his nose as soon as the bamboo and sami trees closed around him. The certainty of his prey's presence struck him hard, as if he were already seeing the cruel, mottled face. He pushed on silently, barely moving his lips as he talked to his enemy. "True, your spoor smells old. But I know you are here. The way I knew the moment my father died. That is subtle awareness. The difference between you and me."

The coming rains made the forest restless. He forced a ray of the consciousness-that-is-hearing to penetrate past the rustling acacia pods and the scraping limbs of yellow pine. His consciousness of scents searched for more than the stink of old tiger wastes and decaying leaves. His vision sought stripes in the shadows.

A branch crashed behind him. Yudishtira spun and shot his two arrows.

Only the wind.

"Stupid!" he cursed under his breath. He drew two more arrows. "You see, Lord Tiger? Better to boast less about my 'awareness'. Pride is always the danger for warriors, isn't it?"

His heartbeats were almost drowning out his thoughts now. The heat in the still thickets was stifling and sweat poured off his face. He pushed farther in. "Yes, some would say this hunt is madness." He was glad no one could hear him whispering to himself like a toothless Nishada grandfather. "But I say that any of my four brothers could kill you alone. And Arjuna is Bharata's finest archer."

He ignored the rustle of a bird on his right. "But I out-shot Arjuna once. Only he knows, but I did."

He took ten more paces, then stopped again. Where were the monkeys that chattered when a tiger was stalking? Driven by drought to the rivers, of course, where the trees might still have fruit.

In his mind he rehearsed the Great Leap Aside. "Leap aside *as* you shoot," Guru Vaja used to shout from his chariot. "Shoot and then leap, and your families will perform funeral rites for you and your opponent, side by side."

In his awareness he saw claws—one of the vivid visions that could come to him without warning.

He brushed the stinging sweat from his eyes. "So you visit my future, Lord Tiger. But only the likeliest future. Vyasa says: 'By seeing the future, one can change it.' *That* is awareness, My Lord."

Above him he could sense the ridge through the trees. He had to be very close to the lair. Yet straight ahead he still saw only bamboo, bilva bush and sami. During Jyaistha, the hot, dry month before the rains, many trees lost their leaves. But in this damp pocket of the forest, with a spring apparently up ahead to feed the rivulet at his feet, too much was still green and growing.

Yudishtira bent low to try to see along the waterway. A branch snapped ahead of him. He aimed towards the sound, his bowstring at his ear. But this time he waited to loose the lovers' ardent whispers.

An animal cry. Yudishtira shot one arrow.

The cry became a scream of pain. No time to exalt. He fixed the second arrow.

But he did not loose it. The scream filled the forest but the screamer stayed where it was.

He took out a new "lover" to back up the arrow in his bow and waited.

Now the sound was only an angry moan. He still saw nothing. Was it dying or only wounded?

He stepped forward. To his left there was a rustle. To his left! He whirled. Orange and black blurred the green. A roar rushed him.

He leaped aside as he shot, his eyes fixed on his target— the white over the heart. The white was framed by claws. The claws of his vision moments ago. And the claws engulfed by flames. *Flames.* "Hear me!" he shouted.

But the roar had stopped. A tiger's body sprawled at his feet, in the spot where he himself had been standing before his leap.

"I am Yudishtira," he heard himself say out loud to his prey. Without knowing why, he glanced backwards, east towards the Ganges River and Hastinapura, but more southeast, towards Panchala.

The sound of wind in the branches broke the spell. He drew two more arrows and drove out the tiger's spirit.

Victory.

Victory! Jaya! He wanted to laugh, to shout to his brothers.

But no. He closed his eyes and composed himself, then began reciting the hymn he had received as he awoke that morning:

> Lord of the forests, forgive me
> Whose arrows have shown you the path
> To the four quarters of the earth.
> Depart for your new life,
> Rejoicing in your might . . .

Suddenly there was the cry from the direction of the lair again, softer this time.

Yudishtira nocked another arrow in his bow, but his hands shook now. He cursed himself for relaxing within three paces of a tiger's lair. He walked forward, not trying to be quiet any longer. Finally he stepped through the last curtain of vines and creepers. Crouched doubled over on a rock, amid the foulness of bones and skins, was a Nishada woman.

3

Never take up a weapon you can not accept the consequences of using. When you aim an arrow, consider its point: Where it goes, you go.

Guru Vaja

He asked me, "Why do your people want rulers, and even your rulers search for a samraj to rule the rulers?"

I said, "Because inside their minds there is an empty throne."

King Kuru

When the Nishada woman saw Yudishtira emerge from the woods, she slipped from the rock and dragged herself as far away from him as her tether would allow. But he was more interested in the injured sound she had just made again—the sound he had mistaken for a tiger. He came and knelt beside her where she lay curled up in the dirt, quivering with fear.

Another Nishada sacrifice, he thought, and they have used up the ugly ones. This one is almost sweet to look upon.

Then he saw the blood beneath her. Given its dark colour, he judged it to be from the stomach, not the heart, although she was curled too tightly for him to see.

The tiger, he thought. It attacked; then I shot towards her scream and its attention was drawn to me.

"Let me see where it clawed you." He hoped she understood Arya.

She shrank away violently. A pool of blood leaked across the earth.

31

"Woman, you live on Arya-conquered land and you are my subject. I am going to look at your wound."

She squeezed her eyes shut. "You kill me," she said clearly in the Arya tongue. The words were articulate with hate.

"Kill you! I killed the tiger to save you."

Now he wanted to shake the girl. Instead he sat back on his heels and concentrated on projecting calm. Moments passed, her trembling lessened, as did his anger.

"Accept my apologies, woman. Of course I have distressed you, having approached you improperly. But you have nothing to fear. I am Yudishtira, the eldest of King Pandu's—"

She screamed and hid her face.

"What kind of crazy Nishada are you?" he blurted out. "Better to have found another tiger than this."

He closed his eyes, displeased by his lack of control. It was despicable to attack even with words a person under one's own protection. In his mind he saw the bloodied ground. But why were there no claw wounds on her face or arms?

There was a crashing in the thickets, then shouts. "You did it! By all Indra's arrows, what a monster this tiger is."

Arjuna and Bhima burst into the clearing. "What's this?"

"A Nishada woman. I was too late." Yudishtira bent down again, a wad of moss in his hand to staunch the bleeding if she would let him.

Bhima stooped beside him. "You aren't going to tend a Dasyu's wound, are you?"

Arjuna walked around her. "She's almost dead, you know. Maybe better to fetch her own people, Yudishtira? Bring her mother and father?"

"Mother?" the woman whispered.

Tears shone on her cheeks now. She's just a girl, Yudishtira thought. He knelt down by her head. Curse this complication.

He ordered Arjuna to bring the horses down, then ride immediately to the Nishada village for their healer and the girl's parents. When Arjuna had gone, Yudishtira demonstrated the girl's reaction to "sons of Pandu". Bhima agreed—her fear of their father's name could only mean that rumours had been spread in advance of them. But it had to have been done the

32

day before, after the Nishada had accepted the aid of Pandu's sons.

And it could have been easily done only by a king, or a king's son.

Bhima was enraged. "We need to know how far this lie has gone. Shall I go to the other villages? In disguise?"

Bhima's whole body was trembling with eagerness to be off and doing something to combat this invisible blow. Yudishtira looked up and shrugged. His most impulsive brother would not have been his first choice. "At least go on foot."

Bhima grinned. "That horse will not worry you again. I will go as soon as I bring your kill here where you can watch it."

With his brother gone even so briefly, Yudishtira felt the desolate spirit of this place where so many innocent women had been torn and devoured. The girl still watched him, but she had withdrawn further into her fear and suffering. He felt ashamed that he had been distracted from trying to help her.

His thighs ached from kneeling. He shifted so that he sat cross-legged. He could not let himself be more comfortable than that while she was in pain. The pool of blood had stopped growing, but it was too large. He knew many kinds of plants could help if she would only let him apply them. He glanced around. He remembered he had been puzzled by something before Bhima arrived. But caring for her wound came first.

"Dear Nishada princess." Princess or not, he hoped she would like that. "You have nothing to fear. Your virtue is as safe with me as your life."

That seemed to help.

"But you *are* pretty." Yes, she liked that.

He aimed for the exact truth, just because he knew it was difficult for himself, an Arya. "You are beautiful. A beautiful Dasyu woman. Now, will you tell me your name?"

"Wood Rose. You killed me." She said the words simply this time, with a trace of sadness but much less fear.

He was about to chide her again when the missing thought came. His inner vision saw his arrow finding her.

He stood up and turned away, sickened. A lament Sage

Vyasa had once recited burst over him: "What I came to prevent, I caused. What I most vehemently denied, that was the truth."

He forced himself to turn back to her, to face what he had done. The blood in the earth made him shudder. "Wood Rose, let me see your wound."

"Prince Yudishtira, I am going to die." Her voice was sweet and unaccusing now.

He gestured towards her clenched arms. "This wound is from my arrow, isn't it?"

She nodded.

Bhima staggered back into the clearing. Through clouded eyes Yudishtira saw an orange and black mantle bowing his brother's broad shoulders. Tiger's fangs swayed at Bhima's breasts.

"A monster," Bhima said. He lowered the carcass near Yudishtira. "You killed him with one arrow. I saw the red heart blood—the other two went in when he was still. Impossible, but you did it. I would like to spread *that* story around about you."

Now tell him I killed her, Yudishtira thought.

No, Bhima will carry no more of my burdens today.

Bhima came and stood beside him over the girl, guessing the essence of his brother's feelings, if not their cause. Since their father had died when Bhima was nine, Yudishtira had been the father to the other four, as dharma required of the eldest. Yudishtira's other brothers had merely needed occasional paternal advice or discipline. Bhima's great, hurting heart had required much more. Being only a year older, Yudishtira had not fully grasped what was actually being demanded, but he had given Bhima his best. At seventeen, Bhima was at last becoming aware of this gift.

"Dearest brother." Bhima shifted his feet, not certain of his words. "It will be very sad if the tiger causes still another death. But please—could you not think a little about how many you have saved by killing it?"

Yudishtira knelt again beside the girl. "If you like. I will try."

"I will like it."

"If you must leave, go now. Journey with the speed of Lord Vayu's best winds."

"And you, dear brother, you remain here with the sweetest peace of Lord Dharma." Then Bhima was gone.

The rising wind loosened shingles from the old palace and sent them flying through the streets of Kampilya, South Panchala's capital. It was the same wind tormenting Yudishtira on his hunt, but in Kampilya the wind was the least of the people's worries. They were already barricaded behind shutters and doors, fleeing from the rumour that there were chariots again on the Hastinapura road. Five chariots. Exactly five.

It was only a year ago that Guru Vaja, the priest-born weapons-master to the princes of the blind King Drita in Hastinapura, had led his students down that same road to defeat King Drupada of Panchala and seize half the kingdom. Since then every king in Bharata was aware that this southern portion of Panchala was ripe for capture. Thus the sight of even one strange chariot started the residents filling quivers and tethering cows. But a rumour of five—five again, on the road from Hastinapura—emptied the streets and the mind.

For of Guru Vaja's thirty or more student warriors, the five sons of the late King Pandu had been the most formidable. And two above all: the princes Yudishtira and Arjuna. Arjuna, the middle son, the archer, had been terrible on that fateful day. Yudishtira, the eldest, had deployed his brothers as if he could see into the hearts of every Panchala defender and knew their secret fears and flaws. To South Panchala's citizens it seemed hopeless to expect that the sons of Pandu would not come again to finish what their teacher had bade them begin.

In her room in the women's quarters the new princess slept in spite of the alarm. Draupadi had been sent to rest after appearing faint at the noon meal. As the sky had darkened with dust and stormclouds and the fearsome rumours were being whispered in the hallway, Panchala's treasured "daughter of fire" had slipped into sweet unconsciousness.

She had rarely slept through the night since her "birth" ten days before. The cruel heat was the least of her torments. Mostly Draupadi lay awake in loneliness, in the emptiness of not even knowing whose voice she yearned to hear and on what part of the earth she ached to walk. The only one who shared her fate and might have comforted her was her brother. But Panchalya was being trained to lead South Panchala's army and she rarely saw him except when he drove by her window in the king's war chariot, a boy being prepared to stop what a thousand men had not.

For all these reasons Draupadi seldom slept. When she did, as she did on this afternoon, her dreams were full of flight and struggle.

The wind banged the shutters of her window. She tossed on her bed, caught in the beginning of a nightmare. A loose shingle tumbled over the eaves. Although her room was far from the palace's outer gates, in her dream those gates now shrieked on their hinges directly beneath her balcony. There was shouting. "The sons of Pandu. Make way." A high-pitched jangling began. Even in her sleep she felt a hurt inside her head from the sound, as if someone were shaking her spine.

The dreamer sat up. In her dream her cloak was beside her on the bed. She drew it on and went to the window. Through the blowing dust she could only see shapes—chariots in the gateway.

In her dream she ran down the stairs and into the courtyard. A war wagon drawn by four white horses had stopped in her path. On the other side of it there was another, larger chariot, drawn by Arya-bays. Three more chariots crowded behind. The wind blew the horses' silver manes forward, unnaturally. The chariots' banners blew towards her also, whipping in the gale. Thousands of brass bells on the harnesses jangled in those tones known to produce terror in an enemy's mind.

The warrior in the chariot nearest her had hair as pale and silvery gold as his horses', and it blew forward around his face like the mane of a young lion. His expression was arrogant, amused, life-loving. Seeing him, she knew as one only knows by instinct that this man desired her. This man intended to plough her field, to leave his seed in her.

But while she watched him with her newly awakened need to be filled by all of life, he looked at her with the self-possession of a warrior who ploughed his kingdom's choicest, and even then only when there was no fighting to be done. He stepped down from his chariot, his eyes now on the palace behind her. Casually he tapped the noses of his war horses, the signal to wait. He strode by Draupadi towards the inner palace.

Yet she was strangely unaffected by his leaving. She stood transfixed before his team of white mares—like them, she did not move from where he had left her. She stared into the dark orbs of the horses' eyes, which were as haughty, wild and overly familiar with her as his eyes had been.

Something in her made her want to touch the white foreheads. These were like ordinary horses as Heaven was to Earth. She raised a hand and she moved it forward, watching herself, and knowing, without knowing, what would happen.

The four horses reared over her. Their hooves carved the space around her head and their harness bells screamed at her. The war team trumpeted neighs that sounded like Death's Deliverer.

She could not move, even as the animals bared their teeth and opened their mouths to rip her flesh. She knew they were trained to kill enemies on foot. She knew she might be safe if she could reach the door behind her. But she could not move.

"Hear me!" The words hurtled at her from the second chariot. The horses dropped down on stiffened legs and averted their heads, their eyes rolled back in terror of the voice.

In her dream, servants now rushed up to pull her to safety. She half heard them whispering, "The eldest son of Pandu. God Yama, save us."

She looked across the empty chariot to the other, with the warrior who had commanded the horses. He loomed over her. She could not see his face through the dust-darkened space, but his clothes were those of a king, not a prince. He said, "I am Yudishtira."

Draupadi woke at dusk. From the normal sounds in the women's quarters around her she knew the chariots had been only a rumour. She fought back the tears that always came when awareness returned, bringing back the relentless confusion. It had been another uncontrolled dream—she knew it even as she felt for dust on her feet and a robe on her shoulder. She sensed somehow, from Before, that these intense dreams were a sign that she was weakening.

But the dream had not frightened her—that indicated a certain new strength. It was only a dream, and if it was of these dreaded sons of Pandu, they could not be the demons the Panchalas made them. She had seen that they spoke and desired like mortal men.

She rose and went to the window. A great drumming was starting on the surrounding rooftops. The first rain had begun.

4

Their warriors want to conquer Earth; their priests to conquer Heaven. Their wisest men say "conquer self". But the Nishada ask, why must they conquer anything at all?

a headwoman of the Nishada

He who understands the dweller-in-the-body to be the slayer, and he who takes him to be the slain, both fail to perceive the truth. He neither slays nor is slain.

Krishna, as recorded in the *Bhagavad Gita*

At dusk the growl of thunder began to spread, like a quarrel in a pack of dogs. Between the dead tiger and its lair, Yudishtira still crouched over Wood Rose, after having put what herbs he could find on the wound and having carefully pillowed her head. The arrow he had left for the healer to remove.

He looked up to watch the clouds finally seal off the last window to the sky. The atmosphere was suddenly hot, dense and motionless. The whole earth was trapped under mountains of clouds that slowly twisted and expanded and pushed closer to the ground. From every tree the cicadas increased their droning. Yudishtira was soaked with sweat that would not dry.

Much as he longed for the downpour that would end this torment, he wished it would wait until Arjuna returned with the healer. After such loss of blood, rain at evening would bring the fever to her.

He glanced around. He could move her under a tree before the downpour began. It would be drier at first. But soon each leaf would be a spout and they would be more miserable there than in the open. They could move under the overhanging cliff that had been the tiger's lair. But he could not bring himself to sit among the unpurified bones of its Dasyu victims. No, the rain would be clean. It was Indra's blessing.

The trees bent under a sudden convulsion of wind. Then the season of storms began.

Yudishtira tried to hold his cloak over the girl but it was useless. In only a moment they were soaked and soon after she was shaking violently. Yudishtira bent down to try to shelter her. She whispered something through her chattering teeth. He bent closer. She said it again: "Hold me."

He gently drew her into his arms and heard himself ask, "Did you have a husband, Wood Rose? Or a lover?"

"No, Prince."

With his free hand he rearranged his bow and quiver, avoiding her eyes, which were watching him. Now his question embarrassed him. She was facing death, and he had sounded like someone seeking *surata* with her.

Still, he could understand in himself what he also condemned. Shortcomings unexamined, so he had been taught, only led to deeper sin. The thought of surata was due to his age and inexperience: This girl, so light from loss of blood and spirit, was the first girl of his own age he had ever touched in any way.

Surata itself he was expert at. He could prepare a woman's field gently or wildly, "for any crop", and plough a delicate furrow or a broad bed. He could pleasure her a hundred ways. Two hundred ways. But his practice had all been with the courtesans his mother had chosen for him—older women who would be most skilful, most responsive, and above all most detached. Except during these lessons, he had never touched any woman in that way. No woman his own age. No woman he liked. Bhima took boat rides with a merchant's daughter; Arjuna had girls reciting spells to win him. But although there were several pleasant and eligible girls pursuing him, the crown prince was expected to control himself—successors to the throne could not be seeded randomly around Bharata, in just any woman's womb.

So for all my caution, he thought, my first embrace is from a Nishada girl, arranged by an arrow.

My own arrow.

If my plough prepares itself for a Dasyu, then at least I must honour her with the recognition of my desire. Admit she is beautiful. Honour that. Admire her smooth skin. The gold in her cheek so near my own. The soft hair on my shoulder.

She must not die!

The girl was shivering. He pulled her tighter against his body. She still watched him. "Rain?"

He nodded. He put his lips near her delicately formed ear so she would hear him above the sound of water pounding to earth. "I'm sorry you are cold."

"I am glad to see the rain." Her face glistened in the twilight.

"Soon you'll see your parents too."

She didn't answer. He studied the subtle fullness of her lips, so near his own. "It tires you to talk, doesn't it?"

She nodded.

"I will ask nothing more of you, sweet Wood Rose, after one question." He swallowed and prepared his heart. "What do they say now about the name Pandu?"

"You destroy," she whispered. "You burn the forests. Kill everything. You love to kill." She shivered. "You bring the 'kali'."

"The Age of Kali? Of destruction? This is not true, Wood Rose. None of it. Someone has deliberately told you lies. And this 'age of strife' the priests speak of—it is a time without dharma, it is—"

Her eyes had closed. He wondered if he would ever see them watching him again. He touched her face shyly with his fingers. "The sons of Pandu only destroy tigers," he said gently.

But hearing himself, he had to correct his words: "Or, if we Arya burn forests, it is because we need to clear land for pastures and crops. There is always more forest."

Again the truth was reshaping itself, in a vision of homeless Dasyu drifting away into smoke and shadows.

"We Arya try to uphold creation by following the path of dharma." He stopped yet again. "At least as we see that path."

Why do I trouble her with such pompous speech?

Arjuna has to come soon. I must somehow keep her aware

41

until her parents come. And their healer. These Nishada can heal anything that happens in a forest.

He felt her shivering stop suddenly. "Wood Rose!" He shook her. Her skin was slippery under his hands.

At last her lips moved weakly. "I understand you, Prince." Shame about his panic swept over him. He should let her go to Yama in peace. He was so uncertain of what to do. After all his education, so uncertain.

Keep her spirit in her body. Talk to her.

"Little Wood Rose. Little Dasyu. What can I tell you? I am an Arya of the Kuru family. But you know that. Kuru because of King Kuru, the first to cross the Sindhu. But there have been three Kurus since. Other kings too. Drita now." He stumbled on, desperately trying to hold her awareness with his will. "You are Dasyu. My great great grandmother was Dasyu. No one talks about that though. Veda Vyasa is my grandfather. Strange, isn't it? His grandmother—Do you know Sage Vyasa? They say he spends time with Dasyu. His enemies say many things. But never to his face. There is no one like him when he speaks of Veda."

With his free hand he rubbed under his gold *niksha*-coin collar at the trickling water. Then he gently stroked her hair. "My father lived in the forest. He went there to save us from the destruction the priests prophesy. This Age of Kali."

Yudishtira fell silent. The blackness of night had finally closed around them. It felt like something heavy, something more than mere lack of light.

"Do you wonder what my father was trying to do in the forest? No, of course you don't. But I must talk to you."

He shifted his aching legs. "It is not a secret. Yet I must beg you not to ask me." He suddenly felt exhausted. "So I must tell you something else. Something that I am indeed very ashamed of."

He was incomprehensibly tired in every part. He thought it was the darkness. Staring into darkness.

"Have you heard of Prince Suyodhana? He is my cousin. A year younger, but raised to be crown prince until I came among them."

Yudishtira stopped. The truth now. "My cousin hates me. Have I caused this? I didn't mean to."

His cousin's face seemed to float among the black slashes of rain. Suyodhana, always at the edge, watching, taunting, tattling. Spoiling the very centre of their lives.

"With all my heart, Wood Rose, I do not want to hate him back."

He felt for her breath. It was faint but even. He allowed himself to fall silent, thinking back as he had a thousand times, reviewing his every behaviour since he had been brought to Hastinapura and set over his cousin as successor to the throne.

But in time his thoughts drifted into half-dreams. Excitement had kept him aware the night before. Then rising before dawn. The hunt all day. Heat. Claws. If only he could sleep a moment. Guru Vaja's face was before him now. "A warrior takes rest where he can. Sitting, standing. If you must, leave the senses awake, resting the parts of the mind you can spare."

In his half sleep he saw on the surface of his awareness the reflection of a net. It seemed as though it was settling over him. He could not see it clearly, but he could feel it. He couldn't move, couldn't cry out.

Terror seized him. He did see through the net now. Faces. Suyodhana. And *yavana* foreigners. Yavanas—those from the west, so cold and sophisticated. They were laughing like jackals. "What kind of *man* follows your 'dharma' in *these* times?"

The net was gone. He pressed the trembling Wood Rose to his heart. "In Indra's name, come soon, Arjuna."

More time passed. Crouched in the darkness and rain, the Arya crown prince rocked the Dasyu girl gently. Near midnight, he finally allowed himself to sleep.

A snarl jerked Yudishtira awake. At first he thought it was the beast in the net, the yavana-faced jackal in his dream.

"Wood Rose!" He clutched at her.

The snarl again. A wolf took form in the rain. Not mere jackals then. The blood from her and the tiger—it had drawn the wolves, even in the rain.

The animal faded back into the blackness. Yudishtira

43

glanced over his shoulder. He cursed himself for not having moved them under a tree where his back would have been protected.

With his free hand he felt through the rawhide cover of his quiver. Eighteen shafts. He removed two, then reluctantly laid Wood Rose across his legs and nocked one arrow to his bow. He also loosened his iron-tipped bone knife.

A pack could easily be thirty. With so few arrows, his best strategy would be frightening them off with a surprise. Perhaps kill their leaders at the outset. Failing that, he would have to wait until the end when they became overly bold.

Either way, protect her.

Protect her? My arrowhead is in her stomach.

Where is Arjuna?

In trouble too somewhere. While I sleep.

Yudishtira scanned the darkness. There was no leaving now. No way to search for Arjuna without abandoning Wood Rose. And dharma was clear on it: First defend the defenceless and wounded.

Nor would this battle end soon. The wolves would be patient. They knew how to wear down prey. There was blood here—that was hope enough for them. Some would doze while others watched. But he could not sleep so safely.

He stiffened with anger. They want her body!

They smell the blood I have spilled.

But I was trying to protect her. Trying to follow dharma.

Intentions. They never satisfied your teachers and they should not satisfy you. He could hear their pronouncement still: "To kill is a sin. To kill someone under one's protection is unspeakable sin."

He watched the darkness, his arrow nocked and his bow half stretched, and let his mind go back to the puzzle. To an autumn afternoon. A keen blue sky and the delirious songs that the birds sang only after the rains. He and his four brothers sat in a half circle on the ground, facing the learned recluses in the forest. He himself was only ten then, Bhima nine, Arjuna eight, the twins seven.

"To kill is always a sin," the teachers said. "Individually and collectively, peace, happiness and prosperity require *ahimsa*, doing no harm. Every person strengthening every other. Ahimsa is the most profitable course too. Action brings reaction, and therefore harm brings harm, but non-harm brings non-harm. Any other principle of conduct is illogical."

To Yudishtira the birds sang more sweetly as his teachers wove the cloth of peace with their speech. The forest fairly shimmered with light and shadow. Until that other voice.

"No!"

It had shattered the day. It came from a figure sitting behind the others, back at the edge of a grove of sala trees. He was an old monk, long lost in the silence of pure being. His eyes were on no one but Yudishtira.

"Ahimsa is only dharma's servant." The voice was hoarse with age, fierce from his long austerities. "Tell this boy that the dharma of a warrior is to protect the weak against evil. Always."

The air itself had seemed to shudder at the old hermit's words. Yudishtira had wanted to flee before the voice could reach him again, but he knew there was no place to hide.

"And a *king*," the voice roared, "—a king must protect the entire world against evil."

The figure faded back into the trees. The other teachers had been quick to say that "only the ineffective king must resort to weapons, however. The strong king eliminates the cause of evil . . ."

Yudishtira could not listen to them any longer. Utterly confused by his elders for the first time in his life, he had felt a terrible tension. He had been certain no one had noticed. But suddenly from the low branch of the banyan tree where he always sat, Sage Vyasa was laughing at him. Laughing at them all. "To prevent the use of weapons, why not begin by teaching children not to envy one another?"

In the darkness and rain Yudishtira cried out, "It's not me who envies. It's Suyodhana!"

"Wood Rose, do you hear me? Listen to me!"

Suddenly a solid form swept in from the liquid darkness. It snatched at the tiger's farthest leg and tugged, testing, growling at Yudishtira. One of its ears stood up alert on the silhouetted head, the other was a jagged stump. Yudishtira awkwardly drew his bow, having to hold it horizontal because he could not stand.

The arrow flew and the wolf sprang back, but the yelping that followed was more angry than hurt. Nothing more could be seen.

"I will have to do better than that. But have no fear, Wood Rose. My brother Arjuna will come soon. Or we'll go ourselves at first light. They'll leave us then." But the slackness of her limbs told him she was not aware of the wolves or the night.

He yearned to move his hands from the bow to feel for her breath. "Keep your awareness on my words, Wood Rose. Listen to me. Let me think. My boyhood. Yes. The woods were all I knew until I was twelve."

He smelled the wolves first this time. Two lunged in for Wood Rose's ankle. He shot after them. There was no snarl, no yelp. Sixteen arrows left.

"My father used to carry me on his shoulders." He could hear his own voice sounding high and desperate. "He sang songs about porcupines and cuckoos."

The one-eared wolf showed itself again.

"But when my father talked to me—"

The wolf watched Wood Rose, the living but wounded one. Testing the prey's strength for the others to see.

"All he would speak of was dharma."

Yudishtira took aim, always talking. Must not miss again. Shoot at a standing animal. Wait for it to stop.

"Then Father died and we came to Hastinapura." He was not hearing his own words any more. "I thought I would faint from the heat. Grandfather Gangeya walked beside me. We all call him Grandfather but he isn't one. None of us calls Vyasa Grandfather. Grandfather Gangeya said, 'Well, Yudishtira, your father wanted to raise a perfect king. Did he?'" Yudishtira nervously checked his bowstring's tension. "I said, 'I can't be a perfect king yet. I'm still not any kind of king.' And he said, 'It's to your credit that you've noticed.'"

Five wolves leaped in. Instinctively he swung his bow to drive them back. "Then he asked me what I knew about women. I said, 'Women?'"

One Ear was back, tearing at the leg of the tiger. Yudishtira shot. The great wet body leaped towards them, an arrow in its chest. Yudishtira blocked the leap with his arms. Jaws snapped in the air. The body dropped beside Wood Rose, shuddered, and was still. He pushed it away with his foot as best as he could.

Now he heard the pack circle behind him. At least six rushed in. He shot two arrows; two wolves fell. The rest faded back into the rain.

Thirteen shafts remained under the cover of the quiver. "You see?" he said to Wood Rose, still lying across his lap. "They run like deer."

It grew quiet. They were letting his recent alarm subside. Letting the deeper fatigue that would follow do their work for them. He closed his strained eyes a moment, using his ears to watch the darkness.

But it all required concentration, and it was his mind that most longed for respite.

He clutched his bow tighter even as his awareness dimmed. Caution!

The attack was from within: it was the old nightmare. He pulled back from it, as he had been taught. "Do not give it your attention," his teachers had said.

Yudishtira opened his eyes, torn by love and anger. It was his father's doing, this dream. This terror of the Age of Vice. The Age of Kali. The forest-dwelling priests taught acceptance —the seasons change, the ages change likewise. But his father had wanted to stop time.

Acceptance was not what Vyasa taught either. Re-create time. See the future, try to shape it. "For the prophecies may be visions of manhood interpreted by a frightened boy."

Or they may be the gods' warnings.

Yudishtira let himself drift. Only to gather his strength, he told himself. The oblivion was sweet. He could hear the wolves padding about in the rain. When they trot faster, then I will shoot. Only rest until then. Sleep until then.

Danger! But this time the vision's grip was too tight: The dice, their cruel eyes, the throw of one—the losing throw, "kali". Then the black chariot with the driver who spread the blackness that killed.

He leaped to his feet, firing arrows into the night.

There was nothing there. The silence said the wolves had moved on.

He sank back down, horrified by his lack of control.

Wood Rose.

She lay in a pool of water. Her flesh was cool, her breath no longer flowed.   Yudishtira caught her up against him and uttered one cry, then laid her out on the earth.

He arranged her limbs and garment, finding his way by touch rather than seeing and so, inadvertently, feeling all of her. All her cold, woman's parts.

He crossed her hands on her heart. Then forced himself to move his palms and fingers back over her in order to find the shaft of his arrow. He gently withdrew it. For a moment blood, still warm, spurted from the wound. Then the cold rain received that too. The young though eldest son of Pandu broke the arrow and threw it aside.

Standing up, knife in hand, he planted his legs and stiffened his spine as a warrior must when keeping watch over a body that once housed an honoured spirit.

5

The gamester goes to the gaming table, radiant in person, asking himself, "Shall I win?"

Rig Veda

Leaving Yudishtira and Bhima, Arjuna had trotted his colt through the dusk along the easily followed path to the village. Which had left him free to think about his eldest brother's feat. Could he have done the same against that tiger? Almost certainly. But would he have agreed to attempt it at all? It annoyed him, but he supposed that in Yudishtira's place he would have had no choice.

The tiger was obviously fat from so many easy meals. Hardly expecting an arrow. Still, the wind and dense growth had made it absurdly dangerous—Arjuna was still bothered that he had not foreseen Yudishtira's insistence on going in alone.

The third-eldest Pandu irritably intercepted another branch before it could slap him. A path used by stumpy little unmounted Dasyu was almost useless to a horseman. He kicked the colt faster.

Suddenly the ground rushed at him. Heavy cords blocked his vision and weighted his back. Above him his horse screamed in pain, thrashing where it hung by one splintered leg. Arjuna fought the web that covered him but it only tightened.

Hearing excited shouts in the Nishada tongue, Arjuna forced himself to lay still. His danger was extreme now—to be netted was bad, but if the net was unwatched one might escape in time, with a good knife. Nishada nearby, however, meant arrows and clubs could only be next, especially if they thought their prey was still conscious. It was a cowardly way to hunt

49

and an honourless way to die. How stupid could he be, riding into a Dasyu deer trap?

His heart was racing. He forced himself to be utterly motionless. But knowing it was growing dark, he risked opening one eye slightly.

They already stood over him—they could move through the forest like spirits. But their nocked arrows still rested on slack bows.

Now he almost laughed with relief. If you could see your stupid faces, he thought—didn't expect to net an Arya prince, did you? You know that if you touch me, every warrior in Bharata will see that you pay.

But they were not setting him free. Or even whining their apologies in garbled Arya. They were tightening the net cautiously, watching for him to try to reach for his knife. When the cords were taut around his arms, they took the weapon, and he was defenceless.

Arjuna had to admit the roasting horse smelled fine. Too bad it was his own white colt, and that his hands were tied so he couldn't strangle the filthy Nishada who had butchered it. Now they were drunk too—he could hear their outlandish singing above the downpour which had begun an hour ago.

I must escape from here, he thought. Now.

"Woman. You do understand me, don't you? Don't lie to me now."

He hardly expected an answer from the girl they had left here in this stinking hut to guard him. But she gave him a polite affirmative in good Arya.

Arjuna was suddenly interested. She was not so ugly as the others either—short and dark like them all, but prettier hair, and round as four melons above and below, narrow at the waist —all the way he preferred. Much like the one Yudishtira was wanting to save, actually. But Arjuna was thinking he would do whatever he must to this one. Anything to return to his brothers before they came after him and walked into trouble.

He studied her carefully, looking for a weakness. "Why didn't your others understand me?"

She explained that she was a headwoman's daughter –

another Nishada habit Arjuna disliked was their way of letting women run things so much. This woman not only knew Arya, but made her children learn it too. The elder Nishada would not learn, though. "They hate all Arya."

Far from angering Arjuna, her daring slightly raised his opinion of her. But he scowled at her anyway. "They didn't mind coming to us for help with that tiger."

"Since you don't allow us our traditional weapons."

"Poisoned arrows? Poison is a coward's weapon."

"A hunter's weapon," she said. "We don't kill humans. Arya do that."

He ignored her. He had noticed his bow and quiver standing against the wall on the other side of the fire. "Have you ever seen a bow like that? Up close?"

She tilted her head and smiled enough to let him know she saw his intention. He looked away. He could imagine Guru Vaja growling over his prize student's predicament: "No weapons? Absurd. If you have a mind, you have a weapon."

And if *I* have a woman, Arjuna thought. He smiled at the memory of the horse-tender's daughter who had told him about the white colt before his cousin Suyodhana could claim it. He fixed his gaze again on the Nishada girl, this time at length and without speaking, in order to make her self-conscious. When the moment was right he smiled sweetly to break her tension. "You're very pretty. You know that? What is your name?"

She raised her head high. "Lotus."

"Lotus, I am wondering how you Nishada expect to keep your skins on you after treating me like this."

"Perhaps we expect a reward, Arjuna Son of Pandu. If we don't kill you ourselves."

"So at least you really do know who you've caught in your net, Lotus the Headwoman's Daughter. And who do you expect to reward you? The king of the demons?"

"Prince Suyodhana will reward us, Stupid Arya Who Rode into a Net."

"Suyodhana will reward you? The Nishada are truly fools. He's my own cousin, and my brother will soon be his king.

Don't you see? You are holding captive the brother of your future ruler."

"We received a warning about you sons of Pandu. All five of you are liars, murderers—"

"'Murderers'? 'Liars'? That's Suyodhana! He's the liar!" Arjuna wrenched at the vines.

"Maybe all Arya are liars."

Again he heard Guru Vaja's sarcastic voice: "Anger and pride, the only enemy a warrior need fear." He controlled his rage and asked questions. The messenger had come only the night before, all but proving Suyodhana's involvement.

"Lotus, don't you see how he's used you? Your people will be punished anyway—you've attacked an Arya and so they'll be forced to punish you. Forced."

She reacted, but she hid it well. "Yes, your cousin must hate you," she said. "Or you hate him." She turned her back. "I care nothing for Arya quarrels."

Arjuna was fully alert to the urgency of escape now—these Dasyu might well decide he could bring a bigger reward dead than alive. What infuriated him was that perhaps they were right. He gave his complete attention to the strategy he must follow. "My cousin's handsome, isn't he?"

"He was handsome enough."

"So he's been here."

"Once."

He saw her stiffen her shoulders. Just how well had this girl known Suyodhana? His cousin was famous for forcing Dasyu women under his plough, counter to dharma though it was. "Lotus, he's an evil man and you know it."

She did not answer. He laughed a little. "At least admit that I'm better-looking."

She turned back towards him and he saw that she had softened. "Yes, you are better-looking."

"And did he kill the tiger for you? I did."

The girl's eyes widened. Arjuna hoped this small lie, only to a Dasyu and a woman, would be acceptable before Lord Dharma. After all, it was to hide his brother.

Questioning her further, he learned that Suyodhana had come to inspect cattle last new moon. Very thin cattle, for the cattle tenders had burned the forests, then brought herds in too soon, so that the rains had washed away everything but the rocks. On this topic Lotus finally lost control. "Didn't your king know about even this?"

"Suyodhana's father, King Drita, is still king in my dead father's place until spring. And he is blind."

"Blind! And you obey him!"

"He has advisers," Arjuna said bitterly. He wondered if he could ever forgive his great grandfather, his grandfather, and his father for the accumulation of mistakes that had put his blind uncle on the throne.

"Lotus, is there nothing about us Arya that you admire? Not our fortresses and cities? Our music and poetry? Our gods? Your gods are cruel, but ours are satisfied with the butter and cakes carried to heaven by Agni's sacred flames. In return they bring us rain, crops and victory. You have to admit that Arya enjoy far more victories."

"You also enjoy chariots, war elephants and iron-tipped arrows," she said. "Give them to Nishada and you would enjoy defeat."

They both heard a muffled cry. Lotus moved to the door and looked out, holding the flap so it did not reveal the firelight. After a long moment she drew back sharply. Her face showed panic.

"What, woman? Speak!"

"The Desperate," she whispered. "Homeless Nishada. They are killing people in their sleep!"

"I thought you Nishada didn't kill humans."

"Not until we're driven from our homes and starving!"

There were more soft cries above the sound of rain. Arjuna recognised the pattern—the invaders would work from tent to tent, killing any children or old people they found, then surprise the rest at the feast and finish off the clan.

"Cut me loose, Lotus."

She stared at him, then drew a knife from her waist and slashed the vines. He snatched up his weapons.

"They may use poison arrows." Her voice was even; her self-control had returned.

"They'll never see me to make me a target."

"I want to help you," she said.

He paused and looked into her dark eyes, then instructed her to stay with her back to his, to be his vision from behind.

Outside, at first it was all blackness and pounding rain. Lotus motioned him towards some bales of thatch. But even here they were easy targets, and in spite of his brave words to the girl, the thought of dying alone among semi-animals terrified him.

Then he began to see the flitting darkness within the raining darkness and his confidence returned. This I can do, he thought. As he nocked his first arrow he remembered how Guru Vaja had tried, for the sake of limiting pride, to keep his best archery student from knowing too soon about his peculiar ability to see in the dark. But one night in Arjuna's thirteenth winter the wind had blown out the light while he was repairing a bow, and Arjuna had discovered his uncanny power.

Arjuna began adding a rain of arrows to the torrents of water, his hands moving swiftly between bow and quiver. As the arrows found their marks the flitting shadows screamed. This finally roused the men and women of Lotus's tribe from their gluttony in the central hut. They rushed out into the night, shouting drunkenly for their children.

Now Arjuna had to be more careful, to discern the weaving, well-fed Nishada from the alert, starving ones. Both sides were screeching threats in their bestial style of warfare.

"Behind you, on the left," Lotus said flatly.

Arjuna whirled and shot. The arrow entered the Nishada's chest.

"Now on your right."

An arrow pierced a throat even before Arjuna had fully turned.

Torches flashed alight throughout the village. In their red circles Arjuna killed five more. Then two by the nearest hut and one Lotus spied behind him. Finally the burning pitch branches illumined only the enemies' retreat, and the only sounds were parents keening, children crying, and rain.

As the tumult lessened the Nishada clan gathered around Arjuna, bowing down in terror of what was coming next. But even if they had stood erect, Arjuna would have been a head taller than any of them, and cowering as they were he was forced to see them only as ignorant children. It would hardly become him to kill them all because they had caught him in a net that he should have avoided.

He let his energy of battle subside, and as he did he felt only one concern: to return to his brothers. They had to be in danger if one of them had not come after him.

But he was uncertain of the way, having entered the village with his head between a Nishada's legs. Now when he ordered them, through Lotus, to lead him back, they refused. Lotus shouted something in Nishada—no doubt that the tiger was dead. Arjuna started off alone anyway. Then he remembered Yudishtira's orders, which he did not dare disobey. "Lotus, with me must come your healer and the parents of the girl you left out there to be killed."

Suddenly they were all coming, falling over each other as they tried to thrust back the dripping branches for him. Others crowded on his heels, determined to hold some kind of rain protection over his head.

Lotus ran beside him. Between breaths she said, "My mother is also her mother—it was my sister Wood Rose they left for the tiger."

"A headwoman's daughter?" He chose not to discuss her sister's injury. Lotus would see soon enough. "Did you ever think of sacrificing deer instead of females?"

Lotus did not answer for a time. "That is not what the tiger desired. Do you Arya toss rocks into your gods' fires when you know they want your cows' butter?"

The men up ahead suddenly stopped, obviously still afraid to go closer to the tiger's den. Arjuna pushed past, feeling more than ever how long he had been gone.

In the dark the white of the tiger's belly caught his eye first. The carcass was stretched out beside the body of the girl. The Nishada following him into the clearing would see for themselves what their tiger worship had cost them. He walked on, searching for his brothers.

Yudishtira was standing under a sandalwood tree, leaning along a great, drooping branch. They rushed to embrace each other. But Yudishtira was stiff in his arms. The eldest explained

Bhima's absence and asked what had caused the delay. Arjuna told him quickly.

"But what has happened here, Yudishtira?"

"I killed her," he said. "The cry that I shot at—it was her."

"I'm sorry she died, Yudishtira. But you also tried to save her. Anyone would have shot at that sound."

"Yes, anyone would have."

The weariness and finality in his brother's voice told Arjuna to leave him alone. He walked back towards the Nishada. When you lead it has to be like that, Arjuna told himself.

No it doesn't. Why doesn't it bother Bhima when Yudishtira shuts us out like this? Arjuna wiped the rain from his eyes. There was something here he desperately wanted to understand. We've shared the same food, the same mother, even the same nightmares. Why can't he share his pain with me?

He can't forget he's the oldest.

Brothers. I would like one real friend.

"Arjuna!"

He rushed back to Yudishtira.

"Arjuna, who attacked these people?"

He described the homeless band. "I don't think they'll cause us more trouble."

"But they will no doubt attack this Nishada village again."

"Excuse me, eldest brother, but who cares if they do?"

"These Nishada are our subjects."

Arjuna did not like the direction this conversation was taking. "Whatever you say, of course. Yes, I suppose we can send back some warriors to track down the troublemakers and finish them off."

"No. We must go ourselves. On foot, as soon as it is light. Please find a Nishada you can trust to take our horses towards home."

"Yudishtira, it's true I drove these people off with arrows once, when they couldn't see me, but there must be forty or fifty of them. This time—"

"Yes, this time we may not surprise them. However, I need you with me."

Arjuna was stunned. "Did you think I'd let you go alone?

Why, even if you commanded me not to come with you—"

"Then you would obey me and stay behind. But I do need you, Arjuna."

It was mid-morning but as grey as before dawn. Draupadi lay awake in her bed. She did not need to go to the window to know the view from her room, for yesterday's storm had not abated. Only the veils of rain were new. Through them she would see four rooftops, a log wall, a field, a dark line of trees, and sky, the same as she had seen the day before and the day before that.

Nor did she need to go down to the dining hall to know whom she would meet. There would be those called priests— whether the wealthy singers and performers of rituals or the mendicants and teachers drawn in from the forests by her "birth". There would be those called warriors, although these included fat barons and silly princes who could hardly string a bow. And there would be those called the wealth-makers— traders, landowners, cattle breeders. The women and family members present would also call themselves "priests", "warriors", or "wealth-makers", for she had seen that all were anxious to be known as anything else but a Dasyu, a servant or a foreign slave.

She disliked almost all of them. They fawned on her and hoped to please her by satisfying her slightest need, without ever guessing her only real craving.

She rose from her bed. She had to be free of walls.

She brushed past the attendants waiting outside her door and strode into her brother's room, which was near hers only because both of them had threatened not to eat if it were otherwise.

He was not there. She took a pair of muddy leggings from the floor and a rough war-tunic from the bed. She pulled on his leather boots and went back out into the hall.

By now a small crowd of servants had gathered. Drawing on the tunic, she pushed past them, descended the stairs, crossed the inner and outer courtyards and stopped before the palace gate, rain streaming off her head and shoulders. "Open!" she shouted.

The gateman peered out of his covered perch on the wall. "For whom?"

"Princess Draupadi. Open the gate."

Silence.

"Have you not heard me? Open!"

An attendant behind her was trying to keep her covered under a sheepskin. "I beg your forgiveness, Princess, but it is not allowed."

She whirled around. "Not allowed? This gate opens fifty times a day. I hear it from my room." She turned and shouted up at the gateman. "This gate opens for the lowest labourer. They call me a princess. Open it."

"He is not allowed to open it *for you*," the attendant whispered again.

"Then I am a prisoner?" she shouted to all of them.

"Not a prisoner." It was King Drupada himself, trotting out to the gate under a canopy held by his personal guards. "We only wish to keep you very, very safe, dear daughter," he panted.

"My brother goes out."

"What would you wish to do out there? No woman goes out alone. No, and even your brother does not go out on foot like a Dasyu. Come in out of the rain, Draupadi. Come to the hall and see the jugglers who've come for your entertainment."

"Let me out!"

She had screamed it. Then she saw the hundred faces staring at her, many from the court itself. She felt shame at her loss of control.

For a moment she imagined she saw in a rain-misted side street the two chariots of yesterday's dream. But they were mere bullock carts, waiting for her to be gone so they could proceed with the work of the day. She was only an illusory princess seeing illusions, an obscurity in the way of real life.

She walked through the crowd with dignity, following a servant back to her room.

The forest was taking on dim shapes and shades in the rain as Arjuna returned to the clearing with Yudishtira's young bay mare and Bhima's grey stallion. The Nishada had taken the bodies of the girl and the tiger and had gone, but Yudishtira was still there under the sandalwood tree. He thanked Arjuna for bringing the horses. Arjuna hunched down into his woollen mantle in response, taking what shelter he could from the rain and his brother's scrutiny.

"Arjuna, the Nishada who will take the horses to the herder's hut—who did you ask to do it?"

Arjuna pulled hard on the reins of the soaked, dejected horses, but there was no escaping now. "The only one of them I know, Yudishtira."

"The one who is Wood Rose's sister?"

"She's better out here than you or I."

"Arjuna, her family has already lost one daughter because of us."

Arjuna turned away to fumble with a bridle. "I know these things with women always happen to me. I understand it less than you do." He turned back, knowing his brother's eyes had never left him. "She saved me from several arrows in the back. Yudishtira, *she begged me*." Arjuna was again seeing the Dasyu girl kneeling at his feet.

Yudishtira nudged a rock with his toe, then looked off into the forest, as if seeing visions again. Arjuna felt annoyed. "Have you some better idea, Elder Brother? At least this one we can probably trust."

Yudishtira's vagueness fell away. "Tell her to order the men to butcher a calf, then leave her alone there. She should cook all the food they have and then just wait for us. I have no wax with which to make my seal, so give her this to prove she carries my orders." He held out his gold wax-stamp.

Arjuna took it carefully, impressed by Yudishtira's excessive concern for a Dasyu. But then he was asking her to look after two good horses.

At mid-day the brothers were crouching in rocks above another clearing, and covered with mud from the scrambling they had done to follow the homeless band without risking exposure in the open. But their caution seemed to have been for nothing. The "desperate Nishada" all seemed to be asleep, huddled under whatever shelter they could find—in the roots of a great simul tree, under a rotting sala log, in a thicket of sami bushes.

Yudishtira gestured towards the single youth standing guard. He was slumped and nodding from exhaustion. Arjuna knew that the clan claiming this land would find these interlopers in a day or two, and in this condition they would not stand a chance. At least this way it would end quickly for them. He fixed his first arrow.

Yudishtira stopped his hand. "Shoot, but *don't* hit anyone."

"Don't hit anyone?"

"I want to alert them, then run for the cattle camp."

"Run?"

"Yes. They won't follow us right away. They'll track us cautiously, expecting us to be lying in wait, and they know your skill. When they finally reach the herders' camp, we'll be waiting for them."

"I can't help but ask my elder brother why we aren't going to kill them here instead of running there to do it."

"Because we can not kill them anywhere. These people are our subjects, and they are homeless due to our burning their forests."

"Let them find new forests."

"Apparently they have not been able to."

"You plan for us to find new forests for them too?"

"That's a possibility—it hadn't occurred to me. I'll try to decide what to do with them as we run." Yudishtira put an arrow to his bow and drew the feathers back to his jaw. It whispered, then struck a tree a hand's width above the back of a sleeping man.

"This is madness," Arjuna muttered to himself. But not to be outdone, he sent his arrow into a log across the clearing, aiming so that the shaft quivered a mere finger's width from a woman's matted hair. She sat up and screamed.

The two brothers ran.

Arjuna and Yudishtira broke out of the forests on to the soggy ground of the cattle pastures. Blood from their leaf cuts ran with the rain in pink streams down their limbs. Their lungs heaved. But the hut was in sight.

They had run the whole afternoon. Even when they could

hear their pursuers, however, Yudishtira had not allowed any panicked sprints.

Now, however, would be different. If the ones behind them had any hope of catching them, any plans for trapping them, it would have to be here.

The soft light of the dying day filtered in low through the rainclouds, giving Arjuna the feeling of being under a woman's skirts. Grey cotton-cloud skirts. He took a fresh, deep breath into his burning lungs. If he had to die, at least it would be in a good Arya cattle pasture.

The brothers had hardly spoken all day, to save their breath. Now Yudishtira panted something. "Your Lotus—" Following his gesture, Arjuna looked wearily towards the hut, "—has a fire going."

"Or someone has," Arjuna panted back.

"Arjuna, if I'm wrong. If they've got ahead."

"Then neither of us—we won't have long to be sorry."

They pounded on. His brother's stamina surprised Arjuna. The rest of them hunted, often running most of a day. Yudishtira generally only hunted lines of Veda. Yet he had breath to spare.

An arrow struck the ground in front of them. Yudishtira leaped left, Arjuna right.

Another arrow, grazing Yudishtira's arm. "Keep on," Yudishtira shouted.

Arjuna felt the terror of losing his eldest brother. In the face of his fear he grasped for a boyhood ruse to keep him running: "Race to the hut?"

Yudishtira actually smiled. "Or I'll run ahead," he shouted back, laughing. "If you're tired. Need to look to Lotus."

Arjuna had to speed up to stay with him. The hut was close now. It was becoming a true race, trick or not and Dasyu or not, and Arjuna willed himself to sprint harder. But he could not pass.

Yet somehow he was first behind the mud wall of the yard. They leaned there, safe, gasping for breath. "Arjuna—the fleet—still the best—" Yudishtira groaned and pounded his back once, dripping blood on both of them.

Arjuna suddenly felt muddled and childish. "Kindly go into

the shed, Eldest Brother. I will check inside. And will you put a cloth on that?"

But there was no immediate danger. Lotus came out, bowing and glancing nervously in the direction from which they had come. His arm wrapped, Yudishtira asked Lotus to bring out the food she had prepared, and Arjuna helped him to carry the dishes farther out into the open, about thirty paces from the hut. On the last trip Yudishtira set his bow, quiver and knife inside the door, then took the bow and quiver from his brother also. "It's a risk," was all Yudishtira said.

Arjuna was too stunned even to argue. He followed his brother back out to the food spread on the ground.

There in the open the faint light cast from the distant hut interfered with his night vision, but he did not need it to know the Nishada were out there.

Yudishtira was calling to Lotus to join them, but she would not come. "I need your help, Lotus," he shouted. "I can't speak Nishada."

She stepped one pace out of the hut and stood with her arms folded across her chest.

"Tell them we have prepared this food for them because we are their protectors."

Lotus started to shout the words, then came out to join them. Her eyes on Yudishtira, she repeated the speech from there. It was met with silence.

The three were easy targets for any Dasyu archer. Yet Yudishtira stepped farther out into the night. Lotus joined him, then Arjuna. Yudishtira told her to say that he and his brother were unarmed and wanted to offer the Nishada a home at Hastinapura. He paused. "And instruction in trades so you can be paid for your work and feed your families."

Yudishtira stopped again, aware that Lotus and Arjuna were staring at him. "Yudishtira, these are Dasyu," Arjuna said quietly.

"So is she. Yet she's helping us."

"Only because I helped her first."

"So you see?"

Lotus considered Yudishtira a long while, then began shouting his words into the dark, empty space. The eldest of Pandu's sons picked up a spit full of meat and walked out into that dark with it. Arjuna ran after him. "Have you gone crazy? Indra's curses, at least let me take it."

Yudishtira let him, and Arjuna strode on. Near a clump of bushes Arjuna set the spit into the ground, then fell back a bit. Lotus and Yudishtira came up behind him.

Suddenly Lotus fell at Yudishtira's feet. "Lord Prince of the Kurus, please take me to Hastinapura also."

Both Arya stared in disbelief. But Yudishtira was utterly bewildered. "And leave your mother, your people?"

"I can not go back. They will not want me now that I have gone away with you." The girl looked from one brother to the other, then bowed her head before the eldest in sweet, well-studied submission. Yudishtira looked to Arjuna for rescue.

"Yudishtira, don't you see it? It was she who begged to come. They'll take her back." Arjuna glanced towards the brush from where, he knew, the Dasyu must be watching. "This is not the time to—"

"We will not destroy Wood Rose's sister too," Yudishtira said. "If there is even a chance that you are wrong, we must take this girl and provide for her." He looked past her. "Provide for all these people."

"Fine. If they don't kill us first. Fine. Bring them all home. This one was my idea anyway. She's pretty enough." Arjuna heard his voice rising. "But should we survive tonight, you had better think about what you're going to say to our uncle about all this."

Even with her head gracefully bowed, Lotus had been watching the shadows in the low trees in front of them. Now she gestured for the brothers' attention. "They are deciding whether this is a trick. Whether the food is poisoned." Her voice was as rational as it had been desperate before. "If they decide it is—"

Arjuna ripped some meat off the spit. "Ah yes, poison— another old Dasyu trick, yes, Lotus?" He walked out a few paces and ate noisily. "It's good," he shouted. "Good food, curse you."

Lotus repeated a shorter version, then added something herself.

Suddenly words were hurled back. Words—not spears. The three sagged with relief.

"We are Nishada," Lotus translated, "and we do not know if we want to live in an Arya village."

"Tell them to eat our food first," Yudishtira said, "then we will talk." Yudishtira grinned at Arjuna in the darkness. "If they come home with us, I think Lotus will have to teach us Nishada, yes?"

Arjuna grimaced as the first silent, gaunt shadow came out to eat the Aryas' food.

6

At this moment my birth is fulfilled. My austerities have born fruit, now that you, manifest and serene, have appeared before my eyes. You have poured forth this whole world . . . creation abides in you and will be dissolved in you. O goddess, you are the ultimate goal.

Kurma Purana

Nature does provide for us.

King Pandu

Draupadi's hands clenched on the window ledge, her fingers biting into the wood, her body leaning left to guide the horses through the intricate manoeuvre. But the horses and the chariot were down on the rain-washed training fields visible just beyond the city wall, and they were driven by her brother.

She knew she had guided horses Before. And shot arrows. Maybe even better than he. But her instincts told her that in another month Panchalya would so surpass her that she would never again, with any amount of practice, be able even to equal him.

She turned away, tears blurring her eyes. She believed she had not cried so frequently Before, but her only certain knowledge of herself now was of someone forever fighting tears. The first days she had had more control. When the wrong thoughts came, she had recited one of her new, hated lessons —the correct flower for each festival or gem for each month, the correct order of applying face colours. But since her dream three days before, and then her humiliation before the gate, the mere wind made her ache to escape, a passing chariot made her wish it would take her away.

She looked out of the window again. On the field Panchalya's wheels spewed mud and his fine grey horses arched their necks, dipped their heads and lifted their muddy hocks high. Their tails were caught up in knots to keep them clean—she had started the braiding herself before breakfast. Until she was caught and led back to the women's quarters.

She picked up the bronze mirror she had been using to practise applying black kohl around her eyes. Her life as "Princess Draupadi", the only life she knew, had begun half a month ago. But she was already different—her body thin, her face gaunt and her eyes staring out from dark shadows without need of kohl. Soon, she thought, I will be useless as a lure in their trap.

She sat down. She had already concluded that it had required great planning and power to put her where she was and to spread the exaggerated rumours of her beauty that her servants repeated for her. Someone desperately wanted her to be the most desired princess in Bharata, obviously so that King Drupada could make a good alliance through marriage and his sorry half-kingdom could be saved. What would this person do if she became so unattractive that the rumours began to call her ugly? Would she be taken away? Or left here for ever?

What troubled her most was whether this goal of someone's should be hers. Or perhaps she was expected to rebel and undo King Drupada's plans. Hoping to discern her correct course, she had tried to listen to everything she could about the politics of Bharata. But the first time she had asked questions, she was told it was "not a woman's business". After that she was sent from the room if she was noticed listening to any intelligent conversation.

It was from the serving girls that she had learned that not all women of the ruling warrior class were so uninformed—it was the king's and queen's prejudice, because of their two mannish daughters. One made a poor marriage and lived in a distant kingdom. The other was rumoured to be actually studying arms and warfare, determined to have revenge on some warrior who had slighted her. Their parents refused even to speak their true daughters' names. But the serving girls swore that in some courts an educated woman's counsel was even more respected than a man's. And in those kingdoms also, most warrior-born women were proficient archers and chariot drivers, hunting alone and at the least driving themselves and their husbands on pleasure trips. Draupadi wanted to believe it must have been in some way like that where she had been Before.

She constantly sought clues in her darkened memory. Who wore the shroud on the day of her "birth"? Why was his voice familiar? What did he mean, "staunch Bharata's bleeding"? "Become their teacher"? How could an empty mind teach people not interested in her thoughts except to change them? Was she abandoned by a madman? Should she try to escape? But then why did she feel so compelled to keep her promise to him to maintain this lie that she had sprung from King Drupada's sacrificial fire?

Above all, she remembered the voice's command to keep her temper, as if he had known her well. It was true—during the first days it had not been sadness that she had needed to control, but red fury. Yet she had never displayed "temper". And with each day it had become easier to hold back the rage. Not because he had told her to, however, but because rage required a person to feel it, and she had gradually realised she was no one. Not the Daughter of Fire. Not the Daughter of the King. She was the Daughter of No One. And so instead of her anger mounting, her very life had been ebbing away.

She heard the door open behind her. As always, the courtesy of tapping first had been forgone, although it would be expected of herself if she entered their rooms. Draupadi did not need to look to identify Yasoda—the queen exuded a smell of overripe wood apples. Scent upon scent upon cosmetic smells upon sweat. The odour made Draupadi weak with sickness in her stomach.

The queen peered into the mirror from over Draupadi's shoulder and shook her head. "Only one eye painted and your father is already asking for you."

Draupadi knew the queen could see she had been crying. Yasoda picked up a comb and began redoing Draupadi's hair.

The movement made the girl smear the kohl again. Draupadi stopped but would not complain.

The queen put down the comb. "Are you pouting because we won't let you dash about the stables like a boy? Your father and I have had enough of such daughters. You will follow the dharma of a princess."

Draupadi felt a sharp pain near her heart. From Before, "dharma" had a deep meaning for her. This use of it violated that. But she could think of nothing to say.

Queen Yasoda sat down, her skirts billowing around her, and searched Draupadi's eyes. These were the moments that drove the girl furthest inside herself, in search of some core that these strangers could not touch.

"Draupadi, you must eat more."

She didn't answer.

"Draupadi? Did you hear me?"

"I am not hungry," she whispered.

"But a marriageable girl should be plump and pretty."

"When you name the date of my bride's choice, I will eat."

She did not know where this sudden defiance came from— she only remembered hearing the sound of Panchalya's chariot. She hung her head, surprised that the queen had drawn back at her words as if struck.

Now Draupadi remembered the washerwoman's whispers while taking her garments yesterday, that it was the right of every warrior-born girl to have a bride's choice—an assembly of eligible warriors at which the girl indicated her future husband with a garland. She might choose on the basis of love, or the man's wealth, status or strength. Or her family's need for alliances. But dharma left it up to her.

Draupadi meant to avoid any more words with the queen, but out on the field Panchalya was calling to his horses, and in her mind she heard another voice shouting, "Hear me." She found herself saying, less softly, "I might also eat more if you allowed me to practise at something besides painting myself."

The queen pushed into this opening. "Draupadi, I really do understand. Your problem is that you were not taught the dharma of women. Women must stay in seclusion more. For their monthly bleeding, for childbearing—"

"I will never be happy inside."

"Watch what you say, daughter. Would you want to be out in the wilderness where any Dasyu could seize you? Indra forbid it. You have a great many bad ways to unlearn." She walked to the window and closed the shutters. "I am becoming increasingly convinced that you would learn faster without this distraction."

Draupadi whirled. "No windows?"

"Your brother has been complaining that he has already surpassed our weapons instructors and needs better training. Your father has been looking for a teacher to bring here. But I think Panchalya should be sent away."

"Away? I could not live!"

"They will not say of my daughter that she pined for her brother in her husband's bed!"

"Whatever they say of your daughter, they will not be speaking of me."

"Take back your words, Draupadi!"

"Never! Hear me!" She flung the mirror at the queen's feet. She saw before her two chariots, their banners blowing towards her, a rage of dust swirling around her. "When I am a queen of queens, you will beg me to forgive you. You will plead for me to remember you, but I will not."

In the silence after her words, Draupadi stood before the queen, aware that something momentous had changed. Why was the queen not shouting back? She seemed so pale and shaken.

"Your father and I await you," Yasoda whispered. "He has a gift for you."

Panchalya stamped into the room, the smell of rain and horses still clinging to him. "Sister, did you see me today?"

Like water striking stone, her anger lost its direction. "Yes. Yes, you were wonderful."

"Mother, I can drive a chariot better than anyone in Kampilya."

"Panchalya," Draupadi said tightly, "your 'mother' thinks it would be better if you went away."

Queen Yasoda reddened. Astonished, Panchalya glanced from one to the other. "But Father would be the one to decide anything like that. He would never separate us without our consent, and we would never give it. Come with me, Draupadi. He wants us to hurry and see the gift he's bought you."

She took her brother's hand and let him lead her. Queen Yasoda trailed behind. Draupadi was finally comprehending that for some reason there truly was a gift waiting for her somewhere in the palace. But in her mind she still saw the two chariots, and she knew that whatever the gift, she had earned it.

The box was bigger than any of the four Dasyu servants who carried it, and was draped with a woollen rug of the Bactrian style. King Drupada strutted around his prize purchase, admiring its size and elegant accoutrements, peering under the rug himself to tease his family, and finally sweeping the covering from the crate with a grand gesture and opening its door.

A person stepped out.

At first Draupadi thought she was seeing a woman, because of the smooth skin on the face and the subtle body curves under the fine woollen mantle. But the unusual height, short dusky hair, rigid bearing and hard expression were, beyond doubt, a man's. When the mantle was removed the strange yellow-toned clothing that covered each arm and leg separately belonged to no class of being at all.

"A *yavani*," the king announced with a flourish. "A woman from the West."

The queen gasped. The twins exchanged looks—this was more than an interesting gift if it was here without Queen Yasoda's approval.

"She is a rare type from some Graikos island in the Northern Sea," the king explained. "The women there are trained to fight like men. They're very popular in Babylon and Sumer, I was told—to guard queens and princesses so no men have to be trusted to it. Isn't she splendid? A trader all the way from Taksasila had heard about our Draupadi and rushed this specimen to me, so I had to buy. You should see this Greek female with a bow and arrow. Do you like her, daughter?"

70

Draupadi did not answer. She was staring into sky-blue eyes.

King Drupada continued his cant, describing the countries the Greek woman had seen, the languages she knew, her fighting skills, her medical knowledge.

"She is rather young for all that," the queen said sourly.

"Not at all. Twenty-six if I was not lied to." The king stopped his rush of words. "Don't you like my idea, dear wife?"

"As a guard for Draupadi? I am only thinking that this yavani will inevitably also be a companion, and our daughter does not need mannish women around her at this time."

The chief priest then offered his opinion, and others gave theirs. But Draupadi was studying this woman whose very bearing was foreign. The woman was a slave. Yet she was so self-possessed. Draupadi had never seen such strength in any woman.

Or perhaps she had.

Draupadi glanced at the king's disputing advisors, then back at the woman, whose eyes had never left her. "Father?"

The one word, never heard from Draupadi before, silenced the room. "Father, may I ask her a question?"

"Of course, dear child. But keep a distance. She must remain in seclusion until we are certain she is not ill or mad."

Draupadi approached the woman anyway. "What is your name?"

"Eos."

"What does it mean?"

"Dawn," the Greek woman said.

"Eos. Dawn. This sounds like our Ushas."

"In many ways the languages you and I learned as children are the same, Princess." The slave's grammar was perfect, her accent charming.

"Why is that, Eos?" Draupadi asked.

"How could it be otherwise?" The chief priest interrupted. "The sound of an object's name structures its material form. Therefore each object can have only one name."

Draupadi whirled around. "Then why do languages differ at all? And why is the Chine language totally different from ours and the yavanas'?"

The priest flushed with anger at being publicly contradicted by an uneducated girl. And where had she learned about the Chines?

"When a chief priest instructs, it is best to listen," Eos said quietly.

The king gave his wife a triumphant look. Draupadi smiled slightly. "I thank you for your insight, Eos. Tell us, could a woman trained to fight like a man also know enough of the feminine arts to teach me how to ornament myself?"

Eos bowed her head, but Draupadi thought she did it to hide a slight smile of her own. "I have spent a great deal of time in women's quarters, Princess, where there is little else to do but practise this art to perfection. Not only do I know your own Bharata styles, but those of Babylon, Egypt—"

"Bharata's will do," the queen said. "It would be enough to begin with if she could learn to steady her hand while painting her eyes, and to braid her hair so it will lie straight down her back and make a proper coil."

"This is easily done, Queen."

"And we do need to protect Draupadi well," the king said. "She *is* the key to our plans."

Draupadi saw that Eos showed new interest. Embarrassed, Draupadi looked away and suggested that the slave woman should be allowed to rest after waiting so long in a box.

"Yes, yes," the king said absently. "But while we are all here together I wish to ask your opinion again about this marriage."

Draupadi started; the king noticed and smiled. Her opinion had never been asked and he knew it.

"I know," he began, "that you, dear wife, agree with our wise priests that the right husband for Draupadi would be the eldest of the late King Pandu's sons."

The sons of Pandu. To Draupadi the walls seemed to fall away, so that she was standing in dark, empty space. Before two chariots.

Panchalya was outraged. "My sister marry Panchala's enemies?"

"Pandu's sons are not truly our enemies." King Drupada smiled benignly. "They only fought for Vaja as payment for their teaching. Except for you, they are Bharata's greatest warriors. That is why my enemy sent them against me. And that is why I will send them against him some day, when they are bound to me through marriage. The only issue is which one should be Draupadi's husband."

The king placed himself before the princess. "It is true that Yudishtira is the Kurus' crown prince—" Draupadi started at the sound of this name from her dream. "Or at least he is crown prince at the moment," Drupada droned on. "But will he ever be crowned? Yudishtira's future depends on others, while Arjuna is the greatest archer in Bharata and depends on no one for his future fame."

Arjuna. Silver. Could he be the other of her dream?

The king still faced Draupadi. From behind him she was aware of the slave's attention on her.

"Your daughter was born to be a queen," the chief priest uttered with finality.

The king was still standing in front of Draupadi. He nodded deferentially towards the priest, but his eyes remained fixed on her. "Of course you must be a queen—and Arjuna can not help but conquer a kingdom for himself before long. Think of the progeny Arjuna will sire, with you as their mother."

The queen drew herself to her full self-righteous stature. "Would you wish your grandchildren all stillborn? A younger brother can never marry before the older without bringing catastrophe to the womb."

"Come now, Yasoda. Yudishtira and Bhima will marry soon. Yudishtira is said to follow dharma like a dog follows a hare, and to keep younger brothers waiting is also forbidden. Especially when the younger brother is so handsome—tall, graceful, powerful. Silver-blond hair, blue eyes. I hear the women of Hastinapura are offering themselves to him like mares in the season when they turn their tails aside."

"He'll be a stallion indeed," Queen Yasoda sniffed. "Never satisfied with one wife, but climbing every filly in the herd."

"Absurd," King Drupada said.

"You can not deny, Husband, that Yudishtira enjoys the reputation of being utterly virtuous, kind, obedient, loyal—"

The queen could not see her husband smiling mischievously. "Well, Draupadi," he said, rubbing his hands as if anticipating

73

a good dish. "You've heard your mother. Which of these two sons of Pandu do *you* prefer?"

Once again, in her mind she saw the two chariots drawn up before her. "I am not certain. I have not met either one."

"But you must decide!"

She looked from the king to the queen, and oddly found that she wished she could see beyond them both to the Greek slave. But it was Yasoda's voice that still nagged in Draupadi's memory, telling her a woman should be content in seclusion.

"Father, I believe I would rather risk life with a difficult stallion than a—a faithful dog."

King Drupada laughed and walked away from her. "Arjuna then, just as I thought, dear daughter. Just as I knew you'd say."

It was only then that Draupadi realised that once again she had merely served to give the king what he desired.

The Greek woman's clothing rustled softly. Draupadi turned to look at her. The slave's eyes were filled with sympathy, as if she, the princess, were the one now in bondage. As if she who had received this expensive gift of a personal slave were the one who actually, now, possessed nothing.

Eos had been guarding the princess Draupadi for two days. She sat at a table mixing a fresh paste of rodhra pollen for painting Draupadi's cheeks. Her bow, quiver and long knife lay beside her on the bench, her dagger was in her belt but loose in its holder.

On a divan Draupadi sat before a carved wooden chest, sorting diamonds, pearls, amethysts and rubies into little compartments. Beside her there was no knife, only a tray of untouched sweetmeats. The window was open to an overcast sky. Today out on the training field Panchalya was practising with the mace.

Draupadi set a large diamond on the embroidered seat of the divan, then looked nervously at her taciturn guard. She liked this woman Eos. Admired her. In fact, had thought about her all night. Yet when she was around, Draupadi felt uneasy. Undecided.

74

Because she's a slave, with no reason for loyalty. Yet I need her.

Then act.

Draupadi put the diamond away and took out a ruby. Put that away and took out a pearl. Then slammed the lid of the chest.

"Eos, with these jewels as my payment, could you take my brother and me to your country?"

Eos glanced sharply at the window, then at the door. She did not answer.

"In disguise," Draupadi whispered.

"Women's fantasies," the Greek hissed. She went to the balcony and looked out. Coming back she only said, "Watch what you say."

Draupadi nodded and bowed her head. Eos had said little thus far, except to warn her yesterday morning, "merely as the person assigned to guard your life", that if Draupadi or her brother did anything to cast doubt on their divine birth and thereby embarrassed the king and queen, their "parents" could easily have them killed and cover up the deed with some myth about the twins "returning to the gods". When Draupadi had protested that dharma would not permit it, Eos had laughed coldly—"I've lived in too many courts where even real parents and children killed each other for power."

Eos was right. An attempt at escape would make a mockery of their "divine origin".

"So you would not help me to run away," Draupadi said quietly.

"Not to run away."

Draupadi considered other measures of the woman. "Then tell me something about the world you will not take me to see. Tell me why everyone worships different gods."

Eos put down the jar of rodhra pollen and picked up her quiver, took out a stone and began to sharpen her iron knife. "You tell me why anyone worships any of them."

"They say it is to increase the good and turn away the bad."

"Good and bad events come when they will—or when humans cause them."

Watching the slave hone her knife, Draupadi said, "Humans

would control both if they saw that they and their gods are all reflections of the one pure light of Brahman."

"Where did you get that idea?"

"I don't know."

"I would keep it to myself." Eos stopped her work. "The gods? I was taken from my home under an Assyrian's arm and heard my mother and sister begging Zeus to save them from rape and axing. Which Zeus, King of the Gods, did not do, of course."

"Eos—"

"I don't care for sympathy. Anyway, you appear to deserve as much as I do."

Draupadi stood up, stiffened herself, then gestured for Eos to close the window.

Eos closed it, watching her curiously.

Draupadi hesitated another moment, then methodically unwound her breast cloth and her skirt, until she stood before the Hellene in her white cotton virgin's shift. "Yasoda says I am not to take this off until I am married. Not in front of anyone."

Eos only nodded.

Draupadi's hands twitched at her sides. Then she clenched the cloth.

Eos watched her but neither moved or spoke.

"I am going to take it off." Draupadi pulled the shift up over her head. She stood naked in the shaft of light coming in around the shutters and looked down at her own golden skin, familiar yet unfamiliar, and her dark, wavy hair, looking so complex against the simple ovals of her breasts.

"You are testing me, aren't you?" Eos asked.

"You didn't try to stop me."

"Is that what you think I'd want to do? But then you have neither memory nor experience of women's quarters, do you?"

Draupadi bowed her head, somehow ashamed.

"That is just as well," the Hellene said gently.

"Eos, will he like me?" Draupadi turned, tossing her hair so it caught the light. "You have seen so many princesses. Will I be good enough for this Arjuna?"

"Perfect." Eos suddenly turned her back. "Now put your

clothes back on and tell me what it is you do want from me, Draupadi."

The younger girl obeyed without answering, then went to the window. Through the crack of the shutters she could see her brother swinging his mace. She thought of Pandu's third son. A warrior would want a warrior's wife.

"I must take some action to help my brother."

"All right, what do you want of me?"

"Eventually King Drupada will ask my brother to fight his enemy, Guru Vaja. Guru Vaja is priest-born, and they say the priest-born must teach any student who comes to him."

"You would have Guru Vaja prepare his own opponent?"

"Yes. And if Vaja refuses, he'll be called a coward. Besides, he'll see that while Panchalya is learning his weaknesses, he will be learning Panchalya's also."

"And given your brother's sweetness, you think Guru Vaja might even refuse to fight him once they are teacher and student." Eos studied her. "So you would send him away even when you have told me you could not bear seeing him go?"

"They will send him away for training anyway. This way, I decide where he goes. To the best."

"The only flaw in your plan is that King Drupada is not clever enough to think of it, and too vain to follow anyone else's suggestion."

"That is why I need a foreign slave to tell him a story of some other court where a king had a son, and an enemy who taught weaponry."

Eos thought a moment. "Yes. Yes, I can do that for you."

It was done. Draupadi lay back on the divan, a pearl still in her hand. Time passed. Yet the incomplete feeling remained. She watched Eos. The slave, Eos. It was unjust. Draupadi had come to accept the attitude at Kampilya that Dasyu were inferior beings, dull and clumsy little animals, and deserved to be slaves. But not a woman like Eos. Suddenly she realised that in some sense she, Draupadi, owned this person.

Draupadi sat up. "Eos, as soon as I find out how, I will see that you are set free."

The slave was feathering an arrow. She did not look up. "Others have also said that."

"No. I will do it."

Eos set down the arrow. "You are too late." Her voice was full of suppressed fury. "I have already freed myself."

Draupadi stiffened, hurt and ashamed, and trying not to lose control. "It was arrogant of me. Accept my apology. You who come and go when you wish, armed as you wish—to be freed by me. I can not even leave this room alone."

The Greek crossed the room and stood over her. When she spoke, her voice revealed she was as close to tears as Draupadi. "I was not honest, Draupadi. I am no freer than you. Nor has anyone ever wanted to free me. No woman anyway, or anyone who meant it."

"Eos," she whispered. "They are going to trade me for an army. That's all they want of me."

Eos turned away. Draupadi, holding out the pearl, reached for her arm with her other hand. "Take this. No one will miss it. Run away."

The Greek turned around. "If they found that on me, they would kill me."

The women studied each other. Eos took her knife from her belt. "You remind me," she whispered, "that I had been planning to give you this. Wear it under your shift."

Draupadi caressed the fine bone carving and the iron blade, worth many pearls. She looked up. "If it's found on me, Eos —"

Eos closed her eyes, then took back the knife. "Whatever we have to give," she whispered bitterly, "they take away."

Draupadi touched her hand. "You are already giving me your experience. And you are guarding my life."

"And you have offered my life to me." Eos took her hand and held it. "You are not like any person I have met, Draupadi. Queens, kings—you are superior to them all."

"I? I am no one." But she could not deny to herself that, for the first time in her short memory, she was feeling what was called happiness. She studied the pearl in her other hand and thought of the sea, which she knew she had never seen, even Before. But yesterday Eos had told her how it felt to be in it: It was silent inside, and looked like liquid light.

"Eos, you and I believe in here, today, and what we can do

—little as that is. But I also believe in another place. A flawless place."

The Greek released her hand. "That is slave dreaming, Draupadi. It weakens you."

"No, Eos, I forget too easily, but I have seen such a place, and I believe you have come to me, not from the northwest, but from there."

7

We came from the north, shedding the Asuras' blood,
From the west, chasing the Dasyu from their hiding places.
Out of the northwest we poured.
Who will come out of the northwest after us,
To shed our blood?

a song

To return from Badari Hermitage to Bharata's kingdoms, Vyasa could travel on the river. Most of the few Arya who ventured into the mountains tended on their return journeys to stay on the banks until they reached the quieter water of the plains. But Vyasa preferred to join certain Dasyu he knew, who, by running the milky mountain rapids in their slim wood boats, could take him down in three days if they travelled continuously.

On this hurried trip especially, the opportunities to rest on shore were few and brief. Still, sometimes the people found him. This time it was on the second night, when he might have lain down a moment while the Dasyu boatmen studied the moods of the rain-fat river before attempting the next passage. But as he dried himself beside a fire he became aware that he had company hiding in the bushes. A priest's son from some nearby settlement, or so it appeared from the gleam of a small white tunic and the feeling in the air of tense and childish awe.

Vyasa rubbed his smoke-stung and sun-wearied eyes, then sat up straight. "You'd best come out, child. There's a tiger up the river. Although when your father arrives, you may prefer the tiger."

The boy darted out of the shadows, then stopped abruptly, staring at the great man he had intruded upon. Vyasa read the child's excited thoughts: Everyone said this one, the famous sage, travelled the rivers like a Dasyu, but who else had actually seen him do it?

"So now that you have found me, what will you do with me?"

The boy made a hasty obeisance. Vyasa gestured him to sit. "I suppose you want me to say something wise?"

The boy nodded numbly, still speechless.

"I'm not sure I feel very wise these days. Do you?"

The boy didn't answer. Vyasa smiled just a little and took out two cloth pouches from his waist band. "Shall we play a game or shall we work?" Vyasa shook black stones from one bag, making a heap on the sand. "Or perhaps we can work and play at once, ruining both." Over the black stones he shook out the other bag. White stones clattered against the black. "Or could that be a false division? For divisions are the question, aren't they? Divisions, divisions."

The boy's eyes were wide. "Organise them," Vyasa said quietly. "Not in separate piles. Put the two colours together. In some kind of harmony."

"A harmony, Great Master?" the boy whispered hoarsely.

"Make a wholeness of them."

"Of rocks?"

"Of black and white rocks."

The boy fingered a stone tentatively. "Do you mean male and female?"

"Perhaps."

"Or good and evil? The black ones are evil!"

Vyasa tilted his head as if puzzled. "Evil? You accuse Brahma of creating evil?"

"Priest and warrior then? Arya against yavana foreigners?" The boy thought. "No. I know it! These are the good white Arya against the ignorant black Dasyu."

Under the folds of his robe Vyasa's fists clenched. He closed his eyes a moment. "You are to arrange them, child, not hurl them at each other. Arrange them so that one does not dominate the other, is not separated from the other or lost from its own. No muddles. A harmony."

The boy began shifting the rocks. He made circles of white around dark, circles of dark around white, patterns of quarters, eighths and sixteenths. Then single pairs. Now and then he would stop and look up. Vyasa would study the design, then shake his head. Finally the boy grew frustrated.

"It's all right," Vyasa said gently.

The boy's father suddenly burst into the clearing. Immediately guessing whose august presence he was in, the backwoods priest-born settler fell to his knees, full of apologies. Vyasa said something reasonably wise and polite about the difficulty of keeping boys at home, and the father dragged his son to his feet to lead him off. But the boy's eyes were still on the pile of stones.

"What is the solution, Master?"

Vyasa picked up a black stone and handed it to him. "We don't know yet."

The lull in the rains had permitted a scarlet sunset. The Northwest Road towards Hastinapura was bathed in red light, and red was reflected back to the sky from long parallel mirrors of water in the ruts of the road. Fourteen leagues west of the city these mirrors were vibrating with the steps of two hundred Dasyu slaves, synchronised by the dull beats of large drums. Twenty slaves drew a wagon. In the wagon were two men. Nothing more was certain to most of those who saw them, for they were frightened and ran.

Eleven leagues closer to the city and resting in sight of its walls were Yudishtira, Arjuna and Bhima (having caught up with his brothers the day before), in the company of seventy-two homeless Dasyu of the Nishada tribe. Seeing the sunlit city against black storm clouds made Bhima comment to Arjuna that it seemed as if Hastinapura was in flames tonight. Their view west along the road, the direction from which they had come, was blocked by a low hill.

The group had travelled slowly, taking three days to cover what one light chariot could have done in an afternoon. But the Nishada were still recovering their strength, and Yudishtira had wished those at Hastinapura to have time to consider the news of their coming, sent ahead by messenger.

The other impediment to speed had been the tiger skin. Bhima had retrieved it when returning to the Nishada village to look for his brothers, and before they had left the cattle camp Arjuna had hoisted it between two poles to announce their accomplishment as they travelled. As a result, at every crossroads there had been crowds wanting them to stop and tell the story, and then to explain again Crown Prince Yudishtira's generous offer to these Dasyu with whom the princes deigned to travel.

Now, in the brilliant, crimson last light, Yudishtira sat on a rock apart from the others. He held the reins of his bay mare while she grazed, and he tried to understand his growing uneasiness. Perhaps it was only that he was tired from travelling and managing the problems of so many people. Or perhaps their nervousness was itself the cause. Now that these refugee Nishada were in actual sight of an Arya city, they were barely controlling their panic, and it had been his awareness of their new mood which had caused him to call this halt.

He forced himself to face his immediate problem: Should he bring them into the city tonight, where he hoped they could be won over with food and shelter—if his uncle, King Drita, had followed his suggestions—or should he wait until daylight, when they would be rested and perhaps feel braver? He looked back at the thin Dasyu women nursing the few surviving children, their men hovering around them or arguing in tense groups. He had learned much about them in these three days, and had come to admire their courage. Thinking honestly, he was not sure he himself could have done what he wanted them to do: advance unarmed, with dependants, upon a fortress controlled by a kingdom which had—on the whole—been exterminating their race as if they were a mere inconvenience.

A runner appeared in the west on the crest of the road. His dress and wild gait said he was not an initiated messenger, but some villager bearing news that was, to him, momentous. Yudishtira felt his vague concern focus upon the runner. He mounted his mare and cantered out to intercept the man. For a moment, as he rode, Yudishtira thought he saw flames in the air around himself, as he had with the tiger. At the same moment his mare had shied.

Yudishtira found the runner distraught. "Yavanas, Prince Yudishtira. West-foreigners. With slaves. Whips."

"Are they bearing weapons?"

"Yes. Weapons too."

Yudishtira controlled his impatience with his own question. "Are they *using* their weapons? Or threatening to use them?"

"No. The Baron. Our Baron Sakuni is leading them."

"The king's brother-in-law?"

"Yes. With a yavana slave. They say he is 'Egyptian'."

The vehicle was pulled by humans—it was this that most disturbed those who saw it. True, those in harness were the lowest Dasyu, the rarely seen bird-eaters from the marshes beside the Western Sea. But not even the cruellest Arya used Dasyu for pulling when horses and bullocks were the very measure of wealth. Therefore this which they were seeing was unnatural and degrading both to those who rode and those who pulled. Or even watched. It violated dharma itself.

Going before the wagon and Dasyu were ten yavanas with drums, pounding out a dull, ominous beat. Behind the wagon came more Dasyu, leading pack animals or carrying loads themselves. Their bundles were covered with strange, rich materials. The pottery vessels on the mules had unfamiliar shapes. Even the baskets were wrong. Foreign.

The taller of the two men standing in the wagon was the Egyptian—a man in his prime, whose face was as still and yellow as sandstone. His name was Zesnor and he was in a sense a slave—he wore the arm circlets; his face bore a slave brand. But even a goat herder could see he was nobly born of some race. In truth, his aristocratic family had dedicated him at birth to Amon-Re, Egypt's most long-worshipped god. Thus Zesnor belonged only to the Egyptian Lord, and in daily life served His Supremely Beloved Servant, the oracle and chief priest at Amon-Re's temple in Thebes.

Beside Zesnor stood Baron Sakuni, King Drita's brother-in-law. He was short, thin, narrow-faced, with pale skin and black hair. One shoulder drooped slightly, due to an injury in youth which had also left him with a limp. That and being short and the youngest among eight sons of a petty king had taught him to use his wits where others used muscle or birthright. Therefore three years before—tired of his brother-in-law's fear and vacillation over the simple act of making his own son, Suyodhana, the crown prince—the baron had left Bharata to see the great kingdoms and empires of the northwest and west.

The procession rolled rapidly east across the river-plain, nearing its goal. Those who saw it were often those who had also seen the earlier group led by the three sons of Pandu, with the homeless Nishada proudly carrying the princes' tiger skin and bragging that in Hastinapura they would be citizens. Although no Arya loved the Dasyu, the conquerors slept more securely when the conquered appeared content. Also to be considered was this new teaching from the Aryas' own forest sages—ahimsa, non-harm. If Crown Prince Yudishtira could make some kind of lasting peace with the Dasyu when he became king, it promised a better life for everyone.

Now the farmers and herders were gathering by the road to watch these other poor Dasyu animals making the journey to Hastinapura, with other fates obviously awaiting them there. The onlookers could not help looking east and speculating. In a few leagues the first group of Dasyu would be overtaken by the second, and those who led them would be face to face.

At the top of the rise Yudishtira stopped his horse to watch the procession, which was still far in the distance. Since speaking with the frightened villager, Yudishtira had decided to halt his own party for the night and expected this one to camp soon also, at which time he could visit properly. But time passed, the sky darkened, and still the group progressed, the drumming continued. A rippling rectangle of torches sprang up around their single wagon. The drums were louder, the wagon closer. Yudishtira's mare, already tense, began to sidestep and paw the ground. He held her firm and sat erect, preparing his mind to welcome Baron Sakuni after his three years of travel.

Arjuna rode out to receive his brother's orders for the night —and obviously to see this which the runner had announced. Arjuna glanced nervously west at the torches as Yudishtira told him in an even tone to camp the Nishada in a distant hollow and leave Lotus to instruct the elders that no one should wander near the road. Arjuna left.

The advancing torches now lit Yudishtira's horse and the surrounding grass. The fresh green turned ugly in the raw light. Yudishtira could see the caravan commander riding up and down; he could hear the man's blows striking flesh. The pack animals at the rear squealed. The slaves took the blows silently.

It was truly King Drita's brother-in-law, Baron Sakuni, standing in the wagon. Beside him there was a tall yavana. Both wore foreign clothing. Yudishtira prepared himself to dismount and give his obeisance to an elder.

But he could not dismount—the mare was simply too frightened to control from the ground while bowing. The drums were in front of the horse and rider now. The noise was deafening. The mare reared and backed, calling attention to them. Yudishtira's royal clothing, if not his face, was clearly visible. But the procession did not slow.

The pulling slaves were even with the horseman now. They were small men. Very dark. Even after so many leagues of pulling without relief, their eyes were wide with fright. Yet each stared only at the whip-striped back of the one ahead.

When the wagon itself passed before Yudishtira his mare could stand no more. Her body was covered with lather. She seemed to convulse with her need to run. Without looking back, he let her take him away.

Three months before, Baron Sakuni had been Bharata's first warrior-born visitor to Egypt. His reception had been less than noble, however. First he had spent three days and nights tied upright to a pillar while his motives for entering Thebes were being considered. Then he had been half dragged down knee-high stone stairs to the chamber of Amon-Re's Supremely Beloved, the infamous high priest, oracle and true ruler of Egypt. At the foot of the oracle's screened dais, Sakuni had sprawled, his clothes caked with excrement, his freedom restrained by a rope held with obvious distaste by a stocky inner-temple overseer. At which point Baron Sakuni had begged the screen-hidden tyrant for an opportunity to speak, sobbing in a manner that would have shamed Sakuni's family. But then, they were far away.

Amused, the voice of the Friend of Ma'at and Witness of the First Occasion had granted Sakuni a few more moments of life, so with his face in an Egyptian floor, the slight, sly little Arya finally had his opportunity to try to strike the bargain his travels had convinced him he must somewhere, somehow make. He would give anything, basically, if he could take back to Bharata a touch of "Egypt's greatness". The response was icy.

"Ah ha! The stinking thing on the floor wants something. Egypt's 'greatness'! You have not heard the jokes, foul little frog? 'Why do Egyptians sleep late? Because they rob the pharaohs' graves all night.' I will tell you because you make no difference to me whatsoever: Egypt is a broken pot held together only by myself, and only because I know how to use temple gold to control mercenaries."

Sakuni raised his head. "Then Bharata will supply Egypt with soldiers! Elephants! Your enemies will be terrified. If Egypt's greatness has stumbled, let a younger son help in return for a father's wisdom."

A shriek of laughter burst through the chambers. "You've heard nothing I've said! Nothing!"

Sakuni had rushed on with a description of divided Bharata, his influence as the king's brother-in-law in the most powerful kingdom, his frustration that the king's malleable son would be overlooked for the throne. "Give me a few troops, some iron weapons. Or whatever you advise! Bharata is yours in return—when I control it."

"You have come a long way to hear the obvious advice: Kill the claimant. Or are you afraid to end a man's life in the name of 'greatness'?" The voice rose. "Tell me why you detest this other prince, this Yudishtira."

Sakuni pulled himself to his feet, grasping the overseer beside him as if he were wood. Rising was not easy for the permanently lamed Arya, especially under the gaze of sound men. "I can control my nephew better."

"This is not the truth." The voice resounded off the stone

walls. "Now listen to the truth. You do not admire 'greatness'. You admire power. Do not confuse them."

"Yes, I admire those who shape nations."

The oracle ignored Sakuni's words. "You want to have this power." The voice grew softer. "Power in *your* hands now, crippled eighth son."

Sakuni's face shone with sweat. He swayed a little, then regained his balance by leaning again on the overseer.

The voice went on: "You hate this Yudishtira because he is all you are not. You would like to see this 'Steadfast in Battle' writhe, hear him scream for mercy the way you have heard our prisoners scream."

The past three days and nights had been too much for Sakuni. The voice was unfocusing his eyes and mind. Sakuni's hands gripped the overseer's cloak.

"All right." The voice was almost sweet now. "Is it not all equal in the end? So you and I will put this Suyodhana in power, and Egypt and Bharata will rule the world."

Suddenly laughter echoed around the vaulted walls again.

"Your Greatness, there is a rumour about Yudishtira," Sakuni whispered. "He was only a boy when I left, but it is said that Yudishtira is the son of the god of Dharma. Duty, Law. And will rescue —"

From behind the screen there was a laboured wheezing. Then a choking sound. With obvious effort the voice resumed. "Then — you will need a weapon, won't you? A slave. He will report to me every two months about you. Do not gape like a stork — it can be arranged. There are faster ways to your 'unknown' land than caravans. When you gain control of your little Bharata, send your best warriors to Egypt, unarmed. As slaves. If they rebel, pick the 'bravest' for examples — have them watch their sons castrated. If you fail, I will have my slave bring your head here to Amon-Re's feet — without that disgusting little body of yours. Now, shall I tell you what the outcome of all this will be?"

Sakuni's head snapped up.

"I see you have not believed I am a real oracle, cynical little Sakuni. I will tell you anyway — two truths! This youth

Yudishtira is not your equal. And any man who would rewrite the laws of Ma'at—what you call 'dharma'—is a fool."

"What do you mean?" Sakuni cried out, his nails drawing blood from the overseer's arm.

"Take him away! This stupid, stupid man! Get him away!" The voice broke. "He sickens me."

A long time after Sakuni had been dragged away, the oracle's laughter had echoed up through the temple's light-shafts and stairwells.

These events had occurred three months before Zesnor's and Sakuni's entrance into Hastinapura.

While the family that had produced Baron Sakuni and King Drita's wife was respected for its pure bloodlines and faultless reputation, its kingdom was only a minor knot in Bharata's great net. In contrast, Bharata's most powerful kingdom was ruled by a family famous for its peculiar matings and violent obsessions. This was the Kuru clan, led for now by Sakuni's brother-in-law, Drita.

Their troubles had begun with the third King Kuru. Although he had married happily and quickly sired an admirable crown prince, Gangeya, Kuru's queen soon died. Years of fruitless mourning ensued. Then the ageing king happened upon the seductive daughter of a lowly Dasyu fisherman and immediately felt love again. Young and foolish love.

The girl was actually only half Dasyu, for she was not really the fisherman's offspring at all. His wife had once attracted her own Arya king. Nor was the fisherman's daughter a virgin, for as a mere child she had rendered meaningless the vows of celibacy of a famous forest-dwelling Arya priest. The fruit of that single day of vacillation had been a dark-skinned, idiosyncratic son called Vyasa.

This time, however, the fisherman was determined that his daughter would not bear a child without a marriage. And when he saw she had captured in her nets the great Arya king called Kuru, the father grew even bolder. First he insisted that only the issue of his daughter's womb could inherit the Kuru throne. And second, to be certain of it, he demanded not only that the bold and virtuous Gangeya, King Kuru's first and only son, should renounce the throne, but swear never to plough a woman's field. Ever. There could be no crop to threaten the fisherman's daughter's descendants.

It was a terrible request. Yet, to give his father some happiness, Prince Gangeya granted it—he forswore both power and pleasure in one absurd and irrevocable oath.

After a few brief years of grateful joy, King Kuru died. He left behind two sons by the fisherman's daughter, and the virtuous Gangeya to oversee the kingdom for them. But one son died in childhood and the other was an evil-spirited youth. Regent Gangeya found two wives for this half-brother of his, but the wastrel died from his profligate ways without leaving an heir. So next the fisherwoman queen demanded that Gangeya plough the royal fields for her—that is, father children with her dead son's widows so that the royal Kuru family would not cease.

Gangeya refused. Although he had made his vow on her behalf, he would not break it for her.

The queen was furious. Then she remembered her own son, Vyasa. Because the Arya permitted a man of the priestly class to father an heir when a king could not, she assigned the duty to the young sage, part Dasyu or not.

Vyasa bent to his mother's will. But he would not pretend to be a bridegroom—he had been performing austerities in the forests and he went to the beds of his mother's daughters-in-law with his wild red hair uncombed and his body covered with ashes. The first girl shut her eyes in horror. When her son, Drita, was born blind, it was immediately rumoured that this was Vyasa's revenge. The second daughter-inlaw was more careful, but could not control her face turning pale. Her son was born with colourless skin and hair, hence the name Pandu, White.

Although the blind son was older, the throne was given to the younger but flawless Pandu. Later, however, some said Drita was the more fortunate. For it was in the few short years of Pandu's reign that certain priests began to prophesy dharma's demise and the gradual destruction of the world. The Age of Kali.

Upon hearing of this approaching season of vice, King Pandu

was determined to protect his people from the horrors being predicted—the diseases, disasters and suffering. But the greatest loss, because it would be the underlying cause of the rest, would be the gradual withering of dharma. Dharma provided law, dictated duty, preserved tradition. From dharma flowed personal intuition about one's proper vocation. Dharma even regulated the seasons, and the number of births and deaths. Most of all, dharma revealed the very meaning of life. All these were given by dharma, all these would be taken when dharma was gone.

But Pandu was a deep man. After long thought he ordered a month-long sacrifice. On the last day he announced his plan for preventing the Age of Chaos.

First his priests told him his plan was impossible. Then they wavered—perhaps it could be done, but only if the king would sacrifice himself and retire to the forest to perform austerities for the rest of his life.

The priests were certain this condition would stop Pandu, but they were wrong. The next day he left his blind brother Drita to rule in his place, with Gangeya to advise him, and Pandu and his two wives entered the forest. They kept silence, ate the plainest foods, and for ten years remained celibate. After which his first wife, Queen Kunti, gave birth to Yudishtira.

The burly Prince Suyodhana, whose hair and eyes were the colour of bronze, sat in his place beside his father's throne on the morning after his uncle Baron Sakuni had returned from Egypt. As father and son waited for the afternoon assembly to begin, Suyodhana studied Hastinapura's vast, shadowy assembly hall rising empty around him.

The banners were pleasant enough, he thought. The seats appropriately ornate. But the columns were what made this assembly hall superior. They had been fashioned from the largest and most auspiciously located sala trees to be found for fifty leagues, then finely carved with flowers and birds, painted delicate colours and crusted with jewels. There was nothing like them in Bharata.

It was raining hard, and Suyodhana found himself recalling other rainy days, when he was a small boy and this hall's corners had seemed crowded with dark mysteries. On such humid afternoons the high ceiling was often lost in smoke from the ritual fires, so that as a child he had foolishly imagined that the hall reached to Heaven itself, the dwelling place of the *pitris*, the Ancestors. And at the end of a long day, during the pitri sacrifice, the painted patterns on the columns would merge into faces. But only for him. He alone knew they were the faces of the dead men whose names were being chanted. And if he were very still and good, the mouths in the faces would move, so that while others might think they were hearing the familiar voices of the priests, he knew they were the Ancestors' voices, sending messages to him from the land of Yama the Fetcher.

But that was childish fancy. Suyodhana looked up at the enormous beams resting in the notched crowns of the pillars and the high-pitched, arching roof that swept down to a man's height above the earth and well out from the walls. It was all merely good construction, even the frivolous carving that awed Dasyu and envoys.

Suyodhana checked again that Baron Sakuni was by the first column, as he had promised. In spite of the baron's dramatic arrival last night, this morning Suyodhana had overheard the same old slights about his uncle: "The king's scheming, crippled brother-in-law" was now a "scheming, crippled yavana-lover". But only Suyodhana knew that Sakuni was not concerned with the comments of these ignorant Arya. For the night before, for some wondrous reason, Baron Sakuni had asked to see Suyodhana himself, alone, even before he took rest after his journey. Sakuni had shared astounding ideas with him, ideas that no one in Bharata had ever imagined. An empire—a great, united Arya empire. And although Suyodhana doubted it could actually happen, Sakuni wanted him, his nephew, to be king over it all. Himself, not Yudishtira. It was worth a try. Very worth a try.

Suyodhana looked out at his uncle, then back at his father beside him on the throne. Rubbing his hands again, the son observed. It was a nervous habit, grown constant during the last year.

"Indra!" His father tilted his head up towards the god called the Showerer. "We thank you for this watery abundance, but more gently please." He turned to his son. "Suyodhana, where are Pandu's sons? They are late." The afternoon assembly of warriors was his father's favourite part of the day.

"Undoubtedly kissing the feet of the Dasyu they brought in this morning."

"Watch your speech, son."

"No one is here yet. Just the priests." For reassurance, Suyodhana glanced again at his uncle by the first column. "Father, are you wondering why Yudishtira and Arjuna chose to bring these Nishada here?"

"We need labourers, of course."

"But you yourself have said we Arya are in danger of being overwhelmed by the dark ones. Now if the Dasyu could be slaves, like Sakuni's—" Suyodhana carefully adjusted his voice to sound shocked and hurt. "Father, I can not hide it any longer: Arjuna is secretly bedding a Nishada."

"He wouldn't dare!"

"Why not, with his eldest brother's example? Seventy-two new Dasyu inside the city and Yudishtira wants them treated like Arya citizens." Suyodhana leaned closer, allowing his bitterness to show now. "And I know why he wants it. Poor self-righteous Yudishtira is trying to atone. I have learned that to celebrate his killing the tiger, Yudishtira himself lay with a Nishada girl afterwards."

Drita scowled. "I do not believe such lies. Yudishtira has always guarded his seed as befits a crown prince."

"Oh, he guarded it this time too—in the morning she was dead. With his arrow in her belly."

Drita only fell silent, his chin raised and his blind eyes staring. It is no surprise, Suyodhana thought, that the people look forward to having a new king on the throne. No amount of finery can make up for their present king's stringy grey hair, flabby body and stupid, bulging eyes. Yet Suyodhana remembered when his father had been a vigorous ruler, settling disputes and directing the expansion of the kingdom, and always telling his son to listen well because "some day you will be king". Then the sons of Pandu had come and made his father a liar.

Finally the old man's lips began to work themselves. "I also know some secrets, Son. When you try to make Yudishtira appear foolish like this, you only give yourself away. Gangeya told me about the message you sent the Nishada the day before your cousins left to kill that tiger."

"Father, your beloved Gangeya is with the others. All of them are hailing your nephews, and Gangeya is saying, 'Why wait for spring to make Yudishtira king?'"

King Drita's face contorted with the old agony. "How can he!"

Startled by the cry, the priests around Agni's hearths in the centre of the room faltered in their chanting. The king sank down in his throne, trying to compose himself. Suyodhana struggled to remember the exact words that Sakuni had suggested next.

"After all these years it's still the same, isn't it, Father? 'Grandfather' Gangeya is the real king."

"Obedience to superiors is dharma."

"Exactly, Father. It's *you*, the king, who should be obeyed. And I, your son! The king's son!"

Drita's hands writhed in his lap. "But I made Yudishtira crown prince."

"Change it. You are the law."

"Dharma is law!" Drita's hands made a sound like sliding snakes as he turned and rubbed them. "My beloved Suyodhana. I know how you feel and my heart is with you."

"Your heart is truly with me, Father. I know why you sent them alone on their tiger hunt."

Drita paled at the accusation.

Suyodhana glanced at Sakuni. "A king should not be ashamed of what he desires." The son lowered his voice. "He should merely succeed at achieving it."

The doors at the end of the hall were thrown open by a white-maned giant. "I will have no more of this tale-bearing and quarrelling. Over Dasyu no less." The voice of Regent Gangeya the Vow-Taker, the last true descendant of a King Kuru, resounded like a conch. "Do you hear me, Suyodhana?" A crowd of warriors came in behind Gangeya, but maintained a respectful distance.

94

Drita's son stood and bowed towards the patriarch, struggling to hide his rage and humiliation. Gangeya was followed by another towards whom the assembling warriors demonstrated unusual respect: the weapons-master, Guru Vaja. Like Gangeya, Guru Vaja was white-haired, although clean shaven, shorter and younger. And while Gangeya was large-boned and loose-limbed, the priest-turned-warrior's body was taut and tightly centred.

"This has decided me," Vaja said. "Their graduation 'tournament' will be an exhibition only, without contests of any sort. They will use it to show the world their cooperation, not their divisions."

Gangeya pointed at Suyodhana. "You above all will use your graduation to demonstrate your complete respect for your next king, Yudishtira. Our enemies relish the thought that you all may yet weaken us by quarrelling among yourselves."

"Wise words," King Drita shouted from the throne. "Full of dharma."

Inwardly Suyodhana writhed. Once again his father was retreating; once again Yudishtira received no rebuke for what was fundamentally his fault. "Curse dharma," Suyodhana whispered.

The king jerked as if hit. Ignoring his father, Suyodhana stepped down from the dais. But Sakuni motioned him to stay.

"Drita," Gangeya boomed, "you must regain control of these princes."

"Uncle!" It was Yudishtira, entering the west door. "Your permission to speak!"

Yudishtira made a hurried obeisance to each elder. "King, I wish to address the rumours, and speak the truth, about my foray."

"Come closer, Yudishtira. This is a matter to be settled privately."

"Privately? In the assembly?" Yudishtira glanced about him towards Gangeya and Guru Vaja, but he obeyed. Standing beside his cousin, he expressed in clear, quiet speech his actions on the hunt, then his concern that the Kurus' Dasyu would never abandon their shrinking forests and labour for the common good if they saw other Dasyu enslaved and pulling wagons like bullocks.

"First tell me if it is true, Crown Prince, that your brother is openly bedding a Dasyu woman." Yudishtira drew back. Before he could answer, Drita said, "You see, your uncle watches you, even if he's blind. I also know about the foolish message my son sent to the Nishada. I am grateful it caused you no harm."

"No harm? Arjuna was netted and lost the white colt."

Drita leaned forward urgently. "Did you punish those Dasyu who dared to do this to an Arya? No. And I know why. Yudishtira, suppose the three of us forget all these matters? Mistakes, disputes, jealousies—all. Forget the past, Yudishtira, and I will make citizens of these Nishada you brought. Not equal to Arya, of course, but some kind of new class of people."

Yudishtira looked from father to son.

"The only evidence you have against me, cousin," Suyodhana whispered tauntingly, "is the word of Arjuna's Dasyu bitch. Quite useless in the assembly."

Yudishtira was white; his hands were shaking. But he merely bowed. "Then for the sake of these Nishada, we will forget, Uncle." Pandu's eldest son turned and left the hall, all eyes upon him.

Suyodhana seized his father's arm and whispered, "Get rid of him! You've tried half-heartedly. Now do it right."

The king rubbed his hands frantically. "A crown prince can not be changed. Yudishtira is a good man!"

Overcome with fury, Suyodhana stood straight and whispered, "I curse you to Hell."

Drita only slumped in the throne.

Sakuni limped to the throne and urged Drita to begin the assembly.

"Sakuni?" There was drool at the corner of the old king's mouth. "Brother-in-law, you have seen so many foreign kings —what should I do?"

"I told you," Sakuni whispered. "Begin the afternoon meeting."

Drita nodded, all his eagerness for it gone.

*

That evening Baron Sakuni stood with Zesnor, his Egyptian slave, on the covered walk between the assembly hall and the palace, looking out at Hastinapura through a light rain.

"This road below us that runs from the hall," Sakuni said in clumsy Egyptian, "is the main avenue. After it leaves the palace it runs through the city to the north gate, ahead of us, where it branches into the major highways crossing the kingdom. Another like it goes south from the back of the hall, behind us. As you see, there are four more avenues to the right, four to the left, and four crossing these. Add the central east-west avenue through the palace and the four behind, and you have a grid of nine by nine—eighty-one blocks in all."

"Are all cities in Bharata similar?"

"As much as possible. Right or west bank of the river on a slope from west to east. The priests choose the site. There are usually practical advantages behind the religious fussing."

It pleased Sakuni to be Zesnor's only source of knowledge. During the disquietingly swift journey from Thebes to Bharata by reed rowing ship and then horses or wagons, Zesnor, the "slave", had been in control. Sakuni, the "master", had been a helpless, ignorant passenger. He had found it disturbing. Although he had no cause, he distrusted his stone-faced Egyptian. To control knowledge is one way to control power, Sakuni realised as he talked, and he reminded himself to give Zesnor no more information than was necessary. Once the Egyptian had mastered the language, even that control would be gone.

"The green spaces are parks and gardens." That was useless enough knowledge. "The city is only thirty years old—it began as a fortress in the area of the palace here. This cleared land you see stretching all the way to the horizon was forest. As you can also see, there is considerable wealth here—excellent residences, shops, storehouses, stables. Of course it is nothing compared to Thebes."

"It is different, Master."

Zesnor's way of saying "Master" particularly disconcerted Sakuni, although, again, he was unable to express the fault in a clear way that could be corrected.

"At least Bharata is beyond the stage of clans and tribes,"

Sakuni continued. "But it is still a hundred petty kingdoms, with weak kings and bickering 'assemblies'. Utterly ripe for our plan. Already there's a title of '*samraj*', but it only means the holder has performed a tedious sacrifice and gained the others' 'consent' to call himself 'king of the kings'."

"Who is samraj now?"

"No one. Jarasamda of Magada has been trying for years. Magada is far southeast of here."

"Interesting."

"Not really. Your oracle, the Supremely Beloved, saw it exactly: My nephew can easily be made the ruler of all Bharata, and can be equally easily controlled by me. An empire here is inevitable." Sakuni stopped. "Inevitable." Involuntarily he looked behind them.

"There are great advantages to a unified country," Zesnor said evenly.

Sakuni noted how the Egyptian rarely showed his true reaction. If he had any. "And as your master pointed out to me," Sakuni continued, "there are equal advantages to the required conquests. They yield slaves, which we need for mining, farming. Those few slaves we have now are mostly women taken in raids." The baron glanced backwards again. "Bharata does, however, have the most beautiful women I at least have ever seen. In Egypt I observed that your master is not against accepting an exceptional foreign woman on occasion — only for Amon-Re's pleasure, of course."

Zesnor also looked tensely around them, while commenting in formal speech on the naivety of Arya. It seemed to him that the populace had been unduly upset the night before at seeing slaves functioning as draught animals. Then there was the king's failure to surround himself with the displays of wealth, ritual and power necessary to properly impress subjects.

"All this will change." Sakuni felt the uneasiness again. "I tell you, it is inevitable."

"Nothing is inevitable." The deep voice came from behind them, where only a moment ago there had been no one. "Why did you come back, Sakuni?"

Sakuni turned to face the sage Vyasa. He wore a coarsely woven robe, but of the costly, pure white Kashmir fleece, and even barefoot he was too imposing. It was his lofty attitude, Sakuni decided. Always the priestly superiority. But with new standards of measure, Sakuni reminded himself, predominance can shift to others.

"Vyasa, it has been so long. 'Why did you come back?' What a pleasant greeting from the Kurus' most successful procreator."

"Why did you come back?" Vyasa repeated.

"Where else would you have me be, old man? Besides gone to Yama, which is not possible even for you to arrange while my sister is the queen here. She is married to your own eldest son, in fact, which makes us family, does it not? Can't you be a little more pleasant to a relative?"

"I will ask you more plainly: If you wanted to practise yavana ways, Sakuni, why didn't you stay in the West?"

Sakuni smiled. "What is it you always say? 'Knowledge without applications is like a cow without milk.'"

"I see it is even harder now for you to speak honestly than it was when you left. Then serve the thin, sour milk of your knowledge far from Pandu's sons."

Sakuni was annoyed that his hands had begun to shake for no reason. "Gladly. I leave their instruction entirely to you."

Vyasa was silent a moment. When he spoke again, his voice seemed to come from several directions at once. "Sakuni, why are you selling Dasyu to Egyptian traders?"

Sakuni drew back, then cursed himself for appearing weak. "You asked me, Vyasa, why I am here. I am here to replace helplessness with strength, so that Bharata can become one powerful nation under one king."

"If that is the only sort of power you saw in your travels, Sakuni, you have received a poor bargain for your time and trouble."

"We shall see."

"I sometimes fear, Sakuni, that you will never see."

Sakuni could not understand his own fury. "You, Vyasa, speaking on the Kurus' behalf? Their king was seduced by your mother, the Dasyu *whore*."

Sakuni recoiled, anticipating a blow for his words, but there was no reaction even in Vyasa's expression. Instead it was

Sakuni who felt his rage mounting. He struck out. But his hand stopped in the air in front of him.

Vyasa had remained utterly motionless. Sakuni dropped his hand.

Again Sakuni saw his hand rise to strike, shaking in the air between them. A horrible pain gripped it. It dropped.

Still the baron could not control his rage. "Defend yourself, bastard. Stupid, stupid old man! I shall—"

Sakuni whirled towards Zesnor. Something physical yet invisible had passed between the sage and the slave. Sakuni turned back to Vyasa, imagining he could almost wrest it from one of them. But Vyasa was striding away.

Sakuni felt nauseated and shaken.

"He is a man of power," Zesnor said in Egyptian.

Sakuni felt the rage come back. "Never speak of him again. Never. What about Amon-Re's power? Speak of that."

"It has no limit."

"Good." Sakuni shrugged himself hard, as if shaking off the webs of poisonous spiders. He stared at his hand. "As soon as you can speak our language and move unnoticed among my people, you will go to Kampilya."

He studied Zesnor. What had happened? The Egyptian could not have understood half of what Vyasa was saying.

"In three months I will be ready, Master."

Sakuni shook himself again. "There is a rumour that this 'man of power' who impressed you so much has sequestered an extraordinary woman at Kampilya. He is pretending she is King Drupada's daughter so he calls her Draupadi. She seems to be quite important, at least to the bastard Vyasa. We will see if Amon-Re likes her as much. She'll be our first gift to his Servant."

8

The mind runs from boundaries,
The spirit refuses all restraint.

> Kunti, Mother of Pandu's Sons

In the three worlds there is no
action which I need do, Arjuna,
nor is there for me anything worth
attaining unattained; even so
I am engaged in action . . .
If I did not engage in action, these
worlds would perish.

> Krishna, as recorded
> in the *Bhagavad Gita*

What shall we do about Krishna?

> Vyasa

A late-autumn half moon was riding over Kampilya's west gate,
as if unaware that night was ending. In an alley by the palace
stables Draupadi, Eos and Panchalya stood at the heads of the
two finely bred bay chariot horses Panchalya had received as
a gift from his father at the same time that Draupadi had been
given Eos, three months before. Eos was dressed in Draupadi's
clothes, Draupadi in her brother's, and Panchalya in a groom's
garb—it was part of their plan. Although to be caught might
mean their deaths, the strong-willed youths chose not to think
beyond their goal. Today, for one day, they would set Draupadi
free.

In the stables a door slammed and a horse nickered. Panchalya nervously touched the ears of the two young mares to keep

them silent—part of the training of all superior chariot teams. The bays obeyed reluctantly, their tiny silver bells tinkling as they shifted and pawed the stones of the courtyard.

Panchalya adjusted a bridle. Eos straightened the cloth which wrapped Draupadi's head in the fashion of some princes. The three clasped hands in the grey light. Then Draupadi stepped up on to the chariot's box and took the reins. The tension in the horses came through the leather to her hands. Their barely restrained energy raced up her arms, straightened her shoulders, and raised her head. She shouted into the darkness, in a prince's voice, "Groom, let them go!"

Draupadi whipped the bays in spite of the blind curve. Curse the curve, she thought. She could not see the gates of the city yet, but she could imagine them up ahead, gaping open in the orange sunset. She cursed the gates too. And whipped again. The red and gold chariot jerked ahead with a fresh din of silver bells and bronze clappers.

The mares were dark with sweat and lunged in uncoordinated leaps now. She whipped them yet again. "Pray Brahma they recover," she whispered. But if the gates closed, she would be a prince caught outside. All attention would go to her. And when her true identity was known and her virginity brought into doubt (no matter how much she protested), she knew there would be no recovery for her or her brother, for Eos, or for all Panchala.

"Curse them anyway," she yelled into the wind. "Today I was free and anything will have been worth it." But she knew it was not true and whipped the horses once more.

The blind curve loomed up and she braced herself. Her red cloak blew open. She snatched for it, terrified of what might be revealed. When she looked up she saw around the bend: Her way was blocked by an ox cart with its bullock down in the road and a crowd gathered around it.

For a few strides of the team Draupadi was aware only of the whites of frightened eyes. As the chariot plunged into the ditch on the right she also saw beside the dying bullock the calm face of an old forest-dweller priest.

The motion stopped; the dust rose around her. One chariot

wheel spun free, clicking with decreasing speed. Otherwise, for a moment, everything was still. She could smell wood smoke from the hot axles of the chariot and dead frogs from the drying ditch. Her hands shook as she fumbled with the reins.

Then the voices of excited peasants began. They were all watching her. She looked up there among them, hoping to see the reassuring face again. Instead her attention was forced to a tall, expressionless man pushing through the crowd towards the edge of the ditch. He wore a black Bactrian robe but she sensed he was not Bactrian, and that he intended to come down to her.

Under her breath she said vehemently, "I will help myself, thank you." But this was only to herself. She could not risk speaking out loud. She felt for the knife in her belt. "Come near me and I will kill you," she whispered.

As if he had heard her, the stranger paused on the bank. She jumped from the chariot and ran to the mares' heads, glancing as she went for legs at odd angles or hooves held tenderly off the ground. The bays still seemed sound, but they were terrified now, rearing and fighting her. She glanced up at the city gates. Too far to run, nor could she just abandon this chariot. She turned back to her brother's darlings and tried to talk to them, but her voice shook.

"I will assist you, *Prince*." The strange accent chilled her. She didn't need to look—the one in black was speaking to her from the embankment.

Try to run, she thought. But leave Panchalya's horses?

"Your assistance is not desired, yavana." This voice startled Draupadi more. She stared up at the speaker, the old hermit-priest. His back was to her as he faced the much taller foreigner. The crowd was retreating. It was partly the word "yavana"—no one trusted the dharma-less foreigners from the west. And partly they drew back because, although neither man was a warrior by birth, both were clearly ready to fight, and who knew what other powers they might possess?

Draupadi felt herself staring, transfixed by the foreigner's eyes watching her over the priest's head. Now he stepped around the old forest-dweller.

The priest did not move. But suddenly his voice was like a spear hurled between the foreigner and the ditch: "In Bharata a yavana does not touch even the chariot of a prince without permission."

The crowd backed away farther. Why take a chance that the curse which the hermit-priest was now sure to utter would be limited to this foreigner? Besides, the yavana's own presence felt like the evil goddess Nirriti's—too dark to be human.

To Draupadi the man in black was like a stone that had fallen from the sky, a stick of dry wood sitting in the rain—he did not belong and he fascinated her. She felt the danger too. Supreme danger. But also such inevitability.

The old forest-dweller priest gestured to the crowd. An angry muttering began, directed at the foreigner. The priest nodded slightly. The crowd shuffled closer to him.

In return the yavana stepped rapidly towards the ditch. Several persons edged in front of him. He pushed them aside. The hermit-priest nodded again. Suddenly fearless, the crowd closed around the tall man and Draupadi could no longer see him.

She blinked a moment and looked back to the horses.

Then, like a good-luck heron, the priest slipped through the crowd and stepped lightly into the ditch, his white robe fluttering around his skinny legs. "Whatever the stories about them," the old man whispered, "united, the Panchala people have always had courage. Now into your chariot, Royal Child, and allow me to serve you at your horses' heads. I have some skill with these timid beasts."

The voice! She saw the dark tent again, the two fires. This was the one who had brought her to Kampilya.

When she did not move, the priest said quietly, "It is my hope that you will resume your good speed." He glanced up towards the road. "Fat bullocks like that one do not fall dead in the road for no reason. Would you have us spend the night out here with that darkness?"

Did he recognise her? Should she hope he had or had not? For the sake of her disguised brother and friend inside the city, she resumed her role. She bowed as a Panchala prince might to his priestly teacher—with as little deference as a youth

104

dared—and remounted the chariot. The old man went to the mares' heads and whispered to them. Then taking one head stall in each hand, he walked between them up the side of the ditch. The chariot tilted wildly for a moment. Then Draupadi was upright on the road.

Her eyes went to the crowd but the forest-dweller moved to block her view of it. There was an intense expression of warning on his face.

But then this old priest with the unkempt hair just laughed. "Best to go now, yes? Next time don't drive so fast that you can't stop what you've started. The gateman always waits when a prince has not returned."

"Who are you?" she whispered. "I must know."

"And they'll blame your teacher if your behaviour is at fault," he said loudly. Then under his breath, "Even though I've been unable to direct your education up until today. Now go. Stop again for nothing."

Reining in by the watering troughs, Draupadi stepped down and stood beside the mares. She was trembling, still hearing the old priest's voice and seeing the tall man in black with the face like stone. Eos appeared, wearing a princess's pink skirts and headcloth and making a touching attempt to look demure.

"You must change clothes quickly," Eos whispered. "In the empty guardroom."

"What has happened?"

"Nothing."

"Tell me!"

Eos swore in her own language. "You are to study Veda."

"Me? Surely my brother, not me."

"Your brother is being sent to study with Guru Vaja at Hastinapura."

"Then I succeeded." She closed her eyes to stop her tears. "There is something else. Tell me."

"Your father has ordered you sequestered under guard until your marriage."

She kept control—she walked back and loosened a girth, her hands shaking violently. "The king found out about today, didn't he?" Draupadi tried to keep the terror out of her voice.

"Maybe not. He's had an important visitor. Some priest. It's not safe to talk here."

Draupadi drew a deep breath. "I will not go back to my rooms."

"You must. Someone tried to stop you out there, didn't they? I saw. Listen to me, Draupadi. If the king thinks your marriage is the key to holding his kingdom, someone else is surely thinking your death is the key to its conquest."

In her mind Draupadi saw the man in black again. She caught the Greek's hand. "With you by me, I can bear any imprisonment."

Eos turned away. "I am not to guard you—or see you."

Draupadi pulled her back around. "Then you are in danger!"

"I think the king does not suspect anything about today. But he knows we are friends now and I might help you to escape. Now let me go before this costs us our lives."

"Eos, I can't go back to those rooms without you."

"The two servants outside the guardhouse—you can trust them. They will escort you."

"Eos, how long before this Arjuna comes for me?"

"Soon, Draupadi. Draupadi, if you cry, I will cry, and that will bring them down on us. Let me go!"

But Eos still held her hand, and in the end it was Draupadi who fled first.

The cry came again from the pallet in the next room. The old monk Urutata trembled. He glanced at the oil lamp at his feet, adjusted it to burn lower, then stared out of the window at the shore of the Western Ocean. The Infinite Water still looked strange to his mountain-born eyes. But the full moon of new winter, the longest night of the year, was familiar. It spread a path of silver across the sea. The old priest wished he and the moaning youth in there could take that path.

I ought to be used to Krishna's suffering, he thought. The others ignore it.

Krishna. "Dark One". Probably half Dasyu with such dark skin. Certainly not priest-born. Not even a real prince—only the son of some Vrishni chief.

Anyway, it is better here for the young man than Badari

Hermitage. Here it's hot all day and warm all night, what he's used to. Noises, stinks. It was foolish of them ever to risk a plains-boy's mind by taking him into the purity of the mountains.

Who am I to question? Some are born for wisdom, some only to serve. To do one's own dharma well, without envy of another's—that is the test.

What of my Krishna's dharma? Why would the gods allot a warrior-class youth this strange knowledge that every priest seeks?

There was another groan and Urutata hunched down against it. He asked himself again why the sages couldn't place their faith in a river or a foothill lake to bring forth the necessary visions. The sea outside there —it was too big to make sense. And salty? A terrible waste of water. Terrible influence on a mind. If they just slept in the same hut with the youth, heard his moans. But no, they talk about him all day as if Brahma himself had been born on earth. Thus, all night, it's only I who hear him, a very mortal boy. Even here when it's only the three of us, the learned one sleeps in the other hut.

Well, that young scholar needs his rest.

Urutata scratched himself. Here was the question that puzzled him: Why did the dark ones always carry the burden? So many dark Arya these days. And everyone asked where they came from. Where did they think? Out of a heron's mouth?

It is punishment for our arrogance, the way these dark offspring of ours shine with the awareness now so rare among the rest of us.

He thought of the woman Aditi at Badari. Named for the goddess, wise in Veda, the mother of twins. Yet dark as the night. The daughter twin they simply called Krishnah, Dark One. Like my Krishna here. Even the great sage Veda Vyasa, Collector of Veda, was first named Krishna Dvaipayana, The Dark One, Island Born.

Three Krishnas. He pondered it. If it continued, half the children in Bharata would be named Krishna, Dark One.

Ah, but Vyasa. The revered Vyasa. A troublemaker, that one. "Veda is structured in awareness. Without that awareness,

Veda is nothing." A fine thing to say to men who've studied Veda all their lives. Urutata laughed out loud.

"Light!" Krishna screamed. The old man jumped up and rushed in with the lamp to chase out the youth's nightmare. Krishna sat straight up on his bed, shaking like a twig in a storm. "It was—it was—" His voice came in broken gasps.

"Like the others?"

Krishna nodded, panting.

"The field of grain cut down? The slaughtered cows?"

"It was men. Sleeping men. Someone came and murdered them. Their spirits rose up and crowded around me. They were crying. The look in their faces—"

"Close your eyes, Krishna." The young man obeyed. "Now tell me—"

The youth leaped from his bed and ran out of the door.

The old man cursed and rose to his feet. Krishna was out of sight by the time his caretaker had crossed the meadow of sea grass and reached the beach. "We ought to leave him alone," Urutata muttered as he ran. "Nothing good will come of this. Now he'll drown himself. That's how this ocean will help him —it'll be his door to the world of the ancestors. I hope they treat him better than we have."

Afraid of the waves but desperate to save his beloved charge, the old man raced in and out with the surging surf, calling in the moonlight. Finally he turned to his left to pace along the beach.

A body down there! The sea had tossed it up. The old man ran. Krishna! The body stood, swayed as another wave struck it, but it was alive. The old man reached him, laughing wildly, and dragged him out.

"You see?" Urutata shouted above the surf. "Even the sea won't have you until you've finished your task."

Krishna leaned on him and let himself be guided up the beach and back into the hut. Urutata washed him and dressed him, then set him back down on the durva-grass mattress for the meditation done before dawn.

Krishna stared ahead for a long time, as if afraid to close his eyes. But finally they closed. The old man closed his too. To meditate of course, but if sleep came—

Urutata jerked upright. Across from him Krishna was rigid and staring. This time he felt Krishna's terror as if it were his own.

The youth whispered, "Destruction. Death. Everyone."

"*Can it be stopped*, Krishna?"

He didn't answer. The old man studied his charge a moment more, then ran for the other hut.

"I think it's happening," he called to the learned young priest whom he served. "Krishna sees clearly now, not in a dream."

The younger monk went from sleep to full command. He was a tall, lean man with glittering eyes, heavy black brows and a long nose.

The two priests—scholar and servant—rushed back to Krishna. But when they entered the youth's presence they dropped to their knees and stared. The youth seemed to glow, to shimmer with his terrible vision.

The two moved over to sit beside Krishna, facing east as the youth did. After letting the air settle and composing his mind, the scholar asked softly, "What do you see, Krishna?"

"Everything is gone. Fire, ashes. Death."

"Yes, Krishna. This is the same—this is the vision others have seen. But is there a way to remake this future?"

Krishna did not answer.

His face seemed on fire. Both monks felt the terror of it. They began to plead. But did the youth even hear?

"A silver one," Krishna finally whispered. After he said the words, a smile suddenly flooded his face.

"A silver one?"

"His back is to me. He says, 'Nothing can harm friends like us.'"

"Who is he? Turn him. Try to turn him towards you, Krishna."

"He turns." Krishna's voice became desperate. "But he can't see me. It's so black, he can't see me."

"Try again, Krishna," the younger monk whispered hoarsely. "Make him see you."

Krishna's face grew calmer. Finally he whispered with awe, "He sees me. He falls down, begging me for help." Krishna

was silent. Then he said softly, "This Arjuna, he will become
our little seed."

The younger monk's body slumped. "It's enough for tonight."

"No," Krishna said. "I must know what to tell him. I must
have more."

The two monks exchanged looks. Both felt the change—
they were no longer teachers but disciples.

Krishna's face was burning and solemn—far more withdrawn
than ever before. His two guardians waited. They waited a
long, long time.

Urutata woke to sunlight and an empty durva-grass mattress
where Krishna had sat.

The young scholar from Badari still slept. Another changed
relationship here, the old man thought, although he would
never tell who had woke and who had still slept on this
auspicious, long-awaited morning. He shook the sage. "Krishna
is gone."

The younger man struggled to his feet.

"Last night he went down to the sea," Urutata said.

"Yes, that's where we'll look, of course."

Out on the beach silver predominated, the sea birds making
silver sounds. Urutata knew he would always be aware of silver
now. Arjuna, the silver one.

Yes, there was Krishna, sitting before the sea, his hair
blowing, his dark face transformed by the bliss of Brahman.
They sat down at a respectful distance. He opened his eyes
and smiled, like Krishna the boy again. "You want to know
what I saw? I saw the water. Golden water."

"Just water?" the younger monk asked.

"It is everything, teachers. It contains everything."

"'In the beginning'," Urutata chanted, "'all this world was
undistinguishable water.'"

"The water was in everything," Krishna said, "like the water
inside the flower and stem and leaf and fruit of the plant. Just
a thought could make anything of that water."

The younger sage continued the verse from Veda: "'That
empty united world which was covered by a mere nothing, was

produced through the power of austerity. In the beginning was desire, which was the first seed of mind.'"

"And the water filled the seed and the world," Krishna sang, composing his own words. "It cooled the fire and ended the thirst. And the sound as it flowed became a name. Yudishtira."

Suddenly Krishna's tone was matter-of-fact. "But the only person I know with that name is a cousin of mine. The eldest son of King Pandu and my father's peculiar sister Kunti. He's fatherless, about my age, has no allies, and he's trying to claim the Kuru throne." Krishna shrugged.

The younger monk frowned. "It is hard to see what plains-politics have to do with Veda."

Krishna scowled at him. It did not occur to Urutata to rebuke this new Krishna for his sudden upsurge of insolence.

"I saw Pandu's sons when they were children," Urutata said. "Yudishtira's younger brother is named Arjuna. Silver."

Krishna and Urutata stared at each other. Urutata shifted nervously. There was something disturbing about this new Krishna. Didn't the young scholar see it?

The younger priest was obviously impressed by the revelations about Arjuna. Reverently he asked Krishna if he had seen more. Krishna laughed hollowly. "The warriors will all die."

"Die?"

Krishna smiled strangely. "I have seen a woman clothed in flames. All those who bear weapons as of today—she will lead them to me. It is I who will destroy them."

Urutata closed his eyes, in search of the inner silence that turns all human pronouncements to whispers. A sea bird screeched.

"*You* destroy them? Not likely," said a voice from behind them. The sage Vyasa strode in among the three like a stray yearling calf invading a solemn ritual ground. "It sounds as if you've done quite enough prophesying for one day—it has puffed up your small-self like a pig's bladder."

The younger monk bowed, Krishna stared, and Urutata fell to the ground, partly to hide his unreasonable delight at this entrance. Only the unequalled and amazing Veda Vyasa could do such a thing. And the honour that he had come here, to only the three of them—

"I speak what I have seen in my visions, great teacher," Krishna answered boldly.

"And I speak what I have seen in mine. As does Urutata here. Visions are merely fancy thoughts, Krishna. Visions and prophecies are all right, unless the future decides to take its own course and leaves you looking the fool. Better to take the reins and drive the future where you wish."

"And the coming Age of Strife, Great Sage?" It was the younger monk, clearly confused by the change in the very air around them—from sanctity to travel sweat. "Pardon me, great Vyasa, but if only you *would* speak what you have seen in your visions. However, you refuse, so we must look to others."

"I've told you many times, and the fact that you don't understand proves it: 'No matter the source of the words, it is the awareness of the hearer that decides their meaning.'"

Krishna's face was lit with pleasure at the debate. "Then, Sage, what is the purpose of words if they do not prepare us for the future?"

"That is exactly their purpose," the sage said with a kind of vehement patience. "But how well words prepare us depends on our awareness—the sleeping man hears nothing, the frightened man hears more than is said. Awareness depends on the body, which is always changing." Vyasa suddenly smiled down at Urutata, who felt a sweet bliss sweep over him. "For example," Vyasa continued, "all three of you look tired. Tiredness produces a certain kind of *unclear* awareness."

The younger monk stood up. "Then you mean the boy is not—"

"The boy *is*, or I would not have spent most of a month travelling to this shore when events demanded my presence in at least two other places. Krishna?" Vyasa took two pouches of stones from his belt. "Take these stones and go over there and arrange them."

"How, Sage?"

"Into a whole," Vyasa said slowly, "without the loss of their individuality."

Krishna's two guardians looked bewildered but their charge struggled not to. When he was out of hearing the younger monk repeated the details of Krishna's vision.

Vyasa shook his head. "The youth's fading health and humility are more important to me than his ability to discern the names of persons whose value I already know better than he does."

Krishna was coming back, having emptied the stones on a flat boulder. He bowed before Vyasa, then pointed behind him. Blurred by distance, the pile of black and white stones seemed grey to Urutata. It also seemed to him that Vyasa did not speak for a very long time. Finally the great sage merely said to the boy, "Prepare yourself to travel."

"Where am I going, Sage?"

"Home, where you belong. You are to stay there, practising your warrior's skills and keeping your mind free of visions, prophecies and things priestly. Stay there until you hear that your cousin Yudishtira is to be married. The brothers must not be divided now, as you will certainly tend to do the day you enter their lives. But once Yudishtira is wed—You do have a wife back at your mother's house?"

"Three thus far, Sage."

The two celibate monks stared.

"Just as I thought," Vyasa said, laughing. "A child prodigy after all. So then maybe when the five brothers marry—in that area of their lives at least—you will be of use to them. Go on now. Urutata? You will also join the brothers after Yudishtira's marriage, as their chief priest."

Urutata felt a wave of misery and fear. "I? Revered Sage, I can not possibly—"

"And myself?" interrupted the young scholar.

Vyasa did not answer immediately, and Urutata's mind was already filling with visions of court priests laughing at his lack of the simplest knowledge of sacrificial etiquette. Vyasa had surely made some mistake.

Now the sage waved his hand at the famous young scholar from Badari. "What you do makes no difference to me at all."

Urutata stared in disbelief.

"But Krishna?" Vyasa called towards a nearby bush. "The fact that you chose to sneak back and listen rather than obey me also makes no difference to me. However, it should be a significant and disquieting sign to yourself."

9

Gods, forgive me.
Gods, protect my eldest son.
May he some day forgive me.

Kunti, Mother Pandu's Sons

Then the world as I knew it ended.
Yudishtira

There had been enough warnings that his world was slipping away. But Yudishtira had chosen to ignore them, because on that day in the assembly hall after he had returned with the homeless Nishada, he had made a private agreement with his uncle that he abhorred: to forget his cousin's attempted murder in return for a home for these Dasyu. And when he could not bear to think about this agreement, he could not bear to think about any of what it implied.

The reasons the young Yudishtira chose not to reflect upon this matter were numerous, and he was aware of them in his heart even if he kept them from his intellect. Most obvious and most conscious was the knowledge that whatever wrong thinking was going on near or upon the throne, he would soon be king and correct it. To make difficult-to-prove public accusations against his uncle and cousin now would be foolish, even tactless, when soon he would be their ruler.

But the deeper thoughts to avoid were all the assumptions and implications behind the bargain he had struck with his uncle. The worst of these was that dharma was not at all clear on an important matter—the Dasyu. Dharma as it was taught by the forest-dwelling priests made no distinction between

Dasyu and Arya. So at Hastinapura, at least, other points of dharma were being applied increasingly. When the Arya wanted a particular piece of land, the Dasyu were considered a type of forest-dwelling animal and it was said they could be forced to move on, but preferably without violence to them. If they resisted as a group, however—as no animal would, it was argued—they were classed as a type of enemy, to be killed or enslaved. Finally, if leaving them alone on land claimed by Arya suited the Arya, as when Dasyu provided materials from the forest that the Arya needed, Dasyu were considered subjects.

Yet Yudishtira knew well that, according to dharma, animals could not be treated as enemies, although perhaps, in some sense, as subjects. Enemies could not be treated as animals or subjects. And subjects could never be treated as animals or enemies.

Yudishtira had gradually become aware through discussions with the palace priests that dharma, the Eternal Law, was not eternal at all, but adjusted itself slightly as new circumstances arose, revealing itself in the awareness of the most revered of the priest-born. But was this the process he was now seeing? At Hastinapura the definition of a Dasyu changed with the priest being asked, so that warriors went for guidance to whoever gave answers that suited them, and the priests would not or could not resolve their contradictory answers.

Although Yudishtira had accepted the unsettling idea of the eternal changing in order to remain eternal, he had frequently wished he could discuss this new concept with someone he respected. But Vyasa rarely appeared at Hastinapura, and never to speak to him alone; he no longer knew the dwelling places of any of the other forest teachers of his childhood; and the priests at Hastinapura he did not respect enough to question on matters relating to dharma's essence. And the fact was that Yudishtira saw it as inappropriate for him to try to resolve matters of law on his own.

Yudishtira found it even harder to think about the many ways his own uncle had violated dharma that day, and the way he, Yudishtira, had essentially abetted it: agreed to strike this secret bargain about the Nishada right in the assembly hall, where dharma required only open debate; agreed to an arrangement that meant an attempt at murder would not be charged; and agreed that this adharmic request be granted in return for nothing more than the fair treatment of subjects. Exactly when did one stop obeying without question one's uncle and king? And had he, the next king, remained silent out of obedience and respect for dharma, or out of convenience?

Finally, Yudishtira was avoiding reflection upon that day because he could not bear to admit his very first error in his encounter with his uncle—his tacit acceptance, through his obvious humiliation, that Arjuna's bedding Lotus was something not merely to be strongly discouraged, but to be ashamed of. When a prince bedded a Dasyu, was it wrong because she was a subject of low status? Or an enemy?

Or was it that she was an animal?

If he admitted that Hastinapura's priests increasingly insisted on this last interpretation, he would again see and feel Wood Rose in his arms. And know clearly that all his understanding of everything was beginning to slip away, like a stick set down on the edge of a flood.

So he did not think. And as a result, for Yudishtira the four months following the killing of the tiger and preceding the graduation tournament were deceptively—dangerously— honey-sweet. Each day brought dryer, cooler weather, and then the winds came from the northwest, sweeping the skies clear.

Of the six seasons—spring, summer, rains, autumn, winter and dews—the autumn months of Karttika and Margasirsa had always been Yudishtira's favourites. After the wild rains they were crisp, rational months. Months when he chose to call the daily whispers, brooding silences and averted eyes throughout the palace normal, given the coming transfer of the throne from Drita to himself. Baron Sakuni's mode of arrival and increasing influence he called insignificant; Suyodhana's treachery, natural. He saw no connection between the discomfort of his uncle's family and the general populace's increasing fondness for himself and his brothers. When stories were told of crowds hailing one of Drita's sons because they thought he was a son of Pandu, and then falling silent when they saw their mistake, Yudishtira was only embarrassed.

With the atmosphere inside the palace so tense, the brothers simply spent more time away from Hastinapura, hunting or merely exploring the realm they would begin in the spring to rule. As their mid-winter graduation tournament approached they also turned their attention to practising their skills. Not that there could be any real competition, given Guru Vaja's decision, but they could still provide a good "exhibition". "Only to impress any potential troublemakers on our borders," Bhima liked to explain.

Yudishtira, however, was beginning to vaguely dread the event. This dread he also might have thought about, but, again, he had preferred to put it aside.

Or he might have contemplated the change in his mother. Such as the night he came upon her at the empty tournament grounds. He had gone out to practise alone in the evening, after his studies were done. He planned only to throw a few battle axes and shoot a quiver of arrows before the light was gone. The contest site was the last place he expected to find his mother. But she was sitting in the stands, staring at the centre of the arena with such concentration that he startled her when he joined her up on the wooden benches.

"A good seat, Mother, but it will be a long month out here, waiting for the ceremonies to begin. Are you that anxious to see your sons proclaimed men so you can have us off your hands?"

But she who had taught her eldest, most serious son the value of humour among family members had only stared at him, then stood and walked away into the dark.

The mother of the sons of Pandu, the small, elegant and imperious Queen Kunti, had always been the most controversial woman in Bharata. Even without her strange ways, her parentage and upbringing would have been enough. She was the daughter of a Vrishni headman, and her older brother was not only the leader now of the Vrishnis but the father of this peculiar Krishna receiving so much attention from the priests these days.

Which had really surprised no one. The Vrishnis were all odd and Yudishtira's maternal grandfather, the Vrishni clan's leader in those days, was everyone's first example of this oddness. This grandfather had had a cousin who was a childless widower, and impossible as it seemed, Yudishtira's grandfather had promised to give his first-born daughter to this cousin. The unfortunate gift child was Kunti.

The old cousin knew nothing about raising girls. He taught Kunti to perform his household rituals, a job most would reserve for a son, and to wait upon his frequent guests, a task definitely better suited to a wife than a maiden daughter. Then this naive foster father invited for an extended visit the peculiar Durvasas, a priest of eccentric and inconsistent vows whose opinions on dharma were extremely unorthodox. Kunti was ordered to please the fussy old man however she could. Apparently she succeeded quite well, for when Durvasas left, he let slip to a servant that he had given the young girl a spell "that allows her to call upon any god she chooses and he will come and make a son with her". The shrewd servant dutifully repeated this everywhere, guessing it was Durvasas' excuse in advance for any seed this wild-eyed priest might have decided it was his dharma to sow in the field that was his host's virgin daughter.

Not only did the little Kunti's reputation somehow remain unstained—Durvasas moved on to Hastinapura and recommended her "virtue and unusual range of knowledge" to the Kuru regent, Gangeya. Within a month she was introduced to Crown Prince Pandu and the following year she chose him at her bride's choice. Thus the reserved and delicate young girl became Bharata's most powerful queen, for four brief years. After which her stranger fortunes returned.

First the noble King Pandu took a second wife, Madri, who was more beautiful than Kunti—at least in the showy ways—but utterly uneducated. This was merely ordinary bad luck for Kunti, and certainly within the rights of a king, who must above all provide an heir. But then her husband caught the priests' and seers' obsessive fear of dharma's destruction and the coming Age of Kali. With his wives, he set off to the forest to prevent this disaster. Alas for Kunti and Madri, surata, sexual pleasure, was among his sacrifices.

Yet somehow five boys were born before the death of both

Pandu and Madri, at which time Kunti brought the five back to Hastinapura. Yudishtira often thought about the courage it must have taken for his mother to walk down the north road to Hastinapura's gates, where the blind King Drita and his sons were waiting under the royal umbrella that she had last seen when her husband had stepped out from under it. And there was the gossip to face about who were the boys' fathers if Pandu had been adhering to his vows. On this Yudishtira felt his mother made a mistake—she insisted that, thanks to Durvasas' spell, the five were sired by the gods themselves: Yudishtira by Lord Dharma, Bhima by Vayu the wind god, and Arjuna by Indra the god of war and rain. She even claimed Madri had borrowed the spell to conceive the twins, Nakula and Sahadeva, with the divine Ashwins, the twin physicians. He could never understand why his mother, so famous for her truth-telling, held to the peculiar story.

But the brothers' paternity was really no issue. The laws of dharma gave a queen's children first claim to the throne of her deceased husband, whoever their father. And in this case their father had been king; their uncle, only a substitute ruling in their father's place. So the title of crown prince was taken from Drita's eldest, Suyodhana, and bestowed upon Yudishtira. In the years that followed, her five sons acquired popularity as easily as grass stains. But their mother remained an unapproachable oddity. At first Hastinapura's royal ladies did try to include her. But whether she felt she had to hold herself superior for her eldest's sake or because she really believed she had bedded the gods, she rejected all overtures from Hastinapura society and kept to herself.

After his encounter with his mother in the empty arena Yudishtira vowed to discuss with Bhima her strange behaviour. But later he forgot, and the days passed. If one feeling—dread —predominated that autumn, Yudishtira's thinking overlooked a hundred causes.

Then at dawn on the morning of the graduation tournament his ever-unpredictable mother at last gave shape to his fears.

He had woken because of a noise. Then he saw her. She was circling his room, waving a branch of the purifying apamarga tree, whose long, backward-turning leaves were said to deflect sin from the sinner. The leaves rustled as she walked; she whispered hoarsely the verses for expiating wrongdoing. The sight horrified him.

"Mother, you've startled me. What have I done to deserve this penance by yourself?"

"Ask what *I* have done."

"I can't imagine, Mother. No sin, I'm certain."

"'Beware of certainties.' You learned that early." She stopped before him. "Yudishtira, this tournament must be prevented."

He did not hesitate—it was his mother's command. "I will speak to Guru Vaja at sun-up."

"Speak to him now."

Yudishtira swallowed, imagining his teacher's reaction. But this was his mother. He rose to dress and go.

Then Kunti cried and threw herself into his arms. "It's too late. I had twenty-five years. Now the penance."

He awkwardly stroked her fine black hair. "For what, Mother?"

She drew back, smoothed her skirt and suddenly looked almost herself again. "No, the tournament must proceed. All the guests. It must be held."

He was speechless, only aware of her profile framed by the open window and crowned by the setting crescent moon. She was as beautiful as his earliest memories of her.

"I wouldn't bother to go back to sleep," she said almost serenely. "King Drita will be asking for you soon."

Yudishtira's fear burst out in annoyance instead. "Why didn't he tell me last night?"

"He didn't know last night." His mother went to the door. "He's thinking of it now."

A few moments after she was gone a servant came to his door: King Drita requested the presence of the crown prince in the assembly hall.

It was an unusually balmy dawn for mid-winter. Yudishtira found his uncle sitting alone on the dais at the far end of the hall, clothed only in a loincloth. The king did not look fresh from an early rising, but more as if he had never gone to bed. A lamp might help his mood, Yudishtira thought. Then he remembered that darkness meant nothing to a blind man.

The king raised his head as Yudishtira approached. His first words were slow, effusive, and sounded rehearsed: "It has been suggested to me, Yudishtira, that I make you and your family a gift of an excursion after this graduation today. Some pleasant and restful recreation before you begin to rule."

"An excursion?"

"Yes, to relax yourselves after today's exertions." Drita waited, but Yudishtira could think of no response to such a strange offer. "Your going will help the kingdom as well."

"That is always my desire, Uncle. A gift of recreation, however, is not necessary. Although I am always grateful—"

"I know you would enjoy a pleasure trip to Varanavata," the king said emphatically. He began wringing his hands.

"Then tell me why I am needed there, my King."

Drita made an impatient gesture. "As you know, the people of Varanavata work the copper ore they obtain from down river and then trade it, all of which makes them rather independent-minded, even though they accept Kuru protection. Since you are so popular with the common people"— the king said that with a disturbing edge to his voice—"your visit will certainly strengthen the coppersmiths' commitment to our leadership. Fortunately Varanavata is a beautiful city in winter—they celebrate the Festival of Light especially well. We can all see that your mother will certainly benefit from the change, even if it fails to interest you."

Yudishtira crossed and uncrossed his arms. To be sent so far away just before his consecration as king was annoying. But it was utterly impossible to refuse his uncle's seemingly innocent request without implying or directly accusing him of some unprovable wrong intention. Nor could he withhold the slightest pleasure from his mother, especially after this morning.

"I am happy here, King Drita. But I will also be happy to obey your command and go wherever you wish to send me."

"I'm not commanding you to go to Varanavata! Can't you just go because you want to?" Drita's hands rubbed each other rapidly.

"I *don't* want to go, Uncle." Yudishtira chose his next words carefully. "But I *will* go. Because you have requested it. We will go whenever you wish."

The king seemed so exasperated that Yudishtira gave up trying to identify the core of unreasonableness he sensed was controlling one of them. He chose his words carefully. "It will be my pleasure to leave as soon as you wish."

Suddenly, again, Yudishtira saw a vision of flames in the air around him.

"Thank you, Yudishtira." The old man seemed to collapse back in his throne. "That's a good boy. Always the good boy. Now leave me alone, won't you, for Yama's sake?" Yudishtira remembered later how much the king sounded, at the same moment, like an angry child and a tired old man.

The stern and famous Guru Vaja stood in the centre of Hastina-pura's royal stadium. The weapons-master wore a priest's white robes, his hair was white and loose, white ointments were on his forehead and cheek, and the white string of the twice-born crossed his chest. Around him were the five sons of the late King Pandu and the four eldest sons of the blind King Drita. In a second row stood ten more of Suyodhana's brothers, plus the new student, Panchalya—the "son" of King Drupada. All were smooth shaven, had their hair coiled at the backs of their necks, and wore the loose white cotton breechcloth of students, with their weapons tied at their waists. Behind them the stands were filled and overflowing on to the high ground around.

Guru Vaja stood in silence, staring at his students one by one, measuring and admonishing each with his eyes. Only when he gazed at Arjuna, his favourite, was there any softening at all.

Now Guru Vaja's eyes left Arjuna and were on Yudishtira, the last. They bore into him, the eldest, the crown prince.

Give it back, Yudishtira told himself. He stared without blinking into the glittering eyes, although he would have preferred kneeling at the man's feet.

"Before we begin," Guru Vaja finally said quietly, so that only his students could hear, "I must tell you the truth: You are grown men with the minds of nursing infants. Your quarrels are dangerous. They could destroy all of you. To me, today is no 'graduation tournament', but the most important exercise I have ever given you. It requires you to wield weapons together and even fight each other, but with the cordiality of men who will jointly rule this country, with Yudishtira at the head as the dharma of succession requires."

"And if we don't?"

Yudishtira could not believe what he had heard. The words were from King Drita's second eldest, Dusasana.

Guru Vaja turned and stared at the stocky youth. "Some of you think you have grown too wise to be students. You want to call yourself 'graduates' in a new way, as if it meant I were no longer your elder and you had nothing more to learn. I see it. This I promise you—whatever I am able to teach you 'graduates' today, it will be your last lesson from me. I leave the rest to Yama."

Yudishtira felt a cold blade pass through him.

"Now let the tournament begin!"

At Guru Vaja's words the musicians began playing and the students marched around the ring, holding up their weapons and personal banners to the cheers of the crowd. Then the individual demonstrations began. Bhima did gymnastic feats in preparation for wrestling, Arjuna shot arrows at moving targets, the twins duelled with swords, Suyodhana twirled his enormous mace as if it were a twig, his younger brother Dusasana did the same with a pike, and so on. Yudishtira was supposed to hurl spears. He believed he did. Afterwards he could not remember. For as he performed, his mind was discovering the forbidding anxiety that comes when those who have always led suddenly cease to proceed reasonably. His mother, his uncle. Now his guru, leaving the fate of his students to the lord of death.

Arjuna's exhibition earned long cheers, to Guru Vaja's obvious pleasure. The weapons-master kept him out in the arena after the others were done, having his prodigy shoot at all the most difficult targets: the iron boar on wheels, a leaf in the spokes of a chariot, a cow's horn which had to be shot into without injuring the goat carrying it around his neck.

The crowd was wild with delight. So, apparently, was the

king. The word was passed until, down at the edge of the arena, even Yudishtira overheard that "King Drita is thanking Indra that the Kurus have Arjuna". Yudishtira saw his cousins' faces flush with rage. Except Suyodhana, who seemed to take it with a strange good humour.

A messenger came to whisper, "Your mother wishes to see you immediately."

Yudishtira hurried up the stairs to her. She was alone, as always, even when surrounded by others. Her expression was no longer anxious, as it had been at dawn—it was rigid with terror.

He bowed low by her ear. "Indra protect you, what troubles you, Mother?"

As if in answer, the crowd roared behind him. He turned to see Bhima and Dusasana, King Drita's second-eldest son, swaggering towards each other, maces in hand and shouting insults. It had happened so quickly—the unveiling of a mature hatred. Some of the spectators around Yudishtira were already waving bits of coloured cloth spontaneously torn from hems and headcloths—blue for the sons of Pandu and red for the sons of Drita.

Only our common enemies have anything to celebrate now, Yudishtira thought.

He moved to go and do what he could to control Bhima. But he stopped. Perhaps Guru Vaja or Gangeya or even Drita could end it, but not he, Pandu's son. He watched Bhima and Dusasana circle each other, feinting and probing defences.

Suddenly an odd sound of rhythmic slapping came from behind the gate leading into the arena. It was an archaic sound and it stirred Yudishtira deeply, although he had only imagined it before, as a boy listening to legends. But he knew it as well as he knew his father's voice—it was the sound of an Arya warrior from the old days across the Indus, slapping his upper arms to announce his intention to do battle, the sound of his palms on his own muscles warning the world of his strength in the clearest way.

Even Bhima and Dusasana paused. The gates were flung open by two fists and a tall, magnificent warrior strode into the arena. He strutted to the centre and shouted, "Arjuna!

Whatever feat you have done, I will better it. Before all of Bharata, I will teach you humility."

The crowd exploded with shouts. The stranger was perhaps ten years older than Arjuna—in his prime and appearing more than able to keep his word. His bearing was wild, his body powerful, his appointments rich if not quite elegant, with gold earrings and shield and an impressive amount of iron on his sword, bow and arrow tips. Above all, his flowing hair—as pale and golden as Arjuna's, but redder in hue—gave his head a crown of red-gold flames. He was a spectacle. And a total stranger to everyone.

Except to Yudishtira, who found the warrior as eerily familiar as the arm slapping. He was like a spectre from the past, a legendary man, an emissary from the ancestors. There was something about this warrior and this moment that Yudishtira knew he would never forget.

The warrior lifted his bow, took aim, but waited to shoot until it became clear to all that he was sighting at the cow's horn around the ram's neck. The animal had been forgotten when Bhima and Dusasana had engaged each other. Now the goat tore at the grass along the edge of the arena farthest from the newcomer. The distance was well beyond any reasonable accuracy with a bow and arrow. The crowd fell silent. The bow spoke; the ram staggered as an arrow entered the cow's horn which it bore.

The stands shook with stamping feet. Even blind King Drita was standing, asking for details.

Yudishtira saw Arjuna step a few paces into the arena, his bow in his hand. But he turned back towards Guru Vaja. Yudishtira was satisfied—in spite of the stranger's arrogant offer to "teach him humility", Arjuna was maintaining his calm.

Guru Vaja nodded to Arjuna and walked out to meet the stranger. Now Yudishtira moved to go down. He did not care for the way this interloper was interrupting a Kuru graduation tourney and pushing Arjuna to the edge of his self-control.

But a man standing next to Yudishtira touched his arm. The crowd noise was too great for talking—the man merely pointed behind them.

Kunti was lying back in her seat, eyes closed and face white. Yudishtira rushed to her, calling for help.

"No! Keep them away," she cried, roused by his shouts. "Tell no one!"

Her serving women were crowding around to care for her, but above their excited voices he heard her say it again: "Tell no one."

Uncertain, he looked back to the arena.

Arjuna was shouting: "Stranger, I will be delighted to compete with you. Let us now announce ourselves according to the rules. Tell us your parents and the great line of warriors from which you must surely come."

Yudishtira saw it even from in the stands—the stranger hesitated. Guru Vaja took a step back from him. "Your lineage, please, young man."

"Are you afraid, Arjuna?" the warrior roared. "Then someone else compete with me!"

"No, I will compete. After we have followed the law and heard your parentage."

"Talk with arrows, Arjuna, before I take your head off in front of your own mother."

The audience gasped. But Yudishtira saw that Kunti had not heard. What kind of haphazard training in deportment had this warrior received?

Arjuna was obviously wondering also. "I'm sure your own mother would highly disapprove of that speech—if you know who she is."

"Hold your tongue," the stranger said. "She is Radha and I am called Radheya, after her."

"Excellent," Arjuna said, as much to the stands as to the man before him. "We are halfway, Radheya. Although I do not know this warrior-born woman named Radha. Now, the name of your warrior father?"

The man's confidence was entirely gone. Yudishtira did not like Arjuna shaming this Radheya about his parentage. But neither could a total stranger be allowed to interrupt the graduation and insult them.

Suyodhana stepped out into the arena. "It is obvious what you are implying, Arjuna—that this man is not a warrior-born so you do not have to risk being humiliated by him. But the old laws say there are three excellent ways to become a warrior other than by birth: One may rule a kingdom, lead an army, or become a champion at arms. If you are afraid to give this Radheya an opportunity to become a champion at arms by defeating you, and since we have no army here, I think we should make him a king. Do you agree, Father?" Suyodhana turned and shouted to the stands: "You can't see this man, Father, but he has just performed an unequalled feat with his bow. Shall we spare him further embarrassment? Suppose we make him king of the Anga?"

The Anga? Yudishtira thought it had to be a joke. The Anga were a small Arya band far to the east, settling a rough, untamed country. Since their king had been captured by Jarasamda of Magada, they had allied themselves with the Kurus.

"Excellent," Drita shouted. "Consecrate him immediately."

Yudishtira ran down the stairs, but Gangeya was already protesting. "Drita, you would give the Anga a king without consulting them? They are our allies—not Dasyu, to be given any master we choose for them."

"There are only a few Anga," Suyodhana shouted. His daring to dispute with Gangeya caused murmuring in the crowd and he softened his tone. "Perhaps they'll be glad to have this man to protect them."

"But not as their king," Yudishtira heard himself shout. "A king must be devoted to his people, and they to him."

Gangeya looked across the stands at him and frowned. Yudishtira was furious, torn again by this conflict between obedience and justice. Behind Gangeya, Yudishtira could see Baron Sakuni whispering something to King Drita. Yudishtira proceeded down to the floor of the stadium and stood by the rail, watching the four inside the arena and trying to maintain his self-control.

"Father?" Suyodhana called. "Shall we become this valiant stranger's patrons? Or turn him away and let him seek some other ally?"

King Drita's voice was a high-pitched croak: "Let him be consecrated. Immediately!"

Yudishtira recoiled. He gripped the railing, then stared out into the arena again. Radheya's face now shone with tears of gratitude. As if in a dream Yudishtira heard the stranger say, "But surely, Prince Suyodhana, you are not going to honour me in this way?"

"Of course I am."

"Prince, what can I possibly give that can match this gift?"

"I merely ask, King Radheya, that you promise me your friendship."

The tournament had been forgotten. The noon sun blazed down on the final rituals of Radheya's hasty coronation. He now sat in the middle of the arena on the traditional golden stool, a royal umbrella over him, the royal yak-tail fan waving. Those who were warrior-borns were filing back to their seats after bending their knees before the new king (an informal courtesy obeisance which the sons of Pandu had avoided performing, apparently without attracting notice). Priests were chanting and the crowd in the stands was enjoying the additional fruit and cakes ordered by Suyodhana in celebration.

The rumour now was that King Drita was praising all the gods for sending the Kurus this Radheya, "the finest archer ever to string a bow". Through it all Gangeya and Guru Vaja had remained frowning but silent, and Arjuna and Bhima had only muttered that the new defender of the Anga had been seen to shoot exactly one arrow. The rest of the audience seemed pleased.

"Now who do you suppose *this* one is?" Arjuna whispered. Yudishtira looked where his brother pointed and saw a sweating, trembling old chariot driver coming through the open gate. The driving cloak that identified his profession was twisted and he leaned on a stick. He nervously tried to cover his bare feet with the dusty end of his trailing loincloth.

Someone was trying to guide him back out when Radheya rushed to him and knelt down, his head still glistening with the consecrating waters. The old man embraced the new king, saying loud enough for all to hear, "My son, my dear son."

Bhima's laugh filled the arena. "A chariot driver. Suyodhana, look! You've made a king out of the son of a chariot driver."

The crowd, many of whom were warrior-born, were not laughing. This old man calling Radheya his son was indeed wearing the clothes indicating an occupation reserved only for the classless offspring of a marriage between the priest-born and the warrior-born. To make a king out of the son of such a person, and in the presence of so many from the oldest warrior families, was in poor taste to say the least. Not that any of them had particularly wanted to be exiled to Anga territory in his place, even to gain a throne.

All morning Suyodhana had been almost calm. Now he lost control. "Bhima! How dare you insult a king!"

"King of the Chariot Drivers," Bhima yelled back, coming out into the open and strutting around Radheya like a peacock. The crowd laughed. The consecration of a king could not be undone—the chariot driver's son had joined the warrior class. At least in return he could provide them some amusement.

"Strength is the only father of a warrior," Suyodhana shouted. "And courage, which has deserted your brother Arjuna."

Yudishtira still stood behind the arena's railing. He clenched his fists, willing himself not to run Suyodhana through with the closest lance.

Bhima screamed back, "I say, the son of a chariot driver still has no more right to a duel with my brother Arjuna than a dog has the right to lick the butter at the sacred fire. And the one who invites the dog to lick is a bitch!"

Suyodhana raised a mace and charged Bhima. Arjuna nocked an arrow. Bhima merely grinned like an idiot at the new fire he had lit. The crowd was screaming the names of all three.

Bhima ducked as Suyodhana's mace sliced through the space where Bhima's laughing face had been. Before Suyodhana could recover from the swing, Bhima was mauling his cousin's face with his big hands. Dusasana rushed to defend his elder brother, his raised battle axe flashing in the sun.

Arjuna's arm drew back, his bow aimed at Dusasana. Yudishtira lunged at him to stop the sinful arrow that would make

Arjuna a cousin-killer. Arjuna flailed backwards wildly, not realising who had stopped him. Yudishtira felt blood on his lips from the blow—blood drawn by his own brother.

"Cease this!" It was Gangeya.

The combatants froze.

Suddenly Guru Vaja advanced and bowed before Gangeya and the king. "I apologise to all Kurus for this display of madness. I have failed to train these children properly. Today I cease to be a weapons-master."

There were gasps and nervous whispers in the crowd. There were far more when Suyodhana shouted back, "How could you ever have been a weapons-master? You're a *priest*."

Guru Vaja flushed under the white ointments, the contrast seeming to make a mask such as Dasyu wore.

"Now," Baron Sakuni stood up. "Apologise to your teacher, Suyodhana," he called down. "Beg him to remain as weapons-master. Don't you recall that he was going to allow this Radheya to show his skill when others wanted to deny him?"

Suyodhana seemed to swell with even more anger, but went down on his knees in front of Guru Vaja, who stiffly accepted his outstretched palms.

"Now," Sakuni said smoothly, addressing the stands, "if all this madness has concluded, I suggest this 'graduation' also be considered concluded."

It was as if a pride of lions had been so agitated by a lightning bolt that a crow was able to order them back to their dens. King Drita tilted his head, then bellowed, "I declare this exhibition over."

The crowd stirred, confused by Baron Sakuni's new authority. They began rising, gathering belongings and filing down the stairs. Yudishtira stood still in the flow of bodies, seeking but unable to find the essence of the cause of the wrongs he had witnessed.

Finally the stands were empty. His elders and his cousins had gone. When he had motioned to his brothers to leave without him, they had also departed. Servants and weapons-carriers were trooping out with equipment. The only persons left were the stranger Radheya and his chariot-driver father. They stood in the gateway, simply staring at each other.

Now Yudishtira made his way slowly towards the gate, for some reason dreading having to pass by the father and son. Yet he was also drawn to them. He meant to go through the gate without looking, but he raised his eyes. The father's back was to him; Radheya faced him. Both were veiled in drifting dust, as if figures in a half-remembered dream. But even so, for the instant when he looked into Radheya's face, it was as if he looked into a mirror.

The two teachers of Veda came daily to Draupadi's room. It was a newly built room, detached from the rest of the palace so that it could be surrounded by guards. But it had a small garden, and it was here that Draupadi was given her lessons.

Initially she refused to attend to these lessons, seeing them as someone's attempt to distract her from her loss of even the semblance of freedom. But gradually the depth of her teachers' discussions and the dimly familiar beauty of the chanted verses of Veda captured her attention.

Of those first, tolerable days of her confinement, one stood out. It was in early winter. The discussion was of Agni, the god of fire, whose name was the first word of Veda. "To some, Veda is a collection of chants for rituals," explained the older of her teachers. "But that is the immature understanding. The seers first heard these sounds deep within their silent awareness. The sounds themselves are the threads of creation, weaving the world we see. And within this first word, 'Agni', all creation is contained as the seed contains the tree."

She could hardly pretend to grasp what all this meant, but, perhaps because she was called Agni's daughter, she drank these words down and they soaked into some parched place in her mind that had not known this water since Before.

The teachers began to chant: "Agni, lord of all . . . bright-blazing and hastening towards the gods, the fierce burning flames . . . ancient, brilliant, omniscient, spreading everywhere . . ."

At that moment a serving girl entered the garden and crept up beside Draupadi. "Mistress, there is news!" she whispered. "The sons of Pandu are taking a pleasure trip to Varanavata. Your father has invited them to visit here also!" Draupadi's

131

heart was pounding. She studied the girl, but the servant did not waver from her story. "Here, Princess."

The chanting had stopped; her teachers had overheard. Their expressions reflected such pain and concern that Draupadi asked what troubled them. But they would not speak or even meet her eyes. They only resumed their singing:

"Royal Agni, messenger of the gods, proceed, scattering the glittering darkness . . . shine with the treasures of Heaven . . . overpower the dark night with brilliant beams. Agni, the Radiant, the Formidable. Agni, the Observer of Truth."

The cottage smelled of fresh wood, fancy lacquers, scented oils and spiced butters. It was charming in every way, as was Varanavata itself. Lying in bed in the dark, Yudishtira still savoured his first glimpse of the town as it had looked in the morning when they had climbed to its picturesque seat on the hill and entered the arched gate in the high crenellated log walls. Throughout the day the breezes had fluttered the city's banners, the people had showered them with flowers and the local priests had chanted blessings with their east-country lilt. Then at dusk the little city had become enchanted, lit by a thousand oil lamps and pitch torches for its Festival of Light.

Yudishtira turned on his side. He knew this lying awake and analysing was foolish. King Drita was right, the trip was becoming worthwhile. The people felt honoured that the sons of Pandu had visited their town. They were already talking more loyally. And the springs and lakes would delight his mother, who had hardly spoken since the terrible outbreak at the graduation.

Perhaps an interlude away from Hastinapura before the coronation was even wise. And by next summer everything would be settled.

The darkness in the cottage pressed down on Yudishtira. He listened. Why then this wakefulness?

It was the puzzle of Gangeya's parting words: "You and your cousin are men now. What was a boyhood quarrel has now become deadly."

Deadly.

Then Gangeya had said, "Consider where the power lies.

There is nothing wrong with running away when you are overpowered, if by running away you gain the strength to take your rightful stand."

But "deadly". The one word kept him awake.

He and his brothers had called Gangeya "Grandfather" since boyhood. If Gangeya thought they were in danger, would he not have said so outright?

Not when it would be an accusation Gangeya could not prove.

Would Suyodhana really attempt murder?

After the tiger hunt he knew it was a boy's question—they were all men now.

So where was the danger? Assassins? To kill all five brothers, even surprised and unarmed, would be a feat. And others would witness the battle, recognise the attackers and trace them back to their employers. The Kuru elders would not allow a king to sit on the throne for a day if that throne had been gained by murder.

Some clever poison then.

No. Suyodhana would not use the Coward's Way.

It was so quiet in the cottage. The walls were thin in the lacy little guest house. Yet all he could hear was Bhima's breathing in the next room. Why no snoring servants in the outer room? *Why no pacing guards?*

He sat up. I might as well have been asleep, he thought, for all my famed alertness. No guards, and I explicitly ordered them.

Now there was a sound outside. But not the confident tread of a sentry. Yudishtira stood. It was very dark. The cottage had twelve rooms, but far fewer windows and only one entrance. Suddenly that oddity felt like treachery. He started for the door of his room.

A figure loomed up. Yudishtira was sure his way was being blocked. A voice said softly, "Can I help you, Master?"

This was not the voice of the servant he had brought with him.

"I want to go out."

There was a red, flickering glow from the left of the open outer door. Its light spread quickly. Now Yudishtira could see this "servant" better. He had the flat-faced features of the local Dasyu and was glancing nervously over his shoulder towards the outside.

Yudishtira's mind was suddenly clear. He shoved the man through the entry room at the front of the house and out of the outer door ahead of himself. From the right someone swung a club and crushed the head that was supposed to have been his own.

From out of the dark hall Bhima hurtled past Yudishtira and grabbed the arm still holding the weapon. He jerked a pale-skinned man into the room with such force that the murderous arm separated from the shoulder. Bhima threw the arm against the wall, then hurled the body down on to the Dasyu with the crushed skull.

Their pale-skinned attacker from the doorway was still alive and clutching at the empty arm socket. Yudishtira recognised the dismembered man as the same unctuous petty official who had welcomed them to the house that afternoon, "a house especially designed for the sons of Pandu".

Yudishtira looked around them. Fire now filled the only door and licked up the lacquered door frame. Kindling was piled on the porch. Just inside stood jars of oil, coils of jute rope and bundles of sandalwood sticks.

"Bhima, try to get Mother and the others out."

Bhima disappeared through the smoke that was filling the room.

Yudishtira crouched over the bleeding, armless man. "Who told you to do this?" The man tried weakly to writhe out of Yudishtira's grip. "We all may die here, but only you will go to Hell. How long you stay there depends on your repentance —*now who told you to murder us?*"

"Secret. Hastinapura."

"The king? Or his son? Or Baron Sakuni?"

"I don't know. Someone came—" The man lost awareness.

The heat of the fire was unbearable. Flames were in the ceiling and even under the floor. Yudishtira groped his way towards the rear of the house, past extra grass mattresses and "gift" bales of fine cotton—more than fifty princes could have used in a lifetime. Yudishtira's throat ached from the smoke.

Where were the others? His mother? How could anyone include her in their plot?

A cry of pain escaped him as he crashed against a stack of tinder-dry carved wooden boxes. More "gifts". He couldn't move any more. His flesh seemed near to catching fire; his lungs felt as if they were already in flames. He crouched low and gulped for the less searing air there. Perhaps because he was already on his knees, he whispered, "Gods, they've sacrificed your gift of dharma in this fire."

At his own words he felt a sense of tragedy so deep that he no longer cared to find his way forward out of the fire. He only thought: How could they? My uncle is a *king*. My cousin a king's son. My own kin. "Brahma, forgive us. Forgive us all."

PART II
THE MARRIAGE

10

I only return to this bothersome suggestion that I wrote the
Mahabharata because my immortality has been the proposed
solution to the lapse of centuries between my participation
in these events and their recording, and I thoroughly sympathise with those in every age (don't let them convince
you it is only yours) who reserve their opinion on immortality until they have experienced it.

Authorship? It is a small-self question, just as one's bodily
immortality only concerns other bodies. I would remind
you that human awareness is infinite. Time and distance
are no barrier to it. Do not be bound by space, do not be
bound by time.

Vyasa

Destroy dharma? Ridiculous.

Gangeya

The ashes cooled, the winds brought seeds, and in the spring
a scattering of flowers grew where the cottage had stood on the
outskirts of Varanavata. The blossoms withered under early
summer's heat, giving way to rich grass after the rains. Winter
frosts touched lightly, then spring came again. Older boys
secretly searched for bones overlooked the year before by the
priests who had come from Hastinapura for the rites, while
their younger brothers played at dying valiantly in a fury of
flames, the way the great sons of Pandu must have died.

Far to the west at Thebes in Egypt, the year and four months
had brought other struggles with death. Amon-Re's Supremely
Beloved Servant, The Oracle of All Knowledge, The Friend

of Ma'at, had seldom left his underground chamber during this year, for he hovered between the Shores, stricken with the Divine Disease. His forty-two years of fulfilling the duty of Servant—eating and drinking the over-rich offerings brought to him in the god's name—had left his body poisoned with excess. The fluids no longer left it, but pounded in his veins and crowded his heart. The smells emanating from him, the stench of his breath—all had the flavour of death.

"Leave this presence!" the oracle was shouting. Raging at the physician most recently summoned. "We know Pharaoh's mother pays you." The words ended in a groan.

"Lord of All, how could you suggest—"

"How could you dare lie in the god's presence! Execute this man. With slow poison, as he poisons me!"

Two of the slaves standing stiffly along the chamber walls now rushed to remove the blubbering physician. The others crept in behind the screen. Dedicated to the oracle from birth, only this Company of Fifty were allowed to see or touch him, understanding as they did that this fleshly body hid the Great One's *Ka* as completely as the jewelled screen hid the body. It was the flaw of mortal existence that both body and screen were necessary for the god to maintain power on earth. The sacred day was coming, however, when the Servant's noble Ka would be free. On that day the Company would be sealed in this stone chamber and set sail with the Lord's Own to the Reed Shore. That was their privilege.

The body's pale and flaccid arm motioned the slaves away. "What is the news?" The voice was a weak whisper.

"In Memphis the Pharaoh—"

"Nothing of him. I will yet bend the boy to Amon-Re's will. What more?"

"The Nubian prisoners—"

"Did I not order them killed? Zesnor. What news of Zesnor?"

The slaves glanced among themselves. Events in the distant place called Bharata had moved slowly—six months to eliminate those five brothers claiming the throne, and since then more than a year had passed, and still the Baron Sakuni's nephew was not enthroned. Surely a blind king could not be so difficult to kill. With lowered heads and trembling voices they shared the task of reporting the lack of news—their master was less likely to punish several.

The sick body panted a moment. "No matter. I do not need him."

"No, Master."

"He is a slave, like any of you!'

The anger was still terrifying, but the voice expressing it was slurred. Those around the Supremely Beloved shifted their feet. Strong as this Ka was, they knew the signs—the body now slipped towards delirium. Soon they would be able to administer the physicians' treatments—the baths, massages, the ointments for the sores—and the blessed *azle* beverage.

"He is nothing to me myself," the voice hissed.

"Nothing, Master," several repeated almost in unison.

"He must return!" The body tried to rise. "We must send him our Love Rope. Yes. For the blind king."

The slaves looked nervously past the screen, concerned that there were spies listening. The oracle referred to an Egyptian cobra, one of any scion of the august family of loyal serpents long used within Egypt's royal household to liberate the Ka of the overly ambitious. The Love Rope had never travelled so far. Or for such a petty purpose.

"I who have never regretted." The voice was fading. "It is that place—those childish people. Simple-minded. Ma'at take them, *I* will show them their *future*." Suddenly the body jerked upward, eyes wide. "Send the snake on the Eastern Sailing!"

In Kampilya during that same soft season of spring, Draupadi sat one evening in the small garden attached to the room where she had been confined these sixteen months. In the morning she would leave the room and the garden, perhaps never to return.

Unless, she thought, tonight I at last die of my grief.

But that had refused to happen.

She raised her eyes to look beyond the garden walls. She had passed most of her imprisonment in this garden, yet she had rarely noticed its surroundings. Tonight she studied with bittersweet love the graceful, airy pavilions and pleasure houses that rose around her. Others called the "palace" at Kampilya, "city of crocodiles", a draughty, leaky disgrace—adequate for an early summer retreat, but never for permanent rule. To her, however, the palace had been the only home she could ever remember.

Her gaze fell back within the garden walls. Yes, she would like her life to end here, tonight. Exactly here. In the first months after she had been told the sons of Pandu were dead, it was here among the lilies that she had cried until she could cry no more. And when she had finally slept a little, it had been there under the arbour of jasmine that she had dreamed of death by fire and rescues by great smiling angels. Then as the months had crept by, with no resolution of her future, it had been over among those strangely familiar plants beneath the dark-leafed asoka tree that she had finally taken a reluctant interest in life again: She had tried to recall the names for their blossoms. Truly, the flowers in this garden had been her only comfort. They and Veda.

But her Vedic teachers would come no more, and today someone had cut half the flowers. Decorations for her "bride's choice". Her mockery of a bride's choice. Still more flowers would die for her wedding. She wished again that she could die with them.

She was not sure why she had not protested more this "bride's choice", for any result promised to be tragic for her. Perhaps it had been her indifference to life, or perhaps it had been pity. King Drupada had been crazed with grief at the news of the death of Pandu's sons—no one had realised how much he was determined to have the third son of Pandu for his son-in-law. But in time he began to deny Arjuna's death and insist that the Silver One was only in hiding somewhere. Out of this mad grief had arisen Drupada's scheme for her "bride's choice". It was not really a choice at all. But the king insisted it was. He believed it would bring back the only man she truly wished to choose, for in this particular stratagem she would be the only prize in an impossible archery contest—a contest that Drupada intended and insisted only Arjuna could win.

At first some found the plan pathetically humorous. But when the desperate king actually began inviting kings and princes, the people of South Panchala were terrified. If the impossible contest truly proved impossible, surely the thousand or more armed men who would gather for it in Kampilya would sack the city and seize the throne in revenge and disgust. For Draupadi that would mean abduction or death at noon tomorrow. And if the contest was not impossible—that outcome was equally menacing. She could not face it. Especially if Suyodhana, the murderer of the sons of Pandu (she was confident of this rumour—of course it was he), were the one to woo her.

So tonight she sat beside her asoka tree, the fragrant red-blossomed tree they called "dispeller of sorrows", and considered the only choices left to her: to live or take her life, and to decide that tonight or tomorrow. At times her mind also turned to fantasies of escape. She knew Eos and Panchalya were in the city. But she had had no contact with them for sixteen months—the outer walls of her garden were as well guarded as the doors and windows.

She stood and paced the little yard. Four paces to the asoka tree, four paces to the arbour of jasmine. Then four to the fountain and four more to the door. Inside her room she heard the servant arrive to prepare her bed. As on five hundred previous nights, her evening meal would be there. Her night cloak.

Suddenly she turned her head. This was not her old female attendant standing in the doorway, but a man. Draupadi could see little of him in the twilight, except that he wore white.

"The guards may have allowed you entrance," she said, intending to sound calm. "But no men may enter here except my instructors."

"I am one of those." In a deep, clear voice he began to chant: "'I bend the bow of Rudra . . . I wage war with hostile men. I pervade Heaven and Earth.'"

She responded with more of her favourite verse of Veda: "'I breathe forth like the wind, giving form to all created worlds.'"

Then she remembered the voice. The voice in the tent, the voice on the road. He stepped into the garden: "'Beyond the Heaven, beyond this Earth am I, so vast am I in greatness.'

The seer of that hymn was a woman, Draupadi. A patient woman. Did you know that?"

Her body was trembling, resentment and fear of him battling with her need for rescue. "This time, *tell me who you are.*"

"I am called Vyasa," he said gently.

Confusion swept over her. "Veda Vyasa? But my teachers say Veda Vyasa is—" She knelt. "It was Veda Vyasa who saved my life when I was in the chariot?" Then she half rose again. "And you who—"

"Took your memories." He drew her to her feet. "Are you angry, Draupadi?"

She nodded, confused and ashamed.

"Excellent." He laughed. "King Drupada said you were dying of grief. But I see you have used this time well—learning Veda and patience. Not excessive patience, of course." He looked around the garden and shook his head. "So small. It is rarely really necessary, this 'protecting' women by hiding them away. A bad Arya tactic that will become worse before it is better. We men become frightened for you, and of you. That is all it is, Draupadi."

She stared at him.

"Have you no more questions for me, Draupadi? You have only asked my name."

"What will happen to me tomorrow?"

"Yes. The question of tomorrow—" He touched her lightly on the forehead. His deeply set eyes were dark, yet bright like fires. "We will approach tomorrow together, Draupadi. After some lessons from tonight."

On the same evening Yudishtira sat on the porch of a mud and wattle house in the village of Ekacakra. The settlement was sixteen months and almost a hundred leagues from the sin of Varanavata. It was just as far from Kampilya and Draupadi's bride's choice.

For a year Yudishtira had been disguised as he was tonight —in the orange robes of a celibate priest. But they did not prevent his remembering Night as the dark-thighed woman who closed her golden doors on the day. Nor did the robes change the month—Phalguna, the month for love.

Yudishtira picked a bud from the vines winding around the porch post and studied the veined inner petals. Then the singing of the returning fodder cutters came to him:

> Tarrying in the forest at eventide,
> One thinks he hears a cry.
> But Aranyani, goddess of forests, injures no one,
> Unless someone injures her.
> Feeding upon her sweet fruit,
> He penetrates at will.

Spring, he thought. And we hide as monks. He tore up the flower in his hand and the evening turned to ashes, as so many had before.

I should have gone back.

But to what—to pretending no one tried to burn us alive? Where would my elders have stood?

Before Varanavata I would have been sure.

I should have gone back to see, to give them a chance.

No. That dawn before our graduation, when King Drita told me to go, *he knew*. And Gangeya. He *warned* me. He at least suspected.

It isn't possible they would have allowed it. I should have gone back to hear Drita's explanation.

I should have gone back to accuse him.

What could I have said—that I let the only witness die in the fire? Suyodhana would have screamed his denials. "Accusations without evidence. Slander!" King Drita would finally have had his excuse to give his throne to his son.

Which he has surely done anyway. Crown Prince Suyodhana. I am dead to them all, either way. Better that Bhima had left me to burn.

Behind him he heard his brothers wrestling—as always, Bhima against the other three. No, whatever his own sinful thoughts on the matter, the great-hearted Bhima had not left anyone to burn that night. Bhima had pushed down the flaming walls, led or dragged his mother and brothers clear, then carried them in relays throughout the night, sometimes two at a time, until he was sure he had put enough distance between themselves and their enemies.

All of which only added to Yudishtira's humiliation that today, as on every day since Bhima had rescued them, although their mother had divided the alms-food in half—half for Bhima and half for the rest—"Wolf belly's" stomach still growled. That was all the eldest could offer the second eldest for keeping them from Yama's gates.

Yudishtira's fists clenched again.

Then unclenched, as he gained control in the manner he had been taught: Locate the anger in the body until it reveals how to overcome what has angered you.

The sensation replacing his anger tonight was the soothing warmth of the brick porch step spreading through the thin orange monk's robe. It was true that he had sometimes been happy here, sometimes wondered if the forest goddess Aranyani was not meant to be his bride.

But the vow-takers' robes were also like iron chains, especially on his brothers. Daily Arjuna risked their exposure, shooting arrows into every tree in the woods. "I must practise," he would cry. In the wilderness south of Varanavata the donning of this disguise—after limited vows to make it not a total deceit—had seemed to be the best means of entering the villages unrecognised and escaping the cold winter nights and wild animals. For the first few months in tiny Ekacakra maintaining the guise had even been a challenge for five warriors. But not for an entire year of their lives.

Yudishtira's attention was drawn to the road into the town from the west. A man was walking in the dusty clouds left by the last hurrying donkey train. Except for his shorter stature and the lesser atmosphere of pure power about him, the traveller was much like Sage Vyasa—old in a strong, ageless way, with wiry limbs and matted grey hair, and he carried a begging bowl on a string around his waist. A true priest-born, not an impostor like myself, Yudishtira thought.

For a year he and his brothers had avoided such wanderers, who were most likely to see through their disguise. But tonight, although he feared it was only out of restlessness, Yudishtira had the strong thought that he should make this man his guest.

He stepped out into the road and bowed. "It's late, Elder, and you'll need to find some lodging in this town. Why not stay here? With us?"

"Are all of you here priests like myself?"

Yudishtira was careful not to lie. "Certainly not like yourself, forest-dweller. But we worship the gods morning and evening, we study the Veda, and we live by the alms we gather, in the priest's way."

The monk, called Urutata, accepted the offer of shelter with simple grace. Inside, Yudishtira introduced him to his brothers, employing the names they had used while in hiding. But nothing could be done to hide his brothers' heated condition after their abruptly ended wrestling match. And seeing his family through Urutata's eyes, Yudishtira noticed new, harder lines on Arjuna's face. Bhima's body, he saw, had become taut with wariness this year. And the twins, Nakula and Sahadeva, were men now, at only sixteen. For all of them, boyhood was over and the mark of some great struggle was on them.

Only his mother, Kunti, seemed younger. She was thin but lithe from their austere life and her silences and sighs had lessened over the year. She went like a young girl to prepare refreshments for their guest.

After the evening rites and meal it was finally appropriate to encourage their guest to talk. Within a short time Kunti had adroitly turned the conversation to what mattered.

"Dear Urutata, all your stories are so interesting. But I do wonder most about my own family's city, Hastinapura."

"Ah, Hastinapura." The old man hung his head. "It is no longer 'the city of priests'. King Drita supports a quarter of those he once did. He says their rites do not prevent misfortune, or else why would Pandu's sons have died?"

"A question he should consider carefully." Kunti glanced at her eldest son.

Next Bhima had to play the bitter game. "Has King Drita anointed his son Suyodhana as the new crown prince?"

The priest glanced around the circle of faces. "I am sorry to say he has." Yudishtira closed his eyes a moment, controlling his anger and disappointment, accepting what he had already known must be. Urutata continued, for some reason in a gentler tone. "Now King Drita seeks a new major alliance, through a marriage for Suyodhana. The new princess of South Panchala is the preference."

Arjuna had been lying back, staying in the shadows. Now he sat forward. "King Drupada has a new daughter?" He laughed. "She must still be nursing, then."

"I hear she is full grown," Urutata answered.

With Arjuna leaning forward the firelight was revealing the calluses on his shoulder and hands, the unmistakable scars of an archer. Seeing Yudishtira's expression, Arjuna lay back again but continued speaking. "So with North Panchala next to them controlled by King Drita's weapons-master and South Panchala theirs through marriage, other allies will join the Kurus out of simple fear. Anything in Bharata not controlled by Jarasamda of Magada will be controlled by King Drita. And then by his son."

"I hope the princess is intelligent," Kunti said. "Her bride's choice will decide much."

"She is very intelligent," Urutata said, "but it will not matter."

He explained the archery contest—which dismayed Kunti especially—and then the prize: "She is called Draupadi, after her father, King Drupada. They say she is 'heart fetching', with a 'waist shaped like an altar, eyes like lotus petals, hair glossy, black and curling'—'a lovely goddess who has chosen a human form'. 'The fragrance of blue lotuses wafts from her for a league around, her hips are broad and well shaped, her skin has the sheen of beryl stone . . .'" The wanderer's voice cast a spell.

Or at any rate, Yudishtira thought his brothers looked like fools in a trance. Could they not see how much these things became exaggerated after endless repetitions such as tonight's?

"I remember the girl's brother. He came to Hastinapura shortly before the tournament," Yudishtira said. "But full-grown twins? Did some mother arrive at Kampilya with her two darlings and demand that King Drupada admit to a boyhood sowing?"

Urutata laughed, then described King Drupada's sacrifice and the emergence of the two youths from Agni's hearth. At the end Urutata lowered his voice. "And the king vowed that his new daughter would marry Arjuna, the third son of Pandu."

"*Arjuna?*" It was Bhima's voice, hiding nothing.

"Yes, it is surprising. But the king greatly esteemed this one who helped to defeat him. Perhaps he thought Arjuna was someone who would not fear the prophecy." Their story-teller hesitated. "But, I understand that I must tell you all."

Puzzled, Yudishtira looked hard at the man. Urutata spoke the words: "'She shall accomplish the purpose of the gods, and lead the warriors of her generation to their doom.'"

Arjuna shrugged elaborately. "Gloomy-sounding for a princess. Anyway, I can't marry before my older brothers." He reddened. "I mean, if we were not—"

Urutata was unabashed. "The fact is, her father has opened the contest to everyone, even priests such as yourselves, if your vows are not for life." He paused. "But unfortunately the contest is tomorrow."

Kunti drew in her breath. "Tomorrow? But Kampilya's at least ninety leagues from here!"

Yudishtira spoke quickly. "It is nothing to concern yourself over, Mother."

"Perhaps she sensed it was a concern of mine," the priest said gently. "I had greatly hoped to go, if only for the entertainments celebrating the event." Their visitor sighed. "But I can not go on alone after dark, close as I am."

"Close?" Kunti asked.

He explained that it was only a few more leagues to the Ganges, where a boatman awaited him. "With the full moon on the river it would have been easy to reach Kampilya by noon tomorrow."

Yudishtira felt his family's eyes on him. It seemed that only he and his brothers could rescue this princess from a contest utterly counter to dharma. And it might result in a valuable alliance—King Drupada's warriors would be at his own command.

It is our chance to return to our world. Whatever that will mean.

But a woman who would lead all the warriors to their doom? Who listens to these wild tales?

He looked at his mother. "A trap?" he asked her softly.

"If it is, this time you will have all Bharata as witness."

Arjuna leaned forward. "Why not let me win this princess for you? It's time you were married anyway."

Yudishtira smiled and glanced towards the still oblivious Urutata. Even so, their disguises could not last long with this sort of talk.

Yudishtira gave in to tense laughter. "Sure of yourself, aren't you, brother? But I'm afraid King Drupada intended her for this warrior called Arjuna."

Arjuna grinned. "Then let him win her. I'm sure he can. And I am equally sure he would not marry before his eldest brother."

"And *I* am sure," Yudishtira countered, "that his older brother would honour King Drupada's desire that Arjuna take her."

"But wouldn't King Drupada prefer his daughter to be a queen rather than a sister-in-law to one?"

Yudishtira burst out laughing. "Enough. Urutata, if we accompany you to the river, may we share your boat to Kampilya tonight?"

The priest bowed solemnly. "That was always my hope, Crown Prince Yudishtira." The old man pressed his palms together in a gesture of blessing that almost seemed sad to Yudishtira. "I am sorry if I have deceived you, Crown Prince, but Sage Vyasa wished you to choose your course in this matter for yourself."

11

Tell your youth that dharma requires one to circle the self relentlessly until all its parts are known, confident that whatever seems definitely missing is that which is most definitely there.

an anonymous warrior

The divine Night approaching looks upon many places with her eyes. She has assumed all beauties.

Rig Veda

The journey by elephant frightened Draupadi. She was certain that her Before had never involved an animal so immense. Nor had she ever travelled in such a hell. It was night, yet unendurably hot. Gnats swarmed about her head. Disturbed animals shrieked. There was no wind and no cooling river— only the rustle and snap of the brush as the elephant forced itself a passage along a footpath.

After some time the heat lessened, the forest thinned and the lumbering motion stopped. Lights shone through the trees. Dark figures surrounded the elephant. Dasyu—the ones called non-humans. They made no sound; they wore no clothing.

Someone leaned a roughly made ladder on the elephant's side. Vyasa went down it, then held it for her. The ladder shifted with every breath of the overheated beast and the swaying seat leaned towards the ground with her weight. She was uncertain whether to climb down facing forward or backward. She made a move to try forward and tripped on her skirts—and she had believed herself never awkward and afraid of nothing. Tears flooded her eyes.

"Draupadi?" Vyasa's voice reached deep into her heart. She turned and climbed down facing the elephant's blanketed side.

On the ground she was surrounded by the Dasyu. But the sage whispered not to be afraid. "You must trust them tonight. They are your people."

She understood—these were Panchala's conquered subjects, even deep in this terrible wilderness.

Most of those nearest her were women. All were shorter than her, but at least as old, for many had full breasts or wombs.

As if he knew her thoughts, he said, "Only married persons participate in tonight's ceremonies, Draupadi."

"And what is the purpose of these ceremonies, Sage Vyasa?"

"To prepare a bride. They believe she should learn she is now free to be as eager for married life as a man."

She turned towards Vyasa, but he gently pushed her forward into the circle of women. "Go with them. *Trust them.*"

Someone shyly took her hand. Other women found other parts of her to hold—a hand, arm or fold of her garment— and they led her across the clearing, moving with her as if they were one body.

They entered a hut. It was lit by only a few oil lamps. Boughs of large, heavy-scented blossoms stood in the corners. At her feet was a bed covered with mounds of fine white cloth.

She remembered the gifts Vyasa had instructed her to bring. From folds of her clothing she removed some—a few sweets and ornaments. The women solemnly accepted them. From behind someone began to undress her. But when she felt they were about to draw off the virgin's shift, she held it down. After her long seclusion, the irrational prohibition against its removal had finally become part of her. Then remembering the sage's command, she forced herself to trust and allowed them to remove it.

They laid her down and their hands lavished on warm oil, rubbing her arms and legs, her head and feet, her breasts, hips and belly. Then the hands moved to her place for love.

She went rigid. Again the prohibitions. And these women —who were they? He had said to trust them. But who was he, even? Why had she believed him so easily? Had she allowed herself to be abducted? Why was she *here*? Confusion stormed her mind.

The hands went away from there. Someone began to sing in her ear. The sounds were meaningless. Nor did their meaning seem important. Perhaps they had none, for they were like wind or running water.

But she *knew* this song. From long, long Before.

Had she had a Dasyu nurse, as certain Kampilya women employed for their children?

A grey-haired woman stood over her. The woman only looked into her eyes—she did not speak. She was unlike any woman Draupadi had seen in Kampilya. But Draupadi saw into Before, and into herself, and was silenced. There was no memory to reassure her, but there was a knowledge in her heart that did more than reassure. It commanded, it spoke of wisdom beyond her own. She lay down again.

Now the hands moved boldly back to her place for love. The singing intensified. Fingers lightly and rapidly stroked her furrow, as if preparing ground for a delicate seed. She felt her awareness drift away to a dark corner, abandoning her body to them. The prohibited sensations were free to come now, but not to her mind. There was a turning and expanding inside her, a warm wet looseness between her legs, and an urgency to lift and open.

Suddenly she was aware again of what she was allowing, and she could bear no more.

But they had ceased. Between her legs she ached for something, and then blushed to realise what it was she ached for. Those watching her seemed satisfied. They stood and helped her to her feet.

Outside a crowd of men came out of the darkness to meet them. Vyasa was far to the rear but watching her. Draupadi wanted to hide her virgin's nakedness but instead she was thrust forward. She kept her eyes downcast, avoiding the sight of the men's long, purplish, curving ploughs, each one ready to spread seed.

The men and women crossed a clearing and climbed a hillock, Draupadi at their centre. On the summit five fires had been laid. Now they were lit. The flames sprang up, illumining a black linga stone. Phallic in shape, it seemed to push up from the stone circle of its base like a man's full plough reaching for a field.

A linga stone—she had heard of these from Queen Yasoda. It was the foulest Dasyu sin, for these people worshipped such stones from the earth, when everyone knew the gods dwelled only in the sky, water or plants. Never in flesh and filth. She saw the rest was true too—instead of cleanly burning their oblations in Agni's fire, they were smearing their oils, fats and perfumes on the thing, caressing it, making it ooze, glisten, stink.

But they also offered flowers and fruits, arranged around the linga's base or in painted vases and dishes. There was a beauty here that she could not utterly deny. The sacred hearth at Kampilya left the giver with ashes.

She turned and searched the crowd again for Vyasa. He met her eyes. What did he want her to do? She could not join in the worship of a linga. She could not.

The women around her were crowding forward, bending down to leave their gifts. Some held her gaze, then glanced towards the black stone as if directing her to join them. She wanted to run, to shield herself from so much evil.

Instead she closed her eyes. She would endure. She swayed with the singing, to give the illusion of sharing their ecstasy. And she waited in her darkness for some sign that her ordeal was over.

But the singing continued. In time Draupadi found a light growing in her mind. At first she observed it. Then she became absorbed there. It coincided with a gentle surging low in her body. This force was like water pushing up between rocks. The fountain rose unevenly, pausing before bursting farther upward, flooding her lower back, her upper back, her shoulders, filling her heart so that it seemed to break open, filling her throat with cool honey, reaching her eyes so that they fluttered as if caught in a wind, pressing against her forehead and finally bursting out from the top of her head in an explosion of dazzling liquid light.

The unexpectedness of it half raised her arms and stopped her breath. Her face was fixed in an involuntary expression of joy, but she had forgotten there were others to see her. There was only the joy.

Slowly she opened her eyes. Tears coursed down her face. Those around her were on their knees. She knelt also. Gifts were being passed forward. Those she had brought appeared. They seemed gaudy here, but like the others, they were met with little sounds of approval. Draupadi felt neither piety nor impiety now. She was only a witness to Brahman's fullness, here among Dasyu.

Another kind of music began to intrude on the soft chants. This was a languid beat on a clay vessel. The tempo was also kept by feet. Taking Draupadi with them, the women rose and went to stand in a half circle around the men stamping out the drum beat.

Dust rose in the moonlight. The music took on more variations and the men's dancing became both strenuous and intentionally humorous. They cavorted and leaped over each other, pretending more and more obviously to mount each other or mate face to face. They took turns playing the role of bashful virgins and eager bridegrooms. Thighs were held tight, to be forced apart. Thrusts missed and sent the thruster sprawling. Or found their mark and caused groans of mimicked ecstasy. The women shouted comments, which caused more laughter, and soon the men were backing into a half circle around Draupadi and shouting retorts. The dance stopped.

Vyasa slipped up beside her. "I must translate for you. This one wants to ask you what you would like between your legs."

"Must I answer?"

"You may do as you wish."

She again felt horribly exposed and ill at ease. But if she responded, perhaps it would all end sooner. She turned to speak in Vyasa's ear. "Tell him, 'a good horse'."

Her answer translated brought gales of laughter. Several clods of dirt were hurled at the one who had asked. Everyone moved about, then sat down, as if relaxing after the easing of some tension.

A young man stood up; Vyasa translated again. "This one says a little girl saw two dogs stuck together after mating and asked her mother if humans stick together like that too. The

155

mother said, 'Only if you can get a net around your man in his sleep.'" The crowd jeered and shouted insults.

To her the stories that followed were no more humorous, but one about a reluctant bride finally made her smile. As soon as she did, the entire assemblage rose and began stamping, shouting, embracing and pointing at her. They closed in around her and now certain men came forward, or were pushed from behind by women. These men's backs were arched to display their very long, very erect ploughs. Their female partners pointed out to Draupadi the fine points of their man's performance, as well as his other excellent masculine features.

These small, dark men and women managed all of this with as much politeness as Arya might evidence while displaying their finest chariots, and Draupadi tried to remain unbothered. Naked men were common enough to her—wrestlers, labourers, and of course her own brother, whose body was as familiar as her own. Even the sight of his prepared plough was familiar to her. Only not held at hand's length in front of her face until she had acknowledged and admired it.

When it was over her stomach was knotted and her throat tight. But surely now Vyasa would take her home.

The crowd suddenly fell back, Vyasa with them, leaving her naked and alone. The only sounds were insects and the snapping fires. The old woman from the hut spread out a cloth on the ground and motioned for Draupadi to lie down on it. Her heart began to pound. She looked towards Vyasa. His eyes and expression were closed. Was this how it was to end, then? Was her virginity of so little use to him and South Panchala after all? Or was she his sacrifice tonight to the Dasyu gods?

She lay down, abandoning herself as he seemed to be abandoning her. It did not really matter. Tomorrow some Arya would have her anyway, by abduction or through her unwilling marriage, and her revenge would be the irreparable impurity to which she would expose him: A Dasyu had ploughed her first. She let them spread her legs, she closed her eyes, and she willed her awareness to leave her body.

But only cool air touched her furrow. She heard footsteps approach, but they receded again. Others approached but also withdrew. All around her now there was quiet, reverent motion.

Finally she opened her eyes. Mountains of flowers surrounded her, each a single offering from a single hand. Between her knees she saw an ageing couple pause, arms around each other's waist, their free hands raised in a gesture of blessing over her field. Over the dark earth that was her womb.

The elephant ambled along through the dusky pink dawn. Draupadi lay back on cushions in the riding box, awakening from a dream. The only evidence of the night that remained was the moist aching. Dreamily she thought of "her people", the small, dark, sweet-faced men and women who had accepted her more totally than she had accepted herself.

"Vyasa, do we treat them well? As our subjects, I mean. We don't ever use that tribe as slaves, do we?"

"No, those Dasyu have never been conquered. The conquered ones are different."

"Then how were these 'my people'?"

Vyasa did not answer her.

"Sage Vyasa?"

When he still did not speak, her logical mind added the implication of his hesitation to "my people". Then added the colour of her skin. Added her undisclosed origins. And the terrible truth closed down on her like death.

But if she was truly a Dasyu herself, even in part, who would want her? How could *she* be chosen in marriage, much less choose? How could she ever escape her imprisonment at Kampilya?

The bitter questions drained the sweetness away.

She looked towards Vyasa, who rode on the animal's neck. Why had he done this to her? Tried to make a princess of a Dasyu?

But his own dark skin, could it be?

Again as if he knew her thoughts, he turned, studied her, and said, "No, Draupadi, I am not your father."

"Then who was it! Some Dasyu animal raped my Arya mother! Didn't he!"

"How quickly you took on the Arya essence. No, it was your

157

mother who was Dasyu, your father Arya. Did you hear the other ridiculous stories? Pure Arya semen falling into wash buckets or being carried off by birds that dropped their load on loathsome Dasyu women? Native nymphs bewitching innocent Arya men? Listen to me, Draupadi. My mother was the daughter of a Dasyu fisherwoman and the great Arya, King Vasu. No bird brought his seed to her. He begged my grandmother to engage in surata with him, just as her daughter, my mother, was begged both by my father, the Vedic Seer Parashara, and then by the third King Kuru."

"Then you are only one quarter Dasyu. And I am half."

He ignored her. "Do you know how they say my mother was conceived? During a hunting trip my illustrious grandfather King Vasu was supposedly thinking so much about his dear wife at home that he accidentally spilled his seed. A fish swallowed it and out came my mother. Everyone in my mother's family, however, knew the Arya seed entered my grandmother by the more usual method, for she was no fish but a dark Dasyu beauty."

"My mother was Dasyu," Draupadi said in a low, angry voice. "You are saying that my Dasyu mother lured an Arya to her bed. My father *went* to her." Draupadi closed her eyes, as if shutting out the scene. "But it isn't true. My people are not out here. My mother is in the north, in the mountains. I know it."

"There are Dasyu everywhere, Draupadi. It seems you think about your mother a great deal." She heard an immense, controlled sadness in his voice.

"My father—was he warrior-born? He must have been if you want me to marry a prince."

"I can only tell you that your parents are extraordinary."

"Then they still live!"

He did not answer.

"Was he a warrior?"

Still no answer. A common man then. Going to a Dasyu. "I hate all Arya."

He shook his head. "Is that a better answer, Draupadi?"

She ignored him. "Yes, I see it now." Her voice sounded high and unreal to her. "Yasoda and Drupada called the Dasyu inhuman, and I believed it. Their Arya priests twist the truth more, calling everything that gives freedom and pleasure wrong. 'That's Dasyu,' they say. They say surata is only for the purpose of children. Singing only for Veda. These people we left—they would die under such restraints."

"So you think now you are their kind."

"I knew I was not Arya."

"There are other Arya besides Drupada and Yasoda."

"The ones who killed Arjuna?" Suddenly she lost all control. She hid her face in the cloth covering the box and cried.

The rocking step of the elephant stopped. The priest-born sage touched her shoulder.

"Say this is a dream," she whispered. "Say I am not a Dasyu."

"Draupadi." His hand lifted her face with firmness. "Every mind is like a broken pot—parts, parts. Every mind seeks to be healed and whole again. But your mind is broken beyond your repair because we had to take your memory to make you a princess. For now, it is very hard for you to see the wholeness around you—which is not Arya or Dasyu, but life."

"I don't want to live, Sage Vyasa."

He was silent a moment. She was dimly aware that he was suffering too. "Listen carefully to me, Draupadi, for I can say no more tonight. There is only one way Pandu's sons could ever be killed. They would have to be divided. Someone would have to destroy their wholeness."

She stared at him, confused. "They were not divided at Varanavata."

"You are right. They were not divided at Varanavata."

The other, fresher horror rushed back on her. "Is my mother like those?" She made a gesture of disgust towards the forest they were leaving.

"I am not certain what you mean, Draupadi. But except for the night your mother conceived you and your brother, she has been celibate."

"Celibate?" When no explanation came she whispered, "But why?"

He did not speak for a long time. "I think the only truly correct way to answer you tonight is to say that all her attention has been absorbed in the attainment of an even greater pleasure."

"Did she intend for me to do the same?"

"And if she did, would you do it? Draupadi, she intended for you to find your own way."

"But to the same place?"

"Yes, to the same place."

The memory of her bliss while standing before the linga stone threatened to return, but she pushed the impiety from her mind.

"Did my mother love my father? And did he love her?"

"He loved her and loves her still." Vyasa whispered that, but now he raised his voice. "Draupadi, you will not speak of tonight with anyone, not even your brother. You have put back on your virgin's shift and your Arya thoughts, and truly you are still an Arya virgin. You will continue to speak the truth to everyone, but select the truth that is sweet to the ears of the hearer."

"Yes, Sage."

"Do not dread tomorrow. It is in the hands of the gods, as has been every other day of your life. And the nights also. Tonight prepared you. Kampilya could not prepare you, for you required a glimpse of a different part of the whole which you are. But you are not just the woman you found tonight either. You are much larger—as large as Bharata."

Draupadi was safely in her rooms and Vyasa was going to his own suite to rest before the bride's choice when Krishna of the Vrishnis stepped out of a doorway and bowed to him.

"So you are here for the bride's choice," Vyasa said wearily. He studied the youth. Had the year changed him so? Brahma make it true—how he needed someone's help.

Krishna smiled. "No, Sage. How could I come for the bride's choice? You intend her for Yudishtira. I came only to be ready to follow your instruction as soon as the condition is met—I will approach Pandu's sons when Yudishtira is pledged to marry." Krishna's face now trembled with excitement. "He is going to become our samraj, isn't he?"

"That seems to be the shortest route to the goal. Except for

Jarasamda of Magada. And the fact that Yudishtira is not yet even a king, and he has not yet married Draupadi, who must be his queen. Or won her. Or even arrived here to compete for her."

"You know they are almost here. And Arjuna will win her."

Vyasa rubbed the hip that always stiffened after elephant riding. "But will they also leave the pavilion alive with her?" he asked irritably. "Do you appreciate the fact that there will be at least a thousand kings, princes, and anointed warriors— led by Yudishtira's own cousins—who are going to do all they can to prevent everything—everything—you have predicted?"

"I will see that Pandu's sons are safe."

"Oh, then I will cease to worry."

"I didn't mean to speak lightly of the danger, Sage Vyasa, but you yourself know the brothers are invincible, especially when I am with them."

"Visions again, Krishna?"

Krishna bowed his head. "The only immediate danger I see, Sage, is that Draupadi loves the wrong brother. Or so I hear."

"I know. I should have foreseen it," Vyasa said. He let his shoulders sag under the same burden.

"Even the best chariot strategies can be laid waste by uncooperative horses," Krishna said gently. "She is a wilful girl— her arranging for her brother to be sent to Guru Vaja was also unexpected, I presume."

Vyasa again saw Draupadi's face shining with tears in the first light of dawn, and almost could not bear to speak of her. "At least I am confident about half the marriage now— Yudishtira will love Draupadi. But we must not let the brothers be divided. Never." Vyasa sensed that his exhaustion and freshly stirred feelings for Aditi's daughter were bringing himself close to weeping.

"I will take care of this also, Sage Vyasa," Krishna said gently.

"You?" Vyasa let himself flare more than he had intended. "You who set out for Varanavata a year ago when you heard the first little rumour, ignoring my explicit instructions for you to stay at home?"

"I should have guessed you would tell my father's priests to watch me."

"No, you should have obeyed me. That was all you had to do."

"Sage, I feared for them!"

"But *you* say they are invincible. No. You wanted to revenge the attempt on their lives!"

"No one else seemed to want to."

"If they had died, not one beam or board of Hastinapura would have been left touching another."

"*If* they had died? You didn't know for certain they wouldn't?"

Vyasa turned away in disgust. "Krishna, if you wish to prove I am fallible, simply ask me and I will give you all the evidence you wish. But that does not give yourself permission to be less than perfect." He turned back. "I need you, Krishna. I need you perfect and I must perfect you even as I lean on you."

Krishna was on his knees, his forehead in the dust at Vyasa's feet. "Forgive me, Master."

For a moment Vyasa saw himself back at Badari, this time to stay—standing in the door of his room, the River Bhagirathi shining at his feet and the holy jujube tree drooping with sweet berries and humming with bees.

But no, he thought, this one is still far from ready to be left on his own. "Stand up, Krishna."

"No! Please forgive me first!"

Vyasa was staring at the knife in Krishna's belt. Maybe there was a good reason why this one was a warrior. "Krishna, I want you to watch King Drita's brother-in-law, Baron Sakuni, and especially the Baron's Egyptian slave Zesnor."

"I've learned everything about them," Krishna said, his face still against the floor.

"That is better—you have 'learned', and not from visions, I presume. Watch for them with your eyes open, Krishna."

"Are visions so wrong, Sage Vyasa?"

"Visions are vision—it all depends on who is doing the seeing and how much their pride in their ability has distorted it. Now listen. Sakuni and Zesnor will not try to come to the bride's-choice pavilion—Sakuni is unable to draw a bow and

Zesnor is a yavana. I think the precautions have been too great for them to attempt a straightforward abduction from the city either. But their scheme at Varanavata tells us what they are capable of. And now they especially want Draupadi."

"They shall not have her, Teacher," Krishna said, still on his knees.

"That would be good. However, the possibility of failure is real and I will not blame you for what you cannot control."

"This existence around me is only my Self unfolding itself. When I control myself, I control what is around me."

"Exactly. And that is why I consider the possibility of your failure to be so real. Now stand up."

"Forgive me first, Master."

"You have no master, Krishna."

The head of dark curls sprang up. The young face showed agony. "No master?"

"We can play at it if you insist. But look at you. I say stand up and you are still on the floor."

Krishna scrambled to his feet.

"Now go. We should not be seen together."

Krishna smiled. "May Veda be as a bride to you, Master, always open."

Vyasa bowed in return. "May your name live among the ancestors and the gods, Krishna. Yes, and even among the foreign gods."

12

The young warriors
. . . with the drunk vehemence
Of rutting Himalayan elephants . . .
Stared at each other in rivalry.
Their bodies bathed in their mind-born love
. . . Their limbs besieged by the arrows of love,
Their hearts gone to Draupadi, these kings of
men
Went down to the pit for her sake
And made even their old friends their foes.

            ancient version of the *Mahabharata*

If only there were a disguise that would hide us
from ourselves.

                            Yudishtira

At mid-morning a chariot bore Draupadi through the city streets. King Drupada drove in front of her. Her brother, who had arrived from Hastinapura the night before, drove behind, but they had not yet been able to speak. Other South Panchala warriors, on foot and on horseback, guarded her also.

As the procession passed through the outer city, crowds went wild at the sight of the "daughter of fire". For a year rumours had passed through Panchala that she had died at the same hour as the sons of Pandu, or in the same flames, or had caused the flames, or had even been the flames—there were many versions. But now they saw that she lived after all, more beautiful than ever, and today she would be betrothed, after the most ornate, exciting and strange bride's choice ever imagined. The shouting never paused.

164

Passing through the north city gate the procession turned northeast. In the distance the new pavilion, built in honour of Agni's daughter, shimmered in the sun. Its walls were white, its pillars lacquered red and blue, and its trellises worked with pounded gold. An enormous yellow canopy billowed over the centre skylight while tapestries swayed in the breeze under the open eaves, and the banners of the one hundred kingdoms of Bharata fluttered above the peaks of the domes.

On the river-plain between the procession and its goal stretched a city of tents. Those visitors who were not among the two thousand invited inside the pavilion were here along the route, observing for the first time the woman who was the prize. She, however, kept her eyes forward. She seemed to see no one, and she so lacked the usual happy plumpness of a princess that, except for the jewels and hundred-pleated linen dress, she might have been a slave or a prisoner of war. As it was, her thin waist accentuated her full breasts and hips, and her obvious anxiety aroused fresh and confused desires in the men she passed. Some shouted and stamped their approval. Others openly cursed a king who imprisoned such a woman and then humiliated her with a "bride's choice" that made her no more than a prize, like a golden goblet, to be carried off by the sweatiest athlete.

The line of chariots crossed the decorative moat surrounding the pavilion and stopped at the royal gate. King Drupada descended and went in. Draupadi turned to look for her brother. Panchalya was already bounding towards her, seeming larger and stronger after their sixteen months of separation. He helped her down and they embraced for as long as they dared, but there was no opportunity to speak in the tumult by the gate. They turned and faced her bride's-choice pavilion.

Through the wide, gilded trellis doors Draupadi saw a thousand warriors in the lower tiers of seats circling the arena. Higher up there were at least five hundred of the priestly class. On the ground, under the stands, there were as many more ambassadors, traders and landowners who had earned the honour of observing. But at every level there were only men, and every man watched her.

Draupadi's serving women had warned her: Women excluded themselves so that the bride would not be compared to another—and so that rejected suitors could not vent their anger with an abduction. None of this was comfort to the lone girl who entered. She clung to Panchalya's arm, aware that she could never have made herself walk through those doors without him.

Then, amid a tumult of shouts and stamping, sister and brother made their entrance. Panchalya led her slowly across the arena and up on to the carpeted dais reserved for them. In front of Draupadi there was a polished sandalwood stand. On it hung a garland of red kimsuka flowers. This she would place on her future husband.

But to reach the dais that future husband would first enter the pit below, string the shoulder-high iron bow now resting in its rack, aim high above at the gold wheel with the turning, slippery golden carp inside, and pierce the carp with five successive arrows. Provided there was a man alive who could do it.

Through the smoke of burning aloe and sandalwood Draupadi searched the upper tiers for Vyasa. She felt faint and ill. The night before, spent in his company, was now a sleepless dream that, far from preparing her, had left her more certain than ever that she had come here to marry Death. A winnerless contest for a dark-skinned girl of unknown parentage? Surely the warriors would have to guess she was half-Dasyu and avenge the insult.

She still could not see Vyasa. There were so many priests, and the air was clouded with smoke. Her head hurt as if someone pressed it into a wall. The shouting was terrible, the incense choked her, the stares frightened her. She leaned against Panchalya and closed her eyes, uncertain if she could remain aware. Now South Panchala's drums pounded too.

Suddenly among the drums she heard in her own mind a roar of bells. Brass chariot bells. She sat up, frantically scanning the pavilion for Vyasa. The jangling of bells increased—they were the bells of her dream in the first days after her "birth". War horses. Hooves. "Hear me!"

With two thousand observing her, she pressed her hands to her temples and cried out, "Panchalya, help!"

He took her hands. "What, Draupadi?"

Frantically her eyes scanned the upper tiers again for Vyasa. Then she saw another. She knew this man. From Before? Not his face, but his stance—among the seated vow-takers he was standing, staring down at her.

Flames filled the air around him. It was the vision again. Not of Varanavata, Yudishtira knew now. Of her. Fire's Daughter.

She was awareness itself—he had seen her true nature the moment she had entered the pavilion. She sat on the dais now. Around him Yudishtira was hearing the words "beautiful" and "graceful" and "sublime". But he saw awareness. The fullness of Pure Brahman embodied in a proud, frightened girl. A woman of great loveliness.

Yudishtira was not aware that he stood until Arjuna made him sit again. "Better not to attract attention to ourselves yet. Yes?" Arjuna was laughing, but he spoke gently. "Even our solemn eldest sees it—she is unequalled."

Yudishtira did not answer. He felt himself burning and crumbling at once.

"And King Drupada risks her in a contest," Arjuna said. "Thank Brahma we came."

Yudishtira saw that Arjuna was flexing his hands under his robes, his eyes going from the target to the pit, calculating.

But I am the eldest, he thought. *I marry first.*

"Panchalya," she whispered, "who is that one?"

But her brother did not hear. He drew her to her feet to accept the greetings of the officiating priests.

"The one standing among the priest-born." She spoke desperately. "Who is he?"

"Better to attend to the princes," he whispered.

She looked into his anxious eyes. They might have so little time together after so long. "Is your Guru Vaja here?"

"No, he has taken the vows that forbid women. Nor does he desire to obtain the other half of Panchala through a marriage to you. He punishes King Drupada with the equality Drupada once denied him. He is a good man."

She felt a weight lift from her: Whatever happened to her, her brother might yet escape death at Vaja's hands.

"Is Jarasamda of Magada here?"

"No, Draupadi. You are safe from him."

"And the murderer Suyodhana?"

But King Drupada had begun shouting the rules. Too soon, the first warrior stood before her. But only to speak. Something about him caused an immediate silence throughout the pavilion. Yet he was as dark as she was, as dark as Vyasa.

"Krishna. Of the Vrishni clan," Panchalya whispered. "A warrior, but the priests consider him some kind of seer."

"But he's dark as a Dasyu."

"Many Vrishni are. He's no darker than you or I."

She recoiled. So my brother and I are further separated, she thought. This fresh reminder of her shame was all the more suffocating because she had been commanded to bear the knowledge of their mother's origin alone. At first she hardly listened to this Krishna of the Vrishni as he announced that his clan would not compete.

"But I personally promise my Panchala friends to protect your princess throughout her life," he declared. "I also offer my alliance, for ever, to whoever marries this fire-born beauty." Krishna turned. The space between her and him seemed to disappear. Yet this intimacy was purer than a brother's. "Princess Draupadi? I am at your service."

The musicians managed to play a salute above the cheering. From his throne up near the roof King Drupada gestured a grand acceptance. "An important ally already," Panchalya said excitedly.

Now the great clay drums were rolling. Under Hastinapura's royal umbrella, someone stood. He was too young to be King Drita. It had to be his son. She was stunned. Suyodhana already dared to take his father's place?

The thick-chested Kuru came down to the pit to compete for her. Draupadi stared up at King Drupada on his throne. If he were wrong—if this task was not impossible—

Suyodhana took the bow, caught up the loose bowstring, and pulled. His arms quivered, for an iron bow of that size was indeed nearly impossible for one man to string. His body shone with sweat. But the bow was strung!

Draupadi could barely control her terror. Her eyes searched the pavilion for routes of escape, but she knew there were none for her.

He took aim. The target swung wildly. The arrows only grazed the outer rim.

Suyodhana looked up at her. For a moment rage distorted his face. She could feel the power of his thought—his desire for the kind of revenge his sort would take on a woman. He smiled mockingly at the crowd, then strode off.

Panchalya had not noticed—he was watching the tiers for the next competitor. Draupadi shuddered uncontrollably, remembering her weakest day, when she had considered giving in to Queen Yasoda's secret counsel and, for the sake of Panchala, marrying this abomination who wore hate like a bronze shield.

Dusasana, King Drita's second-eldest son, also grazed the target. But most of Suyodhana's thirty or so other brothers and half-brothers were unable even to string the bow. None fired an arrow near the golden fish. After King Drita's sons came those who also considered themselves Kurus—distant relatives of King Drita or the late King Pandu or their dead stepfather, King Kuru. Most efforts were pitifully inadequate.

Next came other families: King Virata and his two sons. Then Kings Bagadata, Kalinga and Jayadratha. Rulers and princes from Kosala, Cedi, Videha, Matsya, Karusa and Surasena. But the only other who came close was Salya, uncle to Nakula and Sahadeva. He was one of the oldest present, yet two of his arrows found the mark, earning him a long moment of cheering and stamping, but no more.

Suddenly Panchalya gripped her arm. "This one you must deny. King Radheya of Anga. A chariot driver's son. No, not even that—his parents are unknown."

"As are ours."

Panchalya shook her shoulder. "Radheya is Suyodhana's dearest friend! Is that not enough? Every king here fears Suyodhana, or is allied with him. None wants to see you betrothed to this Radheya. But only you can refuse him."

Anga's king stepped down into the pit. His approach had received hostile murmurs from the tiers and no drum salute. He grasped the bow anyway, and strung it effortlessly. But he did not take aim. Instead he stepped towards the dais and saluted Draupadi.

The tiers fell silent. She looked down on him; she saw the arrogance. She also saw further, down to his fear. Because his parents were unknown, he expected that with which she was about to surprise others. She, the half-Dasyu, almost relented. But glancing up towards King Drupada, she saw instead the young monk in the tiers. Looking down again, she said the wounding words: "I will not wed this man."

The murmuring of the crowd rose as her refusal was repeated and passed back. Radheya's lips parted—not as if to speak, she thought, but as if to cry out in pain. But instead he turned away.

"Never think it was your parents," she said quietly to his back. "It is your friendship with a murderer."

She saw him raise his head even higher in reply. Too high, she knew. Like herself.

Radheya stopped and turned back. "Then I will compete in Crown Prince Suyodhana's name," he announced. "If I win, the princess will marry *him*."

"No! Never!"

Panchalya stood beside her. "Suyodhana took his turn, King Radheya. He failed."

Radheya bowed curtly. "Do not count on it happening again." And he returned to the tiers, where Suyodhana and his brothers were standing, pacing and casting about like men looking for weapons. When Radheya reached them he was embraced. Throughout the pavilion other warriors watched these men under Hastinapura's royal umbrella, ready to follow their lead. And Draupadi watched for Vyasa. Surely he would not abandon her now.

Then from the pit came a voice like a silver flute: "Princess? Have *I* your permission?"

Silver-gold hair, amused smile, arrogant stance. The warrior of the white war horses. The warrior in her dream. His vow-taker's robes were insignificant, like the dust on his bare feet, for he pulled on wrist and finger guards as if they were his second skin.

But the robes were significant to others. Shouts and stamping filled the pavilion. Warriors were insulted that a priest presumed to compete where champion archers had been thwarted, and the priests feared any outcome—that the stranger's lack of skill would remind the warrior-born of their superiority with weapons, or worse, that his ability would injure the warriors' pride and bring down their wrath.

The young man in priest's robes who had come to the pit ignored the crowd, and Draupadi did also. Having obtained her nod of permission, he did obeisance to her, then bowed and circled the weapon he was about to string, doing it honours like an elder.

Then he picked up the bow, strung it, and fired five arrows into the swinging fish.

Priests yelled approval, all reservations gone. Warriors laid hands on hidden weapons, or took up anything at hand. From below her in the pit brilliant blue eyes looked up to meet her gaze. She saw there all that she had seen and feared in her dream. And sweet affection as well.

Her mind was empty, but her heart was finally full. She lifted the garland of flowers, walked down the steps into the pit and placed them over his head. Making the obeisance due a priest-born, she took hold of the hem of his robe as she had seen the wives of priests do. But he took her hand instead.

Those musicians still in possession of instruments began blasting out the triumphal music they had practised, but the war cries were too loud to be so frivolously masked. Through the chaos King Drupada strode down to the dais, the winner's goblet in hand.

For a moment Draupadi was frightened again. What if her rescuer were to learn she was half Dasyu? And with weapons all around them, how could she have allied South Panchala to a begging vow-taker?

Then their eyes met again and her last fears left her. She had made her choice.

*

The four brothers remaining in the stands were exultant; Yudishtira willed away his other emotions. He could see Arjuna in the pit, smiling like the boy he had been too briefly, before their father died, before Hastinapura. Before the tiger hunt, Varanavata and Ekacakra. Before their world had ended, with special bitterness for Arjuna, the prodigy prince.

Now Bhima leaped down the stairs and disappeared into the angry crowd, and Yudishtira sent Sahadeva and Nakula to the main entrance with orders to stay out of any fighting unless the princess herself were being abducted past them. Then he studied the patterns of men forming below him on the floor of the pavilion.

Sisupala, king of the Cedi, moved first, swinging a sala branch over his head and yelling nonsense. "Are we warriors or are we farmers? Is there not a single warrior here whom King Drupada considers worthy of his precious daughter? How dare he despise us so."

"Maybe it's his daughter who despises us," Suyodhana shouted. "Why not make them *both* pay for this insult?"

With encouragement such as that Sisupala advanced on the centre of the pavilion, where King Drupada had joined his son. Warriors gathered around both factions. But Yudishtira's eyes did not leave Suyodhana. Drita's son still hung back, watching Arjuna. And that one, Yudishtira saw, was still in the pit gazing adoringly at his prize.

Yudishtira could no longer delay rescuing King Drupada. Then beside the king Bhima appeared, his orange robes fluttering around him like flames as he tore a three-horse pillar out of the ground. A wad of yellow canopy billowed down, and out of it he stormed, swinging the whitewashed tree trunk. The thickest group of King Drupada's assailants was levelled in one stroke. Several lay still where they fell. Blood gleamed on Bhima's pillar. Yudishtira started down the tier.

In the pit Draupadi was only dimly aware of the struggle around them. She felt its pull upon her betrothed, however. He still smiled upon her, but he also glanced nervously about them. Then from above and behind she heard someone calling, and her beloved laughed. "Eldest, you found us. No need to look so fierce. I will fight for us all."

As he took up the iron bow like a mace and leaped out of the pit, a broad-shouldered priest jumped down and stationed himself with his back to her. Seeing Panchalya on the dais distributing weapons to his men, Draupadi reached for a sword and from behind placed it in the hand of her new guardian. "He called you 'eldest'. Then you must know who my rescuer is," she said. "He has not even told me."

"You have done well for yourself," her protector said, his back still to her.

"Do you know his clan?"

"I do." Suddenly the man turned. "You are betrothed to my brother."

She drew back. It was the face hidden from her in the dream. And now revealed. An intense, impenetrable face. Handsome, yes, but unyielding.

"You are . . ."

"I am Yudishtira."

"'Hear me,'" she whispered. "First you said, 'Hear me.' And he—" Her eyes widened. "Then he is surely Arjuna."

A battle axe sliced through the air near Yudishtira.

"Behind!" she cried.

Yudishtira whirled to face one of Suyodhana's brothers. The axe-wielder strutted at the edge of the pit, still believing he had challenged only a priest.

Suddenly hands gripped Draupadi's arms from behind and pulled her upwards. Yudishtira's back was still to her. She saw King Pandu's eldest thrust, then his blade shine crimson with a cousin's blood. As she rose in the jackal-grip from behind her, she kicked and twisted until at last she could see who she fought: Suyodhana. Then the pain from her arm sockets turned her mind black.

His wounded axe-wielding younger cousin was fleeing, but laughing. Now hearing struggling behind him, Yudishtira turned back. Infuriated by his cousin's guile, he raised his sword to sever the arms of this man who was his only enemy on earth.

Suyodhana released her and sprang back, then disappeared in the crowd. Yudishtira caught the unconscious princess as she fell and held her against him. Her dark hair spilled across his chest. The blossoms in her hair scented the air he breathed.

She is Arjuna's betrothed.

Now her legs bore her weight again. He loosened his grip.

But I can not release her while so many seek to steal her.

Nor can I hold my brother's betrothed.

Her eyes opened. She turned her head and looked up. "Follow Suyodhana. Kill him."

"I can not leave you." He looked away, lifting his sword to guard them with his left arm. She stood erect within the circle of his right.

"If you had killed him, you would be king." Her voice had an awesome calm.

Yudishtira let her go. "It would have been murder. He was not armed."

"Eliminate evil before it can grow."

The argument of his own teachers.

Panchalya appeared above them on the dais. "Draupadi? Are you hurt?"

"I am well."

The brother's sharp look caused Yudishtira to step farther from the woman. Panchalya went away.

Above them the fighting roared; in the pit there was a painful silence.

"Accept my apologies, Princess."

He had meant for holding her. But she said, "It's all right. You will have other opportunities to kill him."

Yudishtira felt a terrible finality descending over him, as if —if he wished to—he could see not some small vision but his entire future. But he desperately did not wish it. He deeply did not wish it.

Arjuna appeared, looking pleased with himself.

Yudishtira slammed his sword blade broadside on the pit's edge. "Come down here! By Indra's curse, protect your prize." Arjuna scrambled to obey. Yudishtira brushed past them both, jumped from the pit, and grabbed two thick legs of a broken chair from the debris on the floor. He rushed towards an opening in the crowd where Suyodhana stood and threw his cousin one of the legs. "*Fight* for what you want, coward! Leave tricks to the beasts smart enough to succeed."

The crowd parted and shouted encouragements to King

Drita's son and the wild monk. Suyodhana hunched down, purple-faced with rage. The two who were actually cousins began circling each other, but Suyodhana still did not recognise Yudishtira. So sure you killed us all, Yudishtira's mind shouted.

Yudishtira threw himself at Suyodhana. Drita's son made a jab and Yudishtira leaped aside. Long aware that Suyodhana habitually led with his right side, Yudishtira whirled past him on their next encounter and smashed down on his cousin's left shoulder. The crowd pushed forward, sensing an inhuman fury in this strange priest.

Suyodhana reached to touch his injured shoulder. Yudishtira struck the unprotected right ribcage, then the right shoulder. While his cousin was stunned, Yudishtira made the strike to the chest, the bent back, the exposed neck. In his mind he heard her voice: "Kill him!"

His arms lifted for the fatal blow. Suddenly he was seized from behind. He fought the hands like a madman, his blood pounding, but too many held him back now. Others were restraining and supporting the bleeding Suyodhana.

Someone was speaking from the dais. Through the sweat stinging his eyes Yudishtira could see it was his cousin Krishna Vasudeva, weaponless and serene. A tremble went through Yudishtira's body, as if his rage could not bear this sudden blocking and his body ceased fighting only at great cost to nerve and muscle.

"Dear and brave warriors," the Vrishni was saying from his higher position. "It seems to me the maiden was won according to the rules we all accepted when we came here. So why are we fighting?"

Yudishtira's body sagged. *Words*.

"Let the winner have her. This isn't worth killing priests over." Krishna laughed. The sound made Yudishtira's head dizzy.

Some were cheering, others growled. But the speech was giving Yudishtira time to think. Kill Suyodhana? Then be massacred, and "fairly", by Suyodhana's brothers and allies? No, take her *out* of here, now, while there's this indecision.

The arms holding him had loosened. He shrugged them off and walked away, catching the eye of Bhima and motioning slightly with his head towards the main pavilion gate, where the twins would be. Bhima nodded and edged towards Draupadi and Arjuna, who were watching.

Suddenly Arjuna swept the princess into his arms and jumped from the pit. The mere physical feat of it kept the crowd back a moment more. Yudishtira ran for the gate, shouting to Panchalya. The twins saw the plan and burst out into the crowd, brandishing knives and opening a path. Arjuna reached the gate with Draupadi as Panchalya plunged ahead to clear the outer entrance. Bhima fell back to protect their rear.

It seemed they were going to make it, but then the twins pushed ahead of Panchalya under the arched outer gate and Yudishtira saw Sahadeva go down.

Yudishtira shoved forward frantically. He almost threw Nakula back into the pavilion and knelt beside the fallen twin.

Sahadeva's wound was only in the shoulder, yet he looked strangely and gravely injured. As Yudishtira examined him, another arrow, from above, felled a horse.

What sort of warrior committed the sin of horse killing? And did it with only a single small arrow in the withers? Yudishtira looked up to identify the archer, and froze.

13

Dharma and kama, lawful action and pleasureful love—the
two duties of those on earth. But kama is first, for it causes
us to love dharma and those for whom we follow it. Without
kama we would not have the strength to put dharma above
desires.

But then I suppose that without kama we also would not
be tempted to do otherwise.

Urutata

Sons, obey your mother. She is truth itself.

King Pandu

Their faces were painted, their eyes were wide like men gone
mad. They were the sort of *rakshasa* demons one saw only in
dreams. All Arya accepted the existence of rakshasa, even if
only in the mind's world—they were the embodiment of evil,
which anyone could see was real. But now for a moment
Yudishtira believed he saw demons in the body's world. Until
one of them aimed at a running woman and missed. Even
rakshasa would not aim at a woman. Neither would they miss.

Shielding himself behind the gate, he leaned out to look up
again. Blue-black loincloths, blackened faces, blood streaking
their arms, filthy matted hair, long nails—so impure they
could never be Arya or even Dasyu. Foreigners then. But who?
And how to escape them?

Bhima bellowed. From inside the pavilion Suyodhana was
leading a foray aimed at retaking Draupadi. Bhima alone stood
between those coming out and Arjuna, who was helpless while
his arms held his princess.

And Sahadeva was writhing at Yudishtira's feet. Poison arrows then! Yudishtira bent over Sahadeva. Nothing else mattered now but his brother.

Suddenly a cloaked form pushed him aside. Yudishtira saw a knife raised over Sahadeva. He seized the arm that held it. The cloak fell away, revealing a woman.

"Leave me be and I may save his life!" she hissed in a yavana's accent.

Yudishtira thought he was losing his mind. But Sahadeva was ashen now. "Woman, if you kill my brother, you and all your family die!"

"First you'll have to find them," she retorted as she knelt and deftly drew out the arrow. "Don't touch that." She cut the wound and began, of all things, sucking it and spitting the blood. "Bring the king's chariot," she ordered. "Drive it here. It has shields. We'll put him in."

Yudishtira set his mind on the chariot, and on the space between himself and it—that it would not admit arrows. He entreated Yama to leave him among the living and ran.

Once in its midst Yudishtira felt the crazed, unskilled nature of the attack. Reaching the chariot, he looked back. Arjuna had set down Draupadi and was shooting at the archers over the gate. Several had leaped down and were slashing with curved knives at anything within reach. But the demons were crumpling as Arjuna's arrows found them. Yudishtira felt a childish relief that these rakshasa had proven to be mortal.

They were also insane—a few were fleeing, but far more seemed oblivious to Arjuna's archery. Only an arrow could wake them to their danger, even as they died.

In the chariot Yudishtira gathered up bows and quivers. Now Panchalya and Nakula reached the chariot too and Nakula took the reins. Crouching down, all of them opened a crossfire.

Suddenly Draupadi was running alone for the other chariot in the entrance yard. A painted body stepped from nowhere and grabbed for her. Her clothing tore and freed her. For a moment her face was blank with fear. Yudishtira took a lance from the rack and hurled it. The nightmare-man fell. The lance Yudishtira had used was only ornamental; its fresh green ribbons fluttered strangely over the stain-mottled body.

Yudishtira saw Draupadi leap into the chariot, heard her shout commands to the team. The chariot swung towards Arjuna and Bhima, still at the gate. Arjuna was killing raksh-asa; Bhima held back the crowd inside the pavilion with only his mace. At Arjuna's feet the strange woman was bent over Sahadeva.

Nakula also began driving, edging their chariot towards the gate as Yudishtira protected their route with a rain of arrows and Panchalya held up shields. This chariot almost collided with Draupadi's as the two drew up to the pavilion.

Suddenly one of Draupadi's team plunged to earth, an arrow in its chest. The other horse went mad with fear, squealing and twisting. Yudishtira jumped out and ran to its head. Someone painted and screaming rushed him. An arrow grazed Yudishtira's arm. From behind the garish head he saw Draupadi hurl a battle axe. The body slumped; the screaming stopped.

"Get under a shield," he shouted at her. He slashed at harnesses until the live horse was free of the dead one. Without its teammate the quivering beast flinched at the hiss of every arrow. But the horse could still save Draupadi, if Yudishtira in turn could save it.

Nakula and the woman were carrying Sahadeva to the other chariot. "Drive them out of here," Yudishtira shouted to Panchalya. "Don't wait. Go."

Their chariot was finally moving—at least the twins, Panch-alya and the woman stranger might survive this.

In the chariot that remained Draupadi crouched under a shield, a battle axe in her hand. Yudishtira turned the single horse away from the pavilion, swinging the rear of the chariot in the direction of Bhima and Arjuna. Those two were still fighting, back to back, but edging towards Yudishtira. The narrowness of the pavilion's entry had worked against the Arya attacking from inside. Outside, the rakshasa were all on the ground now and most were dead. Some still shot from behind the pavilion's pillars. Yudishtira snatched up a bow and quiver from the chariot. When he took aim at the painted faces that remained, the mere sight of another skilled bowman caused the last of them to slip away.

So they are cowards as well, he thought. Or hired killers instructed not to be captured at any cost.

Yudishtira shouted for Arjuna and Bhima. They ran and sprang in. Draupadi whipped the single horse into a trot. Yudishtira sprinted beside its head until it was safely away, then jumped on at the back of the chariot's box. The three brothers kept a stream of arrows flying as the one-horse vehicle careered away from the pavilion.

Out on the plain Panchalya had drawn up to wait for them. As the chariots drew abreast, Yudishtira took the reins from Draupadi. "Your sister is in safe hands," he shouted to Panchalya. "But it's better we don't reveal ourselves. Brothers, are you able to join us here? How is the injured one?"

"Aware and angry," Nakula shouted. He was already helping Sahadeva to step down.

"I am in your debt, healer," Yudishtira called to the cloaked woman still in Panchalya's chariot.

"Your chance to return the favour is coming," she called. "Draupadi?"

"Eos. Seeing you at last—it gave me courage, friend."

"Have no more fear. They will treat you well or pay with their lives."

"We will treat her like our queen," Yudishtira called back.

The woman laughed. "As I suspected, 'Priest'. As I suspected."

They abandoned the horse and chariot at the city gates. Draupadi wrapped herself in Nakula's cloak and, posing as six mendicant priest-borns, they lost themselves in the crowd.

It was a long walk to the alley of decrepit craftsmen's shops near the southeast city wall where the brothers and their mother had found lodgings that morning after the night on the boat. At first the brothers whispered urgently among themselves about the attack, but it surely was not against them personally, for who had known they were there? Nor did it seem to be part of an organised rebellion, or the attackers would have burned the pavilion and killed most of the Arya leadership without a battle. Having reassured themselves of that much, they kept silent to avoid attracting attention.

Alone with their own thoughts, the brothers pondered death. And being saved from death by another. And the beauty around them, even on the back streets of an overcrowded fortress-city—the curve of a bride's cheek, the defiant lift of her head, the mysterious silence of a virgin's modesty, and the subtle sound of her step. They also thought about the order of marriage among brothers.

When they turned into the last lane, which was empty, Yudishtira stopped them. Feeling incompetent, he still prepared to do his best:

"Princess Draupadi, whether it was against us or not, you have just endured an attack. You know about Varanavata too. I must warn you that you marry danger when you marry a son of King Pandu."

He was aware that his brothers were staring at him in awe, as if he had just had the courage to declare war on all of Indra's heavenly troop of *Maruts* at once. He borrowed on their confidence in him to stumble on. "As you discovered in the pavilion, this is my brother Arjuna, my brother Bhima there, and these two are Nakula and Sahadeva. Sahadeva's life was saved by your servant." He bowed slightly. "And mine by yourself, with an axe blow."

When she still did not speak, he braved the worst of it: "Tonight we have little to offer you in return." He swallowed. "Normally at this time of day we would be coming back from gathering alms for our dinner. We have been hiding as priests, waiting until—" He shrugged.

"I understand." Her voice was soft as a forest at evening. "You saved my life today also, Prince Yudishtira."

At that, his chest seem to fill with a radiant warmth. He tried to contain this peculiar joy as he turned and led them down the street to their rooms. At the door he called for their mother, suddenly imagining the delight of surprising her with Draupadi. The brothers understood and nodded their eager approval.

"Are you all safe?" Kunti called back from inside.

"We have had our—adventures. Sahadeva has received a wound, but it has been well tended." The brothers grinned at each other. "And Arjuna's brought home something very precious."

Kunti's voice came from nearer. "Something valuable? Be certain to share it equally."

A current seemed to pass through all six of them. "Share it?" Arjuna called, clearly relishing the joke.

Kunti was in the doorway now. "Arjuna has made a joke," Nakula said lamely. He gestured towards Draupadi.

For a moment their mother stared, motionless. Then she stepped out into the street and Draupadi fell to her knees before her future mother-in-law.

"My beloved daughter," Kunti said, drawing the princess to her feet. "You have finally come into my life." And Kunti embraced her.

Suddenly Kunti looked around at her sons. "What have I said? *Share* her?"

"She's Arjuna's, of course," Yudishtira said. "You can be very proud of him." He was angry to find himself struggling to say his next words. "The rest of us will enjoy her warmth as we do the sun, without calling it our own."

Arjuna shook his head. "Yudishtira, *none* of us can claim the sun. And none of us can claim this woman—especially not while an elder brother has no wife of his own. And there isn't time for that—Draupadi will have to be married immediately, now that she is with us."

"So what are you suggesting, Arjuna?" Sahadeva asked, still leaning on Bhima.

Yudishtira caught the look of embarrassed hope in the face of the twins and Bhima. "I forbid any of you to even make a joke of it."

"The old way allowed brothers to share a wife," Bhima said lamely.

"But only if she was married to the eldest," Arjuna added.

"These are not the *old* days." To talk of it made Yudishtira angry and confused.

"Now that Draupadi is with us she must be married immediately," Arjuna repeated. "She must marry *you*."

Draupadi drew back as if overwhelmed with humiliation and pain. And I am the cause, Yudishtira thought. I am the wrong man.

Their mother led Draupadi to the door. "Stop this. Come in and rest. First a meal, then we will come to a solution."

After the two women and the twins had gone in, Bhima spoke vehemently: "I for one don't care who she marries if I can just look at her and listen to her talk for even one minute a day."

Arjuna shook his head. "Yes, and you'd be happy just smelling a roasted bullock one minute a day—for about one minute the first day. We're human." Arjuna looked at Yudishtira. "She's going to be a source of division among us."

"She will not be."

"She *is*."

"Then you should have thought of that before you won her!" Yudishtira gestured angrily, then dropped his hands. "Forgive me, Arjuna."

"Forgive you? I *forgive* you. *Just tell us what to do.*"

"Somehow Bhima and I will marry tomorrow."

"What does that solve? Do you really think you won't mind when I take this woman off to my room at night and shake the floor you're sleeping on? What pleasant mornings you and I will have. *She is not like any other.* Yudishtira, make her our queen."

"Someone's coming," Bhima interrupted.

A young warrior-born with an abundance of gold niksha-coins jingling on his chest was sauntering down the street, followed by several servants bearing baskets and bundles. Arjuna recognised him first. "It's Krishna Vasudeva."

"Our Vrishni cousin who stopped our fun today," Bhima whispered.

"Helped save our hides," Yudishtira corrected, trying to seem casual as the stranger stopped before them. Under his robe Yudishtira put a hand cautiously to his knife's hilt. "Good evening, Krishna."

Krishna Vasudeva filled the alley with his laughter. "Saved your hides? Yes, and worried-looking hides they are right now, Yudishtira, eldest son of my father's dear sister. You are like five dogs growling over one little rib. Or should I say, one lady pup and five big, hard bones?"

Bhima gave Arjuna a pained look. Yudishtira loosened the blade in its sheath. "You know us then."

Krishna only laughed more. "I think I'm going to find the sons of Pandu amusing friends. Of course I know you. But you are utterly safe with me, Yudishtira. Leave your knife be. Besides my being your mother's nephew, don't you recall that I have sworn to defend both the princess and all those who wed—" He laughed again, with rich amusement. "But *that* is not a matter to be faced on an empty stomach. Would you care to dine with me? I've brought the best Kampilya had to offer, and not bad since most of the warrior-born in town tonight have turned out to be in no mood for feasting. While you five now have *everything* to celebrate."

The sun had set and the only light left was the glow of the coals from the little brazier on the doorstep. Draupadi had fled outside to it with the excuse of heating the last of the dishes brought by Krishna, for she needed solitude and time. Inside her head thoughts and sensations pounded her awareness like heavy rain. If she closed her eyes, as she wanted to so badly, she saw hideous painted faces above blood-streaked bodies. Then sweetly serious faces above naked brown Dasyu bodies. All confused with Arjuna's smile after he had won her, which would bring the horrible jangling of bells again. The howling wind. Dust in her eyes. The way the silver-haired warrior in her dream had laughed at her, had passed her by. And when she had reached to touch his horses, they had tried to kill her—

Her mind always veered away from that. A mere dream. Where was Vyasa? Surely he would come with brides for Yudishtira and Bhima.

Draupadi put her face in her hands. Her shoulders ached, her upper arms were bruised, and her stomach was cramped from the food she had been obliged out of politeness to eat tonight, in spite of her nervousness. And why had this Krishna dominated everything so she had no clear sense of the brothers' plans for her?

Now she was forced to recall what had truly driven her out: those startling, staring eyes. Appealing eyes. But they accused her. And why not? Because of her, he, the eldest, would now have to marry abruptly. The large and gentle Bhima might be satisfied with one of the local warrior-born girls. But not Yudishtira, who clearly could have had any woman in Bharata as his first wife, for he was in fact the most handsome, once one grew used to Arjuna's golden curls. Yudishtira was also a crown prince, which meant he had planned to select a first wife who would make a suitable queen. That choice could hardly be a half-Dasyu, and surely he had guessed by now, even if Arjuna had not.

Nor did the eldest seem to be one who would be happy with a marriage without love. In that he and she were alike, but she would have her marriage of love—Yudishtira would not.

Draupadi forced herself to stand. I must go back, she admonished.

Krishna appeared in the doorway. "Ah, Draupadi, let me help you." He took the heated dish from her, but merely set it down.

Since he had apparently come to speak with her, she risked her question. "They say you know the priests well, Krishna. Have you met Sage Veda Vyasa?"

"Of course. He sent me to you. To you and these brothers."

"Vyasa sent you?" At last she could let the gates of her weariness open.

"Draupadi, you are exhausted. Come and sit. I want you to be the first to hear how your future shall be resolved. It was actually your future mother-in-law's inadvertent suggestion. Isn't that fitting? I have convinced her to adhere to it, and she is convincing them. That they must share you, of course. All five."

Draupadi recoiled as if Krishna had struck her.

Krishna rushed on. "Men can wed more than one. Why not a woman? There *are* precedents too—certainly a girl like you has heard the story of Sri. And the ancestors' way of the eldest sharing his wife with his brothers." He laughed. "I know! Impossible! But it is equally impossible for you not to. This is the only way to avoid divisions. The only way, Draupadi."

Draupadi's mind raced. "Avoid divisions"—Vyasa had said the sons of Pandu could only be destroyed by divisions. Vyasa sent Krishna here, and Krishna came out here to tell me so!

Vyasa would never, never ask this of me.

He would. He took my memories, didn't he?

Krishna was smiling down at her. "A woman's dream come true, isn't it? Five great husbands and protectors, all strong and handsome."

Her mind seemed to roar with thoughts like a river, but she was determined to express herself clearly. "Krishna, you and I do not know each other well. You do not know my mind. How can I marry *five?*"

"You, Daughter of Fire, can do anything."

"But I *love* Arjuna."

Krishna's tone became gentle and reasonable. "You've only just met him, Princess."

"Arjuna has rescued me—that is enough reason to love him. And he is King Drupada's choice. There's very little I can be sure of, Krishna, besides my love. Please leave me this."

"Marry all five, Draupadi. Or marry Yudishtira. The eldest the others could accept. Anything else will divide them."

"Even married to them all, I could not hide my preference. Will that not divide them more?"

"They will gradually accept it as natural that you prefer one and they'll take other wives."

"And dharma?"

"You are Agni's child and may do whatever you like. One won you, but you, Daughter of Fire, chose all five. You can say you took a husband for each arrow Arjuna shot—that sounds godly."

Nakula came to the door. "Ready so quickly?" Krishna asked, laughing.

Inside, Yudishtira appeared shaken. Arjuna's head was down —he was retying a strap on his sandal. She studied them all. Had they truly agreed to this?

Bhima spoke first. "There will be talk, Krishna."

Kunti answered for the Vrishni. "I've taught you to be ruled by dharma, not others' opinions." She looked at Draupadi sadly. "It will be your wife who will suffer most from the gossip. Think of her, not yourselves."

Confused, Draupadi looked away.

Arjuna shrugged. "I think Bhima only meant that we will have to consider the effect on our future strategies. The question of forging new alliances, for example."

"Of course it is always possible," Sahadeva mused, "that other kingdoms would just as soon be allied with 'those bold sons of Pandu' as 'those ever-correct sons of Pandu'."

Krishna laughed. "Exactly, Sahadeva. And Nakula?"

"I think I will be content marrying Princess Draupadi," Nakula said shyly.

All except Yudishtira smiled. Draupadi stared at them each in disbelief.

"We are forgetting," Yudishtira said, "that her father wants her to marry Arjuna." He added more softly. "That is what she wants also."

She finally met his dark, glittering eyes. So it was as she had thought—he looked for a way out. He had not wished this solution either. Especially a marriage to one so obviously of Dasyu origins.

"Draupadi tells me," Krishna said firmly, "that she only wants what is best for everyone."

"I must have time to think," she whispered.

"Of course, Draupadi. Time to become accustomed to your great good fortune."

It was very dark. The twins had woken her by their gentle undressing of her. She sat up. They pulled the virgin shift up to her neck, then very gently laid her back, as the Dasyu women had. Bhima showered her with gifts—flowers, scented oils. Five voices sang to her, worshipped her. Ten hands caressed her.

Then the twins restrained her, one holding each arm. She felt Bhima's broad hands on her thighs, separating them, very gently. He held one leg while another brother held her other. Hands were touching her, searching her, making her ache with her desire for seed. Between her knees, against the darkness of the night, she saw a figure. A man. He came down very slowly, blotting out the night, bringing warmth and weight and breath.

She strained to see his face—Arjuna? Or the eldest one? His hard, curving plough lay in the furrow of her field, ready to plunge deep. But it held back. She struggled, wanting to know who this was. She tried to ask but a hand covered her mouth.

He entered her, spreading pain and pleasure, light and darkness, and his seed, all together. Later she knew there would be surata with the others. But it was the first whom she loved. Although it was only a dream.

For a long time after she woke she lay listening to their breathing. She was wet between her legs, the way she had been the night before, among the Dasyu. Her virginity had become a tangible pain with only one cure. She sat up.

Having only the single room, they had laid her mattress at their feet, out of reach if not out of mind. Kunti was at their heads, where she could hear their slightest need. But Kunti was sleeping soundly. The ones awake were her sons—from years of sleeping with her brother, Draupadi knew the difference. She lay back down. Finally, in her weariness, she dozed off again.

This time it was a dream of men with painted faces. She was trying to run but her legs wouldn't move. Green poison spurted from their fingers. They were reaching for her. She writhed, trying to escape their touch.

The effort finally woke her. Or the sound she heard outside.

The rakshasa! She leaped from her grass mattress, unsheathing the knife Panchalya had slipped her during their escape from the pavilion. But a hand stopped her.

"It's all right, Draupadi." It was Arjuna.

She trembled still more because of his touch, which reawoke the first dream.

"What was that sound?" she whispered, trying to make her violent emotions sound only like fear.

"I was going out to see." He disappeared in the dark.

She listened again to the other brothers' breathing. Yudish-tira seemed restless; the others were finally sleeping soundly. She remembered now that all but Sahadeva had been assigned a period to stay awake and guard them. Arjuna's turn was near dawn. He came back. 'What we heard was someone turning in their sleep. Your brother is asleep on our doorstep and your peculiar Greek serving woman is on the roof."

Eos. She could hear that Arjuna thought it all a bit humorous, but Draupadi's memory of the black-painted faces was too vivid.

"Do not concern yourself, Princess," Arjuna whispered, and explained how the house backed up to the city wall. Rocks he had set along the top would fall on the roof and alert them if anyone came over the wall. "There's no other way up that I can't watch from the window. Your brother is on the porch —I can certainly see anyone aiming for him."

"From the shadows?"

"It happens that I see fairly well in the dark." He laughed softly. "Including your expressions. You don't believe me, do you? But even if I couldn't see those two, they would be safe. Here, come and look."

She joined him at the window. He was right. The moon was full, and reaching any of the shadows would require passing through light almost as bright as day.

She continued to stare long after she was satisfied they were all safe. The patterns of moon and shadow and the brilliance of the very air made the simple street a dream of silver. "Agni has lit our night with his fire," she whispered.

He stood behind her. She could feel his breath on her hair. Even the scent of him was as she had imagined.

She suddenly wished she knew more about men and courtship. Surely he knew she loved him. He knew too well. They all knew he was her first choice. Still, a man should hear it put into well-chosen words.

No words at all were coming to her. She thought of her brother. They had talked about men's ways and he had let her watch his seeder grow hard and ready for ploughing by only thinking about a woman he desired. He had joked that with two thoughts the seed would spill. She remembered Panchalya's embarrassment on the mornings after this had happened because of a dream. She had to be careful—a man's seed should not be wasted.

Arjuna was ready in that way—she could feel it through the soft pleats of her skirt. As ready as she was.

Impulsively she shifted her weight back. Her body rested against his, his plough between her buttocks. It lit a fire there that made her weak with pleasure. She leaned against his length to keep her balance. Her head fell back on his chest; she felt him breathing rapidly on her hair. But her own breath she held, waiting for the caress she would have to reject— they really could do nothing, not even embrace, until they were married.

But his caress never came.

She straightened up, so that no part of her touched him. The silence wore on.

Finally his breaths were even again. He whispered in her ear, "This marriage Krishna proposes would be hardship enough, Princess. Given that none are wed to you yet—it will be better to show more restraint."

His words were so cold, she turned to try to find some warmth in his face. His chest and shoulders were in moonlight but his voice came out of a shadow. "I think it will be best if you begin now to consider yourself my eldest brother's wife, and let him decide the role the rest of us should take with you." He paused. "Now I wish you would look after him. There's something about his breathing that isn't what I am used to."

She was too ashamed to conceive of any response except to do what he'd asked. She slipped away from him, stumbled on some bedding and fell down at Yudishtira's feet. Afraid she would wake them all and have to face them, she crept silently to the eldest's head and tried to listen to his breath. But her tears fell on his tunic. It was a long time before she attended to anything but her own shame.

As the sky began to lighten, Draupadi noticed that Yudishtira's breath had become short and shallow. Reaching out, she could feel the heat thrown off him by his fever. He moaned once and attempted to turn over.

She sat back on her heels. What could be wrong with him?

Leaning forward again, she let her hands follow his body, a little above it, although because of the dim light she could not help but touch him sometimes. Yes, there was more heat on one side. A wound then. More heat near his neck.

She remembered the arrow grazing his shoulder while he ran to her horse during the fight in the pavilion gateway. She shuddered. It had not bled, and like all men, he had undoubtedly arranged his clothing so the tear and scratch wouldn't show, then forgotten about it. But the poison did not forget. Being only a scratch, it had merely needed more time.

Suddenly she felt angry with them all. Little boys, just like Panchalya. No sense at all. What had Arjuna thought—that she would throw him on the floor and stick his seeder in herself in front of his mother and four brothers?

Or was it that he had also guessed the reason for her dark skin?

Now she remembered Eos, up on the roof. She had saved Sahadeva. She would know what to do for the eldest, too.

Draupadi stood and walked to the door, stepping out over her sleeping brother before Arjuna could stop her. "Eos?"

Arjuna grabbed Draupadi's arm. "What are you doing?"

She shrugged free. "You yourself said they were in no danger out here." She turned her back on him.

The Greek woman sprang down softly, as if she had been poised for this call all night. But then, it had been sixteen months in coming. They embraced, Draupadi letting herself hold the tall, strong woman a long while.

They drew apart and Draupadi explained Yudishtira's wound. Eos searched through the folds of her man's-style clothing, drew out a leather pouch, and removed two packages. "Boil water. Brew this one and make him drink half now, half after sunrise. Tear off four pieces of your underskirt. Divide this one in four parts and soak each part inside a piece of cloth and put them one at a time on the wound, changing it when it cools."

"How can you see what you're giving me?"

"Wrapped in different materials. I'm going back up on the roof. Arjuna's clever little rocks on the wall won't work if we're attacked from the roofs on either side."

"How did you know about the rocks?"

"Saw. And listened. I've been here all night." She looked

Draupadi over carefully. "Better drink some of that tea yourself. With five husbands, you'll need your strength."

"You heard that too?"

"It's only a thatched roof." Eos hesitated. "I've been thinking about you all of this night." Her voice was gentle, and Draupadi felt Eos watching in the darkness. "Draupadi, suppose you were to not marry any of them?"

"But what else can I do? Not marry at all?"

Eos took her hand a moment. "You are right. There's very little else you can do." She embraced Draupadi again. "So go and take care of Yudishtira. He'll survive, and you'll be a great success with Kunti."

Rekindling the fire in the indoor brazier calmed Draupadi, as did the preparations with the sweet-smelling herbs. It was not easy tearing the cloth and pouring the water quietly. But she had good reason to try. She desperately wanted to be left alone.

Still, she kept glancing at Arjuna where he kept his watch by the window, his face half lit by the greying light.

A chariot clattered down the street. She saw Arjuna go out to meet it. It was Krishna, back again. "Does that Vrishni never sleep?" she muttered.

The voices had woken her brother. He was sitting up on the doorstep, repeating the greeting to the Sun. Soon the three were laughing quietly.

The chariot drove off with Arjuna and Krishna, so loudly that everyone else began to stir. Panchalya stood guard now. He looked in and smiled at her. She motioned to him not to speak.

The fire needed more wood. She jabbed it into the brazier, then hunched down over the warmth and scowled at the water as it came to a boil and she prepared the brew and poultice.

Yudishtira moaned in his fading sleep. She went to him and slipped his upper garment away from his shoulder. The wound was inflamed but she knew Eos was right—with proper treatment he would heal quickly.

When she put the steamy cloth on his shoulder his eyes opened. Angry at them all, she ignored his confused look. She took a fresh cloth and dipped it in warm water, then began washing his neck and arm near the wound. In the pale light his skin reminded her of pearls, or snow. It was lovely, in an indefinite way.

He was watching her as if she were preparing to skin him alive. Finally out of pity she had to say something. "You have a fever from this scratch you ignored yesterday."

His body eased and he almost smiled. "Then do what needs to be done."

14

Exceptional people do exceptional things.

Krishna

Only the exceptional are remembered.

Vyasa

Arjuna was trying to decide why it was that when this Vrishni
cousin of his drove, there was so much more noise. Maybe
it was Krishna's larger, hard-hooved horses from across the
Yamuna; maybe it was the chariot. But they were banging over
the paving stones so hard that every plank and beam and strap
and bronze fixture rattled against anything within striking
distance. Through it all, this Krishna smiled like the god Yama
the Fetcher himself.

"You are very good with a bow and arrow," Krishna called.
"Brought down quite a prize. I've never seen anything like
her."

"Thank you," Arjuna shouted back. "Where are we
going?"

"Here for the moment." Krishna suddenly reined the team
to a halt in front of the pleasure park at the foot of the palace
wall. "Better to wait for the others. They'll want to be present
when King Drupada finds out who all of you are."

They stepped down, Krishna tapped the waiting-command
on the nose of each horse, and the two young men sprawled
out under a pipal tree—the one dressed still in priest's clothes,
the other in a yellow tunic and green cloak that, worn together,
bordered on gaudy. The sun still had not risen and there was
dew on the grass.

"Panchalya was certainly pleased to know who we were," Arjuna said.

"Why not? His sister is marrying the finest family in the land."

"The entire family. I noticed you didn't tell him it would be all five of us."

"A little at a time, Arjuna. He may take it better than you think, however. Jealousy divided five ways is a bit like a snake cut into five pieces."

"Jealousy? He's her brother, not her suitor."

"Her twin brother. Slept together, played together, suckled the same breast. She's the leader though, as I'm sure you've noticed."

Arjuna had not. It suddenly occurred to him that Krishna had stopped because he wanted them to talk alone. Arjuna rather liked the Vrishni's mild deviousness—it was so utterly unlike any of his brothers. And he too had wanted a chance to talk alone. "How do you know so much about Draupadi and Panchalya?"

Krishna shrugged. "Certain priests. They've taken quite an interest in her. In you and your brothers too."

"And in you, I hear. May I ask why?"

Rather than answering, Krishna looked Arjuna in the eyes. For a long time neither spoke. A cuckoo gave its sensuous call from a nearby fig tree.

Arjuna finally had to look away. "You are a bit like my brother Yudishtira, aren't you? Except not at all."

"Your brother is the water, I am merely the soil. He, the wood; I, merely the flame."

Arjuna frowned. "Do you always talk like this? No wonder the priests like you."

Krishna laughed and rolled over on to his back. "What I mean is, I have a certain energy. Even some power. But your brother is the son of Lord Dharma."

"I see." Arjuna looked away.

"Do you? Your brother will provide a time and place here in Bharata that will allow dharma to take hold so it can never be lost. He will be the water that will keep the plant alive. But you, Arjuna, will be the little seed. With some soil around it, of course."

"The seed? All right." Arjuna found himself flattered. "You are right that I'm good with a bow and arrow, but I admire more your skill with words. Yesterday you controlled a thousand warriors by mere talking."

Krishna touched Arjuna's bowstring-calloused hand, lingering there gently. "But the archer took the woman." Krishna smiled. "He always does."

The touch disconcerted Arjuna. Arya men embraced and touched often, but at expected times. Krishna had done it out of kindness, in response to a moment and a feeling. Although Arjuna could not quite express it, the idea of such spontaneity between two friends pleased him deeply.

"I don't know," Arjuna said. "This morning your ease with words seems the more useful ability even with her."

"Smooth speech does help with women. I take it you have already talked with her alone?"

Arjuna nodded. "She's just so—sudden. I don't mean merely eager. Intense, as if she wanted to devour me. Not just to be ploughed, but more. I do want her, of course. She'll be a fine wife."

"Very intelligent. When she's older, even wise."

"I do like her. More than any woman."

"I understand perfectly," Krishna said.

"It is merely hard to accept the idea that we may all marry her."

Krishna sat up. "Ah yes, but the advantages! This way, when you take another wife she'll have your brothers and won't be difficult."

"I don't have one wife yet—I'm hardly planning on others."

"No? That doesn't fit the rumours about you. But then no one could have lived up to *those* stories."

"You have wives?" Arjuna asked.

"Six. Since you and I are the same age, you have some catching up to do. Women are one of the great pleasures in life, Arjuna. Sweet in every way. No reason to waste time." Krishna laid back down in the grass and asked how Yudishtira had been convinced to accept the marriage.

"While you were out? Oh, there were the same arguments back and forth for a while. Then Mother asked him what he would do if he could simply do exactly what he wanted. Of course first he said what he wanted was to know what his dharma was in this situation."

"Of course."

"So she said, 'But it isn't clear, Yudishtira. So you must decide. Tell us what you would have it be if it were only up to you.' Then he said, 'Share her with my brothers'."

"Share her?" Krishna laughed. "Surely your wise mother did not stop her questioning there?"

Arjuna was trying to understand this question when two royal chariots passed, bearing his brothers and mother, with Draupadi, Panchalya and Eos. The street had been filling with people going about their day's business. At the sight of the chariots they had crowded into the roadway to study the procession, looking for some hint of their kingdom's fate, but the passengers were well disguised.

Krishna stood up to go. Arjuna shook the grass from his priest's robes. "Thank you for befriending us yesterday. And for this today."

"I told you—I'm only soil for the seed. Arjuna, it is hard to celebrate the approach of one's wedding night if one's bride will spend it with another man. You won her. She is yours. If this arrangement angers you—".

"Angers me? But it doesn't at all."

"Only remember, Yudishtira was against it. It has been left up to her. It will be her decision."

Arjuna reached up and put a hand on his arm. "I will remember. I still don't understand this about the seed and soil and water. But I think I understand friendship."

The chariot brought Draupadi, Eos and Kunti to the women's quarters, where a messenger was waiting for the princess. He led her to her old room and garden. And there, once again, was Veda Vyasa.

"Sage, I have decided. I will marry all five, since that is what all of you want."

"You do not choose Arjuna only?"

"*All five is what they want.*"

197

"The words are meek enough, but they do not match either your voice or your past feelings."

"That is what he wants," she whispered. She fell at his feet. "Sage, what shall I do? What will be said about me?"

"All that you have imagined, and more. Could you bear it?"

She sat up, her head high. "I already bear gossip. Do you think anyone really believes Agni was my father? But what if the brothers discover—" Her voice wavered.

"They will not until you or I choose. By then it will be irrelevant. Draupadi, forgive me for not being at the bride's choice." He spoke the next casually: "I was unable to overcome an enemy."

"An enemy? Here in Kampilya? Who?"

"I was tired and became careless. He held me asleep in my room."

"Poison!"

"No, poison I might have fought better."

"It was one of the demons who attacked us, wasn't it? It was the man on the road."

"He is not a demon and neither were your attackers. He is an Egyptian and you and Yudishtira must be especially careful. Draupadi, you look tired. Perhaps you should have more time to think."

Draupadi felt a fresh wave of the anger aroused in her before dawn. "I am especially tired of *thinking* about this. 'Will it be a sin? Or is it my dharma? Will I be happy? Will *they* be happy? What about that horrible *prophecy*?' You—all of you—want *me* to choose." She started to cry and it infuriated her. "*I* must bear the sin."

"No, Draupadi. If there is sin in it, it does not outweigh the good it will do." Vyasa's eyes on her were gentle, but bright with inner fire. "Neither your struggle to do right, nor mine, will ever be called sin."

Hearing the agony in his voice, she felt ashamed of her outburst.

"It is time for me to stop directing your life, Draupadi. It is your awareness I can help with, but the actions that flow from your awareness are your own."

"What about my 'fate'?"

"Your awareness is your fate. If you can see an alternative, you can choose it."

"But I see *none*."

"Then you have no choice."

"But you can see for me!"

His face became infinitely sad. "I see the pain I will cause and this will be no exception, however I decide."

"You think I don't see it too? How can I choose pain for myself?"

"Because something must be done. They are waiting."

She stood up. "Then I will do what they want—what *Arjuna* wants—and marry them all, poor fools. May Indra protect them!"

Vyasa nodded solemnly and said no more to her. They walked in silence through the palace to the assembly hall. There Draupadi announced her decision, and King Drupada raged. He was "delighted" that the sons of Pandu lived, and one of them for a son-in-law had been his "only dream". But five? "It is an abomination! It can only bring us ruin!"

Sage Vyasa walked to the foot of the throne. "King Drupada, we know you must be correct. Yet I ask you to accept the will of your daughter in this. Our concern for these youths should not cause us to forget the larger purpose: Their story must be remembered through a very long age. And now——" At last Vyasa looked at Krishna, where he stood among the five brothers and their bride. In a voice full of anger or mere prophetic intensity—none knew which—the sage said: "Now their fame has been assured."

After King Drupada's capitulation in the assembly hall, Kampilya's palace shook with running feet. Draupadi was rushed to the women's quarters to be prepared for her noon wedding to Yudishtira. No time could be wasted, for there were too many who had reasons to prevent her marriage, whether they thought she was wedding an unknown alms-gatherer or they had recognised the sons of King Pandu. Sahadeva and Bhima went from room to room, directing the gracious removal of every bride's-choice guest within the palace walls except the few whom King Drupada and Krishna had together agreed could safely be allowed to remain for the celebration. Queen Yasoda began frantically organising for the wedding and feast, and decorating the room where the two would consummate this blessed, kingdom-saving alliance.

On the training field outside the walls Arjuna and Panchalya had assembled the best of Kampilya's warriors—not more than eighty unfortunately—and were quickly testing their skills. Given the attack following the bride's choice, Yudishtira had all but demanded that King Drupada create an elite, trust-worthy troop to oversee the protection of the palace and the princess.

Meanwhile Queen Kunti was searching for her eldest son, to bathe, massage, dress and decorate the bridegroom for his wedding. But her oldest walked on Kampilya's ramparts with her youngest stepson. Both were still stunned and bewildered by the decision that had been made in less than a day.

"I think you had no choice," Nakula said. "She has to be wed immediately, you have to marry first, and your wife, above all, has to be a suitable queen. Even Vyasa wanted it."

Yudishtira stopped walking and looked down on the city. "Or did Vyasa acquiesce because I had already decided? I could have refused, Nakula. I feel as though caught in rushing water—" He shrugged and faced his brother. "I could have refused."

Even in their childhood, Yudishtira had felt free to speak his thoughts aloud to the youngest twin. He thought it was perhaps because the dark-haired, reticent Nakula reminded him of himself—as Sahadeva, with his fawn-coloured hair and outgoing ways, was a younger Arjuna. Thinking of all of them reminded Yudishtira again that his decision affected others besides himself. "Nakula, surely you mind sharing your wife with your brothers?"

Nakula thought a moment. "Yes. Yes, I do mind. But having seen her, no other will ever seem the same. Therefore what choice have I? I *must* share her."

Yudishtira looked at him. "That is it, isn't it?"

15

O gods, raise again the man, O gods, who has sunk;
O gods, give life again to the man, O gods, who has
   committed sin.

These two winds blow to the regions which are far
   beyond the ocean;
May the one bring you vigour, may the other blow
   away all evil.

Rig Veda

This time Suyodhana saw that the chariot driver felt his blow.
The driver passed it on fully, slamming his whip across the
backs of the team of four. Still there was no increase in speed.

Suyodhana leaned forward over the rail. "Nirriti take them
to Hell!" The driver turned away and muttered a mantra for
protection; on Suyodhana's other side Radheya shook his head.

"No one's ever made such time between Kampilya and
Hastinapura," Radheya said with maddening calm.

Suyodhana ignored him. "Curse it—Father's probably not
even on the main road. 'So no one will see us.' As if the world
were as blind as he and will not notice him on any route. And
my uncle will be wanting a 'dignified pace'. May Yama devour
him. He said, 'they are *dead*, Suyodhana. *Forget* them, Suyodhana'. So then were they ghosts who made a fool of me in that
pavilion?"

On their right the silver of the Ganges was blinking between
the trees like the eyes of a thousand-headed demon.

"King Drupada planned the entire bride's choice to ridicule
me, Radheya. He knew Arjuna was alive—that's why he held
the contest." Suyodhana touched again the bruises caused by

201

the monk he now knew had been his detestable eldest cousin, then hit the driver again.

"We may kill these horses too, Prince," the driver dared to whisper.

"Kill them and I'll kill you."

"You know you will not, but perhaps he could mind his horses better if you struck him less," Radheya said stiffly. Only now did Suyodhana recall that Radheya was himself the son of a driver.

Radheya. It was Suyodhana's private opinion that the "King of Anga" haggled over dharma worse than a real warrior. But there wasn't another archer like him on earth. If Yudishtira was too arrogant to believe it, that was all the better. Radheya was his hidden weapon, then. And his only friend. He would have to make amends somehow. A bother.

"Your father's chariot," the driver shouted.

"Yes, thank Indra, and Sakuni is with him." He turned to Radheya. "I know you dislike my uncle's ideas—"

"We could still turn back, Suyodhana. Fight them like true warriors."

Now Suyodhana ignored him again. The chariots were approaching each other at a wild speed. Just as it seemed they would collide, the drivers shouted the commands that worked better than bits to turn battle teams aside. It forced Suyodhana to acknowledge that the loss of two full braces of war horses merely by running them to death was wanton waste. Not even an enemy killed war horses. Besides being "innocents", they were as valuable as their weight in silver when captured.

But his uncle's presence made it worthwhile.

Suyodhana leaped down and made his obeisance, circling his elders' chariot and bowing at the four corners. Sakuni and Drita stepped down as another chariot arrived with servants and equipment. Slaves rushed into the trees to prepare a camp in the style the Egyptian had taught, and in the time they once had needed to water a single team.

Suyodhana now respectfully approached his uncle. But he received only a rebuff. "After bathing, Suyodhana, and after a rest. Neither kings nor future kings should ever feel hurried by anyone, least of all their enemies. Don't you agree that your father will think more clearly,"—there was a slight emphasis on the last—"when he has been properly refreshed?"

Suyodhana saw that his father did look even worse than a month ago—like a tree the rains had somehow skipped.

Radheya settled himself at a distance and began his daily contemplation of the sun. Suyodhana, his headlong rush suddenly stopped, wandered fretfully through the emerging camp.

The first thing he noticed was that his father still insisted on the old, pitiful rites, even when travelling. The two priests, who had arrived in a slightly slower chariot, were lighting the sacred fire with embers carried from the assembly hearth at Hastinapura. But they were two of only ten fully trained priests still remaining at the palace—and each of those now had to meet with his uncle's approval. Since most ceremonies required at least seven to officiate, they "earned their rice", as Sakuni put it.

Suyodhana thought with some annoyance that there could have been no priests here today if his father had not weakened Sakuni's test. The priests claimed their rituals "support life", so Sakuni had suggested a year without rituals, to see if in fact a difference could be noticed. But his father, always convinced that some vague catastrophe approached, had all but ruined the idea by insisting that a few always remain near him.

The two priests began to chant Veda. In spite of himself Suyodhana immediately felt less tense, if only because he could not recall a time when the sound had not been somewhere in the background of his life. Veda was preserved entirely in the memory of certain priest-born families, each maintaining its own segment of the hymns by repeating it daily. It was the duty of the warrior-born to support them, and kings especially vied for the honour and prosperity that were supposed to come with patronage of the best families. Failure to give that support, warriors were told, would surely precipitate the dark Age of Kali. Suyodhana was amazed that he had needed Sakuni to point out that all this was more of the priests creating "dharma" for their own convenience.

At last his uncle and father appeared under the king's red and gold canopy. The sandalwood throne was there; the yak-tail fan and white umbrella leaned against it. Suyodhana thought it stupid to drag so much regalia everywhere. He took his place, as did Radheya, and the servants served fresh fruit juices in tiny glass goblets from Babylon, nestled in ice brought by runners from the Himalaya. Suyodhana saw that Radheya was impressed. He would have to remind him that, much as he disliked Zesnor and Sakuni, this was all their doing. If even a little luxury could be displayed before the Anga, Radheya would gain considerable stature.

His father began with a long speech about the sons of Pandu being alive and the influence they would gain through their new alliance to South Panchala. Suyodhana could not believe it when his father finished by saying he wished to invite the five brothers back to Hastinapura and have them welcomed as heroes. "We can not fool the people. They are very fond of Yudishtira especially."

"What great fear of the common people resides among us," Sakuni murmured.

"Not fear, Sakuni," Radheya said. "Respect."

Suyodhana hardly noticed their sparring. "You must be joking, Father. We, welcome them as heroes?"

"We mourned them properly," Drita said in hurt tones. "We thought they were dead."

"Father, you really must be joking. You are very right—we can not fool the people. We have already shown them rather clearly how we feel about those insufferable brothers."

Drita's voice rose. "Yes, I have some idea of how you and Sakuni were involved in that fire at Varanavata. There shall be no more of it."

Suyodhana was furious. "Who helped us by ordering them to go to Varanavata?"

Sakuni sighed. "The past is past. However it came about, Suyodhana has been consecrated as crown prince and it can not be undone. Or so you said, brother-in-law, when Yudishtira was the consecrated one."

"The past *is* the past, lawless as it was," Radheya interrupted. "What matters today is that mortal enemies arose from the ashes of Varanavata. We must send a message to Kampilya today that Suyodhana and I challenge all five of them. Death or victory will be the only outcomes we accept. That action

204

the people will understand. Whatever was done at Varanavata, dharma will cleanse us of sin and our dharma as warriors is to fight."

Suyodhana said something placating to his friend, but watched his uncle, trying to guess his wishes. To Suyodhana's shock, they were the same as his father's—congratulate Yudishtira on his marriage and invite the brothers to return as soon as possible to Hastinapura. Before Suyodhana could reply, Sakuni asked him "to walk a moment away from the *drivers*", his glance falling on Radheya.

The charioteer's adopted son went pale with anger, but held his tongue. Suyodhana stood, unable to meet Radheya's eyes. But as soon as he and his uncle were finally alone and out of hearing, Suyodhana forgot about his friend. "What happened at Varanavata? You said they were dead!"

"And you say they are alive. One of us has made a mistake. I have sent for Zesnor to tell me the truth."

"I would know Bhima anywhere!"

"Except when dressed as a priest," Sakuni said coldly. "Shall we speak no more of past mistakes? Regrets are never becoming."

"Why didn't you tell me you planned this wild attack at the pavilion? If we had been forewarned, Radheya and I could have used them far better. My cousins would all be dead now."

Sakuni frowned and turned away, apparently angry again. Suyodhana tried now to placate him. "I do see your intent, Uncle. It's true that if I'd been involved in any way I might have been blamed. The uproar they caused—using poison arrows, killing women and animals and the unarmed and wounded—it was something Bharata has never seen. With a few more, in another surprise attack, we will be rid of my cousins for ever." Now he broached the more delicate matter. "The Egyptian weapon—you never told me who it was meant for. I took it to the bride's choice, thinking to use it on Draupadi's brother if he remained an obstacle." Encouraged that his uncle was not enraged again by this news, he plunged on. "I have arranged for its use on Yudishtira instead, since you—since the other method failed. It will be my wedding gift."

Sakuni turned. At the same moment the slave Zesnor slipped from the trees. Suyodhana started, as did his uncle, in spite of expecting the Egyptian. Sakuni spoke sharply. "What news have you?"

"In a moment, Master. I am disturbed by what I have just now overheard. I would not have used the 'Egyptian weapon' so near the princess. You had planned"—he glanced at Suyodhana—"other than death for her."

"She won't be harmed, Uncle," Suyodhana said. "I intend to have that one for myself. You, Zesnor, had a year to get her out of Kampilya, and failed. But I shall drive into the city and simply take Yudishtira's poor widow as my wife—and be considered generous for doing so."

But Zesnor insisted he should return immediately and try to reclaim the weapon.

Suyodhana again dared to challenge the yavana. "These demon foreigners of yours are far more dangerous than a single snake."

"Master, I know nothing of these they are calling 'rakshasa' except what I learned in Kampilya's streets, and I will continue to investigate their origins. But during the bride's choice I deemed it most important that Vyasa not be there."

"Then who sent those demons?" Suyodhana asked.

Sakuni's eyes narrowed. "You fear that old man too much."

"I do not fear him," Zesnor said calmly. "But every plan must take him into account. I presumed that with him under my control, your nephew here would certainly be able to win or abduct the princess without my further assistance. Since I believe these efforts at princess-stealing distract us from our central purpose, and since you and your nephew have such numerous and varied"—he glanced at Suyodhana—"plans for her, with your permission I shall cease my concern about that matter and leave her to yourselves. But as for that central purpose, its achievement is now greatly complicated. I studied the sons of Pandu a year ago, before Varanavata, and during the night I have of necessity considered them again, deeply. Yudishtira is easy to manage because of his concern for dharma. But he is hard to kill and—"

"He *must* be killed," Suyodhana shouted.

Zesnor's tone remained utterly rational as he explained that, because of Varanavata, however Yudishtira died King Drita and his sons would be blamed. "I predict that your nephew here would reign for less than a year. He would be murdered in his sleep by some other kin of the late King Pandu."

Suyodhana stepped between Zesnor and Sakuni. "I want Yudishtira *dead*."

Zesnor was silent a moment. "Then perhaps you will yet have your way in Kampilya, for your weapon is more than adequate. But if you do not succeed, and he comes back to Hastinapura to claim the throne, would it not be enough, Crown Prince Suyodhana, if we took it from him and left him humiliated? Caused him to suffer and yearn and live with his failure for the rest of his life? Consider it, Crown Prince. Would that not be enough?"

Suyodhana was suddenly ashamed of his outbursts. "That might be enough. Yes, it might be very satisfactory indeed."

16

The profit-maker does not love work and profit
  for the sake of the work or the profit
  but for the sake of the Self.

The friend does not love the friend
  for the sake of the friend
  but for the sake of the Self.

The mother does not love the child
  for the sake of the child
  but for the sake of her Self.

The husband does not love his wife
Or the wife the husband
  for the sake of the other
  but for the sake of their Self.

Know this: Love expands only the Self.
  All love is directed to the Self.

The "Great Teacher".
Another version is in the *Upanishads*

Kuru Crown Prince Yudishtira and Princess Draupadi of Panchala entered the assembly hall at Kampilya at the moment the
noon sun struck the sacred hearth. They were led by King
Drupada and Purohita Urutata, and followed by Vyasa, family
members and selected dignitaries and officials of Kampilya.
The guests gathered around the hearth and Urutata lit the
ritual fire, made the oblations and placed Draupadi's hand in
Yudishtira's. The bridegroom led her as they took seven steps

around the fire, saying, "I take thy hand for good fortune, that thou mayest attain old age with me as thy husband. The gods Bhaga, Aryaman, Savitri and Purandhi have given thee to me, that I may be the master of a household."

Facing the fire Urutata said, "Pushan, inspire her who is most auspicious, in whom men may sow seed, who most affectionate may be devoted to us, and in whom animated by desire we may beget progeny." Then he blessed them: "May you never be separated. Live together all your lives, sporting with sons and grandsons, happy in your own house."

Kunti gave the blessing to a daughter-in-law: "As Indrani is to Indra and Rohini is to the moon, so be thou to thy husband. Bear live children and be joined with much happiness. Be strict in thy vows and give homage to guests and the holy ones, to children and the old, and to thy elders." Then she added, "May thou soon be anointed queen of the Kurus, and always be favoured with love and gifted with joy. And so shall I bless thee again when thou hast borne a son for us."

Then the consecrating waters ran down their trembling faces as Yudishtira and Draupadi softly spoke the binding words to each other: "May the universal gods unite both our hearts; may the waters unite them; may Matarishwan, Dhatri and the bountiful Saraswati unite both our hearts." And Urutata proclaimed them wed.

Gifts were presented in the large garden. King Drupada gave a chariot worked in gold, overflowing with the latest armaments and yoked with four bay horses wearing gold bridles. Nakula's and Sahadeva's uncle, Salya, gave a lotus-marked elephant blanketed in blue silk and bordered with blue gems. Krishna gave Draupadi gold necklaces set with diamonds, beryls and pearls, plus a cart of unworked gold bullion to Yudishtira.

Afterwards there was a feast and entertainment in the celebration hall, and when the sky was dark and the moon rising, the couple were led to their apartments accompanied by bells, gongs and chanting. Around their necks each brother laid a final garland. Arjuna's was of jasmine. Then they were shut inside together.

As the door closed behind them Yudishtira drew a long steady breath. The room was decorated with jewelled canopies;

flower petals were everywhere. He felt like a fodder cutter at a perfume stall. Facing a night filled with wolves, flames and poison arrows seemed far easier than this. Simpler. His entire body seemed to resound with his heartbeat.

I've lost my awareness, he thought—that is what unsettles me. When I'm around her, I have no vision. Only ordinary sight, and the vision of her.

No, what frightens me is what I am about to do.

Draupadi had gone to the window. She was clothed in white linen—a bodice, a skirt of folded pleats and a border cloth that swept around her shoulders and over her head. All were edged with tiny white sirisa, lodhra and tilaka blossoms. There were gardenias in her hair.

She lifted her head a little in the moonlight. You are trying to smile for me, he thought. Utterly resolute.

He motioned for her to come and sit with him on the bed.

Then he stumbled into it. "The wise say, 'If love is what you desire, first win a wife with words.'" He felt his fists clench as he forced himself to go on. "We're still strangers, Princess Draupadi. We need to fully know each other's hearts and minds before we can think about love."

"Whatever my husband says." He saw now that her hands were trembling.

"No. I want it to be different with us," he said too harshly.

"How shall I make it different, Husband?"

"With me you will be a queen, Indra willing." He paused to consider his words. "I would like to depend on your complete thoughts on every matter. Even those unpleasant for me to hear. I, in turn, will try to give you my thoughts honestly as well."

"Sometimes one does not know all that one thinks or feels."

"Then perhaps we can help each other. For example—" He hesitated just a moment more before beginning what could never be undone. "I think you want your first surata to be with Arjuna."

He saw her eyes fill with tears before she lowered them. "With this help of yours, I will be as honest as I can," she whispered. "You have expressed my secret wish."

"Then I will fulfil it. You and I will have many other nights for surata. I will speak to Bhima about it also."

She looked up, her face shining with more gratitude than he had dared to hope for. Or dared to fear. It was clear—she was truly grateful to him that he would not take her. Elation and anger rose up in him like currents in a flood sweeping along high banks of stone.

"But I ask you, wife, to share my bed tonight." He was startled by his own words, which had escaped on his flood of feelings. But she seemed willing, for she rose and faced the bed, as if almost desperate to gratify him in at least small matters. He observed that he did not mind that.

"Do you wish me to undress?" she asked.

"Only your outer garments."

He watched her. She was graceful, yet unaware of her own beauty. And although the virgin's shift hid her body, her undressing revealed her dark limbs and the full curves beneath the cloth.

He also undressed, then moved on to the bed and covered himself with the delicate materials, which did nothing to hide his arousal. As he turned to place his clothes on the bench at the foot of the bed, he felt her lying down beside him. Felt her eyes on him.

Many women had preferred him to Arjuna. Why not this one?

The blood rushed in his veins, as if he hunted tiger again. He knelt beside her. Her head was on the pillow amid flower petals and a cloud of dark hair. At the centre was her still and perfect face. All around her there was warmth, and scents of more than blossoms. His body trembled, his groin ached.

"I fear a bride should entertain her husband with stories," she whispered, "but I have none. Will you tell me about your own childhood?"

He still stared at her, his mind clouded with desire.

She turned on her side and returned his look. Slowly he lay down, without answering her. Her eyes seemed to soften and grow larger, like a doe's. Her body was nearing his, almost touching his. And it was she who leaned towards him.

Only their lips met, very softly. The fragrance of her skin

211

caught him inside its circle. His body seemed to be on fire. Agni's daughter.

He reached slowly, slowly, towards the bottom of her shift. Then her breath caught; her eyes darted to follow his hand.

He lay back. His plough and thighs and the whole centre of his body demanded this field, while his heart pounded with its fear of losing any chance for her love. And his reason said, prevent this. There is this moment now. There is now. Perhaps she even wants me. But a moment ago she wanted him. And afterwards? When I will be the only reason she can not go as a virgin to her first choice?

He used his warrior's will, he used the techniques the forest monks had taught. He was young—inexperienced and easily aroused—but he used everything at his command. He would not take her. Take her and lose her.

They lay in the moonlit darkness for a long time, in silence. He thought her silence was exactly like the moon's, in fact—it seemed to shout a pure and voiceless light that made him feel clumsy, mortal and crazy with unnameable desires. He had triumphed, perhaps, over his immediate desire. Although he would never trust it while she lay within reach. But a deep sadness now enveloped him. Not at all a feeling of triumph.

Finally he could bear the loss no more. He would share at least his heart. He would talk, about anything.

"You asked about my childhood," he said quietly, evenly. "In my childhood, the priests spoke often of the approaching Age of Kali and the destruction of Creation at its end. They said the age would last thousands of generations, and during it dharma would gradually be forgotten."

No! Why had he gone down this path? Did he mean to tell her *this*?

Yet he heard himself go on, as if the need of his body had taken another form, insisting on release, even against his will.

"My father, as a good king, wanted to spare his people from this age of destruction."

"So he went to the forest," she finished for him, her voice oddly controlled also. "Even I have heard how he went to perform austerities for the sake of us all." She lay very still on

212

her back. "Although I do not know his reasons for thinking his own penance would keep others from sin."

"There was more purpose to his austerity." Yudishtira closed his eyes as if to escape from what was coming. "He reasoned that if the Kurus had a king perfect in dharma—perfect—this terrible age could not touch us."

"But then why did he not keep his throne?" She turned her head. "Everyone says it: Your father should have aimed to become samraj. Then Jarasamda of Magada could never have begun his lawless attempt and—"

Yudishtira's pulse pounded. "It was not himself whom my father expected to be perfect, Princess."

She rose up beside him. Her luminous eyes watched him. He looked away.

"You." Her gentleness gave his heart hope.

He heard himself laugh strangely. "Of course some say my father was merely impotent and his austerities were to hide his shame."

"I know," she said softly. "And I know how they explain his five sons: sons of the gods."

"That's the most flattering explanation. But, no, I remember King Pandu. I am his son."

"Not Lord Dharma's?"

He stiffened. Then rushed on with anything else. "In a way we are alike, you and I. King Drupada had his goal for you; my father had his for me."

He saw unhappiness cross her face and he forgot his own.

"They say you will save Bharata," she whispered. "You know what they say of me."

"Then at least one of these prophecies is wrong—I can not save Bharata if you have doomed me."

But his words were not right—tears shone in her eyes now. He longed to hold her and promise her anything if it would comfort her. But she would not be so easy to soothe. And he knew what would be the result of his holding her.

"My dark skin," she suddenly whispered, "do you mind it?"

He was startled. "Mind? I do not mind." As he answered, he saw Wood Rose in the rain. He pushed the unexpected memory from his mind.

Draupadi was staring at him, studying him, almost crying freely. He tried to think of how to comfort her. "Draupadi, surely you do not believe that prophecy about you?"

"Prophecies!" Now, to his surprise, she spoke with anger. She was truly changeable as a flickering fire. She arose from the bed and stood over him, erect and defiant. "If I decide, right now, to walk across this room, is that my fate? No, it is my decision. And if I am careful not to fall, is that my good fortune? No. Never. It is my skill at walking."

He strove to respond rightly. "Decision and skill must surely affect our fate. Or be part of it. The teachers say one might even avoid one's fate entirely—if one were able to see the whole pattern as well as you and I see this room. But few can do that. Or perhaps no one. Perhaps only Brahma's mind can contain the whole plan for life."

Suddenly she was back in the bed. She took his hand and drew it to her breasts, huddling around his fist for comfort as though it were all of him and it could save her from some terrible danger. He felt her tears on his fingers. "You do not mind," she whispered. He did not understand.

With his other hand he cautiously stroked her hair. Then he pulled her closer—foolishly. For when she came into his arms and lay with her head on his shoulder, crying softly, his desire rushed over him again. But this time his exhaustion and his love blended into a terrible, sweet sadness that changed his body's aching into a vague hurt in his soul.

Bathed in this strange, warm grief, he fell asleep with her, for neither had rested well for many nights.

He woke after night's midpoint, aware that she was awake beside him. But he did not speak or move, for she was still in his arms and he did not want to end even this small joy. Soon, however, the control of his awakening desire demanded all his attention. He lay rigid, his mind focused on blankness.

Then she stirred and held him tighter, as if still afraid. Desperate to stop her suffering, he blurted into the darkness what came first to mind: "I think it is possible to choose not to do harm, even when it seems to be ordained that you must.

This is something even the priests could not teach me. Only my father."

"Lord Dharma?"

How carefully she had observed him and listened. Again he wanted to flee his next words—words he had uttered to no one. And again he felt the insistent need to leave them with her, not merely as comfort, but as the only seed he could allow himself to sow in her.

"It was only a dream," he said into the soft darkness. "I had it on the way to Ekacakra. In my dream it was hot and I was craving water. I came to a lake and found my brothers dead beside it. In the lake there was a crane, standing on one foot. The crane said he had killed my brothers because he had asked them to answer his questions before they drank, but they had refused. The crane said, 'He who takes this water by force will die. But answer my questions, and you may slake your thirst for ever.'

"So I answered his questions. I was dying of thirst, but I seemed to be answering correctly—I was still alive. Then he asked me one last question: 'What is a human?'

"And I said, one is human as long as one follows dharma. Then the crane offered me water. When I had drunk, he told me he was my father. Lord Dharma."

"The harmoniser of life."

"He said that because of my ahimsa, my non-forcing— which he called 'dharma's essence'—all my brothers would live again. And so they did."

"Because of ahimsa?"

"The forest-dwellers seldom reveal it to the warrior-born, but they speak more and more of it. Perhaps because the warriors burn more and more of the forests." He tried to laugh, aware that he, a prince, could hardly aim to avoid causing harm.

Draupadi lay on her back now, staring up at the ceiling.

"Is this dream why you didn't kill Suyodhana when he had me? It's true he had no weapon. But neither did you at Varanavata. And what about righteous anger, Yudhistira? 'The highest virtue of a warrior'?"

He felt a wave of desperation. "Ahimsa was my dream,

215

Draupadi. But in this world of danger I am fully awake."

She lay still, without speaking. He waited. He finally whispered, "Shall we sleep?"

She nodded and turned on to her side, her back to him. But he did not sleep and he knew she did not either.

Some time towards dawn she whispered, "Will the rakshasa come, Yudishtira?"

He felt her hand searching for his again. He took it gladly. "No, we will guard you well."

After that she seemed to rest. But he, although close to sleep himself, could not escape the vague torment of his body's desires and his heart's regrets.

He opened his eyes to golden light and overwhelming sadness. In the clarity of morning he knew without doubt that he did love her, and that she preferred his brother. And today she would prepare for yet another wedding. He would never again have even this illusion of being her only husband.

Now his desire returned, like a stubborn animal. Twice in the short night he had nearly taken her anyway. Then there had been his dreams—tangles of limbs that fell away to reveal women's furrows dark and deep as caves.

He turned to look at her where she lay facing him. Even asleep her spirit emanated everything he had ever desired in his life's mate.

As if she felt his possessiveness creeping over her, her eyes flew open. She sat up, and what she said next startled him more than anything yet.

"This night—I think I have done wrong, Yudishtira. But still it has been the sweetest of my life. For you, my husband and future king, have wanted my thoughts as they are. And you have been truthful yourself, even about matters you had no need to reveal. I am grateful for all you have given. Forgive me for not giving what I owed you in return." She whispered her last words: "Forgive me."

Confusion rushed over him. Immediately the forgiveness she sought replaced what had been lurking there, beyond his awareness until she had revealed it.

Suddenly her face was bright as the sun. "Yudishtira, you

do not know what it means to me to speak freely to someone after sixteen months alone. There is so much I want to know. Who else will you make your allies besides my father and Krishna? Will you go back to Hastinapura at once and claim the throne? Or perhaps I should not ask. It is so unclear to me what women are allowed to know. Will you tell me about dharma, then? How can there be dharma for women and dharma for warriors and—Can you tell me just that much?"

His mind was still whirling, and now it even encountered amusement at her eagerness. "I don't know of anything that women should not be allowed to know. As for dharma—there is so much to say. Each of us has a dharma, according to our character. And each family. Then there is the dharma of warrior, priest and wealth-producer; of women and men, children and elders. And the dharma of all—to reunite with Brahman and—"

Draupadi leaned forward. "Yudishtira, which god came first from Brahman? Would that god be supreme?"

Surprised and pleased by her urgency, Yudishtira tried to instruct her properly. "They say Brahma the Creator came first. He is supreme, Draupadi."

"Yes, I have heard that said, but why is it that they call Dyaus Pitar, the Shining Father, Lord of All? Like Eos's Zeus Pater? Yet he is powerless without Prithivi Matar, Mother Earth. The Queen of All. And who is Lord Varuna, the 'all knowing'? And Indra, whom Veda calls 'supreme'; Savitri, who 'rules all'; Agni, 'lord of all'; Vishwakarman, 'the creator, the arranger, and supreme supervisor'?"

"'Our preserver and parent.' Draupadi, how did you learn Veda?"

"I know very little. I don't even know which god Vishwakarman really is. I believe best what follows in that hymn. 'You know not him who has generated these beings. His life is another, different from yours.'"

He continued it: "'Wrapped in fog and foolish speech do they wander who are gluttonous and engaged in devotion.'"

"Yes! 'Gluttonous and *engaged in devotion*.' Now what does that mean?"

Laughing with delight, Yudishtira struggled to answer, but

only another verse came to mind, his favourite: "'One is Agni kindled in many places. One is Surya shining over all. One is Ushas illumining all this. That which is One has become this All.'"

But he barely noticed what he spoke. How many women in Bharata knew both Veda and politics? Not merely knew, but cherished them as much as himself? Only his mother. And now apparently his wife.

His desire and longing surged again. He could control it. He had before. He had been trained his whole young life to control himself. Even to the point of death. But after the long night, the pain of it was becoming a sickness in him.

"Draupadi," he whispered. "I think we should rise and dress."

Unaware of his mood, she leaped out of bed like an obedient child. "Anything you wish." She laughed. "Only promise we can talk soon, until there isn't a question left in my head. You have given me someone to talk to at last!"

"As you have given me," he said quietly.

"Yes, and now not only will you have someone new to talk to, but someone to help you dress!" She danced to the window and threw open the shutters, then went to the foot of the bed to retrieve his clothes.

He would always remember the next moment. He picked up one of the petals from her pillow. It was bruised and limp, but more pungent than ever. He brought it to his lips.

Then Draupadi fell to the floor, his belt in her right hand. He reached her in time to see the shreds of her awareness slip away and a snake slide under the night's discarded bridal clothes.

17

Although thy spirit has gone far away to the remotest regions, we bring back that spirit of thine to dwell here, to live long.

Rig Veda

"Help in here," he shouted. "The princess." Yudishtira grabbed his knife from under the bed. What had the yavana woman done to Sahadeva's poisoned wound? He saw the tiny punctures on Draupadi's forearm and slit around them, then sucked and spat the way she had.

A servant ran in, then out. Finally the Greek came. "A snake," he said between efforts. "It was in my clothes. Under hers now. Take care."

He heard her walk around the bed. The heap of linens shifted and a blade struck flesh.

She came back and knelt beside him. "With that snake, what you're doing won't help now."

He looked up, frantic. "I must find a snake stone."

"No. Stay here with me." She felt Draupadi's pulse and bent her head over her face to feel her breath. "She's still alive." Eos touched the girl's cheek. "Live, Draupadi! Curse every god, who would do this?"

Then the yavani became utterly controlled again, continuing her examination as if it were anyone. The next time she spoke out loud, it was with cold logic. "The fact she is alive at all is significant, Prince. That kind's bite should have killed her before I ever arrived."

To the servants crowded at the door Eos called for boiling water. She took out her healing bag and removed a package.

219

To Yudishtira she said curtly, "My supplies go too quickly around you sons of Pandu."

She bent over Draupadi and began to massage the bitten arm, pressing away from her heart, then pressing towards the heart along the other arm and each leg. "There's very little we can do, but we'll do all of it. Are you all right, Prince?"

"If she lives, I will live."

"Then you have no sores in your mouth."

He nodded absently. She kept up her talking as she worked. "I don't know why these smaller cobras don't always kill. I know that when they don't, the credit goes to a snake stone. Then next time, when the stone doesn't work, the blame goes to some demon. I think the bites aren't always poisonous. Or the poison does not always enter the wound. Or perhaps these Egyptian cobras"—she looked up at him—"will choose not to kill Arya."

"Egyptian?"

"Egyptian royalty use that kind of snake to kill off rivals. Suggests Baron Sakuni's Egyptian slave, doesn't it?"

"You know this man?" Yudishtira asked.

"I've only learned of him. Zesnor, he's called. There aren't many yavanas in Bharata—we hear of each other."

"Another Egyptian snake to kill." Yudishtira picked up his knife and hurled it back at the floor. The blade stuck halfway into the sala planks.

Draupadi was changing before his eyes, slipping closer to death. "She's breathing so fast. Can you do no more?"

"Faster's better than no breath at all. Do what I am doing on that side."

Yudishtira pressed and kneaded the lifeless leg in front of him. "Make her live, Eos!"

"I am trying." Eos sat back and wiped the sweat from her face. "Unlike yourself, she's all I have." Her voice was even, but Yudishtira saw the break in the foreign woman's wall. She bent back over the bitten arm and massaged it furiously.

There was scuffling at the door—Arjuna and Sahadeva against a wildly flailing Panchalya. "For Indra's sake," Arjuna shouted, "stay out and let them help her in calmness."

But Yudishtira ordered the twin let in without looking up

from his work over Draupadi. Panchalya plunged from the door to his sister's side.

"And me?" The tone of Arjuna's voice caused Yudishtira to turn.

"Of course. All of you, if one will take a turn guarding the door."

But the brothers stayed at the door. Panchalya was clutching Draupadi's fingers to his lips and weeping. "Why murder *her*?"

"Her?" Eos gave them both a sharp look. "The snake was in Yudishtira's clothing, wasn't it?"

Yudishtira drew back, shocked by the obvious.

Eos ordered Panchalya to rub Draupadi's arms. But he only stared at his sister. "I should have stood guard here myself last night."

"I was in bed with her, Brother-in-law, and couldn't protect her. How can you take the blame from me?"

Draupadi's twin stood and fled the room without answering.

More water was brought. Eos was applying cold, wet cloths to the bitten arm, the steaming herbed cloths to Draupadi's head, chest and armpits.

Draupadi's breath gave a great shudder.

"Stay with us!" Eos hissed.

Suddenly the floor shook with running feet in the hall. Yudishtira could hear Arjuna calming the king and queen, urging the priests and healers to let Eos do her work. "The yavana knows your healing methods, and Draupadi will find her more familiar." In the hall a snake stone was already being sanctified with offerings of butter and rice into a brazier of coals from the sacred hearth. Black smoke billowed into the room. Yudishtira saw Vyasa slip through the crowd at the door, go to the window and push the shutters open. The black smoke began to drift out.

"Is Urutata here?" Vyasa asked.

The priests in the hall let the old priest through.

"The necessary chants, please, Urutata."

The old man looked miserable that this awesome responsibility was being given to him, not the priests and healers in the hall. But he sat in the corner, made the appropriate gestures, meditated briefly, and began.

"A messenger!" someone called. "From King Drita himself."

Yudishtira closed his eyes. "No more," he whispered. Then called, "Arjuna, hear his words."

In a moment Arjuna was kneeling beside the eldest, softly repeating the message. "First, our uncle congratulates you on your marriage."

"So fast!"

"And our uncle is so happy we are alive."

"I'm sure. If he—"

Arjuna spoke louder. "He wants you to come to Hastinapura as soon as possible."

Yudishtira sat back.

"It's a trap," Sahadeva called from the door.

Draupadi's body jerked under Yudishtira's hands. He looked frantically at Eos, then returned to his massaging. "Arjuna, I can not consider it now."

"I am surprised. I would have thought this crime against our wife—" Arjuna stopped.

"If she dies, Arjuna, will you want revenge? I believe I will want eternal ashes and silence. I tell you, I can't consider any of it now."

Yudishtira crouched by Draupadi's feet, Eos by her head, and Urutata knelt at her right side, chanting softly. Panchalya sat at Vyasa's feet, near the window. Vyasa was deep in meditation.

Without noticing, Urutata was using the rhythm of Draupadi's rapid breathing for the metre of his chant. Vyasa's attention did not deviate from these interweaving sounds as the sun slowly mounted the sky. Near noon, Urutata's words finally had the tempo of resting life.

"Brahma, we thank you," Vyasa whispered and opened his eyes. The noon sun coming through the window now lit Panchalya, motionless and staring. Panchalya, the neglected one. Vyasa broke the youth's trance gently: "These select warriors you and Arjuna are training seem more necessary now than ever."

The youth heard him but showed no interest.

"Twins," Vyasa said, stretching himself with deliberate casualness. "An interesting condition. I suppose it is quite different for you now that she has wed."

"It has always been different for us."

There was desperate bitterness in his words. Now Panchalya tried to cover it. "I mean, Great Sage, that although I remember nothing from before I saw King Drupada, I know my sister is right—Before, we were always together." He glanced towards the others, to be certain they could not hear, then looked up at Vyasa. "I also know it was you who took our memories, separated us, and had me sent to Hastinapura. But I do not blame you now. In fact, I am glad."

Vyasa did not care to tell him what Draupadi obviously had not—that their separation had been her doing, through Eos. He only said, "But at first you were lonely there."

Panchalya looked away.

"And now you want me to promise that if she dies, you will not have to stay here with King Drupada, but will be sent back to Hastinapura and Guru Vaja."

Panchalya hung his head. "No, I must stay with my father, Drupada. Whatever it is from Before that Draupadi has remained loyal to, I have forgotten it. I have accepted Drupada and Yasoda as my parents. *But why did you send me to Hastinapura?* Didn't you know I would find in Guru Vaja everything Drupada lacks? Yet for my father's sake I must try to defeat my teacher. Try to kill Vaja in battle, take back North Panchala—whatever Drupada desires. While I *love* Vaja!"

Vyasa closed his eyes. "Yes. As if the deepest hate has been bridged by the deepest love."

"The hate bridged? No, the love betrayed."

"Love unites, Panchalya. Even those opposed. Perhaps there will be another way to satisfy King Drupada."

"Besides my teacher's death? Never."

"Vaja knows Yama comes for us all some day. And since he has chosen a warrior's life over a priest's, he knows he has probably chosen to die by another's arrow. What matters to him is not his death, as long as it is honourable, but all that could happen before his death. I've talked with him. He knows your difficulty. He also returns your love. You are not alone in your trouble."

"Will I go back to Hastinapura?"

"You will be with your sister and her husbands."

Panchalya looked at his sister. "Then she will not die?"

Vyasa didn't answer. Panchalya nodded, as if he also finally heard the difference in her breathing. The youth stood, looked around as if he had just woken, bowed to the sage and left the room. Soon in the courtyard below Vyasa heard Panchalya shout, "You there—keep your bow up between shots."

Soon after Panchalya left, shuffling feet drew Yudishtira's attention to the door. Through the opening he could see the messenger with Arjuna, and Bhima behind him, the twins slouching on the farther wall of the hallway. He had promised them a decision by noon, but he still had no message to send. Go to Hastinapura and die in another trap? Fight for the throne? Or perhaps even receive it peacefully from King Drita's contrite hand—it was all irrelevant without Draupadi.

Listlessly he went out into the hall to speak to the messenger, if only to fill the expectant silence. "Kanwa? Were you not my horse-tender at Hastinapura? We meet in more difficult times than when you looked after my beautiful bays. Tell me how you became a messenger?"

The slim young man smiled with shy pleasure. "I have a good memory—I knew the bloodlines of every horse back ten generations. I also have an Arya's skin. All messengers must have light skin now."

"Who says this?" Nakula asked.

"The crown prince." Kanwa looked confused. "I mean, Crown Prince Suyodhana."

"This is no way to help servants to follow their dharma," Sahadeva said.

Yudishtira glanced around at his brothers. "Kanwa, would you like to tend my horses again? I have only four here at Kampilya, but I presume some of mine still graze in the Kurus' pastures."

"Beauties, all of them, Crown Prince." Kanwa looked uneasy. "But I was ordered to return immediately with your response."

Yudishtira felt his patience leaving him. "There may not be a response for several days."

"But there must be!"

"Must be?"

"Baron Sakuni told me in private—" Kanwa's voice died away.

Sakuni. Yudishtira remembered him lit by slaves' torches. Hiding in the shadows of the assembly hall. Letting his disgust show, he said, "Arjuna, tell Kanwa how Sakuni got his limp."

Arjuna laughed coldly and related the story of the chariot axle loosened by Sakuni to fix a race he'd bet half his father's treasury on. When the horses bolted, Sakuni's leg was caught in the wheel.

Now, like a long shadow, the Egyptian Zesnor stood behind Sakuni in Yudishtira's memory. Eos had said it was an Egyptian snake. No longer kneeling beside his wife, he found that the spell of his love and of the fear of her death was weakening. His mind was clear.

"Leave today then, Kanwa—with a message only for Baron Sakuni: Anyone who attempts to kill any of us will wake in Hell and think it Heaven compared to facing my anger."

Bhima smiled and Arjuna's head went up. The twins stopped slumping against the wall.

Yudishtira glanced into the room behind him. The four figures there had not moved. "Yesterday I married a woman who expects to become Queen of the Kurus," he said loudly. "I can not be made king by hiding in Kampilya. Trap or not, we go to Hastinapura." The brothers smiled broadly. Yudishtira did not. "They will not expect us to come very soon after a royal wedding. Therefore we will leave immediately, before they can make any military preparations. We will take these men you are training, Arjuna—those of them who can leave their families and wish to right this wrong. Kampilya's other warriors can remain."

"So we will attack?" Bhima asked.

Yudishtira hesitated. "I will give them two days to set a date for my consecration as king." His voice rose in a cold fury. "My father, Gangeya, Guru Vaja—they all intended me to be king. *I shall be.*"

"And I will be beside you as queen."

Yudishtira rushed to the door. "Eos, did she speak?"

Draupadi answered, her voice distant and strained. "I did. Fix a chariot with a bed. I want to come with you."

"But what about the weddings?" Bhima blurted out.

Yudishtira came in to stand over her. She smiled weakly. "Is it noon yet? Tell Bhima he must put on his wedding clothes."

Bhima came in, moving the way he did when in a small room full of fragile things. "There's no need to rush," he said. "Not for me. You are still ill."

Draupadi tried to answer but her voice was only a whisper. Eos bent over her moving lips. "She says, 'I will be ready. Not perhaps as strong yet as Bhima, but leaning on him I can do anything.'"

Bhima flushed. "That's what she said?"

Draupadi nodded.

Yudishtira stood in an arbour in Kampilya's guest gardens, watching the rushing to and from the rooms where Draupadi was being prepared for her second wedding. He hoped only to catch a glimpse of his wife. To be assured again that she was truly alive.

He had sent for Eos, and when she joined him, he first asked her assistance yet again, for he hoped she would go ahead to Hastinapura, travelling as a man but then mingling with the serving women, and warn him if she found a trap was being laid.

"Gladly, Prince. You can always presume that I will prefer circumventing attacks against you beforehand to repairing your injuries afterwards."

It was said in what he had already learned was her usual unapproachable way, but Yudishtira smiled a little in anticipation of her reaction to his next words. "Yesterday King Drupada gave you to me as a wedding gift. I suppose he knew Draupadi would free you when she could. And that is what I am doing now, in her name. You are free."

Eos's face was expressionless. "This can not be reversed?"

"I give my word."

Eos turned away from him. "Is that all? May I go?"

But she did not.

"Eos, I also wish to thank you for all you have done for us."

"I once vowed," she said in a strained voice, "that if I were ever freed, I would spit in the face of the man arrogant enough to think he had ever owned me."

This glimpse into a slave's heart stunned Yudishtira. He was trying to find words to respond when she turned back. "I should have prepared words of gratitude."

"You need not," he said gently. "It was, after all, an unfair exchange: your one life for two—Draupadi's and Sahadeva's."

Eos was staring at him. "You gave Draupadi her wish for first surata with Arjuna, didn't you? She told me in her delirium. If she had died, you would never have—Did you know you yourself might die by sucking her snake bite?"

"I don't know if I thought of it or not."

She suddenly fell to her knees before him, her forehead pressed to the floor in the Babylonian fashion. "Allow me to continue to serve you, Prince."

Hardly aware of what he was doing he knelt beside her. "Eos, stand up, for Indra's sake. Can't my wife's friend be mine?"

He tried to help her as she rose, but she would not let him. Standing, she was all stiff and proud again. "A yavani and a crown prince, friends?"

He nodded.

"Then, my king and friend, I shall never allow cause for you to regret it."

"We almost lost her this morning," Vyasa said.

"But we did not lose her, Sage." Krishna took a hot barley cake from a basket. They were reclining alone in the fountain-cooled royal dining hall, talking across the remains of a noon feast that had been served close to sunset. The food had been decorated with hibiscus flowers and served on exquisite pearl-grey pottery plates, which by custom would be broken when they were done. And while the food had been late coming, this had been made up for by its abundance, as no one had dared to eat at all but them—the pastry cook having fled after poison and a snake's basket had been found among his abandoned clothing.

"Of course *you* still think nothing can harm her or Pandu's sons," Vyasa said.

"You think differently, dear teacher?"

"There's what my mind thinks and then there's what my heart feels. I think they are protected but I feel the loss I can imagine if I'm wrong."

"An interesting paradox about you, Sage," Krishna said. "You fear they might be killed—you even told me to protect them—yet now you don't think we should be so involved in their affairs."

"And you are now convinced they are invincible, yet meddle in everything they do."

Krishna pointed a finger at his teacher. "It was you, Sage, who intended Draupadi for Yudishtira. What would you have done if I had not helped them to decide on at least this solution? Would you have permitted her to ruin everything because of an infatuation with Arjuna?"

"You really think you know the events that will not, as you put it, 'ruin everything'? You've had your own vision of the end of it, Krishna: Death and ashes. Yet you act as though you mean to prevent that end."

"So do you, Teacher. Yudishtira says you've told him, 'Visions are merely an extension of awareness in time and space. They give us new freedom to shape our future.' I've decided to believe you."

"Were you taught nothing at Badari? Knowledge is different with each style of awareness—the person dreaming, the child, the man of action, the man who pursues wholeness of awareness with his total being. To give the truth of one awareness to another is like feeding grass to dogs and meat to horses."

"So you, Teacher, told Yudishtira a comforting story about shaping a future he really has no control over. Yudishtira above all needs his awareness to be whole. Nothing less."

"Exactly!" Vyasa exclaimed. "That is our only concern. For that he needs to live and to learn much, shedding his old awarenesses like old clothes. But the new garments can not be borrowed from you or me, Krishna."

Leaning back, Vyasa offered Krishna more honeyed mango for his cakes as he asked what the Vrishni had heard about the pastry cook. Krishna loaded his plate with the preserves and asked about this "important" news.

"Only that King Drupada's adviser had criminals tasting the morning's cakes, but it had to be stopped after three died of poisoning."

The progress of a honey cake towards Krishna's mouth stopped.

"Come now, Krishna. Your visions tell you that you and they will have long lives—long enough to cause the end of an age. You have no fear for them. Then why fear for yourself?" Vyasa bent closer. "Or is it that your mind has the visions, but not your heart? Could it be that you have let the sons of Pandu into your mind, but your heart has not yet grown enough to hold more than Krishna?"

Krishna bit, chewed and swallowed with great casualness. "Your point is made. You are still my teacher, Sage Vyasa."

Vyasa stood and walked away. "But do you learn anything, Krishna? Now this invitation from King Drita. Secretly you want them to go, don't you? To walk boldly inside the walls of Hastinapura, outnumbered a thousand to one, in spite of these repeated attempts to kill them."

"An Egyptian snake is sending them to Hastinapura, not I. Shall I stop them, Master?"

"You listen like a puppy on a hunt. I want you to care enough for Draupadi and her husbands to let them have their own fate as well as Bharata's. The former can teach them how to bear the latter."

Krishna's eyes followed Vyasa as he paced. "I'm just trying to help them do what the gods have assigned them, Sage."

"Not what you or I assign them, Krishna? Or is there a difference?"

"Of course there is a difference." Krishna was finally losing his smile.

"But the gods themselves do not guide the brothers? The gods guide us, and then we guide Pandu's sons?"

"You have meddled too, Sage."

Vyasa sat down beside Krishna again. "I hope no more.

Zesnor thought he won by keeping me asleep for a day and a night. He only kept me where I needed to be—out of my small-self, so I could regain my vision of our goal."

They both fell silent. Vyasa studied Krishna's face. "I'm sorry if I've upset you, Krishna. I only meant to see if you had any idea of what you and I are doing." Vyasa started to rise again. "But I see you don't yet."

"If you do, Master, tell me! Or if you don't—Or is it that you don't think I know?" Krishna paused. "*You* don't know, do you?"

"Be quiet for once, Krishna."

Vyasa went to the window. A group of women were winding through the colonnade, from the baths to the princess's rooms. At the centre, veiled and garlanded, walked Draupadi. She leaned on Eos and Kunti, but she laughed and tossed her head. The motion let the wind blow the veil aside, and as she turned her head in his direction the sun caught her face.

She has travelled halfway to the ancestors with Yama, he thought, and returned without even a shadow on her. Only their celestial light.

He turned back. "Do I know what we do? That is a deep question, with many opportunities for feeding meat to horses if it were rushed, and I must dress for a wedding. Krishna, feel free to finish the honeyed mango. But don't eat from the second jar—the one by the lime curds? You've still some work to do for me, and that jar is poisoned."

Prince Bhima, the second son of Pandu, and Princess Draupadi of South Panchala were married at nightfall on the third day after her bride's choice. Urutata lit the fire, made the oblations and placed Draupadi's hand in Bhima's. Kunti gave the blessing to a daughter-in-law. The consecrating waters ran down their pale, glowing faces. And Urutata proclaimed them wed.

Gifts were presented in the garden by torchlight. There was a feast and entertainment. Then, as soon as the moon rose, the couple were led to the wedding apartment—different rooms than the night before. Each brother placed a final garland over the heads of Bhima and Draupadi. Yudishtira's was gardenias. And the couple were left alone.

While her husband crossed the room and opened the shutters, Draupadi leaned along the wall by the door they had entered. Her legs seemed like wood, the snake-bitten arm was throbbing and there was a bitter taste in her swollen throat. Eos had put a poultice on the wound itself and also given her something to drink for the pain and another infusion to strengthen her, but all that had worn off long ago.

"You seem weary, my Beautiful One," Bhima said from somewhere across the room. "Do not fear—there will be no surata. I will reluctantly follow my brother's generous example. But come to the window and let me see you in the moonlight."

"Prince Bhima, would you light the lamp first?"

Flickering oil-light flared up to illumine the room. Draupadi studied the dark corner behind the great bed, then made herself cross to the window.

"This garment you are wearing is as lovely as a lotus pond," Bhima said.

A lotus pond? She looked down, wondering what she wore. Yes, pale pink cotton-silk bordered with begonia buds.

"But beside my wife, all garments and ornaments seem dull. You are the essence of all the flowers, jewels and fine clothes on earth."

She closed her eyes, gathering the strength to respond in a way he deserved. "I've heard of your powers with a mace, but you are skilled with words as well."

"Only as a singer. My metres are merely the rhythms of hoofbeats and rain." He bowed his head. "And as for these speeches, I practised them all day."

She was struggling for a kind answer when the wind stirred the room's curtains, billowing the embroidered cotton. Now dark became light, light became dark, and the room, or her mind, seemed to turn slowly. Then to spin.

Bhima caught her as she fell. But her dimmed awareness returned quickly, and the safety of his embrace eased her body still more. It called up memories of Before, and she clung to him.

He laid her on to the bed, arranging her limbs tenderly. A great weariness came over her.

As she gave in to it she thought, such gentleness from such

huge arms and hands—and perhaps I am the only one to know . . .

She awoke screaming. "Bhima! Snakes!"

He held her tightly. "It was a dream, my love. There are no snakes here." He lifted her up on to his lap. "Every space has been searched and searched again. Do you believe me?

"Draupadi, poor Draupadi—tonight let me make you happy. Please let me try. Tell me, what gives you the greatest joy? What do you love most of all? Eos tells me you're always wanting to be outside Kampilya's walls. Is that true? And you like horses? Then I have something to show you. Shall we go?"

She sat up, clutching at him. "We can't go *out*, Bhima."

"Why not? It's the last place we'd be expected." He began pulling hangings off the wall. "We'll disguise ourselves—you can be my old mother whom I carry on my shoulders."

She stared at him wide-eyed.

"You aren't afraid, are you, Draupadi?" His voice was teasing. "You have to get back on when you fall, you know, awful as it's been for you."

"Afraid?" She slowly stood. "Never, Bhima."

And so, soon, she found herself on his shoulders, riding through the streets.

At the north gate Bhima went out through the low night door, ducking almost to his knees to allow her under too. The guard held it open for them—persons going out now that the palace was sealed were only considered mad, not dangerous.

At least this death will be quick, she thought. Not like the morning. Her muscles had been in such spasms that her very bones seemed to ache from it, still. Eos had said it was the pulling of the tendons, that she was fortunate she could already use her limbs. Until tonight's arrow comes, she thought.

Bhima began to trot north. "No one in sight, Draupadi. Maybe you could hold my hair a little less tightly?"

She loosened her grip. He trotted on. His pace never slowed, even on a steep rise. Then the ground levelled out and there was the acid smell of a horse pasture on the breeze. Bhima stopped. Draupadi raised her head a little.

The world was dancing silver. Moonlit leaves on rustling trees glimmered like silver coins on a king's elephant. The tall grasses swayed their seed heads like the silver spears of a passing army. Among the dappled tree trunks silvered foals were climbing to their feet while dams and sires pranced, every silver eye watching the intruders.

Bhima strode off down the open meadow. Draupadi sat upright on his shoulders, awed by the beauty of what she saw, after her long imprisonment and brush with death. Then, as the breeze caught her hair, she leaned back and threw her arms out. And with the gesture, she felt her terror blow away.

Bhima began to sing. A stallion whinnied an alarm and the horses nearest them burst into a gallop, the dust shimmering round them. A newborn foal, separated from its dam, trotted beside them for the length of an acacia grove, but Bhima outpaced it.

Now she joined her second husband in his song. The lyrics they created together blended into a long, beautiful paean. It filled the meadow and set the whole herd running. But the song rose even above the pounding hooves. It was sweet and wild—the kind of song of triumphant joy that required no skill of them, no practice at all, because it was in their blood.

18

The gardenia bud, hard, tight,
Feels the warm sun for days
Before it cautiously opens
Petals easily bruised and
The fragrance reaches
The flower cutter.

a song by Draupadi

It had been decided that after Arjuna's wedding the five brothers and their wife would leave, taking fifty of the elite "Marut" warriors (named after Indra's celestial troop) who were being trained by Arjuna and Panchalya. The twins' weddings would occur on the road to Hastinapura.

On the morning after Bhima's wedding and before Arjuna's, Krishna himself supervised the packing of the chariots and bullock carts. In the assembly hall Yudishtira, Sahadeva and Nakula offered detailed advice to King Drupada on how Kampilya might be best defended after they were gone. And in the baths Arjuna was being prepared for the noon ceremony by his mother. Draupadi rested in her room.

But sleep was impossible, even after her long night with Bhima. She lay in her bed, forcing herself to face now what the next night might bring. For Arjuna still avoided her. He would not even allow their eyes to meet.

It was that first night when I was too forward—a warrior wants some shyness to overcome. Or perhaps it is my dark skin. He is so fair.

If only I could sleep.

But how can I sleep? Tonight I go to him, and he does not care for me.

234

It was stifling in the room at noon with the shutters closed for darkness. She pulled off the soaked virgin's shift and reached for a fresh one. Then left it off and went to dampen her face with water. The bronze mirror was on the water stand and she took it back to her bed.

She pushed open a wooden slat and in the streak of glaring light she studied her face. Yes, pretty enough, she thought. But so dark. She tilted the mirror to see her breasts from in front, as he would see them.

On an impulse she pressed the mirror high between her thighs. The stripe of sun was warm on her opened flower. How odd, she thought, that they will see me often this way, when I can see myself only with a mirror.

The complications of this flower surprised her. It seemed muddled and uneven. So much the opposite of a man's straightness. A flower that was dark at its centre, disappearing into mystery. She touched the purplish petals and felt the response throughout her body. How was that possible? She closed her eyes and imagined Arjuna parting her furrow with his plough.

But will he want me?

The door creaked. She dropped the mirror and pulled the bed cloth up to her neck.

It was Queen Yasoda. Draupadi wrapped the cloth around herself and leaned against the wall. "It is too hot to sleep."

"And you are too nervous. It seems as though this marriage today is the only one that matters to you and your father. My poor Draupadi. I've seen how this Arjuna is about you. It's just as I predicted. If you would have let me, I would have spoken to him. Or to his mother. Surely he realises he is playing with your affections—after he chose to win you and took responsibility for your happiness."

"Speak to him? No!"

"I knew you would feel that way. My sweet Draupadi. Do you notice? I don't trouble you with 'daughter' any more. If only I never had—then maybe you would look back once at least when you go tomorrow to be Queen of the Kurus at Hastinapura. Perhaps miss even me, just a little."

She thought of Vyasa: speak the sweet truth.

"I will miss Kampilya very much, Queen Yasoda."

"Oh, my sweet little prickly flower. Have you prayed to Indrani for wedded bliss? Or to Anumati and Akuti, the merciful goddesses of consent and plans?"

"I pray only to Brahma."

"Yes, yes, but there are times." She swayed nervously, like a girl. "Today while he went to the baths I threw seeds on him for you. And to finish the ritual, I have made this." From her skirt she drew out a figure with cotton-silk hair and a twig-and-thread bow. She set the little warrior on the floor in front of the bed and took out a handful of crude arrows of sticks sharpened at one end and feathered at the other, and a small bronze box for carrying a burning coal.

Yasoda lit the little arrows, stood erect over the figure, and began chanting a muddled incantation while throwing flaming bolts down on the figure. The burning sticks sparked and went out as they struck the floor.

Draupadi stared, fascinated. In the darkened room the queen might have been taken for a forest-dweller. Or a giantess throwing phalluses made of fire on a helpless warrior.

"Now whisper his name," Yasoda commanded, "and capture his love."

Draupadi broke free of the spell and turned away to face the wall. "I want no 'captured' love, Yasoda."

The queen threw the rest of her stick-arrows on the ground. "Stubborn girl. Then be ready to accept no love at all."

Prince Arjuna and Princess Draupadi of South Panchala were married at noon on the fourth day after her bride's choice. Urutata lit the sacred fire, made the oblations and placed Draupadi's hand in Arjuna's. The two took the seven steps. The consecrating waters rained upon their heads. And they were wed.

Gifts were presented in the large garden. Then came the feast and entertainment, the darkening sky, and the leading of the couple to their apartments, accompanied by bells, gongs and chanting.

Outside the door King Drupada laboriously addressed them all: "Tonight we stand together—Sage Vyasa, the lovely Queen Kunti, Crown Prince Yudishtira, the great Bhima, the skilful Sahadeva, gentle and wise Nakula, our new friend and ally the generous Krishna of the Vrishnis, my dear son Panchalya, my wife and queen, Yasoda, and these two who mean so much to us all, my invincible son-in-law Arjuna and my beautiful gift from Agni, my daughter Draupadi. I do not know if we will ever again all stand together like this." He wiped at his eyes. "May the gods grant it. Now my two precious children, go in those doors and make each other very happy."

Not exactly a speech to make us more at ease, Arjuna thought.

Each family member and guest laid garlands on his and Draupadi's shoulders and whispered blessings. His mother's words were touching. Yudishtira, whose words to him were mostly inaudible, entirely forgot to bless Draupadi. Krishna and the twins made their little jokes. And Bhima was last. He bent close to Arjuna's ear and said, "She's still a virgin, a gift from Yudishtira and me."

Before Arjuna could think of a response, he and Draupadi were shut inside together.

Arjuna stood in the dark, stunned by his brothers' "gift". Draupadi had gone to the window and drawn back the curtain. She turned shyly to him, her face radiant in the moonlight.

"Draupadi." He walked slowly over to her. "This can't be true."

"What, dear Husband?" Her voice trembled.

"That you are still a virgin, 'saved for me' by my brothers."

"It was their wish." She lowered her eyes.

Now the last two days made more sense to Arjuna—Yudishtira's vagueness, his sharp words. He did this for *my* sake.

"Draupadi. I can't allow this." He looked at the door. Could he find his older brother still and bring him in, leave them together?

Draupadi covered her face with her hands. He felt the trap close—whom to hurt, wife or brother? He went to her and took her in his arms—a mistake he felt too late. There was only one comfort her body would accept. She was open to him like a spring field at dawn.

Why not? Her third night of this!

Instinctive sympathy led him to the bed with her. He removed the pale blue cotton covering her head, then the part around her shoulders. He hesitated, but her eyes gave him no choice. He unwound the turn of it around her breasts, leaving her virgin's shift dazzling white in the moonlight. He unfastened the skirt too and let it fall.

She trembled in the short gown, her eyes still begging him. The musky scent of crushed flowers rose off the floor and mingled with the sweet smells of her body. His hands shaking, he untied the bows at each shoulder and the shift fell.

She stood naked before him, glowing darkly. Her hair, falling around her shoulders, caught moonbeams at its edges. The rest he could not look at. I must not take her, he thought. She is his. The eldest's first.

But what will she do if I don't?

She was starting to cry. He drew her into his arms again. "Draupadi, Draupadi."

"Arjuna, I have obeyed you and married them all, but you are the only one I—"

He covered her mouth with his to stop the words. She opened to him and he kissed her deeply. He pulled away. "Say anything, Draupadi, but not that. If you love me, you must love us all." He spoke with the despair of his body.

Can I honour my eldest brother, he thought. Can I control myself with this woman?

And if I do, the twins will have her instead of me.

Let them. It doesn't matter. It only matters that this night not separate me from the rest of them.

But look at her.

He turned to the bed, covered with rose petals, and guided her on to it, laying her down the length of it. He knelt over her, touching her face and the tears on her cheeks and the parted lips still wet from his kiss. He touched her neck as it curved up to him, and he touched the strong yet delicate shoulders and arms. Her breasts, large and round and darkly flowered. Her waist, drawing in from her breasts and flowing out again at her hips. Her broad and abundant hips. And her thighs, like boulders in a river, the stream between running dark and deep.

He put his hand there into the dark place, as he had learned to pleasure women, and she arched up off the bed, her eyes wide and watching him. He lay down, partly on her, partly at her side, keeping his hand where her eyes commanded him, moving it as he moved himself against her.

She's Yudishtira's!

But what will she do if I don't take her?

The rhythm of his hand in the soft, dark waters. Flowing darkness. His body against her side, rocking with her. His plough glowing with heat like molten bronze, aching to be plunged into the soft dark water. To pierce the waters and add his seed. "Soon, soon, soon," he whispered, more to himself than to her.

But not *tonight*.

Except, what will she do if I don't?

She was lost in the sensations he was creating for her, her face transformed. She pulled his body on to her own with a strength some men would have envied. His only defence was his hand, pleasuring her, taking the place his plough would take if he released himself.

"Now Arjuna," she whispered. "No, wait. No, now. Now."

But he waited. He felt the softness soften even more, enclosing his fingers. He opened her to let the flood of her feelings loose, and they ran over him. At last she flowed free in great currents. Now he could let his own flood join hers—his seed spread hot between their bellies.

Then she lay still. He lay very still, waiting. What would she do?

"Draupadi, after Yudishtira, then it will be different—you understand?"

She didn't answer.

The square of moonlight from the window crept across the floor by the bed. Like pottery broken against a stone, the pieces of her love lay about her. There was the deep pleasure he had given her, pleasure she had never imagined. It still echoed through her body, in contractions deep within her belly and in warmth suffusing her limbs. Then there was the deeper hunger, for what she had never had. And there was rage. A killing rage. Finally, there was a need to please him, no matter what.

The pieces would not fit together and the effort to force them left her tired and sick. The moonlight from the window moved on, and still he did not speak or even move, and neither did she.

There's still a chance tonight, she thought.

Nothing I could do would bring him closer. He didn't want me.

No, think of Eos. She warned me about the first night with a man. I should talk to him, make it pleasant.

The need to break the silence finally overcame every other feeling.

"Husband, I know you want me to love the others, but I loved you first and I can only love one." The words came out unguarded, even as she heard them and regretted their lack of subtlety. "You won me. We were betrothed the moment I placed the flowers around your neck at my bride's choice. I will try to seem to love your brothers. But inside I will love only you. Do you understand? Only you."

He turned his head towards her. "Now you must understand, Princess. If you had four sisters whom you loved as much as you love Panchalya, and if I married all of you, and all your sisters loved and trusted me as their husband—their first husband—what would you do if I said, 'It is only you I love, so allow me to forget your sisters and love only you'? What could you possibly say? Except what I have struggled to say, in spite of my feelings for you?"

"Feelings for me, Arjuna?"

"Don't you know? I have known many women, but none like you. None I wanted for a wife. You are the most lovely, intelligent and brave of all the women in Bharata. I admire you greatly. Draupadi, do you hear me? Why are you crying?"

I hear you, her heart screamed. May the gods save me.

But she only said, "Now would you like something to eat?" She rose from the bed. "Or to hear a song? I play the *vina*. Or sleep? Shall I smooth your back first?" She went from the tray of sweets to the lap harp in the window seat to the table with the body oils, her fingers nervously flying to her lips to hold back cries. "Anything, Arjuna. Anything you want."

"I should not have married her." But Yudishtira shared his realisation only with the night. He stood in the garden, supposedly on his way to supervise the changing of the guard, although he had not moved from this spot for a long time. At the other end of the garden, as far from him as possible, was the balcony of the bridal apartment.

One curtain waved languidly in the night wind, shut out carelessly by the inner doors. His thoughts hovered there, rejected by her.

Does he love her half as much as I?

Yudishtira nocked an arrow to his bow and let it fly at the heart of an asoka sapling thirty paces away. The arrow struck deep.

Now the tree will probably die, he thought. He slammed the bow down and strode out of the garden.

19

They made mistakes. Of course they did.
But the eldest of them had only seen twenty autumns.

Eos

As bright as two water-borne jewels . . .
Like two flying birds with forms like the moon.

Rig Veda

The journey to Hastinapura was about to begin. The tension
along the train of chariots was reflected in both its grim-faced
Marut guards and their families, strung out along the line in
the grey dawn to say farewell. Amidst the hushed conversations
and the horses' stamping, Draupadi heard a messenger approach
her covered chariot. He delivered his words without meeting
her eyes.

"Your husband Arjuna says, 'Sahadeva and Nakula will
adhere to the conduct of myself and Bhima. Please inform
Yudishtira after the remaining weddings, at a time of your
choosing.'"

Too stunned to respond to this new coldness, she allowed
the man to go. But her meek acceptance of her humiliation
the previous night was leaving her. Fury was rapidly replacing
subservience. She rose to leave the chariot, at last ready to
rain a fire on Arjuna that would equal his chill.

As she was about to step down, however, the chariot lurched
forward. She was barely able to save herself from falling.
Several of the Marut warriors guarding her rushed to the back
of the chariot to assist her. She rebuffed them.

The train of chariots passed out through the gates. Draupadi
was forced to sit.

The fields and villages she had looked forward to seeing for nearly two years now began to roll by her, unnoticed. Next the dangerous tracts of forest, in which an attack might occur; and they received no glance from her. The rage was gone. She was only frightened by how close she had come to destroying whatever might remain of Arjuna's affection for her. Except for that fear, she felt nothing.

The wedding was at sundown, in a grove beside the Ganges. Urutata lit the sacred fire, made the oblations and placed Draupadi's hand in Sahadeva's, who led her the seven steps around the fire. The consecrating waters were poured, and Urutata proclaimed them wed.

The gifts were announced, or presented when possible. There was a feast and entertainment under the trees. And when the moon rose, the couple were led to their tent accompanied by songs. They were blessed before the door, then left inside together.

Sahadeva strove to be attentive and thoughtful. He admired her garment, which was yellow and trimmed with yellow wood-apple blossoms. And he urged her to be comfortable on the seats arranged by the opened breeze flap.

In return Draupadi thanked him for his kindness and complimented him on his own appearance. For he was fair like Arjuna, although she did not say it. His body was like Arjuna's also, although less mature. But he had the confidence, the grace, the firm stance.

It was the two brothers' habits of thinking that differed. Sahadeva had always been fond of reason and practical learning. Of course a younger brother was limited in how he could use his wits—this in itself required intelligence. Both meek suggestions and direct arguments were less successful than irrefutable solutions based on long observation.

Cattle were Sahadeva's favourite subject for study. But as one of Pandu's twins—the two sons who were both youngest and not Kunti's actual children—he had often gone unnoticed, so that he was free to watch his family, in his keen way, rather than participate. Hence, besides his knowledge of cattle, he had developed a considerable understanding of human nature

—which he emphatically intended to apply for Draupadi's sake, to their wedding night.

First he informed Draupadi that he knew she had had quite enough to deal with since the contest. Tonight it would be best for her to rest. Surata could wait. Then he forced himself to say the rest. That there was one small matter she needed to know before she arrived in Hastinapura. His older brothers must have meant to tell her, of course, but no doubt with their many pressing matters they had forgotten actually to say it: Arjuna had a consort waiting for him in Hastinapura. A Dasyu. No one important to Arjuna, he was sure. Her name was Lotus.

Then, to spare her further embarrassment, he busied himself across the tent, preparing for sleep, and suggested she do the same. "After sleeping everything always seems better," he said. "And you, I know, have slept very little for many nights."

But neither of them slept, as he knew they would not. And some time before dawn he did something he had not planned —he asked her if he could hold her hand.

Nakula and Draupadi were wed on the sixth day after her bride's choice. There was the ceremony, the gift giving, and the leading of the couple to their tent as the moon rose, where they were left together.

"So I am the last," Nakula said, watching her by lamp light.

He slowly unwound the pale green cotton-silk, letting the bordering pale green buds of the sacred barna tree fall about her. When she stood before him in her virgin's shift he touched its hem. Then he drew it off.

Her heart was pounding from more than surprise. "Now you must undress too," she said with false lightness. "Every girl in Kampilya thinks you are hopelessly handsome."

He solemnly obeyed her.

He was thinner than Sahadeva, but actually the more muscled. It was one of the unknowns about him, like his dark, erect plough.

But I am the older of the two of us, she thought. I am responsible. There are others to consider, like this one's feelings later.

She walked to the bed and lay down. "Now you will tell me

all about horses," she said teasingly. "You are an expert, or so your brothers tell me."

He came and joined her in the bed. "Horses." He lay on his back. "There are two thoughts about the breeding of horses —to leave the very best stallion with the mares, castrating the others. Or to leave several of the best with the mares, letting the strongest form the largest bands so that they sire the most foals. However, the fighting is hard on a stallion. And the mares become loyal to their husband, so that when he is defeated, they won't mate with the winner unless he forces them. Did you know that? If the mare is carrying a foal when he does this, she will usually lose it. Some mares will even die of grief, or try to run off with the stallion they feel wed to, only to be kicked and bitten into submission by the new one. You see, even horses love desperately." He turned and looked at her.

She didn't meet his eyes. "No," she said, "you've said only mares do."

"But the stallions are just as bad." Nakula reached out slowly and, under the cotton sheet, his hand touched her breast. "A stallion may have a whole band of mares, but there will be only one he will fight to the death for."

She felt her nipples tighten in response to his touch. "So it is better not to let horses love? To choose for them?"

"That is how many feel. I've watched the stallions, Draupadi —blood running from their wounds—and I used to say, 'I hope I never love my wife the way they love theirs.'" His hand had wandered down to her stomach, then to her thighs. Each of them breathed differently, as if preparing for an exertion, or a battle.

"And what do you say now?" she asked evenly.

"Now I agree with the old men, the ones who bred horses on the northwest plains. They say the very finest foals are born from those pairs who love. Those are the horses with willing hearts."

He drew her to him and she did not resist him. Their bodies simply fitted together, as if space between them was the enemy, not four brothers. His plough pressed with full purpose where it wished to go, but waited.

They rolled gently from side to side, him on top of her, her on top of him. They rolled from one end of the broad bed to the other. They merely rolled like children on new grass. But their bodies were not children's.

Both of them made sounds half hurt, half willing to hurt, all their ache and frustration pouring out. The very tip of his plough was poised where it created the most need in her. She moved frantically, jerking when she was on top of him, pulling him against her.

Their bodies wanted one thing, and their minds were close to wanting the same. Still, the net of lives in which they hung prevented it, so they tumbled with each other instead. The rolling was a movement like that of a caged wolf or monkey, the movement of something wild. It was like a mindless pacing, or a mere rocking if a pace were impossible—an insistence on at least this little shred of what was really needed, which was to devour leagues of some wild world with healthy, straining limbs.

When his seed finally spurted uselessly to the side, it was because both of them had been careful to see to it. She lay along his length, crying softly into his chest. Then slowly rose up, cleaned herself a little, and lay down again, not looking at him.

Some time later she heard out of the darkness, "May I hold your hand while we sleep?"

She gave it to him, as she had given her hand to his twin.

In the afternoon of the day following the last wedding, the sons of Pandu and their companions approached Hastinapura. Long before the city itself was in sight, Yudishtira was straining to see who would be sent to greet them and considering what sort of trap each possibility could signify. But he had never anticipated a single chariot with a white banner bearing a gold palm—the banner of Gangeya.

So they were safe. It was truly Gangeya. Yudishtira could now see the patriarch's flowing white beard. And a terrible tension left him. His sense of dread all day was for nothing then—merely the effect of the gathering of clouds in the sky today, in a month when there should be no rain.

Yudishtira glanced back along the small but well-guarded procession. Krishna was already moving his chariot out of the line to bring Vyasa forward. Vyasa and Gangeya—it was a great honour to have both these elders present today, concerned for him.

The three chariots stopped a few paces apart and all descended. Gangeya came forward and bowed before Vyasa, then embraced. Yudishtira began his obeisance to Gangeya, but the elder stopped him.

"Yudishtira. Alive! I did not dare believe the news until I saw you. The Kurus are whole once more. The people are overjoyed. There is so much to celebrate—not only are you alive, but married. Our chaste little monk of a boy has taken a woman to his bed. May she give you a hundred sons."

"And the Kurus one undisputed crown prince," Vyasa said grimly.

Gangeya turned to him. "No need to talk from the sides of our mouths any more, stepbrother. Your son Drita has promised me that he will anoint his brother's son as king."

"He has said that before."

"Tonight will be 'the long-awaited proclamation'. Tomorrow, the consecration. He has sworn it."

Yudishtira felt relief and joy flood him. He tried to remain solemn, but he could not keep the lilt from his voice as he said he would be honoured to serve the Kurus as king.

"The Kurus will be more honoured," Gangeya said. "At last this shameful situation will be over. Shall we continue into the city? But where is your bride, Yudishtira?"

"At the rear," Vyasa said quickly. "In case of attack."

"Attack?" Gangeya stepped into the chariot after Vyasa, Yudishtira followed. Looking back along the procession, Yudishtira motioned to Sahadeva to drive Draupadi forward. When they pulled alongside, Yudishtira felt another stab of aching love, remembering her in his bed four nights ago. And he saw that even with her red and gold garment so demurely arranged, her beauty was completely exposed. Gangeya stared.

Yudishtira forced himself to control his voice and remain master of his love and pride. "Wife, as you must know, we are safe now. I wish you to meet the most honoured warrior on earth, the great Gangeya. But you may call him Grandfather, as I do." Yudishtira took one even breath. "He tells me that tonight King Drita will announce my consecration as king."

He saw her eyes widen before she bowed low, her folded palms at her forehead. "This honour, and this news, leave me without adequate speech, Grandfather Gangeya."

After Gangeya had bowed low to her, it was Vyasa who signalled Sahadeva to fall in behind them. Then Vyasa formally addressed his stepbrother. "Gangeya, as the only true son of the third King Kuru, you must be the first to be told: This astounding princess is married not only to Yudishtira, but to his four brothers also."

Gangeya recoiled. "To them all? And you approved of this, Vyasa?"

"I did."

"I don't understand." Suddenly Gangeya seemed old and tired. "These times—what do they mean, Vyasa? Arjuna won her, of course," he muttered, struggling with it. "But Yudishtira was eldest and unmarried." He sighed again, deeply. "This will be a shock to them." He nodded towards Hastinapura. "I will explain it. Quietly—not as an announcement. Let it come first to the people as an uncertain rumour."

"As you think best, Stepbrother," Vyasa said.

When they topped the next rise Yudishtira stopped them again. The sun and cloud shadows played across a vast, almost treeless plain that stretched to the horizon on both sides of the looping, silver Ganges. At the centre of this plain there was a city. Its buildings were stark white among green-black gardens and flickering banners of red and gold. Yudishtira turned in his chariot. "The fields of the Kurus, Queen Draupadi," he said boldly, "and at their heart, Hastinapura."

Queen Draupadi. How he loved to say it. And she studied the land like a queen. Like a woman of rare intelligence. She would certainly know that cleared land was the measure of a kingdom's wealth.

Cleared land under an open sky. Fresh breezes after the days in the forest. Treeless land. Sleek cattle, flourishing crops. And open land.

248

Wealth. Tomorrow the kingdom would all be hers—the gift he alone could give.

He saw her raise her head high, as if she knew his thoughts. Then for the first time since their wedding night, she looked towards him and smiled.

Gangeya's single whisper had spread through the crowd under the gaudily decorated arch at the city's gate. Contempt, disgust and the fear that this marriage would curse them—Draupadi could feel it all in their whisperings behind her as she passed up the line of dignitaries towards King Drita and his family. In order to endure it she focused on remembering the faces of those who were most overtly disapproving or rude—those who did not know or had momentarily forgotten that tomorrow she would be their queen.

Finally Yudishtira was bowing before King Drita, and she, being on Yudishtira's right, was bowing before Suyodhana, who was on his father's left. As she straightened up, Suyodhana whispered, "I believe we have met before, Draupadi. At your 'bride's choice'. But you didn't tell us then that you intended to marry not only the man who won you but all his brothers. You should have inquired further—did you not know I had thirty-two to offer?"

Her face went hot. From behind her Bhima said, "Suyodhana, it will be my pleasure to fight *and kill you* at sunset on the north field."

The self-conscious chatter around them stopped. King Drita's face, with its watery, staring eyes and drooping flesh, turned towards Draupadi. "Princess, please accept my apologies for my son's rudeness. We are all so happy that your husbands are alive and back home. Bhima? Please do not spoil your eldest brother's great day by beginning this quarrelling again."

Draupadi saw Yudishtira motion to Bhima to be silent. But he had not motioned to her. "I accept your apology, King Drita," Draupadi said. "But Suyodhana had best remember that when he affronts me, he faces the anger of five. The thought of fighting even one of my husbands should give a warrior of your son's ability ample reason to choose his words with care."

Suyodhana flushed and began a retort, but King Drita's arm struck across his son's chest. The crowd pressing around them stirred at this exchange. Now they know me better, Draupadi thought.

King Drita was beaming blankly at her. "Ah, a fiery woman among us at last. Agni's daughter indeed. What a pleasure. Dear Princess Draupadi, please honour us by proceeding to the palace with the queen and her ladies. You must be tired, and we are justifiably proud of our women's quarters."

"Yes, 'fiery' princess," the wife behind him said under her breath. "By now you must be thoroughly tired of male company."

Someone giggled. Draupadi stepped forward too quickly and stumbled. A hand steadied her at the waist. "Go with the queen, but I've seen to it that you're quartered by us." It was Arjuna's voice, close to her ear. "Don't let these envious women disturb you—you are too brave for that."

She nodded, raised her head proudly and followed the queen into the city.

20

Both of King Kuru's "grandsons" were stubborn, and every one of their children. It wasn't all the fault of their fisherwoman-grandmother's blood either—I was no blood relation to any of them, but just as stubborn. Sometimes the trait was glorified as "perseverance". "Patience". Even "dedication". But we were all simply stubborn.

Now that I am old I think perhaps all Arya are stubborn. We will have what we want—now or later, with or without your permission—and that trait is both our blessing and our curse. Perhaps the gods gave us dharma to bring us under the bit. I often think it. But of course we became as stubborn about dharma as anything else.

Gangeya

Eos's report had shocked Yudishtira. Hastinapura ready to revolt? The people utterly unwilling to be freed of the "yoke of dharma", as Suyodhana and Sakuni now called it? Perhaps this was why Drita had agreed to yield the throne—perhaps he feared that otherwise the people would force it.

Yudishtira lay on his bed, meaning to rest. But he could not help imagining what would take place at sunset: The bell to call them to the assembly, the evening rituals, his uncle on the throne saying, "Tomorrow Crown Prince Yudishtira will take my throne." And all the struggle would be ended. Gangeya said Drita had given his word. There could be no doubt of it.

Then why do I feel this dread?

And why is there this thunder so early in summer?

.

251

The bells woke her. It was almost dark in the room. Draupadi sat up, confused by the sound. Then she remembered the stories about Hastinapura's famous assembly bells. She preferred Kampilya's way—a human invitation made by a chanting crier.

She arose and arranged her own clothes, knowing that Eos would expect her to sleep through the assembly itself—where women rarely ventured—and the palace servants would be elsewhere, helping to prepare for the celebration afterwards. That was all the better, for what she wanted to do. Eos had said the girl Lotus was "just another pretty flower-cutter, except darker". Eos also insisted Lotus had been his consort only briefly. "And long before he ever heard your name, so forget her."

I will, Draupadi told herself as she slipped from the room. Once I've seen her.

One of the Maruts, disguised as a water carrier, stood guard in the hall. When she left her doorway he insisted on following her. "It's Arjuna's order," the man whispered.

She made a gesture of annoyance. "Then stay back. I'm only going to the gardens and I want to be alone."

Thunder passed over them from some distant storm. Draupadi followed the hallway until it crossed another. Queen Yasoda had taught her that all palaces were fundamentally the same: the buildings surrounded gardens or courts, with the women's quarters at one side, then the guest rooms, the royal living areas, the large celebration and feast hall, the smaller dining rooms, and the assembly hall overlooking the city. These last buildings would be near the largest garden, the most likely place for flower cutting before a celebration. She decided on which peaked roof was the assembly and turned towards it.

"The women's gardens are the other way, Princess."

At least she had been right on that. She stopped. If she were too difficult, this man would have to tell Arjuna.

"I prefer to see the famous main gardens," she said quietly.

"Women don't go there alone."

She almost lost her temper. "Married women may go where they please in a palace. Anyway, you will obviously be with me."

The messenger who was sent to escort Pandu's sons brought them late to the assembly. It was almost dark as the brothers ordered themselves by age at the door and Yudishtira stepped over the threshold into the dim interior.

Every warrior rose. Bells rang; flowers showered the five brothers; voices called the traditional phrases of praise. From beside the throne Gangeya himself strode down the speaking floor to join the king's nephews.

Yudishtira made the motion of acceptance of a blessing, palms over head, and then gestured that it was enough. Too much. But the greeting only intensified. The men were cheering now, stamping their feet, all dignity forgotten.

Gangeya whispered close to his ear, "Even your strange marriage seems to please them, Yudishtira. It's bold and it's the old custom—the eldest sharing his wife with his brothers. I think they miss those ways. The last time it was like this among them was the day I made the vow that allowed my father to marry your great grandmother."

Yudishtira turned, forgetting the assembly's acclaim. "Have you regretted it, Grandfather?" It was the question everyone held back. Yudishtira thought afterwards that it was sharing that brief, triumphant moment with Gangeya that must have emboldened him.

"Regret it?" Gangeya's gaze remained on King Drita, in front of them. "I could not have been king of anything if I had not fulfilled my first duty, to provide for my father's happiness when it was within my power. In those days this assembly understood better that there is no kingdom at all without dharma. No warrior or king can do more for his people than demonstrate unswerving devotion to dharma. That is really why they cheer you: They beg you to restore dharma to the Kurus."

Yudishtira looked around the tiers of seats—his relatives, boyhood friends, teachers. Vyasa and Krishna. For some reason even Suyodhana was shouting praises. And Baron Sakuni was not in sight.

Finally it stopped and the sons of Pandu were shown to seats on King Drita's left. Suyodhana and his oldest brother, Dusasana, were on the king's right.

Drita began a pompous greeting of his nephews. Then his

voice broke. "Come let me touch you, boys. I can't believe you are alive." The assembly burst into more stamping and shouting.

There were tears on Drita's cheeks when he spoke again. "Today will be remembered as long as Kurus meet together. Today will see the beginning of a new unity and harmony among all the descendants of all King Kurus. We have much for which to be grateful as we perform the evening rituals."

Aware of every reason to be happy, Yudishtira looked around the noble old hall where he would soon rule and felt an inexplicable sadness instead. Somehow it seemed less grand than he had remembered it. But after all, he was older. The room was too crowded. Nor was it designed for use after nightfall. It was only the smoke from so many oil lamps that created this dingy, dreary look. So it was irrational. But still the darkness and lost beauty weighed on him.

He looked towards the far end where he had seen Vyasa sitting with Krishna, the sage having given up his rightful place near the king and Gangeya to be with the Vrishni. Yudishtira wiped at his eye with the back of his hand—it was hard to see through the haze, but he was certain Vyasa and Krishna were both gone.

From the shadows of a colonnade a voice addressed her. "A bud so beautiful that the others hang their heads and weep. Princess Draupadi, I am so pleased to see you again."

The voice was a man's. He sat on a stone bench in a recess in the towering wall of the celebration hall. In the shadows she could not see his face, but his cloak was a warrior's and well woven. Had she been introduced to him earlier at the city gates?

Keeping her distance, she thanked him for his pleasant greeting.

"It is so refreshing," he said, "to find a woman who does not twitter with the flock, but keeps her own company. Of course you are a married woman now and have that right."

"Princess Draupadi, come," her Marut escort whispered urgently.

"Servants are so protective," the voice from the shadows

said. "But that is just as well when a beautiful woman walks alone. Will you join me here while we wait for the meeting to end? Your zealous guardian there can wait in comfort out by the fountain."

Draupadi motioned the Marut away. But she did not go towards the alcove either.

"I too am unfond of the 'herd'," the voice said, "or I would have stayed to see your husband's consecration announced. It is so interesting to see these quaint rituals after witnessing an Egyptian pharaoh's coronation."

She became more uncertain. "You have been to Egypt?" But this small man would not be the Egyptian Zesnor.

"I fear I have," he said, laughing. "But please don't tell anyone."

Then it would not be Baron Sakuni either—everyone knew of his travels.

"At least, Princess, your voice doesn't bear the usual scorn. 'Bharata is best,' they all say, when they've never crossed the Yamuna. But wait, you have a Greek servant, do you not?"

A motion behind her caught her eye. The Marut was gesturing that he wanted to speak to her alone. She ignored him.

"I have a Greek companion," Draupadi said coolly. "She too has suffered from Bharata's prejudice against all things yavana."

"I'm sure."

"In Panchala," she said, "they've hardly even heard of the Indus River, much less what is across it. 'Egypt' they would probably think was a kind of yavana fruit."

He laughed richly. "Tell me, how ever did you acquire this Greek? Have you travelled?"

Standing nearer the garden, which was still bright with twilight, her eyes were not adjusting to the darkness into which she looked—she still could not see his features. "Unfortunately, I have never left Bharata."

"A pity. The Greeks are interesting people. We Arya share many words with them. Also with the Hittites and the peoples immediately west of the Indus. But the Egyptian, Sumerian, Hebrew and Phoenician languages are different. Not to men-

255

tion the writing, which takes some time for an Arya to master."

"You can do this writing?"

"Anyone in a yavana court for long must learn some form of it. Or at least to read it."

"Even women?"

"Certainly a queen."

"It is a large world out there," she said softly. "And all far away. Have you ever been north, to the Himalaya?"

"Twice."

"Would you tell me about it?"

"With pleasure, Draupadi."

" . . . and above all, the Kurus are blessed with two crown princes, each raised to rule wisely and heroically." There was a rumble of talk from the tiers—after a long, boring speech, here at last was the meat course. King Drita paused to let the murmuring die down. In his lap his hands were clutching and wringing.

"With two such gifts from the gods, we can not cast either aside. Like the divine twins, the Ashwins, my eldest son and Pandu's are 'two fierce, shining fires, hastening to give protection'. Yudishtira and Suyodhana, you doubly fulfil our hopes for greatness." King Drita stopped, then extended his arms up and out towards both crown princes. "Therefore, as of this day, I have decided to divide the kingdom between you!"

The assembly seemed to stagger almost silently to the edge of chaos. Then came the voices, the shouts. Gangeya rose to his feet. The crowd struggled to control itself in order to hear him.

But blind though King Drita was, he knew who would stand first to oppose him, and even Gangeya would not interrupt a king. Therefore Drita rushed on, shouting above the din. "An unusual solution, yes, to our dilemma of two princes irrevocably consecrated." It grew quieter in the assembly. "This dilemma has been doubly difficult because the older, Yudishtira, is of age to rule, and better prepared perhaps, yet I am still alive and obviously the most experienced of all. The younger, my son, will of course not take my throne while I live, but continue to assist me and thus learn the arts of statecraft. Yudishtira, however, must have his own throne without delay. I have discussed all this with my son Suyodhana and he has agreed to my plan." From the other side of the king, Suyodhana smiled and bowed his head slightly towards Yudishtira. Drita still did not risk a pause. "The kingdom has tripled in size since I accepted my brother Pandu's responsibilities—therefore nothing is lost to anyone. I hope Yudishtira will take the advice of an old man who has tried to be a good father to him in his brother's place, and also agree to this plan."

Now Gangeya was gesturing impatiently, but of course King Drita could not see him. "It would also please me, their elder and king, if these two cousins would both agree to stand before this assembly tonight—now—and grasp hands and swear above the sacred fire to abandon—for ever—any show of jealousy towards the other. To live in peace as cousins and allies. With that I will have ended the small troubles we Kurus have faced and assured our future greatness." Drita now stretched out his arms munificently. "Regent Gangeya, we would be honoured if you would give my plans your blessing."

In the pause one could hear the essence of the assembly's response: "A clever solution." Not ideal, but better than fighting.

Yudishtira looked to Gangeya. Save us, Grandfather, his mind cried. This is not dharma. The criminals defend themselves with more crimes.

Standing by the throne, Gangeya seemed to have sagged lower through the long wait for the crowd to settle. Finally he squared his shoulders and let his booming voice override them. "I repeat what I said when we first heard the good news that Pandu's sons were alive. Yudishtira is the rightful king of this kingdom. Here lie unity, dharma and greatness."

There was considerable assent to this, but Yudishtira heard—it was hardly unanimous. Gangeya would hear too.

"I also see the reasoning behind my stepbrother's plan. Too much reasoning perhaps, without enough memory of our history. I have never known division to bring peace—only more war. Therefore of course I give my blessing to Drita's request for this oath between the cousins. I urge them to make it. But as to the division of the kingdom for the sake of peace and unity. That—"

Now Gangeya glanced at the ceiling as if to search for answers among the ancestors. But Yudishtira knew it was to avoid his eyes. "If I were king," the regent said, "I would not do it. Nor will I give my blessing to it. I can not watch my father's kingdom torn in two."

With that Gangeya strode off the dais, down the length of the crowded hall and out of the assembly.

The outburst among the warriors was even more delayed this time, because of the shock of Gangeya's departure. But when it came it was the loudest yet. Gangeya could have forbidden the division. But he had not.

Yudishtira tried to think through this inconceivable turn of events, but Bhima whispered the only possible response: "How could he just leave us! And where's Vyasa? Guru Vaja?"

"Vaja's a priest," Yudishtira whispered sharply. "This is a warriors' issue."

"Ask for time to think, Yudishtira."

Yudishtira nodded, but Drita's arm was stretched towards him, commanding him to respond.

"Uncle, King, and, in my own father's place, Father: Without obedience to king and father, there is no dharma." Yudishtira's eyes were on the door at the end of the hall. It still swung a little from Gangeya's departure. "Without dharma there is no kingdom," he continued.

Vyasa had not returned either. I am left alone with dharma, he thought. Dharma, my only shield and friend. He did not look back at his brothers. Draupadi he forced from his mind.

"Because and only because dharma requires me to obey you, Uncle—" Yudishtira saw the abyss before him. And also, on the other side, he could not help but see his own half of the kingdom. His alone. He saw himself make the irrevocable crossing. "I accept your proposal."

The warriors hailed him this time even longer than when he had entered their hall. But it did not feel the same.

Yudishtira and Suyodhana went before the sacred hearth and took each other's right hand. Suyodhana's face was expressionless; Yudishtira wondered what his own face revealed as he swore by Indra, Agni, Brahma and Prajapati to cease all displays of jealousy towards his cousin.

Yudishtira returned to his seat. Drita began discussing the details of how the kingdom would be divided. "With great precision," he was emphasising to the royal surveyors. "And each half will defend the other and allow free trade and access to roads." And so it went. Yudishtira sat in stunned silence as Drita droned on, giving details obviously thought out long in advance. Many, including Guru Vaja, slipped out, giving their blind king undisguised looks of disgust.

Then came the final words: "Yudishtira's portion will include all land with waters flowing into the Yamuna River and—"

"Uncle!" Yudishtira rose to his feet. "You mean the Ganges. West or east of the Ganges. The Yamuna valley is burned-out pasture and twenty leagues west is the start of the desert."

"It is still half of the Kuru land."

"Because no one else wants it!"

Suyodhana smiled. "A man of your greatness, son of Pandu, will certainly make even the wasteland flower."

Finally Drita's face and tone revealed some trace of shame. "I understand how you feel, Yudishtira, but after all, my son will still only be a crown prince while tomorrow I will make you a king. A king without experience, however, and—"

"No!"

"Sit down, Cousin," Suyodhana said. "*You gave your word.* No jealousy. And everyone knows you will keep it because of course you are not Pandu's offspring anyway, but 'Dharma's son himself'."

"Nineveh, Ur—they are not really so far away, Princess." Seated on a stool a passing servant had brought, Draupadi had been listening intently. "Not so far at all. Why not see them for yourself?"

She shook her head and smiled, wakened from the dream. "Me? Even I know enough to be sure that is impossible."

"Not alone, of course. Under someone's protection. Even in Bharata there are a few world travellers."

She laughed. "Yes, warrior, but it was not my fate to marry them."

"Draupadi, we rule our own fates." She drew in her breath as he spoke. "Standing on the pass into the west, the Indus behind you, the wind blowing and the road winding towards the sun, the caravan beginning its descent, around you the sound of a hundred different chants to the Lord of Light, in languages you've never imagined—suddenly our little wedding rituals here in Bharata will seem as irrelevant, to a woman of vision, as the stones under her feet at the last ford."

She started and rose to her feet. "This conversation has taken a turn I can not approve of."

"In what sense, Princess?"

If he, a warrior-born and her elder, did not know, she was not certain how to make her response stronger.

"Out there," he continued, "there are many travellers. None asks the others' histories. They especially do not ask a sweet-faced woman if she's ever performed some country's marriage rite." He crossed his legs and leaned back farther into the darkness. "If she travels protected by wealth, servants and a knowledgeable man, she is quite safe. Safe and very welcome, wherever she goes."

"I can't imagine why you are talking about this to me."

At last he stood too, and stepped into the twilight. Then she saw that he limped. He smiled and tilted his head. His face was lean, wan and lined from travelling. "I am talking about crossing the line between ordinary and daring." His voice had taken on a strange intensity. "It is unthinkable to live in the same world with Egypt, Nineveh, Babylon—and to die without seeing them."

Suddenly she knew with whom she talked. "Better that than to die dishonoured, Baron Sakuni."

Sakuni stepped closer. "Who determines honour, Draupadi? In Egypt pharaohs call it honour to take their own daughters to bed."

"Then it will be my honour never to see the place." She edged away from him, glancing back for the Marut waiting by the fountain.

"I've shocked you. You are so mature in intellect that I forgot your inexperience. But you'll think about my words. In fact, consider it my invitation, Draupadi."

"Never!" She spat on him. Then ran down the dark corridor. She heard him trying to follow. Another came faster—her Marut guard. Still others were hurrying from the direction of the assembly. As the Marut overtook her, she turned a corner and paused.

"Vyasa," she heard Sakuni say. "And this must be the famous Vrishni they call Krishna."

"Was that the Princess Draupadi running from you?"

"Regrettably, yes. Have you been looking for her long? But I sent my message just when the assembly began. I knew how you worry about her, old sage, and she *was* wandering around the palace alone."

21

Looking back, my life seems most clearly marked by pain. Some were wounds of the flesh, some were injuries to the heart and mind. Some healed quickly, some festered. And some taught me lessons. But certain hurts only left me with a terrible confusion which I feel to this day.

Gangeya

He had dreaded the conclusion of the rituals and mingling with his fellow Kurus. Instead it was easy leaving the hall—the warriors stood and kept a strange silence. Was it due to their awe of his obedience, Yudishtira asked himself, or their own shame?

Outside, the shock of cold darkness awoke his anger. He strode through the halls of the palace, aware of his brothers talking behind him, of Krishna joining them, of exclamations, and Krishna making some apology about causing Vyasa to leave the hall to look for Draupadi. Yudishtira cared about none of it.

At the door to his room he hesitated, aware that courtesy required him to speak to them. But he opened the door without looking back and shut it behind him.

The room was lit by one lamp. Draupadi was huddled on his bed.

"I'm sorry," she whispered. "I'll go. I only wanted to talk to you."

"I want to talk to you also."

She was watching him. "What's happened, Yudishtira?"

When he told her she rose up as if struck. "Only half? You agreed to it?"

"I told you—I had sworn to cease all jealousy!"

"So they chose peace rather than dharma." She began to pace the room. "Panchala villagers say twins are inauspicious. They cut wealth in two. Perhaps I bring you ill luck—I left one half-kingdom to arrive at another." She remembered the broad Fields of the Kurus, the Ganges winding through like a silver scarf. There was enough for two, it was true. Perhaps there was even some wisdom in it. "Which half is yours—from the west bank or the east?"

"Oh, the Kuru kingdom is even larger than what lies along the Ganges, Draupadi." She heard his profound bitterness.

She came up to him. "This half they have given us, where is it, Yudishtira?"

"The land drained by the Yamuna. Uncleared forest and swamp, or wastelands burned and overgrazed by incompetent herdsmen."

"You accepted *this*?"

Yudishtira was impassive. "I should have suspected a plot, but I thought that in front of the assembly my uncle would be fair with me."

"This is wrong. Wrong and absurd. You never would have agreed if you'd known." She crossed the room, then rushed back to him. "Go back and tell them you reject their trickery."

"Did you not hear what I said? I gave my word: I will cease to display envy of my cousin."

"But an oath means nothing when obtained by deceit, Yudishtira."

"Nothing was obtained by deceit. If I had asked what half he was giving me, Drita would have had to tell me. But I did not ask. When a man buys a lame horse or a barren cow, the seller must tell the truth. But only if the buyer inquires."

"I don't care. I really don't care about these fine points of it, Yudishtira." She heard her voice becoming high and wild. "You can speak to me of barren cows? Lame horses? *Go back and tell them you changed your mind.*"

In response his voice became more low and controlled. "I can not do that, Draupadi."

"You can! You can do anything!"

"I *will* not."

"Just tell them you changed your mind!"

"Tell them my wife doesn't like what I've done so she's told me to break my word?"

"Yes! Yes! Tell them your wife can recognise a pack of cheats and liars, even if you can't." She was shaking and ready to strike out. "What about dharma? Always dharma—what about dharma this time? Where was your precious 'Grandfather' Gangeya? Your 'great' Guru Vaja?"

Draupadi stopped her pacing, shocked by her own outburst. "Yudishtira, forgive me. If I have spoken harshly it is because they always seem to find a way to misuse you that you can not fight." She came over to him. "Husband, where was Vyasa?"

"None of them was there at the end, Draupadi."

She slumped down on the bed. "Sakuni. He did this."

"Sakuni was not present either."

She looked up at him, tears streaming down her face. "You were tricked, Yudishtira."

"It is done. We have our kingdom and we will go to it."

"No!" It came out as a wail. "They tricked you." She could not admit her role in it, not even to herself.

"It is over, Draupadi." His voice was flat, angry, controlled.

Then she came at him. "It is *not* over." She grabbed his arms. "Not over! Not over!" Woodenly he let her shake him.

"*Their dharma was to make you king!* How can you call yourself Lord Dharma's son and accept this? Are you afraid of them? Is this perfection?" Her last words stunned them both. But silenced them only a moment.

He jerked free of her easily. "When I came into this room I shut out even my brothers because I wanted to be alone. But I saw you here and I was glad—I had hoped you would give me comfort."

"Comfort? Comfort? Before you wanted my honesty. Remember? Our 'wedding night'?"

For a moment he didn't speak. "You are right. And now I know your thoughts. But next I must go out and face my brothers. Then go to my 'celebration'. If you can not comfort me, then at least leave me in peace."

"Peace? Please lend me some of your peace, Yudishtira. I have to go to the same celebration, bearing the three humiliations which are your glorious wedding gifts: Five husbands, half a kingdom, and a rejected field."

"Then I will see that you do not have to attend."

She walked to the door, shaken too much to reply.

"I will also insist that tomorrow's rituals be brief," he said. "We will leave this city tomorrow before sunset, if we have to camp a league from the gates after departing. We will keep your 'humiliation' as slight as possible. And you can take comfort in the fact that you will probably never have to see Hastinapura again."

Somçone was nimbly climbing the steep assembly-hall roof towards Yudishtira's seat on its peak. It was too dark to see a face, but only one person knew about his boyhood refuge.

"Sage Vyasa?"

"I'm sorry to disturb you, Yudishtira. Their celebration down there is worthy of flight, I agree. Such hearty laughter and earnest congratulations. No, don't rise for me. It is much too dangerous." Vyasa sat down beside him on the spine of the roof.

"I see you still have your ways of finding me, Sage."

"Yes, but among other things, I think you are asking yourself how, with my 'ways', could I have been lured out of the hall by Sakuni's treachery?"

"You merely understood that her safety was more important to me than being consecrated king of all heaven and earth." He buried his face in his crossed arms. "I can understand this had to happen to me. I've been too proud, with my pretending to perfection. But what did my brothers do to deserve this? And Draupadi?"

"Yesterday I talked with a widow whose only child had just died. A good woman. She asked me humbly what she might have done to deserve this terrible punishment. I told her what I know of it: Events are merely events. Certainly not punishments in themselves. For the virtuous such as she and you, all events become useful. The good turn everything to good. In her case, soon she will take in two apparent orphans. She will love them, educate them. Ten years from now the priest-born parents who lost them on the Gomati River will find them in her home. The parents will be so grateful that she will live out her life with the entire family, happier than she has ever been."

"If you knew her future, you must have known mine. Then what was the point of my father's penance, all my studying—" He could not finish it.

"The stars are bright tonight, aren't they, Grandson?"

Vyasa had never addressed him thus before. Yudishtira felt an unbearable sadness fall over him. "The gods are watching, Grandfather."

"Yes, they watch with great interest, I'm very sure. The Yamuna valley was the first place the Kurus settled. It is not infertile land, not under the right hands." Vyasa touched his shoulder, leaving a radiant warmth. "I am going tonight, Yudishtira. So is Krishna. Neither of us wishes our presence at tomorrow's consecration to be taken as approval."

"So you admit they violated dharma. Which means I should have protested. Having failed to uphold righteousness, I have sinned."

Vyasa stood. "You had your own awareness, Yudishtira. You could only see from that. But Drita was aware of other things he might have done. Therefore he is the one who sinned."

Yudishtira could not give it up. "What exactly should I have been aware of, Grandfather? What can I do *now*?"

"If I were to tell you, and you were to carry out my suggestion perfectly, it would be far, far less valuable than what is coming."

"What is coming?"

"That is easy to predict, Grandson. You are going to begin answering more of your own difficult questions." He took something from his pocket and laid it on Yudishtira's knees, then blended back into the night. Yudishtira heard him descending the ladder left against the hall's rear wall. He felt what was in his hands: two little pouches. He removed their contents: only pebbles. In the starlight he could see that some were dark, some were light.

Late the next afternoon the sons of Pandu and their wife departed Hastinapura with their bullock carts and chariots, which had hardly been unloaded during their single day within the city's walls. After them came one Hastinapura family, then another, then whole groups—all choosing to follow the brothers into exile. A large group were the Nishada Yudishtira had brought to the city. But most were Arya. Some of these were truly fond of Yudishtira and angry with the turn of events; some were more dissatisfied with King Drita and his son, or with the changed attitude towards dharma which Drita had allowed in the Kurus' capital; and some simply sought a new life on the Yamuna, in a new settlement. The Arya loved to move on.

From the city wall Baron Sakuni and Crown Prince Suyodhana watched them go with pleasure. To Suyodhana the loss of a few disaffected citizens was a small price for this spectacle, especially Yudishtira's pitiful attempt to hide his suffering. Drita's son was actually glad that the snake had failed to kill his cousin. This was better. "And this season is so pleasant on the Yamuna," he said to his uncle with sarcastic delight. "The rains could be another month coming."

"And Draupadi will only make Yudishtira's failure more unendurable," Sakuni said quietly. But he watched with less satisfaction. Zesnor's plan seemed elegant enough—exile, isolation, then attack. Yet Sakuni could not deny his own reliable ability to observe and deduce human behaviour, and everything he saw told him that this man being banished to the Yamuna was not the youth who had patiently driven off to Varanavata. It seemed too obvious that for once his nephew's first instincts had been right—the only secure route to the throne required Yudishtira's death.

Now Draupadi's cart was leaving the city and Suyodhana was leaning out to watch. "Dark-skinned whore. I will put her in her place yet. Under *me.*"

Sakuni controlled his urge to mock his nephew's boorishness. But it was enough to know Suyodhana would never have her. After the baron's encounter with her the evening before, he was certain she was the only gift they could send to Egypt that would fully embody Bharata's greatness. She alone—by her mere appearance, by her speech, by her spirit. But to obtain her artfully, without destroying her lovely spirit—that was what was taking time.

"So put your mind to that piece of misfortune for these sons of Pandu," Suyodhana was saying.

"Do not order me, nephew."

"Don't order you? Why? Or are you going to give me a lesson now in Egyptian dharma?"

"No, a lesson about power, which you utterly lack, since you have thirty-two other brothers who would serve my purposes just as well. Look out on the departure of your cousins, Suyodhana. They will soon be grovelling for roots in a drought-stricken wilderness because they ignore even the power they have, and obey some principle. Obey the strong, Suyodhana. Or, like your cousins, you will be crushed by the strong."

22

Ultimate beauty:
To taste the pain of love, the joy of revenge.
To see the fire from the inside.

an anonymous warrior

"May I speak with you, King Yudishtira?" It was Eos at the entrance to his tent.

"If you do not call me 'king'. Please sit, Eos."

She, in her masculine clothing, ignored the leather camp stool and sat cross-legged on his rugs. "More people from Hastinapura have joined us, Yudishtira. Some brought food, but Suyodhana had the granaries closed to them when he saw how many were slipping out tonight. Your brothers are hunting, as you ordered, but won't be back until tomorrow."

"I understand. Tell Kanwa to have a bullock slaughtered for them and shift some of its load to other carts."

They fell into a silence.

"I sent Panchalya hunting with your brothers," she said. "Guru Vaja's failure to take a stand has upset him. Although he has a message from Vaja to you—an apology."

"I will speak to Panchalya."

Silence again. "Our king, it seems, is also disturbed."

Yudishtira looked away.

"Is it difficult to have your brothers so dissatisfied with your decision?"

"They say little. They know I could not go back on my word." Yudishtira shifted with deliberate restlessness. Still she did not go. "Something else requires my attention, Eos?"

269

"Draupadi."

Yudishtira picked up a broken leather head guard, then threw it to the ground. "Tell her I am not angry," he said curtly. "I know she has endured a great deal with us."

"Even more than you know. I can not tell you—" Eos picked at the fringe of the rug she sat on. "But you might guess."

"A guessing game, Eos?" Yudishtira let his annoyance show. "What hints do I get?"

"How your wife dresses. Do you notice? For example, what she still wears underneath?"

He was embarrassed, but he did notice, each detail. He nodded.

"Say it, King."

"A virgin's shift. But she isn't a virgin any more!"

"If you were Arjuna, what would you have done when you discovered your older brothers had left her a virgin for you? And the twins, what could they do then?"

Now he remembered Draupadi's third humiliation, a "rejected field". He felt an odd, unreasonable joy, but quelled it. "I will speak to Arjuna as soon as he returns."

"And say what? Tell me, King Yudishtira, whose wife is she? Arjuna's? And the rest of you are her husbands when he's not in the mood? Who takes responsibility for her heart, King?"

"Only you, it seems," he said more gently. In spite of himself he felt he was going to reveal too much of his true feeling soon, if Eos continued. "What I decide about it hardly matters anyway. Draupadi does not even speak to me."

"It can't be left up to her. She has no experience in these matters."

"Dharma says she must be willing."

"Yudishtira, I am only a yavani—I know very little of your dharma. But Draupadi tells me you are forbidden to knowingly cause suffering, and your wife is suffering. Or consider what any observer of court intrigue can tell you—this marriage needs to be properly consummated to protect all of you. That is certainly dharma. And isn't it a sin to deny a married woman opportunities to bear children? 'To let a fertile field lie fallow'? Her fertile time, what you call her *ritu*—it is almost over for this month, Yudishtira. The others are away. But you still have time to avoid sin if you act tonight."

"For a yavani you do well enough disputing on dharma. But I can not force her."

"There are many kinds of force, Yudishtira. Given your vow about your cousin, perhaps it is time to learn about the blowless varieties." She stood up to go. "Therefore, unless you forbid me to, I will send your wife to you tonight."

He did not forbid it.

The night was far advanced but still hot. He waited, tossing stones from the little pouch, slamming them into the clay water vessel across the tent. Black, white, white, black, white.

"Forgive me for keeping my king waiting."

Yudishtira remained in his chair.

Draupadi let the tent flap fall behind her. "It was late when Eos told me you wished me to come."

He noticed the care she had taken, from the wildflower crown to the bells on her ankles. "Please sit here beside me," he said softly. He motioned to the cushioned seat he had arranged. "I hope the heat and dust this afternoon were not too hard on you. We should reach the Yamuna late tomorrow, even with a longer mid-day rest."

He watched her. She still stood; he still remained seated.

You're as angry as ever, he thought. But the fact remains that you have something you must speak to me about. If you won't, then as Eos says—there are other ways to force it.

He looked down at the floor and made himself begin. "You see, Draupadi, after yesterday's consecration I need some amusement. My brothers are all out hunting. So, I thought you and I should enjoy surata together."

"As my husband wishes."

Not an eye blink—the control of this woman!

Except her skirt trembles where she hides her hands. But still she won't say it.

"Please undress for me, Draupadi."

She turned her back and unwound her bodice and skirt cloths.

"But face me, Wife."

She turned back, dropped the upper garment and let the skirt fall. "As you see," her voice wavered a little, "I'm still wearing a virgin's shift." Her chin went up defiantly. "Your brothers chose to leave me as they found me."

"I will not." He meant to speak lightly. Instead he sounded harsh. She hung her head.

"I'm sorry, Draupadi."

Now she looked up and glared at him. "You, Husband, are always sorry. Always with something to regret."

Her words were like a knife stab. He struck back coldly: "Take off this shift too."

She did it in one motion. Her naked body in the lamp light was the colour of gold under the moon, but he only vaguely saw it. "Go to the bed."

She obeyed him, walking the few steps rigidly. He undressed himself.

There are indeed many kinds of force, he thought. Now I'm one of those who use surata to make war rather than sow seed.

He went to where she stood by the bed and he took her in his arms. Her body was rigid and her head was turned away.

No. I will *not* force her, he swore to himself. He reached to turn her head to kiss her, hoping to seem more tender.

She struck his hand. Years of training brought him close to striking back. But she was a woman and he controlled himself, grasping her upper arms instead.

She struck his chest with her fists, over and over. "You're worse than any of them! Any of them," she screamed. "Let me go!" She kept twisting against his hold, her loose hair stinging his face.

When she kicked him, he swept her legs out from under her with his foot, directing her fall on to the bed. Then she kicked up between his thighs. It was the surprise as much as the pain that infuriated him. He fell down on her, pinning her limbs. Growing up with Bhima, he had learned every trick. Now at least he could talk to her.

"Draupadi, speak to me. Are you afraid of the first time?"

"Never."

"Then have I been so unfeeling before tonight? Done something cruel?"

"Nothing!"

She struggled but he held her easily. "So it's that you simply dislike me."

"Yes! Yes!"

Then it must always be like this, he thought. "They expect you to bear me a son, Draupadi. The first time—"

She went rigid and closed her eyes tightly. "Then do it. Do it! Get it over."

With a jerk she spread her legs under him. He rose up a little.

Then she screamed again. "No! Never!" And again she used her right knee to send pain flashing through his groin.

Furious, he shook her, lifting her up off the bed. Then he threw her down, the stupid petals he had spread there tossing around them.

"I hate you!" She spat on him.

"Pretend I'm Arjuna," he panted. "He can have you next time, gladly."

"He wouldn't force me!"

"He wouldn't bother!"

She gasped. He sat back on her thighs, suddenly ashamed. He had lost control—it frightened him that his awareness included this dim pleasure in hurting her mind if not her body. The kohl around her eyes was streaking her cheeks and the red on her lips was smeared. Still, more than ever, she was the most supremely desirable woman he had ever seen.

This is all wrong, he thought. So wrong. He moved to leave her.

She lunged up at him, kicking and hitting. He pinned her again. He was vaguely reminded of breaking colts or bullocks —above all, one never forced them to the edge of compliance, and then backed down.

But he was uncertain that he had the will to finish this. And why was he the one to have to do it? Experience told him too well that the one you forced might never forgive you, even if willing and gentle with those who came after.

Then he let his anger return. "Someone must have surata with you, 'princess', and the others have left you to me."

He swiftly regretted this deliberate wounding of her soul.

Her face seemed to crumple like a leaf in a flame. Her whole body shook with her crying.

"Forgive me" was on his lips. But suddenly he no longer cared. She hated him. Nor did he want her. Not any more.

He moved again to leave her, to let her cry. Then saw between her legs the honey of her flower, flowing like her tears.

So then it's all as Eos said, he thought.

He did not let himself look again at her face or listen to any of her moaned words. He entered her and gently ploughed the field that had been given him by Brahma.

23

Peace permits the heart's subtle growth. The king and I
were forced to fight too many battles.

Draupadi

She still had not spoken to him. She lay beside him in the
blue-grey dawn, her body glistening with perspiration. He had
taken her three times, the last only a moment ago. She had
cried each time, but she had not resisted him again. So it was
only that he was not Arjuna—he forced himself to see it that
way, the truth, over and over.

With the truth came the sadness of his wedding night again.
Even Wood Rose's death, even his father's death—nothing
was like that sadness. He loved this woman. And she did not
love him.

His awareness warned him he would suffer this way often.
He considered taking his life, lawless as even the thought of
it was. To fight it, he blanked his mind and closed his eyes.
But the image of death came again.

Suddenly there were shouts and the bright, sickening flickers
of flame reflected on the tent walls. He sat up. A woman cried,
"Rakshasa". Then the voice was cut off.

Yudishtira threw himself from his bed and seized his bow
and quiver.

"Your armour," Draupadi said from the bed.

"Not now."

"Yes. They will have poison arrows." She was up, naked,
gathering up the heavy leather chest and arm protectors,
handing him the leather helmet. An arrow shot through the

tent wall and lodged in the pillow where she had lain a moment ago.

He took the armour from her. "Get under the bed."

"No, you can't put it on without help." Her hands began fumbling with the stiff ties.

Other arrows flew by them. He moved to shield her. She kept working. The tent lurched around them. One corner sagged, then burst into flames.

"Done," she said breathlessly.

He picked her up. She was still naked and he was strangely worried that the bronze rivets of his leather armour would hurt her. He held his shield over her and ran from the tent.

The camp was chaos, yet some order was emerging: The Maruts were standing in the carts and chariots, shooting arrows to cover the women and childen as they ran for protection between the wheels. But some carts were burning. Flame-tipped arrows then, as great a sin in battle as poison.

He carried her to his chariot. Although it lacked horses it was more easily defended than the carts. Five of the Maruts assigned to Draupadi had followed him to help protect her. He gave her the driving cloak lying on the seat. She stared at it, then realised she was naked and covered herself.

He wanted to stay. But he could see the slaughter around him—countless rakshasa it seemed, against fifty Maruts trying to defend the several hundred unarmed Arya and Dasyu from Hastinapura who had joined him. Who had sought *his* protection.

And he had sent his brothers hunting!

"Look to Urutata," he shouted to one of the Maruts. Then he took a battle axe from the chariot and ran in the direction of the horses. Mounted, he would be more effective.

A mare charged at him from out of the smoke of a burning tent. It was one of his own bays. He called the command to stop but she was too panicked. He caught her broken tie rope and ran beside her while pulling back to slow and circle her, then leaped up on the dipping shoulder.

From the greater height he saw why he heard screaming horses and oxen—a score of rakshasa were in among the tether lines. The black-painted arms above the hideous face-markings hacked at the livestock with curved knives. Their blows were random—blood spurted in fountains from necks, withers, haunches.

The Maruts around the carts were protecting human lives and did not see the concentration of the enemy among the animals. Yudishtira forced the mare in among the horses and smashed one demon face, then another. The crazed men hardly seemed to know a blow had struck. Others ran screaming and fell among the kicking, mutilated horses.

The brave mare was cut in several places but the rakshasa were largely gone from among the livestock. Yudishtira turned her and galloped for the carts and tents. Near the first tent an arrow entered the mare behind the ears. She dropped under him, dead.

He jumped clear, touched her forelock in gratitude, then threw down his battle axe and took his bow and quiver from his back. From over the horse's belly he began raining arrows on everything painted and bloodied that moved. The smoke was intolerable but he stayed there near the tents, for now and then a woman or child would bolt from a mass of burning skins and under the cover of his arrows run for the carts. He tried to shut his ears to the screams of those trapped under the collapsing tents or cut down by a knife as they attempted to escape.

His quiver began to rattle emptily when he reached for arrows. Glancing down, he counted five. He could use them carefully or shoot them all and be done with it—either way he would be defenceless soon. And his enemies knew it. Even now he could see the crouching figures watching him, holding back, waiting for him to spring out and take his death stand when he was finally unarmed except for a battle axe.

He looked back at the carts and chariots. They were well stocked with hundred-arrow quivers. But how many poison arrows would be aimed on him if he went for more weapons? Despite his leather shielding there were many exposed places, and any clean hit anywhere would kill him.

The Maruts were watching him too. Soon, he sensed, one would be chosen to give his own life to try to save the king.

"I know your thoughts," he shouted. "Stay where you are. Too many of us have died in this already."

A rakshasa took advantage of his turned head. A grotesquely painted, blood-splashed body leaped over the dead horse. A knife slashed Yudishtira's ear. He jerked and twisted the arm that had wounded him and the rakshasa died on his own weapon.

Three more were coming. He dropped them with three arrows. Two arrows left. And two more coming.

Skilled archery from the chariots and carts was helping to protect him, but he was out of their most effective range. He grasped his battle axe and stood, his back to his men.

A sudden hard shove from behind knocked him face down on to the bloody mare. "Forgive me, King." It was the Marut named Vimada. He had five quivers under his arms. "It seems I made it, though."

Yudishtira grinned. "It seems you did. I am grateful."

Both men began shooting. The crouching figures immediately began to fade away among the burning tents. Someone cheered. A bullock bellowed anxiously. But mostly Yudishtira heard his people weeping.

Draupadi walked beside the cart that still carried the gifts Yasoda and Drupada had given her for her weddings. The gifts, never unpacked since Kampilya, had somehow escaped being burned in the morning attack. For some vague reason she needed to guard them. Or perhaps they guarded her.

The dust rose around her in a yellow wall. She only knew where to direct the single bullock by goading it into the thickest cloud. The heat was another wall she faced. And her thirst. Her garments—muslin cloth from some hamper—were soaked with her sweat.

Some time in the mid-afternoon her brother, Bhima, Arjuna and the twins had caught up with them after their hunt. Their horses had come in stumbling under their loads of game. But there was no lack of meat now—Yudishtira had already seen to the roasting of a hundred dead oxen and horses. And the cremation of almost a hundred persons. The smell of burning flesh still clung to her. Some of the survivors ate the cooked cattle flesh as they walked, knowing it would soon spoil. Others, she knew, would never eat meat again.

The returned brothers were almost as stunned as those who had survived the attack. But they were practical men—they had quickly harnessed their horses to ease the work of the remaining draught and chariot animals, and rode or walked in silence, hurrying the survivors on towards the Yamuna where a permanent defence could be organised.

Immediately after the attack about half of those who had followed Yudishtira out from Hastinapura had chosen to go back, taking some weapons but refusing an armed escort. They feared that the rakshasa meant to exterminate the sons of Pandu and anyone appearing to be with them.

At mid-morning the only survivor had returned—the others had been killed on the road.

Now the rumour was that anyone allying themselves in any way with Pandu's sons was doomed, whether with them or not. But when others from Hastinapura asked to go back, this time under the Maruts' protection, Yudishtira would not divide his forces. They accepted that, too stunned to argue, too relieved to hear certainty of any kind from anyone. So "King" Yudishtira's few remaining "subjects" trudged on towards the death they expected to come at any moment out of the dust wall in front of them.

Draupadi could hear Eos's comforting voice—it was what kept her walking, and she was not alone in that. Eos was in the cart ahead tending some of the burned and wounded. She was able to help some; they stopped often to bury or burn those she could not help. But in every case she gave courage and kindness.

Behind Draupadi a chariot pulled by a single horse was overtaking her.

"Draupadi, stop. You must not walk any more in this heat." It was Arjuna.

She halted, mostly because she'd been told to. The single horse with its heaving flanks drew up beside her. "Get in," he said.

"Your horse is too tired," she said dully. "You should find another."

"It will be glad to have you—you'll keep me driving slower." His easy tone seemed strange to her. But then he hadn't been there.

She stepped up and sat on the seat. Within moments she was asleep.

The jolting had stopped. She started awake. The dust was drifting to the side and shadows reached across the road—it was late afternoon. Yudishtira stood where Arjuna had before, speaking encouragement to the same single horse. He had evidently halted to let it rest a moment. Now he was urging it back into motion.

He saw she was awake. "I'm sorry," he said. "Arjuna is at the rear, meeting with the remnants of the Maruts."

"Sorry?" she repeated.

He did not explain himself. She stood up beside him, dazed by the passage of most of a day and by the memories of the morning which flooded back. They were on a slight rise and she could see the train of bullock carts and chariots in front of and behind them, none pulled by more than two weary animals. The uninjured people were walking beside the animals to spare them extra burdens.

"So many died," she whispered.

"After they trusted me to protect them," he said.

"But the Maruts came from Kampilya to protect me, and how many of them died, Yudishtira—sixteen?"

"Eighteen now. Many of the rest were wounded or burned." He put out his arm to catch her as she swayed. She leaned against him, her face in the curve under his shoulder. "Now we near the Yamuna," he said. "One can tell because the biting insects are growing worse." He pulled her headcloth up around her face. "The King of Yamuna Land approaches his kingdom," he said bitterly. "Yudishtira, Lord of the Sami Bush and Thorn Tree."

She pulled away and bowed formally, palms together, as best as she could in the jolting chariot. He laughed harshly. She shook her head. "No, I'm not mocking you. I beg your forgiveness. I was unspeakably cruel in Hastinapura and during the night, yet in the morning you saved my life."

"You also saved mine by insisting on the armour, and it is I who must beg for forgiveness for the cruelty that occurred between us."

"No, a wife should be willing—"

"My wife should be honest, as I asked you to be. And no wife should be frightened and forced."

"But I struck first. And I was not honest— I don't hate you. You have only been generous to me—on our wedding night and—always."

They rode in silence.

"Please speak plainly, Draupadi. It was because I was not Arjuna, was it not?" She looked down, not denying it. "And because I allowed our kingdom to be divided, yes?"

"And because I could not bear to admit my own guilt."

"Draupadi, Sakuni would have created some other lie to remove Vyasa. And that assumes Vyasa could have stopped Drita anyway."

"Vyasa could have."

"If he had chosen to. Draupadi, do not blame yourself."

"But you blame yourself," she said. She reached up and very gently touched his swollen ear where it had been cut by the rakshasa.

"I don't know if Drita's treachery towards me even matters compared to what has happened to these people who followed me."

She leaned against him again, unable to stand. "Who really attacks us, Yudishtira?"

"I don't know. I too find it hard to believe that Suyodhana and his uncle would tolerate the use of poisoned and burning arrows, and knives used on women and children and animals."

"But at Varanavata—"

"I know."

He fell into a long silence. She still leaned against him. Finally he whispered, "We have difficulty with our nights, but they are nothing compared to the mornings after." He laughed a little wildly, as if almost out of his head. "We will have to warn everyone when we take to our bed so that extra guards can be set out."

She found herself feeling the same wild need to laugh. She,

at seventeen, was only two years younger. "But set the guards far from our quarters, King of Yamuna Land. I'm afraid every one of your subjects heard me shouting that I hated their ruler."

"I fear they heard a different song from us later, Queen of the Quick Sands." Their laughter still sounded half crazed.

The horse suddenly shied. A chariot drove out of the trees on their left. "Krishna!" Yudishtira shouted.

"King, Queen! I left that stinking Hastinapura and started home, but decided I could not miss this moment. It will be a story to tell my great grandchildren—the day the sons of Pandu came to the Yamuna to found their unequalled city of Indraprastha, Indra's home. So myself and a flock of Vrishni priests have been studying the land and have found the most auspicious site—at a broad ford, west bank, sloping sharply—"

"So. The site and the name—have you left anything for the rest of us to do?" Yudishtira asked dryly, but with affection also.

Krishna hung his head. "Of course nothing is final without your approval, King Yudishtira. We must also consult your wise chief priest, Urutata. But what is this? By your livestock and condition I surmise that you have encountered some difficulties. I see all your brothers back there, and Panchalya, but others are missing—is Urutata well?"

"He is. He rests in the rear."

"Give thanks to Yama."

"But many others died in an attack by those same demons."

"My condolences to their families. Remind them, 'He is not slain when the body is slain, but is eternal, unchanging, imperishable.'" Krishna hardly stopped for a breath. "Yudishtira, these past two days I have had some small huts built for you on the far bank, so you could grow accustomed to the site. Actually your hut, Queen, is a bit more than that if I do say so. Of course there will be no problem for anyone with biting insects—there is fine-woven cloth over every bed. Garments, food, bedding—all fit for royalty. And fit for the devoted men and women who have accompanied you—persons awake to dharma and to the Kurus' true future. They should be well rewarded."

"Few of them are left, Krishna."

"But this is very generous," Draupadi said.

"All from my father. After all, Kunti is his own sister. And more is on the way from him. The Vrishnis are very pleased about being your first allies. Also about sharing your southeast border. The priests I brought expect their usual gifts in return for services, of course, but the Vrishnis are honoured to advance a bit of gold to please them. And wise to do it too, as my father was first to say. For Pandu's sons will soon be rich, he said, on such fine and fertile land. It is easy to see King Drita is blind to have parted with it, and that his son Suyodhana is unacquainted with husbandry. Yes, when the five sons of Pandu are rich they will pay us back ten times over. But that is Yudishtira's way—generous to a fault. Or so some would say. *I* say, at Indraprastha unstinting generosity will become a warrior's virtue once again. Allies will gather from all over Bharata to bask in the glow of your dharma. Ah, it is good to see you and your queen smiling again. Yes, I see it has been a tragic journey for you. But all your troubles are over, sweet Queen Draupadi. Yes, put your sorrows behind you, everyone. An auspicious day, truly an auspicious day."

PART III
INDRA'S PLACE

24

One man indeed seeing Speech has not seen her; another man hearing her has not heard her; but to another she delivers her person as a loving wife, well attired, presents herself to her husband.

Rig Veda

Bharata's hundred kingdoms reeled with the waves of news about King Pandu's sons. Given that after the brothers survived the fire they had gone into hiding, they surely must have suspected treachery from some quarter. The contest and their winning it in disguise suggested others had also suspected a plot and had seen to it that Pandu's family would have at least one secure ally, through marriage. And not just any marriage, but one to this rumoured Daughter of Fire. Yet still King Drita had not given up his throne to his nephew. (The "division" fooled no one.) Could it be that Drita would dare to flout dharma? But the newest rumour was that the division was a punishment for the brothers' own violation of dharma, by sharing one wife. And so opinion vacillated and in the end Pandu's sons received neither help nor hindrance on the Yamuna.

Not that dharma had never been ignored before even by kings and princes. There were entire bands of Arya who scoffed at the laws. But these rogues tended to fight each other into extinction. That was the real danger of abandoning dharma —not sin, not dishonour, but that your enemies could abandon it too. Every thoughtful person east of the Indus and south of the Himalaya knew that if Arya warriors were free to obey only their impulse to conquer (and if certain Arya priests could be free with their greed), the hundred kingdoms would devour themselves as well as the Dasyu in a storm of wars, raids, hoarding, stealing and guile. Or unspeakably more sinful behaviours. It was not only Yudishtira who considered dharma his friend and shield and only recourse. Dharma was the protector of all those wishing to live in peace or unable to win in war.

The problem for the Arya was that, compared to greed and violence, dharma was so frail. When an individual stepped outside dharma and began cheating in the marketplace or attacking the unarmed or hunting female animals bearing young or burning competitors' fields, others naturally felt that in order to survive they had to do the same—and do it first next time, if possible. And when a king or prince stepped outside dharma the danger was far greater—to every Arya and Dasyu, every cow or deer or fish or bird, even every crop and pasture.

Still, a king and his kingdom could be conquered. The most terrible threat was one that all felt at all times, yet none had a name for. It was that somehow the entire reservoir of tightly restrained belligerent impulses might break within them all one day, might flood them all. Some of this swelling supply was unleashed on the Dasyu. But never, never enough. And so it was that the most urgent aspect of all the rumours about the sons of Pandu was any news about those who now embodied this fear of the loss of dharma—those who had attacked the bride's-choice pavilion at Kampilya and then the train of settlers following Yudishtira to the Yamuna.

Yet, oddly, few Arya were curious about who the rakshasa actually were, or who might have sent them, or why. These questions their inner minds had already answered: the rakshasa came from the Arya and for the Arya, as punishment for all that the Arya wished to do, even when the Arya did not do it.

Sakuni shivered in spite of the hot night. The chill of fever. A hateful season, this before the rains. Impossible to breathe. Not a time to go without sleep or decent food for three days. But all worth it if Zesnor had really found them.

Zesnor's bent form led on through the drought-dead forest.

The deer path they followed required walking in a crouch. To straighten up meant a slap in the face by crackling thorn branches. Sakuni's face already bled from such slaps, drawing biting flies. He was dizzy, dry-mouthed and nauseated, and his lame leg ached from the pounding required to keep up along the hard, uneven ground.

Still worth it, he thought. If Zesnor can really control them. The treacherous, sick old wizard in the bowels of Egypt would be patient only so long. Yudishtira and his brothers had survived a month on the Yamuna; they would survive longer. The rumours he had planted would stop allies from joining them—especially that anyone daring to offer the six sinners help would be shunned themselves. But Yudishtira was growing more clever—he had refused the warriors King Drita had offered to "protect" the Kurus on the Yamuna. He intended to have a kingdom or die. Sakuni understood well that degree of determination.

But determination was nothing beside power, and the rakshasa could provide that power. Uniquely. Since destroying the caravan of Pandu's sons better than he could have imagined himself, the "demons" had slaughtered an entire Arya village —raped women, mutilated children, smashed skulls and hacked off the limbs of the wounded and dead alike. Even kings would grovel before the man able to direct the attacks of these demons.

A scream cut off Sakuni's thinking. A woman begged, in the Arya tongue, then screamed again. He looked ahead and could see firelight through the trees. Zesnor motioned to come up beside him. In a clearing, naked men weaved and stumbled around a linga stone, phallic shaped and bloody. A Dasyu rite then, outlawed by the Arya. Witnesses caught would be killed. Did Zesnor know?

Zesnor gestured towards the captive Arya woman. Like the stone, she was bathed in blood—apparently her own. "They took the bait I have offered."

"Then *these* are the rakshasa? But they are not foreigners. They are mere Dasyu."

"Mere Dasyu, desperate with hate. I thought it best that you see for yourself." There were also Arya deserters, unbelievers and criminals, Zesnor explained crisply. And the woman was a courtesan from Hastinapura, paid to travel with only one frail escort and a flask of a beverage Zesnor wanted the rakshasa to have.

"I did not know any other way to deliver it to their lips but to have them steal it from a traveller. Of course she was tortured. That is the azle. They are releasing their hatred of your people on to her."

"Rescuing her is going to be difficult."

"It will be impossible," was all Zesnor said.

There were more screaming pleas for help. Sakuni demanded to know the slave's plan. Zesnor explained that when the woman was dead and the rakshasa were in a stupor from the azle beverage, he would gather their weapons, aim one of their poison arrows at the leader's throat, and come to an agreement with them: Help in conquering the Arya and more of the beverage in return for accepting Zesnor as their leader.

"If they are not in a stupor when we go to them?"

"They have taken too much from the flask. I know the effects of the azle. It is with this—the azle—that we will truly control them. Once one feels invincible, the craving is difficult to resist. I now grow it here in Bharata."

There was yet another horrible shriek. Sakuni covered his ears; Zesnor turned away and began meticulously cleaning an area under a sami tree. "Soon, Master, you will have control of a very dangerous weapon."

Before Sakuni had thought of a suitable response the Egyptian had sat, closed his eyes, and assumed an expression Sakuni had seen before. The yavana would say no more until circumstances demanded his response.

Sakuni found a place for himself leaning against the trunk of an acacia. He too tried to close his eyes and silence his mind—he had had the Badari priests' lessons once. But soon ants were crawling through the sweat under his arms. And the screams came so often.

I must wake him, he thought. Demand he somehow stop this screaming!

No, let the Egyptian teach you. She was a courtesan. Ten

more will fill the bed she's emptied. People die screaming every day.

Still he shivered violently when she gave her death wail. He had thought he had heard her screech it many times. But in this one he heard everything that it meant.

But at least afterwards the night was quiet.

Draupadi lay on her bed on the porch of the hut Krishna had had built for her. Through the thin cotton netting that gave protection from insects she watched the tops of the towering, dazzling rain clouds in the east. They had appeared three days ago, but still stood aloof from the valley of the Yamuna River.

"Kampilya's roofs will be shining with rain," she said to Eos. "In Hastinapura the people will be dancing wet in the streets. And here we shrivel like toads on a hot rock."

The Greek was inside, unpacking hampers. She offered no comment.

Draupadi's view east was across the marsh and open river. Nothing about the scene had changed since she had lain down listlessly after the morning rites. Now it was afternoon. The most interesting event today on the Yamuna had been the coming of the new watch—two men had slipped into the shadow of a tree, two others had gone away.

As if their silence had mattered, she thought. The Yamuna valley rang all day and night with bird cries, insect chatter and hyena howls. The sound of a man walking could hardly make a difference.

"Could you sleep last night, Eos?"

"No. They told me the very loud sounds were a leopard killing a water buffalo."

"This morning while I bathed, I watched a marsh deer giving birth. It's as if we weren't here."

"The drought makes them desperate," Eos said. "They lose their fear of us."

Eos came to the door but said nothing. A monkey threw another mango stone on the roof, making a sound like a mule kicking wood.

"Eos, I hate this place."

"You hate that we are here and Suyodhana and Sakuni are in Hastinapura."

Draupadi sat up. "Why not? They sit in cool garden houses sipping ices, training pet monkeys and laughing at Yudishtira's understanding of dharma."

"That is their bad fortune." Eos studied her for a moment. "Perhaps you should prepare now for the assembly?"

"An assembly seated on durva-grass mattresses under a rush roof?" But Draupadi arose and began tying back her hair. "No wonder Yudishtira is encouraging me to attend—with all the rest wrong about it, why not invite women too?"

"He said anyone instructed in Veda may attend Indra-prastha's assembly," Eos said evenly. "Unless a woman is in her monthly bleeding."

"I am not yet. But soon." She bit her lip and tossed her head a little. "One sowing does not make a crop."

Eos brought out a shimmering blue skirt embroidered with flowers and cuckoo birds. "So by going today, you'll show them you are still available for surata."

"They won't want me tonight either."

"Not want you? True it has been over a month, but a difficult month for everyone."

The girl dropped down on the bed. "Eos, forgive me. I complain like a child. But I can't stop it. Why can't I accept this? Yudishtira has."

"Your husband is water," Eos said quietly. "You are fire."

Draupadi hid her face in the mattress. "My husbands have good cause to avoid me, Eos."

"What good cause? Bhima and Arjuna even agree with you."

"How do I know what Arjuna thinks? He won't even speak to me. And Bhima I only make restless to go back and fight when I know Yudishtira forbids it." Draupadi pounded the bed with her fist. "Where are the allies Krishna said would come?"

"It takes time for envoys to be sent. Stand up and let me help you dress."

"Eos, there's no one on the Yamuna but Nishada!"

"I think there is nothing wrong with Nishada." Eos handed her the blue headcloth that matched her skirt. "But there is something wrong with you today. Yes?"

"Yes," she hissed. She went to the flap of cloth that served as a door and watched her brother coming slowly up the path to escort her to the assembly. "For fear of rakshasa I can't even walk alone. It's worse than Kampilya." She stamped out.

Some predator had killed a peacock in the yard, leaving little drifts of iridescent feathers matted with dark blood. Draupadi stopped and faced the fluttering cloth covering the doorway, and the woman behind it whom she could not see. "I'm sorry, Eos." Then she joined her brother.

Draupadi took the lead in the walk to the main part of the encampment. As always since they had left Hastinapura a month before, Panchalya was spiritless. Today she felt no sympathy.

"Brother, you grieve too much over Guru Vaja. Don't you see it yet? Even if Vaja had spoken against King Drita's division of the kingdom it would have made no difference."

"There is no honour in silence," he said dully.

"Maybe." Draupadi slowed because of the heat. "We're being burned alive out here! Where is the wind? There's not even a breeze on this river." Her skirt caught in a sami bush. "You see? Do you see the joke we are? Why dress like a queen to live in a jungle?"

Angry at her own childish tone, she jerked the material and it tore. Her brother knelt to untangle the long skirt, then stood. She let him embrace her and press her hot face against his shoulder. "I'm sorry it tore," he said softly.

"Forgive me," she whispered. "I hate myself today." She held on to him, glad of his familiar smell. "And I'm afraid to go to an assembly."

"Then I'll stay beside you, Draupadi." His voice rose a little. "And do what little else I can to make you happy here."

They walked out into the roughly cleared area surrounding the banyan tree Yudishtira had chosen to be the heart of his "Indraprastha". Around it were the rude huts housing the brothers, Urutata, Krishna, the Vrishni priests, the thirty-two surviving Maruts from Kampilya and the twenty-seven remaining Arya and Nishada from Hastinapura who had not gone back or been killed—all that were left of several hundred. And

293

now there was a new structure, the roofed shelter for the ritual
fires and for their assembly.

For now, however, the brothers were seated in a half circle
under the banyan tree, facing a woman—a young, handsome
Nishada. As Draupadi approached, the five men and the girl
all stood. Arjuna and Sahadeva seemed ill at ease.

"Queen," Yudishtira said, "it gives us great pleasure to have
you join us. This blue garment you wear, Draupadi—you seem
fresh as autumn."

She smiled and bowed her head, hiding her shock at Yudishtira's appearance. He was gaunt and his eyes were shadowed
with weariness.

She tried to speak lightly. "But you must rest in this heat,
husbands. What are you able to do on such a day?" Remembering Eos's rebuke about Nishada, and her own night with
another clan of Dasyu, Draupadi tried to nod pleasantly to the
stranger.

"We are learning the names of the common trees," Sahadeva
said with gentle meaningfulness. "Lotus, will you resume?"

Lotus. Lotus. Draupadi went rigid. Arjuna was seated nearest
the woman, of course. His head was down, his pale skin turning
red.

Draupadi walked away abruptly; Panchalya followed her.

Under the new shelter Draupadi leaned against one of the
pillars and tried to breathe evenly and control her loathing.
So the woman made Arjuna bring her into exile with us,
Draupadi thought. Why has no one told me, his wife, that his
consort has accompanied him? That would have been only
courtesy. Only ordinary kindness.

Draupadi hardly noticed Panchalya beside her. Or Urutata
before her, preparing the hearths of the three fires. Still, both
presences began to calm her a little. Especially the old chief
priest's.

There was something about Urutata that brought back her
strongest sense of Before. Perhaps it was only his priestly
activities, which she already knew she had watched many times
as a child. The laying of the sacred woods on the three hearths
—the libation altar, the northern fire, and the southern fire
for warding off evil. The digging of the shallow trenches around

each. The spreading of the delicate barhi grass to the four corners. The arranging of the vessels carved from palasha and ashwattha wood containing the curds, purodasa cakes, grain and butter. And the setting out of the seven seats for the seven priests, the most propitious number for royal rites. Obviously the priests brought by Krishna from Dvaraka had left these mundane preparations to old Urutata, who was "used to serving". But he was content, for none of this work allowed jealousy or pain. Only order, calm and love of the gods.

As she came in closer under the roof she smelled the incense, the lilies from the Yamuna, the melted butter and roasted barley. Urutata was reciting Veda to himself—the song to Speech: "'I am Speech the sovereign queen . . .'"

He slowly straightened from his work, a hand on his thin back, and considered her.

She stepped back. "Perhaps you would rather I went away, Urutata."

"That I would never want, Draupadi." He continued his singing. "'I am Speech, the sovereign queen, the collectress of treasures, cognisant of the Supreme Being, the chief of objects of worship.'"

She went on with the verse, which flowed from her memory like cool water: "'As such the gods have put me in many places, abiding in manifold conditions, entering into numerous forms.'"

Now Panchalya took up the hymn: "'Those who are ignorant of me perish.'"

"But Urutata," Draupadi burst out, "they also call Brahma Speech."

"Then my queen misunderstands Speech, not Brahma," Urutata said gently. "We speak now of the first movement of Pure Consciousness within itself—vibrating within itself—and from that sound springs all that is. This first stirring is the Sovereign Queen and Mother of All. Personified Brahman. The god Brahma can create only from Brahman. From the mother."

As if hearing a challenge to their last words, the three under the shelter were suddenly aware of the five brothers approaching, their footsteps loud on the sunbaked earth. Panchalya stepped closer to his sister, as though to protect her heart.

Yudishtira entered first and took the "throne"—a chair of rough-hewn sandalwood. The rest took their seats on the ground by age, including those fourteen Maruts who had studied Veda and were not on guard today. None had seen more than twenty autumns except Urutata—and the Vrishni priests, who came in late, their robes hitched a little higher than usual, as if the soil at Indraprastha was somehow a little dirtier, or the warrior-born more inexperienced.

Draupadi avoided Arjuna's desperate efforts to catch her eye, but she glanced back twice at the banyan tree, where she thought she saw Lotus still sitting in the black shade among the great twisted roots and hanging offshoots. A handsome woman, Draupadi thought again, and hardly darker than myself.

As soon as the ceremonies ended, the discussion began. Draupadi noted the simple, direct tone Yudishtira set. The assemblies of long ago must have been like this, she thought—a mere meeting of the educated for the purpose of governing their clan. She remembered how some of the ordinary people had called Yudishtira "he who takes us back". Or so they had said before the rakshasa had attacked.

The first topic was cleared land. Arjuna and Bhima spoke adamantly on the need for room to build, plant crops, graze animals and, above all, to see enemies coming. "There is only one way to clear," Arjuna said. "And it isn't with axes and hoes. It is the ancient Arya way. Feed Agni. Burn as much of this forest as will burn. Before the rains. The fire will move rapidly and the trunks of the larger trees will remain useable for building."

"Isn't that how some of this country was ruined?" Yudishtira asked.

"By grazing too soon after a burn," Arjuna said. "Isn't that correct, Sahadeva?"

Sahadeva stood and explained that by sowing the seeds of the local grasses after a fire, and keeping large herds off the land for two seasons, the river valley could be turned into excellent pasture and farmland.

The subtle Vedic chants still in her awareness, Draupadi heard herself say, "The forest animals will suffer greatly in a fire now."

Arjuna made an impatient gesture. Draupadi imagined his thoughts: It's one thing to allow a woman to be present, another to let her speak foolishness. A second silver arrow lodged in her heart beside the one already hurting, and she vowed to say no more today.

Nakula expressed concern about the local Nishada as well.

"Both of you raise important concerns," Yudishtira said, giving Draupadi a nod of appreciation. She was grateful but hid it.

Arjuna rose, clearly annoyed. "I say, both the animals and the Dasyu will escape. They are going to lose this forest to us anyway. We can take it in a day, or make it slow and painful for both sides, our people picked off by Nishada arrows out of the shadows."

Several Maruts nodded in approval. But Panchalya sided with Nakula, pointing out that the Nishada were in the process of deciding how to respond to the Arya's arrival. To burn their forest would surround the new settlement with Dasyu enemies.

Now Nakula stood. "Fruit, roots, game—it is all close by to feed us, unless we burn it. Why do we burn it? To gain pasture and farmland. But we have only forty-five horses and bullocks. Also three heifers—but no bull. And two farmers sound enough to work the soil." He glanced around. "Besides ourselves of course, if King Pandu's sons plan to follow a plough now."

It was a strong speech for Nakula. Draupadi noticed that Yudishtira was trying to hide his satisfaction.

He looked towards the Vrishni. "Krishna?"

Kunti's nephew smiled his sweetest. "Isn't it odd? Just before I left my father was saying to me, 'Krishna, I know our horses out-race everyone's and have the intelligence of men, and our cows give so much milk that we've had to drain a lake to store the excess. But I'm starting to wonder if these beasts are crocodiles in disguise—eating up everything in the land. Get rid of them—if not next year, the year after—even if you have to drive them into the sea,' he said. Of course I could never do that. So I think you will not lack for horses when you want them, Nakula, or milk cows either, Sahadeva."

Everyone was waiting for his thoughts on clearing the land, but Krishna only smiled benignly.

Yudishtira bowed his head in the gesture of gratitude. "We would be honoured to do the Vrishnis a favour in return for all their generosity by unburdening them of some of their famous horses and milk cows once our pastures are ready. But should your father change his mind, we will certainly understand."

"No, Yudishtira, he was quite adamant. He'll be delighted to be rid of them. You will do him a great service." Krishna's device to persuade Yudishtira to accept another gift had brought grins—including Yudishtira's.

The Marut Vimada asked to speak next. "Those of us from Kampilya have a new king—yourself. We fought the rakshasa with you."

"And you saved my life with a quiver of arrows," Yudishtira said.

Vimada looked around, obviously embarrassed. "We do not wish to offend your brothers. But we want you and you alone to decide, Yudishtira."

There was a faint roll of thunder, reminding them that soon the rains would make any decision about burning irrelevant. "No one here is offended by honest, thoughtful argument, Vimada." Yudishtira paused. "We will all think on this question, but it must be decided—I will decide—tomorrow for certain. Have we other urgent problems?"

"I believe you do," Panchalya said. The thunder came again. The young warrior stood up.

"Five of you have married my sister." Draupadi drew in her breath. "But Eos tells me that still only one of you has bedded her, once. It has been over a month now. How are you going to arrange among yourselves to satisfy her right to children?"

"Not here!" Draupadi whispered.

He did not look at her. "I bring this up here because the decision the five of you make will affect Indraprastha's future, and because it must be clear among yourselves—and among the rest of us as your witnesses."

Yudishtira looked at Arjuna, then Bhima. Krishna cleared his throat but said nothing. The twins stared into their laps.

Draupadi trembled with embarrassment, but she could not blame her brother, for he was utterly correct to defend her position in her new family.

"All right," Panchalya said. "I have a suggestion. Each of you husband her field for three months, then wait one to see if she is with child."

"What does it mean to 'husband her field'?" Bhima asked. "When she is with one of us, does she still see the others? Speak to them?"

"Try to prevent her," Arjuna whispered loudly. Draupadi's face grew hotter.

The discussion went on. Draupadi's hands were shaking, though she kept them folded in her lap. When would they stop talking as if she were a cow to be bred?

Sahadeva stood to speak. "We ought to have a rule that when she is alone with one brother, the others can't come in for any reason." He looked around at his older brothers, waiting for the arguments, or at least the teasing.

"Fine," Arjuna said, palms raised. "If any of us walks in on his brother and Draupadi unbidden, for any reason, he has to leave our fair Indraprastha for a month and wander the forests bewailing his fate. If he bursts in on them during their surata —well—"

"He should leave for an entire year," Krishna said, unable to control his laughing. "Tearing his hair and moaning his stupidity."

Arjuna laughed too. Draupadi was furious now. She vaguely heard Yudishtira whisper, "Enough."

"But who will bed her first?" Nakula asked.

Krishna grinned. "The same old thorny thicket."

"It's obvious," Arjuna said. "Yudishtira must be first, since he has already begun. Then Bhima, then myself, each in order of our birth."

Draupadi stared ahead of her, fighting to contain her anger. That night with him—his promise of "soon, soon". All lies. It would be six months. Much longer if she conceived with Yudishtira or Bhima.

She stood up, shaking uncontrollably with rage. "Arjuna says 'Yudishtira and Bhima first' so he can seed his lotus pond in peace."

Arjuna's face made a display of surprise and pain, but she did not believe it. When Krishna whispered something to him and he smiled, Draupadi lost all control.

"Five ploughs," she said in a low, bitter voice. "Five ploughs, and all of them made of willow wood. I'd rather be sown by the wind than by any of you. All right. Yes. I will *take* Yudishtira first. For three months? Then three more with Bhima? It's said and it's done. My pleasure. Arjuna may have his Dasyu consort." She was shouting now. "But it is *I* who takes each of *you*. I will take you as I please. And *none* of you tonight." She ran from the assembly.

25

Black buck, gazelle and wild buffalo. Ranku, ruru, musk, marsh, spotted and black deer. Leopards, lions, tigers, gavials, crocodiles and cobras. Wolf, jackal, bear, fox, ferret-badger and hyena. Iguanas, hedgehogs, tortoises, frogs, porcupines, snakes and bumblebees. Camel, boar, rhinoceros, monkey, mongoose, otter, frog, elephant and wild ass.

Peacocks, cuckoos, wild geese and ducks. Moorhens, pheasants, woodpeckers and "love-their-youngs". Cakoras, cranes, gallinules and parrots. Cataka, ciccika, cakra bird, osprey, quail and pigeon. Vulture, falcon, owl, eagle, starling, sparrow and curlew. Turtledove, karandava duck, kokila, plava and bhulinga birds.

Sahadeva, "Animals and Birds of Indraprastha"

Where is the new Agni born? He is present in the old plants and in the wood, grey-haired, smoke-bannered . . .

Rig Veda

Arjuna rubbed his eyes and tried to focus again. Look for black figures moving among black trees on a black night. Never stop looking. Could attack any time.

Even I who "see in the dark" see nothing when this tired. Doesn't Yudishtira know it?

"Make your eyes move," Guru Vaja used to say. "Stare and see nothing."

Think and see nothing. Think of a woman and invite your enemy in the gate.

If we had a gate.

A gate to her field, dark and sweet.

Think of defence.

I'm only human, curse them all. I can't stop sneaking beasts without some cleared land around us.

"What about the animals?" she asks a room full of warriors, looking pretty as Saraswati herself. *Women* in the assembly. Why not invite our cleverer servants too?

We must clear. To Yama with these Nishada and every other kind of animal.

Growing lighter. Here come the river mists. Extra care now —they could attack right now. Think it: Right now.

He drew himself up off the trunk of the tree where he had let himself sag. Bad example. Stand straight when change of watch arrives. Thank Indra, it's coming at last.

The chariot was rolling towards him out of the mist. But a white team?

"Krishna!"

"Here with your relief. Since when are you standing guard the whole night?"

"Someone has the fever. I'm today's watch captain—I do what I must."

The replacement took his place behind the tree and Arjuna stepped in beside Krishna, who was holding out a pottery flask. "Something to go home on?"

Arjuna uncorked it and the musky scent of honey wine came out to greet him.

"I know, Arjuna—your eldest Brother doesn't like you drinking madhu. But he doesn't forbid it. Have some to keep me company. You look terrible."

Arjuna took a big swallow, then another. The sweet fire improved his mood considerably. "A difficult enterprise, guarding them all in these woods."

Krishna nodded and snapped the reins. They trotted south into the encampment, where the fires burned low. Krishna stopped and picked up a pot, set a few coals into it with bronze tongs, then returned to the chariot.

Arjuna was dizzy with madhu added to fatigue. "Why are you doing that?" He heard the slur in his voice but could do nothing about it.

"Thought we'd do our morning sacrifice to Agni down the river a league."

They drove on through the waking camp, then into the silence of the mists along the shore. The ground under the trees was hard from the drought and carpeted with dead leaves. The brush was eaten down to almost nothing, so the horses could trot briskly. The wheels squeaked a little, the harness clinked. Otherwise it was quiet. It was as if no Arya had ever passed here before. Only deer melting away into the fog, and resting buffalo and rhino that seemed like boulders until they stood and faced you with lowered heads, their skins shivering off a cloud of flies. Out in the reeds along the shore a group of elephants stopped their bathing to watch the chariot. A cakra bird scolded from a bamboo thicket.

Arjuna glanced at Krishna. Our Vrishni smiles to himself even more than usual, Arjuna thought. Up to something. Arjuna took another drink of madhu. Whatever it is, I'm ready. I'm sick of being their "city walls" by night and hacking at thorn bushes by day.

"Can't do it, Krishna," he blurted out. "Going to have to take them all back to Hastinapura until we've built some walls here. Can't see a cursed thing out there. Rakshasa could have walked right past me last night. And in the rains that are coming? These mists? Hopeless."

Krishna nodded.

Arjuna was beginning to notice the jolting of the chariot and of his stomach with it, when both stopped. They were on a grassy bluff over the river. Krishna stepped down. Arjuna blinked at the bright rising sun and followed the Vrishni, half falling.

Krishna was gathering wood. Next the wood was in a pile in a thick patch of dry grass and Krishna was saying, "Now, my woods-raised friend, which way is the wind blowing?"

Arjuna oriented towards the breeze. Even drunk he knew weather signs. "From southeast and rising. Don't light a fire there or our little sacrifice to Agni could—" Arjuna stopped.

"Yes, Arjuna? You must know what has to be done this very morning, before the rains, and who are the only ones who can possibly do it. He never forbade it. He only said we should all

303

think it over. I have, so have you. There is no other choice, but he can't make it. Don't you see? His dharma is to protect *all* his subjects—Nishada, Arya—why, he probably even counts the cuckoos and ferret-badgers. But our dharma is to do what he needs done. You see? Very logical."

"No, Krishna, can't do that. Can't do it."

"Here, more madhu. Yudishtira wants the land cleared far more than I want it for him—you can see it in his eyes. But how to do it? I have to teach him: One has to take supreme steps to reach supreme goals. I also have to teach him that if one moves fast, the change hurts less. You and I will give him the first lesson."

"But Draupadi will—"

"Draupadi wants her beautiful city too." Krishna took a coal from the pot and dropped it into the middle of the dry wood. "Now sing a fine hymn for Agni."

Arjuna ran to the pile of wood and stared helplessly into its depths. A tiny blue flame sprang from a curled-up pipal leaf. Arjuna reached down into the pile but his fingers couldn't stretch to the leaf. He looked up at Krishna, feeling terror and awe.

Krishna smiled benignly. "You won't sing a hymn to Agni? All right, I will have to sing one." His voice soared in a drunken waver, dipping deeply for emphasis in the metre. "'The great fire at the beginning of the dawn has sprung aloft—'" He gestured grandly. "'And issuing forth from the darkness has come with ra-a-a-diance.'"

Arjuna recognised the sacred hymn which began the tenth cycle of *Rig Veda*. Krishna kept it up: "'Agni, the bright bodied, as soon as born, fills all dwellings with light.'"

It was like a dream—the fire crackling, Krishna singing with strength and seriousness now. Arjuna heard his own voice joining Krishna's. "'May He, who as soon as manifested is vast and wise, defend me, his third manifestation . . .'"

Krishna sprang into the chariot. "And we'd better help him to defend you. That fire is about to burn your buttocks off."

Arjuna sprang after him without looking back at what they had begun. Krishna urged the horses into a trot and continued south. "Time to move on, birds and beasts," the Vrishni shouted, waving the madhu flask. "This is Indraprastha now!"

They stopped again. Krishna dropped a coal into a dead karnikara tree. Flames appeared almost instantly. Krishna pointed back along their path. Smoke was rising from the entire river bluff. The undulating black cloud finally roused Arjuna. "The camp!"

"The fire will move northwest and leave the camp unburned just east of it. Or"— he shrugged—"we'll build another camp."

Arjuna stared at him. The dead karnikara tree was alive again, blossoming with orange flames. The horses were trying to back off from the heat. Krishna reached out and pulled off two unlit limbs and thrust them into the heart of the fire. They caught. He handed them to Arjuna, then whipped the horses hard.

"Light something," the Vrishni ordered. "For Agni's sake, *let us clear this land.*"

Arjuna obeyed without thinking. He reached out and lit a drought-dry acacia as they passed it. Krishna smiled approvingly and turned them east towards the river.

"Are we crossing?" Arjuna yelled.

Krishna nodded.

"But there's no ford here."

"We'll swim then," Krishna shouted. The horses were already up to their bellies, too panicked by the smoke in their nostrils to notice the madness of it.

The water came up over the horses' backs and into the chariot. Krishna held the clay pot on his head.

"Are you sure you know what you're doing, Krishna?"

The white mares were indeed swimming now, the chariot beginning to float and drift downstream, turning the horses upstream.

"I'm sure I know you had better jump out on the down side and kick a little." Krishna put the madhu flask to Arjuna's lips again and tilted it until he choked on the wine. "Keep you going. Now into the water. A little faster, please?"

The cold water cleared Arjuna's head. He saw the whites of the mares' frightened eyes and their vain struggle to obey the snaps of the reins. Arjuna swam in the lee of the chariot and gave it a great shove upstream and shoreward, then another.

"Hiya, white beauties, we'll do this one together. Swim, ladies, curse you. Swim now."

The mares felt the help and redoubled their efforts. One struck shore and lurched up into the shallows, then the other. Water poured out of the chariot. Krishna had the reins hitched into his belt, the madhu flask in one hand and the pot of coals in the other. "Get in, Arjuna. What are you doing in the river like that?"

Arjuna cursed him back under his breath and jumped in. "Could have killed all four of us out there—two dumb warrior-borns and a couple of fine battle horses."

"Not possible."

"I don't know why," Arjuna grumbled. The poor mares were being pressed into a gallop again. They raced up the slope of the river bank, spraying water from their whipping tails. Krishna pointed them due east. At the first dead tree Krishna again threw in a coal, waited for flames, lit dead branches, handed two to Arjuna, and drove on. Whenever something dry came within reach now, Krishna lit it. Arjuna leaned out with one of his own branches and touched it to a thicket of bamboo as they raced past. It burst into flame.

They swept by a thorn thicket. Arjuna lit it. "There's some I won't dig out with an axe!"

They both laughed. Krishna shouted another verse from Veda— "'Come, youngest of the gods, to the presence of those desiring thee.'"

Since they had begun west of the river, crossed heading east, and were now turning north, they were leaving a long trail of fire south of the camp and now on its eastern flank. If the wind out of the southeast held, the fire on the west side of the river would burn northwest and leave the camp in an unburned wedge along the west bank. On the eastern side, where they were now, the fire would burn northwest to the river and stop. Maybe.

They had mounted a north-running ridge. Arjuna could see the river shimmering far away through the smoke that filled the broad valley. It would be an enormous expanse of cleared land. Vast as those other Fields of the Kurus.

Krishna drew up for a moment. "See this? This is Indraprastha, receiving Agni's blessings. Agni, the destroyer. Agni, the showerer of benefits. Destruction, all-consuming darkness. Black smoke and black land. We spread it like seeds on the wind." Krishna laughed like someone gone mad. "*We* spread it. You and I, Arjuna the son of Pandu, Arjuna the little seed!"

The horses bolted forward. "Shout it, Arjuna: Agni, eat! Destroy it all." Krishna waved a burning branch, spewing sparks into the grass.

Arjuna dipped his own and a row of trees burst into flames behind them.

The horses stopped again, breathing hard and trembling. The fire seemed to be all around them now. Arjuna felt a moment of fear. "The wind is straight from the south now. The fire on the other shore will go into camp!"

"If it doesn't, maybe we'll start one there ourselves. We have to cross anyway."

"But our people, the huts—"

"I built the huts and gave you most of those possessions. I give, I take away. Then I'll give you better."

"But my brothers are down there!"

"Everything intelligent will go into the river. Nothing is permanent in this world, Arjuna. All is change. Didn't the forest priests teach you anything?"

Krishna started the horses again and they plunged down the slope, running due west towards the river. Krishna no longer bothered to light fires or urge Arjuna to, for Agni was feasting everywhere. Deer and wild boar were running on both sides of them. Birds collided in the air. Porcupines and snakes were skittering across their path, making the horses snort and shy.

Then they saw their first Nishada—women carrying babies, men carrying older children. Arjuna thought of the likely reaction of Yudishtira and Draupadi. Curse this Krishna!

The horses raced on until the river was in sight, then the Vrishni stopped them. "Out, Arjuna. Into the river. Swim across and help your brothers."

"Where are you going?"

"To pay my debts." The chariot disappeared into the smoke.

Arjuna ran through the margin of marsh and plunged into open water, only then remembering the crocodiles and gavials.

He seized a drifting trunk and pushed it in front of himself. Hanging on with one arm, he unfastened the sheath of the knife in his belt with the other. A sambar buck swam by, then its doe, and finally the fawn, slipping under every wave, terror in its brown eyes. Arjuna shoved it up on to the log and started kicking.

Somehow he made it to the other side, but the sambar buck and doe were gone. Carrying the fawn, he ran into the trees, veering left to catch the trail that followed the river south to their camp. He ran along, dodging animals that darted first towards the river for the safety of water, then away because of the wind-blown smoke coming from the far bank.

Finally he was among the huts. He heard women's shouts, children's terrified screams, men's orders that no one listened to. Draupadi appeared in front of him, wrapped in blue cotton-silk as if she were headed for a feast. "How did this fire start, Arjuna?"

"South of here."

"How?"

"No time, Draupadi. Can you give this fawn to one of the older children? Get everybody in the river."

"The river?" She looked towards the flames she could see, which were on the east shore.

"The fire won't cross. Don't try to save anything. And don't let them try to run away in that direction." He gestured inland. "More fire out there. Just go to the water. This is moving fast."

Bhima ran by carrying old Urutata to the river. Draupadi gave Arjuna a fierce look, but took the fawn.

Arjuna trotted on, then walked. Project calm, he reminded himself. "Into the river, everyone," he called. "Into the river. Don't worry about the huts. Help the children. You there, help turn those horses back. Make them go into the river. That's it.

"Hello, Yudishtira."

His eldest brother was driving his two bays, his chariot filled with some of the remaining families from Hastinapura. "Arjuna, have you noticed? Our forest's on fire." Arjuna had never seen Yudishtira so coldly furious. "Most of the bullocks have run off. Nakula's trying to get the horses into the water but I doubt he'll save many. Was this the work of rakshasa?"

"'The imperishable energies of thee, Agni, the devourer, rush forth like charioteers.'"

"This is no time to chant Veda, you fool. Go and help Nakula to save the horses."

Arjuna bowed his head beneath what he suddenly realised was the worst shame of his life. "May I harness a chariot and try to save some Nishada instead?"

Yudishtira pointed across the river at Krishna unloading a family into the water. "Why not? You have quite a few Nishada to impress with your tender mercy. Arjuna, if anyone dies in this fire—"

"It will be fewer than the rakshasa were going to kill if we couldn't see them coming! I swear it."

A hare dashed between them, its fur on fire. "Get out of my sight," Yudishtira said.

Arjuna ran for the chariots. Nakula and most of the Maruts were there, trying to lead horses out of the circle of carts that had been their stable. Nakula had his four browns, two lead ropes in each hand, but they were dragging him back towards the woods.

Arjuna took two of them from him. "Tie those others. Let's harness these two to a chariot." He turned to the Maruts. "Harness them all if you can, then drive them into the water."

Nakula was grabbing harnesses. They began bridling the browns. The horses were calmer the minute the familiar trappings were across their backs. As Arjuna finally stepped into the chariot and took up the reins, fire appeared at the southwest edge of the camp.

He had planned to drive west, to look for Nishada trying to reach the river. Now he chose northwest—visualising the wedge north of the camp that would still be unburned, and crowded with people. As he drove among the huts he was trying to remember enough Nishada words to say "go to the river".

Suddenly he saw Lotus leave a hut. "The river!" he yelled to her. "Go to the river." But she had entered another hut and was trying to drag out a screaming old woman.

He was driving after her when he saw Draupadi and Eos

beside a bullock cart loaded with Draupadi's possessions from Kampilya. "Are you all mad? For Yama's sake, leave that and get to the water." The two women just stared at him.

A burning tree crashed down a cart-length behind them. Eos glanced back, then obeyed him, apparently assuming Draupadi was behind her. But Draupadi stayed by the bullock's head. "Go on," she said. "I saw. Rescue Lotus. I can take care of myself."

A tree overhead cracked. Arjuna jumped down, hurled her over the side of his chariot, and shouted for the browns to run.

The abandoned bullock bellowed.

"Don't leave that ox," Draupadi yelled.

"I can leave what I choose."

"Lotus! Go back for your Lotus."

"She made her choice," Arjuna shouted as he whipped the horses.

"So did I! The ox and cart!"

He stopped the horses at the edge of the river. "Just save yourself, Wife." He lifted her over the chariot's side and into Eos's arms, then had the horses trotting as soon as they were free of the deepest mud.

Up on the west ridge Arjuna found a small encampment of Dasyu—ten or fifteen, now huddled around a sala tree. "To the river," he said in Nishada. They tried to escape him by running west but their children slowed them down. He caught several of the smallest and yelled in what he hoped was good enough Nishada, "If you want to see these babies again, go to the river." The adults obeyed him, running east down towards the Yamuna. He put the children in his chariot.

He used the same method with other groups, until he saw that soon it would be impossible for anyone to make it back to the river except through a wall of flames. The chariot was loaded with hostage children but it was all downhill and the horses sensed his plan—to race around the front of the flames as they moved up the valley.

But the fire's heat was unbearable as they neared its head, and the flames jumped faster than he had ever seen before. The horses veered away, racing along beside the fire wall. They dodged thickets and crashed over ravines. Arjuna was terrified of losing a wheel. But speed was their only hope, and there was no need to whip the horses. His efforts were better spent keeping children from falling off the back.

They passed through a shower of sparks from a thicket of trees exploding into fire. The horses' manes and tails caught, then his own flowing hair. He beat out the flames on himself but could do nothing for the mares. But even with this new fright, they did not gain on the front of the blazing storm.

The smoke blinded him now—the horses were on their own. How soon before they made a mistake and ran the chariot down a gully too steep to come out of? "Agni, defend us!" he shouted.

A burning sala tree crashed down in their path. The horses leaped aside, up a short, steep slope. Arjuna held on to the children as best he could. At the top he could see a little better. The hillock they were hurtling northeast along was level, grazed clear, and ran straight for the river. But the fire was so close behind and on their right—left now too—always reaching for their path.

"What's your name?" he shouted to the oldest boy at his feet in his stumbling Nishada.

"Fruit Fox."

"Hang on to them, Fox. Don't lose any." The boy seemed to understand and gripped the arms of the youngsters around him.

To the horses Arjuna shouted, "I've seen what you can do, daughters of heroes. Go to the river." Their ears were back, he knew they understood.

He jumped, rolled, and came to his feet running. The chariot had leaped ahead, lighter without his weight.

Now, he thought dimly, how much of a sacrifice does Agni demand?

The air he breathed burned his lungs. He ran as he had never run in his life. The river was close but the fire was closer. His clothes smouldered, his lungs seemed scorched. He veered off the hillock where the fire had breasted it, then cut an angle down towards the river, leaping rocks and logs and bushes until he struck mud and crumpled from the sudden change in footing.

Now he crawled. Dry reeds all around, fire roaring down on him. Finally shallow water. Steaming water. He flattened himself face down in it. The water hissed in his ears. He rolled over to expose his other side and saw an orange tent of flames above him. With his feet he shoved himself out into deeper water. More of the blessed fluid closed over him. Cooler here. He pushed again and saw blue sky over him.

Satisfied at last with him, Agni passed on.

The chariot was upstream and farther into the water, thoroughly stuck in the mud. The horses were twisting and snapping at their smoking manes and tails. He staggered over and splashed water on them. Then checked the chariot: all the children were there, staring up at him. Their people stood in the river upstream. He picked up the oldest, Fruit Fox, and carried him to the shore. "The forest is gone," Fox whispered in Nishada.

Arjuna looked up. The larger trees still stood, each trunk wrapped in smoke instead of branches. The plants and smaller trees had left this world. It was true—the forest had vanished. The loss of so much life of all kinds stunned him.

There was a shout from mid-river. Krishna's two white horses, their faces now grey with ash, were swimming towards him without chariot, harness, or reins. Krishna was on one and a grim, ragged stranger on the other. The mares hit shallow water and stood, then bounded up to the browns and stopped to touch noses and nicker.

Arjuna waded out to them. He stopped by the Vrishni's horse. "Why did we do this, Krishna?" he asked softly.

Krishna didn't answer for a long time. "I don't seem to know, Arjuna."

"Oh."

"What happened to your hair?"

"Agni took a fancy to it," Arjuna said. "How many were you able to save?"

"All the Nishada I saw, plus Lettermaker here." Krishna gestured to the other rider. "Lettermaker, this is my dearest friend on earth, Arjuna the son of King Pandu. Lettermaker has this name, Arjuna, because he can make the signs for words, the art we Arya have avoided. But Lettermaker is also an architect. He is from Babylonia."

"No, Phoenician-born, actually," the stranger said in a passable accent. "But, yes, I was last in Babylon."

"I found him in the forest. Can you imagine? In your forest? The very man who built Babylonia's great cities?"

The man frowned. "I am *not*—"

Krishna interrupted him. "Since he is so grateful to me for saving his life, he has agreed to help us build Indraprastha. Here." The Vrishni stretched out his arm towards the blackened western bank.

"This part is correct, Prince Arjuna," Lettermaker said. "In return for saving my life, I will grant his request and help you."

26

When the times require change, all means gather around
the one who is ready to change.

a Videha saying

They had been hiding among the smoking stumps or standing
in stunned silence on the banks of the Yamuna. But now they
sat in the open, in the ashes—hundreds of angry Nishada men,
women and children, coaxed out by Lotus "to hear the Arya
king".

Yudishtira stepped on to a rock and looked down at Lotus.
Once again his life—perhaps all their lives—depended on her
ability to change his Arya words into Nishada.

"My name is Yudishtira," he began. "I am the son of King
Pandu, and myself a king of the Kurus. This land that has been
burned was claimed by King Drita of Hastinapura, who gave
it to me to protect. I am deeply ashamed of what has happened." He had chosen his words carefully, and ignored the
stirring they were creating among some Arya, including his
family. "This destruction was caused by one of my own brothers
and by my closest friend. You have every reason to hate us.
You outnumber us here today, and if you choose to, you can
try to kill us."

Try? he thought. You can kill us easily. If you've saved
anything from the flames it will be your weapons. Only don't
let me die without a warrior-born's right to fight back!

"But you must first consider your past sad experiences with
Arya. You lack our horses and our hard-metal weapons." He
paused. "You also lack our strange greed to own Prithivi Mater,
Mother Earth."

314

Yudishtira was aware of every Arya staring at him now—his family, the Maruts, the Vrishnis and those from Hastinapura. Speech like this was treason.

So let them think I am talking my way out of a massacre.

"You Nishada will be pushed west into the desert, or north and south into the mountains, or east into places already settled by others. This *will* happen. Kill us and others will come. Or you can live *with* us. Some of your people already live among the Arya."

"As slaves," an old man shouted, using the Arya word. Beside him someone used a ruru deer's skin to hide the stringing of a bow.

"There will be no slaves in my kingdom of Indraprastha. But we wish to build a great city. Perhaps we have no right to build here. However, if you choose to join us, I will see that you live comfortably among us, in your own villages, and I will see you are taught occupations that will make you important to us, so that you will be needed and well paid. You will want to discuss this among yourselves. In the meantime, please camp with us."

Please don't hide in the dark and then attack us in our sleep the way you have every right to.

"And share the food we are preparing for tonight. The rains will begin soon—if you are willing, we can help each other to build shelters. Thank you."

He stepped down, turned his back and walked away, motioning for his brothers to do the same.

Bhima came up beside him. "They've weapons," he whispered.

"I know. Many more than we have."

"Can I bring out our bows now?"

"No! For Indra's sake, give them room to think."

Bhima seized his arm. "At least let's die fighting."

"That way we die for certain," Yudishtira whispered. "This way—"

"We leave it up to them!"

"Exactly, Bhima."

Yudishtira walked on alone towards the river, controlling his urge to look back. He stopped on the shore, the only place of beauty left in his kingdom. How sharp the edges on the things in this world, he thought, when those behind you may be nocking an arrow to send you to the next one.

Well-spaced rocks invited him to step away from the blackened shore.

The wind's rising, he noticed. Soon the rains will begin.

I should be angry. But I can not die angry at Arjuna.

Indra, if I must die angry, let it be in a fight with Suyodhana, who sent us to this place. And let me take him with me to Hell!

He stepped farther out on the rocks. He thought of the piles of charred arrowheads—all that was left of their vast supply of arrows. He remembered the exhausted faces of the Maruts going out to stand guard. Either these Nishada will kill us now, he thought, or the rakshasa can do it tonight or tomorrow, when they learn we are all but defenceless. To die now might even be better—we would be spared a night out in the rain.

He tensed. Something moved on his left, behind a clump of river grass.

Then from behind he heard a bow twang. An arrow split the water by his foot.

He froze. There were shouts behind him in Nishada. Not to move to protect himself required more effort than any Great Leap Aside. But he stood still.

He thought of Eos: If I can not impress the Nishada with one kind of force, I will show them another.

A movement on his left again. He stepped slowly forward to look.

It was only Urutata, kneeling on a rock while performing the water rite. The priest glanced up, an eyebrow raised.

"Better not to stand just now," Yudishtira said quietly.

Urutata went on chanting and pouring the water from vessel to vessel. So far there were no more arrows from behind.

When his Chief Priest was done, Yudishtira whispered, "I regret our continually placing you in danger, Urutata."

"I will admit it is not how I had envisioned my final years."

Yudishtira was almost certain the priest was smiling. "If it had not been Vyasa's wish that you come with us—"

"But, alas, it was."

"If they shoot me, Urutata, dive into the water."

"I have considered that plan already, King."

Yudishtira felt a new wave of anger—that he was in such helpless danger himself, and so without resources that he could not protect and support even one priest.

"Forgive me for failing to give you proper attention since our arrival, Urutata. Have you had what was needed for the rituals?" He felt his jaws tighten. "Not that I can provide anything now."

Urutata shrugged. "With all that Agni has carried for us to the gods already, I think we need offer no more for a while."

Yudishtira looked out across the grey water, still waiting for the arrow that would enter his back. "I suppose you are going to comfort me by telling me not to feel responsible for this fire —'the gods give, the gods take'. Or 'destruction is inevitable'."

"I had not thought of those words. Good ones, though."

"I should have guessed they'd start a burn."

"Probably so."

Yudishtira laughed tensely. "A strange time for my counsellor to offer humour—when Yama is standing on my heels."

"You see? I say all the wrong things. I really make a poor chief priest."

"And what makes a good one?"

"I don't even know."

Yudishtira crossed his arms. "Advise me anyway. If we survive the next few moments, do you think I should punish my brother and Krishna? But perhaps it is unfair to ask you— Krishna was a year in your charge and you are fond of him."

"Who isn't? But I am fonder of my king."

"That is not—" But someone was approaching from behind. "Do not move," Yudishtira whispered.

"I think half of them stayed, Yudishtira." It was only Nakula.

"And half left." Yudishtira's body sagged with relief. A terrible exhaustion replaced the tension. "Then at least the Nishada won't attack us in the night, with some of their people among us. Which only leaves the rakshasa."

"Krishna says not to worry. Enjoy the storm eve. He will see to everything." Nakula rushed on, ignoring his brother's sharp glance. "I feel the same as you, Yudishtira. You know I

317

was opposed to the burning. But perhaps he and Arjuna were in some small way right if now the Nishada will join us."

"Of course they were right, curse them!" Yudishtira rubbed his eyes, feeling a sting from the smoke. "We must take care, Nakula, or Suyodhana and Sakuni will defeat us without ever having to swing a mace. All we have to do is fight among ourselves."

"Yudishtira, the rest of us understand that you had to accept this land."

"Do you? Tonight *I* would rather ride back and strangle our cousin in his sleep."

Nakula and Urutata stared at him.

Yudishtira laughed bitterly. "If you were Arjuna and Bhima, you would be fetching me a horse and speeding me on my way to my murder of a defenceless sleeping man."

From the shore Sahadeva was shouting to them. "You must see this—the Phoenician is like Brahma the way he creates from nothing."

The three on the rock looked back. Every pair of branching, burned tree trunks within sight had a third trunk lying horizontally between it, rested in the lowest forks. Smaller fallen trees had been leaned along these horizontal beams. The skeleton of a village had already arisen.

Nakula pointed to the marshes upstream. Nishada men were scything rushes with Arya battle axes. Their women and children were carrying bundles of reeds to the tree-huts, where the Phoenician was supervising the thatching. Meanwhile, the Arya women were finishing the roasting of one of the bullocks on which Agni had begun.

"Sheltered and fed after all," Nakula said. "For one more night. Perhaps even in the Age of Kali, the season of forgetting, the gods will remember us."

Yudishtira was watching the dark and light bodies weaving in and out among the blackened trees as they worked together. The twilight and the ashes they kicked up made them all appear grey.

Then the first large, gentle drops of rain struck him. He looked up from the camp to the western sky. There was a faint glare of red in the due west, shining in under the clouds. The last of the fire? Or the setting sun? He thought of the yavana whom Krishna had found. Lettermaker was his name. A man from the ashes. A man from the west. And Eos was from the west. And Sakuni's slave. And Sakuni's snake. It suddenly seemed to Yudishtira, as he watched that streak of red sky, that some dream world was trying to wake him to its presence.

That night when the Yamuna's burned soil drank in the first rainfall of the storm season, no rains fell on Egypt. Yet the Supremely Beloved Servant of Amon-Re lay wet and shivering in his bed chamber. It was sweat that soaked his linen bedding again, even though the cloths had been replaced three times in the night.

The illness was still fed by the poisons of excess, but this feverish agony was new. Ten of the Supreme Servant's Company of Fifty knelt around his couch, faces averted from the sight. But they could not avoid the inhuman sounds from the obese, diseased body.

"One of you," the voice commanded between groans. "Tell me something amusing."

Although panting from pain today, the oracle's voice had its old terrorising power. The slaves looked among themselves and silently came to an understanding as to who would accept the risk of speech. "Lord, the pharaoh's mother—"

"That scheming whore is no longer amusing."

"Supreme One, the Assyrians have ordered every Phoenician city north of Joppa to send to Assur once a year the weight in gold of every citizen of every city."

"So the murderers rob the thieves! But Egypt suffers when those filthy pirates can't set sail. And Amon-Re suffers—" There was a retching sound, then a cry. "Azle!"

One of the crouching attendants darted to a carved cask and decanted a little of the tawny liquid. Returning, he offered the cup with shaking hands. Young hands—one did not grow old these days in the service of Amon-Re's Chosen.

The groaning stopped. "The news from Bharata?"

The room was still. The slaves tensed. "Very little, Lord."

The voice was silent a long time. When it came again the words seemed chosen to mask the suffering of both body and soul. "This Sakuni's 'woman of unsurpassed beauty'—when is she to arrive?" He shifted his bloated belly with his hands. The inevitable crude scents were passed. "She and this corpse of mine in love sport—*that* would be almost amusing."

The slaves crouched lower around their master, waiting for the inevitable question.

"And Zesnor?"

"There is a letter, Lord, but it was only from the Sakuni of Bharata." The slave explained the baron's "demon army" —the collection of criminals, runaway slaves and rebelling tribesmen, supplied by their fellow conquered peoples with spies, food, and enough inebriating beverages to make them bold.

"Of course." The voice was stronger now, the azle was easing the pain. "May this foreign imbecile see all the possibilities in that."

"Zesnor is using the azle to control—" The slave stopped himself, shaking with fear.

"Say it! To control them. It can only be that way with the uninitiated. Never with Amon-Re's Own."

"With azle Zesnor controls them, Lord."

The great body lay back slackly. "Zesnor must see something of great value in this Bharata, to use the secret beverage of the initiated. But then he knows that oaths of secrecy only invite violation by turning knowledge into a precious commodity. I truly gave too much when I sent Zesnor with that ugly little man."

"Divine Servant, Zesnor has stopped the demon army's futile, wild attacks. He is training them. Then, the Sakuni says, 'Each of their lives will cost their enemies fifty.'"

"How many are in this army?"

The servant cringed, afraid for his own Ka, then forced a laugh. "He says eighty, Supremely Beloved."

"Eighty? Eighty persons or eighty phalanxes?"

"Ma'at's Friend, he says eighty persons."

The body raised up.

The slave was shaking violently. "Perhaps it was amusing, Divine Voice?"

"Is the baron's nephew now king?"

320

The huddled figures around the couch froze as if watched by a lion. "Lord and Master of Amon-Re's Home, he is not yet king." One of them finally whispered the worst, that the five brothers still lived after all, and that the Love Rope had been used and had failed.

"Failed? Failed?"

"But the five are exiled." The slave spoke rapidly. "These 'demons' especially hate them, for the demon army's leader had two sisters, and one sister was killed by the eldest, the other was enslaved by the middle brother. And this exile will certainly be the end of—"

"No," the Great Voice roared. "This is not to be tolerated. Never. Send Zesnor this message: 'Sakuni will control Bharata in six months. By winter. Or you will bring the man's ugly head back here to Amon-Re.' And after you send that message to Zesnor, you who are not worthy even to hear his name will be tortured until you die. Here, before the God's Own."

The servant lost all control, falling to the floor in a heap. There was an obvious odour of fresh faeces about him, but those near him left him to lie where he was, afraid to draw attention to themselves.

Yet the odour had a strange effect. "When he wakes," the voice said dully, "send him to Nubia for the rest of his life. Even his suffering wearies me."

27

I am the goddess who assumes all forms . . . Ignorant of my true nature, all you gods glory in your omnipotence to no avail.

Shiva Uma

On the day after the fire the Yamuna flowed red-brown with the soil being washed away by the first hard rains falling on the barren earth. The others at Indraprastha could watch the sepia river rise as they moved logs to build some rough defence. Draupadi only heard the river, for at dawn she had begun her monthly bleeding and so she was in seclusion.

Some explained the need to confine a menstruating woman with the mystery of a bleeding that does not bring death. Others understood the blood was not a haemorrhage at all, but only the sign of an unseeded field, rejected by the gods. When the dark and odorous blood was gone, the woman's past failings were gone. It even removed the sin of unfaithfulness, a purification no man enjoyed. But because sin is ever attracted to sin, while this wondrous shedding of error was occurring it could attract undesirable forces—an obvious fact given the woman's unpredictable moods—and so it was best she remained alone.

Draupadi, however, had ceased to question the reasons. She knew only that today she was confined, and not merely confined but forced to lie in bed, for the rough hut built at yesterday's twilight was too low to stand in and the floor was ankle deep in water from the leaking roof. She knew she ought to be grateful—hers was the only bed in "Indraprastha". Bhima had built it during the night, working outside the door of her hut in the dark, the rain streaming down his face. But he had known that without a raised bed she would not sleep, for fear of the snakes the fire and rain had sent hunting for dens across the bare ground around their shelters.

But even on her bed, she had not slept last night or today. In her mind she was still seeing the forest devoured by flames. Every possession—everything from Kampilya, everything Krishna had brought—devoured. The fleeing, falling animals —devoured. An entire world gone.

Yet after all that devastation, today her husbands shouted encouragement to each other as they rebuilt. The others from Hastinapura laughed at their princes' jokes. And even the new Nishada were softly singing work chants or talking quietly, learning the Arya tongue from Lotus.

Draupadi understood. Life went on and there was work to be done. Only she remained inside, alone and feeling too much.

"Daughter of fire." "Control your anger." "She will destroy them."

She twisted on the bed, her womb cramping. She could not escape her thoughts. Impulsive anger had caused her to agree to this miserable marriage. It had also caused her to search for Lotus at Hastinapura and so allow Sakuni to prevent Vyasa from stopping the division of the kingdom. It made her lash out at Yudishtira both when he had sought her comfort after the division and again during their first surata. Anger had caused her to shout her rejection to Arjuna in the assembly and lose him for six more months. And then to rage at him last night about the fire, until Krishna had had to explain that Arjuna had really only watched as he himself had done his mischief. Anger had devoured her life.

And she was being punished. Last night Eos had sworn that when Arjuna and Lotus were reunited at Hastinapura, Arjuna had refused to tolerate Lotus as anything but a servant. But since she, Draupadi, had accused him anyway of bedding Lotus, and had caused him to wait six months until he could bed his own wife, one could only expect him to do what he had done near dawn. What she had *heard* him do, in one of these huts so close to every other.

I will *not* be angered.

She struck out at the roof over her head, then crouched upright on her "bed" of rushes and logs. She was frantic from the dripping of water on to her head. Devoured by fire yesterday, tortured by water today. Nothing was dry. Nor was there any clothing besides what they were wearing when the fire began—no spare skirt to be dried over a fire, no spare cloth with which to wipe her face. Everything had been eaten by Agni. There were only these piles of branches to crawl under, and a few metal weapons and tools with which to rebuild. They had become like the animals they had destroyed—Arjuna crawling like a snake to a woman. Slithering through the rain. To any woman but herself.

I will not be angry. I will be still, without anger, without pain. Like the sages in the forest. No flame, no fire. Nothing.

Bhima's broad, beaming face appeared at her door. "Beloved Draupadi, we have a gift for you."

She wanted to scream, but she only ignored him. Eos stepped in, crouching down, and Bhima went away. "They've finished a better hut for you. It is hot inside because of the fire I lit to dry it. But it has no leaks."

Draupadi now felt tears spring to her eyes, shaken by the unexpected kindness. She crawled out of the hut behind Eos and stood unflinching in the downpour. "How could I have been so cruel? *Again?* And to dear Bhima? I will truly control my anger, Eos. Always."

The rain pounded down on the two women. The Greek merely nodded at the daughter of fire.

The days of Draupadi's seclusion finally ended and she emerged from her hut, bathed, and asked to be put to work. Perhaps trimming logs, for the high wall of defence that had to be raised to secure them before anything but the rudest huts could be built. Or cooking, under the tents that had just arrived from the Vrishnis. Everyone who could move at all had been put to some task—their survival required it. She was eager to join them.

But it was a unanimous decision by a quickly called assembly that Draupadi could not be put to work. Even Eos agreed. Draupadi was a queen.

Furious as their queen was, however, she accepted the decision graciously. She told no one that if she was not allowed to do something useful, she would go mad. That if she listened one more night to Arjuna passing her hut to go to Lotus, she would die by dawn.

Then that afternoon Yudishtira had asked Lettermaker to discuss with her the plans for the palace's royal apartments. Draupadi presumed the Phoenician was sent only to amuse her, but she politely studied the drawings the Phoenician had made on smoothed planks of wood. And she was fascinated. Suddenly Queen Yasoda's boring instructions about the management of a palace gained meaning. But unlike Yasoda, or almost any other Arya with an intact memory of how things ought to be, Draupadi alone could listen to Lettermaker's yavana ideas about palaces without prejudice, while adding her own thoughts from what she had admired and disliked at Kampilya and Hastinapura. By nightfall Lettermaker was calling Draupadi indispensable to the work of building the palace, and the young but dour foreigner said nothing that was unnecessary and certainly nothing that was merely polite. Draupadi had gone to her bed happy for the first time since they had arrived on the Yamuna.

More days passed, and her work with Lettermaker became increasingly satisfying. But then, like the shoots and buds forming in the rains, her fertile time came and grew to fullness, and it forced itself upon her awareness. She was still unbedded, and this month it was her own fault—another result of impulsiveness and anger. On the day before the fire she had dared to decree to the entire assembly that she would choose the time. Now all day they watched where she went. All night they kept the cloth door coverings of the closely grouped lean-tos open, "for coolness". And to listen for her to go to Yudishtira, she was certain.

Which she could not bear to do, not while they waited to watch and make their jokes that she finally wanted a ploughing. She who had screamed so all could hear the last time.

Besides, she told herself one grey but rainless mid-morning

as she stood in her hut's doorway, I could not go to him when he is so tired from building the wall. She had just watched him plod back to his shelter through the mud. What had Eos asked this morning before she went out? "Have you considered Yudishtira's feelings?"

Draupadi reached inside the door and listlessly took off the wall the new bronze mirror Krishna had brought two days ago. It had come with clothing, salt, spices, cooking oils, tools, bedding, harnesses—fourteen bullock carts of essentials, all cheerfully sent by the Vrishnis. All of which reminded her of the debt her husbands owed Krishna, and she thought that perhaps Yudishtira was dejected as well these days, not merely tired.

She looked in the mirror and remembered wondering the day before the fire if her husbands wanted her at all because it had been over a month since one of them had bedded her. Now it had been much longer, and her face looked still wearier, rested as she was.

Like his. My face looks like *his*.

Then suddenly, clearly, it came to her: *He thinks I don't want him.*

She sat down on the bed. The days pass, I said I would choose the time, but I don't send for him. During our first surata everyone heard me scream I hated him. Everyone knows I don't go to him. *Don't want him.*

She went to the door and looked out across the churned mud between her doorway and his. I may have conquered some of my anger, she thought, but pride has replaced it. Pride and Yasoda's twisted modesty.

She dropped the bronze mirror into the mire at her feet and ran barefoot out into the rain.

At his door her certainty left her. But he lifted the door covering before she could decide whether to leave or ask entrance.

"I saw you come back just now," she said. "You seemed so tired that I feared you were ill."

His expression was impossible to read. "No, I am not sick, Draupadi. Do you choose to come in?"

She looked down at the mud halfway up her calves. "Krishna

only brought me fancy shoes. I go out like this and wash when I am on dry ground."

He nodded. "Shall I help you? With your feet? Or will you go back now?"

"No." She was confused. "I will wash them myself."

She used water from the collecting jar under the overhanging eaves of rushes. He watched her. She felt nervous, and her legs looked darker splashed with mud. Why hadn't she first dressed properly?

Finished, she followed him inside. "Yudishtira, it is my opinion that Eos and I have too generous a hut for only two women, even if I am a queen." She swallowed. "With your permission, I will leave it and ask two of the five widows to stay there with Eos."

"And yourself?"

She knelt and continued drying her feet, afraid to look up. "Yudishtira, you understand dharma better than I. Can you tell me why some priests say surata must not take place in daylight?"

He stood over her, large and still. "Vyasa has told me," he said, "that these rules—surata without speaking, only indoors, only at night—they all serve to protect the couple from danger or difficulty. For example, surata in daylight is forbidden only because one can be seen to be inattentive to danger."

"So if the two are inside, alone and well guarded?" She stood up. "As we are now?"

"Then the rules serve no purpose." He touched her face. "They do not apply."

"Our experience tells us we must also guard against each other," she said quietly.

"I think we are wiser about each other now." His hand came down to her shoulder cloth.

"And this time will not be my first." She moved cautiously towards him.

He took the wet cloth off her back and arms. "No, not your first."

Suddenly she drew back to look up at him. Her clothing fell to her waist. His eyes were on her uncovered breasts. All the weariness in her face was gone.

In her mind's eye she saw a sky filled with stars. Against it, between her open thighs, a Dasyu couple blessed her field—a field damp with rain and aching for seed ever since that night when it had been prepared. No, not merely for seed, but for something much more, that her woods-people's blood had understood best. As she opened her arms to this man and saw his serious Arya smile, she heard a soft, warm laugh, almost of victory, and it was her own laugh and her own victory.

28

Yavanas? They are very strange people, much like ourselves.

Yudishtira

It was autumn. The rains were ending, the new year beginning. The little band at Indraprastha had no rain-season rice, sesame or millet to gather for a fall harvest, but they were at last ready to make a small winter planting of the spring-harvested wheat, barley, peas and linseed—now that their most important crop, a high, circular log palisade, had grown up strong around the area that would become the royal palace.

The process of building the wall had produced other achievements as well. A web of roads had been laid out to bring in the logs without disturbing the seeded grassland, and when the outer city wall with its much longer perimeter was built later, these orderly tracks would become the city's streets. The villages of the various Nishada clans that were growing up at the meeting points of the roads would be its districts.

Inside the walls, those few buildings that were easy to construct because they were against the wall were also standing: the granary, which was Draupadi's apartments for now; the guardhouse, Yudishtira's temporary lodgings; and the armoury, which was the only building already being used for its intended purpose. It was filled with maces, spears, shields, battle axes, composite bows and simple bamboo or wood bows, plus five hundred baskets of arrows—all gifts from the Vrishnis.

The palace walls also enclosed the rude huts built after the fire, the staked-out foundations for the new palace, and five large, bright-coloured tents, again provided by the Vrishnis. The tents kept animals, tools and building materials dry, and permitted the citizens of Indraprastha to gather as one people for celebrations.

The first of these celebrations had been conceived in ashes and elaborated during long days of work in deep mud; if they survived—if the wall was up before the rakshasa found them —they would have a magnificent holiday on the very day the last log was lowered into place. On that day, for the first time, they would fly the blue and white banner of Pandu's sons from the watch towers of a kingdom's capital, lay the first palace floor-beam, plant their first winter-crop seeds, thank the gods, feast and rest. And they would remind themselves that everything begun that day would have long consequences thereafter.

That day had finally arrived. During its daylight hours all were free to do exactly as they wished. And Prince Arjuna had chosen to drive out with the queen to survey the flooding of those fields nearest the swollen Yamuna River, and to enjoy with her the new fresh, dry weather.

The king, however, unused to such freedom, chose duty— overseeing the games and entertainments inside the walls. Which left him, as the day ended and the feast was prepared, with nothing to do but stand with Eos near the tent where the evening rituals were about to begin. From there he kept his eyes on the palace gates, finished only yesterday. Yudishtira was waiting for his brother and his wife to return.

The three months since the fire had changed King Yudish-tira. Everyone noticed his vigour, his unfailing attentiveness and gentleness, his ready laugh. There had been endless debates while men stripped bark from logs or women gathered herbs —was it possessing a kingdom or a wife that made the king so happy? But then, as someone would point out, the test was coming, wasn't it? His three months with his wife were almost over.

But Yudishtira knew his time with her was actually not over. Soon there would be no more surata, but she would be in his bed—for almost nine more months. Perhaps it was for this reason that he had rarely indulged lately in the sort of misery he felt this evening.

Tonight, however, he couldn't help himself, and fond as he

was of the Greek woman beside him, he wished she was busy elsewhere—she was much too aware of moods.

When he finally had to break the silence, he made a brave effort to sound perfectly indifferent. "I am sure they will come soon."

Eos only stamped her foot.

"Eos, you are not responsible for her. Nor am I her only husband."

Eos still said nothing.

"My wife's days are her own." Yudishtira slammed the new stone cistern they stood beside with both fists. "It's just that now that we finally have these walls, you'd think Arjuna would keep her safely behind them."

Eos looked at him sharply.

"At least she seems happy, Eos."

"Very happy, Yudishtira. And everyone adores her. She is confident, patient, kind to everyone. And why not? She has everything she wants—her nights with you and her days with him."

"The nights that she gives me are far better than I had hoped for, from any woman," he said quietly. "And now she is going to give me even more. She has hidden it from me, but I know it: The queen is carrying my child."

"No one else's."

"You don't need to reassure me." He was surprised by the irritation in his voice. "But why hasn't she told me, Eos?"

"She says she waits in order to surprise you. But can't you guess the real reason? She fears your 'dharma of women', which instructs her to forgo surata until its birth. Which makes me think you also give her more at night than she had hoped for."

The great gates began to creak; then in the open entrance Arjuna's team of four whites was prancing prettily—a new trick he had taught them. They trotted through with their free grace, the queen and the prince standing side by side in a gold-leaf wedding-gift chariot, each driving a pair of the horses. Draupadi waved as the team turned towards the stable tent.

"Yudishtira!" Arjuna called. "Congratulations!"

Draupadi shouted a rebuke to Arjuna, then laughed. And they were gone.

Yudishtira felt an irrational anger grip him. "She has told him before me, it seems."

"Or perhaps he guessed, as you did," Eos said with sympathy. "Will it please you to have a child?"

He answered with great control: "Immensely, whether a son or a daughter."

"If you can't have the mother, you can at least have her offspring? And keep her in your bed for nine more months, where no one else can touch her?"

Yudishtira stiffened as she forced him to look again at the truth. But he could obtain a small revenge. "Now that you have stirred up certain uncooled ashes of mine, my dear friend Eos, shall we discuss your own smouldering fire? Does your quick temper lately have anything to do with the Phoenician architect? Or is it the full moon? Maybe you can even tell us why he is so secretive, Eos."

She glared at him. "Secretive? It has nothing to do with me —he is only a runaway slave or a criminal, I'm certain. But if you want to know more, I will make him talk tonight. As easily as you make babies. You think I can't? I will force him to tell you more than you ever wanted to hear, Yudishtira. As for the full moon, I think it has you seeing two people in every bed. Now find your wife and let her explain herself to you, and leave me be."

At the feast, Draupadi took some of everything. She had felt slightly ill in her stomach earlier, but now that the hot breads, boiled and roasted meat, river rice, and tubers with herbs in broth were all being offered to her, she was almost frantic with hunger. Then came the barley cakes soaked in madhu. She had to have not one but two. And only a little spoonful of the curds, as there was as yet so little milk. But the sweet fresh cheese appealed to her even more than honey.

A child. She calculated it again. Perhaps seven months until she gave birth. Perhaps a month, maybe two, before she went to Bhima for three. Eight months and three months—Eos said she would probably not conceive while she nursed a child— and then the month to be sure. Next year at this time, Arjuna.

Not that she had been the least unhappy in Yudishtira's bed.

Not at all. And with him, at least, she could speak freely.

She looked from Arjuna to Eos, seated next to him. Her Greek friend was glaring back across at Lettermaker, who was on Draupadi's right. Before entering the tent Eos had whispered, "I feel strange tonight, Draupadi. Stay by me." Now she sat erect and stiff, her fists clenched, her face lovely. Draupadi wished she knew what to do for her.

The taciturn Lettermaker, on Draupadi's right, was also handsome tonight, in his white tunic, with his sun-darkened skin and his flowing red-brown hair and beard.

Draupadi was about to speak in the hope of breaking the odd tension among them when Eos said loudly, "Lettermaker, it is time for you to tell why you left your homeland."

Her abruptness silenced the others in the circle—the five brothers, Krishna and Panchalya. The demand was rude, but Draupadi knew they were not shocked, but merely thought they were observing the strange way yavanas spoke to each other. And with the meal almost over, they were ready to enjoy a story no matter how Eos coaxed it from the man. Both foreigners were being honoured tonight for their help since the fire, and curiosity about them was stronger than ever.

Lettermaker's young but weathered face bore its usual expression, a mask of unimpressed caution. "You know I do not speak of my past."

"Why did you leave your homeland?" Eos repeated loudly.

As moments of awkward silence passed, Draupadi sensed them all wondering what the yavana was so ashamed of. Was he a criminal then, as Arjuna had first feared? But Lettermaker had ignored the opportunities to rob them artfully arranged by Arjuna and Sahadeva. In fact, the yavana worked as hard as any of them, not only at planning the city but also at hauling logs and digging foundation trenches. Draupadi saw that she would soon have to end the painful pause in conversation, much as she herself wanted to hear his answer.

"My father was Phoenician." His voice was level but too loud. "My mother was his slave."

Draupadi smiled across at Arjuna—Eos had won.

But Eos still pursued him, like a badly trained hunting dog.

"Just say you are a yavana. You say 'Phoenician' to try to make them feel ignorant, don't you?"

"That is never my intention. It would not be polite." His voice made the suggestion about Eos's own conduct very clear.

Eos scowled. "Go on."

"My father purchased my mother at a port at the western end of the Great Sea."

The Greek interrupted again. "He means the sea of my homeland. You of course have your own sea."

"Thank you, Eos," Lettermaker said. "I'm sure you are right."

Draupadi almost smiled at them both. She offered the Phoenician a honey cake but he kept his eyes on his apparent opponent as he continued. His father had died when Lettermaker was twelve. His mother had been freed, but being a concubine, she and her daughter and Lettermaker were turned out of the house. However, like the sons of all wealthy Phoenicians, Lettermaker had already been taught to read and write. This made him a valuable commodity, so his mother sold him in order to buy passage for herself and her daughter to return to their homeland. "It was that or sell herself, but I was worth more." He shrugged. "And I was glad not to be going to live with her barbarians."

The mask had become more rigid—Draupadi was beginning to understand.

"A Phoenician who knew my father bought me and took me to Egypt, where my owner enrolled me in a scribes' school so that I could learn the Egyptian style of writing and conduct his trading affairs at Memphis."

"So you are a runaway slave," Eos said.

He ignored her. "In Egypt I was able to indulge my real interest, which was architecture. Tyre, where I lived my first twelve years, was constantly being designed and redesigned to make it more impregnable. And all Phoenician children grow up watching ships being built. So I had approaches to construction that the Egyptians had not imagined. Pharaoh's vizier eventually noticed my talent and purchased me, at a sizeable profit to my first owner."

The Phoenician went on to describe being sent south to the king of Nubia, as part of a large payment intended to keep the Nubians from invading Egypt. "They did anyway, more or less, but I was already in their miserable country, building poor copies of Egyptian temples for the pious Nubian nobles, who worship Egyptian gods more fervently than even the Egyptians do. That is when I ran away.

"First I had to hide in the desert until my hair and beard had grown out to cover. Pharaoh's slave brand on my cheek and neck." He spread his beard to show them. "The eye of Horus. Then I worked on river barges back to Egypt and joined a caravan to Sumeria as a pack saddler, for I was determined to see Babylon and Ur. The caravan took the longer but easier route, north through the land of the Hebrews and Arameans, then down the Euphrates River. The caravan master swore he'd paid the proper Assyrian officials, but we were taken in a raid anyway."

"Very Assyrian," Eos said under her breath.

"Somehow I was able to demonstrate a talent or two before all my skin had been flayed off, and so I saw Assur first, before Babylon. I saw Assur for several years, in fact—every brick of it—while I was a slave, a slave overseer, and then the king's chief architect, building yet another new temple to Ashur, their supremely boring god."

"Assyrians," Eos said. "Mean and dirty, all of them."

"There we agree, Lady Eos. Were you someone's concubine in Assur?"

Draupadi controlled an urge to smile—the foreigner could attack as well as defend.

"Probably the same man that whored with you," Eos hissed.

Several at the table were discomfited by such harsh speech, but Lettermaker's face remained utterly without emotion. His eyes were fixed on Eos. "I finally had my wish," he said softly. Then he looked around at the others. "I was sent to Babylon. This city is south of Assyria, in Akkad. And Ur is south of that, in Sumer. All the cities of Akkad and Sumer are much weaker now than the barbarians all around them in the hills. So one year some of these cities 'invited' the Assyrians to help rule them—that is, protect them in return for servitude—

rather than see their beautiful palaces, temples and libraries further ransacked."

He told how the Assyrians were constantly struggling to appear as cultured as their sophisticated but declining southern neighbours, so were proud to help the cities. "And I was part of their first effort. Initially, of course, we had to refurbish the decrepit forts and enlarge the Babylonians' temples to Ashur, usually taking stone from the other temples. But we were allowed to do a little restoration on the most sacred of the old buildings. Mainly Marduk's temple in Babylon, then Nanna's temple in Ur."

"What exactly is a temple?" Bhima asked.

In spite of Eos's accusations, Draupadi saw that Lettermaker, far from trying to show them up, was embarrassed at having assumed too much. He explained the belief, prevalent in the northwest, that the gods wanted elaborate homes, food and clothing. "Your Dasyu feed their lingas and tree gods, do they not?"

"But other western people are like yours, Bhima," Eos interrupted, "and give their offerings under the sky, or in their own homes."

"How do you persuade a god to stay indoors?" Bhima asked.

"You don't, actually. You worship its statue. Ordinary stone or wood."

"You did well to run away, then," Eos said. "You can't say that in Ur and live long, the ignorant pigs."

"Apart from their religion, I found them highly learned, Eos." And for Sahadeva's benefit Lettermaker described the Babylonian method of calculating the volume of cisterns and reservoirs. "You, Yudishtira, will be more interested in the Assyrians' inventions for defence."

Sahadeva grinned at his eldest brother. "Oh, Yudishtira enjoys mathematics as much as I do—especially adding points on dice."

"Our king is well educated and enjoys many arts and sciences, Lettermaker," Eos said. "He needs nothing that Assyria would have to offer."

"I am aware of that. Bharata's astronomy and healing arts are far more advanced than even Babylon's. Many aspects of your agriculture and metal-working have impressed me too, as well as your astonishing way with wood."

"Therefore they have no need for things Assyrian," Eos concluded emphatically.

But Lettermaker went on as if she had not spoken. "One remarkable weapon of the Assyrians, Yudishtira, is the very hotly flaming substance one can put on arrows or float on boats or toss down on to those pounding on your gates."

"The Arya have banned fire from warfare," Eos said coldly.

"They also have battering rams," Lettermaker added. "Siege houses, tunnelling equipment, and armour for horses as well as men."

"I could have told him all that," Eos said.

Arjuna was leaning forward. "But you didn't. Why?"

"She did tell me," Draupadi said.

"I did not think that new ways of killing would seem important to Yudishtira," Eos said. She glared at Lettermaker.

There was a long silence. Draupadi asked Lettermaker about his name.

"Whatever the language, I use its words for 'a man who writes', so my value is instantly recognised."

"Except in Bharata," Sahadeva said. "Where many useful things go unrecognised."

Lettermaker laughed. "But Sahadeva, I could easily teach you to write."

Sahadeva looked at Yudishtira. Krishna, who had been silent all evening, suddenly broke in. "If you are not going to tell us why you came to Bharata, you can at least finish telling us how you came."

Lettermaker looked around at them. "When I'd seen enough of Ur I told my overseer that I needed to see it 'from a distance', for architectural reasons. I walked to the top of the nearest mountain, took my look, then just kept right on going, south-east."

Krishna persisted. "Why not back to Phoenicia?"

"In Ur I heard of your philosophers who teach harmony among citizens and rulers. No one weakening another."

Yudishtira spoke for the first time. "Ahimsa, non-harm."

Lettermaker nodded. "Warriors protecting the husbandmen

337

and priests, priests guiding the warriors and the husbandmen, the husbandmen feeding the warrior and priest. And the king serving them all. *Serving* them. So I came to see if it was actually being lived, or was only philosophy." Lettermaker bowed slightly towards Yudishtira. "It lives."

"I think you need to explain to the king more exactly why it is so important to you," Eos said.

Lettermaker lowered his eyes.

"Go on," Eos insisted.

"In most of this world—what I have seen of it—the strong persecute the weak. Subjects live in fear of their rulers."

"Now we are closer to the truth about yavanas," Eos said. "If you are going to tell them about the 'glories' of their mathematics, you must tell them about the rest."

"In Assur I saw a king order a human pyramid," Lettermaker said quietly. "People are piled on to other people with cranes. The ones on the bottom kept in place at first by knife point, until they can no longer move. Then they begin to scream from the weight." He picked up his cup and drank. "I have also seen persons flayed until their skin was gone. Ripped apart by horses galloped in opposite directions. Castration of course, often. Eyes poked out with hot irons. Babies cut from living wombs."

Lettermaker looked sideways at Draupadi and shrugged. But in the gesture she saw his struggle to stay unaffected. "Persons bricked inside pillars or walls. That's a favourite death for architects who do poor work. I watched several acquaintances end that way. Bad cooks are tied out in a field to be eaten alive by insects and birds. And almost anyone can be burned alive."

"The evil face of the Age of Kali," Yudishtira said softly.

"The face of the West," Eos said. "It's true the yavana have one or two interesting inventions. But when you open the door for a peacock, the vulture can also fly in."

"I consider myself neither a peacock nor a vulture," Lettermaker said. "Perhaps a quail."

"You bring the possibility of these things just by talking about them!" Eos shouted.

"All this he's described is terrible, of course," Arjuna said.

"But if we adopt those yavana weapons not forbidden by dharma, they might make all the difference some day."

Eos stood up. "Fools' talk. Your 'Age of Kali' will seem like a wedding compared to what happens when you welcome a few more yavanas like this one into Bharata." She strode from the tent.

Draupadi had hardly heard Eos's words—she had been watching tears filling her friend's eyes for the first time. Draupadi stood to follow, but so did the Phoenician, who gestured for her to stay.

"*You* are going after Eos?" Bhima said to him. "Better to send a jackal to soothe a hare."

"It's all right," the yavana said. "This is more like one porcupine comforting another."

He found her leaning against a tent pole, crying softly.

"Who did what to you?" he asked.

"*I do not talk about it.*"

"In there that was my defence, but you forced me. Now I will force you. Or should I assume someone somewhere did their very worst to you, and then forget what I can imagine?" He shook her by the shoulders. "You are free now—it's you who must forget."

"Never." Hatred burned through her tears. "You weren't a *female* slave."

He loosened his grip and merely held her. "You are right. I was fortunate. So you'd best talk about it after all. Let's start in the present and then go into the past. Which one of the five brothers enjoys you?"

She tore out of his hands. "None of them, you filthy yavana!"

"So they don't bed 'filthy yavanas'?"

"I don't *want* a man."

"Where were you before you joined up with the sons of Pandu?"

"I guarded women."

"And took your lovemaking with women? How very Greek."

"Phoenician men have their own reputation," she said coldly.

"When we are at sea we do what we can. And we're as long

as our boats. But we bathe more often than men from Ur."

"Men from Ur smell like they bathe in faeces."

He studied her. "So they were the last men to have you?"

"The last men who will ever have me. I will die first."

"That's very sad for you."

"But it's true."

"Do you use the herbs to prevent childbearing?"

"I was a slave woman who lived past fifteen, wasn't I?"

He kissed her quickly on the mouth. She struck him. But only after some hesitation. He made no move to protect himself.

"You would be a happier woman with a lover," he said.

"No, you would be a happier man if I agreed."

"Yes, I would be. I admire you more than any woman I have ever met."

"Admire!" She turned away from him.

"What shall I say? If I praise your beauty, you will be reminded of some slave market. If I say I need you, you will tell me to vanquish needs."

"I hate a man's touch," she whispered.

"I know. Ur."

"It's not Ur. I hated them all."

"You hated every one since the first time."

"He killed my mother. I was only twelve."

"Was he Phoenician?"

"Assyrian."

"Was it only one the first time?"

She bit her lip. "You know the answer to that."

"And it hurt terribly, so many," he said. "But what was worse was that suddenly you had no family to avenge your shame. You might die and no one would know. You even wanted to die. Except you were afraid to."

She nodded her head.

His tone was still even. "But never any Phoenicians?"

"No."

"No?" He dared to touch her hair, just a moment.

"No Phoenicians," she said. She stared at the hand she had allowed to touch her. It came back to wander down her cheek and caress her neck. She drew back but it came with her, gently.

"No Phoenicians? Then we're all right. Phoenicians live by the sea and write with pens, just as the Greeks do." He took her hand and kissed it. "Most important, Phoenicians are not men at all. Don't you remember anything from your childhood? 'A Phoenician at sea—half fish, half boat.'"

She was trembling and wanted to run. But the rhyme from the past stopped her. She stared into his eyes, seeing a clear, blue-green sea. "'Half fish, half boat,'" she repeated. "'and the girl who nets him has one year's good luck.'"

"With your permission, Achaean girl, your year starts tonight."

29

A hope can be as confining as an oath—tomorrow's walls
rise from today's wishes.

Draupadi

How many fires are there, how many suns, how many
dawns, how many waters? I address you, O Pitris, not in
rivalry. I ask you, sages, in order to know the truth.

Rig Veda

Lettermaker left Eos at dawn for the dining tent. After the
feast the night before, only Sahadeva was up and breakfasting,
for both he and Lettermaker preferred their work over sleep.
The Phoenician ate heartily and hummed a tune to himself.
Feeling generous, he again offered to teach the young prince
to write.

"I thank you for your offer, Lettermaker," Sahadeva said. "I
hope I shall continue to learn more from you. But my brother
forbids anyone to learn. The priests say the use of writing will
be another sign of the loss of dharma. The coming Age of
Kali."

"But does Yudishtira fully comprehend the possibilities? Or
is it that the priests don't wish to lose their role as the sole
source of knowledge? After all, if what they've memorised were
in writing—"

"I know. Please do not remind me."

Lettermaker served himself more steamed barley and sesame
paste. "But what are their arguments? Perhaps you could refute
them."

"Never. They say the writer makes a symbol of reality, losing

342

the reality itself. Each reader sees the symbol differently—each one distorting reality."

"But this is equally true of those who hear speech, Sahadeva."

"With writing, the symbols are strung together in a chain of errors which are spread far from the mind of origin, where no reader can question that mind and clarify any misunderstandings."

The Phoenician slammed down his cup. "But the advantages!"

Sahadeva ignored him. "In time persons who obtain their knowledge by reading will lose all ability to question a source of knowledge deeply."

"Yet the knowledge that could be preserved! Made widely available, anywhere, any time."

Sahadeva stood, his hands shaking. "I tell you, don't speak to me of what we lose. I feel it more deeply than you."

With minimal courtesies, the Arya youth left the tent. But instead of going to his work he went to the stables to obtain a mount and ride out his frustration.

Meanwhile Arjuna had gone straight to his task that morning —overseeing the day's construction. And since Indraprastha's defences were his chief interest, he had chosen to inspect the archery platform above the new palace wall. Krishna was with him.

"Excellent," Arjuna said to the Nishada carpenter. "A small outer opening. But the slots have to angle down more, Badger. Imagine shooting at rakshasa right below—you may be doing it soon. Don't be shy with your chisel—a good sharp angle down."

Arjuna turned to the Vrishni. "We need allies, Krishna. If only I could go and talk to some of our old friends. But this afternoon I take my turn overseeing logging. Tomorrow I plant. I can't believe Yudishtira makes *everyone* plant. I've barely shot a practice quiver in three months."

Krishna smiled his own particular smile. "Then there's been your responsibility to your wife and queen, to show her each blade of grass as soon as it sprouts."

Arjuna was ready to protest but Krishna waved his hand. "Why not? The outings do her good. I do notice Sahadeva doesn't plant, however, although he does work in the ground. Of course he would pound us both if he heard us even mention it out loud."

They both glanced down at two Nishada crossing the court-yard carrying a litter of shovelled earth from the tunnels. The idea of underground passages was Lettermaker's, but it was Sahadeva's personal project. Although the Yamuna Valley lacked stone for building a true yavana fortress, at least this particular yavana solution to flaming arrows and other lawless forms of attack could be used at Indraprastha—provided the tunnels remained a secret.

Krishna pointed below to the armoury, which was built against the wall. "Speaking of secret escapes, it seems the happy couple who brighten our nights with their love-sounds now look for a little daylight privacy. Imagine, Yudishtira not working for two days in a row. But of course that's because Draupadi was so occupied yesterday, and today she's free, since you are busy elsewhere."

This time Arjuna felt he had to protest, but Yudishtira and Draupadi were already almost under them, walking quickly hand in hand towards the armoury. "I only take her out *because* she spends her nights with him," Arjuna whispered.

Krishna raised his eyebrows.

"I enjoy her company now. *I like my own wife.* Is that wrong?"

"You've convinced me. Convince me more and I'll doubt you."

"She's very curious, never forgets anything I show her. I swear she could take over any of our jobs."

"And would if you let her," Krishna whispered back. But the couple had gone inside the armoury, out of hearing. The Marut Vimada took up his position at the door beneath them.

There was a distinct giggle and sound of struggle from beneath them. Krishna smiled at Arjuna.

"Surely they aren't still doing it now that she carries a child."

"Time of year, Arjuna. 'After the rains the Arya plough their fields'."

344

"But not once a woman is with child," he repeated frantically.

"I've heard you went to Lotus last night."

Arjuna flushed. "I suppose everyone knows she carries also."

"Not yet. Send her home, Arjuna."

"I can't! No Nishada would marry her now."

"Then send her to Hastinapura to serve the queen. It would be fairer. What life can she have here? She's a Dasyu in love with a prince."

"Maybe I could go and serve the queen too," he jested almost bitterly.

"Tired of Indraprastha so soon?"

Arjuna looked away.

"Or tired of this?" Krishna referred to another spate of laughing coming from the armoury. There was a cry of pleasure and the planks they stood on trembled. Arjuna was about to vent his surprisingly strong annoyance when the appearance of a guard's head at the top of the ladder at least explained the shaking.

The Marut guard rushed to them. "Sahadeva says rakshasa may be up on the plain. He saw smoke from a campfire."

Arjuna raised clenched fists. "The chance to catch those hyenas in camp. Krishna, want to go hunting?"

"Definitely." Krishna smiled his broadest. "But you'd better take a big party and arm them well."

Arm them. Arjuna turned to the guard waiting for orders. "Go down and ask Vimada to tell my brother we need to go into the armoury."

The Marut reddened and hesitated. It was already a saying that "there are no secrets in Indraprastha".

But Arjuna insisted, and he and Krishna watched the two Maruts conversing in whispers below them. The outcome was clear: Yudishtira had given his own orders not to be disturbed and a king's orders overruled. Now if these rakshasas had actually been seen—

Arjuna went for the ladder. Krishna was right behind him. The two guards left the armoury doorway to them gladly.

"I'll knock," Arjuna said decisively. But he didn't.

"Maybe they aren't in the main room," Krishna whispered. "You could just go in quietly and take what we need."

"I'll have to try." Arjuna opened the door and slipped into the shadowy room.

Draupadi's scream ran through Pandu's third eldest like an iron shaft. Then there was Yudishtira's shouting.

Arjuna backed towards the door but Krishna had come in behind him. "Gone this far, may as well collect the arms," Krishna whispered.

"I can't *see*," Arjuna cried, caught between Krishna in the light behind him and this before him in the dark.

"Krishna? Arjuna? Is it only you?" Yudishtira sounded equally confused.

"Yes, we need more arms. Sahadeva thinks he's found some rakshasa."

Staying outside, Krishna reached past Arjuna and opened the door wide. In the full light Arjuna saw Draupadi and Yudishtira struggling up off the floor, their garments lying around them like flower petals.

The terrible silence was broken by Krishna's low laugh. "Well. I think you'd better prepare your chariot, Arjuna. You seem to be going travelling for a year."

"What do you mean by that?" Yudishtira demanded. He was on his feet, pulling on clothing.

"Wasn't that the rule when one of you walks in on another during surata?"

"This was not yet precisely—" But Yudishtira didn't finish.

Draupadi came and stood behind Yudishtira, pale gold cloth loosely wrapped around her dark gold body. "What's happened?" she asked softly.

Arjuna thought she had never been more beautiful. He glanced away while his brother answered her.

"Arjuna needs arms so he's come in. And you know our agreement. A year of exile."

"But that was a joke!"

"And Arjuna was trying to do his duty," Krishna said, following Arjuna in. "This is one agreement best ignored."

Yudishtira glared at the Vrishni, then turned his back on them all. Facing a wall of spears, he gave his judgment:

"Arm twenty. We'll go immediately. As for our 'joke' of an agreement, it served an important purpose. Can we weaken ourselves with exceptions right at the start?"

"There's also your military weakness if you send him away," Krishna said softly.

"Indraprastha can be defended without him," Yudishtira said with some annoyance.

"I agree," Arjuna said, his head lowered. He could only think how badly he wanted to run from this place and this time. "I will collect the necessary arms."

"Wait!" But Draupadi fell silent as soon as she heard the desperation in her own voice. They all felt it, like a blow— her deadly power to divide them.

"Draupadi—" Arjuna gestured helplessly.

She shook her head, as if more words would undo them, for she was almost crying openly. Arjuna moved to take down some bows.

"No, Arjuna," she whispered. "Don't go."

He stopped. Yudishtira turned around and stared at her. To Arjuna the room had the atmosphere of a battlefield the moment before the conch blast ordering the advance.

Again the Vrishni's laugh ran through the room like water on a fire. "It seems I'm the only one to gain—I must return home tomorrow, and it would be a great comfort to have Arjuna accompany me. There could be worse exiles, Arjuna."

"It's not up to me," Arjuna whispered, his eyes on Draupadi. "Right now all I know is that I need bows and quivers." He walked to the racks.

Krishna mumbled something about gathering the men needed for the foray, and left. Draupadi stepped slowly out into the light to finish arranging her clothing. Without meeting her eyes, Yudishtira went to help Arjuna.

But after stringing one bow, the eldest dropped it. "Arjuna, you should not have come in," he whispered.

"And you should not have brought her here!"

"Better to an armoury," Yudishtira whispered back, "than what you did yesterday—taking her out where rakshasa could kill you both."

"What are you accusing me of?"

Yudishtira looked shaken. "Yama save us, I hope I'm accusing you of nothing. But I don't know."

"Curse it, Yudishtira," Arjuna whispered, "*I don't want her. I'm glad to be going.*"

"Glad? And who will she blame for your going? But then, if she did blame you, she never stays angry with you anyway," Yudishtira whispered bitterly. "You can bed your consort almost before her eyes, burn a forest, treat her like—"

"She's young!" Arjuna's voice was almost a wail. "She only *thinks* she loves me—"

Yudishtira slammed his fist into the rack of spears. "Stop it! Arjuna, what in Brahma's name are we doing? I'm sending you from us for a *year*."

Arjuna bowed his head.

"We can not quarrel now." Whispering again, Yudishtira put his hands on Arjuna's shoulders. "Listen to me. Maybe not now, but some time this year you are going to wonder if I held you to this agreement to be rid of you."

"Why would I think that?" Arjuna broke free and grabbed another bow. "I only hope we kill every one of those demons today. If you're attacked while I'm gone, I will—"

"If we're attacked, we'll save one for you and finish off the others on our own. Arjuna, do you understand? That you're going gives me no satisfaction?"

Arjuna stared at him, then set down the bow and faced him. "Do you understand that it pleases me very much that you and Draupadi are happy in your surata? It pleases me even more that she carries your child."

They both looked at Draupadi. She stood alone in the square of bright doorway.

Arjuna snatched up a quiver, wishing he could slam it on the floor and let its hundred arrows fly. It was the helplessness he could not stand—the feeling that a moment ago it had not happened, and now it was done. He kicked a basket of arrow tips out of the way. "Make her take some of the blame," he whispered. "You came here together—it takes two wheels to move that particular chariot. For that matter, blame me. I knew you were in here and I could have waited. Tell her all that. Or I will." Arjuna turned around, but Draupadi was gone.

Outside the armoury the sunlight was blinding, but she did not have to see to feel the stares of the labourers. Everyone had known her rooms were being painted and Yudishtira's were being floored; everyone had seen her and him rushing to the armoury, laughing; everyone would have seen Arjuna come to the door. She finally turned and ran from their eyes, through the open main gate.

The Nishada working in the fields had been frightened by the rumour of rakshasa and were streaming in. She pushed through them. Someone was coming out after her. She ran faster but her sandals were slipping in the mud. If it were Arjuna—

But they were Yudishtira's arms that caught her as she stumbled.

She waited for the questions: Where are you going? Have you no concern for yourself? For those who must guard you? *Have you no concern for my child?*

He didn't say any of it. His embrace felt oddly gentle rather than restraining. The pleasures she had been enjoying with him a few moments ago crossed her awareness like smoke.

But there could be no pleasure with Arjuna gone. Certainly no pleasure with the one who had made Arjuna go. This fool of unbending *rules*.

Someone else came. It was Eos.

"The Maruts are asking for you, King. And none of us should be out here if rakshasa are nearby."

Draupadi slipped free of Yudishtira without meeting his eyes. Finally he had gone.

"I heard," Eos whispered. "But you must come inside."

Draupadi followed her numbly back through the gate. Krishna fell in step beside them. "I'm sorry, Draupadi."

"You are *not*," she said fiercely. "You goaded them into it. Your 'one agreement best ignored' and 'Arjuna is badly needed here'!"

Krishna looked again but did not refute it. When they came to Draupadi's rooms and Krishna followed her in, she told him to leave her presence.

Instead Krishna closed the door behind them. "He wanted to go anyway, Draupadi."

"No! He loves me."

"He loves you but he still wants to go."

Draupadi walked to her bed, recalling Arjuna's previous signs of restlessness and feeling the truth descending on her like a sickness.

"Why are you telling her this?" Eos said.

Draupadi lay down. "Did he do it on purpose? Tell me, Krishna. He didn't, did he?"

"He took a chance because he needed the arms. He hoped you were not in the front room."

"He knew we were in the armoury?"

"He also heard your lovemaking."

"Why in all the gods' names are you telling her all this!" Eos yelled.

"She would find out anyway. She sees too far into things." Krishna reached for a chair but Eos grabbed it from him. He ignored her. "It was fate, Draupadi."

"Fate?" Her hate for the word pulled her off her bed. "Some are already saying 'fate' started the fire that burned our forest also. Is fate now named 'Krishna'? You *chose* to start that fire. Well, if I wish, I will choose to follow Arjuna."

She saw Eos recoil. "I will, Eos. On foot if I have to."

"You will not do that to Yudishtira," Eos said.

Krishna bowed. "As she says, she will do it if she chooses to."

Eos looked from one to the other. "You're possessed, both of you. It would kill Yudishtira. And destroy the five brothers' trust in each other. It would all be over."

"It is all over whenever she chooses to end it," Krishna said. "It will always be that way. Anything she can imagine, she can do. But will she? Knowing her origins, I think not."

Draupadi stood up and came to him, feeling she was a fly caught in a spider's web. "*What do you know about me?*"

"What I know doesn't matter. The past is a waste of time, Draupadi."

"How dare you decide for me. Tell me!"

"You will be told, at the right time. If and only if you stay here with Yudishtira for the entire year Arjuna is away."

"You demon! How can you bargain with my love?"

"It is the only way to bargain with you at all, Draupadi. You and I have our own rules, don't we? For us there's really only love. I've learned to love you, but I've learned to love these two husbands of yours just as much. I will do all I can for all of you. This is why I must bargain with your other love—your old love for these childish memories you have lost."

The three stood in silence.

Eos recovered first. "You don't have to accept any bargain, Draupadi. But don't go. It's only a year. You'll be bearing, then occupied with your baby. There will be Bhima before Arjuna anyway—"

"It's not the nights with him that I crave now, Eos, but the days." Her voice broke. "I can't hide this grief from Yudishtira. I can't."

"Hiding the truth from Yudishtira," Krishna said quietly, "is like hiding the sky from an eagle. He loves the truth, even the bitterest kind."

Eos took her hand. "It's true. Yudishtira already knows."

"The child will be your comfort," Krishna said. "Once women have babies they forget men."

"I will *not* forget." Draupadi came close to him. "You said yourself I am different. I know it better than you. I *must* understand my true birth. If I stay, are you promising I will know my mother's name and origin?"

"It will happen. I promise."

"Within a year?" she demanded.

"Or soon after."

"Be certain of this, Krishna—a hundred children will not make me forget your promise. Or make me forget Arjuna. This child? It will mean nothing to me in comparison."

"Remember your words, Draupadi."

"Remember your agreement, Krishna."

The twenty warriors drove back at dusk, silent and vile-tempered. There had been no rakshasa—only the campfires of herders from Hastinapura looking for stray yearling calves. On the way the warriors had found Sahadeva and learned that the entire foray had gone out in error: Sahadeva had sent a log cutter with the message that he had wanted one of his brothers to join him because he had seen a suspicious fire. That was all. Nothing of rakshasa. The message had been confused by the frightened labourer. Sahadeva had to struggle not to speak of the obvious—that a message sent the yavanas' way, in writing, would have prevented Arjuna a year of exile.

Back inside the walls Yudishtira found a royal messenger from Hastinapura waiting for him, with three more troubles.

The first was a message from Guru Vaja to Panchalya, Crown Prince of South Panchala, inviting him to come to North Panchala's capital of Ahicchatra at the end of the winter. "Please ask my dear student King Yudishtira to forgive my request that you leave him while Indraprastha may lack sufficient warriors, but it is urgent that you come."

So here was the unpleasant possibility no one wanted to mention—that the invitation was some kind of trap set at Hastinapura to draw Panchalya away. But Panchalya himself was so pleased to hear from his teacher that treachery could not even be discussed.

The other two messages were to be spoken only to Yudishtira, so he went alone with the man to hear the words.

One was from their mother, Queen Kunti. She had left Kampilya for Hastinapura, "hoping to be of some help to my brother-in-law, King Drita". Yudishtira understood this to mean that his mother was trying to bring Drita to his senses about the division, his treatment of his priests, the discipline of his son, the enslaving of Nishada and many other issues.

"But," the cautious message continued, "I find matters here are as your message indicated, and am concerned by what I see around me. False rumours continue to be spread about you. Although the rakshasa seem to leave you alone, do not let down your guard. I am anxious to join you, but my being here also has its advantages. Do not trouble to send for me before your mind can be at ease about my safety there."

Yudishtira had studied the envoy, hating having even to consider the possibility of treachery. A messenger's dharma was truth and confidentiality—to think of this one lying was to doubt everything. That was the hateful effect of Sakuni.

Yudishtira finally had to conclude that his mother and Guru Vaja would have chosen their man carefully. He was even more confident of it when he heard Vyasa had sent the third message.

Vyasa. His heart ached with love for his teacher, his grandfather. After so long, and then to send a message when it was most needed. So the day held some good after all.

Or so he thought until he heard Vyasa's words: "They are only three, King. 'Learn to write.'"

Yudishtira drew back, as if struck by a friend.

30

Winds from the southeast—
We are warm, wet and bold.
Winds from the northwest—
We are brooding, dry and cold.

a children's song

As winter cooled Indraprastha's days and nights, the small planting of wheat and barley sprouted and grew green. The floor and some walls of the palace were finished, and even certain rooms. And the queen began to show that she was bearing a child. Yet the small city was subdued. A first child, a possible crown prince, was never to be celebrated until it was safely brought to light. And everyone could see that the queen and king were not in a happy mood. It was understood that they missed Prince Arjuna. Very much.

Arjuna, however, was missing Indraprastha not at all. He and Krishna had spent the rest of the autumn travelling to the Vrishni capital of Dvaraka. Although the distance was not so far, the weather had been pleasant. Thus it had seemed worthwhile to take their time and cautiously explore a few of those locales where the rakshasa might have been hiding, as well as to visit some of those sacred fords and holy bathing places most recommended by the priests. Still, it was not until the night before reaching Dvaraka that the two young warrior-borns were caught out in a frost.

But the weather was no great problem. As usual they bedded down their war horses in a circle around their camp, trusting the wise animals to warn them with a nicker if they sensed an intruder. They built a fire, roasted a haunch of autumn-fat marsh deer, baked bread from grains purchased in the last village and drank a little madhu wine. Then, Arjuna found the courage and told Krishna his intention not to enter the Vrishni capital in the morning, but to live in a true exile, in the woods, alone. "My brothers are working hard back at Indraprastha. I at least can perform a proper penance."

Krishna merely shifted to make himself more comfortable. "An error done with good intentions deserves a gentle punishment."

"Then I should at least serve my family by visiting a few of our neighbours and forming some alliances with someone besides your father."

"Arjuna, do I have to say the bad news outright? You won't find any allies. Some very unpleasant lies have been spread about all of you. And even if a king lets you through his gates, you will hardly look like the envoy of a prospering new kingdom after living out of your chariot for a few more months."

Then Krishna tried to tell him that his forest sojourn would be unsafe. But Arjuna was adamant. He would go on foot then, disguised as a wood-dwelling monk, the way they had all done in Ekacakra. He would go and hear the lies being told, and he would find some way to dispel them.

Krishna made a disgusted sound. "I believe you are simply afraid to meet my sister Subhadra."

"Subhadra again. Why do you always say these absurd things that confuse me? Krishna, you can not tempt me into your comfortable city with your sister. I must—"

"Suffer? Fine, go suffer. But wherever I am, you are always welcome, Arjuna. Always. In fact, I will expect you tomorrow night. One day's suffering should suffice anyone."

But, in fact, one day did not suffice Arjuna. He did not return to Dvaraka until the spring.

The coming of winter also brought a change in Egypt. As Amon-Re's Beloved slipped closer to death, Pharaoh's mother attempted to name the oracle's successor. Her choice was the High Priest's own son—a man whose loyalty she owned, an enemy of his father. And the only one whom the God's Own could trust to do what had to be done to stop her was a slave far away in the place called Bharata. A man whose messages had become terse and infrequent.

Begging Thoth and Osiris not to judge him yet, the High Priest and Friend of Ma'at sought to regain control over his slave. He sent word to Zesnor to turn Bharata's "demon army" into true demons by initiating them into that secret society "from which there is no return". Only another who had done the Deed would know what he meant. And Zesnor knew.

Meanwhile, winter came with irritating slowness to Suyodhana in Hastinapura. The stories about "Indraprastha" had to be only rumours. But nothing pleased King Drita's son once these tales had come to him. Not the outrage he was able to arouse over the sons of Pandu sending the Dasyu girl Lotus, fat with Arjuna's bastard child of sin, to serve Hastinapura's queen. Not Guru Vaja's increasing petulance about the division of the kingdom and the rift finally growing between the weapons-master and the king. Not even Radheya, who had stayed on at Hastinapura at Suyodhana's request and remained loyal even when Suyodhana had to shout at him to stop his endless lectures about dharma. ("Loyal as a dog" was how Suyodhana's younger brothers and half-brothers put it. But Suyodhana noticed that even Hastinapura's dogs avoided that troop of troublemakers.) No, not even Radheya's faithfulness pleased him any more. Nothing. He had to see if it could be true about his cousins. He had to see this Indraprastha for himself.

He might have gone alone or in disguise, but as the winds blew colder he began to imagine something better. Something to make their exile truly miserable. Something to remind them of the ridiculousness of their little log-fort "palace".

Not that this plan was born of envy, he told himself. It was merely important to be certain that his cousins, who had left Hastinapura with such bitter expressions on their faces, were not indeed building something truly large. For that would imply a well-disciplined following of Nishada whom the sons of Pandu might arm for revenge after all, oath or not. The real danger, Suyodhana swore, was that they, his cousins, were feeling envy and preparing to attack *him*.

So Suyodhana went to his father for the formality of obtaining his permission for a luxurious "cattle inspecting expedition", on which a few of their allies could be invited, to impress them with the Ganges-Kurus' holdings and sumptuous way of travel. King Drita barely heard his son's request, so anxious was he to warn Suyodhana again that they had all made a mistake—that "good fortune goes with my brother's sons" and the division of the kingdom had been a sin. Suyodhana ignored his drooling, hand-wringing old father. To his uncle Sakuni he told nothing.

A crescent moon of cold silver rocked in the bare trees along the river bottom. Bitter north wind or fog—it seemed to Sakuni that there had never been anything else. He wished he could feel warm one moment more before he did this which might be his last act.

He drank the sip of azle that each night allowed him to slip into his nightmares and rest his body. But instead of lying down in his furs, he picked up his knife. Best to do it now, he thought. Or to try.

He crept to Zesnor's hammock. As always, the breathing was slow and light. Sakuni raised the knife.

"Yes, Master."

Sakuni jerked back. Then leaned forward over the slave. "I know what your messages have said," Sakuni hissed.

"Because I leave them where you can read them, Master."

Sakuni's hand trembled—he might still be able to hurl the knife at the slave's heart. "He gave me six months, Zesnor. It has been six—I do not yet control Bharata."

"Not even Hastinapura," the Egyptian said coolly.

"Soon you must obey him and kill me."

"Unless you take my life first?" Zesnor asked. "But I assure you, if I had thought it served him, I would have killed you already. Certainly I would have when I sensed you were hoping to kill me. But here in Bharata I am the best judge of what will satisfy Amon-Re. He would have it so."

Zesnor's voice seemed to come from a cave now. That was the onset of the effect of the azle. Sakuni stared at the knife in his hand. "*They* are the demons," Sakuni whispered. "Outnumbered by Dasyu. They burn the Dasyu's forest. Then somehow enslave the same Dasyu. Without weapons. They build during the rains. They grow stronger every day." Sakuni began rocking uncontrollably, forward, backward.

The voice from the cave said, "There has been a new instruction today." The voice was cold, black. "If the struggle is for the better control of the Dasyu, we shall now win."

Sakuni shivered. "What will you do to them?"

"It does not matter. You will go back to Hastinapura tomorrow."

"Why? What will you do?"

"It is the god's own instruction to me. This I can not disobey."

Sakuni pressed his hands to his ears to shut out the words, but they found him. They entered through his eyes and mouth and nose, one word after another. "This sacrifice changes them," the voice said. "They will do anything else after they have done the unthinkable."

Sakuni swallowed hard to stop his nausea. Always the nausea and the pressing inside his skull. "What about Eagle? He will not even drink your azle now."

"If Eagle refuses, he must go."

"But so many follow him."

"None of those belong. And many more are coming now." The voice was cool and dark, like the wind from a shadowed place.

"But you. You belong!"

Then there was a face in the cave mouth. Its mouth dripped blood. Sakuni doubled over, sobbing. "A boy or a girl?" he shouted, and huddled under Zesnor's hammock, screaming.

The cold, hard ground finally faded his vision. He looked up at Zesnor. Behind the Egyptian the crescent moon hung like a horn. "What have I seen?" Sakuni whispered.

"It is only azle. Go back to your city, Master. You are ill and useless here."

In Indraprastha on the same night, Yudishtira lay awake in the bed he shared with Draupadi. Through an open window the crescent moon faintly lit the room. It was a new room, part of the first wing of the palace. The room was spacious, delicately painted, hung with fine weavings—and cold as the moon. Cold as his heart.

She was awake also. He always knew. But silent. And he could bear the silence no more. So he formed the sentence he would speak, arranging the words as he might have arranged chariots for an attack. Attacks were something he understood.

"Do you ever sleep any more, Draupadi?" He instantly hated the crudeness of his approach.

"Do you?" she asked.

"Is it that my own wakefulness keeps you awake? If you wish to sleep elsewhere—"

"I am content here."

"Content, but—"

"I am content here." Her tone told him to ask no more.

So he was silenced, but he could not sleep. He tried to understand. She was large early with her bearing. It would be hard if it were himself, this doing nothing except waiting for something to come.

It is a message from Arjuna that she waits for. It has been four months and she has received no word from him.

He planned another foray of words. Dangerous as it was, it was better than waiting. Defending.

"Draupadi, perhaps you should rest more. Eat more." His voice sounded loud and large in the dark.

"I eat enough for the child."

"I know. You do all your duties."

"But you've heard a waiting mother's mood must be light? Then I shall smile more too. I will start tomorrow."

"To me I'd rather you shouted."

"About what?" she asked evenly.

"About my sending him away."

"He wanted to go."

"Wanted to go?" Yudishtira was stunned. But of course it could be true. The evidence had been everywhere—Arjuna's restlessness after the rains, his complaining, his eager packing. He had even said it himself, in the armoury that day.

"If he wanted to go, I could still have ordered him to stay. For you."

"So he would hate me?" Her bitterness was burning.

I should stop this sparring. There is a clear shot right before me, and it is called the truth.

"You love him. More than anyone. I understand this feeling, too well."

"I love you all, equally."

"No! Say anything to me if it is honest. But don't play with your words. Not to me. I am too unhappy myself. I can't bear it."

She did not respond. The wind wailed on across the small, sharp moon.

In another new room at the far end of the new wing of the palace, the shutters also stood open to the night. Under sheepskin bed rugs Eos cried softly, her head on the Phoenician's chest and her tears falling into his beard.

"Why am I always like this afterwards?" she whispered.

"You cry for all the times you couldn't cry before."

"That would be many, many times."

"You must cry for each."

She huddled closer against him.

Then she pulled away, trying to retrieve what she had allowed to escape her. "No, I think I cry for the times I won't be allowed to cry in the future."

He stroked her hair. "Why do you insist you must cry in the future? Haven't I promised to stay? Or take you if I go?"

"There is more future than you and me, Lettermaker. Nor do you know what you can promise. And I don't know if I could leave with you."

"Then it is I who should cry. But I don't."

"No, you never do. You are as cold as the moon."

"And you are as moody as the wind."

She rose up on an elbow and looked into his eyes. "I tell you my stories of pain, but where are yours? You were a slave just as long."

As always, her question drove him into silence. He closed his eyes and his face became still as death. If pressed, she knew he would claim that nothing came to mind. Or he would tell her some painful scene, but with no pain—only a cold blankness that sucked in every thought so that soon he would fall back into silence.

Eos rolled over on her back, too familiar with the chasm she had forced him to cross again. Or at least she was familiar with her side of it, where he left her so often. It continually proved what she knew anyway—that for all his control, he was a man out of control. He would have to leave her, to seek outside in the world what he had lost within. For all his promises, he could keep none.

She looked up into the darkness above their heads. "Yudishtira needs some kind of victory," she said, knowing the subject had to be changed. When he didn't respond she continued. "Do you know, Lettermaker? I almost wish the rakshasa would attack. We're ready for them. We'd defeat them. Where are they?"

He finally stirred. "They won't disappoint you, little Achaean warrior. The longer they wait, the stronger they'll be. Only, why do they attack a king who cares so deeply about what's best for his people?"

"The rakshasa don't seem to care, and not all Bharata's kings think as logically as you."

"Then you also expect *Arya* to attack Indraprastha? Not even Arjuna expects that. He says his people don't attack cities. 'Innocent noncombatants might be hurt.' I tell you, this is civilisation such as Egypt and Sumeria can only dream of!"

"But once someone breaks these laws," she said quietly, "Bharata's kings will be as crazy as any others, and Bharata itself will be gone like dust on the wind."

"Therefore you think I should teach nothing about yavana warfare in Bharata. And Sahadeva and I think I should teach them everything I know—so that Yudishtira remains the victor in every contest."

"Most of what you want to teach violates their 'dharma'— Yudishtira would never use it. He knows that the purity of Bharata's devotion to dharma is its best protection."

"I too believe in the power of their righteousness, Eos. I do. I don't think anything can really defeat them."

"Equally foolish. You've seen Ashur's armies—what good would dharmic warfare be against them?"

"Then what do you propose, Eos? Leave them innocent? Or teach them what to expect so they can defend themselves?"

"I don't know."

"So you hover near them like a mother partridge, hoping to rescue them if your former yavana masters ever come here to hurt them."

She felt her tears coming again. "I feel too much pain and you feel too little," she whispered. "Something is wrong with both of us."

Lettermaker drew her close and fondled her breasts. "Then we'll cure it."

"I fear this is no cure, but the beginnings of another bout of sickness."

"You know our lovemaking has changed you. It has changed me also. I have never cared for anyone the way I care for you."

"Make your love, but please do not speak it. Not to me, Lettermaker."

"I must."

"You must not." She rose up out of the bed.

"You're freezing us." He grabbed for her.

She came down on him, forcing laughter. "Shall I show you what my mother used to do to my father?"

"You Hellene whore. You watched your parents?"

"She made a hole in the wall, just for me. She considered herself very talented."

"Maybe for an Achaean. All right, I am more than ready —try to show this Phoenician something new."

"New? No, very, very old. Something from long before men and women learned how to hurt each other with love."

The wind wailed louder, the moon sailed west, and the room belonging to the Greek woman was filled again with stirrings and sighs. While in the king's apartments the winter night remained unrelenting in its cold stillness. Near dawn Yudishtira decided to rise even in the darkness, to inspect the watch, or anything. But then she spoke.

"Forgive me." Her hand searched for his and found it. It had been four months since they had touched.

"They say love is one of life's duties," she said softly. "But I think it is a great sin. It makes one blind to dharma, to others' feelings, to everything that's beautiful. Until Arjuna left, Yudishtira, I was happy with you."

He did not try to deflect the hurt—he let it in, because now she spoke the truth.

"And you were happy too," she whispered. "Now, with Arjuna gone, you are not. Will you ever talk freely to me again? Or laugh with me?"

"Whenever you wish, Draupadi."

"I can hardly hear you."

"Whenever you wish."

"Then I wish it now."

But neither of them spoke again for a long time. They merely lay still, each with a hand upon the other's heart.

The crescent moon was fading in a grey dawn before Draupadi turned and asked her husband what more troubled him.

"Panchalya is on his way alone to Ahicchatra," he said wearily. "And I must consider that Guru Vaja might plan some treachery there. Also I dislike these lies Sakuni has spread."

"And that Vyasa doesn't come?"

Yudishtira did not answer.

"Hasn't he even sent you a message?"

It was as if she were watching the thoughts pass through his mind. He had ached to share with her the news of the instruction he had still failed to obey. He had also dreaded it. But especially now that she had asked, his feelings about it did not matter—there could be no secrets between them.

"He did send a message. Three words. 'Learn to write'."

"Write!"

He closed his eyes. "What hypocrisy it would seem to Sahadeva if he discovered I was secretly learning what I have always forbidden him to learn."

"But only you will know how to avoid its dangers."

"Will I?"

"Yes. Or Vyasa would not have ordered you to do it. When a horse is known to be dangerous, we put the best rider up to bring it under control."

He looked at her in the morning light. She smiled. "Shall

I say it clearer? You, dearest husband, are our best. It has always been so."

He gestured to deny it. But it seemed to him that all the comfort and beauty he had ceased to hope or ask for was pouring upon him like the sun suddenly shining into the room.

"If writing could be used for no purpose but to praise you, my wife—so that others could read about you everywhere, for ever—then I would learn to write today and never stop."

She touched his face—just his face—and life ran through his deadened body, awakening it to joy again.

A barefoot Nishada was running along the hall. There was a violent pounding at the door. "King Yudishtira! Hundreds of people at the gate, asking for you. They wish to be your subjects."

"Where are they from?" Yudishtira called, trying to keep his hope from being revealed in his voice.

"They are Nishada, King. My people. All asking for you."

Yudishtira reached for his clothing. "So. It seems I am still only king of the Yamuna Dasyu," he whispered, his disappointment barely hidden. "I am sorry, Draupadi."

After a moment she spoke solemnly to him. "Then I am their queen. Which is more fitting than you know. And they are, after all, the ones who seem to need us most."

31

Celebrate all your victories, whether they announce themselves at your gates or creep in under the stable fence. You admit every defeat—admit every victory too. This is your duty.

Gangeya to Yudishtira

"They carried the daughter off alive." The Nishada headwoman spoke in broken Arya. Another woman stood beside her. "This one's son fought to save his sister. We found him with his feet and seeder cut off, and with this spear through his belly."

The spear the headwoman held up trailed a blue and white ribbon, like all Indraprastha's spears. The mother beside her stared into space, already dead from grief in the old Nishada way.

"Do you know which Arya family goes to battle under blue and white?" Yudishtira asked.

"The sons of Pandu."

"And you've come to us?" Bhima asked.

"We are not stupid people, Prince Bhima. Rakshasa did this."

"We hear that some of them seem to be Nishada themselves," Yudishtira said.

"They want us to have to fight you—to kill ourselves on a million Arya arrows." The headwoman hung her head. "I know. My son is among them."

Now Yudishtira recognised her. "You are Lotus's mother. And Wood Rose's."

"Also Eagle's, who has led the rakshasa against you. And now against his own people."

Because the kidnapping and atrocity had taken place early that night and some distance away, Yudishtira saw little value in going to the site. His immediate concern was for the unprotected Nishada in his kingdom. But the headwoman assured him there were none. "We are here or we are dead. Or gone south to our new 'king'." She used the Arya title, for Nishada lacked it. "He prepares the Nishada to fight the Arya in the Arya way. He says in the future the Nishada will revenge every tree that is burned in our forest."

"What is this leader's name?" Yudishtira asked. "I must speak with him."

The Nishada shifted nervously, but the headwoman revealed the name. "They call him King Does-Nothing-Yet-Gets-All."

Bhima laughed.

"No, it's a wise name," Yudishtira said. "There is no better trait in a king."

Sahadeva came out of the crowded darkness with a youth at his side. "This one says he saw cattle on our eastern lands tonight—thousands of cattle."

Rakshasa, and now ravaging numbers of cattle. Yudishtira looked east across the river. A large herd could return all their newly seeded fields to wasteland.

Bhima shouldered his way closer to Yudishtira. "It's Suyodhana's doing, I know it. And I will personally strangle every cow of his and send the ears in a basket back to Hastinapura."

"You will need more like a thousand baskets," Sahadeva said. "It sounds like Hastinapura's entire western herd."

"Sahadeva, could this be only careless cattle tending?" Yudishtira asked.

"No, I sent a warning to their western herdsmen. They understood."

In the dawn light Yudishtira stepped up on the rim of the courtyard fountain and began speaking in Nishada, formally extending Indraprastha's protection to the refugees in return for working one sixth of a day, month, or year for the kingdom. "Some day I will avenge this crime against you. But I can not today. If there is to be enough food and wealth to sustain us here, I must correct another wrong."

In the Arya tongue Yudishtira ordered every chariot prepared, and every warrior into them or on horseback except the five eldest Maruts, who would defend Indraprastha with the newly trained Nishada bowmen. Vimada would command those left behind.

Yudishtira put a hand on Vimada's shoulder. "It seems I am always asking too much of you. But this herd may well be out there to lure us away from our walls.

"The rest of you? Do not forget cattle whips!"

A meagre assembly of nine two-horse chariots and fourteen outriders left the fortress, directed east by the Nishada youth who had seen the cattle. At mid-morning the warriors reached the herd—a multi-coloured, twitching, stamping body creeping across the burned-off plain. There were no herdsmen in sight.

"Sahadeva," Yudishtira called, "how much damage would a herd this size do now, pastured back by the Yamuna?"

"Some of our land there would tolerate it—what we'll plant next year. For only one season the well-controlled presence of cattle might even improve it."

"Bhima, do you see any herdsmen?"

"None at all."

"Then these must be wild cattle, yes?"

"Definitely. Or abandoned."

"Then gather them in and drive them home!"

Giving directions from his chariot, Bhima eagerly split the company into two arms, which moved out to embrace the herd, then turned to face west. The older cattle on the margins of the herd considered this odd threat, the whites of their eyes showing, their hooves pawing and shifting.

Conchs blared; spears banged the sides of chariots. The edge cattle turned, their tails up and their ears back, and began their panicked shoving. Soon thousands of black, dun, grey, bay and spotted cattle were running before the chariots. Nakula was driving Yudishtira's chariot and took the lead, heading Hastinapura's herd precisely towards Indraprastha. Both were laughing. Cattle raiding was an Arya sport as old as Veda.

Suddenly Nakula reined in. Far out on their left a messenger ran on foot. He carried Suyodhana's red and gold on his envoy's belt.

They turned aside and drove out to meet the man, who was speechless from his effort. "Help. Nishada. Captured!"

Yudishtira and Nakula exchanged glances. "The trap," Nakula whispered. "This man may be an initiate messenger, but these are strange times."

"Would he look so afraid, Nakula? Envoy, where are they?"

He pointed south. "Five leagues. Suyodhana and twenty warriors, the herdsmen, and drivers and servants. Fighting off hundreds of Nishada."

"Hundreds against our nine chariots?" Yudishtira grinned at Nakula. "Our Maruts will enjoy those odds. If we can divert them from this sport."

Nakula sounded his conch. Across the plain the chariots left the running herd and turned slowly towards them. Even the horses were reluctant.

"If they are annoyed now, wait until they hear the rest, Nakula." Yudishtira took a blue and white ribbon from a spear. "Envoy, you are under my employ now. When the chariots reach you, say, 'Yudishtira commands: The outriders will take the herd home and the chariots follow me south. Suyodhana and his allies have been captured by Nishada and we, his kin and allies, must rescue him.' That will tangle their reins. Now we must hurry, Nakula. If it is a trap, better to arrive sooner than expected."

The run south tired the horses, even with Nakula's excellent driving. Finally forced to halt, he stepped down and walked ahead cautiously, then motioned for Yudishtira to drive after him, to the top of the next rise. From there they were still hidden, if only by sami thickets, but Yudishtira could see down on the battlefield.

The scene was satisfyingly chaotic. A surprise attack during the noon meal, given the fallen canopies strewn about between trees, the tables overturned, the chariots still harnessed but to dead horses. It must have all finally finished just moments ago, for the Arya were being disarmed, moved to the centres of knots of Nishada, and restrained under nets. One Nishada, on an enormous, shaggy, red-roan horse, was obviously directing the mayhem.

"These can't be rakshasa," Nakula whispered. "The Arya are still alive."

"I'd say that's King-Does-Nothing down there," Yudishtira said, "living up to his name—he's taken it all."

Yudishtira looked back. Indraprastha's eight other chariots had quietly arrived. Perfect, he thought—the second surprise of the day for my cousin. Yudishtira signalled the chariots to move up. Then he shouted for a charge, beginning it himself with an Arya battle cry.

The chariots bore down the slope like nine angry bulls. But the Nishada were not so easily panicked. They assembled around their king, hostages pushed in front of them as shields, arrows drawn.

Yudishtira gestured and Nakula pulled up sharply. Indraprastha's warriors arrayed their chariots behind them. Yudishtira had learned from his new subjects that the shorter Nishada shafts and bows made their arrows accurate for only half the distance of an Arya's. In the forest, where surprise from close range was the first weapon, this disadvantage was minor compared to having bows and arrows that were easy to hide and to handle. But on an open battlefield the mere sight of a distant row of Arya chariots with Arya bows drawn would signal defeat to a reasonable Nishada leader.

Suyodhana stood by the Nishada king's horse, wrapped in net like a honey cake. Radheya was with him under the net, his gold earrings gleaming and his expression one of even more bitter humiliation.

"Bhima," Yudishtira said, just loud enough for those behind in the chariots to hear. "The rest of you as well. Do not taunt our cousin or King Radheya. We will not shame them further. Besides, we have some rumours to dispel. I'm sure you've noticed that many of Hastinapura's long-standing allies are here—most of whom were once our good friends. Suyodhana may be presenting us with a useful gift, provided we don't damage it with taunts."

Yudishtira stepped up on to the driver's seat of his chariot.

"Hail King Does-Nothing-Yet-Gets-All!" His near-perfect Nishada caused a stir among both the captives and captors. "I am honoured to finally meet you. I am also in your debt— these warriors you have punished were allowing their cattle to stray on to my land."

"*Your* land, Arya?"

Yudishtira was satisfied with the tone in Does-Nothing's voice—his gibe was mostly for the benefit of his people. He knew his hopeless position, both today and in the future.

"I am King Yudishtira, and I consider the cleared land drained by the Yamuna to be mine. The forest land I leave to the Nishada to enjoy in their traditional ways, provided they will learn certain skills at Indraprastha and serve me during two months of each year, or pay a reasonable tribute to me instead. In return I will strive to protect them from all types of misfortunes"—Yudishtira gestured slightly towards the captured Arya—"and I will consider them my allies."

There was a stir both among the Nishada and in the chariots behind him, where many spoke the Dasyu tongue, but Yudishtira watched the captured Arya.

"Dasyu, your allies?" the Nishada king repeated with exaggerated doubt. "And these Arya warriors I have captured— what about them?"

"Most are Kuru allies and therefore my allies, by oath. But even allies must be punished if they break the law, as these have done, or attack those I protect. And I suspect you know what has gone on between myself and that one beside you under the net."

Does-Nothing grinned. "Shall I kill him for you?"

"Let him," Bhima whispered. "Let's just drive away and let him kill them all."

Yudishtira gritted his teeth. *Must it always be I who restrains them?*

"My prisoners don't understand us," Does-Nothing shouted. "You can speak the truth."

"Thank you, King, for offering me such liberty," Yudishtira shouted back, still in Nishada. "But whatever the language, I try to speak the truth. We Arya obey dharma, not the passion of the moment or our personal ambition. Dharma requires that if you, King, try to injure a disarmed man, a prisoner, or a relative or ally of mine—including my cousin Suyodhana—I must fight you, and I will."

Yudishtira saw Suyodhana stiffen at the sound of his own name. But he had not understood—his eyes had stayed fixed on the ground. A true Kuru, Yudishtira thought. He's not going to beg me to purchase his release, or even ask me. If he'd known his messenger would reach *me* with his call for help, he would have preferred death.

"When we are allies, Does-Nothing," Yudishtira said clearly, "dharma will require that I defend any of you just as fiercely."

In the eight chariots around him there were whispers. The laws of dharma applying to Dasyu allies?

Look at them, Yudishtira wanted to shout behind to his warriors. Think of what you've seen at Indraprastha. These Nishada are at least as brave as you, as loyal as you, and even more determined when their people are threatened.

"What did my cousin do to offend you, King Does-Nothing?" Yudishtira asked.

"Men from this party set a fire in the forest."

"Was this fire more towards the Ganges or the Yamuna?"

"Towards the Yamuna."

"Then they were on my land and taking an action against me. This violates a vow made before King Drita, the father of this party's leader. Therefore, as his father is my elder, I will have his father deal with it. Let Suyodhana and the others go. It will not happen again."

The Nishada warriors shifted about, tightening their grips on the nets that held their captives. Twenty Arya plus numerous servants would have brought a large ransom at Hastinapura.

"Let them go," Yudishtira said more sharply, lifting his bow very slightly. "They're on foot now—your forest-watchers can see that they behave. Then let us camp together and talk, King, and form our alliance. These Arya warriors are no threat to you—they can't even keep watch over a herd of cattle. This morning we had to take their entire herd to the Yamuna for watering."

Finally he saw the response for which he'd prayed to Brahma, Lord of Speech. Subala, one of the five Kekaya brothers and a loyal Kuru ally, looked up sharply: Subala was reacting to this news of the loss of half of Hastinapura's cattle.

It was the herd that I should have been given, Yudishtira wanted to shout to Subala.

But there was a more pressing problem: several hundred armed Nishada, edging forward under the protection now of shields, and still considering doubling their number of captives rather than releasing these.

Does-Nothing was conferring with several of his warriors. Yudishtira knew his own warriors would have liked the same opportunity. He thoroughly shared their reluctance to die defending Suyodhana and Radheya.

I obeyed my teachers, he thought—*I stopped gambling for wealth. But now I wager with other men's lives.*

Suddenly King Does-Nothing began removing his net from Suyodhana and ordering the other Nishada to free their prisoners also. The game was won.

Behind him he heard the grips on weapons relaxed and the stamping of horses whose reins had been loosened. Out in the chaos of the destroyed camp, Hastinapura's allies were shaking themselves and gathering up what belongings they could find around them. The first of them began walking northeast.

Nakula whispered in Yudishtira's ear, "I hope our cousin and his friends can guess what you've done for them."

"They won't have to guess." He could barely contain his excitement. "Today we have given Suyodhana's allies an interesting new story to spread about us, in detail—for Subala of the Kekayas understands Nishada."

In the becalmed palace Draupadi waited for the men to return. She spent most of the long day on the walk above the walls, looking east, her Nishada serving-woman fussing near her. Eos came up several times but saw Draupadi was in no mood to talk, so left her alone.

This thought kept returning to her: now both have left me. Both are in danger. And she saw that together the man gone today and the man gone four months ago held her as much a captive, in her heart, as King Drupada had at Kampilya. Thus as she leaned her body, heavy with bearing, upon the top of

Indraprastha's log wall and watched for the return of at least one of her two husbands, she thought deeply about each of them.

As Arjuna's absence lengthened, she was increasingly unsure of what he had ever felt for her. Although she had learned to be careful of what she said in his presence so that he would not think her unintelligent or petty, still Arjuna had often seemed indifferent to her, even mocking. Then at other times he had been kind and tender, as if some wall had fallen, so that he could treat her not as a woman but as a friend. For it seemed to her from small things he said that he did not truly like women, any women. Even though he also appeared, both from her experience and from his reputation, to crave women's company, and for more than surata.

If Arjuna was critical of women, he clearly despised Dasyu, in spite of his growing tolerance of those Nishada he actually knew and the common knowledge of his own slight Dasyu taint through his grandfather Vyasa. But she had to face the truth: he might well openly disown her if he knew she was half-Dasyu.

Thus she again had to ask herself how she could love Arjuna so deeply. So frantically. How she could take that risk. And most of the answer lay in that moment when he rescued her from the terror of the bride's choice. Ended her imprisonment. Carried her through those gates.

The rest of the answer came from those last days before he had gone—those brief, sweet, autumn-fresh days of green after the rains when he had taken her driving every afternoon and their hearts and minds had been like blossoms on the same branch. It surprised her, but her body had really desired him very little, perhaps because she was already bearing. What she saw she had craved from him then was a certain lightness. An actual light-headedness that had come as they had driven across open fields of swaying grass. A light way of laughing, after so much grief.

Then there was Yudishtira. The source of the child in her. Of the heaviness of bearing, of being a queen, of feelings so tangled she could not have a single clear thought about them. Feelings such as her shame that she had not hidden her love for Arjuna from him. And at the same time gratitude, that she did not have to hide it, or anything, from Yudishtira. From Arjuna she had had to hide so much.

And she felt a need. A need and a fear. Need of the kind of surata she had had with Yudishtira; fear that these unspeakable emotions they had called up in each other during their love-making could never, never come again. Not with anyone.

And, then, an even greater fear, that someday he would finally retaliate for all her wrongs towards him. He was a king, after all. How much would he tolerate from his first wife? Dared she forget his fury during their first surata?

That memory brought shame again for her behaviour, yet also a wave of the need, of the sweet frenzy, such as she seldom felt now that she was bearing.

In her vision of them long ago Arjuna had offered his body, yet had left her standing alone. And Yudishtira, his face hidden, had loomed over her, rescuing her. Rescuing her from Arjuna even.

But in the world of reality Arjuna had rescued her, while Yudishtira had taken her body for himself and left her inner spirit to stand alone before these feelings that struck and tore at her.

At dusk, when the news finally came that Yudishtira was safe, and Hastinapura's great, milling herd spread out along the Yamuna to drink its fill, Draupadi finally allowed her serving woman to lead her to her bed, for she was exceedingly tired.

32

There was darkness covered by darkness in the beginning . . .
that empty united world which was covered by a mere nothing
was produced through the power of austerity.
In the beginning there was desire,
which was the first seed of mind;
sages having meditated in their hearts
have discovered by their wisdom
the connection of the existent with the non-existent.

Rig Veda

Zesnor stood at the edge of the clearing. It was dawn and
around the ashes of the Twelve Fires two hundred and twenty-
six rakshasa lay in a stupor. Blood was on their lips; the
food-that-never-leaves-one was in their bellies, and the unforgivable sin was crouching in their confused memories, ready
to drag them back to this tainted fellowship should they ever
hope to rejoin humanity.

And one more unimportant life had been sacrificed to
Amon-Re's purpose. A "mere Nishada", as Bharata's Arya put
it. Who were mere Arya to an Egyptian.

Zesnor turned and walked into the forest. There were new
messengers from Thebes to meet.

Suddenly he stopped. The girl-child's dark, terrified eyes
were watching him from the winter-still woods.

Then he went on. It was only the dead girl's Ka, wanting
revenge but of course utterly incapable of it. That he had even
noticed this flimsy spirit was a weakness in himself that he
scorned.

But as he walked the familiar path, he could not escape the
memory of her, and it no longer seemed entirely a weakness.

Changes in his soul, however, had taken place before on this path. For example, here at the stream there was usually some quieting of his mind.

This time it was a dead calm.

And now here at the yandava grove he would often forget some of his concerns.

This time he felt a blankness.

Passing the banyan tree brought the greatest change. Here he could expect to feel the rock of regret deep inside himself.

Today it was an enormous and immovable grief, for the child and for himself.

But on the slope afterwards such feelings would generally soften, in spite of the years he had carried that rock in his heart.

Today, suddenly, the rock melted. It was not the tears from his eyes that surprised him, but the inner trembling and despair. Yet he allowed the strange emotion to come, without any attempt to control it—that was also an effect he had observed along this path.

Here, as he came up the meadow, his thoughts would always finally come home to Osiris and all earthly matters would be behind him. This moment, this peace, made all the rest acceptable.

Today that peace was exactly the same.

Then he was standing at the door of the Teacher's hut. This old priest was no one well known, even in Bharata, and he never left the vicinity of his dwelling. It was not an especially charming setting either, or a place frequented by the powerful. Yet today Zesnor knew the truth: He had not chosen this place to hide his arriving messengers because of its convenience, or its isolation, or the useful information this truthvowed priest supplied—but because here at this hut his own Ka was nourished. No place in Egypt had nourished his soul as it was nourished here.

The Teacher's hut was round, made of bamboo, and thatched with palm fronds. It had one door and one window. In front was the hearth for the sacrificial fire, kept smooth and cinder-free by his students and protected from rain by a small pavilion.

Today the little compound was deserted and the fire gave only a thread of smoke, so Zesnor proceeded to the river behind it. There the old priest and his four students were bathing in the water—icy snow water from the far mountains. But they played like children in a warm pond.

On the bank were the two Egyptian messengers. New ones, their staring eyes revealed—they had lived an entire life in two months. First the frantic drive to the eastern sea, then the rapid voyage by reed rowing ship. The ship would be crowded with galley slaves capable of revolt and the coast full of hidden rocks and pirates, but the open sea which the captain probably chose after a day or two was infinitely more frightening to men like these. Finally the landing in this unimaginable place; the rapid march through the desert with its strange animals; followed by the beast-filled Bharata forest, horrible to an Egyptian, with its wet air and rotting life.

But even without seeing their blank faces, Zesnor could be certain the messengers were new. The Supremely Beloved let no one see the secret route twice. They would start back today with his message, and upon arriving in Egypt they would take their final journey, to the Reed Shore of Osiris, where they could repeat nothing about landmarks and passages on the secret route southeast by sea. Zesnor also knew they would consider themselves fortunate that they had died in Egypt, not Bharata: In Egypt their Ka would receive a proper Opening of the Mouth.

Somehow frightened by what he saw of himself in these messengers, Zesnor looked to the Teacher instead, until his self-control returned. Then he addressed the pair.

"Good day, Servants of Amon-Re. I have a papyrus to be taken to His Supremely Beloved Servant without delay. And the one you brought me?"

Even the news of their imminent departure did not remove the blankness of journey-confusion from their faces. We Egyptians are not very flexible, Zesnor thought. Consider those Arya in their frigid river. Perhaps it is that the Nile lacks these extremes of warmth and cold to harden us.

One of the Egyptians handed him a scroll. "It is from Pharaoh's mother, not our master." The man lowered his eyes.

377

"They say Amon-Re's Supremely Beloved is too ill to send messages to a slave."

Zesnor frowned. He wanted to ask the man if he believed that lie. If he had gone himself down to the oracle's chamber. But there were countless reasons why asking would be futile and dangerous. Zesnor walked to the river bank without even looking at the confusing absurdities this scroll from his master's enemy would provide if he were stupid enough to ever read it.

From the water the Teacher watched him. Zesnor felt afraid for a moment, for in those grey Arya eyes he thought he saw endless change. He turned back to the familiar Egyptians.

Behind him the monk was laughing. The monk and his students came out, dripping, into the chill of the winter morning. From the corner of his eye Zesnor watched the old man's body. It had a refined strength that Zesnor, even in his prime, greatly envied. It was rumoured that when the best of these priest-born Arya forest-dwellers died, their bodies refused to decay. Zesnor found that almost humorous. In dry Egypt the body was preserved by adding costly substances to it after death, while in wet and rotting Bharata—if the rumour were true—preservation was carried on during each day of life, from the inside. Surely the eternal existence on the Farther Shore was better with a body untouched by the embalmer, its organs left in place.

The Teacher led them all back to the hut. His students added wood to the indoor brazier and brought their master a deerskin to wrap around himself, shirts of bark-cloth for themselves.

When they were seated, the priest wasted no words. "You are troubled today, Zesnor."

The Egyptian glanced at the others. The students never spoke and the messengers did not understand the language, but still he hesitated. The Teacher merely looked around the hut and it was enough—students and messengers left.

Still Zesnor found it hard to speak. But today it was also impossible not to.

"I have always obeyed my master."

The Teacher nodded, as if he had already guessed the essence of the problem.

"I have never even wished not to."

Another nod.

"But last night—" Zesnor stopped. "I wish I had disobeyed."

The old man closed his eyes and said nothing. They sat in silence. Finally Zesnor also closed his eyes, and found himself slipping away into a soft darkness. He had no idea how long it was before he heard the Teacher's voice.

"What confuses you, Zesnor?"

Zesnor was surprised to hear his own voice answer, "I am confused by your gods." It was as if they had been having a conversation all along, but he himself had only now opened a door and begun to hear it. "Not only their number confuses me, but their character—bodies of light that thunder and flame and flash, in the water, the stars, the sun."

The Teacher inclined his head a little. "We each serve the god with whom we are in greatest harmony."

"I serve Amon-Re, you the god Brahma." Zesnor fell silent.

"But you wonder," the Teacher said quietly, "what created Brahma and Amon-Re, for That would be supreme over any god. That you could still obey without question. Only That."

"Yes. Here is my confusion."

"I could tell you what you seek and you could believe me or not. But the better way is to know it." The teacher picked up a twig with one dry leaf on it, then set it before Zesnor.

The Egyptian felt something in him tremble and he stilled it rather than let it show. But the old man nodded as if he had seen. "Nothing in its essence is evil, Zesnor, not even you. For everything arises from That. And every action—*every* action, whether we intend it to be or not—is our best attempt to *be* That."

The Teacher gently touched the leaf on the twig that lay before them. "But let's speak of your immediate concern— whether a master can ask a servant to do something because the right thing will be for the servant to find the courage to choose not to do it."

Zesnor was shocked. "But then every time a task seems difficult, the servant could say, 'My master asked me but he really meant for me to refuse.'"

"That is why in Bharata we teach children to obey dharma

without question. Only when they are parents of children do we teach them the exceptions to dharma. And when their children have children, if we are very fortunate, some will come to us in dismay and say, 'In my old age I am becoming a sinner, for I find I must do what I do, regardless of dharma.'"

"You call that a teacher's good fortune?"

"Without these old ones to change dharma, it would become like laws made of stone—and then shatter under the blows of change." The priest picked up the twig again and studied its single leaf. "What did you wish to disobey, Zesnor of Egypt?"

Zesnor felt the trembling well up in him. He couldn't answer.

"But you didn't disobey?"

"I have trained myself not to allow such thoughts."

"But you fear that next time you will disobey anyway."

"This desire is very strong."

The Teacher plucked the leaf from the twig. "The Self divides and divides like existence, into many selves. One can favour one self so long that another seems evil, but deny any part of the Self continuously, even to please a master, and there will be rebellion."

Zesnor could listen very little now because of the effort to control the trembling.

The Teacher spoke near his ear. "For Bharata's sake, I will hope that your neglected side is freed. Now you wish to go. That is no discourtesy to me. For those accustomed to bearing weapons, a self momentarily weakened by inner warfare is a private matter."

The Teacher set the single leaf upon the brazier's fire.

In the spring Arjuna returned to the gates of Dvaraka, still wearing a forest-dweller's garb. The winter months had left the bark-cloth hanging in tatters over a thinner but still strong body, for Arjuna could never cease to practise archery, even when he had nothing left for a bow but a branch and vine, nothing left to nock but a stick.

The winter had been hard, however, in much graver ways than mere hunger. Alone with his thoughts, he had only seen more clearly what Krishna had often said—*she* caused the conflicts, she caused him to lose control. She caused them all to lose control. She was making a fool of every one of them. Even Yudishtira. After three months Arjuna knew one thing for certain. Or almost for certain. Somehow, he should have insisted that Draupadi marry Yudishtira and Yudishtira only.

But Arjuna had also seen in his solitude that he was pulled to Draupadi as he was to no other woman. It was this unusual feeling for her that, above all, he had considered and reconsidered, with no better conclusions than on the day he had first seen her walking into the pavilion at Kampilya.

On some days of his forest exile he thought it was that she challenged him. That she was unpredictable. Or that she was uniquely lovely, with her strangely dark skin yet her body more perfect in its subtle curves and proud stature than women of the fairest complexion.

Other days he was sure it was merely that she was not his alone, to have when he wished and ignore when he was busy with something more interesting.

Whatever the ultimate source of his feelings for Draupadi, by the second month he had decided they had to be cast off. Therefore, like the priest-born forest-dwellers, for his third month he set his mind on tranquillity and non-attachment. And at the end he was able to believe himself liberated from the Daughter of Fire.

So, pleased with his austerities and their results, he was back at Dvaraka's gates to celebrate with Krishna and finish his sojourn away from home.

It was not Krishna, however, who met him under the painted arches of the city's entrance, but Krishna's enormous older half-brother, Balarama. Although the Vrishnis had no true king, they did have a more-or-less leader in war and adjudicator in peace, and this was Krishna's and Balarama's father. Being the oldest son, Balarama would some day take his father's place. For now, he served his father as his spokesman among the far-flung, stubborn Vrishnis. Given his size and strength, and his good humour to balance them, Balarama was a persuasive administrator. It also helped that, like his father and most of the Vrishnis, Balarama was fond of drink. And his final important trait, also shared by all the impetuous Vrishni clans, was an absurdly sentimental fondness for forest-dwelling monks. Incapable themselves of the slightest austerities, they worshipped without discrimination those who did perform them.

Thus it was that, upon seeing Arjuna and without knowing who he was, Balarama immediately fell at his feet and a huge crowd gathered. After Arjuna's months of silence and isolation, the situation left the third-eldest son of Pandu speechless, and he soon found himself being carried on Balarama's shoulders into the heart of Dvaraka. When he was set down in the Vrishnis' assembly hall, Krishna was finally at his side. But far from clearing up the matter, Krishna only whispered, "Thank Indra you finally came, and just barely in time. Continue your silence. I will explain later."

Arjuna obeyed, and his silence only endeared him more to Balarama, the Vrishni elders, and then to the father himself. They admired his composure, his rags, and his "unbounded awareness". They also, without seeing any inconsistency, loved his "obvious strength and handsome appearance". They showered gifts on him, and then proposed an entire celebration to welcome the stranger, for they still had no idea that their heart-fetching monk was the third son of Pandu.

In the midst of his hosts' headlong rush to prepare, Arjuna, in a state of considerable confusion, turned and beheld a young girl approaching him. She wore a plain, finely woven virgin's gown and carried a simple refreshment of water and fruit. She bowed, left her offering, and departed before he could speak —or remember not to.

After that he tried to watch for her in the crowd. Everything about her had pleased him. She was as perfect as her choice of a gift—she had known he was hungry and thirsty, but that he was not ready after the forest to eat the rich foods others were trying to serve him. When he drank the water she had left him it seemed sweeter and purer than any he had ever known. The fruit he ate without noticing, his eyes still searching for her lovely face and dearly curving body.

Instead he saw Krishna. The Vrishni approached with a gift of incense and whispered, "I see that my ripe-for-marriage sister has pleased you. Didn't I tell you?"

Krishna's sister! Arjuna wanted to shout that it did not

please him at all. Not at all. His austerities gave him too clear a vision of what could be, and one scene he did not care ever to see, in his mind or in physical space, was himself returning to Indraprastha with a second wife.

Some time later he found himself alone at last with Krishna and free to protest. Or free if Krishna had been willing to yield a moment's silence.

"Thank all the gods you have come, Arjuna. Subhadra's bride's choice is imminent and Father and Balarama have asked her to choose this old buffalo who happens to be Balarama's best friend. She of course is going to be the good daugher and do it. I arrived here to find it had all been arranged down to the last garland and honey cake. My sister, wasted on an ageing wart hog. So I immediately thought—but I knew it was impossible—but still, if Arjuna returned in time—if you could make her love you. Of course, with you dressed as a priest and my sister so proud of her warrior family, she's not going to want you. Is she?"

Arjuna just stared at Krishna.

"Is she?" Krishna repeated. "Arjuna, I would like to make a wager with you. I will bet, Arjuna, that you can not make her love you. But if you succeed, I will personally help you to abduct her out from under my father's and brother's noses."

"Abduct her?"

"She can hardly choose a priest in a bride's choice, can she?"

"It's been done, and I was the priest."

"Not this time. No, my father and brother would not stand for it."

"But they wouldn't object if I abducted her," Arjuna said with grim humour.

"You'll do it by night. Once you are gone, I will explain. When they learn it is you, they will be delighted."

"Why not tell them who I am now?"

"Then what do they say to this rhinoceros of a bridegroom they promised her to? No, this is best. But I will not have my sister frightened to death by an abductor she does not know or would not have chosen for herself. You must first make her fall in love with you—and in your disguise, so she is not forced to lie to our father. If she has a girlish infatuation with a celibate, silent monk, they will only call it charming. And when she and everyone discover you are Arjuna, son of King Pandu, they will call it the most joyful day of their lives."

"Krishna, perhaps you have simply forgotten Indraprastha, and all that happened after we walked in on Draupadi and Yudishtira in the armoury."

"I have not forgotten," Krishna said softly. "But do you or do you not want Subhadra for your wife?"

Arjuna walked away. Then returned and stood before the Vrishni, pleased with his solution. "If I were to decide to attempt this, it would not be your help in abducting her that I would want. I will never marry any woman without my eldest brother's permission."

For once Krishna seemed almost dismayed.

Arjuna laughed. "It's all right, Krishna. I couldn't ask Yudishtira either. Can you imagine his reaction when he realised he'd have to tell Draupadi?"

Now it was Krishna who laughed. "No, Arjuna, I will keep my word—if you win her, I will ask him."

"Keep your word? You never *gave* it. No, it has hardly come to that."

Krishna stood before him, his eyes dark and cold as iron. "But of course it has, Arjuna. Unless you are so afraid of Draupadi's wrath that you plan to be celibate four fifths of your life."

Winning Subhadra demanded as ridiculously little effort as winning his first wife had required his utmost skill. Krishna's father and brother insisted on the honour of sheltering "the great young seer" in their household. And, as was the custom, the eldest daughter in the family was appointed to serve him. She was Subhadra.

Arjuna spent his days in the garden, under a blossoming citron tree, his every need attended to by the graceful, intelligent young girl. But for the first nineteen of those days, Arjuna kept his eyes downcast or in meditation whenever she came to serve him or play the harp. This was no callous strategy to tease her. He simply could not bring himself to take the irreversible step that would draw this sheltered, exquisite child into his life and make her a target for rakshasa, or for Sakuni and his Egyptian, for Suyodhana and Drita, or perhaps even for Jarasamda of Magada. Nor did he want to expose her to Draupadi's anger, and protecting her from that was what he was least confident he could do. From that he might not even be able to protect himself.

When Subhadra entered the garden on the twentieth day, in spite of all his concerns Arjuna's love mounted too swiftly to be ignored—he would have to declare himself today, before he shocked her with his unchaste desires. But when she knelt before him to leave his food, instead of rising again and taking her seat at a distance, she suddenly whispered her own declaration.

"Dear sage, I know you can never return my love, but if you will offer it on to the gods through the power of your austerities, this unworthy girl will be grateful for ever." Then she turned and fled, her headcloth pulled across her face to hide her tears.

Arjuna sighed and motioned to a servant to find Krishna. There were certain explicit instructions about the negotiations with Yudishtira that would have to be clear.

Standing beside Krishna's chariot outside the gates of Dvaraka, Arjuna urged his friend to perform his errand quickly. "You are leaving me here in a very awkward situation."

Krishna promised to return before the rains, and with Yudishtira's permission.

"But you will not insist," Arjuna repeated.

"I will follow your orders exactly."

"How I hate to do this to him."

"Arjuna, your brother has other, larger matters on his mind."

"Of course." Arjuna felt foolish. Then curious. "Have you heard some news?"

"None at all. But don't you think he is bound to begin thinking about becoming samraj? King of the Hundred Kingdoms?"

Arjuna started. "Krishna, you have one absurd idea after another. He has no allies. He would have to fight Jarasamda—"

"Someone must defeat that filthy butcher. But be easy,

Arjuna—I did not mean Yudishtira *is* thinking about becoming samraj. I only meant to suggest that this news about your winning Subhadra will seem like a small matter because he has so much to think about *like* becoming samraj."

"Krishna, after this with Subhadra, I am completely wise to your tricks, and if you love us at all you will not suggest to Yudishtira that he attempt to become samraj. Do not even hint of it with your 'of course you are too busy to consider trying to be samraj' or some such."

"Why Arjuna, could it be that you are finally feeling a little jealous of your eldest brother's potential power?"

"That is crazy! How can you say such a thing? He is the *eldest*." Arjuna searched frantically for words. "Yudishtira would be a perfect samraj!"

"Your brother would be an unsurpassed samraj, and such a samraj does not need prompting—the gods make their choice and the one chosen knows when this happens. For that reason, and because I do love all of you, I will have neither cause, desire nor need to suggest it to Yudishtira myself."

Krishna touched Arjuna on the shoulder, then shouted to his team. Arjuna watched the chariot speed northeast across the pastures of the Vrishnis, while his mind tossed in waves of loneliness, annoyance, love and confusion.

But not complete confusion. On one point he knew Krishna was utterly wrong—he was not jealous of Yudishtira. It was only that the sort of conquests required to become samraj demanded something exceptional of a man, something Arjuna had always thought he himself possessed in abundance. Arjuna flexed his arms. He would have to deal with this wedding bother promptly. Yudishtira would need his help.

33

You all want more. Always more.
                    the oracle of Amon-Re at Thebes

We had opposed writing because, when the intelligent
expand their influence by writing, they become spoiled
by pride, and when the ignorant expand their influence,
everyone is spoiled.

   Yet writing had to be risked in Bharata.

   Besides, no force in creation can stop the Self's expansion. So, like any wise teacher, I made mandatory what I
could not prohibit.

                                                    Vyasa

It was spring in Indraprastha. The seed heads of the winter
grains were fat and the palace now had a full complement of
sleeping apartments, as well as certain buildings for other
purposes. One of these was the king's new council room.
Yudishtira had chosen a round design, at the suggestion of the
Nishada—in a round council hut, they claimed, the worthy
advisers can not be edged so far to the rear by the sycophant.
The room's windows looked out upon the new gardens, where
some of the plantings were already blossoming in the warm
spring weather. The king was fond of the view.

   Outside the walls the villages were being built under Draupadi's direction now, since she had seen that no one else had
time to look to their design. At first, as was proper, she
preferred not to go out too often among the Dasyu herself.
After all, she was bearing a child. But within a month she had
entirely ceased to be proper in the matter, driving to the

387

villages almost daily, until the hot spring weather caused even soft-hearted Bhima to insist she must stop. So on warm days like today she stayed inside the walls and walked her gardens with the slow grace and tilt of the bearing woman, using pot shards to mark where trees should be planted.

Her walk was her only resemblance to the usual plump, boring serenity of a future mother of Arya royalty. She refused to even taste the dishes a bearing woman should eat. To everyone's delight, even when the king himself had been asked to try to coax her to eat the stuff, she had tossed it out of the window. And then the royal couple had laughed. These days they often laughed.

For Yudishtira the spring had been marred by only one trouble, which he was finally facing this particular sunny morning. He had done it—just after dawn he had found the Phoenician and told him, in great secrecy, that he wished to learn to write. They had agreed to begin after breakfast. And now Lettermaker stood in the doorway of the council room.

"You wish to proceed then, King? You haven't changed your mind?"

Yudishtira only glared back at him from by the window. The Phoenician might use a less cheerful tone, Yudishtira thought.

Lettermaker did not even wait for an answer—perhaps knowing how much his student hated assenting again to this particular question. "Well then, King. What would you like to write?"

"'Like to write'?" He thought about it. "I suppose I would like to write to my mother, so no one else at all would know the contents of my messages to her. That assumes, of course, that she could read."

"That assumes she would be the *only* one able to read, King."

Yudishtira flushed. "Concerning reading *or* writing, I try not to think beyond myself. Lettermaker, you must teach none of this to anyone but me, and tell no one I am learning. Also please desist in calling me 'king' and 'lord' when we are alone, even if Draupadi does make me sit on this throne."

"She is right, as always. The world belongs to kings."

"And apparently also to scribes."

"More to kings, and it should belong entirely to one as

virtuous as yourself." Lettermaker laughed. "Yes, I know you don't like compliments, but as payment for my instruction you must listen to my ideas."

"If I am virtuous, or appear to be, it is only because I was prepared for my responsibilities from birth."

"Where I've been, it's these ablest sons whom their ruthless relatives kill first."

"Are there no priests to teach the consequences of such absurd behaviour?" Then in his mind Yudishtira saw Varanavata's flames.

He rose and went to the window. The clouds were gathering into knots. A shower was coming. Perhaps the last one before the summer wait for the rain season. He closed the shutters and turned to face Lettermaker. The room was dark after the brightness of the day. He did not like any of what shuttering the window implied.

"Lettermaker, shall we keep to the task?" He made himself say the words again. "I must learn to write."

"I hope to make the tasks of writing and ruling less separate in your mind, Yudishtira." Lettermaker studied him a moment. "But all right, we will begin with the easier one."

The Phoenician described the three writing forms. The first used a wedge in wet clay to form different designs—several thousand of them—each standing for words or parts of words. The Egyptian mode employed ink on papyrus to draw standard pictures or, in the new style, simpler versions of those pictures plus some word parts and sounds. Finally, there was the Phoenician method—each symbol representing a sound, and a string of these symbols making a word. Lettermaker sat back. "Which may seem less efficient than having a single symbol for a word—"

"But you would have to know many, many symbols for all the words. And you would have no way to agree on how to show a new word."

Lettermaker stared at him. His incredulity made Yudishtira look away, embarrassed. "Exactly," the yavana said softly. "Although it took us much longer to see it. We make signs for the sounds of speech—there aren't so many of those. Once you learn them, new words are easy to add."

"Less like drawing pictures, more like speaking."

Lettermaker smiled. "And anyone can learn it quickly. No years spent in a school for scribes. Would you like to see how I would write your name?"

"Just to see it," Yudishtira said, then rebuked himself. "After that I will try."

Lettermaker took out the bits of bark and the writing tools he always carried and made some marks. "Your name—Steadfast in Battle."

"So a Phoenician seeing this would know I exist."

"If we could get it to him. But first I would write much more." Lettermaker made additional marks, reading each out loud as he formed it. "'In Bharata there is a king who is the true servant of his subjects. Implore your gods that kings everywhere follow his example.'"

Yudishtira stared at the marks with distaste. "Phoenician, with all the wonders the yavanas command, how in Indra's name do they curb the impulse to think they are gods?"

"I don't believe many of them see it as a problem, Yudishtira."

Yudishtira felt something almost frantic rising in him. "But pride can blind a man to sin, and his sins will keep him in Hell."

"Or a man can create Heaven on Earth, for others as well as himself. It is called Indraprastha, and the reason it works is your ahimsa—your desire to do what is good for all beings. That should be in writing, Yudishtira."

So Lettermaker understood his real desire. Was this also Vyasa's reason? Yudishtira felt his mind rebel; his very body revolted at the thought. "But it won't help!" he shouted. "One may as well address one's words to the wind as to a man who has gone mad with envy and greed."

"You refer to your cousin?"

Yudishtira stood, his sense of inner privacy deeply disturbed. "Show me again how to write my name."

"That will be too easy. Let me give you a whole line. 'Dear cousin: I have taken your cattle. My wife bears my child while you are still childless. Indraprastha now outshines Hastinapura. And a crowd of your former allies is pounding on my gates.'"

Yudishtira gave in and smiled a little. "So our clever Phoenician knows what I'd like to write. But besides inciting Suyodhana to break his vow, this message isn't true. I'm afraid the allies are not at the gate yet and we're still a little short of 'outshining Hastinapura'."

"What does Indraprastha lack that is of any importance? Perhaps an assembly hall? I know—now you will tell me you don't need it, for you have so few warriors to meet in it. But in Phoenicia we say, 'Prepare for guests and they always come.' How would you like it if your new hall were roofed with arches?"

Yudishtira shook his head at this yavana's audacity. "And how would you put arches over something so large?"

"It is true that wood lacks stone's weight to counter the tension pushing outward. But why not try securing each wood arch at the base with tension inward, just like bows?"

"A warriors' meeting place constructed in the manner of bows."

"Exactly. I am also interested in your pottery glazes. I would like to tile a floor in the centre of your assembly hall—one that shines like water. Blue, green, gold—depending on how it is seen. A place where speakers will stand to say their thoughts and, looking down, see their own reflection."

"Reminding them that their words reflect on themselves. Lettermaker, your plans always have an appealing boldness."

"I'm glad you agree." Lettermaker came and stood beside him. "*King* Yudishtira, it is my intention to build an assembly hall fit for a samraj consecration."

Yudishtira started. Lettermaker laughed at him. "I have read your mind like a piece of my own writing, haven't I?"

Yudishtira flushed.

"I have found out all about this matter, Yudishtira. A samraj has the sworn loyalty of every other king in Bharata and—"

"He must *obtain* that loyalty," Yudishtira corrected. "Kings may challenge him to duels or full battles if they do not wish to consent. That means the candidate must have an army at his command. Warriors with chariots, not a mob of Dasyu bowmen. For that reason alone there can be no samraj consecration at Indraprastha."

"Or a samraj might receive the kings' consent simply by being well respected," Lettermaker countered. "Your greatest have not demanded tribute, yet they've been showered with gifts. They have not called themselves generals, yet commanded all others in battle. You will be such a samraj."

Yudishtira recoiled. Lord Dharma, protect us. These yavanas have no sense of what is best left unspoken. "This is hardly the time for me to consider becoming samraj."

"But you have considered it, haven't you?"

"Only in foolish dreams. But my reputation has been slandered. I have no allies, no armies—"

"You have your brothers, your father-in-law in Panchala, and Krishna with all his Vrishnis."

"Listen to me, yavana!" Yudishtira paced the room. "Given certain grandiose plans which everyone knows my father had for me, I must at all costs avoid arrogance, and—"

"Arrogance is your least fault! What about your willingness to ignore Bharata's need for a samraj dedicated to dharma?"

"Lettermaker, I invited you here to teach me to write."

"You are proud of your honesty, Yudishtira. Can you honestly tell me Bharata does not need the wisdom you have been trained to share?"

"Bharata has been without a samraj for a full generation. A new attempt now would upset a delicate peace. It would certainly bring out Jarasamda of Magada, a dangerous man who has been trying to gain the consents lawlessly for twenty years."

"I have heard about him. Here is another reason for you to act."

"*Enough.*"

Draupadi suddenly burst into the room. "Forgive me. But I can't believe it. There's a message from Panchalya. Guru Vaja has given him North Panchala!"

"Your father-in-law rules South Panchala," Lettermaker said under his breath, "and now your brother-in-law rules North Panchala. Allies, Yudishtira."

Draupadi stared. "How did you know? This same envoy brings word from the Kekaya brothers." Forgetting Lettermaker, she went to Yudishtira. "They want to discuss forming

an alliance with you. And coming here to dwell! Here, Yudishtira—to Indraprastha!"

Lettermaker smiled. "While you are responding to Panchalya
and these Kekaya brothers, I will go to begin the plans for your
hall. Only, please tell me, how large must it be to accommodate
a truly grand samraj consecration?"

Yudishtira saw Draupadi look from Lettermaker to himself,
her eyes wide with fresh excitement.

"It is only a joke we've been making," Yudishtira said. "Only
a joke."

The same news of Guru Vaja's gift to Panchalya reached
Hastinapura under similar warm spring skies. Upon hearing
the announcement, Sakuni left the assembly hall almost at a
run. He crossed the gardens, stumbling over nothing, and fell
against a column along the covered arcade.

North Panchala to Panchalya! To the jackal's own brother-
in-law! And Vaja is the jackal's bitch—giving it to him.

Sakuni dragged himself upright, clutching the painted pillar.
They look at *me* in there. Blame *me*.

Of course. I am their only hope. Pitiful, pompous old
monkey-men. No wonder I was sickened by them, after the
company of my rakshasa. *They* kill freely, without this mask
of "dharma".

Yudishtira plots to kill me. I know it. His spies were in
there. I felt their eyes.

Sakuni burst into a shuffling run again, his stiff leg dragging.
Then he collected himself, falling against the next column.

No need to run. Yudishtira isn't here.

But he is preparing his revenge. For Varanavata, for the
snake, for his exile—

Yudishtira is on the Yamuna, starving.

He is on the Yamuna with half our cattle and a new throng
of allies! While nothing happens here. Nothing! Curse Zesnor
to Hell for ever.

He searched the folds of his clothing for the azle flask. But
he had left it in his quarters, afraid it would be discovered.
And afraid of the way terror overtook him whenever he tried
to do without it. He began to run again.

I must simply kill Yudishtira. Before he kills me. That is not unreasonable. He stopped at the next column. But no need to run. The man has a thousand vulnerable places.

"Uncle!" It was Suyodhana. Sakuni spun around.

"How could you leave the hall? Did you even stay long enough to hear Guru Vaja's message to us?" Suyodhana's large face, beaded with sweat, peered into his. "Are you sick, Uncle?"

"Zesnor has tried to poison me. But no more—I will take no more of his 'azle'."

"What do you mean, Uncle?"

Sakuni straightened up, summoning all his strength. His nephew was bad enough, and now the headache had begun, and the trembling. He spoke as curtly as he could manage: "At least I finally know on what side your 'guru' stands, Suyodhana. And why he went off to Ahicchatra and only now prepares to return."

The baron was relieved to see that he had distracted the youth. Suyodhana had begun gesturing wildly, almost speechless with anger. Sakuni used the time to gain greater control.

"Our 'guru' is *afraid* to return here," Suyodhana ranted. "After giving his kingdom to our enemies! To that two-faced Panchalya!"

Sakuni resumed his walking. "It was his to give." Suyodhana's absurd fluster was so familiar it was almost calming to his uncle.

"Vaja may as well have given it to Yudishtira himself!" Suyodhana shouted.

"Vaja only follows your example. You gave Yudishtira half your cattle."

"Nirriti take you to Hell!"

Sakuni stopped. "At least Yudishtira does not let himself be conquered by a few Dasyu wood rats."

"If I had not risked the defeat, we would not have known that Yudishtira had already turned all the Dasyu west of the Ganges against us and instructed them to disobey dharma. We were a party of peace-minded princes inspecting our lands when we were attacked by rebels incited by Yudishtira."

"I have also heard a different version."

"Those Kekaya brothers are all liars." Suyodhana grabbed his arm. "When will I be rid of Yudishtira, Uncle?"

"My rakshasa can not walk through fortress walls. We have to know Yudishtira's weapons stores on the Yamuna, his defences for the city." Sakuni began walking again. "It is a pity you were incapable of finding out any of *that*."

"But I can now! From Guru Vaja himself."

Sakuni stopped, his mind suddenly alert. Why hadn't he thought of it himself? When the pompous Guru Vaja returned, in decided disfavour for what he had done, he might easily be persuaded to go to Indraprastha and observe its defences.

"I mean it, Uncle. I can make him tell us now. His old servant has told me—under threat, of course—that the great, celibate, dharmic, honourable priest-born weapons-master once bedded a Dasyu woman. If it were known, it would destroy him."

Sakuni walked on. "Fool! No one would believe you. Meanwhile Vaja would have an excuse to take his very considerable military abilities to Indraprastha."

"This old servant says Vaja still loves the woman."

Sakuni stopped again. "That is another matter. He still sees her?"

"He doesn't still see her—he doesn't know where she is. But the old man swears Vaja dreams about her. Prays to her like a goddess. If we could find her—"

Sakuni was disgusted. "Find her? Why bother? Merely say we have. *Think*, Suyodhana. Good, then. Yes. Obtain the plans for Indraprastha's defences. Especially their tunnels. They'll have them—it is a favourite yavana trick, and they have that yavana who is building for them. We must have a way to put rakshasa inside." Sakuni's head felt clear at last. "And yes, bring down the arrogant Vaja. That in itself would please me greatly."

"Uncle, it will be my pleasure."

With Suyodhana gone, Sakuni went to the women's quarters, feeling well for the first time since winter. Plans whose vague shapes he had felt for two months were suddenly obvious, ready to be carried out. He tapped with his toe on the heavy yandava-wood door—a wood that Arya used only for chariot wheels and the barriers to women's apartments—and smiled to think how easily gold turned their yandava wood to sponge bark.

The door opened a crack, then, for him, swung wide. "Bring me the one called Lotus," he whispered to the female guard. The large, flatfaced woman took the coins with the ease of habit and showed him into an empty room. He watched her go, her arm and calf muscles bulging against brass circlets, her short bronze sword slapping her leather skirt.

Lotus came in and knelt at his feet. He was pleased with her appearance: gaunt, frightened and unwell. In short, receptive. Her kind of Dasyu never lasted long inside a city like Hastinapura. He was suddenly utterly sure of himself, the fog of the azle completely gone. She would be his weapon. Even Zesnor would be impressed by his plan. A woman would not be suspected or opposed when she approached her "beloved king" at Indraprastha, and from what he had heard of her story, this one could easily be made desperate enough to do anything.

"Baron Sakuni," she whispered. "You have called the wrong serving woman. I am unclean after childbirth."

"Unclean means nothing to me. But if you thought I might wish surata with you, that would be impossible anyway." He smiled warmly. "You and Arjuna are too much in love."

He could see her conflict on her face: He had pleased her, yet she did not trust him. "How can you, an Arya, say unclean means nothing?"

Sakuni shrugged. "If the king, my dear blind brother-in-law, insists on my presence later at his silly butter and rice burnings, and if I'm 'impure'—that is not my fault."

"You are here when all the other men are at the assembly?" She was confused. Good. Then he would make her reel.

"They bore me," he said, "with their storming about the loss of some useless cattle and land."

Lotus's eyes darted absently around the room, as if she were trying to orient herself. "But all Arya want land and cattle."

"For what? A few buckets of milk from every square league

of scrub. Taken from places that should never have been cleared anyway. I'm sure we agree on that."

Pressing her hands to her forehead, she didn't respond. Next he asked her about her baby, replacing her confusion with despair as he might play different notes on a flute.

"He was born sick," she whispered. "I had the sickness of the swollen limbs before his birth. Now he is sicker than I."

He sighed. "Another victim."

Still on her knees, Lotus suddenly clutched at her stomach and doubled over. "Whose? Whose victim?" she panted.

"Yudishtira's, of course."

She stiffened. "In Indraprastha they use your name to describe stable filth." Then her pain overtook her again, causing her to crouch lower on the floor.

He merely watched her. "I think Yudishtira should not have made you travel while you were bearing."

She was crying now. "No. Not Yudishtira. It was Arjuna who sent me here."

"Because Yudishtira wanted to be rid of you."

"No! Arjuna was going away too."

"Then he must have sent you to keep you safe from Yudishtira. After all, Yudishtira killed your sister."

"No. By mistake. He came to save her."

"Yudishtira shoots an arrow blind, from deep within the forest, and 'by mistake' it strikes your sister? No, he used her for surata to celebrate his tiger kill, then killed her to hide his deed. You and your people are too trusting, Lotus. Yes, Yudishtira protects the Nishada—because on the Yamuna they outnumber him. Once his city is built and his allies gathered, Yudishtira will have all of you killed."

"No." She covered her ears.

He took her hands away and drove home the last barbs— that Yudishtira could never rule the Kurus until he proved to Hastinapura that he hated all Dasyu. That Yudishtira was jealous of Arjuna because of Draupadi. Jealous, too, of Arjuna's happiness with Lotus. "How Arjuna must long to see that spiteful Yudishtira dead."

Lotus was crying and shaking her head, but no longer arguing. "Lotus, I tell you the truth: Arjuna will have to kill

Yudishtira some day, or be killed by him." Sakuni straightened. "But if Yudishtira were the one to die—as would be justice— Arjuna could be king."

"King? Bhima would be king."

"That of course must be prevented. When you kill Yudishtira—"

"*I?*" She clutched her head now, not her stomach.

"—then I will remove Bhima from your way. Arjuna will be king and you, as daughter of a Nishada headwoman, will be Arjuna's queen."

"But Queen Draupadi!"

"Draupadi I will remove too. Arjuna will forget that whore and marry you."

"No!" Her voice was frantic with confusion. Her face had gone from pallor to a blotchy flush. Sakuni drew back, afraid of the fever's presence. "No," she kept moaning now, "Yudishtira has saved my people."

"Has he?" Sakuni risked bending towards her, to stare deeply into her eyes. "Decide when you see whether your helpless child lives or dies."

She sprang up and rushed from the room. He could hear her running, shouting for word about her newborn. Then the afternoon quiet of the women's quarters settled around him. To celebrate, he could call for another woman now, for pleasure. But Lotus had given him pleasure enough.

Only a few questions remained. Would she herself live, and when and how could she be returned to Indraprastha? Perhaps Suyodhana really could learn of some secret entrance. But knowledge of their tunnels would be best saved for an attack. And during an attack Yudishtira would be alert and no doubt harder for Lotus to kill. This weapon would work better during the confusion of some sort of celebration. But no one from Hastinapura would be invited to Indraprastha for anything. It would require patience. First, he must hone his weapon properly.

He went to the door. The guard came to him, anxious to please. "How the Nishada woman suffers," Sakuni whispered.

The flat-faced woman nodded agreeably. Obviously Nishada did not concern her much.

"Her baby will die, of course." Sakuni sighed heavily. "All the portents are clear about that. So why not end her waiting?" He handed a gold-heavy coin bag to the woman. Suddenly she looked interested. He smiled. "The mother must live—give her better food. A healer. But the baby's misery must be ended. I want you to see to it yourself. I'm sure you understand me. Do it tonight."

34

Do not presume to understand a child's fated life span. Consider Gangeya's birth. His mother, River Ganges, took a woman's form to bear the eight divine Vasus, who were sentenced to a life on Earth for a divine misdeed. Ganges' adoring mortal husband was instructed never to inquire after his offspring, but he could not contain his curiosity. Following Ganges after each birth, he saw her drown her own infants, not knowing she did it to shorten their punishment. He interceded for the last, and so Gangeya was forced to live and suffer as a human being.

a Kuru legend

Moving within Herself,
She gives birth to consciousness.
She is the Creator.

Aditi

"*No*. I'm dying." But Draupadi did not die this time either. Instead the pain eased. She felt it was testing her. How much could she bear? Next time it would go quickly to what she found unendurable, then add more. Next time she would die.

"How much longer?" she whispered to Eos. "Tell me again that every time brings the end closer."

"Every time brings the end closer," Eos said quietly.

This time Draupadi heard the words differently. "I'm going to die, aren't I?"

The eldest priest-born woman from Dvaraka appeared over her. "Stop your words, Queen. You draw demons to you with your sounds."

Draupadi started to cry and gripped Eos's hand, but did not speak again. She had broken her silence only twice today— the first had been a scream three pains ago. Or four. It was too hot to think. It was a hot day—late spring. Or was it summer already? The *sutikagni* fire to purify the room was so large. Was it so impure here? But it was evening now. The end was coming. Eos had promised over and over since dawn—an end had to come.

Dawn had been so long ago. The first sharp, tight feeling had come and gone just as Urutata was singing the morning ritual.

She might never hear him sing again.

She knew she had been patient at dawn though, just as she had promised to be. No use exciting everyone for nothing. Ten cycles of pain. Then tell Eos. Don't excite the priest-born women from Dvaraka for nothing.

For nothing but death—all their preparations had been for death, not for birth. Ritual upon ritual, and this was the result. Not an infant. Only this. There had been sacrifices by Urutata to Aryaman and Pushan. More sacrifices by the Vrishni women to the goddess Sushana, who loosens wombs, and Bishkala, the fertile. It was all a confusion in her memory now. They had purified and sanctified this room over and over. She could see the white cloth hung everywhere. The wreaths. The corners made benign with vessels of water, the floor strewn with tinduka wood, mustard seed and kusa grass. Every knot in the palace had been untied— horses stood loose in the stables for fear the presence of even a halter knot would knot her baby's cord. All for nothing.

The pain toyed with her, delaying. Then rushed in. She bit her lips to keep from making a sound. She tasted blood afterwards. There was fresh blood between her legs too, where she knew there should not be.

Her mind flickered like a lamp in a draught. She wished she could see the sky again. She had been sequestered during the best month of spring, all for nothing. Shielded for so long from any shock—harsh words, loud sounds, strong tastes or smells. For nothing. She wished her skin was not so waxy from the massages with clarified butter. She wanted her husbands to remember her differently.

Yes, and she wished the women would bathe her again. Earlier today they had been bathing her so many times. Warm, scented water. They always began with her right-hand braid. She also remembered the four portions of the dregs of clarified butter being poured into a pail. The four munja-reeds on her forehead, pointing east. So much care had been taken, for nothing.

The chanting had stopped in the afternoon. The three priest-born women no longer burned hyena teeth and red he-goat hairs, no longer bathed her or made signs on her forehead. They only peered between her legs. Or felt her stomach, her pulse, her forehead. Every touch hurt. A jarring of her couch began another pain. But she forgave them, for she had troubled them so much. For nothing.

"Can you see it yet?" one whispered.

"Nothing. By Indrani herself, something is the matter."

"Don't you think we know that?"

Another pain came—this one did not build but clutched her suddenly. In spite of herself she screamed.

When it had passed, no one even admonished her. "We've sent for other healers," she heard someone say.

"And the king's mother is on her way."

"I'm going to die, Eos," Draupadi whispered.

"Don't say that."

"No. I must not say that. Must not say that. Not say." She could hear herself raving. "Not say. Not say." The pain knifed through her again.

After that one, her mind was strangely clear. She marvelled that others around her, in other bodies, were free of this pain.

Another came. This one did not stop. She heard herself screaming on and on, and shouting the names of the goddesses. "Indrani. Rohini. Aditi. Aditi."

Finally there was an opening in the red that filled her mind. "Yudishtira," she whispered. "I must speak to him."

"He is performing important rituals for you," a voice said.

"He's outside, Draupadi," Eos said. "I will bring him."

"You can't allow the husband in here!"

Eos bent beside Draupadi. "First try to shove inside your belly, Draupadi, like I told you."

She tried and the pain roared back. "Eos," she said through tears. "Tell me again about the slave women. 'The babies always get born.' Isn't that what you said? It just takes longer the first time?"

"Push it, Draupadi."

"I can't," she panted. "It makes the pain worse."

"You fight it. Don't fight."

"Can't bear it, Eos."

"Stand up, Draupadi."

"No!" The eldest of the Vrishni women went to Draupadi's head on the other side. "The woman must recline. Demons find the standing ones."

"Curse you, they already have. She needs to bear down."

"What would help would be more hyena teeth. I told her husbands there were not enough."

"Husbands," another said. "There is the cause. Five—it's unnatural."

"Mind your speech in front of their wife."

They fear for my death, Draupadi thought. My end comes. I must think.

The pain again. She arched up with it. Now she saw the birth-bed demon. He was there. His red-spotted face flew past her.

He was gone.

I will die here, she thought.

"Stand up," Eos repeated. "Draupadi, I want you to sit down on your heels."

"You endanger her," the midwife repeated.

"Someone must do something."

"It is up to fate now, yavani."

"I can't get up," Draupadi whispered. "Bring me Yudishtira. I must speak to him before I die."

"Up." Eos was lifting her shoulders.

"Please, please, bring him here," Draupadi cried, eyes closed against the pain.

"The husband may not enter," a voice commanded again.

Draupadi hid her face between Eos's breasts.

403

"Give me a chance to help her," Eos said, "or I will have the king remove you all."

"I'm so hot," Draupadi whispered.

"You must put out the fire now too," Eos ordered. "She has a fever."

"Never," someone said. "Extinguish the sutikagni and the demons will take the child too."

Another pain. It climbed and climbed. "Yudishtira!" Draupadi screamed. "Yudishtira!"

"I'm here." The voice was cool, clear.

The demon shimmered before her eyes and was gone again. There were other voices. When the pain let her open her eyes, she saw she was alone with Yudishtira. The sutikagni fire was out, the window open.

"I'm sorry," she whispered. "I don't know what's gone wrong. Your child—"

"He will live and you will live."

"No, I'm going to die, Yudishtira."

He buried his face in her wet hair. His voice was soft, crying. "What needs to be done? Tell me. I'll do anything. My mother will be here soon too—Nakula has gone to meet her at the ferry. Kunti learned birthing in the forest, and she never fails. Never. Let me help you, Draupadi."

With a shaking hand she touched his face, where tears shone. "I want you to know," she said with great effort, "that I love you. With a love that is different than—the other. But very great. Great. I only pray that I will not be punished for ever for my unfairness—" She started to cry. "But that I will some day join you in Heaven—" The pain crept closer. "Forgive me, Yudishtira!"

"There is nothing to forgive. But I will forgive anything if you will only live."

"Find my mother, Yudishtira. Vyasa—"

The pain struck. She clutched his arms, tearing at him with her nails, trying to keep back the screams.

Afterwards she stared at the blood on his arm.

"You must live," he whispered. "If you live, I will see that you and Arjuna are never separated. I will make you queen of all Bharata—"

"Stop. No. I want nothing but to live for you. For *you*."

Eos burst into the room, a steaming cup in her hand. "Sit up and drink this. Raise her up, Yudishtira." The two obeyed the yavani like little children.

Another pain consumed Draupadi. This time Yudishtira's arms were around her upper body. She strained with all her strength against them but they held. The hot liquid in her stomach spread around her belly and through her limbs.

"Lie back, Draupadi." Eos knelt at the foot of her bed. "Yudishtira, I think the head is turned. Keep her still while I try to straighten it."

"Can you do that?" Yudishtira asked.

"I don't know. I've seen Babylonian midwives do it. And I've straightened out the legs of a foal or two."

Draupadi heard herself laughing strangely. Alone with Eos and Yudishtira—if this was her end, this was how she wanted it.

"Good, Draupadi," Eos said. "Laugh at us. Come here a moment, Yudishtira. What do you think?"

Yudishtira went to look, no shock or revulsion, or even fear, on his face. He spoke softly with Eos, gesturing.

The pain came again. She felt his arms around her once more. The demon danced at a distance.

When the pain retreated Yudishtira nodded to Eos. In Draupadi's ear he said, "Now, my sweet wife, nine months ago we started this trouble together, perhaps together—"

Draupadi screamed. "Stop! Stop it."

"Hold her!"

"Only a moment, Draupadi."

"Help me, gods. I can't, I can't."

"Help her, Indrani."

"Aditi, mother of the gods! Stop!"

"Push, Draupadi."

"Aditi, I can't. Can't."

"You are. Again."

"Mother I can't bear it!"

"Again. I've turned it, Yudishtira. I've done it, I think. It's coming now. Good. Again, Draupadi. Again. Again."

"No. No. No."

Yudishtira's hands were gripping her arms so tightly that this pain almost blocked out the other. Neither hurt let go of her any more for an instant. They simply climbed. Ate at her mind. She knew she screamed with all her breath—it didn't help but she couldn't stop herself. The red-spotted demon had her dancing with him.

At last she was above it. The unendurable pain happened to a body, but not to her. The demon leaned close, smiling. So this is death, she thought. So quiet.

Then there was unbearable noise again. Rushing feet. Eos was shouting, "Bring the priests also. Yudishtira, look! Push, Draupadi. Yudishtira, you have a son! Again, Draupadi. Good, good."

The demon rippled and dissolved.

The pain in her arms stopped. Then the other pain faded too. Her eyes had been staring, but now she saw a red, wet thing in Eos's arms. Yudishtira bent over it, blew three times, and whispered in its ear.

A golden spoon appeared in Yudishtira's hand. He put it to the creature's lips. "I wish you Veda and prosperity and long-life," he said to it. "Intelligence, strength and the protection of the gods." Was he speaking to her? No, he would not, for she had loved Arjuna more.

The room was crowded. Now Mother Kunti held the creature. "I dedicate you to warfare . . ." Draupadi struggled to focus what she saw, for it was too much like a dream. Kunti and the baby were watched by every eye. "May you die a glorious death in battle . . ."

Battle? Die in battle? But Draupadi could not grasp it. She only wanted to study Yudishtira. Only Yudishtira. Her heart was filling with a kind of love she had never felt before. She wanted to see everything about him. Know everything about him. There was something so important to remember.

But she was already forgetting. Eos whispered in her ear, "Don't fight it—go to sleep." All of it disappeared.

Vyasa reached Aditi's cave before twilight. As he approached, two women suppliants faded into the mists and stunted trees like shy does. He laid out his gifts of food and soft woollens beside theirs of fruit and fresh water, and sat down at a distance, assuming the posture for meditation.

He had thought all day that he would resist his need to come up to this place where he had never come throughout the long three years since Aditi's withdrawal. Then in his room at Badari Ashram, in the late afternoon, he had had the clear thought that just because his small-self wanted to come and be near her, out of habit he had refused its demand. And that was only one more distortion of awareness, keeping him from realising that today required him to go to her.

But by the time he had straightened out his mind, he had arrived too late in the day. Aditi emerged at dawn and dusk, but only when she was alone on her mountain—this was part of her vow. To stay at this hour and keep her inside would be a serious discourtesy.

He closed his eyes for one sweet moment before going. "For how long?" he whispered. "How long, Aditi?"

Out of the silence of his mind, she spoke as clearly as if beside him: *For as long as is best for my daughter.*

He felt his heart lifted up as he responded. "She is labouring too long at the birth today."

It has just ended. She and her son are well.

"Can you know everything about her?"

Only what she feels.

"Then you suffered as much as I today. Can she feel what you feel?"

She can not. We made her forget me. No, do not blame yourself again. I need to ask you difficult questions and I can not if it adds to your pain.

"What do you want to know?"

My daughter has been despondent. Is Yudishtira not the man we thought?

"He is more than we ever hoped, yet she has preferred Arjuna."

When she was a child, I would send her out searching for the most potent herbs. She would come back with some pretty flower.

"I fear this one will not bring her joy."

She has divided her heart because we have divided her

407

mind. Five husbands. Her brother. Today a son. The child's grandmother also. She is too young to give to so many.

"Aditi, knowing she is Dasyu also disturbs her. Perhaps I should tell her of her priest-born father?" He heard his small-self in the question, testing to see if he spoke to the real Aditi or his own need.

The long silence itself was an answer.

You know I always wished them to know. Otherwise my son will be sacrificed to this secret.

"Perhaps not. The mending holds—Vaja gave the boy North Panchala."

Kaliyuga will tear apart every mere mending—only the truly whole will remain. If my son and daughter are to be accepted as royalty, they must seem warrior-born. Their priest-born father must not be known. You see, Vyasa? The divisions deepen everywhere—warrior and priest, Dasyu and Arya.

"The Age of Discord. The Age of Kali."

I create and I destroy, in order to create again. A greater wholeness.

He opened his eyes, certain she was in front of him now. But the entrance to the cave was still empty, black and cold.

Yet he heard her voice: Now please go before we weep.

Draupadi woke to bright sunlight. Her baby slept in a basket beside her. She remembered that his name was Prahara, "Fighting". The name had been chosen by her husband and Urutata.

Had the tiny child been at her breasts two times in the night? Or three? And what did he look like? She could barely recall.

Eos appeared with a steaming cup but did not speak, nodding as explanation towards someone on a divan in the corner. Draupadi saw it was Mother Kunti, lost in thought, her eyes open yet not seeing.

Eos gestured for Draupadi to drink what she had brought. Draupadi sipped the bitter liquid.

She had meant to express her gratitude, to ask questions— but she was already slipping back into the shelter of the sleep-inducing herbs.

When she woke again it was twilight. Eos was placing

Prahara beside her to nurse. When Draupadi moved to offer her full breast to his searching mouth, she was aware that she felt tired, awkward and proud. Eos was smiling down on them.

Behind her Draupadi saw Kunti again, sleeping on the same divan in the corner. "You must encourage my mother-in-law to rest in a proper bed," Draupadi whispered vaguely, adrift in the pleasant sensation of Prahara's lips tugging gently at her breast.

"It has been two days since the birth and this is the first time she has slept at all, Draupadi. It is as if she has gone to another world. I can only think that her stay in Hastinapura was a great hardship."

In the quiet room Prahara's sucking sounded noisy and eager. A bee buzzed where it was trapped in the fold of a curtain.

Hastinapura. With effort, Draupadi thought about it. Of course Kunti had suffered there, among her sons' enemies. She should have been sent for sooner.

Prahara struggled with some vague frustration. Draupadi offered him her other breast. More alert now, she stared at her own son with wonder. Kings and kingdoms. Would this little one rule all the Kurus one day?

She forced herself to admit that her child might not even rule the half kingdom of Indraprastha if King Drita and Suyodhana had their way—Indraprastha's new allies, honest men such as the Kekaya brothers, had said enough to make that clear.

Draupadi felt her love crowded out by fear. Perhaps Baron Sakuni's Egyptian would try to kill her child even before he was grown.

Or perhaps this child would die avenging his father.

She looked again at Kunti. How had she willed herself to make her suckling babes into warriors who walked with Yama? But then, what had Kunti said over this very child? "I dedicate you to war . . . May you die a glorious death in battle."

Gripped with this new anxiety, Draupadi looked up at Eos, who offered the cup of herbs again. Draupadi drank, and slept.

When she woke again it was almost dark. A baby was crying near her. Yes, her child. Prahara.

"I am seeing to him," a strong voice said.

Draupadi looked. Her mother-in-law held Prahara; her expression was serene and purposeful.

At dawn Draupadi woke yet again. Mother Kunti slept on the divan with Prahara, her body at ease at last. Eos stood at the door. The Greek woman looked at the resting Kunti and her grandchild, then at Draupadi. Draupadi saw sympathy in her friend's eyes, and an honest acknowledgment of what had come to pass and what would have to be.

Draupadi felt a sorrow and an acceptance. The child was after all a vague new being to her. If he could heal Kunti, Draupadi could never deny her that balm.

Still, her heart felt a new wound. But one that ceased to bleed too quickly, for the sake of the whole body's life.

35

What we really want is what we always do.
Baron Sakuni

In the month after Prahara's birth the weather on the Yamuna became breathlessly hot. Indraprastha's grain fields ripened until the heads bent low, and were scythed, threshed, winnowed and stored in cool jars. The Nishada carpenters were glad to be shaded by the twenty huge wooden bows that curved over what they all thought had to be the most magnificent assembly hall on earth.

Draupadi spent the month in seclusion, recovering from the birthing, and Yudishtira occupied himself with the many plans, problems and disputes that arose in a growing kingdom. Still, he was often reminded by the hot and dusty days that his wedding had been at this season a year ago. This would bring memories of his dangerous, bittersweet journey to the Yamuna with his beloved, which in turn would remind him that his time with her was very nearly at its end. And then he would plunge deeper into his tasks. But it is difficult to avoid one's own wife. For example, on the last day before the full moon, the day before Draupadi would become Bhima's for three months, Yudishtira had retreated to the half-built hall to show Nakula the tiles Lettermaker had fired for its floor. Then, after admiring the samples strewn about like squares cut from a clear lake, Yudishtira had led Nakula to the side of the hall that overlooked the garden.

"Out here will be the real pond," Yudishtira explained. "Same tile floor and kerb, but filled with water."

"Like the same object seen in different realities—awake and

411

dreaming." And then Nakula pointed to their right, where Draupadi and Lettermaker were rounding the corner of the hall, debating the location of a small latticed pavilion four labourers were carrying in their wake. Nakula stiffened. "Two more realities to discuss."

It was Draupadi's first day out of her rooms. She was holding the month-old Prahara, jiggling him to the rhythm of her conversation. When the infant cried, she absently gave him a finger to suck.

"Lettermaker has more ideas than I can understand," Nakula whispered, "and she has more moods." He laughed too loud. "And I think your Prahara will learn early to compete. He will have to fight for her attention with the rest of us."

Kunti emerged from a doorway and took the child. Yudishtira turned his back on the scene.

Nakula shook his head. "The reality I thought should be discussed was her intention to go to Bhima's bed only one month after such a difficult birth."

"Everyone asks *me*." Yudishtira did not bother to hide his annoyance. "But no one asks her."

"You are right—it is not your place to question it."

But Yudishtira could not stop himself. "She has four other husbands, but I'm supposed to tend to this. Even Mother won't speak to her. But you all expect me to."

"Yudishtira, we know you can't. None of us can, when we all know she's only doing it so that she can be with Arjuna as soon as he returns."

The hopelessness in Nakula's voice startled Yudishtira, so that he studied his youngest brother for several moments. "You also love her that much, Nakula?" Then Yudishtira turned away. "In spite of all our precautions, it seems she has divided us."

"Our hearts, but not our minds. Not our loyalty. Never doubt that, Yudishtira." When the eldest turned back to respond, the youngest had fled.

The morning wore on. Yudishtira tried to lose himself in the remeasuring of distances and the examining of materials before they were employed for roof or floor. The feeling of distress that would not dissipate he attributed to his feelings about the day, and to his conversation with Nakula, until he went to his council room at noon and found Krishna waiting for him.

"How did you come in without anyone announcing you to me?" The Vrishni had never seemed so exhausted or tense. Yudishtira was immediately concerned. "Have you news from Arjuna? He has sent us only one brief message in nine months."

Krishna stood and bowed, then sat down again. "I'm sorry if I startled you, King Yudishtira. I assayed one of your tunnels. As for the Silver One"—the Vrishni's voice was noticeably strained—"he is in Dvaraka right now, performing great austerities."

"Austerities? My brother? Krishna, what in Indra's name is going on?"

"Very little, really. Only that your brother wants your permission to marry my sister Subhadra."

"*Marry?* He's already married!"

"Now calm down and listen to me, Yudishtira. I knew you wouldn't listen."

"Curse it, Krishna. This is absurd. In all fairness, have I ever not listened to you?"

"No. But listen to me now also. Your brother wishes to take a second wife, and I assure you, Subhadra is—"

"A marvel of womanhood, I've no doubt, if she is *your* sister."

Krishna grinned, but Yudishtira thought it was the strangest, most strained smile he had ever seen. Pandu's eldest paced around the room, finally sitting on his throne, as it was the only decent seat left now that the Vrishni's legs were sprawled across the others.

"Arjuna hasn't even consummated his first marriage. Krishna, you do not realise what you are saying."

"I know—Draupadi feels strongly for Arjuna."

"You do *not* know. You can not, and say what you are saying. Draupadi's grief would endanger her very body and mind."

"I do realise that."

"Then how in Indra's name can you be smiling again?"

413

"Only that it might also be the very best thing for Draupadi," Krishna said.

"Never."

"Anyway, it is a fact—Arjuna is madly in love with Subhadra and says *he* will not survive without her."

"*That* I don't believe."

Krishna laughed. "Well, at any rate, he is enjoying himself. Come now, Yudishtira. You know she'll turn to you for comfort —that won't be so painful, will it? Anyway, it's really between the two women. First wives are always jealous of the next ones. Surely she knows that a king and his brothers are expected to take other wives—or she needs to learn it."

"But one can take other wives and still leave it clear who has one's heart, Krishna. Draupadi might understand if only Arjuna came home first and—"

"Subhadra has his heart!"

Yudishtira went to the window.

"It's a wonderful story of how it happened, Yudishtira."

"I don't want to hear it."

"You are the only one Arjuna wants informed until he can tell Draupadi himself. You see? He does want to spare her feelings."

"How gracious of him!"

"I am planning a nice, rowdy Vrishni wedding for the couple. All that is needed is your permission."

Yudishtira still stood by the window. He could see Draupadi sitting alone at the far end of her beloved gardens, in the shadows of a coral tree.

"Yudishtira, you must not worry about her. Arjuna has a plan to make her accept it."

"No plan of his can make her accept it, and if he thinks he has one, it proves how little he knows of her."

"Arjuna and I will see that no word of the marriage leaves Dvaraka ahead of him, and he will not return until his year is over. But Yudishtira, Arjuna must marry Subhadra soon. You see, he has already, well—"

"So now he *has* to marry Subhadra. Is that why there will be no bride's choice? Why do you two even ask my permission?"

"You know why. Arjuna would forget Subhadra in an instant

if you told him to. It is I who plead—my sister would suffer terribly and our family would be humiliated."

Yudishtira slammed the window shutters closed. "Subhadra is your family, I have my own."

Krishna suddenly looked exhausted again. He stood, bowed and made the formal gesture for permission to be excused. Yudishtira granted it in the rudest way—the signal used with servants. Then he shouted, "By Indra, you are a cursed nuisance! How can I send you from me like this?"

Krishna shrugged innocently. "Just do it, I suppose."

Yudishtira spent the afternoon observing a demonstration of the leather shields Lettermaker had suggested be placed on chariot horses. Krishna rested. Yet when they met again to eat together in Yudishtira's apartments, he thought the Vrishni looked more troubled than ever. This time the subject of Arjuna and Subhadra was not alluded to. Instead Krishna had another team to harness.

First he congratulated Yudishtira for his cleverness in sending back half of Hastinapura's western herd. "What you lost in cattle you gained in reputation. A masterly move."

Yudishtira denied any "masterly moves", reminding Krishna that according to dharma those who avert a cattle raid receive half the cattle saved. When Krishna suggested he might have been conducting his own perfectly legal cattle raid, Yudishtira countered that one does not raid one's own kin or allies.

Krishna laughed in an empty, discomfiting way again. "King Drita tried, but he could never make you see a division where there was once wholeness. I'm sure you've heard that Suyodhana blames you for the whole thing. You are 'encouraging the Nishada to rebel by treating them as equals'."

Yudishtira was furious. "How can you even repeat such a preposterous thing? The Nishada are joining King Does-Nothing out of anger at all Arya and out of fear of the rakshasa, whom we Kuru would have eradicated by now were it not for our silly disagreements and this weakening division of our country."

"Nishada have also joined *you*, Yudishtira."

"They are no threat to Suyodhana."

"Unless you arm them."

"Which you know I have done—only for their own protection, because we lack Arya warriors to defend them. What, do you agree with Suyodhana?"

"No, I hope you do more of the same—form a vast Nishada army, build your unequalled assembly hall, make many alliances."

The two lapsed into an uncomfortable silence. It occurred to Yudishtira that Krishna's strange, almost grief-stricken mood might be because he somehow knew writing was being practised at Indraprastha. Yudishtira tried to bring it up vaguely, referring to Lettermaker. When the Vrishni showed no reaction, Yudishtira changed the subject—and stumbled into the Vrishni's nets.

"Lettermaker actually thinks I should attempt to become samraj."

Krishna nodded as if he already knew. "But of course you have not considered it."

"I have considered it."

"But only because Lettermaker suggested it."

"And I had considered it before. Only because it was my father's dream for me. Before we were humbled by reality." And Yudishtira reviewed the reasons he could not make the attempt: First, the lack of allies, warriors and chariots; and second, Jarasamda. "Flouting dharma, he kills those he defeats, except the ones he supposedly chains in caves to be used later for sacrifices to Rudra, Magada's god of war. The latter outcome I doubt ever really occurs, but either one would mean I had denied my people my protection."

Krishna protested that Yudishtira would eventually have to lead an expedition to defeat Jarasamda anyway, since no one else was doing it. Or Jarasamda would attack Indraprastha, expecting an easy victory.

"But we are discussing now an attempt to become samraj, Krishna. And even if we could defeat Jarasamda, and even if we gained the allegiance of all those he's imprisoned or angered, and provided we could win against those who would not give their consent without a fight—"

"Let your brothers handle them. Make them examples to

the rest. It will bring you peace in the long run. The most quarrelsome wolf pack is the one with tail-wagging leaders."

Yudishtira sat back. "There is still my uncle and my cousin."

"What of them? Suyodhana has sworn to forgo his jealousy. At least publicly they will all have to act pleased that a Kuru is samraj. Any Kuru."

"Privately, it will increase this taking of sides by everyone."

"Which you can't stop. Look beyond that," Krishna said harshly. "Far beyond."

"I have. I will admit that I have also wondered whether it wouldn't stop the quarrel. If Indraprastha were invincible and I were samraj, is it possible that my uncle and cousin would be forced to rest content?"

The Vrishni's face showed no agreement, no disagreement. Yudishtira asked again. Krishna only shrugged.

Yudishtira was confused. Had he been mistaken in thinking the Vrishni was for this madness? "So, enough of this dreaming."

"Enough of this dreaming," Krishna repeated.

"Only tell me, Krishna, why did you even bring it up?"

"You brought it up."

Yudishtira felt ready to shout some curse. "Krishna, I could use your help. These are difficult decisions—this absurd suggestion of Lettermaker's, this matter with Arjuna—"

"Why not merely do what you want about these things?"

"I must do what dharma dictates. You know that."

"Which is what *you* always want."

"Stop your jokes."

"'When dharma is unclear, let a righteous king decide.'"

"But am I righteous enough!"

Krishna shrugged. "I suppose we'll know when we see the results of your decisions."

"Oh, for Indra's sake get out of my sight."

Krishna stood and made a servant's obeisance, communicating hurt feelings in every motion. Which only confused Yudishtira more when the Vrishni turned at the door and his face was lit by the first unclouded smile since he had arrived.

That night a nearly full moon lit the palace. It poured through windows left open in the heat and silvered the room where Eos and Lettermaker lay naked across the bed.

"We're white like snow," the Phoenician said, running a finger along his lover's hip.

She moved away. "I sometimes wonder if I will ever see snow again."

He caressed her hair instead. "The Himalaya are said to have snow. Why not go and see them? Or go home to your beloved Greece. You're free."

"Is that what freedom is like?" She let her voice be bitter. "I am not as used to it as you."

He sat up. "What bothers you tonight?"

She rolled on to her side, her back to him. "I don't want to talk about it."

"You don't want to do anything else either."

"Don't I? How do you know?"

"You are being strange and difficult." He ran his hand gently down her back, then turned her towards him. She kept her eyes closed. His hand searched between her legs. She waited.

Instead he stood and went to the window. "Why don't you just ask me? You know a messenger came for me today."

"I don't care."

"Yes you do. He brought a papyrus and you know it. So you think it is a letter calling me back west."

"'Go where you want. You are free.'"

He ignored her. "It was from the Baron Sakuni of Hastina-pura."

"Then you should have put it in the dung pile."

"Sakuni and his Egyptian slave may be the only persons in three thousand leagues who can speak and write the languages I am fast forgetting. No one told me this about Baron Sakuni."

"When describing the cobra, it is easy to forget to mention the colour of his eyes."

Lettermaker came back and sat down on the bed. "Sakuni has invited me to visit him."

"Go if you like, free man."

"I don't intend to leave you, Eos. But it would be possible to drive me away. I only know so many ways to circumvent your hate for the men of your past. I am not one of them."

"Do you really know who you are, Lettermaker?"

"And can you admit you are jealous because I spend so much time with Draupadi?"

"I could if I were. I don't like it only because her husbands are certain to notice, and there are four too many of them already."

"I do like her, Eos. Because she is like you. And like myself. We are horses left behind by mistake when the caravan moved on. The customs and traditions that bind others are for us merely shreds of bridles that will be easily rubbed off on the next high pass."

"That is not Draupadi or me. That is only you." She turned away, hearing the anger in her voice. She felt sick inside. Yet he could change. She stared at her hand and imagined reaching back to him, saying what might still heal him. What he wanted to hear: "I care for you. I love."

She could do it. Just do it.

Suddenly he was on top of her. All night she had expected this. Still she fought him. But with half efforts. She who could kill a man with a blow had never dared resist this—the men had too often been her masters.

He thrust into her. She bit back the scream of hatred that was right behind her mouth. Her throat ached from the urge. But she would not give him even that much of her.

He rose up a little and smiled the conqueror's smile. She spat at his mouth. He laughed and finished his deed, making soft victory cries.

She lay rigidly still afterwards, waiting for him to go.

He finally rose and stood over her. "I wish to all the gods in all the heavens that you had screamed out loud what you were screaming inside. For I know that only after you do that can you begin to love me. But I will always treasure the taste of your spit—a small gift from me to you."

On the same night Draupadi walked boldly through the moonlit garden. After all, he had invited her. Besides, there was no reason not to be going to Yudishtira the last night before Bhima's three months, as long as there was no surata. Since

Prahara's birth they had not had a single moment alone together.

Still she slipped into his council room without waiting for an answer to her tap, anxious to be out of sight of Bhima, the twins, Kunti, Eos, Lettermaker, Urutata, the newly arrived Krishna, the new allies and their families and hundreds of others, including dogs, parrots and monkeys, who were all forever curious about her and everyone else in their small city.

Yudishtira was seated beside a lamp, examining varieties of seeds for the rain-season planting. She cast her eyes down and waited. Her purple skirt with the border of gold thread and jewels glittered in his lamp light.

When he did not speak she moved sideways into the room, closer to where he sat on his throne. Now she could feel him watching her. She made the formal bow to a king, falling to her knees, and remained on her knees near his side. Within reach.

"There are some things I want to discuss with you," he finally said.

She nodded, her heart pounding. She could hear in his voice that he also had his barely controlled hopes for tonight.

"I thought now would be better than tomorrow," he said. But when he did not begin, she looked up. She was surprised that he appeared deeply troubled.

"I have to tell you that Krishna—" He stopped. "I want to make you happy, Draupadi, and I am very uncertain what will serve you best."

"I am happy now, Yudishtira."

"But in the future." He came down to sit on the floor in front of her and took her hand. "When you almost died I made you two promises, Draupadi."

As it had at Prahara's birth, her heart filled with love for him. But she could not find the words to express it. She lowered her eyes. "I did not accept those promises, Yudishtira."

"But I might still make one of them as a gift. I must decide. I will also speak to my mother and Urutata about this, and eventually our assembly. But except for Vyasa's opinion, which I doubt I will receive, yours is the most important to me, and you are the first to hear: Draupadi, I am considering attempting to become samraj. Making you what I said that day—queen of the world. Or at least of Bharata."

She caught her breath. Yudishtira as samraj!

Then she remembered all she had heard of Jarasamda of Magada.

"It would require a clever strategy," he was saying. "Army against army would be difficult, with Magada's slaves. Although there might be some who would join us for this particular purpose. But if a small party could go, right after the rains—"

"And surprise him," she said. "No one has challenged the man himself in years. Bhima could defeat him. I know it."

"So you would not, after all, completely oppose this wild idea?"

"I would be afraid for you." She wondered if he knew he had already decided. "But I would approve it."

His satisfaction reminded her of Panchalya's in some Before time: In her mind she saw a bow in her brother's hand, a white hare and a winter sky.

"If we succeed against Jarasamda," Yudishtira was saying, "we send out my brothers. Bhima will go east. East will be difficult, with Kosala and Videha. Sahadeva south. He can deal with the Cedi and Karusa. Nakula west—Rohitaka shouldn't be a problem for him." He hesitated. "And Arjuna might go north for me. But only if you agreed."

"Whatever is needed," she said calmly.

I know what you expect, she thought, but I am no longer a weeping, lovesick girl—Arjuna will have time for conquests and for me also.

But you, a samraj!

"The way you look at me," he said, "I may myself go out and conquer all of Chine and Bactria for you alone. Consider the celebration we would have for a samraj consecration— every warrior-born, every king and prince in Bharata, all here at Indraprastha." He was laughing. "They will say, 'Anyone with gardens like these, designed by his own wife, must definitely be samraj.'"

He had taken her hands in his. Now their touching stopped their laughter. He quickly drew his hands back, but this drawing back said more than the reaching. "To have you consecrated beside me," he whispered, "as queen of Bharata—"

"To have you speaking truth before the hundred kings. Yudishtira—" She gestured helplessly, her eyes lowered.

He did not answer, but his hand came to her cheek, then caressed her breast. It seemed to burn where it touched.

"Draupadi," he whispered. "I must hold you."

He lay her down and pressed the length of his body to her with a kind of wild despair. His hands searched for her breasts and hips and thighs, undressing her swiftly, as if for the first time. "Daughter of Fire," he whispered. "Queen of my world. I cannot bear to lose you."

"You will never lose me. Never." Her voice was choked. "And you will be king of the whole earth."

The length of his plough pushed hard against the gate of her field, and she ached from wanting him, yet that was only a small part of her surging feelings. The love that gripped her was that love she had felt since their son's birth, and it made possible the forgoing of even the most intense desire if he would suffer for it later.

Her hand found his plough, and she began to urge it to accept a different pleasure. She moved from under him, turned him, and crouched between his thighs. The priests at Kampilya had told her lovemaking such as this which she wished to do was sin, but she was also Dasyu—she knew other laws. Taking his plough in her palms, she caressed it until she received his burst of seed.

Afterwards she allowed him to ease her longing also. But even after they had each found some satisfaction for their bodies, their hearts still caused them to cling to each other. There was a despair remaining that she had never imagined. They kissed again and again, as if on the eve of some hopeless battle.

At last they lay unmoving in each other's arms. Draupadi fought an emptiness rising from the depth of her being. This was not the emptiness of a wife's field unparted by her husband's plough or even the emptiness of farewell. She sensed that some profound lesson was being ended, just as she was learning to listen for its truths.

They rose and slowly dressed each other, reluctantly, as if

putting away something precious to be sent a great distance and perhaps never seen again. He kissed each part of her before it disappeared under cloth; she outlined him with her finger as if to paint him in her mind. Finally there was nothing more to do but say goodbye.

Eos crouched in the garden, hiding in the shadows from the moon that made the night as bright as day. She had not meant to see Draupadi leave Yudishtira's council chamber a moment ago. Or to see Yudishtira come out shortly after and hurry towards Krishna's suite. Troubled by her unintended intrusion into their private world, Eos was rising to go back inside when she saw Nakula.

"So much coming and going tonight," Eos said with a forced lightness.

He nodded. He was looking up at the sky, as if watching for an attack from the stars themselves.

"A bad night," she said.

"Only an odd one, I think."

"But you feel it coming too, don't you?"

He didn't answer.

She shuddered. "What is it? Can you name it?"

"I am not certain, Eos."

"It's coming for them, isn't it?"

"For them?" He looked at her oddly. "For all of us," he whispered. "For us all."

"Krishna, are you awake?"

"This is a question? When a king asks, I am awake."

Yudishtira came in. Unable to see in the shuttered room, he stood by the door. "I've decided to try for it, Krishna. After the rains."

"Samraj?"

"Yes. For her sake. Perhaps it will make up for Arjuna. You may give him my permission to marry."

"You will not become samraj for yourself, of course. No matter—the water brings life, whatever the reason it flows."

"What did you say, Krishna?"

"Nothing."

"But tell Arjuna he must not come back with Subhadra until his year is up. It must be after the rains. That will be after Bhima's three months too. Bhima must have those undisturbed."

"Of course, although I would have thought Bhima's marriage happiness was Draupadi's responsibility, not yours."

"This is my decision!"

"So be it. Excellent, in fact. I see you are leaving. Good night then. And may Lord Dharma protect Bharata's next samraj."

36

I possessed her body for one night. She possessed my mind
the rest of my life. It is as if I can only want what I think
she would want, only do what I think she would do.

Guru Vaja

The heat was all the more oppressive because of the rain clouds
darkening the sky, rumbling, promising relief. But it only grew
more still and hot. Suyodhana walked slowly on his errand,
wanting time to think. Yet when he arrived at the door of the
weapons-master's small house near the armoury he knew there
was really nothing to consider.

Looking in through the window, he saw Guru Vaja's old
servant had been right—the priest-born warrior had not yet
returned from his errand. Childhood inhibitions tried to re-
assert themselves—"the privacy of a teacher is sacred to a
student". But Suyodhana reminded himself he was no longer
a child or Vaja's student. The weapons-master had ended that
himself. Suyodhana opened the door and went in.

It did not take long to find what he sought—the house was
bare of decorations or furnishings except for a wooden sleeping
platform, a cooking hearth and a bench and table. The furni-
ture was of the best woods and well made, but Suyodhana
found them absurdly plain for a man of Vaja's stature. But
then, the man was not royal or even warrior-born, Suyodhana
reminded himself, but the son of a priest. This would be
important to remember. And Vaja was not only priest-born,
but he had taken the vows of austerity, including celibacy, in
order to increase his awareness. He was formidable.

But this time his cherished austerities would be his downfall, for they formed the white background that would make the one smear so shocking. Like the one exception to the sparseness in this room.

Suyodhana approached this exception cautiously. It stood on a shelf built into the wall. It was a statue of the goddess Aditi, the Unbounded, the Infinite, the Absolver, the Mother of Gods. Around it hung a garland of flowers crumbling with age. At its feet was the evidence of many camphor-light and sandalwood-scent offerings, and one fresh sprig of orange oleander. All very interesting, since Guru Vaja was sworn to Indra.

Suyodhana had never actually seen a statue of any god before. He would not even have been certain that the clay figure was meant to be Aditi had it not been for the symbols associated with her, such as stars and apamarga branches.

Suyodhana made himself touch the thing. When nothing happened, he flicked it smartly with his first finger snapped off his thumb, as one might test a fruit. After all, according to Vaja's servant this weapons-master did not consider his statue to be of a real goddess anyway, but of a living woman Vaja had once known. Suyodhana studied the statue a moment longer, then sat down to wait.

The weapons-master came almost immediately—Suyodhana heard him striding through the gravelled yard. The priest-born thrust open the door, then stopped. "Suyodhana, one does not enter a house without its owner's permission."

Suyodhana was annoyed by the paternal evenness of his teacher's voice. But he could change that. "I'm sure *my father* will not mind."

Still Vaja controlled himself, and Suyodhana saw that he should have done the same. Undoing that remark would cost more time. Belatedly he rose to his feet in the presence of his elder and offered his apology. "But when I realised today how much I needed your advice, I came straight here."

"Your obligation to ask for my advice before acting ended with your graduation."

"And also your obligation to advise? I hope it has not ended, for I fear that no one but you can help me. You know I swore to cease my enmity with my cousins. But I can not forget

Bhima's gloating face, or Yudishtira's self-righteous silence when he accepted half the kingdom, all the while plotting to build a nation of rebel Nishada on the Yamuna." Suyodhana came closer. "How do you forget something which has made a mark on your mind like a carver's tool on stone?"

Behind the weapons-master Suyodhana could see the statue's face, smiling from the centre of her dusty garland.

"One keeps one's vow," Vaja said flatly.

Suyodhana fought to keep from laughing. "Have you never broken a vow, Guru?"

"No, Suyodhana."

"A pity. It would be a comfort to know that even you, who seem so perfect, could weaken like the rest of us, now and then. In a way you are more my father than Drita is. Yet I have no memory of you ever making an error—or letting me make one."

Vaja frowned. "You made very few—with weapons. If I failed to praise you sufficiently—perhaps you are right, perhaps it was what was required after all."

"It was very difficult with my cousins," Suyodhana said. "But you did what you could. Only now, with my own troubles, do I appreciate that you might have had yours also. Which caused me to question your servant about your contentedness with your position here."

"You should have come to me."

"But I am, now."

"I thought you came for advice."

"That too. Guru, I want you to know that I admire you for giving your kingdom to Panchalya. I am sorry that my rigid envy caused you to go off to Ahicchatra to consecrate Panchalya, when rightfully we should have all celebrated your magnanimous act here at Hastinapura. I have always liked Panchalya. He is much like my Radheya—both are great warriors, committed to dharma, loyal, with their parentage intriguing mysteries."

"You did not come here to praise Panchalya."

But Suyodhana was certain that his teacher was privately pleased. "Others may laugh at you and me, Master, because

427

we make so much of persons of uncertain birth. But it is as if now and then the gods hide an exceptional being where least expected. Even among the Dasyu."

Vaja did not seem to understand him yet. Suyodhana pressed on. "For example, I myself have taken to bed a Dasyu woman or two. Your great Arjuna has even admitted to fathering a child on one—although the gods killed the abomination."

Vaja recoiled. Suyodhana clenched his fists in frustration at these slips. "Not that all the offspring of Dasyu are unworthy of life. But when a prince—I think you would agree that Lotus is a simple woman. Whereas the type of Dasyu woman I speak of—Guru, your life has been a lonely one. Who could blame you for loving a woman?"

"What are you talking about? I have taken vows."

"And you've *never* had a woman?"

"Before my vows, yes."

It was disappointing, but to be expected. Suyodhana was pleased, however, with the confusion crossing Vaja's face. There was clearly some guilt here to be used. He begged his weapons-master's forgiveness. "But I am still sure she must have been an exceptional woman."

"I never compared her to other women. She and they would have no resemblance. None at all."

Suyodhana was delighted. Vaja was turning as soft as a love-smitten boy. "Do you ever think of seeing her again? I mean, perhaps there was a child. Sired before your vows. What a blessing that would be to you."

Vaja walked away. Suyodhana saw that he was facing the statue of Aditi. "I have sometimes dreamed of a child. But of two, not one." He turned back. "Which is impossible—I was with her only once. And since she would not tell me her name, even if there was a child, she did not wish me to have more to do with it."

"But if she had known you would possess a kingdom? You might have given North Panchala to your own son! Even now, Panchalya would give it up if you asked him to."

"*If* there were a child, and *if* it were a son, and *if* I knew where to find his mother."

"Just to see her again—" Suyodhana said softly. "Those

Dasyu women—it's true what they say about their 'river land' fields being dark and moist."

Vaja turned white with rage. "Whatever your reason for coming here, Suyodhana, I see it was not the reason you gave, so you have lied. I see your interest in this matter as a defilement of her memory. Leave my lodgings."

"Of course, Guru." It was enough—Suyodhana had never before seen Vaja truly shaken. The trap was laid and the bait was clearly fresh, for all its years of ferment.

Radheya stormed into the apartments of the crown prince shortly after Suyodhana had returned from his visit with Vaja. "Samraj. Your cousin Yudishtira has had the audacity to attempt to become samraj."

"Where did you hear such a lie?" Suyodhana felt his stomach knot tight. A lie? All his dreading and doubts told him it was true.

Radheya pounded the wall. "We should have fought them long ago. You can't protest your own cousin's bid for samraj."

"I can do what I wish."

"Then invite him to battle before he begins it!"

"Why bother?" It was Sakuni, standing in the open door. "Suyodhana, let Yudishtira—or Jarasamda—do your work for you."

"What work?" Radheya glared at the lame warrior whose head came to his chest.

"The work of conquering Bharata," Sakuni said coolly.

Radheya stepped between uncle and nephew. "Suyodhana, this time you will not listen to this man. Your allies are leaving you. To win them back, you must eliminate the rakshasa. Only that. Defeat these rebel Dasyu, *with whom your uncle sides*. Do not feign surprise, Sakuni. Anyone can hire a spy."

Sakuni stood his ground. "Emotion blinds you both. The rakshasa have attacked no Arya for months. I have told you, Suyodhana—take *credit* for that. Tell your allies you have the rakshasa at your personal command and that you will loose them whenever you wish, against anyone you choose."

Suyodhana lost control. "I do not *want* that rakshasa filth at my 'personal command'. I don't believe they are at yours either."

"Use them!" Sakuni shouted.

Suyodhana gestured for Radheya to go. Sakuni laughed openly at his nephew's attempt at self-control and Radheya's stiff departure. "Suyodhana, that driver's son would be a more suitable friend if you put a harness on his big back instead of listening to his mouth."

Suyodhana flushed. "You have insulted a king."

"Stop raging and sputtering. Tell me your progress today with Vaja."

"What difference does that make? If Yudishtira is to become samraj? This is Vaja's doing. I hate that man. Yudishtira would never have dared to try to become samraj without a united Panchala on our east."

"You froth at the mouth like a mad jackal. Vaja is essential now. It is true—this news changes everything. If Yudishtira succeeds, you will soon be samraj—all it requires is Indraprastha's plans."

"Samraj? I am not even a king!"

"That is obviously another step to be taken."

"But my father is still alive!"

"So he is." Sakuni turned away. "As are Yudishtira and Bhima, to your everlasting regret. But events shall turn all three regrets into joy, little warrior. Your regrets into joy."

"What are you talking about?"

"It does not matter at all. It only matters that if there is actually a samraj consecration at Indraprastha, you have persuaded Vaja to learn about their defences. For we, as his Kuru relatives, will all have to be invited there."

"Uncle, what are you talking about?"

"*Control Vaja.*"

Suyodhana stared at his uncle. "I will break the man."

"Turn! Thrust! Turn!" The training hall resounded with Guru Vaja's commands and the clash of bronze axe blades.

"Parry! Close! Back! Back!"

Suyodhana ignored the warning and met the priest's crashing blow with the handle of his axe. The wood shattered but he drove the useless butt into Vaja's unprotected stomach, stopping just short of injury.

The two men glared at each other, panting. "In a real battle I would have worn a leather protector there," the weapons-master said. "You did well to return to me for a review. Never let an opponent raise his axe above your head unopposed."

"In a real battle," Suyodhana sneered, "I would have handled you differently. I did not seek a review, Vaja, but an opportunity to talk where you could snarl more freely when I said something which displeased you. Shall we try the mace next? Or are you too tired?"

"I am twenty years your elder but I will outlast you." Vaja selected a mace from the rack on the wall. "Because I do not waste my energy on anger."

Suyodhana swung his mace to loosen his arm. "Because you have nothing you are angry about. Yet." The mace was iron spiked and heavy as a summer calf.

"What makes *you* so angry, Crown Prince? Soon the Kurus may have the honour of a Kuru samraj." Vaja thrust menacingly at the younger man. "Tell me, Crown Prince, what more can a Kuru prince hope for?"

Suyodhana swung suddenly, with an expert's speed. The weapons-master backed down the hall's row of columns, countering blows that could have killed him.

"What, Suyodhana? What do you wish for? What more sin do you wish to incur? Do you hope Jarasamda defeats him?"

Suyodhana's wildly swinging mace crashed into a column a finger width from Vaja's head.

"What do you *want*, Suyodhana?"

Suyodhana stopped, sweat pouring down his face, his breath coming in gasps.

"A samraj—who is loyal—to his own family."

The weapons-master stepped out from the column and swung. Their two maces met in mid-air, causing both men to stagger back.

"A samraj who does not arm himself in secret and command his rebel Nishada to trap me," Suyodhana said, drawing back and swinging again, slowly and with his full strength.

Vaja easily countered the obvious blow. "You are angry because he doesn't send you daily messages about his doings?"

Suyodhana stopped the parry, doubled over from the effort. "I am angry—because he keeps secret—the defence plans for Indraprastha. Is that the behaviour of a loyal family member? An ally? If he were attacked, how could we help him?"

The older man stood perfectly erect. "How sweet your concern, Suyodhana. If you were really concerned you would worry about how Yudishtira can possibly defeat Jarasamda, who will probably kill all your cousins for you."

"But if he does win. Consider the invitation he may soon send, to his 'great samraj-consecration sacrifice' in the dry winter month of Karttika. Every warrior of Bharata *inside* a wooden city."

"No Arya would fire a city."

Suyodhana leaned in over his mace and described Yudishtira's Phoenician architect, and how yavana cities were famous for secret entrances and other lawless defences against lawless attacks, and why those who followed dharma would be slaughtered in such a place if they did not know the secret ways out. "King Does-Nothing could attack. Other rebel Nishada. Foreign enemies. What better time for them to strike us? If you refuse to save Bharata, my father will command it."

"Command what?"

"After the rains, go to Indraprastha. Offer to help them with Jarasamda. And ask to see their defences. To improve our own. If they permit it, they are allies. If they don't, their secrecy will speak for itself."

"They will not be able to deny me. I was their teacher."

"Exactly."

Suyodhana walked around Vaja, holding his mace up at shoulder level, directed at the weapons-master's eyes. Suyodhana's arm shook from the display of strength. "If you will not do it for my father, then do it for her. I have found her."

"You have not."

"I have. I can take you to her."

"I do not believe you."

"Yes you do! You know I could go to her and tell her

anything I wished—that you still remember that night with
disgust, that if there was a child you would kill it—"

Vaja swung his mace wildly. Suyodhana jumped aside. "'*I
do not waste my energy on anger*'. And didn't I just see the
great Vaja swing at a man's knees? An utter disregard for
dharma, Teacher."

Vaja had regained control. "I did not realise your capacity
for cruelty, Suyodhana. I am profoundly ashamed of you."

"I will do it. I'll go to her."

Vaja walked away, his face contorted by the effort to contain
his grief and rage.

"Vaja, I will do everything I have said!"

"Fear for yourself that you will."

"Fear for her, Vaja. Fear for never seeing her again," he
shouted. "After the rains, Vaja. Then I'll go to her. I will!"

37

One of my wings is on high;
The other I dragged below.

Rig Veda

The rain season fell upon Indraprastha with thunder, down-pours and dark days. But the palace was finished; there was food; and the rain crop of rice, sesame and millet was in the ground. Seeds of other kinds were also being planted. The first seed was buried deeply.

Draupadi went to Bhima's bed without realising the intricac-ies of her own feelings. She had shared surata with Yudishtira; now she supposed she would simply share it with Bhima. But when he approached her the first time, she felt a strange revulsion—she thought she would not be able to bear his touch. Worse, when he entered her she was gripped by breath-taking pain. She hid it as best as she could. But this fear of pain added to her dread of him on the second night.

She was fond of Bhima. She tried to want him, or to seem as if she did. Which forced her to find a way: On the third night she discovered she could pretend he was Yudishtira.

The solution shamed her, but the effects did please Bhima. The problem was that she began to have trouble sleeping. Sometimes she lay awake most of a night thinking how she might yet become used to Bhima, but by then she would go to Arjuna. Her time with Arjuna she imagined often—it would be like Heaven. Except too brief, because then would come Sahadeva and Nakula, each so different. And Yudishtira, waiting to steal her heart again. Then Bhima again, and these feelings of coldness towards him to be reconquered.

There were also other causes for her trouble in sleeping—

the simple changes in her nights. Bhima adored Prahara and insisted he sleep with them. Bhima himself fell asleep quickly when their nightly lovemaking was finished, too tired or too painfully shy to lie awake and talk. Prahara, however, slept lightly and had to be attended to often. Thus even if she did fall asleep, she was soon wakened again.

After a few more weeks she had even more to keep her awake: It became clear that Yudishtira was avoiding her. Especially after their final night together, his indifference now left her distraught. Perhaps this was for Bhima's sake, perhaps for something more that she could not grasp. But it tormented her.

Meanwhile, the twins followed their eldest's example and spoke little to her, and Eos during this busy time was always working when she was not sleeping with her Phoenician. Everyone seemed determined to leave their queen to Bhima. During the day Draupadi could stay occupied out at the villages. But after her year with Yudishtira she was used to sharing her thoughts with someone at night. Instead, she was utterly alone.

Thus, for all these reasons, sometimes she would arise, throw on her shawl and go out into the night. Nodding to the guards, she would pace the covered but open-sided halls, making a complete circle of the living quarters. The falling rain would be lit by the lamp light of only two rooms—Yudishtira's council chamber and Lettermaker's work room.

She would stop first at her husband's door, sometimes for a long while. She missed him greatly.

But she would not beg.

So she would go to the second lighted room. There she was always welcome, and control did not matter because desire did not exist. To the Phoenician she was a queen first and always, and as he had put it, "A queen's friendship is far more useful, enjoyable and safe than a queen's desire." Sometimes they would discuss the villages, sometimes compare yavana and Arya ways. But it was always merely a way to be less lonely.

Thus another seed planted these nights was simply an observation: From the window of the other lighted room, Yudishtira was often watching as Draupadi found her companionship.

The next seed was even more bitter for Yudishtira.

·

"What is this, Sahadeva?"

"Writing, Yudishtira."

"I know that. Whose writing?"

"Mine, Yudishtira."

"Yours." The eldest paced around the council room, his knuckles white from gripping the marked plank of wood. "Do you recall what our forest-teachers told us about writing? Or was my little brother too young to listen? And did you know Lettermaker was forbidden to teach you writing?"

"He told me he was teaching you."

"He told you that?"

"I begged him to teach me also."

"You did not realise that I did not want you to learn? Did I have to explicitly forbid you?"

Sahadeva's head sank lower. "No, I knew you did not want me to."

Yudishtira dropped the plank at his feet. "This is a grave error."

"I know."

"How am I to trust you?"

"Please, Yudishtira. Punish me, do whatever you want. I am so ashamed. I swear I will never write again. Never again without your permission."

"Which you should not be looking for. It is a dangerous knowledge. Yes, I have learned it. Because Vyasa commanded me to. But it gives a disastrous illusion of power. Leave me now. Tell Eos I wish to see her immediately."

Yudishtira had half hoped that the Greek would defend her lover, to whom they all owed so much. But she would not.

"No, it is not a matter of his misunderstanding our ways. I know of no land where a guest can expect to remain welcome after doing something the host has forbidden. But he is a strong-willed man, Yudishtira. He likes to imagine himself above law and custom. Especially when he thinks he knows what needs to be done."

"In other words, he lives without the guidance of dharma," Yudishtira said softly. "It is like a disease, isn't it? Creeping

436

into Bharata by many routes. Do I protect us by sending him away? Or by trying to cure him?"

Eos touched his shoulder lightly in sympathy. "Yudishtira, Baron Sakuni has invited Lettermaker to Hastinapura."

"Surely he wouldn't go to our enemy."

"Hastinapura is the only other city Lettermaker knows; Sakuni and his slave the only other persons who speak and write all of his precious yavana languages. He will intend not to reveal anything, but—"

"But Sakuni is devious," Yudishtira finished for her.

"Lettermaker does not know himself, Yudishtira. Sakuni will trap him with his own desires, his own self-delusions."

"Those can trap us all."

"It seems they can." And she left the king to his decision.

Thus it was that on a rainy morning the Greek woman watched the departure of the Phoenician man, the man who had received her first love and her first unguarded hate. Her tears blended with the grey, slanting rain as she saw him go. "Half man, half fish," she whispered. "The girl who nets one has one year's good luck." The year was almost over.

Six days after Lettermaker's departure Draupadi tossed in her bed again beside Bhima, trying to stay asleep through the pounding of another rain shower on the roof. A dream had been gripping her. She was in the air over Bharata. The ground writhed as if covered with snakes. But when she dropped closer, the movement was of human bodies. She flew away in horror, and a king flew beside her, wearing the robe of a samraj, and he guided her to a forest, wild and empty like the Yamuna valley before the fire. She was happy here, soaring in the warm updraughts. The samraj said, "This is our favourite part. We discourage the people from coming here and bearing children. We tell them, *'We must keep one part wild.'*"

She tried to hold the dream in order to stay asleep through the pounding rain. She had struggled like this all night— trying to sleep rather than wake and think about the writhing in her stomach. The writhing nausea that came most in the mornings.

Another dream came. Someone handed her a baby wrapped

in cloth. She held it to her breast and heard a hissing. Throwing it from her, she saw a snake fall to the ground.

Draupadi sat up, fully awake. It can't happen while I nurse. Eos said so.

Draupadi felt her loneliness assault her from the darkness. Arjuna, Panchalya, and now Lettermaker, gone. Eos grieving and Yudishtira still so cruelly aloof.

Yudishtira will challenge Jarasamda when the rains end. Which of them will die? Bhima? Arjuna? Or Yudishtira?

I must speak to someone!

There is no one left to speak to. No one at all.

The next birth might be worse.

I could not survive worse.

But a woman's dharma is childbearing.

It is bad to have another so soon.

But children are a woman's wealth.

My body will coarsen. Arjuna will hate me. I've been free for less than two months!

Bhima will be happy.

I don't want another child!

Stop! Eos said it can not happen.

Yudishtira will challenge Jarasamda when the rains end.

She started to cry silently, rocking herself. "I could not bear it. Indrani, I could not bear it."

Yudishtira sensed Draupadi's suffering without knowing the cause. He longed to comfort her, but he dared not see her alone, and if they were seen in public together he was sure their feelings for each other would be too obvious and Bhima would be hurt. Most of all, however, it was Arjuna's approaching return that left Yudishtira speechless when he was even near her. What could he say to prepare her without violating Arjuna's demand that she not be told before he arrived? What could he say when he knew that later she would see every conversation in which he had not told her to have been deceitful? For he had wanted honesty between them above all else.

What he was certain of was that whatever Draupadi's grief now, it was a mere whisper of the pain that would shout to her when Arjuna returned with Subhadra. Yudishtira, however, felt this pain already, as if it were his own. It was, paradoxically, this pain which was revealing to him how much his joy truly depended on her happiness. How much he was one with her. And that in turn told him that however much or little she loved him—however much or little either of them wanted it or were hurt by it—they were bound by the strength of his love alone. This he wished her to know.

Thus yet another seed was planted in the rains.

To the east, in North Panchala's capital, Ahicchatra, Panchalya also worried about his sister's suffering. He had received a message from her which was so vaguely sad that he could not ignore it. So he had sent word to Guru Vaja at Hastinapura that he would be leaving for Indraprastha for an extended visit. The response was immediate and unexpected—Panchalya should of course go if he was needed on the Yamuna, and Vaja himself would pay a visit there when the rains were over. The next seed had fallen into the furrow.

For the moment it was not raining in Dvaraka, but it was very dark. Krishna led his sister to the servant's door of the women's quarters, told her who stood in the chariot in the alley, hushed her gasp of surprise, then lifted her in beside the third-eldest son of King Pandu. Arjuna snapped the reins and the team trotted out of the women's courtyard, through the palace gardens, out into the palace gate-yard, through those gates and down the royal road to the gates of the city of Dvaraka.

It was when he neared these city gates that the alarm was sounded—conchs from the palace walls and shouts from the palace-gate guardhouse. Afterwards Krishna swore it was not he who alerted them. Or if it was, it was only a wedding prank.

Arjuna whipped the horses and shouted. They charged the gates, which were already shuddering on their hinges as they began to groan closed. Arjuna threw off the cloak that hid his bow and nocked an arrow. His hands occupied, he could only shout his command for more speed. But the team was unfamiliar with his voice and the closing gates were causing them to slow.

He aimed at the gateman, but dearly wished not to have to shoot a Vrishni tonight.

Suddenly soft hands took the reins from where he clenched them between his thighs, and Subhadra leaned out to whip the backs of the horses. They leaped towards the gate. Faced with such determination, the gateman stopped the closing and the horses pounded through, splinters flying from the grinding of gate wood against chariot wood.

In the open, under the protection of darkness, the horses galloped along the smooth city road. Arjuna stood to the rear, his bow ready should it be needed. His driver's hair flew back on the wind, her slim figure seeming to rise and fall a little with each lunge of the team. She commanded the horses like a man, yet better—she understood them. She was a true warrior-wife.

The sight of her, the sound of the hooves, the rushing through the night towards anything but Indraprastha because it was a little too soon to go there—he wished it all might never end. But no one stops time, and his year was nearly over.

And so the full crop was sown.

PART IV
THE CONQUEST OF ALL SPACE

38

When I awoke from youth and dreaming
I saw everything as two:
Laughter, crying; praying, lying;
Good and evil; me and you.

And now we have seen other summers.
You and I have other lovers—
Family, household, travel, trade;
Glances back, attempts well made.

Yet in every blend and faction
We can also see the source,
Know the stillness in the action,
Feel the one united force.

So why do I awake in darkness
Hating yet still loving you?
My heart, a mockery of Oneness,
Revels in this pain of two.

                                                anonymous

It is always the first knot that comes loose on a load.

                                        a Panchala saying

"Zesnor!"

The voice shouted it every day now, as if the slave had merely gone up to the library or out to the horse yards. As if he had left yesterday, not three years ago.

It was the effect of the illness, his attendants whispered. Yet as the oracle's Ka approached the Farther Shore, they saw it prophesied more now—when the voice could be understood at all—and with fearful accuracy.

"Send for Zesnor." The Company of Fifty could only shiver in the face of the command, for there was no new word from Zesnor. Most had never even met this slave, for they replaced others—this particular service to Amon-Re took more and more lives.

"I see you, Zesnor!" cried the God's Voice again. "There, among their strange trees, wearing their ugly clothes. Wait. I see *him*! Is this Yudishtira the one who tries to steal you from me? What causes you to forsake our Egypt?

"Whatever it is, it will be destroyed. Beware, Zesnor. Time itself will destroy your Infinity."

There was a gagging and retching. Those waiting in the shadows now ran to do what they could. If only the body would remain aware enough to ask for azle. They poured more each time, unable to bear the waiting. But they knew it was futile —the god was immortal, and so, it seemed, was his voice.

"I have seen *her* also," the oracle whispered. "Send a god's daughter to destroy me, will you? These two may try to guard the laws of Ma'at in Bharata, but Amon-Re—" The voice rose. "Lord, spare me. *I will destroy them.*"

The sky over the Yamuna valley was clear of rain clouds again. The earth was black with moisture. The crops and grasses were a blaze of tender, reassuring green. It was autumn, season of relief—relief from heat, relief from rain.

At Indraprastha it was also the season when the queen had begun to smile a little again, upon the arrival of the new King Panchalya of North Panchala, who was none other than her beloved twin brother, returned to her. Furthermore, if Queen Draupadi still ate too little and slept too much in spite of his return, and if King Yudishtira still seemed too sad and thought-ful in spite of his new plans and allies, then surely Prince Arjuna's homecoming was all the royal family lacked to be happy the way they had been before. And it was now, in autumn, that Arjuna was free to return.

There were, in fact, already signs that Queen Draupadi eagerly anticipated the arrival of her exiled husband. For the

last three mornings—since her time with Bhima had ended—
she had risen almost early, dressed in as much of a queen's
proper finery as she had ever tolerated, and then had emerged
to sit in the gardens or stroll the walks or pace the entrance
street above the main-gate courtyard where, when the gate
stood open, one could see the broad road down to the river.
The queen stood before the gate often.

And why not? She would not even have the month of
waiting between one bed and the next, for she still nursed
Prahara, still had not had her bleeding time, and therefore
surely had not conceived while with Bhima. Why ask her to
wait past the very day of the Silver One's return?

For Draupadi, however, these rampant speculations were
her one satisfaction, because for once they were utterly wrong.
If she stood before the open gates, it was more to see the
peaceful, freshly green pastures and the gleaming new thatch
of the villages. And if she arose from bed earlier these days,
and strove to appear well and cheerful to her serving women,
it was only to prevent their guessing. For to her the outward
signs seemed more and more obvious that she was bearing, and
that she was both sick and miserable from bearing too soon.

It was important to her that no one know, for when she was
rested she bore this lonely knowledge with reasonable courage
and acceptance, but at other times she searched frantically for
an escape from the trap her body had laid for her. And the
only escape her mind could consider was denial. Somehow it
seemed to her that if no one knew—if even she did not admit
it too often even to herself—it would not be true.

There was also the fact that, until they knew, they would
let her have surata with Arjuna, and everything would be as
she had planned. After the long year she could only dimly
re-create the feelings that had given her so much despair over
his leaving, for this new despair seemed so much greater. But
she clung to her old plans and desires as something familiar,
and to be Arjuna's had been the goal towards which her life
had always moved, as a day proceeds towards sunset.

Some hidden thought even hoped surata with Arjuna would
somehow change this other, for she dimly recalled Nakula's
explaining that a breeding with a new stallion could cause a

bearing mare to lose another stallion's foal. Anyway, there would be time enough to tell them it was Bhima who was the father when it became inescapably true and obvious that she was going to be a mother.

Her sheer loneliness, however, could not be so easily denied. Much of it was the result of this denial. The two most ready to sympathise were themselves too preoccupied to guess Draupadi's trouble. Eos was hiding her own grief, about Lettermaker, in a storm of work: after the new allies finally coming to Indraprastha were officially welcomed and feted by Pandu's sons, it was Eos who arranged their comfortable settlement, or the terms of their continued communication with Indraprastha if they were returning to their own kingdoms. And similarly Panchalya, who had arrived full of worry for his sister, had drifted away from her on a wave of preparations for a visit by his beloved Guru Vaja, once she had failed to give him a reason for her grieving.

There was only one person Draupadi truly believed could have comforted her, and she asked herself many times a day what Yudishtira would say if he knew. He had witnessed her suffering with Prahara. But he would also want Bhima to have the joy of a child. But however he might have reacted, she could not discuss it with him—she would approach Yudishtira last for anything. He continued to avoid her, and he continued to prepare to challenge Jarasamda, which she increasingly understood would probably be her husband's doom. How could he help when he was the cause of her two other griefs?

Loneliness, fear for him, rejection and the burden of bearing too soon—these were what had really forced her from her bed again on the fourth morning since she had left Bhima. She had dressed and come as usual to the gate courtyard, where a number of Nishada were waiting to speak to her about the building of the villages now that she rarely came herself to view the work. Badger was there with his sons, offering her the first cheese from his goats and the last word on the council house being built in her favourite village, the one by the river, Sukshetra. This was also the village of Lotus's mother, and the headwoman had come to discuss ways to ease the lingering fear and loss of those Nishada who had come to Indraprastha last, after the attack of the rakshasa. Draupadi suggested a pier built into the river so they could fish without the dangers of going out to the small Sister Waters of their old territories or of drowning in their flooding Mother Yamuna.

As the queen and the Nishada headwoman planned the details, Draupadi heard a chariot emerge from the stables to her right. It bore bells—decorative silver bells, for a pleasure outing. She raised her head to listen, then turned when the driver stopped close behind her.

The occupant was alone in his vehicle. He loomed up over her, the sun behind his head so that she could not see his face. But it was this—his face being hidden—which most brought recognition. Her heart began to pound for no reason.

"Yudishtira?" she called.

He nodded once. She looked about her, confused by his sudden presence after he had avoided her so long. But what he said next was more of a command than a question, and it was clear.

"You will drive me, Queen?"

With so much that each wished to say, they rode in silence. At the ferry the mares were difficult to load, coming down the bank stiff-legged and rearing when the ferrymen tried to take their bridles. But Draupadi encouraged them through the reins and spoke to them as if they were Prahara until they turned their heads towards her, arched their necks like fine ladies, and stepped on to the boat's deck. Yudishtira thought he saw his queen smile a little.

But mostly she did not smile, and he could not give her any cause. Today he could only give what he had—a small dry cloth to stop a flood.

Yudishtira stepped down to talk with the ferrymen, but in the end said nothing to them. He only stood at the rail, breaking a twig into halves and halves again, tossing the pieces into the swift-sliding water.

Around noon Draupadi drove the team to the top of the eastern ridge. Yudishtira tethered the horses to graze, then led her to a clear viewpoint under an acacia tree.

League after league of autumn-green pastures stretched away

447

west to the Yamuna. Scattered across this expanse were the herds—some from the Vrishnis, some from Hastinapura. Thatched herders' huts and log cattle pens were clustered beside pools made by damming the west-flowing streams. The few larger houses, of smoothed planks, belonged to Indraprastha's new allies.

But inevitably it was the city itself that seduced one's senses. It seemed to dance in the sun on the western bank of the river, its surfaces undulating in the heat waves, its banners snapping in the wind. Its flooded moats and white walls reflected the blinding noon sun like a dancer's jewels. The raised trellis gates made bold black patterns against the palisade. And on every tower polished fixed-javelins, turrets, pikes and hundred-killers glittered. It was a fortress dancing away towards the west.

It gratified him to know that those walls and defences protected beauty: the palace, the assembly hall, and, most precious, her gardens. In those she had directed the planting of each mango, asoka, breadfruit, sala, palm and jasmine. Her own hands had released every duck, peacock, cuckoo and cakravaka goose. Danger had been averted because of his fort; but Heaven had been brought to Earth in this wasteland because of her garden. Because of her mysterious spirit.

Yudishtira closed his eyes a moment, requesting help from the gods. Any god. Then he knelt there at her feet, between her and her city.

"Draupadi, I dedicate my married life to you. I vow to take no other wife for as long as you live and there is a son to replace me."

Then he stood and walked away from her. He neither wanted nor needed to know her reaction. The vow was all he could give. It was what he felt; it was what he was. Even if it meant nothing to her, it was his vow.

She followed after him. "I don't understand."

He turned. "I can not imagine another woman your equal. Therefore I wish no other."

"But a king—"

"Should be able to do as he wishes."

Her eyes were still wide with disbelief.

"You have had a great deal to fear since you first met me,

448

Draupadi. I wish to remove at least the fear that I will take a second wife, should that also trouble you, now or in the future."

She still seemed only shocked.

"You will understand soon," he said, with a confidence he deeply regretted.

Yudishtira drove back. He spoke to the horses once or twice, but never to her. When they reached the ferry the bays were foamy under their harnesses and darkly streaked with sweat on their bellies. Yudishtira descended immediately and joined the ferrymen, but again said nothing to them.

Draupadi had hardly noticed the rough, galloping return to the river. Her other husbands might have her as their only wife if they chose, but the king? Perhaps the samraj? It bordered on violating dharma. What would they say she had done to cause this? What did it mean? Surely he could not value her this much if he could be so cold to her even now. It made her head ache, and her heart even more.

On the ferry she began composing a speech to him in which she would express her deepest gratitude for the honour of this vow, although she would admit to not fully understanding why he had made it. Then she would try to express her confusion about his aloofness, about his moods.

Suddenly, looking towards Indraprastha, she noticed chariots at the gates. They were not just a few, pausing to enter, but many, tied or held, as if too numerous even to be accommodated in the unharnessing yard.

Guru Vaja and his entourage? Or Arjuna and Krishna? It seemed that perhaps it was all of them.

In her excitement she turned to call to Yudishtira. But she was distracted by a young woman emerging from the shelter at the centre of the boat. She was in the dress of a milkmaid, but this was obviously some disguise—her skin was too white, her arms too soft.

The young woman looked about her, as if a little frightened, then approached the bow where Draupadi stood.

"May I ask who you are?" Draupadi said impulsively.

Her obeisance could have been a milkmaid's, but her response was too quick. "I am merely one who has come to serve the queen."

"But I am the queen." Draupadi had a feeling the young woman already knew that very well.

The stranger smiled nervously and made another little bow. A very feminine woman, Draupadi decided. She might do very well with Prahara. Or with my wardrobe, which Eos and I never seem to keep straight any more.

But this one will be no serving maid, even to a queen.

"Tell me your parents, young woman."

"I beg your patience, Queen, but may I answer you when we are inside the city?"

This bit of mystery only added to her charm.

"Then tell me how you came to be here on this ferry."

"I have been travelling to your city from Dvaraka, but I chose to see your lovely villages first, and so crossed on your ferry for the view from the eastern shore."

"You came today from Dvaraka? Was my husband Arjuna with you?"

She lowered her eyes. "I came with him. He is a man without equal. And I have heard him call you a woman without equal." Now she looked boldly at Draupadi. "His words still do not do you justice."

Draupadi flushed. She was not used to this sort of praise from a woman her own age. "Your words are sweet, and your service would please me I am certain, but even in your milkmaid costume you can't hide that you are of royal blood yourself, or soon will be by marriage."

Then both were distracted by the ferry docking, and Draupadi all but forgot the stranger when she saw the Vrishni banners on the chariots and Arjuna's white horses just inside the gate.

Still, Draupadi was not overcome with anticipation, and she was pleased with herself for that. She would not act the fool over Arjuna ever again. She even calmly invited the Dvaraka woman to ride to the gates with the king and herself. The stranger said she would be honoured, although as Draupadi led her to the chariot she again noted that it was not the impossible honour a milkmaid would have felt.

"Yudishtira," Draupadi called, with a nervous gaiety in her voice that she disliked and tried to remove, for his sake. "Did you see? Krishna and Arjuna have arrived. And this charming woman came with them. She says she has come to serve me, but the rest she is keeping a mystery."

Draupadi thought Yudishtira regarded the Vrishni girl as if assessing the possible disease of a yavana courtesan.

"I have invited her to ride with us, Yudishtira."

To Draupadi's amazement, Yudishtira merely stepped into the chariot, turned his back, and took the reins. "Then tell her to climb in."

Draupadi studied him as the chariot rolled off the ferry and the team began trotting up the slope. Then she forgot both Yudishtira and the woman: Arjuna had come out of the palace gates.

Seeing him too, Yudishtira pulled up sharply, as if expecting her to jump down whether they were in motion or stopped. But she made herself descend with proper dignity.

"Draupadi!" Arjuna's voice was like a shaft of sun out of a cloud. Her head lifted with pride. "Draupadi, my extraordinary wife." His voice was tender, playful and excited, as it had been one year ago, when it had been he who had driven her out across the green plains. She allowed herself to run the last steps to him.

They embraced, and with his touch the whole long year was gone. "At last our time has come," she whispered.

He laughed. "Yes, our time has come. How I've missed you, my exceptional, amazing, beautiful Draupadi. There is no one like you." The voice speaking into her ear had a passionate despair to it and he pressed against her in a way he never had before. "I can say it for certain now," he whispered. "No wife can equal you, anywhere."

"And I am still yours and yours alone," she heard herself whisper back. "I know, 'Don't say that'. But you'll see—I've changed. None of your brothers will ever doubt my love for them again."

Arjuna slipped out of her arms, but with reluctance, as if it was only that he was remembering they were in public. He took her hand and led her solemnly into the city—without a word to his eldest brother, Draupadi noticed. She looked back at the chariot as it entered the gate behind them. Yudishtira was talking heatedly with the woman from Dvaraka.

"Arjuna, don't you wish to greet Yudishtira?"

Arjuna stopped. She had never seen him look at her that way before. What was this? Hurt? Shame?

The tired bays trudged up the slope to the gate. Yudishtira reined in when the rear of the chariot was beside her and Arjuna. He turned in the chariot box. "Arjuna, enough of this."

"In a moment, Yudishtira."

"No! Now."

Draupadi looked from one husband to the other. Arjuna reached up and took the milkmaid's hand and helped her down. He bowed low. "Draupadi? I wish you to meet my bride. My second wife. Krishna's sister Subhadra."

Panchalya was in the garden with the newly arrived Guru Vaja. "Yes, particularly in building our defences, Lettermaker gave us many ideas we've never seen in Bharata. If you have the patience, I will show you everything." Panchalya glanced away. "Except for certain details."

"Of course." Vaja shrugged.

"No, it shames me. If I could have my own way—"

A scream startled them. Both men ran towards it, knives unsheathed. Unreal as the sound had been, Panchalya knew it had come from his sister.

But Draupadi was deathly still when they reached her. She was facing Arjuna and a pretty child-woman in milkmaid's dress.

"It is always the first knot that comes loose on a load," Draupadi said with venom. "However well tied."

Panchalya had never heard his sister's voice sound so deadly. Then he understood, and instantly also knew that no two women could ever be more different.

Draupadi now faced Yudishtira. "You knew, didn't you?"

He spoke very softly. "I knew and I gave my permission."

"How long did you know? You knew all day today, didn't you?"

"I've known since before the rains."

"But you didn't tell me."

"Arjuna requested me not to."

"And today? All this today?"

"He asked me to see that you were not here when he arrived. He hoped to let you know in a painless way."

"Painless?" She spat the words at him. "Is that what your words were about today?"

"They were not 'words'. They were a vow."

"Made to soothe me."

He looked her in the eyes. "I had hoped it would be a comfort to you."

Draupadi backed away from him. "And make things easier for Arjuna. Everyone fears I will divide the five brothers. I think they love no one but each other. Whatever makes Bhima happy, whatever makes Arjuna happy. Is this why your three months of not even speaking to me, Yudishtira? After I bore your child? Of the five of you, I do believe *you* are the cruellest."

Yudishtira did not move or even allow his face to change expression. But Panchalya saw he was rigid, like a warrior determined not to admit to the mortal wounds that would disqualify him from battle.

Guru Vaja stepped forward, seemingly oblivious. Panchalya put out a hand to stop him, but the priest-born did not notice. "Draupadi, allow me to greet your husbands. My dear Yudishtira! Bhima. And Arjuna. And Krishna too?"

All the men addressed began trying to adjust to the demands of proper behaviour. Krishna was quickest with words of welcome. Arjuna followed, but his eyes, like the skilled hunter's, never left the one he had infuriated with pain. And Panchalya saw that his sister was trembling, ready to strike.

Yudishtira, still shaken, tried to cover up for Arjuna's inattention to his most beloved teacher. "We are overjoyed that you chose to come, Guru Vaja. Myself especially, with this task of preparing for the samraj attempt."

"I will help all I can, Yudishtira, although I think a few more spars like that with your wife might be the best preparation."

Panchalya cringed for him.

"You, Vaja!" Draupadi whirled on the weapons-master so

that the battle-scarred man almost fell backwards. Yet she had hardly raised her voice. It was the pure fury that had struck him off guard.

"*You* were my husbands' teacher. Therefore *you* are most responsible for this. This lack of honesty, of feeling. This lack of *reason*."

She stalked around him, her expression so full of hate that Vaja could not seem to take his eyes from her. "But why am I surprised?" she said in a low, bitter voice. "For a warrior the arts of war serve to protect the weak. But for you, a priest lost from his dharma, teaching the art of killing is just a way to earn food and lodging. That is no surprise either. We all know how you treat a 'friend' when he is a little foolish—you order your own students, who have no grudge against him, to steal half his kingdom merely to satisfy your need for revenge. Do you have any idea how much suffering you caused by dividing Panchala? My brother and I are both being sacrificed to your selfishness."

She stopped circling him and took a step closer to look him in the eyes. "And all of us here have suffered at the hands of your prize student Suyodhana—with your 'wise teaching' you have created a murderer! My husbands may not have the sense to bar you from this city. But I know you should never have been allowed through the gate. You came here to spy!" She spat at his feet. "Well, your students deserve what you will do to them."

Panchalya saw his teacher shudder. Draupadi did not even notice. She had turned to Krishna. "How thoughtful of you to send your sister to us, you conniver and destroyer. Your sister will certainly be happier here, away from a place that breeds men like yourself."

And to Subhadra she only said, "So he would make us rival wives?" She looked around at the sons of Pandu. "And now they expect me to bless you." Her gaze fell on Arjuna. He paled. She said with deep bitterness, "I wish you well with him, Subhadra."

Draupadi walked from the courtyard.

•

Somehow Panchalya and Vaja made their way back to the garden through the confusion of the removal of baggage from chariots and the unharnessing of horses. The older man's face seemed almost scarred by Draupadi's words.

"Will you ever forgive us?" Panchalya whispered.

"She did me no wrong."

"No wrong? Her words were unforgivable."

"Forgive her."

Panchalya's voice softened a little, out of obedience. "I only know my sister has loved Arjuna from the first time she heard his name. She's endured much—much more than I. She did not know what she was saying."

"She knew."

"No. There was no truth in any of it. We trust you completely. Even Draupadi. We are twins; I know her thoughts like my own. She only spoke impulsively."

"Your sister's eyes tell me that her impulses are wiser than the longest thoughts of most others."

"Not about this!"

For the first time the teacher appeared old to his pupil. "Can you take me to my quarters so I may rest?"

Panchalya felt desperate. "Do you understand me, Master? We trust you completely."

The weapons-master exploded with anger. "Why? Why trust *me*? Open your eyes, Panchalya. I might have stopped this rivalry between Yudishtira and Suyodhana at its very start. I was there. I was their teacher. But it was difficult; I did not make the effort. It isn't going to stop with a samraj consecration, Panchalya. Even if he can defeat Jarasamda. Don't be lulled here within the circle of these new sala-log walls."

"*You did all you could,*" Panchalya cried. "You're as trapped as I am. I trust you with my life more than anyone on earth. Even my sister." His voice lowered. "Come, let me show you something."

"No!"

"I must. I *will* show you."

"I refuse!"

But in spite of Vaja's continued resistance, the younger man could not be stopped. "Come or I will never forgive my sister. There is no other way. No other way now to show you my trust."

39

After its beginning at the time of Pandu's sons, the Age of Kali came gradually. Each generation hardly noticed the loss of dharma, peace and wisdom; beauty, space and plenty. Like winter days, lives merely grew shorter, darker.

In the darkest times "enlightenment" always seems like talk of rain in the desert. Yet these are the best times for liberation from the small-self. Nothing else is a hundredth as charming. For those few fortunate ones who turn inward, Kali's Age will not exist.

Vyasa

Bhima stood over the bed where she had slept with him four nights ago. All those nights of sweet warm rain. Where was she now? Not with Arjuna where she belonged, not with himself either. Taken to somewhere in the forbidden women's quarters.

He touched the place where she had lain, then lifted the gossamer sheet to his cheek. It still smelled of her perfumes, the flowers she had worn in her hair their last night.

"Did you ever tell her, Bhima?" It was Eos, speaking from the door.

He shook his head without looking at her.

"You should have told her. Not just that you loved her. About your hurt from it. I know her well. She's divided so many ways, but she would have found a way to take your pain away."

He didn't answer.

"I'm on my way to her. Shall I try to tell her for you?"

He shook his head hard.

"Do like Arjuna, Bhima. Take another wife."

He shook his head again and wiped his eyes.

"Why didn't he tell me? He should have just told me."

Draupadi tossed on her bed while Kunti and Eos sat on either side, wiping the sweat off her face, shoulders and breasts.

"Yes I preferred Arjuna," she said, almost delirious. "But I've been good. Haven't I? Haven't I, Mother Kunti? I married them all, didn't I? Didn't I wait for Arjuna's turn? Didn't I let them send him away? Didn't I act as if I didn't even care? But the year is up. Isn't it, Eos?"

"Yes," Eos said, stroking her brow. "It's over now. You have a fever, Draupadi. Be still."

"Arjuna took another wife, Eos." Draupadi tried to sit up.

"It happens."

"Why didn't he tell me?"

Eos changed the poultice on Draupadi's head and felt her stomach again. Hard like a stone. "They are afraid of your anger, Draupadi," Eos said quietly.

"I will never forgive him."

Eos sat back, uncertain whether to tend first to Draupadi's body or to her spirit. "I tell you, he couldn't send you word because he was afraid of you, Draupadi. That's why he chose Subhadra—her kind never angers. You'll forgive Arjuna in time."

"Arjuna? I will never forgive *Yudishtira.*" Draupadi cried out softly, then turned her head away. "Those vows—merely to soothe a child."

"Always Yudishtira, isn't it? You call for him when you hurt, or you blame him for it." Eos wiped her brow dry yet again. "Yudishtira told me he was beside himself when Arjuna sent word about this. Yet how could Yudishtira have refused him?"

"They do what he says. They all do what he says. He is samraj."

"Not yet, Draupadi."

"Don't let him go! Jarasamda will kill him!" Draupadi clutched Eos's hand. "What happened to me? I'm so hot, Eos. Eos, I ran at him. In front of them all. If only I had kept control!"

"Nonsense, Daughter." Kunti had been massaging Draupadi's hands, keeping her thoughts to herself. Now she stopped and leaned over her daughter-in-law. "Your only error was disobeying the dharma of women and not resting properly before and after giving birth. And my error has been being too preoccupied, too reluctant to cross you and my sons—I should have kept you in seclusion much longer after such a bearing. You've been satisfying Bhima by night and building Yudishtira's Nishada villages all day." Kunti stood up straight. "But that is a cow already milked. The question now is what is the trouble and its cure."

Eos felt Draupadi's brow again, then her pulse, then her stomach. The Greek woman shook her head and looked at Kunti with worried eyes. Draupadi's face stiffened from some cramping pain, but it seemed not to touch her awareness. "I love him, Mother," she whispered. "Why did he do this to me?"

"His father did the same," Kunti answered. "How Pandu and I loved each other, yet he had to take Madri. Madri was like Subhadra—sweet and pliable. Some women are too much for certain men, Draupadi."

"Indrani, make me less!"

"Take that back," Eos said.

Kunti shook her head. "I prayed it too. It was a waste of my breath, and Arjuna will be like Pandu. You will always be on Arjuna's mind. He will always come back to you, trying to master himself through you. He will want you to raise his children, even hers, just as I raised Madri's. But he does not dare give you full power over his heart."

Draupadi's face clouded with pain again. "Are there not ways to vanquish a rival wife?" she whispered through clenched teeth.

"Never think of such a sin," Kunti said.

A much stronger pain gripped Draupadi. Eos felt Draupadi's stomach, then lifted the muslin sheet. Fresh blood was flowing.

Draupadi's whole body became rigid, fighting something. Eos had the feeling of reliving a nightmare. "Draupadi, could you possibly be bearing a child?"

"I can't be—I never—" Another pain came rapidly on the one before.

Eos asked Kunti what knowledge she had for stemming the loss of a child. Kunti glanced at her and cited the dangers of carrying another child to its full birth time so soon after Prahara.

There was another pain, another gush of blood.

"I'll never forgive him," Draupadi cried. "Samraj! Brahma forgive me. Forgive me, Mother—I didn't want it."

"And it seems you may not have it," Eos said evenly, selecting herbs from her bag.

"I'm being punished. 'A woman's dharma is bearing.' All of it is punishment. I didn't want it, Eos. I didn't want it."

"Listen to me," Kunti said. "If you lose this child, it only means that Brahma also did not want you to have it."

"Yudishtira!" Draupadi shouted. "Come to me! No. No. Tell him I will never forgive him. Never."

Eos took her hands and held them tightly. "Let go of it, Draupadi. Let go of all of this."

Draupadi closed her eyes. "No!" She started to cry. "It was going to be a son for Bhima," she whispered. "I know it."

"Panchalya, please have three chariots prepared for an excursion—mine, Bhima's and Krishna's. Tell Nakula he will drive for me, the Marut Vimada for Bhima."

"Gladly Yudishtira. But Krishna has gone."

"Gone?"

"At dawn. He went to the river with Urutata, and Urutata said that after the rituals, Krishna simply crossed and—"

"Indra take him. He delivers us into Hell with his sister, then leaves when I need him. Two chariots then. Tell Nakula and Bhima we go immediately."

"Not Arjuna?"

"I leave him to his women! Will you take charge of defences here for me?"

"Of course. May I ask where you are going so I may select the right equipment?"

"Anywhere. To some empty forest. No, better say 'hunting'. Give my regrets to Guru Vaja. My many regrets. Sahadeva should take on my duties. And tell your sister—No, tell her nothing."

"We were all so happy, Arjuna. Then this. She won't even answer a message." Bhima's voice was frantic. "Why, Arjuna? Why did you marry that Subhadra?"

"I like her. I was away a long time, Bhima."

"You 'like her'? You were lonely?" Bhima pulled on a wrist guard, then stared at it. "'Hunting.' He wants me to go 'hunting'. He should have warned her. He should have *stopped* you. Now they say she is sick. I don't want to go 'hunting' until I talk to Draupadi."

Arjuna slammed his fist into a leather shield. "Why doesn't he let *me* go? Bhima, he isn't going hunting. He's found the rakshasa."

Eos came to the door of the armoury. "Prince Bhima?"

Arjuna started out past her. "I was leaving anyway."

She stretched her arm across the door. "Better to stay. Bhima, Draupadi has lost a child. Your child. I'm sorry."

"My child? She carried my child? But—how could she lose it? She didn't lose Yudishtira's." He started to grab Eos as if to shake her, then threw up his hands. They came down on Arjuna's shoulders instead, trembling from the effort to resist doing more. He stared into his brother's face. "See what you've done?"

"It was just too soon after the last," Eos said. "It was no one's fault, Bhima."

"Is she suffering?" Bhima asked.

Eos looked hard at Arjuna. "She is suffering less now."

"I must see her." Bhima shoved roughly past Arjuna.

Eos stretched her arm across the door again. "Your mother has ordered that Draupadi stay in seclusion in the women's apartments at least until winter." Eos glanced at the pile of quivers on the bench. "I hear the king is going out. Bhima, please protect him for us."

Bhima bent over his other wrist guard to hide his tears. "For you I will, Eos. But I have no heart for it. Not for anything."

"I know, Bhima."

"Eos, why do I want to blame someone?" Bhima's expression was confused and contrite now. "It's only that we were so happy yesterday. Yesterday my baby was inside her. My baby!"

He stared around him. "Today it is all so different." Bhima went to his brother. "Why, Arjuna?"

Arjuna turned his back on both of them and began packing more arrows into quivers. Eos finally answered instead. "It's only change, Bhima. Only some change."

From the walled settlement of Indraprastha on the banks of the Yamuna two chariots equipped for hunting drove out in the clear morning light.

At the same moment twelve leagues northeast a man wearing the Vrishni colours entered a clearing and waited for the shadows moving in among the trees to decide whether to kill him with their poison arrows or to welcome him as their leader.

40

When roughly handled,
even the gentle bird pecks.
an Anga saying

The night was half finished but Yudishtira still lay awake beside
the coals of the cooking fire. It had been three days now—
one to reach the end of the cleared land, two more wandering
in the uncleared north. Still he had not escaped his pain and
anger.

Yesterday, when the forests had finally cooled his rage, he
had just felt foolish. He was dragging Nakula, Bhima and
Vimada around the wilderness on an aimless hunting trip,
without servants, eating wild fruit and half-cooked meat, and
for what? To forget Draupadi and Arjuna.

Today, however, his flight had turned from foolish to dangerous—all four had sensed during the afternoon that they were
being followed. Rakshasa? That would make it a worthwhile
hunting trip. If they survived.

He turned over. But the gliding shadows they'd seen today
probably had more to do with the huge Dasyu woman who had
offered her services yesterday as a hunting guide. No doubt her
people were waiting for some signal from her. He would have
to continue reminding everyone to stay alert. If all of her tribe
were as large as she, a fight would not be a simple matter.
And since joining them she had done more watching of her
employers than of game signs.

She especially watched Bhima—as if she were figuring how
best to fit him on a spear. But at noon, when Yudishtira

had warned them more strongly, Bhima had only grunted something about it making the day interesting.

Bhima. He was standing guard with his back to Yudishtira and the others. He had said about twenty words since they had left Indraprastha. Two more than myself, Yudishtira thought.

He hasn't been this angry with me since he was ten. Why, of all the things I might be blamed for, does Bhima pick this? How was I to know Draupadi was bearing again and Arjuna would choose such a poor way to be "painless"?

Yudishtira drew the furs around him against the autumn coolness. Bhima heard him and turned a little, then looked away quickly. It annoyed Yudishtira that Bhima still wore a red sash of Draupadi's, knotted together at its ends so it hung like a garland. It was becoming dirty and was often in the way, but he refused to take it off.

Now, as if watching a dream, Yudishtira saw by dim firelight a large hand reach out and grab the red cloth. Bhima was yanked almost off his feet. Yudishtira sprang up.

But it was only the Dasyu woman, who called herself Hdimba. She was tugging violently still, but Bhima was holding his own—Hdimba was even taller than Bhima but not quite as thick. And very handsome in her way, Yudishtira thought. Neither of them had noticed him rise from his bed. He was finding their struggle rather amusing.

"Hush!" Bhima hissed. "Want to wake the others?"

Hdimba tugged again anyway and said something in Nishada, but she only spoke a few words of that Dasyu tongue and Bhima wasn't understanding her. Her efforts were growing frantic. Yudishtira was about to intervene and try to translate when Hdimba screamed.

Rocks the size of small boulders came hurtling into the clearing, followed by three Dasyu men even larger than their woman. Yudishtira was knocked sideways off his feet. But not by a rock. Vimada had hurtled past him. A stone had struck the Marut on the spot Yudishtira had stood a moment before.

Yudishtira crawled towards the short sword beside his bed furs. Suddenly a huge naked man stood over Yudishtira, laughing. He lifted an axe; its rough-hewn flint head gleamed dully.

In one motion Yudishtira grabbed the rock that had hit

Vimada, swung back, and hurled it down on the giant Dasyu's foot. The man howled as Yudishtira rolled away. But the Dasyu axe only raised higher.

Suddenly an arrow dropped the man. The axe flew wide. Yudishtira turned in time to see Nakula's bow flying from his hand—a mace thrown by another giant attacker had caught his brother's arm. Yudishtira leaped on the mace-swinger from behind. A lesson from Guru Vaja flashed—with fingers in the fat throat, Yudishtira rode the man until he collapsed, dead.

Bhima was engaging the third and largest, with the help of Hdimba's scratches and kicks. Yudishtira wondered if she considered these to be her people after all. He surveyed the camp for weapons. The short sword was by his furs. Bows and quivers were by each bed also, and in the chariot.

But Bhima's opponent suddenly kicked Bhima in the groin—a move that obeyers of dharma could forget to defend against. While Bhima staggered doubled-over, the giant picked up Hdimba and threw her on to the coals of the fire, then backed towards the trees and laughed.

Yudishtira rushed to drag the woman out. Then he collected himself before pursuing their remaining attacker. The man could see any move he made—taking up a weapon would only cause the giant to do the same. But the man was too strong to pin—he had handled Hdimba like a piece of firewood. And there would be no help coming from Bhima, who was groaning, or from Nakula with his arm dangling. Vimada lay motionless.

The giant began ranting at Hdimba in their peculiar Dasyu tongue. Hdimba broke for the woods at a run. The man started after her, but had to pass Yudishtira and hesitated. They glared at each other. Yudishtira crouched slightly, prepared to leap forward.

Suddenly Bhima rose up behind the man and seized him around the hips. He lifted the huge, flailing body with a horrific shout, then pounded the Dasyu down spine-first over a log. Still furious, Bhima again raised him, though he was limp now. Then smashed his head on a rock.

A heavy silence followed, from which the sound of the cracking skull would not fade. Bhima stared at the crushed head, the brains in the mud. Yudishtira wanted to say something to make it all right, but no words came—only the memory of his brother raising the body the second time.

Hdimba came creeping back through the trees. She stood over the body Bhima had broken. "My brother," she whispered in Nishada.

Bhima recoiled, horrified. But Hdimba took his hand. "Don't be sorry. A bad brother, Sweet Bhima."

Yudishtira looked over at them. "'Sweet Bhima'?"

The second eldest flushed. "Last night. We only talked. She likes me, Yudishtira."

"Then what was all this about?"

But Hdimba had guessed the question and tried to explain in her bad Nishada. "Two days passed. I heard my brother and the other two. I was supposed to help them, but when I saw all of you closer—"

"Saw Bhima," Yudishtira corrected, almost smiling.

"Saw Bhima—I wanted to save you instead."

Yudishtira could not help himself—after all this, and with the tall Hdimba embracing Bhima now, so that he seemed almost small—Yudishtira laughed out loud.

Hdimba clutched Bhima harder and glared. But Bhima thrust her aside and came at Yudishtira. "She's beautiful. Even you can see it!"

"She is. I'm sorry I laughed."

"You're always saying they're so smart and we should treat them like Arya."

"I know."

"A Dasyu was good enough for Arjuna."

"Yes, Bhima."

"She was trying to save all our lives. Against her own brother. And you laugh at her!"

"I said I was sorry. It's just a touch of battle madness. You know it."

Suddenly Yudishtira remembered the others. He rushed to the Marut first. Bhima went to Nakula, then came and knelt at Vimada's other side. "We're cursed fools," Bhima muttered. "We argued while they needed us."

The prone man's eyes fluttered. "It's the second time he's saved my life," Yudishtira whispered.

The Marut tried to speak. His nose began to bleed.

"I'll bring herbs," Bhima said curtly. "I don't know about Nakula's arm. Look to him."

Yudishtira frowned at being ordered, then saw the tears in Bhima's eyes and obeyed him.

On the same night, at Indraprastha, Draupadi lay awake with a fever. Her body had cried out for rest after the loss of the foetus and the storm of changes it was wreaking inside her. Now some infection had taken advantage of her weakness. Yet still her mind could not let her fall completely into the black emptiness of sick sleep. Instead it dodged questions that flew like boulders coming out of the night. They came too quickly to answer forcefully in her dull state, but threatened to crush her if she let down her vigilance.

Why do I blame Yudishtira? Why this rage? What choice did he have?

She tossed, trying to ease her injured field, where Bhima's child had been.

Yes! Why did he make me go to Bhima?

It was the revulsion of that first night with Bhima that always rose in her. Bhima was a good man, a gentle man, but he had violated her. Her field belonged to Yudishtira, the father of her son.

Then why did the gate to my field open for Arjuna the moment we touched?

Whom do I love?

Before he let Bhima have me, Yudishtira could have kept me for himself. Only half awake, she began to cry uncontrollably. *I'd had no surata with any but him. Why did he make me go to Bhima? How can I be his only wife if he is not my only husband?*

A feverish convulsion racked her. Then she lay still, her mind clearer for a moment, so that the truth was sharp as a sword: *This marriage to five is my fault, for I preferred Arjuna.*

She cried out with the pain of it. *But if Yudishtira had even once—*

What? Loved me in return? Why should he?

But his vow!

It means nothing. Yudishtira will find his heart's mate in some consort.

She sat up, but dizziness forced her down again.

Then is love the same as surata?

No!

But is surata bearable without love!

And how can I love when I can't forgive?

At dawn they burned the three Dasyu bodies, after Hdimba had performed a few simple rituals over them. At least we're not saying rites over any of us, Yudishtira thought. Nakula's sprained arm was in a sling and his expression easy. Vimada was dizzy and unable to remember how he had been struck, but otherwise all right. And Bhima was still nursing nothing more than hurt feelings.

Yudishtira had spent the last hours of the night keeping guard and thinking about vows, skulls and the different kinds of love. It had all been unclear, out there standing watch in the dark. Now, after lighting the cremation fires, he at least knew what he was going to do today and tomorrow and ten days hence.

The idea had come suddenly, with the first flame of these hot fires. Then it had unfolded as a complete plan while he watched the burning. This morning the smell did not even disturb him. He hoped to smell it again soon. In Magada.

Yudishtira waited impatiently for a decent amount of flesh to return to its elements. Then he made his announcement: "Today I go south. To Jarasamda."

Bhima and Vimada were too stunned to respond. It was Nakula who reached the heart of the matter: "With only the four of us here? And without Arjuna?"

"Or I'll go with less than four."

"I want to come," Nakula said with vehemence. "Don't stare at my arm. I am coming."

Yudishtira nodded slightly. "You told me yesterday that Guru Vaja said we must avoid engaging Jarasamda's armies at all cost. Since he can't bring out a large force against one or two men without looking like a coward, if we go in this way he will be forced to accept a challenge. I am best with spears, but—"

Bhima interrupted. "Vaja said our only chance was a 'battle of breath'. Long-duration wrestling." He smiled. "My speciality."

"If you choose to come—"

"Of course I'm coming!"

"—then you and I will prepare ourselves while we travel. You will need a wrestling partner."

Bhima nodded eagerly as Yudishtira began outlining the details. They would hide the chariots and leave the teams with the last herders they had passed coming north. In disguise, on common horses, they would ride east to the Sarayu River, avoiding villages. Then hire boats and go down the rivers to Magada. Speed was essential—the longer Indraprastha's king was observed to be away, the more suspicious it would seem to the inevitable rumourmonger spies.

"Now listen to me. The most likely result, still, is that I will end up chained in one of Jarasamda's caves, or dead. In that case, I can only hope he'll be satisfied with my life and let those with me go. But perhaps he will not. Having one or two more along will make little difference to the outcome." Yudishtira turned and looked at Vimada. "Do you understand?"

"Yes. You think you're leaving me behind. And I'm getting the harnesses."

The worst part of running through the woods with a sala log across his shoulders was swinging it sideways to pass between close-growing trees. Every muscle ached, every breath was a gasp, and still Bhima was the same five paces ahead. And then to have to turn the log for a tree.

Today Yudishtira's pain was so great that he no longer even felt the inevitable slaps from branches that parted for Bhima and closed on him. It was important to take this beating, to stay behind. That way Bhima would not notice he had changed logs along the way and carried one twice as large.

At the moment when Yudishtira was certain he would have to lose awareness and fall, Bhima stopped. Yudishtira dropped the log and collapsed down on it to hide its size. Bhima stood over him, panting.

"Yudishtira?"

"Yes?"

"I wish—your permission—to marry."

Sweat was pouring into Yudishtira's eyes so that he couldn't see. "Marry? Are you joking, Bhima?"

"Joking?" Bhima's face suddenly filled with rage. "*Joking?* Arjuna took another wife. It nearly killed Draupadi. It did kill my baby. But you didn't laugh that proposal away. You didn't stop it. You 'had to say yes'! But me? 'You must be joking, Bhima'!"

Startled, Yudishtira stood. "You are going to do what you blame Arjuna for doing, Bhima?"

"Yes! Yes I am!"

Then Bhima's expression was transformed again. "No." He hung his head. The anger was gone, overcome by the deeper feeling that had fed it. "Draupadi doesn't care what I do." He was nearly weeping now.

"But Hdimba does care," Yudishtira said softly.

"Hdimba loves me."

"Then for Hdimba's sake, wait. Would you marry her and abandon her the same day?"

"She's been following us. I want to take her with us."

"With us? Bhima, Vaja says Jarasamda is stronger than any man you or I have ever seen. We must put all our attention on endurance, Bhima. Strategy. And travel quickly, before we are located."

"No one will recognise us with her along."

Yudishtira reached up and touched Draupadi's red sash that Bhima still wore. "There is simply no place right now for more women in our lives, Bhima."

"I can train and love her too." Bhima stepped back, his expression frantic. "I can love someone too, Yudishtira. You think you're the only one Draupadi hurts? The only one who wanted a child? Well, you have yours. And when you grow sick of hurting and want another wife, that will be easy for you also."

Yudishtira looked away.

"But I've never had a woman love me—never ever like Hdimba does. She likes how I am, my bigness. She—"

"Stop, Bhima. Forgive me. I will marry you and Hdimba tonight."

Even though they were in disguise, Yudishtira insisted on avoiding well-travelled routes. But they still moved fast—reaching the Sarayu river in five days. Each day after the morning ritual, Hdimba, Vimada and Nakula mounted the three scrub ponies they had purchased, and Bhima and Yudishtira began running. The two ran until Bhima, the heavier man, could run no more. Then Yudishtira would taunt him about using up his manhood during the night, and they ran farther. Yudishtira would permit no rest until he was sure at least one of them was on the verge of collapse. Only then would he take Hdimba's horse and let Bhima walk slowly with his bride.

After the mid-day rest the two brothers would start again. In the evening they would wrestle. Every moment they could catch their breath enough to speak, Yudishtira questioned Bhima about holds and wrestling strategy—until late at night when Bhima would become so angry and desperate to be with his bride that he would challenge Yudishtira to a final match and attack so wildly that Yudishtira would be pinned and turning purple from a choke hold. "Go on," Yudishtira would gasp. "Go to her."

"You admit I'm stronger than ever?"

"I do."

"She doesn't slow us?"

"She doesn't."

Then Bhima would let go and slip off with Hdimba to the nest she had made in some low tree, where they slept among the flowers and leaves like two Dasyu of the most far-removed tribes. Yudishtira would sit by the fire and look up at the stars.

Disguised as traders, they bought a boat and floated four days down the Sarayu until it met the Ganges. On the boat Yudishtira arranged a tent for wrestling in secrecy, and for Bhima and Hdimba to spend their mid-day together.

It was during their last afternoon on the Sarayu that Yudishtira finally permitted himself to talk to Nakula about Draupadi. Vimada was steering, the married ones were still in the wrestling tent, and Nakula sorted arrow shafts while tending a fishing line. Having had twelve days to think, Yudishtira now understood what there was about their last day in Indraprastha that had to be discussed. He sat down beside Nakula and asked as lightly as he could, "What did Arjuna say to you before we left?"

"He asked me to request that you forgive him."

Yudishtira nodded. "Sahadeva sides with him in this, doesn't he?"

"Sides?" Nakula studied him. "Sahadeva only sympathises. He thinks Arjuna did the best he could. That Arjuna believed Draupadi would understand if she saw Subhadra first. Or at least that if he told Draupadi himself, in person, he would take the blame instead of you."

"I suppose Bhima also talks to you."

Nakula looked away, embarrassed. "It's only that I'm quiet."

"No, you listen and you are discreet."

"Bhima is angry at both you and Arjuna." Nakula looked sideways at his eldest brother. "It's too bad that none of us has the courage to be angry at our wife."

"Nakula, I promised her I'd never take a second wife." He blurted it out like a child confessing a blunder.

Nakula didn't speak for a long time. He sat very still, brushing away an insect now and then. Finally he said, "Are you angry that it didn't appease her?"

"Maybe it did. Maybe otherwise she would have taken my knife and stabbed herself. Or me."

Nakula silently baited a new line and threw it over the side. "I think you almost wish she had done the latter."

"Nakula, if it turns out that you must return from Magada without me, you must promise me you will make her understand that in the end my vow had nothing to do with Arjuna taking a second wife. The event only determined the day I spoke of it—a terribly wrong day, I see now. Will you tell her?"

"I think she'll realise that soon."

Yudishtira laughed bitterly. "Anyway, Gangeya would be proud of me—I've practically sworn celibacy, having promised

472

to be faithful to her in the same hour she made her own preference clearer than ever and simultaneously ceased to want anything more to do with me."

"She'll have more to do with you. You don't see it, but the rest of us do."

Again Yudishtira barely listened to him. "I should have faced Draupadi. Faced Arjuna too. I should have led the five of us together to Magada. That's what you think, isn't it?"

"It is hard to rage at those we love."

"No, my fear of their raging back is what turned me into a coward."

Again his younger brother did not respond for a long time. "About this 'cowardice'," Nakula finally said, "only you know your heart. But please remember, Eldest Brother, that where you are going, no one goes out of cowardice."

On the fourteenth morning, on the south bank of the Ganges, which was the northern border of Magada, they burned the boat and donned the robes of vow-takers. All except Hdimba, who stood apart. Yudishtira said nothing, but Bhima glowered anyway, anticipating the obvious. It was Hdimba herself, however, who said the painful words in her broken Nishada, and not the words they expected.

"I will go no farther." Bhima was offering her a trader's garment as a disguise. She threw it down. "I would not see you killed because your attention was divided."

"What?" Bhima asked, incredulous.

But she had more to say. "Bhimasena, I carry your child."

"You are sure? My child?"

"I am sure. And I will not risk it down here in evil Magada."

Bhima beamed and looked at Yudishtira, as if to say they all should have expected she would be the most practical, the most wonderful, the most fertile woman on earth. "Then we will come back to this spot within three days, sweet wife." He glanced down. "Or you may make inquiries. You will be safe alone here."

"I will go back to my people."

"Go back?" Bhima looked frantic.

"I will raise your son to be a warrior and bring him to you when he is ready to serve Pandu's sons."

"No! You must come to Indraprastha with me."

"I do not wish to, Husband."

"You will!"

"Bhimasena, something dies in a Dasyu when she leaves the forest. You would no longer love me."

"I will love you for ever."

Like a hare caught before a hunter's lantern, Bhima watched helplessly as Hdimba took off her belt—an intricate weaving of dyed grasses studded with ocean shells and tigers' teeth—and laid it at his feet. "I have no fear for your safety, Bhimasena, for you will wear this of mine."

She turned majestically and walked northwest along the bank of the river.

Finally he ran after her. "You can't just walk back two thousand leagues. How will you cross the river? Don't leave me! Hdimba!"

Yudishtira, Nakula and Vimada started south into the forest without him, sensing the outcome and not wanting to add their witnessing of it to his misery.

Bhima caught up with them later, alone. Around his neck Hdimba's belt was now intertwined with Draupadi's red sash.

41

It was, at last, a deed he did entirely alone.

Vyasa

Draupadi started from her sleep. She sat up, shivering in the cool night. Eos came to her from a bed across the room.

"He's going to Jarasamda, Eos."

"He wouldn't without more men. What's troubling you? Has your fever returned?"

"He has gone," Draupadi whispered. "I saw him there. They will kill him."

"You truly saw that?"

"No. I only saw him there." She took Eos's hand. "The rest comes from my fear."

Eos did not answer.

"He offered me something precious and I lost it in the mud."

"Then forgive him, Draupadi."

"I want to." She closed her eyes. "*I cannot.*"

"Anger is bad for healing," Eos said softly.

"Then I shall never heal. Indra protect him!"

Yudishtira led them southeast through the forests of Magada towards Jarasamda's fortress-capital of Girivraja, but soon found their pathless route to be impossible, for only a few leagues south of the Ganges the land became swamp. If they were found wandering in that, it would certainly raise more questions than anything observed about them on the roads.

Or so it seemed until they were on the roads. Exposed under the noon sun, they were miserable with worry that under

475

their vow-takers' loose robes their muscles and bowstring scars shouted their warrior identities.

After a league Yudishtira drew them off the road into a thicket to talk out some of their fear.

"We're going to be recognised," Bhima said with doom in his voice.

"Maybe one of us alone could do better," Vimada said with the equanimity of a warrior eight years older. "We need to find out exactly where Jarasamda is today, see his defences."

Nakula frowned. "And if that person is caught, he must be rescued."

Vimada squared his shoulders. "I don't intend to be caught." Yudishtira began to protest. "King, allow me to speak my mind. You and Bhima can not go in there asking the things we need to know. No monk would have muscles like these you both have now. And even if it were safe for Nakula to go without the use of one arm, his sling would provoke curiosity and, given our accents, we only want to ask questions, not answer them too. No, it has to be me."

"I don't like it," Bhima said.

Vimada looked out at the road. They all felt the threat from it—the route to Magada, its white stones glaring in the sun. "I am warrior-born," he said tightly. "I have a right to risk my life for others when I choose."

Yudishtira could only nod—it was good strategy. "We'll continue slowly, then. Until the travellers on the road grow too numerous, or we can actually see the place. I want to be close if you need help. Don't go inside unless you must. If we leave the road, we'll leave crossed sticks at that point so you can find us."

Reluctantly the three said goodbye to their fourth and watched him disappear around a curve. Then they began walking the highway at the sedate pace of mendicant students of Veda.

In another league they topped a rise and entered a portion of the road that ran downhill through an alley of evergreen lodhra trees. Their soft grey trunks and the carpet of their fallen yellow leaves would have given the scene an air of peace, were it not for the Magada fortress called Girivraja, suddenly visible between the two rows of lodhras. The fort was massive and ugly, with squat log walls, taller sooty buildings of rough-hewn lumber, and bowmen's windows cut everywhere, like staring eyes. At its base a marsh-moat spread unevenly out to a plain, where at least several hundred chariots, horsemen and foot-warriors were practising military manoeuvres with a precision that independent-minded Arya warriors seldom displayed.

The three on foot suddenly heard bells and shouts from behind them. Six bellowing, bulging-eyed, well-decorated cows were trotting down the road, planting their feet wide but still sliding in the muddy places, and tossing off loose flowers, garlands and ribbons like rain as several hurrying priests ran to keep up. Yudishtira motioned the other two back among the trees until the frantic parade had passed.

"So they worship the Roarer here in the old way," Yudishtira whispered.

"Rudra the Old One," Nakula said. "The Avenger."

"You mean those were for cattle sacrifices?" Bhima was horrified. "Have they no priests who are forest-teachers? I've never even heard of horse sacrifices any more except the Royal Horse Sacrifice itself."

"Magada is a strange kingdom." Yudishtira shrugged, trying to seem unaffected. "There's more fever out here. For three months of their year the rains hardly stop."

"No reason to sacrifice animals," Bhima muttered. "I think we're close enough to this snake den."

They fell silent as they chose places to rest among the lodhra trees that would keep them in view of the fortress and road. The afternoon wore on.

Nakula was the first to see Vimada. But Nakula motioned for them to stay back, for the Marut was not alone.

Vimada and the man they watched coming up the road were about the same age, although at first the stranger seemed much older because of his stooped posture and halting gait. He was also very thin, if not ill, and wore the clothes of a labourer. Observing him, Yudishtira felt a tremendous uneasiness. There was more hopelessness here than even the distress of half-starved servitude could explain. Was this their first glimpse of the inside of Girivraja?

As soon as Vimada had left the road at their crossed sticks Yudishtira stepped out to meet the Marut and this person he had retrieved from Magada. Yudishtira was immediately aware that Vimada was uneasy also—as if he had seen something that greatly disturbed him and was determined not to show his fear.

When they were all well hidden in a field overgrown with creepers and thistles, Vimada introduced the man as Prince Sini, the youngest son of King Saibya Ausinari of Usinara. At once Yudishtira saw that much of his own discomfort, at least, came from the contrast of the man's royal features with his haunted, half-mad face. He tried to remember what he could of the kingdom of Usinara. It was south of the Vrishnis, and had been harassed by Jarasamda almost out of existence.

"Your country and mine both enjoy the banks of Lady Yamuna, I believe, Prince Sini."

"I have not seen the Yamuna since my tenth autumn, King Yudishtira. Only this swamp." Sini gestured towards the valley and its slough. "*It* has no name."

"Your father is imprisoned in Girivraja?"

"Imprisoned in Magada's hell." The man's voice wavered like an agitated boy's, tears appeared in his eyes. "And my two older brothers with him."

As the prince described his sixteen-year watch, Yudishtira, feeling pity, whispered to Nakula to light a cook fire and make a drink of the sedative herbs Hdimba had found for them after the fight with her brother.

"So, like a loyal son, you have waited here for your father all this time, Prince?" Yudishtira asked.

"I waited with my mother and sister, until my mother died of grief. When my sister was old enough, they took her."

Yudishtira glanced at Bhima. It was hard to be raised as a warrior and a prince, and then to have failed to protect one's own sister. Even if one's attempt had to fail, one was expected to die trying. But Sini would have been so young, and would have lacked his father's and brothers' guidance—only the memory of their expectations of him.

"It seems an evil place, this Girivraja," Yudishtira said.

"They took her to make her a gift to Rudra," Prince Sini said in hollow tones.

"Meaning?"

"Meaning she was a summer sacrifice."

"And that means?" Yudishtira glanced at Nakula. "I'm sorry, but it is important to me to know the nature of the sins of our common enemy."

"It means they raped her and then they killed her. They fed her to Rudra. They burned her alive in his fire."

The silence after his words was long. Finally Sini whispered, "I live in disguise but I miss nothing. I've watched this road for sixteen years, for the king who would kill Jarasamda. I know what you need to know. He has hundreds chained in his caves. Fifteen kings. Many more of their families. And anyone else who has dared oppose him. Forty-three have been sacrificed in these sixteen years. Even priests. Does that help you? I would go with you to rescue my father," Sini looked away, "but I am no warrior now."

"You have endured like a warrior," Nakula said gently, "even if you lacked the means to protect your family."

The prince's look of childish gratitude made Yudishtira avert his eyes. He could only think of Jarasamda now. Of this sinner's flesh between his hands.

Nakula had finished preparing the brew of herbs and handed it to their visitor. "In your opinion, Prince Sini, is this king possessed?"

The rational question helped to restore the man's senses. "Jarasamda thinks he himself is Rudra's incarnation. But in other ways, his mind is too clear. Beware of him."

Yudishtira suddenly felt impatient. They now had more than sufficient reason to attack, and he did not care to hear anything else from someone who had lived sixteen years in defeat. Still, he would have one more use.

Yudishtira motioned for Vimada and his brothers to move well out of the prince's hearing. Taking a long breath, Yudishtira asked the Marut to stay behind with the Usinara prince. It was a hard request, but an essential precaution against the chance that Sini had been forced by Jarasamda to survive by spying. And although Vimada was beside himself, he was a warrior—he would not delay them with arguments when he saw the sense in a plan.

Yudishtira instructed Vimada to return to Indraprastha if he did not see a signal of victory from them within a day. "Arjuna and Sahadeva must be warned that if Jarasamda has defeated me, he will try to seize Indraprastha. Perhaps other kingdoms as well. 'The insulted snake squirms out of his hole and strikes at everyone he sees'."

Yudishtira led them back to Sini and, asking if there was a crown prince of Magada, received a description of Prince Sarasa. "He was once Jarasamda's pride," Sini said. "But now he spends his time with the imprisoned priests."

Perhaps the rotten city had a healthy core after all, Yudishtira thought. He asked where they would find Jarasamda and how monks were treated in the city.

"He's in the 'House of Rudra', at the very top. Vow-takers are greeted with rich food and madhu drink. Jarasamda corrupts them until they are performing sacrifices to Rudra, just like the others."

"He'll find these three are not like the others. Brothers, shall we visit Old Roarer?"

The city had a foul smell of refuse and faeces that came out to meet them from the moat. The guards at the drawbridge showed a strange complacency, allowing the three brothers to pass under the first sinister log portico without challenge. "I see crocodiles," Bhima whispered, staring down from the bridge into the weed-choked swamp.

"Excellent," Yudishtira whispered back. "A place to dispose of Jarasamda's unrepentant followers."

His brothers smiled a little. Good, he thought. Confidence would help. He had never felt so utterly responsible for their lives as today, walking unarmed into this city. He whispered to them to imitate whatever pose he assumed, then began striding imperiously up Girivraja's steep Royal Way, his arms folded across his chest and his head high.

Both this "royal way" and its side streets were littered and dirty, the windows in the house walls shuttered. And although a few people stared at the strange, swaggering ascetics, they attracted little sustained attention. Jarasamda's subjects seemed anxious to leave and be left alone.

As they neared the end of the steep street, the gates of the palace itself loomed over them. In their shadows there were a few stands selling garlands, honey cakes and caged birds, all apparently for rituals to Rudra. Silently asking Lord Dharma to forgive him for any sacrilege, Yudishtira stepped between two racks of garlands, kicked one over and cleaned the other of its contents, which he used to decorate himself and his brothers.

"Unclean!" the seller shouted. "You've made them unfit. A day's work!"

Yudishtira serenely turned to face the two guards trotting towards them. "In the name of Brahma the Creator of all," he said in his best imitation of his grandfather Vyasa, "I say your 'Rudra' is not divine at all, but a demon who takes *human lives* as sacrifices. You two guards! You will function as my envoys and take my message to King Jarasamda—exactly as I speak it, should you have forgotten the dharma of a messenger. Say, 'We wear the robes of vow-takers and have come to prove you are ignorant and unfit to rule. We do not come as guests, but as attackers of sin. Therefore we scale your palace walls rather than enter by your gates. Prepare to be judged, Jarasamda.'"

Yudishtira glanced at Nakula and Bhima. "No, better, say, 'Prepare to be judged, *coward*. For we hear you hold even priests as hostages in order to maintain your faltering power after failing in your effort to become samraj.'"

The guards cringed.

"Deliver my words!" Yudishtira shouted.

To the brothers' amazed relief, the pair of guards obediently ran off through the palace gates. Yudishtira slipped a gold coin to the garland seller—enough to buy every garland the man had probably ever sold. Then he took ropes from the stall's tent. "Now we scale the palace wall."

"But the gate is wide open," Bhima said. "These people will think we are mad."

"Would three sane priests create awe? Kindly throw this noose up over that spike, Bhima."

As they descended inside the palace a half circle of royal guards waited for them. The brothers painstakingly re-coiled the rope and sent it back to the shopkeeper, then allowed themselves to be escorted into the palace. They were taken up countless flights of steps, through long halls and finally across an inner court to the entry room of the House of Rudra—a very large and very ugly edifice of logs and stone. But Yudishtira noted that every door they'd passed through had borne considerable quantities of ornately carved sandalwood, the kind of tiresome work done by slaves, prisoners and others with years of time at another's disposal. He also saw that his brothers were looking increasingly awed themselves—which they could not afford.

"Still mourning your lost love?" Yudishtira whispered to Bhima. "Or are you ready to fight?"

Bhima stiffened and bared his chest, pointing to the tattered red sash and the grass belt wound together under the pile of garlands on his broad neck. "My love will make me strong. Very strong."

Yudishtira hid his satisfaction at the effect of his taunt. "We'll see."

They entered a large room that was almost pleasant. The walls were white and covered with artfully dyed hangings. Long low windows looked out over Magada's four quarters and let in a cool breeze, although not enough to clean the air. But in many ways Rudra's house was elegant, and Yudishtira vowed to remember that here in Girivraja things might not be as they were supposed to seem outwardly.

In the middle of the room a huge, lumpy body sat naked on a raised platform. Yudishtira's first thought was that this was Rudra the Avenger after all. His face was merciless, his body enormous, and his torso and limbs revealed no evidence of decline—only the definition of muscle and vein that comes with years of training and merely adds to the impression of strength. True, with his age and weight, his breath might well be his weakness. But how important could endurance be if one could crush an opponent in the first contact?

Jarasamda's flesh shone with the warm oil being slathered over him and rubbed in by four serious young monks. They treated each segment of musculature independently and with great reverence as the king flexed it and offered it for anointing. Additional oil vessels rested on stands at the four corners of the platform and were drawn from frequently. The excess oil drained down into a pit beneath the greasy throne. The whole room reeked of sweat and rancid fat.

Bhima giggled. "Like a big baby being oiled," he whispered.

Yudishtira glanced at him, then laughed out loud. "Like a big baby being oiled," Yudishtira repeated clearly.

The nearest guards and servants flinched as if expecting Yudishtira's imminent death. But the object of the insult and of their abject fear appeared not to have heard.

Yudishtira came closer. No more words came to him. He could not take his eyes from this man who was his fate. One of them would not leave this room alive. And Jarasamda was even larger than Bhima.

Yudishtira silently aimed his mind, then strode forward and kicked over the closest oil stand. "So you are 'Rudra'. But I don't see any god here—just the coward Jarasamda."

The guards stepped forward this time, but with hesitancy, Yudishtira noted. They were obviously unprepared for a display of either confidence or intelligence around their king, and probably had lived in terror of the day when a true sage, with the full powers gained by long austerities, would come to punish their king for his forbidden acts.

"It is my policy," Jarasamda was saying evenly, "to honour any vow-takers who come to my city. But I believe you are in disguise. Monks don't wear flowers, climb walls or hurl insults."

Yudishtira was worried by the rationality in this response—something else here that could not be predicted from appearances.

"You are right. I am not a monk. I am King Yudishtira of Indraprastha, son of King Pandu of the Kurus. These are my brothers, the princes Bhima and Nakula. All warriors, Jarasamda."

Now the guards did rush them. Nakula yelled, "A *king* should fight a king, not a king's guards."

Jarasamda shouted for the guards to withdraw. "I have heard

of you, Yudishtira—you are the king of the Yamuna Nishada and husband to a dark Dasyu whore."

Yudishtira held Bhima back with an arm across his brother's throat. His own heart pounding wildly, Pandu's eldest made his formal accusations. But as rudely as Yudishtira worded them, Jarasamda kept control.

"I know what you want, little Yudishtira. You fear my armies so you goad me personally to make me challenge you. All right. I do challenge you. Now."

It was so ominously simple. "And I accept the challenge, Jarasamda."

Yudishtira glanced at Bhima. He had not yet guessed. That was good.

"And the weapons, Yudishtira? What type of combat, little weasel?"

"Battle of breath, no blows below the waist."

"Excellent. To the death, with you and the other becoming my slaves when I win."

"With the consents of all kings transferred to me if I win," Yudishtira returned. "All prisoners freed, and the future worship of the gods here—and Magada's future itself—entirely at my discretion. If I wish to burn this termite hill to the ground, I will."

Jarasamda stepped towards the rush wrestling mats that Yudishtira had noted were a permanent furnishing of the royal audience room.

"Have you so forgotten dharma, old warrior, that you do not consecrate a successor before a battle so your kingdom will not suffer after your death? Who knows, I may even let your successor actually rule."

"If you wish more time, merely ask for it," Jarasamda said. "I will not die, so I have no need for such foolishness. But you shall see that I do honour the old code. My son will be anointed." He made a gesture to the guards. "Your brother may make any arrangements he needs before he dies."

"You challenged me, not my brother," Yudishtira answered.

Bhima began whispering and tugging on his sleeve. "Yudishtira, I am the wrestler. We prepared *me*."

Jarasamda had overheard him. "Wrestling you, Yudishtira,

does not interest me at all. Let this one fight in your name, Whoremaster—he's young, but at least he'll give me some fame when I kill him before your eyes."

Yudishtira's arm was receiving a hard shaking from Bhima. But as Bhima felt Yudishtira's muscles under the orange robe, his eyes first reflected disbelief, then recognition and horror.

"Your back was always to me," Yudishtira whispered gently. "I always carried extra weight."

"I beat you in every fight!"

"At the end it was only because I let you. You taught me all your secrets. Now let me use them."

"You want to spare me. But I'd rather die myself than watch him kill you."

"We may all die here. Better to be sin-free, however it comes—which means you must obey me, your elder and king." Yudishtira shook himself free of his brother. "Anoint your son, Jarasamda. I will anoint my brother Bhima."

Naked except for a loincloth, his hair cut short and his body oiled, Yudishtira faced Jarasamda on the mat. The man he intended to kill bowed low before him. "In the name of Rudra I offer this small king's life."

Yudishtira bowed in return. "May Lord Dharma remain my shield, if I deserve that honour."

Jarasamda's chief priest signalled the beginning of the contest that would not end until one of them was dead.

Jarasamda howled and leaped for Yudishtira. For a moment the great body was high above him. He stepped aside and Jarasamda crashed to the mat, sliding on his greasy hip. But the Magada king seemed to have intended all that—he was grinning as he rose up again, turned his back, and flexed his arms for the audience of priests and guards.

Yudishtira jumped on top of him from behind, even though knowing he was expected. The oil made them both slippery —Bhima had not used oil. Jarasamda merely played with Yudishtira's efforts to upset his balance, then shrugged him off. In this aspect of Magada there was no illusion: The man was clearly stronger.

But as they danced around each other, slapping and grunting, Yudishtira was seeing possibilities. The goal of death changed a wrestling match. Impressive moves did not matter. A head had to be pounded hard on the floor, a strangle hold had to be sustained a long, long time. Neither had a hope of doing that much harm while the other was fresh. It was a battle of breath after all. And a battle of wits. Perhaps that was really why Guru Vaja had told them to challenge Jarasamda at his speciality—the old king might be overconfident.

Now when openings appeared, Yudishtira deliberately ignored or misused them. Jarasamda pinned Yudishtira and began to pound him. Yudishtira broke free, spun and took a strike at Jarasamda from behind as they separated. But it was only a glancing fist blow when it could have been a damaging side-hand attack. Jarasamda was smirking when he turned around.

Yudishtira began concentrating on conserving his own strength while keeping Jarasamda moving and making himself look as inept as he safely could.

But judging that margin of safety grew more difficult. Or Jarasamda had guessed his tactic. Suddenly Yudishtira was caught in a pin. Many blows battered his head before he could break free.

He reeled off the edge of the mat. But Jarasamda's back was turned to receive more adulations from his priests and guards. Yudishtira stumbled back in and tripped him with a leg sweep.

Jarasamda stayed on his knees a moment, and Yudishtira left him alone on the mat. Water—that was his only thought. Nakula held it up to him.

"Why didn't Lord Dharma give you any sense?" Bhima muttered, wiping him down.

"Don't know," Yudishtira panted.

"What were you doing out there?" Nakula asked.

"Strategy."

"Well, find a new one please."

"Wait." Bhima was standing between Yudishtira and the mat. "Now listen to me—he's saving his energy too. You can't outlast him."

"Can't I?" Summoning all his strength, Yudishtira bounded back on to the mat.

The display made Jarasamda, plodding forward to save his breath, look old.

"Tired already, Elder?" Yudishtira shouted.

Jarasamda took the bait and leaped the distance between them. Yudishtira did not step aside this time, but landed a blow in his face. Bhima howled his approval. The fight went on.

On and on. Lamps were lit. More persons, in greater finery, wandered in. Even food was served—Magada's priests and nobles had apparently seen other long fights. If that were true, Yudishtira vaguely realised that the strategy of gradually wearing down Jarasamda must have been used often before. And Jarasamda had never been defeated.

The fact was that if anyone was being worn down it was himself. He effected blows, but the Magada king's blows were crushing. Yudishtira's head and abdomen ached from them. One knee was sprained so that every step was agony. Both calves were cramping. A finger hung useless at its middle joint. Then there was just the dreadful thirst. And the simple aggravation of constant sweat in his eyes.

He came out again to Bhima and Nakula.

"You're holding your ground so far," Bhima said, avoiding his eyes. "I'm not even sure I could do better." Yudishtira knew Bhima was finally afraid for him.

"You two go," Yudishtira whispered, panting. "No one—no one will try hard to stop you. Take care of her. Draupadi."

"No." Nakula dropped the cloths in his hands. "Never. Ask anything else. Let *me* fight for you."

"It was always my plan." Yudishtira swayed and Nakula caught him. "For you two to go. If he was too good. I have left a son—it is enough."

Bhima grabbed Yudishtira and shook him. "Drink some water!" Then Bhima released him, his big hands now tenderly helping him to hold the water gourd. "And rest a moment, dearest brother. Look, that fat pig is even lying down. You're going to finish him any time now, and live a long life with ten wives and ten times ten sons."

"Only one wife," Nakula muttered.

Bhima glanced at him. Nakula shrugged, tears in his eyes. "He vowed it the day we left."

Bhima looked from one to the other. "That's crazy, Yudishtira. Crazy."

"It is." Yudishtira suddenly stood erect and stumbled back to the mat.

The sweat still stung his eyes. He wiped and blinked, then shook his head. His ears rang. He began to talk to himself as he circled his opponent. "Crazy. This is crazy. What am I doing? Do I just want to die?"

He dreaded every contact with Jarasamda now. His mind's effort to avoid a blow or pin was even more exhausting then his body's struggle, but more crucial—his body could take no more damage.

Then he was flying through the air. He hit with a horrible force. Jarasamda was on top of him. They thrashed and struggled, but Yudishtira was defending, nothing more. Closing openings. Curling tight.

There was a shift and Jarasamda had him in a choke. Purple crowded his brain. I'm going to die here, he thought. I'm going to lose. Everything. Bhima. Nakula. Draupadi!

Yudishtira wrenched upward and broke the hold. Bhima shouted, "Kill him!"

Kill him. Yudishtira thought the words sounded strange. Familiar. He turned to follow Jarasamda's recovery. The Magada king leaped at him, sure that his work was almost done. Yudishtira managed a feeble mockery of a Great Leap Aside. But this time he dropped to his knees beside his fallen opponent and struck his ear, his nose, his neck, using almost childish blows.

Jarasamda turned on him in a rage. Yudishtira struck at the leering mouth, the eyes. He punched the oily, heaving stomach as it rose up over him. And no blows were returned.

As Jarasamda came down, Yudishtira rolled backwards out of reach, stood—and tripped on his own feet. He scrambled out of reach yet again. Sweat blinded his eyes now. But blood blinded Jarasamda's.

"Here," yelled Bhima. "Good. That was good. Here, tie this around your head."

Yudishtira saw dyed grasses and the red of Draupadi's sash swing before his eyes. He drew back, staring at it. "No."

"Why not?" Bhima wiped the sweat from Yudishtira's eyes, then tied the twist of cloth and straw around his forehead. "It's a good use for it, and may all those who rage at each other in the name of love flourish in Hell. Now go for his face and stomach again. He doesn't like that."

Jarasamda came back energised with anger. But even if he only imagined it, the wad of belt and sash around his head gave Yudishtira a foolish hope of living.

Instead of a quick climax, however, the battle wore on into the night. Neither could maintain a good hold for long; both stumbled often, as if drunk. Once Jarasamda hit Yudishtira hard on the side of the head. But he recovered. Once Yudishtira knocked Jarasamda down with a footsweep and gave him another series of blows. But he was too weak to follow it up and pin him. The circling and the straining embraces went on and on.

The room was growing grey with the light before dawn. But the room was now overflowing with people. The soldiers and nobles of Magada sensed that the end was near.

Something about seeing daylight drained Yudishtira. It seemed to him that he had nothing left. Could have nothing left if he had fought all night.

Bhima called him off the mat again. "Curse this place, Yudishtira. They're already measuring us for chains with their eyes. For Indra's sake, you've got to drink more water. You have to come out more often when you fight this long. Now think of Sini's sister and kill this snake!"

Yudishtira nodded vaguely. He staggered back towards Jarasamda. The Magada king was also reeling, and jabbering: "How does he keep fighting, Rudra? What is his secret? A little man against me. A little man."

Yudishtira closed in and pummelled him feebly. Jarasamda exploded with new energy, throwing and pinning him. He had been faking!

Yudishtira was trapped, his arms twisted behind and cracking at the shoulder sockets. He could hear Bhima's shouts. "Try.

489

Push. His foot. Watch his left hand. Keep it from your throat. Live, Yudishtira! I can't live without you, Brother."

Yudishtira yanked up and out on something. Jarasamda's left arm. Air rushed back to his lungs. He arched up with his back and neck. Jarasamda shifted. Yudishtira strained upward again and was free. He began pounding the huge body crazily.

Bhima was screaming: "*Kill him*, Yudishtira."

Jarasamda was cowering down. He was only a heap, curled up against vicious blows. Yudishtira found it odd—his own arms were delivering those blows. He reached down and watched himself lift a great weight, heavier than any sala tree during his training. But like a sala tree. Except that this object grunted and struggled. Bhima was screaming, "Kill it, kill it."

Yudishtira took an agonising step towards a stone bench near the mat. Another step. Then hurled the weight off his shoulders. There was a crack—an echo of something he had heard once before. He reached down and lifted one end of the thing up and smashed it against the stone.

Bhima was yelling, "Jaya, jaya, jaya, jaya! Victory!"

Priests and warriors were running from the hall. Nakula was blocking their way, giving orders: "Bring every prisoner here. The kings first. Obey and you have nothing to fear; try to escape and we will hunt you down. We'll learn who was here from others and hunt you down. Prince Sarasa? You will be consecrated king. Yes, now. It is King Yudishtira's desire. You will answer only to him, your next samraj."

Yudishtira heard as if it were all going on outside a room that he was locked inside of. He looked around him but his vision was strange, distorted. Now Bhima took up the raining of words. "You there, take this orange robe of my brother's and hang it from the flagpole—we have warriors to signal. Here, bring in those kings. We want Jarasamda's war chariot prepared—the large one you call Pushkala. And its pennant —bring that to me immediately."

Nakula whispered, "You were fighting for fifteen hours. And at the end you lifted twice your own weight."

Yudishtira nodded. An old woman was prostrate in front of him, forcing jewels into his hands. "You have saved us, you have saved us," she kept sobbing.

The room grew vaguer. He was trying to think. Trying to remember. Something he had realised. Couldn't forget it. He felt himself falling. Bhima's arms caught him. Nakula's face was hovering before his own.

"To make my wife love me. Stupid of me. I did it because —so she'd love me the most."

Only Nakula heard him. "Is that why, Yudishtira? But she wasn't even here."

42

You never appreciate
a bowl until it is broken
or a person until they are out of reach.
                    a Panchala saying

The two chariots returned at twilight, thirty days after they had left. Yudishtira had sent his message of "jaya" from Magada, and other messages as they travelled back, so they were expected. At the river they were greeted with banners, flowers, musicians, chanting priests—everything Eos, Kunti and Sahadeva could think of.

Yudishtira had attached Jarasamda's pennant to his chariot pole as they crossed on the ferry. When he entered Indraprastha's gates he bent the pole and removed the flag. "Take this to the queen," he commanded a woman servant.

Then he saw he was addressing Subhadra. She bowed to him. "I will see it is done, King. But best not by me," she whispered, "if it is to please Draupadi."

"So my wife is still angry?"

The girl's expression was one of obvious misery. "Will she ever forgive Arjuna and me for our love?" She turned away to give the pennant to an attendant.

For some reason it bothered him deeply that for an entire month others had considered this woman his sister-in-law, and he did not even know her. He was a stranger here.

For a whole month Draupadi had hated him.

Yudishtira was overwhelmed by a feeling that he would never be happy at Indraprastha again. It would never be as it

492

was. He made himself admit the exact truth: It would never be the way it had been while Arjuna was gone.

He forced himself to address the cheering crowd. "Yes, dharma has been restored in Magada, but Jarasamda died bravely." Yudishtira also still bore a peculiar sadness for the man with whom he had struggled through an entire night. "And he left a good son. That strange king I have defeated will gain Heaven yet, with Rudra's intercession."

Bhima snorted. "After a long rest in Hell." The crowd laughed.

"You should all know that Bhima was the real hero," Yudishtira continued. "Without the skills he taught me, I would not have survived my fight. Now I must send him and my other brothers off on another dangerous errand. Many of our brave Maruts will go with them. Until they are all safely home—" He looked out at his mother, Arjuna, Sahadeva, Panchalya, Eos and Subhadra. No, she was not among them. His wife was either not able or not willing to greet him after the most important victory of his life. "Until then, I fear I can not celebrate."

After bathing, Yudishtira searched for Arjuna. He found his brother in the first place he looked—the armoury. The same armoury where this had begun.

"Arjuna, we must speak honestly before I can send you out to defeat kings for me. I wish to ask your forgiveness for my rude departure and for not summoning you when we went to Magada."

"None of it matters, Yudishtira. As soon as you were gone I realised all that really mattered to me was your safe return."

"I find that hard to believe. If I had been left behind I would have been angry."

Arjuna shrugged, obviously not expecting such frankness. "You had good reasons."

"I had some reasons. You did have a right to a second wife, and it was necessary to ask my permission. But you did not have to humiliate her in public."

"Other first wives accept a second."

"Some do." Yudishtira took a deep breath to contain his

desire to shout. "But we did not wed an ordinary woman. Arjuna, I will try to no longer concern myself over who you love or who loves you."

"Is it that simple, Yudishtira? Pardon me, Eldest Brother, but I don't think so." Arjuna picked up an arrow, sighted down it for straightness, then threw it down. "Draupadi hates me now."

"She has forgiven you before."

"This is different."

"Does it bother you that much, Arjuna?"

Arjuna looked sharply at Yudishtira. "I love her. I wish I didn't, but I still do."

Yudishtira suddenly felt very uneasy. "So much that I suspect you would travel two thousand leagues in order to kill someone, just for her. As I did. Do we love her, Arjuna? Or is it more that we can't love ourselves when she doesn't love us?"

"*I* love her."

Yudishtira walked away. After a long time he turned and said, "So maybe it would be better to talk about who you'll be facing in the north. I wish Krishna were here to advise us."

At that Arjuna's face became even more drawn and Yudishtira felt a stronger wave of irritation. "What, are you worried about the Vrishni? You know he's safe. He'll come back when the mood strikes him."

Arjuna's jaw tightened. "Perhaps. All right, where do you wish me to go, Yudishtira? I am eager to win back your respect. And to be away from here."

Yudishtira sighed, wishing he could walk through the armoury door again and this time say only simple, forgiving things to his younger brother. Gently he said, "First you will enter Naimisha. They have already invited us, but their neighbours the Bhadrakara . . ."

Their four chariots faced the four quarters. Behind each were four more accompanying chariots, each containing a Marut and a driver. The three sacred fires were kindled by Urutata and the five oblations poured by the seven priests from Dvaraka.

The east-facing chariot was led forward a step by Bhima's weapon bearer. A hymn was chanted to Vayu, Bhima's "father", lord of the wind: "'I proclaim the greatness of the impetuous Vayu; his voice spreads thundering around; he moves along sweeping the sky, tinting purple the quarters of the horizon . . .'"

Then the north-facing chariot, and a hymn to Indra, Arjuna's "father", the god of rain, raining arrows, and the invincible thunderbolt: "'Worship him who is exhilarated by the sacrificial food, the mighty Indra, the leader of men . . .'" Arjuna's blue and white banner with the gold monkey figure slapped in the brisk wind.

The twins' chariots, facing south and west, were led out, with a hymn to the Ashwins: "'You both demand the oblation, you spread out the ceremonials as two weavers stretch cloths . . .'"

Yudishtira stood at the centre, representing the nadir of earth, while the gods in Heaven fixed the last of the six directions, the zenith of the universe. He glanced at his mother, who stood beside him representing his father Pandu. She was smiling.

Good then, he thought. The ancestors will be satisfied with the beginning.

He addressed his brothers: "Go and conquer in my name. Envoys have been sent—may your conquests be nothing more than welcoming celebrations. But should you be defied, conquer without anger. Accept no tribute or titles. Ask only that the defeated king accept my sovereignty and appear at my consecration. Do not approach a king with even the slightest anticipation of opposition—leave your weapons in the racks and wear your festive garments. The kings have heard how I defeated Jarasamda, released his royal prisoners and respected his son's rights. They are even beginning to appreciate my patience with my uncle and cousin. I think they are ready to consent. So wits rather than whips, yes? Send me messages more often than I sent them to you this last month. Now go with great speed. You have less than two months in which to conquer one hundred kingdoms."

The chariot teams reared and leaped forward in their best displays of battle behaviour. Each squad of chariots took a direction—the north and south river roads, the northwest road to Naimisha, and the road east to the Ganges and beyond.

Yudishtira, Urutata, Kunti and Panchalya watched until even the chariots' dust had settled. Then Yudishtira turned to his mother and brother-in-law. "I wish to remain in seclusion. Please see that I receive every message as soon as it arrives." As he walked through the gate he saw Jarasamda's pennant flying from a window in the women's quarters.

Messengers arrived almost daily from his brothers. Mostly they reported that the brothers were being welcomed and showered with consents. When it was otherwise, he received messages like Arjuna's: "Here in Kanakhala King Bhagadatta and I played with bows and arrows for eight days before he saw my point of view. He has some interesting warriors from Chine."

Or Nakula's: "In Rohitaka I was able to practise my skills with the Mattamayuraka champions. If they'd been Guru Vaja's students they would have spent a month in the small-boys' class after making the mistakes they made against us."

In the assembly hall at Indraprastha Panchalya hung a ribbon on Yudishtira's ritual lance every time a king's consent was gained. The lance was soon rippling with colours.

But except for one terse, formal expression of pleasure that he had survived, the messengers who came back from the women's quarters bore the same repetitious news of defeat. Finally Kunti came to speak to him.

"She is still ill and overwrought, Son. She has lost a child!"

"What about Prahara? She still has him."

"She sees him daily. What you mean is, what about Prahara's father? She's hurt. Angry. And I say, be grateful. Better anger than simpering or pining away. Amarsha, the passion that flares up angrily and avenges an insult—it is a noble trait in a warrior's wife. It is the sign of a magnificent discontent, a never-resting demand for something more, something higher. Amarsha is essential in a warrior. And in the mothers of them."

"Including yourself, it seems," he said. "Are you telling me that you are also angry with me? You have never given me your own thoughts on my acceptance of Drita's division of the kingdom. Perhaps it is time."

"That is over and Indraprastha is a great kingdom. No, I am telling you to appreciate your wife."

"I'm trying to send her love messages every day!"

"Maybe that is not quite the same thing."

Jarasamda's pennant hung limply in the still air of twilight. Draupadi absently touched it to her lips. "Four thousand leagues there and back, Eos. He crossed twenty kingdoms to do his brave deed. And I haven't left this room."

"Anger is a strong prison." Eos had just entered to bring Draupadi her evening meal.

"Kunti says I must stay in."

"You know you can leave at any time. You can leave when you are well, and you will be well when you leave—so go out. Talk to him. Honour him for what he has accomplished."

Draupadi came from the window. "It's this 'dharma of women' that I hate."

"It allows for travel. Just not when your awareness is like churning butter. Have you heard anything I have said?"

"You think I should read his messages, don't you?"

Eos walked back with her to the window. Both women were lit by the deep, clear blue-green light before darkness.

"It's only that I'm the one who must see Yudishtira's face every day, Draupadi. Full of sadness."

"He only worries about his brothers."

"He worries about you. He needs you to forgive him."

"Does he say that?"

Eos frowned. "Anyone can see it."

Draupadi slammed the shutters. "And if I'm being unreasonable?" She closed her eyes and whispered, "I can't believe his kind messages and *I can't face him*."

Eos lit a lamp. "Because he witnessed you swooning in Arjuna's arms after he vowed his life to you. That's your real difficulty. You are ashamed of yourself. But Yudishtira has already forgiven you. I know it."

"Forgiven *me*?"

Eos sighed. "Draupadi, you are not the first to be blinded by an infatuation. What matters is how you repair your mistake."

Draupadi did not respond, but her face was drawn and pale.

"So maybe staying in your rooms a little longer is wisest after all." Eos came over to her. "Only don't become angry with yourself when you stop being angry at them. You've felt the shock of pain, that's all. But something good is always born of it. Something bad is always shed when it is gone."

Yudishtira and Panchalya were lit by the same twilight, high on the walkway above the armoury. The two young kings were looking out over the palisade towards the Yamuna. The smoke of the cooking fires in the villages made a band of grey across the blue-green evening.

"Panchalya, I feel as if parts of me are scattered all over Bharata."

"You've never been separated from all of them before, have you? I know how it feels: Pulled in two."

"Krishna's gone also—no one knows where. I haven't seen Vyasa since we left Hastinapura. Nor Gangeya. Guru Vaja seemed like a stranger when I left here, and was gone when I returned. I even miss my uncle, Drita. Even my cousins."

"And my sister? Rest assured that she refuses to see me also."

"Draupadi most of all," Yudishtira said quietly, "and she is nearest. We are all parted."

Yudishtira turned to go down to the assembly hall, where another envoy was waiting to speak a message from a distant brother. "I feel so much weaker without them, Panchalya. I feel weak and tired." He stopped for one more look across his darkening kingdom. "You never appreciate a whole until it is broken, do you?"

"Nor a person," Panchalya said, "until they are out of reach."

Vyasa hurried through the twilight—she had sent for him. She had ended her vow of silence and sent for him. His heart beat hard from more than the effort of the climb in the thin air— this summons had to mean that she had felt the changes too.

He stopped when he could see the mouth of the cave. He took his seat on the same spot of ground he had taken the last time and closed his eyes. But he could not still his mind. Suddenly his eyes flew open spontaneously.

She stood before him, alive and real, but outlined by sunlight as though the sun had not yet set.

"Aditi." His emotions would not allow him to say more.

She bowed, then seated herself cross-legged, young like a willow, and as earnest about their task as when she had been his student. Yet now it was he who felt the awe of the presence of Pure Veda.

"The danger to my daughter is increasing."

Her long-stilled voice was like water blown on a breeze, like damp ploughed earth, like fire. Yet utterly reasonable.

He strove to match her calm. "I feel it too—they are all in danger. Yet he has been magnificent. She will be the wife of Bharata's samraj."

"The danger increases, none the less."

"Perhaps it is the Egyptian."

"I believe he, at least, is taken care of." Aditi smiled a little. "No, what is needed next is that you take her my message, and that you tell her who it is from."

43

In that leafy tree where Yama drinks with the gods,
there the progenitor, the lord of the house,
invites us to join the men of old.
At first I beheld him with anguish
inviting me to join the men of olden time,
and walking with that fell design;
but afterwards I longed for him.

Rig Veda

"He's done it!"

"It's true, Suyodhana. I also heard the envoy. Your cousins have gathered the consents."

Lettermaker looked up from his writing to listen to the voices on the other side of the guest-garden wall.

"You've heard Vaja's report on their defences, Suyodhana —send our challenge now, before he performs the samraj rituals."

Of the several voices Lettermaker could hear along with King Drita's eldest son's, Lettermaker recognised only this last one, King Radheya's.

"Radheya's right," another warrior said. "We still can bring a bigger army to the field. What do they really have yet besides Nishada? The Panchalas and the Vrishnis—they are nothing. Magada is too far away and no other kings are required to fight for him until after the formal vows."

"Now, Suyodhana," said another. "Challenge him now."

Suyodhana only laughed. "Friends, brothers, take your ease. Attack my cousin? On the contrary, I have sent word to him that I am delighted that a Kuru is near to becoming samraj. I've promised him the support of all of our allies. That way he need not approach them on his own." Suyodhana's tone changed. "In fact he can not, without seeming to doubt our word. Of course, at the consecration itself, if it turns out these changeable allies have altered their thoughts and do not give their consent—"

The others paused. "Then every king's consent will be gathered," said one. "All ready to bow down—except for those held back by you. All Bharata's kings subdued—"

"And armed, and inside his walls," Suyodhana finished. The group of them was walking away now.

"No more trickery!" It was Radheya. "Suyodhana, challenge him today. You have *every* reason."

"I have one more important reason not to . . ." The voices turned a corner and were gone.

"Sad, isn't it?"

Lettermaker started. It was Baron Sakuni, speaking from behind him.

"Not for you, it seems, Baron. Your nephew as samraj? Yet he isn't even a king, am I right?"

"Being familiar with courts, I'm sure you can imagine the rest of his plan."

Lettermaker picked up his writing implements and vowed to say no more. There had been too much said between him and this sly Arya already, always with the same start and end: Sakuni's invitation to meet would repel him and he wouldn't answer, but somehow they would meet anyway, converse wittily in elegant Egyptian, invariably agree—and afterwards Lettermaker would still feel revolted, as if he had succumbed to something he should have resisted, or at least said some small thing more than he had meant to. But it would not happen today.

Sakuni sat down beside him. "You find me disturbing, don't you, Phoenician?"

Lettermaker looked up quickly.

"Do you know why, Lettermaker? Because you still see me as Yudishtira's enemy and feel you must protect him. But he can't be protected, and that is what really disturbs you. From here at Hastinapura you see it is inevitable: The sons of Pandu are doomed. Yes, Yudishtira is almost samraj, but he has merely done Suyodhana's work for him. So now, what concerns me —and you, I think—is his queen's fate in all this."

"The brothers will not be defeated so easily."

"No, not easily. They'll fight to the death to defend the city you built them and the subjects who will have sought shelter inside."

Lettermaker shook his head, not speaking his thoughts— that in the end Yudishtira's 'dharma' had trapped him.

Sakuni smiled with complete understanding. "It is always dangerous to cling to old ideas when those around you have moved on."

"No, Sakuni. I believe that Yudishtira's way of ruling will be adopted some day. Somewhere. Not because it is just, although it is, but because it destroys the least life and wealth."

"Of course. This 'ahimsa'? Non-harming? Each supporting the other? It is the very basis of society. But you are right, ahimsa requires a different environment. In fact, I would say it has a far better chance under Suyodhana's rule than Yudishtira's."

"That's absurd."

"Not at all. If Yudishtira really could have become samraj, Bharata's barbaric warriors would have constantly challenged him, just because of ahimsa, and all his time and wealth would have gone to warfare. While under the gracious Suyodhana, peace will be enforced and learning will flourish, including ideas like ahimsa. It's the Assyrians who are rebuilding the libraries of Babylon, yes?

"You can't deny it, Lettermaker."

The Phoenician didn't answer.

"But you and I must concentrate on the essential matter," Sakuni said. "Getting Draupadi out of Indraprastha alive— and then seeing that the world has a chance to appreciate this woman who is Bharata's single greatest treasure. Good, you are at least listening. We have so little time left—the gathering at Indraprastha is less than a month away. I will have a comfortable slave box built, with a strong lock—"

Lettermaker stood. "I refuse to listen to this."

"It is merely the safest way to remove her from Indraprastha unseen."

Lettermaker was furious, lavishing on Sakuni all the accusations he had ever heard made about the man, and all his dislike of him since their first meeting. Finally he broached even the subject of the fire at Varanavata.

Sakuni was unfazed. "I'm accused of so much, Lettermaker. Yavana ideas are looked upon with great suspicions here."

"Burning a house with six people inside, including a woman, does have a yavana flavour," Lettermaker said sarcastically, "but I think Bharata already had fire before your travels."

Sakuni laughed. "What about the things they say of you here behind your back? That you corrupted Sahadeva by teaching him to commit the horrible sin of writing? How much we always have in common, Lettermaker. But we've no time left for pleasant debates. We must think only of Draupadi, trapped in a burning city with husbands doomed to die."

Lettermaker assured him that no one would ever convince Draupadi to abandon her husbands, much less her child. Nor did he think her fool enough to put herself in a locked box, for any reason. He moved to go.

"Have you heard that Arjuna took a second wife?"

Lettermaker stared, then slowly sat.

"Yes, he has wed Krishna's sister."

"Krishna and Arjuna wouldn't do that. Nor would Draupadi allow it."

"They did it and she had no choice but to allow it. She also conceived with Bhima—two months after giving birth to her previous child. I assure you that she is already looking ahead to her future as a combination brood mare and rival wife. And when she then sees the brothers on the verge of defeat—"

"She will be more loyal to them than ever."

"Unless you can make her see beyond Bharata and this petty rivalry. Or maybe it doesn't even matter if she agrees to leave. Just bring her out of Indraprastha and then make her understand."

Lettermaker protested that the very idea was ridiculous. Even in the box, Draupadi would be as trapped inside the city as anyone else.

"You will escort the box out through the tunnels."

Lettermaker breathed in sharply.

"You look surprised. Spies, Lettermaker. Their precious teacher Guru Vaja told us about them—in order to save as many lives as possible during the battle he knows is coming."

Sakuni then unfolded the version of the events to come that he had prepared for Lettermaker: How Suyodhana wished to burn Indraprastha to the ground and put his brothers at the gates and tunnel entrances inside the walls, where those escaping would be free to choose to die or to submit to him for life. "A clumsy plan, but I fear it will work well enough. My problem is that I would like to enter through the tunnels' *outside* openings, to bring in litters on which to remove the injured."

Lettermaker smiled grimly. "I see you don't quite know all about the tunnels. And you will learn nothing from me."

"You still fear that I might help to destroy Pandu's sons? Does it really sound as if that task requires my help? You know what a city's defeat means. Do you want that for her? Think carefully, Lettermaker."

"I left more friends at Indraprastha than the queen, much as I admire her. I could not betray them."

Sakuni leaned closer. "I will allow you to save the Greek too—the two women, and yourself."

Lettermaker closed his eyes, overcome with painful memories.

"You would like to believe that Eos will escape without anyone's help," Sakuni whispered. "But you can't be sure. She'll probably try to save others. Or she could be injured and unable to move. Tell me the entrances, Lettermaker. We must save the women!"

Lettermaker stood. He wished there was even one god he believed in, one god he could take strength from. But he'd encountered so many, and in the end he'd seen that survivors like himself had not prayed, but planned.

"Give me time to think, Sakuni."

"Your moment of triumph is coming, Lotus."

She didn't look at Baron Sakuni, but stared out at the night.

"We leave in two days for Indraprastha. You will accompany Suyodhana's party."

She still did not speak. Did she know about Subhadra? That was his concern.

"You must take hold of yourself, Lotus. Look prettier."

She glanced at him sharply.

He smiled. "Good. You are quiet, but you haven't lost your anger. Draw it back in silence then—it will fly all the farther when released." And he gave her his final instructions: to ignore the confusion on the day she would strike; to merely go where he would instruct—no one would bother to protect Yudishtira from a 'mere Dasyu woman'—and to beg to speak to the king. "Wait for his back to be turned. And kill him." Then, again, Sakuni recited his lies. To her it was that when she had revenged the needless death of her child, Suyodhana would have his revenge and kill Bhima, and Arjuna would become king. "Perhaps even samraj, why not? And you will be his queen."

She didn't answer.

"Have we agreed, Lotus?"

The silence was long. Finally she said, "I will go to Indra-prastha."

"Uncle, I want to know exactly what will occur at Indraprastha. I must know my role."

Sakuni smiled. "Wear a red cloak, Suyodhana. And prepare two speeches. The first can be anything—you will give it during the last hour of Yudishtira's life when the assembled kings will give him their consent. You will speak for your absent father. The second speech should be for when *you* are anointed samraj."

"Samraj? But I'm still not a king. Then you'll convince my father to step down?"

Sakuni turned his back on him. "In that speech say that events now make it clear that Bharata needs a large, permanent army under the samraj's direct control."

"What events will make such a thing clear?"

"The events that will have occurred."

"But what must *I* do to make them occur? Obviously I must try to convince the unallied kings that Yudishtira is unfit to be samraj."

"In the end their opinions will be as insignificant as ashes." He turned back to face his nephew. "But, yes, do try to sway them. It will take up all your energy and attention."

Sakuni laughed. "And I will have that much less to be bothered with."

Sakuni met Zesnor at moonset under Hastinapura's eastern wall and gave him his orders like a true master—for Sakuni had rehearsed this moment often. "Return to them tonight and divide them into nine troops, four for Indraprastha's four gates and five for the outer tunnel entrances." He could barely control the pride in his voice. "I obtained their location myself."

Zesnor only nodded.

Sakuni went on with his plans. His true plans, carefully wrought. An attack on one village at noon of the first day, to start a panic. But only one village—more would arouse too many of Indraprastha's Nishada against them. The rakshasa were to focus not on burning but on killing everyone trying to escape the city, especially through the tunnels—for those who knew of the tunnels would be the brothers themselves or their most loyal followers. The rakshasa were to allow only Lettermaker and his box to leave, the Greek woman warrior if she was with him (to be killed later), and Suyodhana, who would be with Sakuni. "Lettermaker, Suyodhana and I will wear red cloaks and use the password 'soma'. Absolutely no one else should leave alive."

"If Radheya is with Suyodhana?"

"I repeat, no one else."

"Not this woman Lotus either?"

"She knows nothing about the tunnels."

Again Zesnor only nodded.

Sakuni explained that he would signal from the tunnel mouth nearest the river when he was ready for the rakshasa to set fire to the fortress. "The fire must not begin before I signal. Pick good leaders for the nine troops—tell them not to drink the azle themselves—and give all these instructions carefully, for you will not be with them."

"Where, then, shall I be?"

"Tonight you will give me the necessary herbs to cause King Drita to be too ill to travel when the others leave tomorrow for Indraprastha. After you have arranged the attack, you will return here and kill my brother-in-law."

Sakuni explained that the news of Drita's death had to arrive. at the same hour that Indraprastha was destroyed. Suyodhana would then emerge from the smoke as one of the lone surviving members of Bharata's royal families. When it was made clear that Suyodhana—only Suyodhana—could control the raksh-asa, those still alive would plead for him to accept the burden of samraj.

"Master, you have planned elaborately."

Sakuni barely hid his satisfaction.

"Of course the timing of your part is especially delicate. I will see that in Egypt you receive equal credit for its success."

"I would prefer you should have it all."

"You see a flaw?"

Zesnor did not answer.

"Tell me. I will admit it—I need your opinion."

"A king is a god, Master. Even this Drita."

"That's true in Egypt." Sakuni strained to see Zesnor's expression in the darkness. "And in Egypt pharaohs are murdered as regularly as the Nile floods. But you are right—we must add this idea to 'dharma'. It will greatly facilitate the rule of these stubborn people. Although watching anyone worshipping my nephew will require all my patience."

"As always, you see the smallest scale on the cobra, Master." Zesnor spoke the next slowly. "Then your plan will be the one."

"As soon as you have killed King Drita, I want you to concern yourself only with Draupadi. Kill Lettermaker and the Greek woman and take Draupadi to Egypt. Deliver her as our gift to Amon-Re. She will impress even your cold Egyptians. I know it."

Zesnor turned away, stopped, and turned back. "My first lesson in the service of the gods was to properly carry the water vessels used to wash the steps of the house of Amon-Re. All day long I was taught to repeat one thought: My treatment of the gods will one day be the gods' treatment of me."

"Meaning what?" Sakuni asked.

"Whatever one hears, Master."

44

The samraj does not rule kings only. He has achieved
digvijaya, the conquest of all the quarters of space itself.
And space is everywhere, both outside and inside the samraj
and his people.

Vyasa

For three days Bharata's one hundred kings came. Dust towered
to the sky along the winter-dry roads that led to Indraprastha
like spokes to a hub. The royal entourages piled up at the
gates, waiting to be escorted in. For, without mentioning
"rakshasa", King Yudishtira's orders had made it clear that
everyone of any importance would be housed inside the walls.
Three thousand or more people would be living within the
palisades—some within the palace itself, the rest in the buildings and courtyards between the inner palace and the outer
walls.

When their turns came, the kings' chariots paraded in
through the streets, each with a blue-uniformed Nishada at
the head of their teams of four, to direct them to their lodgings.
Over three hundred additional four-wheeled, four-horse, heavy
war and hunting chariots rolled in between the north gate
towers, crowded with Bharata's other outstanding warriors.
After them, four times as many two-wheeled, two-horse, light
war chariots brought queens, crown princes and other members
of the royal families. Every vehicle flew clan and kingdom
banners and sported long garlands of flowers. Wheels creaked
ominously under jewelled ceremonial weapons loaded on at
the last moment from ox carts left outside the gates. The
horses had also been groomed just before their entrance—they

pranced under blankets of flowers and circlets of gold bells.

Next the bullock carts began squeezing into the city, carrying the elaborate gifts, plus the requisite clothing, gear and animal feed for family groups who had been travelling for up to ten days. A few kings had brought their royal elephants as well—an imposition inside a city, but preferred by some for the impression they made. Usually the owners were ageing monarchs who needed all the display they could muster—so much so that some young warriors were starting to use the phrase "an elephant kingdom" to signify a territory ripe for a raid.

In the days of the ancestors, a *rajasuya*, the consecration of a samraj, meant a true confrontation at the winter cattle-counting, when the "kings" of semi-nomadic clans vied for the title of supreme ruler. Now the kings ruled settled kingdoms scattered across two thousand leagues, and the contests were frequently political and always fought beforehand, in courts and assembly halls as often as on battlefields, and mostly by representatives of the samraj candidate, not by that preoccupied man himself.

All of which changed the rajasuya ceremony also. Yudishtira would call himself the conqueror of the four quarters of Earth and the one above him in space after merely taking a step in each direction and one upon a golden stool placed on a tiger skin. Then he would drive out, yes, but not to armed camps to subdue his remaining opposition. He would merely shoot a few arrows at an imaginary enemy as the priests chanted and the crowds cheered. Nor would he gamble for more territory in an all-night dicing game—he would play a pleasant round for gold coins, or if he chose to please the priests rather than his fellow warriors, he would forgo the gaming entirely and simply give gifts. It was all ritual now, with a significance that no longer belonged to this world.

One aspect had not changed, however. At no point in the rituals or in daily life was a king or a samraj treated as if he were a god, or god-given, or even divinely blessed. Both king and samraj ruled by consent and could, in principle and quite often in practice, be overthrown by their subjects or exiled for misconduct. They were given wealth in order to perform their duties, both administrative and spiritual, and because it reflected well on their subjects when their palaces were luxurious. They deserved respect, especially if they followed dharma and their kingdoms prospered. They were even obeyed in battles, provided they were bold enough. But gods they could never be.

The function of the samraj was to represent the Arya—to the gods through rituals, and also to themselves. Like the laws of dharma and the teachings of the forest-dwelling priests, a samraj tempered the Arya aggressive streak by reminding them all of the whole which the parts damaged if their destructiveness should be directed towards each other.

There had not been a rajasuya ceremony while Yudishtira was alive, or any other gathering of Arya as complete. As he observed the arrival of these arrogant kings, swaggering warriors and vivacious women—many of whom he had only heard stories of—he was awed by what he had accomplished, almost inadvertently. He had wanted to be samraj some day only because his father had expected it of him, and he had understood since the morning of his victory in Magada that the day had come so soon more because of Draupadi than Jarasamda. Thus he had never thought about the meaning of every king in Bharata agreeing to bow at his feet and revere his leadership for as long as he lived.

This fervent bestowing of esteem seemed almost a mistake, much as it moved him now that the kings expressing their respect were here in Indraprastha, speaking to him over a cup of madhu or walking with him through the stables. Didn't they notice he was young and inexperienced? He supposed the older kings were mostly responding to the memory of Pandu and the greatness of the Kurus, and the younger kings were following their elders' lead. Of course certain events could have impressed them as well, especially the defeat of Jarasamda. But in Yudishtira's opinion nothing obvious made him worthy to be the sole embodiment of his nation. Yet that was what he would soon be—the only king in Bharata able and expected to see the quarrelling Arya people as one wholeness.

The irony, to Yudishtira, was that he himself had never felt less whole, for his queen was still "unable to go out", although it was promised she would appear for those rituals requiring her. Nor had Vyasa come as yet. Or Krishna. Not even his father-in-law, King Drupada, would be coming—not with Guru Vaja present. Panchalya would represent Panchala as one kingdom. His uncle, King Drita, claimed illness, although Yudishtira could imagine several more likely reasons. And although his four brothers were back, they seemed almost like strangers, with their adventures to share with each other, to which he could only listen.

Yet if he was upset, he hid it, for he was about to enjoy the honour of becoming samraj and could hardly complain of loneliness or envy. His reactions only caused him to wonder again why he and his fellow human beings were so contrary. The gathering inside the walls had created problems of water and cleanliness that had been simple to solve, thanks to Lettermaker's ingenious system of channels, floodgates, springs and cisterns. But the problems of protocol would not flow away with a tenth of the ease. The housing steward had resigned, dejected and ashamed, because he could not solve a quandary involving a prince from Cedi who had developed a fresh hate for the king of Matsya which had made it impossible for the men or their families, friends or servants to sleep within three streets of each other. Hundreds of persons had had to be rearranged to circumvent the invisible storm.

Where did these winds come from, Yudishtira asked himself again as he made his final preparations for his rajasuya. Why are my people so difficult? Why do their hearts shed rain and their thoughts hurl thunderbolts?

And why do I still love her? And love all these who have gathered inside my walls? For I ache with love for them. I ache with love.

At dawn on the "illustrious and auspicious day" a hundred kings and at least six hundred more warriors all strode out through the gates and down the trampled fields to the banks of the Yamuna, where they bathed and performed their morning rituals in silver river mists. Then they came west a half league, walking in silence to the area laid out by the priests for the morning sacrifice. At the moment when the three fires flared up, the chill valley fog parted to reveal Ushas the Dawn, her skirts flashing as she opened her doors. A good start, many whispered to each other.

They returned to the city in single file, eldest first, and entered the now famous assembly hall of Indraprastha to formally yield their consents to Yudishtira. Standing in silence under the arches, none of them failed to recognise their own magnificence. There had never been a meeting like this in their history. The ancestors were great, but they the living were greater. Their fathers and grandfathers had cleared and fortified a hundred rough-hewn kingdoms. But this generation was bringing those lands to their full glory, even while new princes looked farther east and south to satisfy their Arya urge to conquer. Yes, the assembled warriors were thinking to themselves, we are a people born to rule.

"And it is only through dharma," Yudishtira was telling them in his welcoming speech, "that we were able to conquer a harsh land, and still be at peace with each other. Our warrior ferocity, which defends and expands our nation, is tempered and guided by the priests' wisdom about dharma and nourished by the prosperity of our farmers and herdsmen. Priest and husbandman benefit us as we benefit them and they benefit each other. This harmony, this balance, is a delicate thing. Feuds, floods and famine may come and go, but we keep our balance. How? Because dharma shows us the way to live in peace. I tell you today that what we have conquered is not our lands, but our selves."

Bells rang, flowers were tossed, and feet pounded the floor in agreement at every pause. Whether the listeners grasped the full thought or not, they knew they could be proud that they were presumed to. It *sounded* noble. As Yudishtira went on, some even used the ancient, rougher form of approval: crossing their arms on their chests, slapping their upper forearms, and shouting various descriptions of how they would dismember anyone who disagreed with the speaker.

It pleased this well-muscled crowd to think of themselves as wise and disciplined—as protectors of their raw young land, not just its pillagers. This satisfaction spread to become strong approval of their collective decision to let such an eloquent, handsome, clever young man be their samraj. Enough of old, crafty, bloodthirsty, uneducated plunderers. This Yudishtira was the future of Bharata. Intelligent. The man to whom they had given their precious consent.

Several speakers followed, each outdoing the one before in flowery praises addressed to Yudishtira and his brothers. All their feats were retold, from their appearance with their mother at Hastinapura down to the defeat of Jarasamda, the release of a good many of those present from subservience to that tyrant, and the rapid gathering of the necessary consents by the brothers. The drama of Draupadi's bride's choice was retold at least six times, with the brothers' skill at arms becoming more miraculous with each version. Soon heads were nodding in the hot upper tiers.

But they leaned forward again when it was Suyodhana's turn. Here was the potential for something.

Everyone smiled when they saw Suyodhana hesitate to step on the polished blue tiles—several speakers had done the same, unable to overcome the impression that the floor was really a decorative pond, or at least still slippery from a washing. But it was much more interesting to see Suyodhana looking foolish while his cousin was being praised. Not disappointing them, Suyodhana looked up and glared at the few who risked a tentative laugh.

Rather than addressing Yudishtira, Suyodhana spoke to the assembly: "I am happy to join you in congratulating my cousin on his many successes—this settlement, his new son, the defeat of the ageing Jarasamda, and the consents his *brothers* have obtained for him this last month." Everyone noticed the innuendos, and the omission of the most important cause for laudations, this rajasuya ritual and celebration. It was really quite humorous to most of them that the samraj aspirant was acclaimed by all but his own stubborn clan. The crown prince of the eastern Kurus could hardly bear the king of the western Kurus becoming samraj. So much for dharma. When would the open battle begin?

"It is a pity that Yudishtira's queen is not at his side to enjoy his moment of triumph, since I understand he permits women in his assembly. Yes, we all regret not seeing the seductively beautiful Draupadi at his side. And it is here that I encounter my difficulty with feeling real enthusiasm for his becoming our samraj." The whispering began.

Suyodhana raised his voice. He also looked frequently at the main, north door. "For of course we all know why she isn't here—she is not just his wife, but wife to all five. This is a point of inevitable embarrassment to Yudishtira, and therefore to all of us if he is to be our samraj. I have heard that they have kept her from being a total whore"—Bhima stood but Yudishtira very reluctantly motioned for him not to violate a speaker's rights—"by taking three-month turns with her, but this means Yudishtira has no queen at all for the moment. Of course a king only needs a queen in order to have a son, and that he has by her. Or at least I presume we can narrow the father down to five."

It was Gangeya who finally stopped him—the gathering's eldest being the only one who could properly interrupt a speaker on the assembly floor. "Do you deliver your father's consent to your cousin's sovereignty or not?" the old warrior bellowed.

Addressing the revered Gangeya, Suyodhana could only keep his tone polite. "I am of course honoured when a Kuru becomes samraj, Grandfather Gangeya. *Any* Kuru."

Guru Vaja stood up beside Gangeya. "Then give your consent and those of your allies, which you told Yudishtira you would present to him today."

"I believe the choice of a samraj is up to the warrior-born," Suyodhana said sarcastically.

Vaja was pale with anger. "I am requesting you follow the procedure, Suyodhana—which is my duty as a priest-born and a teacher, regardless of whom the warrior-born have *already* made their samraj." Vaja sat down. The pulsing of the veins in his temples could be seen.

"These are unusual times," Suyodhana continued, as if Vaja and Gangeya had never spoken. "No warrior has ever let four others marry his wife, then tried to become a king, and after that expected to be accepted as samraj."

The whisperings were loud now. "Tried to become a king" —here was the reference to the real dispute. And Suyodhana still watched the main door like a dog waiting for its master.

It was also obvious now that he was stalling for some reason.

"Of course for purposes of inheritance and succession to the Kuru throne, Yudishtira considers my father, his uncle, to be his own father's representative. In fact, nothing more than a substitute for his father. Yet for purposes of receiving guidance and blessings before a marriage, *my uncle, his father, was never consulted.*"

"Give your consent, my *child*," Gangeya said in a quiet, deadly voice that carried well.

Suyodhana's head raised defiantly. "All right, old *Grandfather*. My *father* is honoured to consent to Yudishtira's consecration—since even he must obey you, his *elder*," he said bitterly. "And my allies will also consent. But as for myself, I am no king, so my consent should make no difference. Correct? Correct, Grandfather?"

Lotus crouched before the cave. It was only a league from Indraprastha but as yet no Arya had found it. For if they had, it would have been gone. The white ones always desecrated the Goddess's places. Overturned the sacred stones, cut down the holy trees. They said, "The gods do not live in rocks and caves, but in the sky! Let Agni take your gifts!"

She crept forward into the cool darkness with her offering. The Goddess's gold ornaments glittered in the shadows. "We will see whose gods are stronger," Lotus whispered.

The Merciless Queen of Endings smiled from under her blanket of dying flowers, her shining veil of oils and essences, her crown of fawns' skulls.

"Mistress," the Nishada whispered, "you who give us meat and unburden the Mother Earth of our numerous bodies, destroy my enemy."

Lotus laid flowers before the Destructress. "You who shorten the days and light the killing fires, destroy my enemy."

Now she drew out a gold wax-seal. It was Yudishtira's, given to Lotus the day she had first met him, the day she had helped him, the day he had accepted her, a Dasyu, into his Arya world. Long before he had gone mad with jealousy. She set the small gold cylinder in the statue's outstretched arms, beneath its staring, glass-bead eyes. "Mistress, loan me your sharp teeth and your urge to purify. Mistress, strengthen my will and darken my heart. Darken it as you will darken us all when you close the tired eyes of our Mother at the end of time. And today, destroy my enemy."

The woman drew a coal from a fire box and touched it to the pool of oil at the idol's feet. A flame appeared, austere and steady as the eye of a cobra. She set more flowers around the fire, and arranged honey cakes from the palace around the flowers. Then she backed out, bowed, and ran—afraid of what she had called up in the cave or in herself.

The south gate of the fortress they called "Indra's home" was shining in the sun, open, waiting for her. Soon the Arya men would be leaving the assembly.

In spite of Yudishtira's protests that she take Draupadi's empty seat beside him on the dais, Kunti had chosen a stool far from him, well hidden behind the musicians. It was not who would see her that she feared, but whom she would be forced to see. Still, she could not keep her eyes off the one she dreaded. Which meant watching and listening to Suyodhana too. Until her brother-in-law's eldest son dared to slander Draupadi and she could stand no more. Then she fled to Draupadi's rooms to repeat all she had heard.

Draupadi's response was adamant—her husbands would not allow Suyodhana to say such things. But the usually self-controlled Kunti only pulled the hem of her headcloth across her face to hide her weeping. That was proof enough of her report.

Draupadi paced up and down the room. "I should have gone. I should have. They see us divided and dare too much." She stopped at the window and whispered, "I've stayed behind these walls too long. Now I don't even know—can I go out into that world again?"

Eos ran through the halls, cursing herself that she'd spent so much time on the trivial preparations for this event without thinking through what mattered. She had obtained partial reports of what was happening in the hall, and Suyodhana's bold speech and door watching had to signal a plot—she had witnessed too many court conspiracies.

As she stepped from sun to shadow, a hand caught her shoulder. For a moment Eos could not see the face behind it. Then she pulled back. "Do not touch me."

"Please," Lettermaker whispered. "You must listen to me."

"To have entered these walls, you had to come in disguise or in hiding, which means treachery."

He caught her hand again. "Can't it mean love?"

She closed her eyes, willing away the feelings that came with only his fingers embracing hers. "You have let Sakuni become your friend."

"What makes you say that?" he whispered.

"I have my ways to know what happens in Hastinapura. Don't lie to me, Lettermaker. Spare me that." She drew her hand free. "I must go."

"Wait. Yes, I've been with Sakuni. Enough to know his plans and that no one—no one—is safe here today. There will be a fire."

"When?"

"Very soon."

"We must warn Yudishtira."

"It is too late."

"Too late? Why didn't you come before?"

"As you say, I am not allowed in at the gates. It wasn't easy—"

"Stop your excuses and tell me what's to be done."

"Take me to Draupadi."

"Draupadi?"

"Trust me, Eos."

She glanced towards the hall where Yudishtira sat deep in a crowd of warriors. She, a yavani, would not even be able to get a message to him. She took Lettermaker to Draupadi's room.

The three stared at each other, while Kunti sat in a corner, motionless. Finally Lettermaker broke the silence. "Events will not go as your husbands have planned, Draupadi. Therefore I wish you to consider something."

"What?" Eos asked for her.

"Allow me to speak it. But I request that neither of you respond now. I will speak and leave, so that you may consider carefully my proposal."

"Of what?" Eos repeated coldly.

"I want to take you both away from here. Today. We'll find Draupadi's home. Then perhaps go west."

Eos closed her eyes just a moment. When she had recovered her full resolve, she said. "Get out of here."

He ignored her, as she realised now that he would. He had come for Draupadi. "Queen, I beg you to think—"

"Get out! The tunnels—you told Sakuni, didn't you? Now you distract us to give him more time."

"I came to save you. I'm the only one who can. Eos, the tunnels were irrelevant. Yudishtira let his enemies in by having this foolish rajasuya."

"*You* are the enemy. Get out of here."

"Look." It was Kunti. She stood at the window, drawn there to look for the cause of a curious darkening of the noon sky.

"The villages!" Draupadi shouted.

Three were in flames, three more flew banners of smoke from their thatched roofs. Nishada were running from the city and from village to village. Livestock circled their pens wildly, their sounds of distress rising above the shouts from the watches on the city walls. Here and there in the smoke the women at the window saw dark forms.

"Rakshasa," Draupadi whispered.

"Rakshasa," Eos echoed. "But hardly demons from another world. Not when they choose to attack Yudishtira today of all days. I say they are being directed from the heart of this rotten world right here."

They looked back into the room. Lettermaker was gone.

45

May thy unbroken weapon, Indra, proceed against our foes
like the banner of the shining dawn. Like a stone cast down
from Heaven, pierce those whose friendship is deceitful
with thy consuming, loud-sounding weapon.

Rig Veda

The guards on the palace walls were shouting something.
Yudishtira, leading the procession along the colonnade from
the assembly hall to the noon Feast of Consent, was aware
that he stopped a thousand men in order to listen.

The call came again: "The villages are on fire! Rakshasa!"

Arjuna and Bhima, on Yudishtira's left and right, ran to
confirm the report, and shouted its truth.

Her villages! Willing aside his horror, Yudishtira turned
to address Bharata's finest warriors: "Attacking today, these
rakshasa challenge us all. Shall we eradicate this scourge?"

Their answers were war shouts, and orders for weapons,
shields and chariots that were answered eagerly by servants
watching the procession from the garden. Yudishtira broke
into a run towards the stables. His young Nishada shield carriers
jogged beside him, presenting his leather body protectors,
helmet and wrist guards. He girded himself as he ran.

One image would not leave him—a green-tipped poisoned
arrow. Arya burned Dasyu forests without feeling partly because
of the Arya terror of the writhing death brought by these
short-flying arrows. To be slain thus, without the opportunity
to fight on until blood was gone, was to be consigned to Hell.

Yudishtira knew that if he warned these men behind him, he would lose them.

But if I fail to warn them, he thought, I lose Dharma's protection.

"Sahadeva," he shouted, knowing his brothers would be beside him now. "Have the north street cleared and archers ready to cover the gate when it's opened. As chariots leave the yard, have a trustworthy man instruct each driver to stay half an arrow's flight from all rakshasa. Say exactly that.

"Panchalya. Stay inside the walls and see to our plans. You understand me.

"Arjuna? Our defences. Keep the Maruts inside with you."

Arjuna seized his arm. "Not this time. Let me go out!"

"You returned only yesterday, Arjuna. This may be merely a distraction. You understand me well." Yudishtira ran on without meeting his eyes. "Bhima, you'll drive on my left. Nakula, my right."

They pounded into the stableyard. "Yama protect us! First, little horseman, straighten this out!"

Confusion bordered on riot as hundreds of servants fought each other to be the first to get horses to chariots, weapons in weapon stands and masters in good positions near the gate.

Nakula dived into the mob. "Make way. My brothers' chariots first. Then take places by rivers. The kings west of the Yamuna, then Ganges, Gomati, Sarayu, Sadanira and Gandaki. Then other warriors, same order. Everyone, help the kings leave first, then the rest."

"Our shy brother," Bhima said, jumping into his chariot, which had been freed to move thanks to Nakula's orders. Bhima would lead out of the stables, since he would drive on Yudishtira's left once they were entering battle.

Suddenly Arjuna and the Nishada carpenter Badger appeared. "The Nishada want to go out to protect their villages," Arjuna yelled above the uproar. While their people and most of their weapons were outside the walls, the celebration and rituals had kept the Nishada men inside, to serve as guards, runners, cook and all the rest.

"Send out Nishada when we've so many Arya chariots?" Yudishtira shouted back. The Nishada men were now adept bowmen. Still, all the reasons not to allow it raced through Yudishtira's mind: Lives wasted trying to put out hopeless fires; Arjuna having no large, secure force inside the city; the Arya confusing them with rakshasa; and the Nishada women and children being safe anyway, thanks to the tunnels.

Clearly angry, Arjuna had shrugged and run off. Badger still stood motionless before his king, the confusion moving around them like water around two rocks.

"All right, Badger, arm your men. But stay inside. Protect the gates. Whatever can be done outside will be best done from chariots."

Sensible as it was, Yudishtira hated asking the Nishada men not to fight for their women and children. Not waiting to see how the order was taken, he leaped into his chariot.

The Marut Vimada stood in the driver's place. "Do you mind sharing another adventure with me, King?"

"Mind? I am honoured." Even delighted, Yudishtira thought, as they paused to take on extra quivers.

Except it's her villages we must defend.

He imagined her high up at her window above the north entrance to the inner palace. Unlike his fight with Jarasamda, this one she would be watching.

To the boy holding the horses he shouted, "Fox, take a message to the Queen. Tell her I will try to save the villages. Or die."

Try or die? An idiot's message. But Fox was gone and Vimada couldn't hold the four excited bays any longer. They thundered out of the yard, racing to catch up with Bhima's team.

Along the street leading to the north gate, crowds were shouting encouragement. Behind them Yudishtira could see lines passing water buckets to wet the roofs. Clever Panchalya —only last month he had distributed twenty movable sheds to hold fifty wooden buckets each, and trained water captains to form these lines. Although privately Yudishtira had feared the effect would be like spitting on a bonfire. To burn dwelling places! Only demons did it.

Like heroes, Bhima's horses were charging the huge fortified gates. As they'd practised, the gatemen swung them open only at the last minute. Nishada bowmen on foot rushed out on

Bhima's right to protect the open gate as he swung left to make room for Yudishtira. But suddenly Bhima's chariot careered right again. A horse was down, a single arrow in its neck.

"Poison," Bhima shouted. "By Yama, right at the gate."

Vimada reined in the bays, also shouting the command to stop. Behind them drivers were cursing and horses neighing in fear of collisions.

Nirriti take them! Yudishtira glanced down. Still in their racks—the horse shields Lettermaker had had made for him. Too much weight, Yudishtira remembered saying, but the Phoenician had insisted. And his reward had been exile.

Yudishtira grabbed the shields and sprang down. Vimada followed, more familiar with and always more approving of the shields than he had been. Three Nishada bowmen rushed to their assistance.

Yudishtira glanced around as he steadied the two mares on his side. Several Marut warriors from the walls were helping Bhima and his driver to free the three live horses from the dead one. A half circle of Nishada bowmen protected these two chariots outside the gate as well as the ten or more stopped just within. The bowmen wore leather protectors and knew the far-flying Arya arrows they used would drive the rakshasa back. Still, the Nishadas' stand took courage.

"We'll clear the way out," Yudishtira shouted to those crowded at the gate.

"Have you more shields for horses?" a king called back.

Yudishtira didn't answer. He had heard all that the question meant; he would not beg for their help.

Towards the river swirling black smoke was covering the sky.

He would kill every one of the inhuman beasts who had torched those villages! Alone, if necessary.

"Hurry, Vimada. Shields on just two. We'll unharness the other two."

"Four, King, for speed."

"I yield to your wisdom."

"Almost done, Yudishtira."

At the gate many were turning back. If only there were more horse shields.

Yudishtira turned again to face the burning villages. Attack
and punish the arsonists? Or defend and save lives? With so
few willing to come out, any punishing would probably cost
the punishers' lives. "Bhima," he shouted. "Try to defend the
walls. Don't come out farther."

His great red-maned head towering over his team of blacks,
Bhima only nodded as he worked at the reharnessing.

Finally Yudishtira's bays were ready, their shields in place.
Shouted into a gallop, they tore around the far end of the
protecting circle of bowmen. Suddenly Yudishtira and Vimada
were alone on the plain—one chariot pursuing a horde of
black shadows.

Gangeya's and Vaja's chariots had just rumbled out of the
stable courtyard, claiming precedence as regent to Pandu and
teacher to Pandu's sons. They were followed by Radheya. After
heated whisperings with Suyodhana, the King of Anga had
insisted on a position ahead of the others waiting to leave,
claiming the "right of amarsha"—the fury that disallowed all
other considerations. Many heads turned when he shouted,
"Every rakshasa I destroy will be killed in the name of my ally,
friend and benefactor, Crown Prince Suyodhana."

Most of the kings and warriors were still preparing to leave
when Baron Sakuni stepped up on the rim of the central
fountain to address them. "There's word the palace is on fire.
Some should look to the safety of wives and dependants."

The news brought panic. Arya had always built from wood;
no one broke the prohibition against burning habitations.

Now Suyodhana joined Sakuni up on the fountain wall.
"I've heard these 'rakshasa' are nothing but rebel Dasyu. And
Yudishtira himself has been arming these Nishada! Has he not
created his own troubles?"

"Poison arrows outside the gates!" a battle runner shouted,
bursting into the yard. "Shield yourselves! Protect your horses!"

"How do we protect horses?" someone yelled. "Why didn't
Yudishtira warn us? We can't lose war horses to poison arrows!"

"This is not a dharmic battle. It's a trap."

"If it burns, this where we stand is a bigger trap," another
called.

Sakuni used the moment of chaos to verify the rumour that all the villages were burning. It angered him that his plan had been marred, but the important thing now was to begin a rush for safety. "We must leave," he shouted, "and regather at Hastinapura to discuss who shall be our samraj."

"Nonsense!" Sahadeva ran in among them and leaped up on the fountain rim, shouldering Sakuni aside. "'Discuss who shall be our samraj'? What are you saying, Sakuni? Is this dharma? Your brother-in-law's nephews have just driven out of the gate into a battle."

Sakuni started. This failure of the rakshasa to follow his orders was more critical.

Sahadeva continued to shout: "Listen, all of you—if your chariots stay a half-arrow's flight from the enemy, you can advance and defeat these rakshasa for ever."

"Sahadeva," Sakuni pleaded in his most reasonable tone, "first let us take the women and servants to your *tunnels*, so we can be sure they escape before your fortress burns."

Sahadeva hid his shock as best he could. "It will not burn. We have—"

"It's wood. Wood burns," Sakuni retorted loudly.

"We *have* a way to put out fires. Not a spark will touch the walls if these brave Arya drive out to defend their families."

"Why not first see those families safe in your tunnels?" Sakuni yelled. "Or do you refuse to reveal to these men the secret escape routes you have planned for your own women and children?"

"If they wish to run away, they can use the gate," Sahadeva retorted. "And our bowmen will cover their *retreat*." The son of Pandu stepped down. "Or come to the armoury for arrows and fight like heroes."

"To the gates then," a king shouted as soon as Sahadeva had gone. "Tunnels won't let our horses out."

Others argued for standing by Yudishtira, who had freed many of them from the caves of Girivraja. But for most their fear for their families and of fire was too great.

Taking advantage of their wavering, Suyodhana began shouting about Yudishtira's "treacheries". He was hardly heard over the first frantic orders to servants to assemble dependants.

"Be still and maintain your dignity," Sakuni hissed at Suyodhana. "Their opinions don't matter. No one will escape by the tunnels, very few by the gates. You can convince those remnants later. Shortly, Suyodhana, I will give the order to burn this place you loathe."

"*Burn* it?"

"As soon as Yudishtira returns. The fool escaped us. But no one else will. The stupid animals did just what I feared—couldn't stop with just one village set to the torch, and so they left the gate under-guarded at the start, when it mattered most."

"What are you talking about, Uncle? Surely you do not intend to keep the warriors inside and burn the city? Do you mean for all Bharata's warriors to die here?"

"Not yourself. Or me."

"But these are kings and princes!"

"Obstacles!"

"They'll go to Hell if they die without weapons in their hands when they could have—"

"Stop your mouth and listen to me. You must immediately put on the red cloak I gave you and go out through the tunnel that runs east from the smaller pantry at the rear of the celebration hall. Say 'soma' to those guarding the exit, then—"

"If I don't?"

"You will be killed, as will anyone you take with you."

"This stinks of cowardice and I'll have none of it. I'll lead Bharata's heroes out of the gates."

"Bharata's bull-brained fools," Sakuni said to the broad back which Suyodhana turned to him. "Suyodhana, do as I say. Suyodhana!"

When she heard that the city was in danger as well as the villages, Draupadi's first thought was of Prahara. But Eos insisted that there was a plot behind the torched villages, and a queen wandering the palace with a crown prince in her arms would be too easy a prize. Eos helped Kunti to disguise herself and sent her with servants to Prahara. Then Eos herself went to prepare for the burned and wounded who might make it in through the tunnels, instructing Draupadi to stay hidden as long as she safely could—not referring directly to the threat of fire.

Draupadi went back to the windows to stare at the burning villages and at her people running for the hidden tunnel mouths. And being slaughtered there at the entrances. It had been a worthless, deadly plan. She knew now she should have forbidden it. Every Nishada woman and child should have at least been inside these walls on this day—not these guests, but her own people.

"Queen?"

She turned from the window. The Nishada stable boy Fruit Fox had not left after bringing Yudishtira's message, but was backed up against the door, trying to hide his trembling.

"Your King Yudishtira is fortunate," she said to him. "At least he will die fighting from a chariot, not burning in his room."

Always her devouring anger. And why had she said such a thing to a child?

"Come here, Fox. The king will not die."

"I know, Queen Draupadi." The boy came and sat beside her on the window seat. "He will save us all. Indra will help him."

"Indra? Is he a Nishada god now?"

"Indra is the god of rain and thunder. The rain falls on everyone the same. The king says so."

"And Indra brings arrows, which fall on all our enemies the same," she said. "Do you know which villages are burning? I cannot see any more."

"Some say all of them, Queen Draupadi."

"Look and tell me. I can't."

"I see the king's chariot. The painted ones are following it!"

"Enough news of that. The villages."

"I can't see past the smoke of Sukshetra, Queen."

"I know. Sukshetra is burning," she said softly.

"The one you call the prettiest. You make the others jealous, you know."

"I should be more careful," she whispered, brushing away tears.

She set him on his feet and stood up. "We can not merely sit here. We must do something."

"Yes you must." Lettermaker stood in the open door.

"You enter without my permission." She tried to sound like a queen in command of her world.

He answered gently, like an old friend. "Soon there will be no room in which to enter, Draupadi."

"Address me as Queen."

"Queen, Bharata's 'brave warriors' are refusing to risk defending Indraprastha. It will soon be in flames."

"No warrior-born would dishonour himself this way!" But she had already guessed otherwise, having seen only three more chariots leave the city after Bhima's and Yudishtira's.

"They plan to abandon Yudishtira and select a new samraj at Hastinapura," Lettermaker said. "That is the truth."

"Arya are cowards," Fruit Fox said, his own shoulders squared like a hero's. "Most of them, anyway."

"The ones who are not cowards are doomed," Lettermaker said. "Go and see what you can do to help them, boy."

Fox ran out.

"Shake yourself free of this, Draupadi," Lettermaker said softly. "Come with me."

"With you? *You* caused this!"

"You know that isn't true. But unlike your husbands, I have been where I could learn the truth about your situation. I truly regret I did not realise it before, but encouraged this disaster, for Yudishtira has never stood a chance. Suyodhana has all the allies. All the power. Your husbands can stay here and defend their city if they insist, and you know they will. But why you? I promise you, everyone who remains within these walls will burn. If you leave, it will only be as someone's booty. Listen to me: *I alone can save you.* You don't belong here, Draupadi. Your future is as empty as your past. Your life in Bharata has been a dream. Wake up!"

Draupadi stared at him, then turned back to watch the black smoke eating the square of blue sky she could see from her window.

·

Arjuna rushed into the stable courtyard. "Nakula, bring me a chariot. I'm going out there."

"He told you to stay inside."

"He needs me and I'm going out."

"He would send for you if he wanted you."

"Bring me a chariot!"

"Arjuna, you must ask someone else to do that."

"Curse you." Arjuna rushed across the yard towards a stable boy leading horses.

Nakula called after him: "Does it really matter if Indraprastha stands or falls if the souls of its rulers are destroyed?"

Arjuna stopped.

"Arjuna, it was not your blind uncle Drita who commanded you to stay inside. It was Yudishtira."

Arjuna whirled around. "He wants to do everything *himself*!"

"Then he needs to. And we need to obey him."

"Indra take you." Arjuna closed his eyes. "Curse it!" But when he opened them again, he spoke with control. "Forgive me, Nakula. Have you sent Panchalya all the quivers from the chariots? He needs every weapon up on the walls."

46

To some death comes as Yama
the First to Die, the Fetcher,
the King of the Ancestors.
To others Nirriti comes,
as Misery, Nightmare, Decay.
Or Mrityu enters, as the End.

anonymous

Yudishtira had gone back to the gate to pick up four of the
best Nishada bowmen. They were crowded in with him, each
facing a direction and covering the chariot's progress with a
steady stream of arrows as Vimada drove Yudishtira on a hunt
for demons among the burning fragments of the kingdom of
Indraprastha.

The last village had burst into flames a short time ago,
in spite of all the efforts of Bhima, Gangeya and Guru
Vaja—and the efforts of none of his allies, none of Bharata's
kings.

No, Yudishtira remembered—Radheya was out there somewhere too. But there was no way to know whether the king of
Anga was fighting the rakshasa or helping them to defeat
Indraprastha, and no one to send to find out. Bhima had just
been forced to withdraw after losing a wheel, breaking both
his bows and receiving several wounds, apparently unpoisoned.
Gangeya and Guru Vaja were at some distance, fighting
bravely, but as much to save their lives and unshielded horses
as to defeat rakshasa.

So her villages are gone, he thought numbly. His body still
did its rapid work—shooting, spearing, commanding, scanning

the plain. But inside there was a stillness like death. Draupadi.

As if to haunt him, her villagers' bodies were everywhere—mutilated, their hearts cut open, their blood drunk and smeared in the dirt. It was difficult to look. But it was necessary—rakshasa hid among them, feigning death in order to spring up and shoot poison.

It was even more difficult for Vimada to avoid running over these forsaken bodies. Vimada cursed and cried over them, both at once. Yudishtira could only hope they were, after all, completely without life.

"Better they die anyway," he whispered, "than live with the memory of what they've seen done today. Indra, where is the arrow for me?"

No, he commanded himself. Control the mind. Because they do not—they are crazed and therefore a controlled mind can punish them. Chase one down alive—that is the goal. Identify their leader and make him suffer for this.

Now Yudishtira found himself having to fight spontaneous images of coldly torturing this demon of demons.

But I am gaining skill at hunting demon men, he thought bitterly. They hide, and I flush them like mice under a plough.

He took up a lance and aimed it at a fleeing figure which Vimada was unable to turn the team in time to follow. The lance dropped the rakshasa. He was still screaming when Yudishtira took up another spear, but the distance was now too great to finish him.

Yudishtira shouted the right-spin command and the horses swerved into the path of a painted body just as it was breaking from cover. The eldest Pandu's spear severed his leg.

This time Yudishtira jumped down, an arrow nocked and aimed at his captive's heart, an eye on the knife the demon held between them with a trembling hand.

"Drop it or you die," Yudishtira said in Nishada, although he still could not believe that the rakshasas could be even a distant Dasyu tribe.

The knife thrust upwards. Yudishtira loosed the arrow at the arm. It creased the elbow, showering blood into the ground. Yudishtira groaned from the intimacy of the suffering he had caused. He doubted he could bear this day any longer.

Yet the painted face above the arm showed almost no expression.

Drugged, Yudishtira realised. The only explanation. I would gladly sip the same oblivion.

"Who leads you?" He repeated.

Hate-filled silence.

"Answer or die."

"Die!" The uninjured hand shot from under the painted body. Only the Great Leap Aside saved Yudishtira. But the rakshasa's face was all but gone. There was only a head, gushing with blood from the arrow. Behind Yudishtira one of his horses lay dead from the poison dart meant for himself. It had entered one of the unshielded hocks. The other bays were too exhausted even to shy.

Yudishtira helped Vimada to unharness the horse. "Find me another rakshasa," was all he said to the Marut. His mind was stunned. The final word of that one—"Die!"—had been spoken in Yamuna Nishada.

Vimada begged him to go back to the city to tend his wounds. "They may be poisoned."

"I'm still alive, so they aren't."

"But the loss of blood! Let me drive Arjuna out in your place."

"Vimada, you are wounded too. Let me take you back and get another driver."

"Never."

"Then say no more to me about it."

They drove on with only three horses now. Outside the next ruined village they came upon a rakshasa hiding between the furrows of a field. He bolted. A lance dropped him. But this one also had to be killed.

The third they captured, however, was different—neither near death nor demented by the drug.

"*Who leads you?*" Yudishtira demanded in Nishada, a knife on the painted throat. The smell from him was as ugly as the black and white patterns on his body. Blood was caked under the long nails. Fresh blood was around his lips. Yet Yudishtira sensed some bizarre integrity under it all. He was near his goal. If this one did not die first, for Yudishtira's spear was in his stomach.

"Who leads you!" Yudishtira pressed the tip of his knife into the dark neck.

"One of your *own*." Beneath the illusions of the painted mask, Yudishtira saw hate, satisfaction and an enormous effort to hide great pain. And he spoke Nishada exactly as Yudishtira had learned it.

"An Arya?" Yudishtira could not believe it. "Sakuni? Is that the name?"

"I betray no one."

Yudishtira stared at his spear protruding from the man's belly. A jerk of the shaft was the way to get the answer.

I will not stoop to demon ways, he swore. Lord Dharma, protect your son from sin.

"You will betray 'no one'?" Yudishtira bent over him. "But you have betrayed your own people today. Those are Nishada women and children. Dead. All around us. In a moment you will pass to the other world. I would not want what waits you there."

Yudishtira saw that his guess was right—the man had the intelligence to look beyond this world. "I will make a sacrifice to Yama in your name if you help me to stop this slaughter. Tell me who leads you."

The prisoner still did not answer.

"The gates of Hell swing open for you."

"The Dark One," the rakshasa whispered.

"Who leads you!"

"The one you call Dark. The Krishna."

"Krishna? Krishna Vasudeva of the Vrishni?"

"Vrishni, yes."

"You lie. Who told you to say this?"

The man's eyes flared with some recognition. He tried to sit up. "So kill me like the liar and murderer you are, Yudishtira son of Pandu."

Yudishtira recoiled. And if he knows me by name, he could know others of us, Yudishtira thought.

Krishna!

Yudishtira took his knife away from the man's neck—it seemed depraved to threaten a dying man with death. And depravity seemed the true enemy now.

Krishna? The accusation was absurd.

The demon's eyes in their painted circles bulged. The whole body shook with the death rattle.

Krishna. Where was he? And why had he acted so strangely during his two visits? Why had he left so suddenly after bringing Subhadra?

Yudishtira moved to sheath his knife.

Then the Leap, the exchange of hissing blades.

But it was an arrow that killed the Nishada demon— Yudishtira's own knife had only struck the rakshasa's shoulder. The Nishada's knife still hummed with his life where it had penetrated the earth at Yudishtira's feet.

Yet even now, Krishna was all he could think of.

A roughly made chariot rattled up, pulled by two energetic, dun-coloured mules. King Does-Nothing-Yet-Gets-All stood beside a dishevelled Dasyu imitation of an Arya chariot driver. The king's bow was already nocked with another arrow.

"That was Eagle you and I have killed," Does-Nothing said.

"You make it sound like something more than the slaughter of a raving beast."

"It was."

"Anyway, you and I did not kill him." Yudishtira saluted his rescuer. "It was you only. You saved my life."

"I shot the arrow," the chief said. "I leave the greater burden —of the cause of his death—upon the king of the Arya."

"Who leads these rebels?" Yudishtira braced himself for the answer.

"What does it matter? An Arya—that much I have learned today. He has made them stupid with your 'soma', taught them to perform human sacrifices to your gods, and worse. If I were a lying Arya, I could break my oath of alliance with you sons of Pandu. But being Nishada, I am here to fight for you."

"I thank you. Does-Nothing, this man said Krishna of the Vrishnis leads them."

"This Krishna I do not know. There are already too many Arya to remember."

Yudishtira remounted his chariot. King Does-Nothing signalled for his own to move on, then halted again. "Now that you have learned who leads them," Does-Nothing called with disgust in his voice, "perhaps you would be willing to help me kill them, 'Ally'. My men are trying to save your people—Nishada, Arya or whatever. But many of the women and children gather at certain places where the rakshasa wait to kill them. This I don't understand. Look over there!"

Yudishtira didn't need to. The tunnel entrances. The rakshasa knew about them, then.

Krishna.

Yudishtira stood wordless beside Vimada. Lacking other orders, the Marut directed the chariot to follow King Does-Nothing's. Ahead of them the king was already engaged in the first real battle they had seen. It was around the southeast granary, the once-secret entrance to a tunnel. Rakshasa were shooting from behind mounds of Nishada bodies. Nishada who had trusted my orders, Yudishtira thought.

He began shooting furiously into the black swarm, but from well beyond the range of their pestilent arrows.

Does-Nothing, however, had been more careless. One of his dun mules was down and dying and his driver was crouching, trying to reach forward and unharness the beast. The Nishada king, however, was upright and shooting.

But he was outnumbered. First the driver was hit, then the second mule.

"Drive alongside," Yudishtira ordered. "Take cover, bowmen."

Vimada did not hesitate—the bays rushed up and Yudishtira seized Does-Nothing by his leather tunic and pulled him part way out of his rickety chariot. The Nishada king managed the rest, scrambling over the railing. In Yudishtira's ear he said, "In the future I shall remember not to insult the only other warrior fighting with me."

"No matter. You Nishada are new at this madness."

Vimada had returned them out of range. Their bowmen in the chariot were raining arrows on the rakshasa around the granary. Now the king's Nishada warriors were rushing in also, to avenge their leader's losses.

Yudishtira was turning to find a bow for Does-Nothing when the man groaned. Yudishtira looked anxiously for an arrow wound but the pain was of another sort: the man who had been leading the king's advancing warriors was sinking to his knees, then crumbling to earth, a battle axe in his back.

Yudishtira looked behind the row of advancing Nishada. Gangeya was giving a victory shout. From a more distant chariot, Guru Vaja was diligently spearing others of Does-Nothing's men, having obviously discovered that their arrows lacked poison.

"You Arya can't tell one Nishada from another," the Nishada king said with bitter disgust. Vimada turned the chariot to intercept Gangeya and Vaja.

Beside Yudishtira, Does-Nothing suddenly jerked and stiffened. Yudishtira and the Nishada both stared at the arrow in the latter's side. Livid green dotted his skin around the wound.

As if the discovery was his real undoing, Does-Nothing slumped against Vimada, his dark hands still trying to put an arrow to his bow.

Yudishtira eased the king to the floor and knelt beside him. "You saved my life and tried to save my people," Yudishtira whispered. "We will meet again where the heroes dwell as immortals."

"You also saved my life. And now, you try to save my people." The king's eyes were closing. "Take them in. Tell them they too go to this place where these immortal heroes dwell."

"They will go in glory."

The man shuddered and died. Yudishtira stood and signalled the Nishada messenger still faithfully trying to keep near his king's position. Yudishtira and Vimada passed down the body and left them on the battlefield, one dead and one living.

Yudishtira fought the feeling of hopeless loss. Krishna. The villages. The deaths at the tunnel mouths. The needless killing of brave men by Vaja and Gangeya. And now this good king, sacrificed trying to save his Arya enemies.

Vimada's efforts to intercept the two Kuru champions turned out to be needless. Both had turned back towards Indraprastha, having sustained too much damage in their last advance. "Come in, Yudishtira," Gangeya shouted. "Perhaps at least the fortress can be saved."

Yudishtira did not follow, but neither did he provide Vimada with other orders. The Marut stood silent beside him. The horses' flanks heaved, but their ears were still turned back in readiness for the next command.

"Standing still is dangerous," Vimada whispered.

"Then we'll try a little longer," Yudishtira said wearily. "Drive to the walls."

Vimada coaxed the three bays into a trot.

Time passed but Yudishtira knew only shouting, the hunting of dark figures, the directing of the chariot around bodies, the flames and the smoke. Two of his bowmen were killed in quick succession. Their bodies were left lying on the floor of the chariot because Yudishtira could not bear to put them out. The two remaining Nishada bowmen were now protecting the rear and sides of the chariot while Yudishtira shot from the front. Both Vimada and Yudishtira bled from many cuts and wounds, none apparently poisoned.

Somehow they were found by a trembling messenger, trotting on foot through the smoke. "Krishna Vasudeva says: 'Abandon Indraprastha. The rakshasa intend to burn it. Rescue all who matter to you, the most important first.'"

Yudishtira felt an urge to shoot the brave messenger. Yet his heart cried out: Obey! Go back for Draupadi and Prahara. Run away with them, far from all this.

But she had four other husbands to rescue her, if the message was not treachery anyway. He remembered the prophecy: "She will lead the warriors to their doom." If she had appeared before the kings with him, would it have averted this?

No. I summoned my own doom with my arrogance. With a hundred selfish choices made in dharma's name, a thousand subtle evasions of the truth.

He would not even allow himself to look back at his beautiful Indraprastha and the window from which she must be watching. He ordered Vimada to drive the circuit around the walls again, in a futile effort to stop the rakshasa who would sneak close enough to shoot the first flaming arrow. But he knew he gave the order only to move closer to her. To save her if he could. For himself. Not to save his brothers, his mother, his people. Only to save her, and save her only for himself.

On the south side he came upon Radheya. The Anga king's horses were dead, his chariot overturned, his driver nowhere in sight, and he was surrounded by rakshasa. Those who were able fled when Yudishtira's chariot approached.

"Have you spare arrows?" Radheya called formally. "If you have, the south wall of your palace will be safe as long as I have breath."

"My quivers are nearly empty. Go back in, King Radheya."

"Warriors do not retreat while enemies threaten the unprotected."

"Nor do they allow themselves to die without an arrow in their bow. I thank you for your efforts. Go in."

"After you, King Yudishtira."

Yudishtira drove closer. "As commander on this field, I order you in when these arrows are gone." He signalled Vimada to toss Radheya one of their remaining quivers, then had the Marut drive off.

But Yudishtira made Vimada stop again. Pandu's eldest son turned around. "You are a valiant warrior, King Radheya."

On their next circuit the king of Anga was fighting his way back to the south gate.

It was almost dark when Panchalya galloped up on a black, half-broken stallion. At Yudishtira's orders, Vimada was driving the chariot up and down before a burning calving shed not far from the palace walls, futilely searching for those who had set it on fire.

"Vaja betrayed us," Panchalya shouted as his horse reared and plunged in the heat. "They have found the tunnels."

"It was *not* Vaja," Yudishtira called above the roar of the burning barn. The pitiful bawling of the cows tormented him, but he concentrated on his answer to his brother-in-law. "Vaja fought out here with me today. He can not be the traitor. Panchalya, does Indraprastha burn yet?"

Again the black horse tried to throw his rider. "Your brothers do all they can to control the panic," Panchalya shouted. "And Indraprastha will not burn as long as I am alive. I tell you, I revealed its secrets to Vaja—I will save it."

Vimada whispered, "Finish this talking, King. We are the only prey left and a still target is an easy mark."

The black horse danced backwards, Vimada edged the chariot forward. If Panchalya was right about Vaja—Yudishtira felt a sudden strange despair. Reveal no more treachery, Brahma. Please, no more.

"Panchalya, there was a message to abandon Indraprastha. Pay it no heed. None at all. It came from the real traitor. Gather all dependants at the gates. Do not leave until it seems hopeless."

"Yes, Yudishtira!"

"And do not blame our teacher for this!" But Panchalya was gone, carried towards the gates by his own black demon.

The sudden appearance of one of those he loved, and his sudden departure again, made the fear of losing them all too real. Yudishtira saw finally that their end had come.

But his mind, trained for war, refused to give in. Better to die while swiftly nocking an arrow than standing rigid with grief.

Of the eighty quivers they had brought out with them, there was only one left. He would use it well. But alone, if he could find a way to force his bowmen and the Marut to go in.

"Vimada, drive near the gate. I wish to protect some loyal companions."

Then, at the moment Vimada moved to obey him, an arrow pierced the Marut's throat.

Not now! Yudishtira caught him as he fell. Another arrow struck the railing beside Yudishtira's hand. He lowered Vimada and took up the reins. "See to him!" he shouted to one of the remaining two bowmen. "Both of you, get down."

"He is dead." The words rose from the floor of the chariot like grey doves.

By voice Yudishtira drove the stumbling horses hard after those who had shot the arrows. He screamed the commands for speed. Instead, one mare fell.

The chariot ran up on the team. As trained, the other two turned to protect the one down. Blood ran from the mare's nostrils. The two Nishada looked up at Yudishtira, finally frightened. He himself was shaking uncontrollably.

"I would take you back to the gate, but I'm not sure we would make it." Control, he commanded himself. Make the mind control the heart. "I would rather we died advancing than retreating. Have I your permission?"

They nodded, their eyes wide.

"Only one of you stand at a time," he said. He handed the reins to the one who rose. In a voice he did not recognise he said with perfect calm, "You see? Our third horse is back on her feet. She only stumbled. You will drive now. Go slowly, though. We must show the mares some mercy—they have been brave. And I will kill our enemy, showing no mercy at all."

Through the long afternoon Draupadi had kept her watch at the window. For a time there were four chariots, but by twilight only his. The worst times were when he was out of sight in smoke or behind Indraprastha. But then he would appear as if from a cloud, like Indra. Vimada would be leaning out over the horses, the Nishada bowmen firing arrows, and Yudishtira wielding every weapon he possessed, his wrath as visible as his shields. They would chase a dark figure or hurtle in among some fight, and for a moment their vigour would give her hope, until her eyes went back to the villages and tunnel entrances, where the rakshasa still did their destroying. When the demons were through there, she knew they would come for him. And then for the city.

She had meant to go down to the gates by now. The serving women had begged her to. Kunti was there, in the armoury with Prahara. But all Bharata's warriors and their families were huddled at the gates also—she would not join cowards.

Although the kings had refused to go out to help Yudishtira, they had tried several times to break out to save themselves. Each time the rakshasa had appeared outside the gates, the Arya women and children had screamed and their men had driven the chariots back. "Not until we must, not until there's fire," she'd heard the women shouting at their husbands. Cowards.

But *she* had Lettermaker's box to leave in. It stood outside her door. He had come back twice; both times she had refused to speak to him. Through the door, however, she had heard enough. "And if you will come," he had said the last time, "so will Eos."

540

Draupadi doubted that, but not the rest. It appeared that Lettermaker had purchased her life with his knowledge of the tunnels. But why? Vague answers came to her, each depending on how thoroughly Lettermaker had succumbed to Sakuni. Which she herself had almost done once.

And what did it matter? All that mattered was that one way she lived—and might avenge this day. The other way she died.

But now that it was twilight, her time to decide was running out. What was happening to Arjuna? Panchalya? Bhima and the twins? She thought of Vyasa's first instructions to her: "Teach them." And of the sounds a burning city would make. She imagined Arjuna's laughter. And the pounding of rakshasa at her door. Then her mind would fill again with Lettermaker's offer: "I can get you away." Over and over she heard that.

But most of all she saw Yudishtira's face. Above or beneath her own in the night, floating in moonlight or lamp light, whispering, sighing. Or she would relive memories of him trusting her with his secrets; listening to her opinions, then favouring them over his own; echoing her voice in disputes. Saving her life. Holding her at Prahara's birth. And, finally, driving into their city with Jarasamda's banner on his chariot. The banner he had sent up to her, that now hung at her window.

Yet Yudishtira was doomed. As was the serene world they had made together behind these walls.

Her life seemed so short to her now. A few years of memories. Of the few men she had known, she had respected only Vyasa and Yudishtira. And they had believed she was someone superior. Not merely beautiful, but essential in some important future. Something inside her had been on the verge of showing itself. Now it would die.

There was a tap at her door. Not leaving the window, she turned towards it.

It came again. She shuddered and hid her face.

It came again.

"I have seen the box," she cried out. "I must have more time!"

The tap insisted. Others could come besides Lettermaker. The inexperienced young guards had fled, promising her they would be watching the stairs, but from the safer ground floor. She walked slowly through the gloom towards the tapping. Her hand shook as she withdrew the bolt on the door.

It was Vyasa.

She fell at his feet. "Sage, dearest Sage." She could say no more, but clung to his ankles and kissed the hem of his robe.

"Dear Draupadi, let me come in."

She half rose as he rebolted the door. "Dearest teacher, you should not have come for me. We're going to die. Yudishtira may already be dead. The villages—This waiting! Letter-maker—"

"Has made his offer." Vyasa's voice was utterly unperturbed. He pulled her to her feet. "His box for you does look as if it will survive a long trip. Although one probably sees very little in such a conveyance."

His gentle teasing helped her to recover herself. What, after all, had happened to her? "Being shut up here so long," she whispered. "It is lonely, waiting to see if one will die."

"Still lonelier waiting to see if someone you respect will run away from things that are hard."

She stared at him.

"I have been in the next room, Draupadi. From its windows I've seen a few rakshasa, the regrettable loss of your tidy villages, the returning of some innocents to their ancestors, and a great deal of spectacular fighting from one particular chariot. What I have not seen is even one of these 'demons' within an arrow's shot of the walls. I believe someone is holding them back, while sowing panic downstairs like mustard seed."

"Then you think we might be saved?"

"I think Yudishtira has already saved you. But soon"—Vyasa gestured towards the window—"he will return down there to far greater danger."

"You can stop it, I know."

"That is not for me to do."

She turned away. "Then nothing has changed. And I would only add to his peril if he tried to save me."

"I repeat, he already has."

"I've only divided them, Sage Vyasa."

542

"Divided them? Or caused them to stand alone when necessary?"

"I have weighed all of that, Sage. I am his doom!"

"You weighed this against what, Draupadi?"

"All that I had longed to see and be," she whispered.

"And you are still weighing that."

She rushed at him. "You are going to say Yudishtira needs me. But if he survives, you can not deny that he would be happier with a different queen. He would. He should have someone like Subhadra."

"Subhadra. Arjuna found your weakness, didn't he?"

"I am full of weaknesses, Sage." She walked to the window. "I don't want to see my husbands' dead bodies."

He followed her, sitting down with her on the window seat, the sunset and glowing fires behind them.

"Draupadi, I bring you a message."

His voice had an intensity that startled her. "From whom, Sage?"

"Your mother."

"Mother? Queen Yasoda?"

He did not answer, but took the tone of an envoy. "She begins, 'Your pony Orchid still waits for you under the pines at the head of the meadow trail. He misses you as much as I.'"

At the first words, Draupadi began to cry uncontrollably. Her head ached, her body trembled. And the spotted pony poked its nose into her mind, looking for wood apples.

Now behind Orchid there were three peaks, the middle one higher but farther away and lit by Ushas the Dawn.

Vyasa took her hand. "Your mother is like no other woman you will ever meet, Draupadi. The light fills her like the sun, yet she is as humble as her Dasyu parents. They were simple people, and they conceived a woman as close to the gods as we dare aspire. There is a lesson in that for all of Bharata."

"What is her name?" Draupadi whispered.

"When she came to us as a young girl craving Veda, we named her after the goddess Aditi."

Draupadi closed her eyes. "I knew this."

"Yes, you did. But don't look inside for your father's name

—you've never known it. Yet he is also a person to be proud of."

"A warrior?"

"I can not say—the risk is too great. Indeed, everything I tell you today can only be shared with your husbands, your brother, and Prahara when he is old enough to keep it private at all cost. It is important that you and your brother always be accepted as Drupada's and Yasoda's children, and be seen as fit to be royalty. In fact, however, you are fit to be much more. Besides your parents, you have a rearing like no other's, in Badari Ashram on Mount Kailasa of the Himalaya."

"I see Badari," she whispered. "It was all of stone. Deep snow in winter, flowers and berries all summer." She looked at him, excited.

"I know your thoughts. But do not go there until she sends for you. Yes, that day will come." He looked out of the north-facing window. "Your teachers, Draupadi. Remember them now?"

"Chitramahas. Kavasha. He was very strict. The shy physician Bhishaj with his herbs."

"Your schooling was unique." He smiled a little. "Although it made you more difficult for Drupada and Yasoda to handle than I had foreseen."

Draupadi shook her head. "Why?" she whispered. "Why a Dasyu's children?"

"Listen to me! Forget these words—Dasyu, Arya. If you must, separate people by their excellence, Draupadi. Didn't I tell you to *teach*? To correct rather than learn Bharata's blundering ways? You were raised for one purpose—to heal this land. But I am wasting our time. I came because you needed her message, not my own." Vyasa stood and stiffened himself again like a messenger. "Your mother wishes me to tell you this story:

"The gods were once fighting an army of demons. They fought divinely, but were losing the world to evil. Suddenly a goddess appeared among them and defeated the demons. Afterwards the gods forgot her and bragged of their victory. Then a tower of fire rose over them and they were terrified. None of them could bear its heat. And it spoke to them: 'I am the goddess who assumes all forms. Ignorant of my true nature, all you gods glory in your omnipotence to no avail. As a magician makes a wooden puppet dance, so do I, the Dark Mother, make all creatures act. So recognise who I am, and renounce your pride!' Then the gods abandoned their arrogance and worshipped her, as before, and as was fitting."

Draupadi had studied him while he spoke, but had seen her mother's face.

"And your mother sends this message," he said. "'Consider the two kinds of strength—that of seeds and that of axes. Love and anger. Truth and deception.'"

Draupadi knew she had heard this Before. Or had been born with it. She was crying softly as he went on. "'Both strengths are part of her creation. The Age of Kali is only the season when axes, anger and deception predominate.'"

Vyasa spoke slowly; Draupadi heard and set each word in place, as if each were a clear glass bead on a string.

"'Neither creation nor destruction can alter the eternal dharma. But it can be lost to human awareness. Your husband Yudishtira was born to prevent its complete loss during this time while destruction reigns. And you were born to prevent his despair. Creation and destruction have a single source, daughter. Find that source.'"

When Aditi's last word had died away, her messenger and her daughter remained in silence. Memories were returning to Draupadi like crowds of hungry dependants. But she could give them nothing more substantial than her passive attention.

Finally they were still. And from among them she saw the only one who mattered.

The room was almost dark. Below the window torches were being lit. She heard babies crying, men shouting, hooves striking paving stones restlessly.

As if he knew which memory ruled her thoughts, Vyasa stood and walked to the centre of the room. "He's coming back now, Draupadi."

"I know."

"The lock on that box of the yavanas is very strong, Draupadi. But do not underestimate the dangers outside it either. They are formidable. Tonight especially."

She looked below at the crowd of milling warriors. "Should

I go down there, then? Is that what she would want me to do?"

Behind her Vyasa did not answer.

"Tonight I will say it, Sage Vyasa: I am afraid."

When he didn't answer, she turned around. He was gone.

47

Consume, affluent Indra, the foe that is like thee in might
. . . We long for the universal Aditi.

By his laudable strength Indra supports my limb; thou
Brihaspati art the prolonger of my life . . . We long for the
universal Aditi.

The divine force of Indra is well constructed; Agni abides
in our dwelling, the praiser of the gods . . . We long for
the universal Aditi.

We have not done any great evil in secret from you, nor
any open action causing the anger of the gods . . . We long
for the universal Aditi.

Rig Veda

Draupadi threw on a plain grey shawl and held her headcloth
over her face below the eyes, as if she were unclean for some
reason and to be avoided. Her hands shook as she opened her
door a finger width. The guards, new Arya youths, were
definitely gone. If someone had been watching her rooms they
would know she was alone now, and even in her disguise she
would be followed. Unexpected speed was her best defence.
She slipped into the hall and ran, never looking back.

The women's gardens were dark and empty—her guards had
not kept their watch here either. It was their terror of rebellious
Dasyu and burning buildings. And it was older. It was the
ancient Arya fear of demons and of being trapped inside, of
dying far from the beloved plain.

But we with Dasyu blood don't mind a few shadows, she
told herself. Or footsteps behind us.

She ran on through the halls to the main courtyard, fighting down her panic. It's Yudishtira who's in danger, she repeated like a chant.

At last she was among other people, where a woman being abducted could raise an alarm and count on a response.

Forced by the crowd to slow down, she listened as she threaded her way through. Mostly there were servants here, encamped among their employers' belongings and engaged in tense arguments. What should the kings have done? Was there a fire in the stables? Were there a thousand rakshasa surrounding the walls, or two thousand? Yudishtira was mentioned often, never in a tone of sympathy.

From the palace entry she came out into the short street leading to the north gate. The street and the gate courtyard were poorly lit by a few torches and thronged with chariots, horses prepared for riding, shouting kings beside grim-faced queens and many uncomforted children. An elephant was squealing off to her left—some sovereign was determined to save it if escape became possible, even if the frightened beast trampled other men's families. Draupadi was disgusted with everything she saw.

Finally she reached the gate itself. Gateman Murdanvat, one of the Maruts whom she had known since Kampilya, was at his station halfway up the wall, from where he commanded the opening of the doors. But he was under siege—half the warriors around the gate were shouting to open it immediately, half threatened to shoot Murdanvat from his perch if he considered opening. The grim gateman had positioned two guards at the foot of his stairs. Their swords were drawn and pointed towards the crowd. Murdanvat himself was using his watch-hole to look outside the walls and gave the mob below him no notice.

Draupadi was about to call some word of encouragement to him when he gave the order for opening. In their rush not to be exposed, the warriors forgot the gateman himself. He, in turn, turned his back on them.

Draupadi was left in front as the great wooden doors parted and gave way to cool darkness. A single chariot approached her out of the night. Its team of three remaining horses limped on chipped and cracked hooves, blood streaming down their legs. Their heads went up with a pathetic eagerness at the sight of the opened gate, but they could not increase their speed. Over the railing of the chariot she saw the bodies of four Nishada bowmen. Her husband stood erect behind them. But his eyes seemed to see nothing.

Draupadi walked out and stopped the team. She heard the shouts warning her of rakshasa but she ignored them. They had to be gone or dead—Yudishtira was coming back defenceless.

She mounted his chariot and gazed down at another body —Vimada, who had been dear to her. She touched his brow by way of farewell. Then took the reins from Yudishtira.

The horses felt the fresh energy through the lines and stumbled into a trot. The gates finally closed behind the chariot. And Vyasa's warning came back to her: he faces even greater danger inside the walls.

She tried to judge the extent of her husband's wounds. None would be heavily poisoned since he still lived, and she saw no large amounts of fresh-flowing blood. Calling up to Murdanvat, she obtained the use of his lodgings, which were near the gate and, out of respect for the Marut's difficult job, had not been used to house guests.

Eos and Nakula were both beside her now, helping Yudishtira down, taking charge of the horses.

Draupadi noticed that the crowd around her had fallen silent. Then she heard someone whisper that it must be safe to leave. Another answered that it must also be safe to stay.

"Jaya," a voice shouted. "Jaya. Victory." And then the ancient song of praise to a samraj was taken up. It spread through the courtyard as she led her husband through the parting crowd. The hymn uplifted her, despite her anger with these warriors around them.

But Yudishtira ignored their adulations, breaking his silence to whisper only two words: "Treachery, everywhere."

Inside the gateman's lodgings, Draupadi and Eos found what was needed most—a wooden bathing tub behind a curtain that could be drawn. Eos ordered hot water, bandages and fresh clothing, selected herbs for Draupadi to use, then asked leave to go back to tending the wounded. "Nakula is looking to the king's brave mares," she said. "I will set guards outside the door. There is a back door here that opens out by the gate, should our king wish to leave without dealing with those fawning 'warriors' waiting in the front."

He was facing away from them, still standing where Draupadi had left him, rigid with fatigue. "Deal gently with him until he has talked about it freely," Eos whispered, close to tears.

"Stay with us, Eos."

"What you can say to him will heal him better than I," Eos whispered fiercely. "Besides, I can not bear to see what those out there allowed to be done to him."

As Eos left the room, Draupadi felt an unreasonable dread. She turned to her husband, bowed formally, and began slowly removing his leather body protectors.

"I failed you." His voice was flat. "The villages are gone. So many are dead."

Her mind raced wildly. There was so much to say, so much to be careful of, and now it seemed Nirriti's spell threatened to steal his mind.

"Certainly not all our people are dead," she said. "And you saved Indraprastha, just as you saved Magada from sin. The kings want you to be their samraj more than ever. Through your influence many other Dasyu will live."

He didn't respond.

"You must rest, though. Let the kings wait."

He couldn't respond, she realised. She saw him glancing warily around him, unable to trust safety and rest. When the servants came with the hot water she gestured for them to finish quickly and go.

She began removing his clothing. Everything was coated with drying blood—she saw him trying to find the words to protest her touching such impurity. "All of it is sacred today," she whispered. "You are our samraj."

She eased him out of the rest of his clothes.

"What room is this?" he whispered. "I'm lost."

"You are not lost. These are the gateman's lodgings. You let him plan and build them himself—you have never been here."

His body sagged. She brushed her lips across his forehead. He was fighting the loss of all control—his face trembled and tears shone at the edges of his tightly closed eyes. "Here I feel I am in Heaven," he whispered.

"Except you haven't died. This is your city of Indraprastha."

"Krishna." He shook his head. His voice was full of misery. "Vaja too?"

She didn't understand this.

"The kings did not come out to my aid," he said. "But I must not think about that. Treachery is our nature."

"Certainly not yours." She put her arms around his waist to lead him to the bath. "And you will change the rest of us."

He didn't answer, but she thought he only looked sadder because of her words.

She helped him into the warm, scented water. They both looked down at his naked body. Every unprotected area oozed blood from a multitude of wounds. His right shoulder and hip and left calf were bruised black. He tried to lower himself into the water as if to hide from her, but she had to inspect the wounds first. One still contained a barbed arrowhead. When she touched it, his fingers brushed hers aside, then pulled out the head by the shaft's stub almost roughly. His body recoiled at this, but his lips remained silent. She staunched the bleeding with fresh cloths.

Finally she eased him down, satisfied that none of the wounds were poisoned. He felt like a child to her. And she felt like a child also—wanting to beg his forgiveness, to share her memories, to voice all her fears. But none of that belonged here.

"Close the doors of perception," she whispered in his ear. "Rest and forget. Later we will talk." He obeyed her.

Draupadi sat down on the floor beside the tub. When she had been small and had had some little hurt, she remembered she would rush to one particular monk at Badari. He would tell her that: Close the doors of perception; rest and forget. Now the words would heal Yudishtira.

So much kept crowding her memory. But there was no time for it now. Krishna had been right after all—the past did not matter when the present threatened to run away with you.

There was a tap at the door. She looked at her husband. He seemed asleep with his head up, but she knew his mind had gone much further than sleep. Reluctantly she left the curtained alcove, hesitated at the front door, then remembered it had to be safe because guards were posted, and slipped outside in order not to disturb Yudishtira.

It was Subhadra. "Draupadi, forgive me. I have seen something. It must be nothing, really. I am sorry to trouble you."

Draupadi had a vision of a radiant milkmaid against the green of late summer. The Vrishni princess was now thin and pale. Why not, after three months of being the stranger, the newcomer? The alleged cause of a miscarriage and the object of hatred by a rival wife who was a well-loved queen? For a moment Draupadi disliked herself. "Teach me the first kind of strength, Mother," she whispered.

"What did you say, Queen?"

"Tell me what you saw, Subhadra. It must be important if it has upset you so."

"The woman Lotus. Arjuna's—the Dasyu—"

"Arjuna's Nishada consort. She is here at Indraprastha?"

"She came with Suyodhana's servants. I have been watching her today because she is acting strangely and I feared for Arjuna's life. Now I think she carries something hidden in her skirt and she is asking directions *here*—to the gateman's house."

Draupadi glanced at the door. Only these two Marut guards, and none by the rear entrance to the house. She considered sending Subhadra for more men, but if there were some plot unfolding against Yudishtira, Subhadra would be most easily stopped. So instead she ordered one of the two Maruts to the rear door and sent the other for reinforcements. "Subhadra, you will kindly guard the front and inform me if anyone at all approaches."

Draupadi went back inside, but there was a tap almost immediately. "She's out here, Draupadi!" Subhadra sounded frantic. "Lotus is hiding in a doorway."

"Come in, Subhadra. More guards will be here soon." Draupadi closed the shutters on the windows in the front part of the house.

From behind the curtain Yudishtira called for her.

"All is well, dear Husband." Glancing around, Draupadi saw Yudishtira's knife on the floor in its bloody sheath.

Beginning softly to sing a love song to reassure him, Draupadi slipped the stained knife from its sheath and handed it to Subhadra. The girl's eyes widened but she took it. "It will be all right," Draupadi whispered. "She would not dare to come in."

Draupadi was crossing the room to rejoin Yudishtira when the front door creaked behind her. She turned towards it, staring with horror at the bolt that hung free of its hole. How could she have failed to lock the door?

Subhadra, nearer to it, reached to push the bolt home. But too late. She sprang behind the door as it swung open.

Lotus stood on the threshold. She asked for King Yudishtira.

Draupadi saw that the Nishada's hand was hidden in a fold of her skirt. Her whole body shook as if fevered.

"No." It was all Draupadi could whisper.

"Who is there?" Yudishtira asked dully. Draupadi stepped so as to be more in line with him behind the curtain. She kept her eyes on Lotus, knowing that even a glance at Subhadra might give away her single hope.

Lotus took one step forward. Draupadi's hands twitched at her sides. Mother, she thought—which kind of strength defeats a knife?

Lotus took another step.

I don't care, Mother. I will never be without a weapon again.

Lotus swerved and plunged towards the curtain. Draupadi stepped in her path as Subhadra leaped from behind. The three women fell. Draupadi felt a violent spasm shake Lotus. The Nishada was screaming into Draupadi's chest. The knife Subhadra had thrust was between Lotus's shoulder blades; a Dasyu knife was embedded in the floor a finger's breadth from Draupadi's left breast.

Lotus was still aware. Draupadi slid out from under her and drew out the knife from the Nishada's back. "I think you will live, woman," she whispered. She felt dizzy with the remnants of fear. "Why, why did you attempt such a thing?"

"He killed my sister. He killed my baby."

"Who?"

Lotus raised her head. "The King. Yudishtira!"

"What?" he called. His voice still lacked alertness.

"It is nothing." But Draupadi heard him stepping out of the bath. Subhadra took back Yudishtira's knife and knelt next to Lotus, still wary of her. Draupadi rolled the Nishada on to her side to examine the wound.

At this display of concern from Draupadi, Lotus suddenly began to cry. "Sakuni," she whispered. "Baron Sakuni told me to kill Yudishtira. Beware—he wants to kill Prince Bhima too. Then Arjuna will be king. And I—I will be consigned to Hell!"

"Not if you come with us before the kings and tell them what Baron Sakuni told you to do," Draupadi whispered back.

She could hear Yudishtira dressing. She rose and went to the open front door. Still no guards. She closed the door and bolted it, folded her skirt so the splash of blood did not show, and calmly observed that her hands did not work very well because of their trembling. Nodding to Subhadra, Draupadi went behind the curtain.

"Who is out there?" He stood naked in the lamp light.

"Don't trouble yourself with it." She began drying him with a cloth. "More guards are coming. But perhaps it is better that you go, although I wish otherwise, for you have lost too much blood. Yudishtira, you must be extremely careful wherever you go. Take with you the guard at this back door. Promise me."

Yudishtira said nothing. He was drawing on the fresh garment, shrugging away her assistance. He moved stiffly, but with self-possession now.

Lotus might have killed him, she thought. Or me. And he would never have known my thoughts.

"Yudishtira?"

He raised his head.

"I have wronged you," she whispered. "Over and over. Forgive me."

He faced her, his eyes unclouded at last, so that she could see far into the depth of the injury to his spirit. And she saw she had caused much of it.

Without speaking, he bent down and kissed her roughly, then turned for the door.

"Wait," she said. But too many words crowded into her mind to speak any of them.

He left, closing the door hard behind him.

Draupadi wanted to call him back and beg his forgiveness. Beg for his love. But she knew he would not return.

She went back through the curtains, determined to learn from Lotus all she could about the threats facing him.

"Subhadra, see if the guards are outside yet. If they are, find Eos to help with this wound. Keep the knife with you."

Draupadi knelt beside Lotus again. Then, as the Vrishni girl walked to the door, Draupadi heard the bolt being moved with some tool from the outside. Subhadra gave her a terrified glance, then slipped out of sight of the doorway again and raised the knife over her head.

The door flew open. In the rectangle of darkness stood Baron Sakuni.

Draupadi froze. She still knelt beside Lotus. The baron did not enter, as if he knew Subhadra was behind the door.

"Yudishtira still lives, Lotus. You have failed." Sakuni's tone was chilling; the Nishada's eyes were glazed with fright.

Draupadi wanted to stand, but couldn't. Instead she drew the prone Nishada to her and clutched her tightly.

A blade blurred in the air. Lotus jerked in Draupadi's arms.

Then scarlet seeped through the Nishada's upper garment around a silver knife. Her eyes were open, but rolled back in death.

From the corner of her eye Draupadi saw a movement in the doorway. There was another knife in Sakuni's hand. "Draupadi. You will now come."

"Never." Her own low fury startled her. Yet she was aware that she laid Lotus down tenderly.

Sakuni raised the knife. "The box is in the alley." Sakuni stepped forward.

Subhadra struck, hitting the back of his head with the butt of the knife. He fell face down over Lotus's feet.

The two women rushed for him. Subhadra felt for his breath. "I wanted to kill him," she said rapidly. "But with her dead, I think we must somehow make *him* tell the assembly the truth about Suyodhana's plots."

Draupadi looked at her, amazed by such rational thinking. Now Subhadra was searching Sakuni for other weapons. For Draupadi's inspection she set out darts, small blades, a vial of greenish fluid, and sticks for fire starting.

Draupadi was shaking so hard she could hardly speak. "Subhadra, guards?"

The Vrishni girl went to the door. "Still none."

"Find them?" she whispered.

Subhadra touched her hand. "If he had come for me, I would also be speechless."

Draupadi did not answer. Subhadra went out.

Draupadi very slowly lowered her eyes from the door to Sakuni, who lay without awareness a hand's width from where she knelt. She told herself she only had to be alone with him until the guards came.

For my husbands' sake I must kill him, she thought.

They would not. Not in cold blood.

Lettermaker's box. It was really Sakuni's. Lettermaker told Sakuni the tunnel entrances. *This* man burned the villages. *This man.*

She took up the knife and held it over his heart.

But she could not plunge it into his flesh. She dropped it.

Her eyes closed a moment out of exhaustion. Suddenly fingers brushed her skirt. She started.

Sakuni's hand flailed at his side. His eyes opened.

She struck out. Her clenched fist hit an open eye. Her other fist slammed against his mouth, the teeth hurting her. She struck harder at his head. Then pulled his hair. Beat his chest with all her strength.

He recoiled only once, then his body went slack. She went on pounding anyway. Then scratched him with her nails. Blood appeared at his nose, at his mouth. Her own hands hurt and dripped blood, both his blood and hers. Yet she could not stop. She poured on him all the hate and anger she had held back since the moment she had stepped through King Drupada's fire. She hated like the world-devouring Dark Mother. She was destruction Herself.

Then she leaned back, her hair falling down around her, and she cried. For under the rage was the grief, the terrible grief that evil had taken her villages, and now herself.

It was to this that Subhadra returned. She stared at Draupadi. "Bring in the box from the alley," the kneeling woman said hoarsely.

In a moment Subhadra had two Marut guards dragging in the box. They glanced anxiously at the blood on Sakuni and their queen, but the Vrishni girl sent them back out without a word of explanation.

Draupadi slid open the door of the box and motioned for Subhadra to help her to roll Sakuni into it. Draupadi slid the door closed hard, locked the intricate iron lock and turned away from the box. "Now, Subhadra, you must find me Eos."

Eos looked around the room, peered through the box's slats and nodded with grim satisfaction. "Subhadra told me what happened, Draupadi. As I have said before, women do make the best guards."

"Maybe in Greece," Subhadra said politely. "I will go now, Queen."

"Subhadra—" Draupadi stopped. Her eyes went to Lotus's body. "I owe you my life." •

The Vrishni princess bowed. "I know you would have done the same for me." And she left, closing the door quietly.

Eos and Draupadi stared at each other across the dead Nishada woman and the box where Sakuni lay, perhaps dead also.

Finally Draupadi spoke. "Vyasa has returned my memories."

"And what do you remember?" Eos whispered.

"My mother best." Her voice caught. "But he said I must not—"

"Your past never mattered to me, Draupadi."

"Eos, what about Suyodhana? Will he try to kill Yudishtira now?"

"Your other husbands watch him. He bellows like an ox without his driver. This one was the master demon, Draupadi. And you have defeated him."

The two women came together and embraced. At last the

tears of relief were free to flow. The endless day was over, the rage exhausted, the danger locked in a box.

A long time passed. Someone knocked. When the women did not answer, the person went away. But Draupadi knew she could delay no longer.

"Eos, beloved friend. I must ask you a service. Deny me if—"

"I can deny you nothing," Eos whispered fiercely.

"Don't say that, for I wish very much that you would deny me. You see, Sakuni may still be alive. I need you to go to Lettermaker. To tell him I changed my mind—that it is I in this box. Say that after seeing Yudishtira safe, I felt free to go. And Eos—when he thinks he takes me, go with him yourself." Draupadi held her tighter and spoke faster. "Pretend you changed your mind also."

"And when he discovers who is really in there?"

"That is why you must be with him—to convince him to go on anyway. To take Sakuni far from Bharata. Tell him he is lucky, that this is my gift to him—that Yudishtira will hunt him and kill him if either of them stays. Or tell him I forgive him and beg this favour. Tell him anything that will make him go far, far away. And then, Eos, come back to me."

Eos pulled away. "Exile is not safe or sufficient punishment for traitors."

"I can not believe Lettermaker meant to cause so much destruction. And Sakuni is an unarmed and wounded cripple now. To kill either in cold blood would violate dharma. I can not ask it of you."

"Then I will arrange to have to kill them to defend myself," Eos said coldly.

Draupadi did not protest, but pulled Eos to her again. "Mother, forgive us," she whispered. "Sometimes it is the only kind of strength we can find."

"What did you say?"

"I can not speak of it." Draupadi slipped from her arms. "I must find Yudishtira now. Will you be careful, Eos? And return to me quickly? You must, you know. As queen I demand it." Draupadi backed towards the door, her vision of Eos becoming clouded by more tears. "Promise me, Friend!"

48

You ask why Brahma created evil. This illusion arises from
the fact that anything created has dimensions—some parts
are near, some far. Those near seem to belong to you, to
support you. Those far from your understanding seem strange
and dangerous. Evil. So you find you must fight them. They
are real to you. *Evil is real.*

But unlike Brahma, Brahman is both source and goal,
both substance and design. Brahman is omnipresent. At
rest in Brahman, nothing is distant. We are one. *That is
also real.*

Vyasa

Yudishtira stood in the deserted main-gate courtyard. Above
him lamp light played from every window of the palace. In
some he could see servants busy with garments and jewels, as
a hundred kings and their queens prepared for the evening's
feast and ceremonies as if nothing had happened.

"But nothing can be the same," Yudishtira said out loud.
"Guard!"

The sentry who had followed him from the rear door of the
gateman's house rushed to him.

"Act as a messenger to the crier. He must announce this:
'Indraprastha's king commands that because of the dead, there
will be no celebrations tonight. Those Nishada inside the walls
may go out now to tend their wounded and fallen. Bharata's
warriors shall accompany the Nishada and protect them.'"

The guard ran off, replaced by several more from around the
gate. "Another message, to my brothers: 'Have the Maruts

see to Vimada's body, then meet me in the assembly hall immediately.'"

Yudishtira walked up the short street towards the palace. The great arched hall rose above him in the gathering mist of a winter's light rain. On either side of him a scattering of princes fell in step with him, but in the shadows, at a discreet distance, each hoping to be the first to regain his favour after their cowardice during the day. And under his feet the slick paving bricks shone.

Leaving twenty or more warrior-borns behind at the door with only a cold look of disdain, Yudishtira entered the empty hall alone. He was hurt to find the place gave him not the smallest comfort. It was as hollow as everything else. Only Draupadi seemed substantial now. Her few words: "I have wronged you; forgive me."

But those too might prove to be an illusion.

He wanted to promise himself that he would never need anyone again. Never draw near, only to be cut.

Yet this hall reminded him he could never be alone, or even self-sufficient. Another man could be a forest recluse for a month or a lifetime, wandering alone into the comforting trees to heal himself. But dharma tied Indraprastha's king to this throne on the edge of the speaking floor, surrounded by a thousand seats.

Surrounded by burned villages, grieving Dasyu, and traitors.

He remembered his return from Magada. And his return from the tiger hunt of his youth. This was the third return after a "victory" that had seemed more like a loss. Would they always?

Bhima arrived first. "Thank all the gods you are alive. Nakula told me, but I could hardly believe it."

More numb than he had realised, Yudishtira could only respond curtly. "Yes, 'alive'. What is your report?"

Bhima assured him there were no rakshasa in sight of the walls. Within the city the day of interminable, needless panic was finally over, and Suyodhana had been humiliated for having helped to create it. Now there was only an almost hysterical eagerness to celebrate the consecration of the next samraj, the man who had saved them.

How dare they think of celebrating, Yudishtira thought. But he said nothing. He walked out on to the gleaming speaking floor. Although the lamps were unlit, the reflected light of moon and stars from the high windows made the hall strangely bright. Yudishtira turned and asked with elaborate casualness. "Bhima, have you seen Krishna today?"

"Yes! But only from a distance. He was coming in the west gate. The way he looked, I thought he had been out fighting alongside you."

"Find him, Bhima."

"No need." Krishna entered from the south portal, behind Yudishtira.

The eldest Pandu turned and the two men faced each other for a long moment. Without looking away from the Vrishni, Yudishtira stretched out a hand towards Bhima. "Your knife, Bhima. Krishna, are you armed?"

"No, nor do I wish to be. I stand before my samraj."

"Then your 'samraj' wishes you armed."

Bhima stepped between them. "What are you talking about, Yudishtira?"

Yudishtira pushed Bhima aside without answering. The Vrishni's eyes were circled by shadows, his cheeks were sunken and hollow from some deep strain of the spirit as much as of the body, and his skin was smudged with black paint that had failed to come off with the hard rubbing which had reddened the cleaner parts. The evidence could not be avoided.

Sahadeva and Nakula entered.

"One of you, give your knife to Krishna," Yudishtira ordered. "And see he has no poison darts hidden on him."

Bhima groaned. "Poison darts on Krishna? Are you losing your senses, Brother?"

"Beg Indra that I am. But my eyes see the same black paint on his face that I have seen all day on others. My nose smells the same rotten smell. And my ears have heard a rakshasa call Krishna his leader."

Krishna only bowed his head.

"You do not deny it then." Yudishtira turned his back on him. His voice broke. "Krishna, how could you wound me so? What of our dream of dharma ruling here at Indraprastha?"

He heard the cry of pain and rage in his own voice and did not try to hide it. What reason was there left even for maintaining control?

"What has Krishna *done*, Yudishtira?" Bhima begged again.

"He led the rakshasa in the burning of our villages and the killing of our people. I don't know how long he's led them. But how often was he with us when they attacked?" Yudishtira could speak no more.

Bhima slowly backed away from both men. "I can not believe this!"

Arjuna entered through the north door. Bhima whispered to him their eldest's accusation.

"Is he possessed?" Arjuna shouted.

"Only with sadness," Yudishtira answered numbly. "The Vrishni will give his convoluted explanations, then I must turn my sadness to rage and try to kill him."

Arjuna begged Yudishtira to put down his knife. When Yudishtira refused, Arjuna reached for it.

"Interfere and I will remove your hand, Brother. Choose today—do you stand with the Vrishni or with me?"

Without pause Arjuna stepped beside Yudishtira. "I welcome any opportunity to make my loyalty to you clear. Krishna, I beg of you, explain away his charge and make this nightmare end!"

The slightly-built youth appeared almost childlike in the huge empty hall. But as the Vrishni began to speak, alone on the darkly shining floor, his voice seemed as large as space itself.

"You worried about those dark demons, Yudishtira. But I *hated* them. They were a threat to all I cared for. So I set out to find them. Yet when I did," he said with sudden bewilderment, "I only pitied them."

Krishna's voice had been low. Now he raised it. "Our 'demons'? They were our own runaway servants, their backs scarred from old whippings. They were Nishada husbands who could only court death after their wives had been stolen from before their eyes. They were Dasyu sons who had lost all respect for their fathers after seeing them humiliated by us time and time again. Youths eager to please any leader who would teach them to fight back. All the rakshasas' rumoured sins were real, Yudishtira. But we Arya were the ones who sent them to Hell. In their eagerness to regain some sort of manhood, they encouraged each other to greater and greater cruelty. But their worst sins were done in the name of Lord Soma himself, a god they had no more understanding of than infants, though as our dependants they ought to have been educated at least about what is truly sacred and what is filth. But we did not teach them, so it was easy for Baron Sakuni and his Egyptian slave to give them a 'soma drink' from the yavanas that turned their awareness to living death."

"Sakuni!" Bhima growled. "I knew it. I will cut off his body parts and feed them to the Yamuna's gavials while he watches."

"These 'living dead' called you leader, Krishna," Yudishtira said coldly.

Krishna's face now reflected an even deeper agony. "Some of Sakuni's rakshasas finally rejected their life of defilement when the Egyptian insisted on even worse atrocities. Eagle—"

Yudishtira stiffened. "Tell me about this one."

"He was Lotus's brother and also the brother of your Wood Rose. He wanted to avenge the one's death and the other's 'degradation'."

Yudishtira drew in his breath. He looked at Arjuna. The latter lowered his eyes.

Krishna did not notice them. "When the Egyptian began to use the rakshasa for Sakuni's purposes, Eagle's faction saw through it. So I arranged to meet them in the forest—they had already accepted one non-Dasyu leader, and I am dark, I recited them Veda—"

"Veda?" Bhima said. "To Nishada?"

"Surya's hymn: 'He who has drunk thinks that the herb which men crush is the Soma; but that which the priests know to be Soma, of that no terrestrial being partakes—'"

"Why didn't you come to *me* with this?" Yudishtira interrupted.

"I intended only to use these rakshasa to learn Sakuni's plans. But when the information most needed was about to come—the details of this attack—Eagle separated his men from Sakuni and begged me to actually lead them."

"Against us?" Arjuna asked. "And you agreed?"

"I saw Eagle's men could not be stopped, but perhaps diverted. Eagle knew Sakuni planned to attack during the rajasuya. Eagle, however, could see that Sakuni did not plan to improve the Dasyu's lot, but only wanted to use them to replace one Arya, yourself, with another, Suyodhana. Therefore Eagle planned to attack you today on his own and to burn Indraprastha. I was able to learn that Sakuni's group had been ordered to burn the villages and kill their inhabitants, but to begin with only one village and to spare the fortress until Sakuni gave some signal. Above all, you were to be kept inside by attacks on the gates. Knowing the villages would be lost anyway, I encouraged Eagle to attack before Sakuni's group— to set fire to the villages and draw you out 'where he could fight you like a hero'. And where I knew you would not die uselessly, in flames."

Arjuna's face mirrored Krishna's misery. "But the villages were full of women and children."

"They were going to burn anyway! And if they had torched Indraprastha, you would have defended her until you and she were ashes! Sakuni's rakshasa were not to strike without every one of you inside. I knew you would defeat them if only you came out to fight them. As for Eagle's men, I thought I could intervene once you were outside the walls, grant them the usual privileges and protections you offer Dasyu, then bring them before the kings to accuse Sakuni and Suyodhana."

Krishni looked around and above, as if expecting to find their Dasyu spirits high up under the dark arches. "But I could not stop them. Except for Eagle, they drank the Egyptian drink after all. And then King Does-Nothing came. And you, Yudishtira. Later I searched—I believe they all are dead." Krishna bowed his head. "That is my story. Believe me or not—I am ever your servant, Samraj Yudishtira."

"It is not a matter of belief, Krishna," Yudishtira said guardedly. "Who told them about the tunnels?"

"I do not know."

"Panchalya now suspects Guru Vaja. After your treachery, why not?"

"It was Lettermaker," Draupadi said. She came out of the

darkness of the west entrance. "Sakuni's work again." She also described to Yudishtira how Sakuni had convinced Lotus to kill him, and how Subhadra had prevented it.

Yudishtira was trying to grasp this news when he saw Radheya enter behind Draupadi.

Bhima made a threatening gesture, but Yudishtira was remembering Radheya's stand near the south gate. "Let him speak."

"On her way to find you, your wife heard me insist to others that Sakuni had controlled the rakshasa. She wished me to report it all to you. I have had Sakuni followed—I can prove his slave Zesnor led these rebel Dasyu."

"Be careful, 'King of the Anga'," Arjuna said hotly, striding up to him. "You have loaded so much evil on the cart of your arch enemy Sakuni that many will be asking how it could have moved without your dearest friend Suyodhana in the same harness."

Radheya pushed past Arjuna. "You think Suyodhana knew of these treacheries. But when I have tried to tell Suyodhana about Sakuni's dealings with these rakshasa, he has not believed me."

"I wonder why you are telling us this now?" Arjuna asked with disdain. "And why did you wait so long?"

Radheya looked at him coldly. "I waited for the sake of justice—such an accusation, especially against a king's brother-in-law, demands strong proof. And I tell you now only for the sake of justice. I do not seek personal power at the expense of Bharata's peace, as your brother Yudishtira does with this rajasuya. All I came here to say—for the sake of justice only, if you care about that—is that Sakuni has violated dharma in his plotting against you. And as you seem to blame your troubles on this Vrishni here, I am also bound by dharma to bear witness that Krishna could have done little to prevent the attack today." Radheya turned and left the hall.

Yudishtira slowly released his grip on the knife. It clattered against his foot. He turned his back on all of them.

Arjuna went to Krishna and shook his shoulder. "If you had only come to us with this, Friend! We could have brought in the villagers, blocked the tunnels, imprisoned Sakuni—"

"You could have tried, and possibly failed," Krishna said dully.

"So *you* tried something else." It was Vyasa's voice filling the hall from the east door. He walked slowly out on to the night-blue speaking floor.

Krishna rushed to him and bowed deeply.

"Meddling again, Krishna? Who is about to become samraj? Can you remember?"

"Yudishtira," Krishna whispered.

Vyasa's voice filled the room. "In your vision, who provides the sustaining water? And what do *you* provide?"

"Nothing." Krishna, bent in his bow, seemed to sag lower.

"You have let fear, expedience and your own small desires overshadow dharma." Suddenly his voice was full of compassion. "The very tragedy you sought to avert."

The hall was silent. Finally Yudishtira spoke. "Dear teacher, I saw it dimly on the battlefield and again when Radheya spoke. Hearing your voice, dear teacher, now makes it clear. Do not accuse Krishna of acting to please himself. Accuse me."

"You, Grandson?" Vyasa's voice was kind, but he watched Pandu's eldest with a detached, almost amused interest.

"Please hear me out." But Yudishtira went to Draupadi instead. "So much of this tragedy began when I decided we five would marry this woman—counter to dharma and her own wishes—only so that I could possess her too." His voice rose. "I sent Arjuna away for the year and Lettermaker away for ever —not for dharma, but to have you to myself, Draupadi."

"That isn't true," Bhima wailed.

"I did not know it then, Bhima. But it is true." Yudishtira still faced Draupadi. "I allowed Arjuna to marry Subhadra for the same reason. I fought Jarasamda alone, putting my kingdom at unnecessary risk, because I wanted you, Draupadi, to think that I am braver than Arjuna and Bhima. I ordered Arjuna to stay inside today rather than help me to defend your villages —for the same reason, I see now. Above all, Radheya was right—dharma did not truly concern me when I chose to become samraj. I wanted the honour, and that only to somehow make you love me. I believe now that, in part, the gods have put this desperate love for you in my heart to force me to see my own arrogance."

He finally met her gaze. When her eyes failed to accuse him, but instead filled with tears, he turned away.

Walking to Krishna, he said, "You once told me that when dharma is unclear, a righteous king's desires indicate the way, implying that I was such a king. I am not in any way."

"You exaggerate," Arjuna said softly from behind him.

"We are all like this," Bhima cried.

Yudishtira whirled around. "Yes! Yes, we are. Someone tell me, who is better? I will bow to him immediately. Vyasa, tell me who does not disguise their small-self's desires as righteousness? Look at the behaviour of Bharata's 'heroic' kings today. None of them are better than my uncle Drita. And I am no better than he." Yudishtira came back to stand before his teacher. "I have dedicated my life to preserving dharma, Beloved Sage. But I believe I preserve an empty shell."

"You are making progress, Yudishtira," Vyasa said with great gentleness.

"Progress? No! Teach me!" Yudishtira cried out in anguish.

"You know the answer. When your self is larger, your desires will be larger."

"But what is dharma? I don't understand it any more."

"Good."

"But tomorrow I am samraj! My father—" Yudishtira stopped.

"Gave up everything for you," Vyasa finished. "So that you could prevent thousands of years of horrors, and you don't know how to do that. Yudishtira, the Age of Kali is merely another season—fearsome only because, like any season, it will require us to change. Change a great deal. But that means *we* will decide how terrible it will be, according to how much wisdom we can bring to bear upon it. For that, we do count on you. But you are only twenty-two!" Vyasa's voice seemed close to breaking; his expression was filled with pity. "And those years in which you will be forced to change so greatly are approaching too swiftly as it is. Be easy for an hour, grandson."

Vyasa came closer to him. "If you want advice, this much I

will give: be at least as afraid of humility as you are of arrogance. They are a team, and they will gallop you off the nearest cliff. See yourself, Yudishtira, as you are."

Yudishtira was reflecting on Vyasa's words when he was forced to notice Krishna walking from the hall.

"Krishna!" Yudishtira shouted. "Where are you going? Don't you understand? I forgive you."

"Go with Vayu's speed, Krishna," Vyasa called softly. "Take your time there."

Yudishtira fell silent, ashamed of his outburst. Draupadi stepped closer to his side. He saw her face was trembling with emotions.

"So many innocent deaths," the eldest Pandu said quietly. "So much pain."

Now Vyasa moved towards the north entrance. Yudishtira allowed only his eyes to beg his teacher to stay.

The sage paused in the doorway. "Not as many innocents died as you think, Yudishtira. As for the pain, there was no path with less or I would have shown it to you."

49

As this spacious earth supports these trees
so has Agni placed thy spirit in this body
for life, not for death, but for security.

The wind blows downwards,
the sun burns downwards,
the cow yields her milk downwards,
so be thy sin cast down.

Rig Veda

She stood in the garden, tears coursing down her face. Before her the black arches of the assembly hall stood against the sky. In there, had he not seemed to say it? He regretted it, but in some way he loved her.

And now he must know the truth. Vyasa expected it of her —he'd said to inform only her husbands and brother. Nor could she believe in Yudishtira's love until he knew.

But he had fled the hall without her. And now a messenger approached her from the direction of the gate. "Queen, Krishna of the Vrishnis gives you this gift."

She took the parcel. It was heavy, yet contained a sheer cloth—a long length, it seemed, folded with precision, and utterly different from any of the hundreds of lengths of cloth the Vrishni had brought her before. This was so soft it seemed to be spun of spider webs.

"Did he tell you what this is?" she asked.

"He said 'silk'. From 'far Chine'. And he gave this message: 'You stayed the year and now you know who you are. Our agreement is fulfilled. But I owe you other debts, and the villages are but one. Some day I will endeavour to repay you.

Until then, I leave you with this gift—you will know when to wear it. And I leave you with the love you and Yudishtira now share, discovered during that hateful year I made you spend with him. In the future remember that at your bride's choice I swore to protect you. I always have and I always will.'"

The messenger walked back into the darkness. Clutching the parcel with one hand, Draupadi picked a stalk of moon flowers with the other and held it to her cheek. "Can you protect me, Krishna, from what Yudishtira must feel when I tell him I am half-Dasyu?"

After the day's fighting the guards would not consider letting in the tall, strangely accented yavana who appeared out of the dark. "Egyptian" he claimed to be, a new kind of demon to them.

Nor would they comply with his laughable request to have one of Pandu's sons come out to the gate to speak to him. He would have to use a messenger, like anyone else, and the king or his brothers would decide if they wanted to hear a foreigner's words.

But Zesnor refused to trust an unknown servant with his thoughts out loud. He considered writing—Sakuni had said the Phoenician had taught Yudishtira to read—but merely bringing out pen and papyrus in front of these guards might cost him his life. He felt light-headed due to his earlier decision and made the next one impulsively.

"I am sick of all of you," he shouted. "Sick of your palaces, your petty plots. Send for Suyodhana then! I don't care. I will speak to *him*."

Unfamiliar with Zesnor, the guards failed to run for their lives before this unprecedented outburst. But the foreigner was still worrisome. He had asked first for the sons of Pandu—he was unlikely to be a traitor. He was also losing all patience and it might turn out he had good reason, and guest rights as well. So the guards reluctantly complied, provided Crown Prince Suyodhana agreed to go outside the city's gates to speak to him.

King Drita's son took his time, driving up in a freshly prepared chariot. Zesnor watched him through the night gate, the small door within the larger wooden barriers. Suyodhana stepped down and came out to the Egyptian, demanding to see his uncle.

Arrogant as ever, Zesnor thought. "I do not know where he is."

"But you are his slave!"

Zesnor straightened his spine and prepared his Ka for death. He had made up his mind—tonight he became free.

"Your uncle ordered me to kill your father."

Suyodhana only grew red-faced. "Did you, Egyptian? Is my father dead?"

"No." Zesnor felt his Ka safer, but his sense of disgust was overwhelming him. "Is it that you wish I had?"

Suyodhana moved to strike him, then stopped himself. "No, I have some affection for my old father."

"Then why aren't you rushing to kill your uncle for ordering such a thing?"

"First, I don't know where my uncle is. Second, I suspected that was his plot anyway. He wouldn't tell me, of course, but it was logical. I'm sure I could not have stopped him. If my uncle wished to make his sister a widow—well, let the old ones quarrel among themselves."

"And in the process, make you king and then samraj."

Suyodhana shrugged. "I understood that to be an undertaking you and my uncle were both involved in. If your loyalties have changed—"

"You fear I will reveal your plots to others."

"My uncle's plots," Suyodhana said coldly, taking a step back, "not mine."

Zesnor saw Suyodhana's hand going to his knife. Suddenly the Egyptian wanted to live very much. But he knew the danger of letting such weakness show.

Instead he shrugged. "I am sick of you all, Crown Prince Suyodhana. After tonight I will be telling nothing to anyone—I have found a teacher in your forests and at dawn I take the vow of silence, to keep the evil that I have seen and done from poisoning the air through speaking of it. I am here tonight to tell the Arya what I have *not* done. First, I did not kill your father."

"I am sorry, Egyptian, but in Bharata we do not give rewards for such accomplishments."

Zesnor ignored him. "Second, I tried to prevent the burning of the villages and the killing of innocents. The rakshasa were under my command and I might have avoided the entire attack. But other rakshasa obeying the Nishada called Eagle began the burning of the villages. They were responsible. After that I could not control those under my own leadership."

"Only Dasyu died, Zesnor. Do not be troubled by it."

Zesnor was looking past Suyodhana now, to the night gate. "From my teacher, who knew them as children, I understand that King Yudishtira is a good man, Queen Draupadi an exceptional woman. I do not wish to be remembered as their enemy."

Suyodhana stepped closer to the Egyptian. "Something has gone wrong, hasn't it? Everything failed! So now you protect yourself by praising Yudishtira. Where is my uncle? Curse him, must I bow down to my vile cousin after all? Zesnor!"

But the yavana had walked away into the night.

Suyodhana turned around. Guru Vaja stood in the night gate.

The younger man started. "Vaja. Listening to private conversations now?"

"He saw me and could have held his speech."

Trying to recall all that had been said, Suyodhana brushed past Vaja and stepped through the night gate. The weapons-master followed.

"Guru Vaja!"

It was Panchalya, a raised battle axe in each hand. Two servants with torches stood behind him. To one he shouted, "Find Yudishtira and Draupadi to witness a challenge."

Suyodhana made a gesture of contempt. "Vaja, it seems you have more than one disillusioned student. Are you only now finding out, Panchalya, that your beloved Vaja came to see you here after the rains only so he could spy on you? He had to, you see, because he was afraid I'd tell his secret courtesan—"

"I've heard enough!" Panchalya shouted; his voice was pitched high with anguish.

The three turned towards the sound of running feet. Yudishtira burst into the circle of light, followed by Bhima and Sahadeva. All quickly honoured their weapons-master, who merely stood in stunned silence. And from the direction of the gardens Draupadi appeared. At the same moment Suyodhana slipped away.

Panchalya bowed to Yudishtira. "Because I am within your walls, I ask your permission: allow me a duel to the death." He turned towards Vaja. "I would have you try my teacher as a criminal, were it not"—he bowed his head—"that I am equally at fault."

Yudishtira gestured in utter frustration. "Stop this, Panchalya. My foolishness with Krishna was evil enough. Are we always to be fighting *each other*?"

Panchalya seemed not to hear him. "You may try the winner of the duel. That is your right. But I myself want to be as generous as I can to this man"—Panchalya was near to tears —"who has always been so generous with me."

Yudishtira stretched out his hands to take the battle-axes from Panchalya. "Panchalya, only three drove out to help us defend this city today. Our teacher was one of them." Yudishtira stepped closer to his brother-in-law. "Nor could I bear to lose either of you." His voice was strained. "Not tonight."

"Do not try to stop me!" Panchalya shouted. Then he fell at Yudishtira's feet, the battle-axes clutched to his chest.

Draupadi knelt beside him. "You trusted Vaja with the knowledge of our defence because of *me*, Panchalya. Because of what *I* said to him in anger. I am equally to blame."

"Hundreds died at the tunnel entrances," Panchalya whispered. "For that, I alone am to blame." He looked up at Yudishtira. "Allow me the duel," he thundered. "Or try *me!*"

Now Sahadeva knelt before Panchalya. "Panchalya, Guru Vaja only revealed the locations of the outlets *inside* Indraprastha. This is true. It was the Phoenician who betrayed us."

Vaja, at first unwilling to defend himself, finally told how, when Panchalya had shown him the outer entrances, he had made a point of not noticing any identifying features. And how Suyodhana had threatened him. And why he had succumbed enough to those threats to reveal the inner openings.

Panchalya clenched his fists. "Why, why do you not side clearly with Pandu's sons?"

The teacher stood over his student. "I am sworn to serve all those who come to me to learn. To do that I must remain in the middle-ground. Even if it opens and swallows me."

"But righteousness is here, in Indraprastha!"

"Panchalya, a teacher is only as good as his worst pupil. I must try to change Suyodhana, not abandon him. And hope Indra prevents your father demanding that you attempt to kill me." Vaja lowered his voice. "But if I should meet death by your hand, I will consider it an honour." He now studied both Panchalya and his sister. "Even anger—from either of you— is more pleasing to me than the love that might come from others."

"Then act according to your love!" Draupadi cried.

"I try not to act according to any of my feelings, Queen. But according to what my intellect judges to be my dharma."

His words bore into her. She turned away, stunned by a simple thought that seemed to accuse the core of her.

The king of North Panchala stood, after laying the two battle-axes at his teacher's feet.

Yudishtira's eyes were searching the shadows of the torch-lit courtyard. "Where is Suyodhana? I will tolerate no more of this. No more."

After the others had gone, Draupadi felt compelled to stay longer with Panchalya. Only she could comfort her brother now, and it was not until he seemed in better control that Draupadi could follow after Yudishtira. And still she could not yet search for him, for there was important news to be heard from the carpenter Badger. After that, with so much more to tell the king, she sought him everywhere, but no one could tell her where he had gone.

Finally she found him, back near the gate again, in the alley between the armoury and the gateman's house. She heard his voice raised in rage. "Where is your brother, bitch's whelp?"

Straining to see down the dark alley, Draupadi watched Yudishtira shaking King Drita's huge second-eldest son like a pillow.

"I don't know," Dusasana whimpered. "I will make an oath of it! Don't kill me, Cousin. I beg you."

"An oath? Do you keep oaths like your brother?"

But Yudishtira suddenly dropped Dusasana. "Killing you, Dusasana, would not satisfy me enough."

Yudishtira stood over his cousin, but talked now as if to himself. "I threaten cousins. I weigh the sins of Krishna, my friend. Vaja, my teacher. I vow to kill Suyodhana, my ox of a cousin. But who *planned* this attack? *Sakuni.*" He plunged towards the farther alley entrance, head down and shoulders hunched.

"Wait," she called.

He stopped. "Draupadi? Is it you?"

"Yudishtira," Draupadi said quietly, "Sakuni is gone."

"Gone? Gone where?"

"I took my own revenge for the villages—and other things."

Yudishtira sagged against the wall of the alley. "Then how will we prove that Suyodhana was behind all this with him?"

"It seems we can not."

"You should have left him for me, Draupadi."

"You were exhausted and he was too dangerous."

"No, you should have left him for me."

The strain of her own day and night, and of what she still had to do, broke her now. "Then you should have had me guarded better or left me alone less."

"Left *you* alone less?"

"Since Prahara's birth you have been in my company twice."

"Since Arjuna returned that has been your choice, Queen. But I thought that was past when you spoke of your forgiveness such a brief time ago."

Still she raged on, out of control. "How fortunate you are that at least a few of us ignore your orders to do nothing but *watch* you. Sakuni would have killed you if we had. If you want to be angry about people not obeying you, by sitting still to observe you in awe, begin with the carpenter Badger. I've just seen him. He disobeyed you and went out during the attack. He has rescued three hundred of your people."

"A Dasyu?" He grabbed her hands in his excitement. "Badger saved hundreds?"

"Yes, a Dasyu!" she shouted. "Yes! And he did it by disobeying you." Suddenly she threw herself at him and began pounding his chest. "This *Dasyu* said, 'I'm sorry, Queen, they were excellent tunnels, but Nishada do not like holes in the ground.' This *Dasyu* said, 'We decided instead to seek safety among Mother Yamuna's reeds along the shore.'" Her voice went flat. "About half the Arya went to the river and many more Nishada. They were all saved."

Yudishtira simply stared at her.

"You see, we Dasyu have a talent for surviving: we merely disobey." She looked up at him, her voice becoming wild again. "We Dasyu. Do you hear me? Only my father is Arya, Yudishtira. And he's not even a warrior. My *mother is a Dasyu.*"

Yudishtira still did not speak.

"You might have guessed!" she was shouting again, and crying. "I'm as dark as half of these Nishada. I remember everything now—Vyasa brought it all back for me. You think you've made mistakes, Yudishtira? I remember my mother telling me over and over, 'You were meant for only one man.' Just like you, yes, Yudishtira? You said, 'You will be my only wife,' yes? And she said: 'He will love only you. And you must love him the same way, with all your heart.' Every night she said it. Oh I obeyed her, didn't I? I did love with all my heart." Her voice became wild. "I loved *Arjuna.* Loved him until now you must hate me. Loved him when I might have had your love, at least for a year. Until I had to tell you I am Dasyu. Yudishtira, do you know whom she meant I should love? She used to say it every night. 'The *eldest* of the five, my daughter. *The samraj of all Bharata.*'"

Draupadi started to run out of the alley, but Yudishtira caught her and held her while she cried.

Yudishtira led her through their palace's gardens, his arm still enfolding her, while she told him her memories, each one like a stitch in a seam binding her life to his. Through it all he did not speak.

Finally she stopped and raised her head. "And my name at Badari was Krishnah, Dark One. I am half-Dasyu. Have you understood me? I am what your own brothers call 'an abomination'."

Yudishtira kissed her gently, then led her on, and in the darkness of midnight another dark night came back to him: He began to speak quietly of Wood Rose, and the strange story of her wounding and death.

"I kept it from you, Draupadi, because I was ashamed—not of having cherished a Dasyu woman, but of having killed her while meaning to save her. That, however, is a shame I have multiplied today many times over."

He stopped and turned to her. "But now I can believe that Wood Rose's death, at least, was not without some purpose— if it eases your heart at all."

She touched his cut and bruised face tenderly, wanting to take away every pain that had ever touched him.

"So once again it was my pride which caused you grief, Draupadi. For if I had only told you sooner, you would have known long ago that your mother's origins made no difference to me. No, that is not true—what you tell me of her tonight gives me still more reason to love you."

They walked on, revealing, as lovers do, all their great and small fears and misunderstandings of each other. Draupadi felt light as a flying bird.

Until she remembered Arjuna. Then, impulsively, she took Yudishtira's hand and spoke her new and deep desire. "Beloved husband, ask your brothers to do as Arjuna did and find new wives. I beg you, allow me to be only yours, as you are only mine."

He stared at her. "Allow you?" he asked in dismay. "If only it were mine to allow. But they *love* you, Draupadi. How can I tell them I now take you for myself?"

She clutched his arm. "You must not make me go to Arjuna tomorrow!"

He did not answer.

Slowly she let go of his arm. Then turned away, her love for him making it difficult even to bear the sight of him while also so fully aware of what must happen on the following night at this hour.

"I had thought," she whispered, "that when two people

577

married, they only needed full hearts. But a marriage to five requires a clear and cold mind."

She held her head high. "Of course it may be that he will not want me, a half-Dasyu."

"He will want you." The agony in Yudishtira's voice made her ache.

Suddenly he reached to caress her face.

She stopped his hand.

"Shall I leave you alone, then?" he asked hoarsely.

"No, never. I could not bear that either."

He studied her. "No, neither could I." He turned and began to walk; she fell in beside him.

"So perhaps Kama will allow us to be lovers for only brief seasons, Draupadi." He took her hand firmly, ignoring her fear of his touch. "But Brahma will make us friends for life."

At dawn Arjuna still walked the torch-lit halls of the royal quarters, searching for peace. He had overseen the funerals of too many people tonight. Been shorn of too many heroes —Lettermaker, Krishna, Vaja. Lotus. And, in some sense, Yudishtira.

He felt that only his two wives had behaved heroically. Subhadra had been brave, but then she was the daughter of the man the Vrishnis had chosen to lead them. But what mighty warrior must have sired Draupadi?

Tomorrow night he would bed her. He felt his heart pound at the thought, but not so much from desire. Draupadi, he knew, was the only person he would ever fear. Even his very first surata had seemed less awesome. Less dangerous. He had been so sure he had put this woman from his heart, but the moment he had seen her that autumn day in the chariot between Subhadra and Yudishtira, her tyranny over him had resumed.

Yudishtira should just keep her, he thought.

Then his whole being rebelled. For a moment he had imagined his life ending without ever having united with her. It made his existence seem dry, wasted.

He walked on. Was it her beauty? Or the challenge? The same old questions.

Or was it that she was not his alone?

She divides us—he thought it again. Yudishtira would never have kept me from the battlefield today. The agony of it— that Yudishtira would do that—still tormented him.

Yet Yudishtira had suffered more for it. The vision of all those dead Nishada came again. Anyway, could he himself have really prevented any more of those deaths?

Only if I had trusted Lettermaker less.

And Lotus, who was totally my own mistake, and she nearly murdered Yudishtira.

"It's all madness," he cursed.

A man approached along the walkway, then emerged from the shadows. It was his eldest brother.

They stood in silence for a long time. In his mind Arjuna saw today's dead again. Raced again beside this brother of his towards a herder's hut. Played again as a child in a forest clearing, secure within the sight of him.

"What has gone wrong with us, Yudishtira?"

"Could it be we have grown up?" The eldest son of Pandu asked gently.

"I don't know! Tell me!" Arjuna suddenly gripped Yudishtira by the shoulders and shook him. "Tell me! Tell me!"

But his older brother did not answer. Instead, somehow, the shaking turned into an embrace. The two held each other for a long, long time, and Arjuna cried tears of exhaustion, tears of fear, and tears for other feelings he believed he would never comprehend.

50

I think I have left some questions unanswered. Such as, who did write the *Mahabharata*, and why? Is it a true story? And if so, why all these versions?

A mother sat down by her children before they slept, wanting to tell them a story. She knew their favourite— the one that best closed their eyes, opened their minds and stilled their night fears. And this story was a true one. It had, in fact, happened to herself. Yet because her children were always growing and changing, she had to change that story with every telling.

Yes, I suppose I wrote the *Mahabharata*. My large-self was recording the events "to preserve dharma". My small-self was simply re-telling a tale from a brighter time, to ease my fear of the dark.

Vyasa

After an hour's rest Yudishtira performed the ritual dawn bathing beside the river, then returned to the assembly hall to make oblations to his ancestors and the gods. As Urutata guided him through the ceremonies he tried to put his awareness with the meaning of each sacred act. But his tired mind often wandered to all that was wrong about this long-awaited day.

The funeral pyres beside the river. The land empty and burned again. Krishna gone. Vyasa apparently gone too. Bharata's warriors humiliated.

Prostrate on the sacred barhi grass where Urutata finally left him, he closed his eyes and saw the day roll away before him like a slow-moving chariot.

The procession waiting for him—his mother and brothers;

his friends, relatives and allies; the kings and princes and all their wives and mothers and daughters and sons, all in gaudy chariots moving through Indraprastha, out through the main gate, circling the city and returning. Aloe and sandalwood burning everywhere along their path. Garlands of flowers and arches of greenery trembling in the wind. Banners of coloured cloth, swaying, snapping. Strings of beads, gems and pearls tapping on the white walls. All as planned, before yesterday had removed so many of his reasons to celebrate.

Then the procession on foot through the palace, through the gardens, under the covered breezeways to the north door of the hall. In at the great doors and up to the throne. The assigning of ceremonial duties to his kinsmen. The lighting of the six fires by the priests. The offering to Anumati, Goddess of Consent. Then more rice, butter, barley cakes, curds, to all the divine company.

At noon the unction ceremony itself. And Draupadi beside him at last. A single radiant light in the greyness.

The lustral fluid dipped and filtered. Water from the sister rivers, the great oceans, the sacred fords, pools and lakes. With honey, ghee and the waters of today's calving cow. If any had survived.

The anointment itself, of both him and his queen, and the bestowal of the remaining consecrated water on Bhima until Prahara was old enough to become Crown Prince.

The hundred consents repeated. And then the recessional. The stepping in the four directions of space, plus the fifth above them towards which he would step on the golden stool. The drive around the outer walls in Jarasamda's great chariot. The arrows sent flying into space. The walk to the river, the bathing at the removal ceremony. The ritual dicing hall, where he would instead bestow gifts. The solemn evening rituals. The feast.

Tomorrow the Departure, each chariot carrying a garland from Indraprastha, each king leaving a last gift, making a last vow of loyalty. Driving away, but remembering.

And Suyodhana still unpunished, still envious, still humiliated.

As Yudishtira lay there where Urutata had placed him,

between earth and heaven, the future samraj knew it was this with Suyodhana that could not be left unaltered. For the sake of peace, this was what he had to change.

But accusations would solve nothing—they would have to be made at Hastinapura, before Drita, who was responsible for Suyodhana's behaviour. And Drita would still see Yudishtira as a nephew, and believe nothing. A samraj could not begin his reign by bickering with his uncle and cousin.

Yet Suyodhana had clearly violated dharma in numerous small ways, if not in ways large enough to bring before an assembly. And even his allies suspected he had played a deeper role in the attacks, given his closeness to Sakuni. But that simply could not be proven.

Then there was the oath—both his cousin's brazen speech in the morning meeting and the versions Yudishtira had heard of his harangue in the stable courtyard seemed to contradict at least the spirit of their mutual vow to display no jealousy. How would it seem if the new samraj ignored and forgave so much in an opponent? For everyone else saw them now as opponents, Yudishtira knew, however King Drita would like to view it.

Yet with Sakuni's influence removed, Suyodhana might yet recover his reason—whether Suyodhana liked it or not, he would probably not have the courage to attempt any further trouble. Or it might also be that, since he himself had gained virtually everything to which he had aspired since the kingdom's division, while Suyodhana had gained nothing, the slightest further jostling of his cousin might shatter his pride and bring more violence to the Kurus.

However much it went against Yudishtira's deep fury towards this man, and however politically risky it might be, from the larger view of both justice and strategy he knew he must let the past go.

"Prahara, I must go in there now," Draupadi whispered.

Half asleep, the six-month-old child blinked up at his mother. She held him tighter. "There are a hundred queens in that room behind me. What shall I say to them?"

From a balcony Draupadi looked out across her gardens,

where kings now walked in twos and threes before the ceremonies. The mid-morning sun shone on the dark foliage of the paravata and citron trees. She could see princes stopping to admire her peacocks.

She turned to face the open balcony door. Its fluttering curtains brushed her white linen gown. "Mother," she whispered, "sustain me with your first kind of strength." Then she entered the room.

The queens and princesses gathered around her, praising her child, her dress, her palace and gardens. Then they nervously asked her about life "in this isolated place". Sensing their real concern, she reassured them that the rakshasa had been eliminated. "But you still allow so many free Dasyu here in your palace," a queen exclaimed.

"Yes we do," Draupadi said flatly. Then, thinking about it, she smiled a little.

A princess asked her if it was true that she had studied Veda. "I have asked our priests to teach me, but—" The princess glanced around her and shrugged.

In her mind Draupadi heard Vyasa's first instructions to her, so long ago now it seemed, and she saw the fires she had walked between. Then she gave Prahara to Kunti and took a seat, inviting the others to join her, indicating places near her for those who were eldest. She paused, then began:

"If you remember nothing else, remember that Veda resides in awareness, not in words or rituals or priests or even gods. As for the hymns, think of them in two ways, as sound and as meaning . . ."

Listening to her own voice, Draupadi seemed to hear a woman who had been far away but had finally come home.

The procession was forming. Yudishtira waited under a canopy while kings and princes lounged by their chariots, whispering. But Suyodhana and Radheya stood apart from everyone, as if disowning the procession itself.

Forcing himself to see the two without prejudice, Yudishtira recognised in them the essence of the warrior-born, whatever Radheya's parentage or Suyodhana's sins. Indeed, he thought that if it were not for himself, his cousin and his cousin's loyal friend might have been two faultless kings.

At that moment the hundreds in the procession and the two thousand waiting in the garden to watch it saw King Yudishtira walk the five paces to Crown Prince Suyodhana. Their rumoured words were repeated for generations after.

But they were simple words. Yudishtira thanked Suyodhana for performing his kinsman's role of accepting the samraj's gifts. Suyodhana observed that it was his assigned duty. Yudishtira spoke of peace, Suyodhana said he had already sworn it. Yudishtira mentioned recent trouble between them, Suyodhana replied that he was unaware of any. "And if I raised certain objections yesterday," Drita's son said stiffly, "it does not matter—others did not agree. You have every consent you need."

"Perhaps, Suyodhana, it is that I wish to apologise to you for destroying the future you and your father had planned."

"You have destroyed nothing." Then Suyodhana asked his cousin's leave to go, and received it.

His face expressionless, Yudishtira next turned to the King of Anga. He first thanked Radheya for his help the day before. Radheya called it his duty. Yudishtira said that duty was not always clear, as it had not been yesterday to any kings but the two of them. Radheya said duty was always clear.

King Yudishtira looked into King Radheya's eyes and remembered his graduation tournament, when seeing Radheya was like looking into his own self. But today Yudishtira saw an earlier self, whose sharp edges had since been ground away. And he recalled Vyasa once saying, "The truly wise do not drown the ignorant in truth—to wet a person, a drop will suffice."

"Radheya," Yudishtira said gently, "if Suyodhana were to violate dharma in some extreme way, could you absolve yourself of your vow to stand by him even to your death?"

"An oath can not be broken."

Yudishtira contemplated the space between them. "There is an awkward thought, Radheya, to which I am still trying to give birth. It has to do with the paradoxical way in which even those laws and behaviours we have always called dharma can violate dharma." But then Pandu's eldest stopped. "Why must it be that we are an arm's length apart, King Radheya, yet it feels like a league?"

For a moment Radheya's eyes softened. "It will be an honour for Bharata to have you as samraj."

Then the moment had passed. "But if you wrong Suyodhana, you can expect to fight me also."

"May Brahma preserve us from each other's arrows," Pandu's son said quietly.

King Yudishtira then left King Radheya and walked back to his place at the head of the procession. The priests gave the signal, the music and chanting began, and the chariot of the next samraj of Bharata advanced.

She stood beside him, like a bride. Yudishtira could hardly listen to Urutata, for his awareness was with his queen.

"Today is a wedding," Urutata was saying. The words may have been traditional, but to Yudishtira it was as if his chief priest had known his mind. "A samraj is wed to the land of Bharata as a husband is wed to his wife. Thereafter they are one. The husband is nothing without his wife—who can be a husband if he has no wife? Likewise, who can be a samraj without the land? And if this king is nothing as a husband without his wife the queen—then I declare this husband and wife to be samraj together. As they love and protect each other, may they love and protect this land."

There were shouts, songs, drums, cymbals and a rain of flowers that seemed never to end. But Urutata proceeded with slow dignity, pouring the consecrating fluids. "To thee this kingdom is given for the development of agriculture, for the common good, for the prosperity and nourishment of the subjects . . ."

Then the remainder of the fluids fell upon Draupadi, covering her black hair with a crystal veil. "For the sake of peace allow no man but your husbands to touch this consecrated hair. For the sake of wealth encourage your people's happiness. For the sake of . . ."

Yudishtira saw only Draupadi's face. He felt only his heart

filling with light, warmth, and joy. Filling with fire. He and she were samraj.

The "yavana gift" came in the evening, before the feast, as the full moon rose. The messengers were breathless with excitement—the thing had come from Egypt.

Arjuna ordered the package opened at a safe distance from Yudishtira and Draupadi, even though Sahadeva insisted it was merely an Egyptian written message.

When Sahadeva was proven right, he bowed before Yudishtira and offered him the papyrus scroll, his emotions concealed.

But the samraj knew his young brother's feelings. Yudishtira took the object and turned it in his hands, reflecting how, on the day before, the Nishada had proven to be the bravest warriors in Bharata. What other of the Arya's precious "truths" might be turned upside down by the coming Age of Kali? And this belief of his that he must prevent the spread of writing—that he personally could prevent the coming age, even if the gods willed it—had that been his ultimate arrogance? Or, had it been his stubborn rejection of what might even be a disguised gift from the gods, meant to compensate for the decline of awareness? Was that not the essence of Kali's Age—a failure to recognise what was truly narrow, and what was boundless?

Samraj Yudishtira asked Prince Sahadeva to accompany him to a private place. There, although the oldest son of Pandu could have managed to read the papyrus himself, he asked his younger brother to read it for him.

In simple words, spoken in Sahadeva's trembling voice, the oracle of the god Amon-Re of Egypt conceded "victory" to the "Great Yudishtira" and the "Divine Draupadi", claiming himself defeated by ". . . That which, for the moment, blesses Bharata with its infinity. But there will be no easy ending to the battle you have engendered among the gods. Creator and Destroyer, like rivalling kinsmen of the same family, can never vanquish each other. They can only cause the havoc we call mortal life."

At the same hour that its message was read, beneath the temples of Thebes, beyond the full moon's light, the Ka of

Amon-Re's Supremely Beloved Servant departed for the Other Shore. The Company of Fifty had forgotten how many days the last oracle of Amon-Re had been fighting his leave-taking. Day and night had meant nothing, for the sunrise, noon and sunset deliveries had ended. No emissaries had come from Pharaoh, no suppliants or inquirers of the god. What was needed desperately had been sent down. That was all.

The oracle's last words had been uttered two months ago, to a scribe —a message of nonsense sent to that petty, distant Bharata which had so tortured their master. And still he had lingered on until this hour of convulsions and haemorrhage. But at last it was over. The eldest of the Company announced the death to the darkness: "The Ka of Amon-Re's Beloved has departed His body." And more softly he said, "May we please Him, may we find joy in our service to Him when we join Him today on the Other Shore."

One began to sing, "He flies now. He flies away from you, you men. He is no longer on Earth, He is in the sky."

Others took up the chant. "He rushes the sky as a heron, He kisses the sky as a hawk. And His heart will be weighed by Osiris. He will be led by the hand before the judges by Horus and His heart will be laid on the scales of Osiris. Attended by Anubis, while the wise Thoth calculates, His heart will be weighed. His heart will be weighed against Truth. May the scales find their balance. May Truth be served."

In the gardens behind the assembly hall Vyasa waited. He did not know why he waited. It seemed that nothing could warrant the return of his old premonitions and dreads. In there at the rowdy feast some were even saying that the Age of Kali was simply impossible with such a samraj. So it seemed that finally Pandu's stubborn faith in a son of dharma had ceased to be a joke.

Then why do I wait here in the dark?

He made his way through the asoka grove to the reflection pool and stood on its tiled kerb. He still waited—for something he could not name. There was not a single ripple to disturb the reflection before him. The lights of the feast shone as if he were looking directly at the celebration hall, not down towards their twins at his feet. Voices intoxicated with madhu and joy skipped across the bright space, dappling it with sound. But the water at his feet waited, dark and still except for the lights it gave back.

More laughing voices. And now they came. The five brothers and Draupadi, and Suyodhana, who was very drunk. "Good cause to drink tonight, my misbegotten grandson," Vyasa whispered.

All evening the five warriors had struggled to be amiable with the sixth. To heal the split in the Kurus' royal line. Now they were letting Draupadi lead a tour of her gardens especially for Suyodhana. Encouraging her to be witty and charming only for their cousin's delight. But as she led them out among the trees, and as her sweet words fell around them, the five brothers were the ones who hovered closer, like bees at the centre of a flower. Suyodhana only lurched and staggered—the bee caught in the web of the spider.

Vyasa felt his awareness pulling away, as if he were watching from a great distance. Or through a cloud that had no substance, yet separated him from them. The separation was time—theirs was brief, his was infinite. He remembered his teacher's name for this which he had never himself known before: The Breath of Brahman.

"Here is the pool I described, Prince Suyodhana," she was saying on the far side of the cloud. "Just like the floor in the assembly hall, except that here there is real water. Wonderful, isn't it? Yudishtira says the floor inside is to remind us to speak the truth, but this one here is to remind us that the truth can be slippery."

"Did I say that?" Yudishtira asked, laughing.

"Yes, you did."

"That is not water!" Suyodhana's drunken voice shouted to Vyasa across the centuries.

"No, I'm sorry, Suyodhana, but I'm afraid it is." How charming she is being, Vyasa thought, even to this one. How she laughs.

"Bring the torch closer and look."

Now she leans forward.

And now Suyodhana does come closer, his body near hers,

his lips over hers. But she does not back down. "It is water, Suyodhana. Step there and you'll become our best entertainment tonight."

Vyasa saw Suyodhana whirl to face his cousins. "No, when I *don't* I'll be your entertainment. You want to make a fool of me. You succeeded in the assembly hall, with your ponds that only *look* like water." He turned towards the pool. "Not again." And he stepped—so slowly, it seemed to Vyasa—on to the black stillness.

The dark water shattered into infinite arrows of light as Suyodhana fell through it. He rose from the pool like an angry animal. He fell again. He rose again. And fell again, too drunk to stand on the polished bottom. Still something goaded him to try. He fell yet again.

Yudishtira's face reflected the danger he saw. The others only laughed. They shimmered with laughter. Shards of their laughter shone in the space over their heads until even the eldest was forced to smile. For the pond had gone wild with light; the water was leaping its walls. This was truly the dark night's most fond entertainment, the cause for even oblivion to sparkle.

Vyasa saw Bhima offer Suyodhana a hand. The hand was spat upon. Arjuna and Sahadeva received the same.

Then Draupadi took her husbands away. She walked with one arm around Yudishtira, who looked back but was, after all, as helpless to change this moment as a river was helpless to change its course. Her other arm was lightly through Arjuna's. The remaining three brothers leaned close, trying to impress her with their imitations of their cousin. But it was her laughter alone that rang all around Vyasa now, in distant places and between the stars, as if Brahma himself were enjoying Suyodhana's fall.

The victim crawled to the edge of the pond, stood, teetered, and stepped out with effort. His curse was ugly but not loud. Then he went away.

A cara bird chattered in the simul tree on Vyasa's left. Someone called across the garden that the jugglers had arrived. The seer stood alone in the dark, watching the pond return to stillness.

THE CHARACTERS

Sometimes the traditional epic version of the *Mahabharata* uses several names for the same person, although one prevails. However, in earlier drafts I found this most-prevalent name for a character often sounded and looked too similar to others – for example, readers confused Bhima with Bhishma, Gangeya's usual name. Other names, such as Dhritarashtra and Dhrishta-dyumna, seemed too foreign and awkward. Therefore sometimes I substituted a character's less common name, or shortened his or her common name. In these cases the common name is given in parentheses in the list below.

If a character is not found at all in the traditional version of the epic, the name is followed by an asterisk.

Aditi* – Draupadi's and Panchalya's mother. Also the name of the goddess of infinity, who is the mother of many of the other Arya gods.

Amon-Re's oracle* – also called His Supremely Beloved Servant; high priest of the foremost Egyptian deity of that period and historically the most powerful man in Egypt.

Arjuna – middle brother of the five sons of Pandu, and a great archer.

Badger* – a Nishada carpenter and leader among his people at Indraprastha.

Balarama – Krishna's brother.

Bhima – the huge second eldest of the five sons of Pandu.

Does-Nothing-Yet-Gets-All* – king of the Nishada and a leader of a Nishada rebellion.

Draupadi – wife to all five sons of Pandu, "born from King Drupada's sacrificial fire", and prophesied to be the one "to lead the warriors of Bharata to their doom".

Drita – King Pandu's older brother. After Pandu's abdication, Drita became king in spite of being blind. Suyodhana's father. (Dhritarashtra)

Drupada – king of South Panchala and "father" of Draupadi and Panchalya after he obtained them from his sacrificial fire. Enemy of Vaja, who took half his kingdom.

Dusasana – King Drita's second born and Suyodhana's full brother.

Eagle* – leader of a splinter group of rakshasa, son of a Nishada leader, and brother to Wood Rose and Lotus.

Eos* – a Greek; first Draupadi's slave, then her friend.

Gangeya – Kuru patriarch; regent and "grandfather" to both the sons of Pandu and of Drita; sworn since boyhood to celibacy for the sake of his father, King Kuru. (Bhishma)

Guru Vaja – see Vaja.

Hdimba – Bhima's second wife, a Dasyu.

Jarasamda – King of Magada.

Kanwa* – a messenger, also the supervisor of Yudishtira's livestock.

Krishna – the charismatic friend of Pandu's five sons, especially Arjuna. He is Subhadra's brother and Kunti's nephew.

Kunti – King Pandu's widow; mother of the three eldest sons of Pandu and stepmother to the twins, Nakula and Sahadeva.

Kuru – a deceased king; Gangeya's father. Kuru is also considered Pandu's and Drita's grandfather because they were the offspring of the widows of one of his sons, although Vyasa actually begot Pandu and Drita with those widows, after Kuru and his sons had died. This is the third King Kuru. Kuru is also the name of the kingdom and its people. (Santanu)

Lettermaker – a Phoenician architect and Eos's lover for a time. (Based on the character Maya in the epic.)

Lotus* – Arjuna's courtesan; daughter of a Nishada leader and sister to Wood Rose and Eagle.

Madri – King Pandu's second wife; Nakula's and Sahadeva's mother. Died with Pandu.

Murdanvat* – a Marut; gatekeeper at Indraprastha.

Nakula – one of the two youngest sons of Pandu; Sahadeva's twin.

Panchalya – King Drupada's "son" and Draupadi's twin brother, he was "born out of the sacrificial fire" to kill Guru Vaja, King Drupada's enemy. (Dhrishtadyumna)

Pandu – King of the Kurus until he left his throne to his blind brother, Drita; the father of Yudishtira, Bhima, Arjuna, Nakula and Sahadeva.

Prahara – son of Yudishtira and Draupadi. (Prativindhya)

Radheya – the adopted son of a woman named Radha (hence his name, Radheya) and her husband, a chariot driver. Made king of the Anga by his friend and patron Suyodhana. (Karna)

Sahadeva – one of the two youngest sons of Pandu; Nakula's twin.

Sakuni – Suyodhana's maternal uncle and King Drita's brother-in-law.

Salya – uncle to the sons of Pandu (Madri's brother, so actually Salya is only Nakula's and Sahadeva's uncle).

Sini* – prince of Usinara encountered at Magada by Yudishtira.

Sisupala – King of Cedi.

Subhadra – Arjuna's second wife and Krishna's sister.

Suyodhana – King Drita's eldest son. (Duryodhana)

Urutata – at first Krishna's guardian, then Yudishtira's chief priest. (Based on Dhaumya in the epic.)

Vaja – a priest by birth but skilled in warfare; the weapons-master and teacher to Panchalya and the sons of Pandu. The sworn enemy of King Drupada. (Bharadvaja, Drona)

Vimada* – a Marut fighting companion of Yudishtira.

Vyasa – "the collector of the Veda" and a revered Vedic seer said to have written down the *Mahabharata*. Pandu's and Drita's actual father. Also called Krishna Dvaipayana.

Wood Rose* – daughter of a Nishada leader; sister to Lotus and Eagle.

Yasoda – Queen of South Panchala and wife of King Drupada.

Yudishtira – oldest of the five sons of Pandu.

Zesnor* – an Egyptian slave.

GLOSSARY

Agni – god of fire.

Ahicchatra – capital of North Panchala, originally capital of all of Panchala.

ahimsa – action that does no harm in any way.

amarsha – righteous anger; the refusal to tolerate an insult or wrong; ever restless striving. A virtue in the warrior-born.

Anga – a kingdom in eastern Bharata, which Suyodhana gave to Radheya to rule.

Anumati – goddess of consent.

Aranyani – a goddess of the forest.

Arya – "noble"; the Sanskrit-speaking Indo-European people.

Aryaman – a god called the "Friend" and the "protector of the good".

Ashwins – the twin gods, the physicians, the horse riders and honey drinkers who rescue and grant long life; found in the morning twilight, which is half light and half dark. Said to be the fathers of Nakula and Sahadeva.

azle – a fictitious name for what could be one of a number of plants and beverages employed since prehistory for their strong effects on the mind.

Bactria – roughly what is now northeastern Afghanistan.

Badari – an ashram or hermitage in the Himalaya Mountains. Today called Badrinath.

Bharata – Arya India. Originally it was the name of a king who was the common, distant ancestor of all Kurus; then the name applied to their kingdom, between the Yamuna and Ganges rivers; and finally it acquired a much broader reference, as used here.

Brahma – the Creator. Originally the root word referred to certain powerful ritual utterances said to be capable of creating, altering or destroying material objects. Eventually it also came to refer to one who uttered these words (a brahmin or priest), to the god who first uttered them (Brahma) and to the infinite energy and order giving rise to and pervading material existence (Brahman).

Brahman – the unbounded oneness of pure energy and order said to move within itself to create Creator and Creation (much as modern physics describes the creation of physical matter as fluctuations of a nonmaterial field of pure energy and order).

Brihaspati – god of wisdom, the priest and teacher to the other gods.

Cedi – a kingdom south of the Yamuna.

Chine – China.

Dasyu – the aboriginal people the Arya encountered as they pushed into the subcontinent from the northwest.

dharma – Eternal Law, natural law; the long-standing legal codes and traditions prescribing correct behaviour for all humans, as well as for each individual (according to personality and heredity), each social role and each class. Additional guidance and interpretations can come from elders, sacred hymns and good examples, but dharma is ultimately known only through the direct cognition of Brahman.

Dvaraka – the Vrishnis' capital.

Ekacakra – the village where the widow and sons of Pandu hid for a year after the fire at Varanavata.

Ganges River – a river flowing southeast from the Himalaya, through north central India.

ghee – butter fat or clarified butter, made by heating butter and separating the fat from the froth and settled milk solids. It does not spoil as rapidly as unclarified butter.

Girivraja – the capital of Magada.

Hastinapura – the Kurus' capital, on the Ganges River.

Indra – god of war, rain, thunder. Said to be Arjuna's father.

Indrani – Indra's wife, or else his female form.

Indraprastha – the capital of the half of the Kuru lands given Pandu's sons by their uncle, King Drita. It is on the Yamuna River (where Delhi is today).

Indus River – northwest of Bharata.

jaya – Sanskrit word for victory.

Jyaistha – mid-May to mid-June.

Ka – Egyptian term for a person's spirit or soul.

Kailasa – a vast mountain, or mountain system, in the Himalaya. The peak itself is in modern Tibet.

Kali's age – an age in which dharma declines, war increases, the population explodes and natural balance is destroyed; said to have begun with the events in the *Mahabharata* and to continue into the present. Kali refers to the losing throw of the dice, equivalent to what we call "snake eyes".

Kama – love; sexual pleasure; also the god of these.

Kampilya – capital of South Panchala.

Karttika – mid-October to mid-November.

Kurus – the descendants and subjects of any King Kuru.

linga – a phallic-shaped stone.

Ma'at – the Egyptian goddess of truth and justice.

madhu – honey wine.

Magada – an Arya kingdom south of the Ganges in eastern Bharata, ruled by Jarasamda.

Manu – the first sacrificer and sometimes thought to be the first human.

Maruts – the fictitious name given to the select group of warriors recruited at Kampilya by the sons of Pandu and named after the "heavenly troop" of gods associated with Indra.

Matsya – a kingdom in southwest Bharata.

Mrityu – goddess of death.

niksha – gold coins, carried in the form of necklaces.

Nirriti – goddess of misfortune, misery, decay and destruction.

Nishada – a major Dasyu people.

Panchala – the kingdom in central Bharata which is southeast of the Kurus, on the north and south banks of the Ganges River.

Phalguna – a month (constellation) in spring.

pitris – the "fathers" or ancestors in Heaven.

Prajapati – the god of creation in the form of the Golden Egg.

Prithi – Mother Earth, "the broad one", the goddess of earth and heights, who supports the mountains and forests.

purohita – chief priest.

Pushan – the "glowing god" of prosperity who protects property and pastoral life.

rajasuya – ritual consecration of a samraj or "king of kings".

rakshasa – demons; the fictitious name for the renegade Dasyu employed by Sakuni.

Rudra – a mighty god with a reputation for anger, yet a healer; later Rudra evolved into Shiva, god of destruction, in the triad of Hindu deities which is Brahma, Vishnu and Shiva.

ruru deer – a kind of deer.

samraj – the king over all kings; title gained by attaining the consent of every other Arya king.

Saraswati – a beautiful goddess of learning and wisdom.

Savitri – the golden god who impels the sun and dispenses good things; the "stimulator" and supreme lawgiver.

Sukshetra – a fictional Nishada village in the environs of Indraprastha.

surata – passionate, pleasureful sexual union.

Surya – god of the sun.

Thebes – a major city of Egypt, site of the temple to Amon-Re.

Ushas – goddess of dawn.

Usinara – a small kingdom south of the Yamuna near Cedi and South Panchala.

Varanavata – a town between Hastinapura and Indraprastha, and site of an infamous attempt to kill the widow and sons of Pandu in a fire.

Varuna – the god upholding natural and moral order.

Vayu – god of the wind.

Veda – literally, Eternal Knowledge. The hymns cognised by certain seers during meditation; the knowledge or Intelligence which structures all creation (including the human being, the knower, through whom knowledge is able to know itself).

Videha – a kingdom in eastern Bharata, north of Magada.

vina – a stringed musical instrument with a long, fretted keyboard and a soundbox of gourds.

Vrishnis – a highly independent group of Arya, having chiefs rather than kings. Krishna's people.

Yama – the god called the "fetcher"; the King of the Ancestors.

Yamuna – a river in central Bharata.

yavana – those from the west, especially Greeks.

yavani – female yavana.

BIBLIOGRAPHY

This is a selection of scholarly works on ancient India used to research *Samraj*.

Auboyer, Jeannine. *Daily Life in Ancient India*. New York: Macmillan, 1965.

Basham, A. L. *Aspects of Ancient Indian Culture*. London: Asian Publishing House, 1966.

Bhargava, P. L. *India in the Vedic Age* (2nd ed.). Lucknow, India: The Upper India Publishing House, 1971.

Dimmitt, Cornelia, and van Buitenen, J. A. B. *Classical Hindu Mythology: A Reader in the Sanskrit Puranas*. Philadelphia: Temple University Press, 1978.

Griswold, H. D. *The Religion of the Rig Veda*. Delhi: Motilal Banarsidass, 1971.

Gupta, S. P., and Ramachandran, K. S. *Mahabharata: Myth and Reality*. Delhi: Agam Prakashan, 1976.

Kosambi, D. D. *Ancient India: A History of its Culture and Civilization*. Cleveland: World Publishing, 1969.

Meyer, Johann Jakob. *Sexual Life in Ancient India*. Delhi: Motilal Banarsidass, 1971.

O'Flaherty, Wendy Doniger. *Sexual Metaphors and Animal Symbols in Indian Mythology*. Delhi: Motilal Banarsidass, 1980.

Puri, B. N. *Cities of Ancient India*. Meerut, India: Meenakshi Prakashan, 1966.

Renou, Louis. *The Civilization of Ancient India*. Calcutta: Susil Gupta, 1954. *Religions of Ancient India*. New York: Schocken Books, 1968.

Roy, Brajdeo Prasad. *The Later Vedic Economy*. Patna: Janaki Prakashan, 1984.

Subramaniam, Kamala. *Mahabharata*. Bombay: Bharatiya Vidya Bhavan, 1980.

van Buitenen, J. A. B. *The Mahabharata, Books 1–5*. Chicago: University of Chicago Press, 1973, 1975, 1978.